THE LT. KATE GAZZARA SERIES - BOOKS 4 - 6

THE LT. KATE GAZZARA SERIES
BOOK 2

BLAIR HOWARD

From Blair Howard

The Harry Starke Genesis Series

The Harry Starke Series

The Lt. Kate Gazzara Murder Files

The Randall & Carver Mysteries

The Peacemaker Series

The Civil War Series

From Blair C. Howard

The Sovereign Star Series

This one is for Jo, as always

SAPPHIRE: CASE FOUR

A LT. KATE GAZZARA NOVEL

BOOK FOUR

BY

BLAIR HOWARD

1

TUESDAY, SEPTEMBER 8, 1987

Bolton County, Ohio

Ohio State Trooper Dan Walker rolled his cruiser off the road onto the grass shoulder. Well, to call it grass would be something of an exaggeration. It was, in fact, a dry patch of dirt, deeply rutted and surrounded by tall weeds and grass-like undergrowth skirted by unfettered woodland: low-lying vegetation, small trees growing beneath large trees, dense and impenetrable...or was it?

Dan really didn't care. He needed to take a whiz in the worst way, and he knew this was as good a spot as any; he'd used it many times. A quick pee just inside the tree line where no one could see— then set up the radar and wait. *Yeah, sit and wait, that's what I'll do,* he thought dryly and chuckled, knowing full well a nap was in his near future. He turned off the engine, exited the cruiser, locked it, and then ambled off through the weeds.

He unzipped, tilted his head up, closed his eyes, and sighed deeply as he relieved himself. For maybe two minutes he stood there, enjoying the moment, then shook it vigorously. *Only three times,* he thought grinning—*any more than that is considered playing with your-self. Ahhh*—and then he zipped up.

He was about to turn and go back to his cruiser when he spotted something.

He squinted through the flickering sunbeams that filtered through the treetops. *Hmmm,* he thought. *I don't remember seeing that before.*

It was just off to one side, maybe fifteen feet away.

It's a box, a wooden box. What the hell?

He looked around. He didn't like leaving his cruiser unattended, but it wasn't as if this was the interstate. It was, in fact, nothing more than a rural two-lane roadway, little traveled and quiet.

He turned again and squinted at the object of interest.

Dumped. Rolled down the slope. Whatever it is, it's big. Okay, so let's go take a peek. Aw shit, my damn pants...and my friggin' leg.

His uniform pant leg had snagged on a bramble of some sort, tearing a triangular hole in the material and scratching his skin.

Damn, damn, damn! He almost turned back, but he didn't. Why he didn't, he wasn't sure. What he was sure of was the uncomfortable, itchy feeling at the back of his neck.

He stumbled through the underbrush until he finally reached his objective.

Yeah, it's a box. Solid. Well made. Good box. Why would anyone... He stared down at it, his stomach rising to his throat. He had a horrible feeling that he knew what it was. The box was maybe four feet long by twenty inches by twenty-four and made from three-quarter-inch plywood. He looked around, taking in every inch of the terrain.

If this is what I think it is... He kicked the side of the box. It moved slightly. *Hmmm, not heavy. Maybe not, then. Okay. Now what? Better call it in, I suppose. You never know.*

He turned and struggled through the vegetation, back up the slope, and out onto the dirt patch where his cruiser was parked.

He slid into the car and keyed his mike.

"11 to Post 44. Signal 3."

"44 to 11. Go ahead."

"Show me Signal 3 on a large wooden box off the road on Highway 52 Northbound, Milepost 333. No vehicles or persons nearby."

There was a pause, then:

"44 to 11, PC Allerton advises caution."

The post commander? Geez!

"Okay," Dan replied but waited for a moment, thought about what he wanted to say, then said, "11 to 44. The box is a large wooden container, sealed. There is no apparent name or label present. What do you advise?"

"44 to 11. Lieutenant Allerton is sending Sergeant Beavers to your location to assist. Do not attempt to open the container until he arrives."

"11 to 44, copy."

And so he waited, closing his eyes after turning off the radar, and he didn't open them again until Sergeant Billy Beavers arrived some thirty minutes later.

"Whatcha got, Dan?" his voice boomed through the open window of the cruiser, startling Dan awake. "Caughtcha nappin', did I?"

"Er, no. No! I was just restin' my eyes. Sun's bright today, Sarge."

"Restin' your eyes, my ass. You were asleep. I catch you again—an' I'll be watchin'—your ass will be grass. Understand?" He didn't wait for an answer. Instead, he asked, "So where's this box, then?"

Dan led him down the slope through the undergrowth to where it lay, just as he'd left it. Sergeant Beavers crouched down beside it, stared closely at it, leaned in close and sniffed at one corner. He stood and said, "No smell. It's what, four feet by two by two? Can't be anything much. You should have a pry bar in your unit. Go get it. Let's open this baby up."

He did, and they did, but neither one of them was prepared for what they found inside.

The top came off easily enough; just a few nails, bright and shiny in the sunbeams. Inside was what appeared to be bundles of old clothing wrapped in a colored blanket.

On their knees now, they leaned over the open box, heads almost together. Beavers reached tentatively over the edge and touched the blanket, poked it with a forefinger, then took hold of an edge between finger and thumb and pulled. The blanket moved easily enough; he dragged it back some more, revealing...

"Oh shit!" Beavers gasped, dropping the blanket and reeling back, landing on his butt. He could still see the empty eye sockets staring balefully back at him.

"Holy crap! Leave it alone," Beavers said, grabbing Walker's arm and scooting himself back away from the box. "Don't touch it, Dan."

"Don't worry. I ain't."

Together they stared, mesmerized, at the partially revealed skull. Then still staring into the box, Beavers said, "Go back to your unit and call the sheriff. Be careful how you walk; disturb the scene as little as possible. Have Milt get his crime scene team out here. When you've done that, call Allerton and let 'im know what we got. Then wait at the roadside. I'll stay here."

BACKUP ARRIVED QUICKLY, IN LESS THAN FIFTEEN MINUTES. The first to arrive was Bolton County Sheriff Milton "Milt" Grambling—known fondly to his deputies as "Grumbling Milt." Grambling was quickly followed by the crime scene "team," which consisted of Bolton County's only forensic tech Deputy Rufus Watson. The next to arrive was Deputy Gene Drake, one of the county's two full-time detectives. The part-time coroner who was also the full-time funeral director, Lawrence "Birdie" Cackleton, arrived a few minutes later; he was driving his hearse. He parked the vehicle on the shoulder, barely leaving enough space for other vehicles to pass. Then he flipped his keys to Dan Walker, still on the road by his cruiser, and joined the others now standing in a wide circle around the box.

Cackleton, acting as coroner, stooped down beside the box and stared at the partially uncovered skull, shook his head thoughtfully, then said, "This one's been dead a long time..."

"No shit," Deputy Watson let slip.

Cackleton looked sharply up at him, opened his mouth to speak, but changed his mind. He stared into the box, thinking for a moment, walked slowly around it, his hands in his pants pockets, and then shook his head before gently moving aside the remaining coverings.

Slowly, carefully, he uncovered the rest of the skull, then paused and leaned back so everyone else in the group could see.

"Holy shit!" Deputy Drake said in an awed voice.

"No shit," Cackleton said, dryly, and then resumed stripping away the blanket and rolled-up items of clothing beneath it.

As he worked his way down from the head, because of the size of the box, he began to think he was dealing with what once had been a little person, a "dwarf," but it soon became evident that that wasn't the case. The legs had been severed at the knee and the lower leg portions, having then been wrapped, were placed neatly beside the hips.

Finally, the coroner stood, legs akimbo, hands stuffed deep inside his pants pockets, head bowed. He remained motionless, staring down at the skeletonized body.

"As I said, been dead a long time; completely dried out: every-thing—blanket, clothing, bones. What little tissue's left is like leather. Ain't no way to figure time of death; two...three years, maybe more, maybe even five or six. Has to be a homicide. Someone chopped off the damn legs; her fingers are missing too. But here's the thing: the box is clean—looks like it might have been made yesterday. It ain't been out here more'n a few hours, a day at most. See the grass under it?" He stooped, grabbed a corner of the box and lifted it a little; the grass underneath it was crushed flat, but fresh and green. "So where the hell has it been? Where did it come from?"

He lowered the box, stood up, stuck his hands back in his pockets. "We should probably get the bones to Doc Lewiston. He's done this kind of thing before. Maybe he can determine the cause of death," Cackleton said, looking at Sheriff Grambling. "Unless you want to turn it over to the BCI, that is?"

"The Bureau of Criminal Investigation?" Grambling tilted his head and stared at the coroner. "Hell no. No offense, Sergeant Beavers," he said to the state patrol officer.

Beavers rewarded him with a sloppy grin but said nothing.

"We can work it, right, Gene?"

Detective Gene Drake looked decidedly uncomfortable but nodded anyway.

"Yeah, course we can," Grambling said to no one in particular. "Okay! It's your case, Gene. I suggest you start by checking missing persons for the past six years... What?"

"Sheriff," Drake said. "We don't even know if it's a man or a woman. How'm I supposed to do a proper search without knowin' that?"

"How tall's the body, Birdie?"

"Hell, how should I know? It's in pieces, for Pete's sake." He paused and stared thoughtfully down into the box, his lips moving silently.

"At a guess, five-two, five-four."

"So a woman, then?" Grambling asked.

"Could be, could also be a kid, or a short guy."

"Damn it, Birdie. I need better'n that. What about the hair? It looks long, so a woman?"

"As I said," Cackleton said, "you need to get the bones over to Doc Lewiston. He'll be able to tell you for sure."

"Okay, do it, but wait until Rufus gets finished examining the scene," Grambling said. "Now, everybody else get outa here and let him get to it. Birdie, you wait up on the road until he's done, then take it all to Lewiston."

And that's what they did.

It was later determined by the local GP, Dr. Lewiston, to be the body of a young woman aged between twenty and thirty. He identified the cause of death was due to manual strangulation—the hyoid bone was broken—and estimated it had occurred sometime between three and six years earlier.

Detective Drake initiated a three-state search of missing person reports for the years 1980 through 1987, but to no avail. Eventually, the investigation stalled and, though he worked the case diligently for more than a year, the woman in the box remained unidentified. The case went cold and was eventually shelved and forgotten, until...

2

Chattanooga, Tennessee

It was cold that Thursday afternoon back in May 2015 when Assistant Chief Henry Finkle walked into my office. The heating had been off for hours. Finkle's arrival, however, added a new chill to the surroundings: the never-ending unwanted attention I received from him was, even then, becoming almost unbearable. It finally came to a head... Oh, but that's a story for another time.

My name, by the way, is Lieutenant Catherine Gazzara, Kate to my friends. I've been a cop since 2002. Today, I work homicide in the Major Crimes Unit at the Chattanooga Police Department, have done so for more than ten years. Well, except for a stint with the Cold Case Squad back in 2015 when all this took place.

As usual, Finkle barged into my office without knocking, startling me...

Assistant Chief Henry "Tiny" Finkle. Tiny? Yeah, tiny in both stature and mind, but no one had the guts to call him that, at least not to his face. He was a diminutive little man: just five-eight and slim, maybe a hundred and forty pounds. Nobody knew how old he was—

he kept it a closely guarded secret. I figured him to be in his early-to-mid forties; his brown hair had yet to show the first gray hair. His thin face, high cheekbones, thin nose, and beady black eyes all reminded me of a possum. Rat might have been a better description. Though his signature shit-eating grin made him a dead ringer for Disney's cat in Cinderella. He was also a bigot and a misogynist. I put up with his asinine remarks and pathetic attempts at flirting because I had to. If I could, I'd report him for harassment, but he was smart, didn't do it in public. Someday I'd figure out how to stop him...

"A-hah," he said, lightly. "Caught you napping, did I?"

I looked up at him, sighed, then said, "What do you want, Finkle?"

"What I want is a wild night between the sheets with you. How about it, Kate? How about we get out of here, rent a sleazy little motel room for a couple of hours, and I—"

"Give it up, Finkle," I interrupted him. "First, I'm sure a couple of minutes would be more than enough. Second, you're married. Third, I hate your guts and would rather die than let you within ten feet of me. But you knew all that, so what do you really want?"

He grinned the grin, seemingly unperturbed by the rejection. "The chief wants you and your partner in his office, now."

"What does he want?"

He leered at me, turned to go, hesitated, then looked back at me. "Nothing good, I hope."

I watched the door close behind him, pursed my lips and shook my head, exasperated.

I sat for a moment staring at the several piles of paperwork on my desk, gave a sigh, rose to my feet and headed out of my office, through the situation room toward the elevator. Chief Johnston's suite of offices was on the first floor at the far end of the building.

I threaded my way through the maze of jumbled desks to where my newly minted partner, Sergeant Lonnie Guest, was seated at his desk, his eyes mere inches from his computer screen, and tapped him on the shoulder.

"What?" he said, without looking away from the screen. "Can'tcha see I'm busy?"

"Busy doing what?" I asked, looking at the screen over his shoulder. "If that's porn..." I could see that it wasn't, but I'd already learned that Lonnie was quite addicted to the sad side of life. *He needs a good woman*, I thought as I looked down at him. *He's not a bad-looking guy. Maybe if he lost a little weight... Nah! A lot of weight.*

He rolled his seat away from the desk and looked up at me, smiling. "Not this time, LT. What's up?"

"The chief wants us. Let's go." I turned away, gesturing for him to follow me.

I always thought the long walk along the corridor to the chief's office must be something akin to the condemned man's last walk to the execution chamber. I'd been a cop for more than thirteen years, and I'd taken that walk many times; nothing good ever came of it.

So, it was with a feeling of deep trepidation that I walked into the great man's outer office that day. Cathy, his secretary, looked up and smiled at me, somewhat sympathetically, so I thought.

"You can go on in, Lieutenant. He's waiting for you."

I nodded and pushed through the heavy soundproof doors into Chief Wesley Johnston's inner sanctum.

Johnston was seated as he always was behind his desk, his back ramrod straight, bald head shining in the weak sunlight that shone in through the window. The shaft of sunlight had an almost ethereal effect. I wouldn't have been surprised to hear heavenly music playing softly in the background.

Johnston was—still is—a big man. Not overly tall but hefty, powerful. Probably from being ex-military. Marines, I think. His uniform was pressed, the creases sharp, perfect. A gold clip held his tie precisely in place. The gold stars on his collar glittered as he moved. His big head was round, shaved, and polished to a shine; the huge white eyebrows were a perfect match for the Hulk Hogan mustache. And he had an air of authority about him, not arrogance... Well, not exactly, but he was used to getting his own way, and he expected unquestioning obedience from his staff and the entire department.

Assistant Chief Henry Finkle was at the right side of the desk, his arms folded across his chest, the ever-present grin belied the narrow chips of ice that were his eyes. I looked from one to the other. Johnston had already adopted the pose: he was now leaning back in his chair, his elbows on the armrests, his hands curled into fists except for his forefingers which were steepled together at his lips, chin lowered almost to his chest. I'd seen it so many times before. Finkle? There was no way to know what was going on between his tiny ears but, from the way he looked me up and down, I could guess.

"Good afternoon, Lieutenant Gazzara," Johnston said over his steepled fingertips. "Please sit down. You too, Sergeant Guest."

I sat down on one of the two seats in front of the desk; Lonnie sat in the other.

Johnston stared across the desk at me. I had a feeling he was waiting for me to speak. I didn't. What could I say?

Finally, he broke the silence.

"How long have you been with the department, Lieutenant?"

That took me by surprise.

"Thirteen years," I said, wondering what the hell he wanted. He knew good and well how long; he knew everything about me, and about everybody else in the department, but there was more to come, a lot more. He began to question me in depth, about both the professional and personal aspects of my life. Questions about my career were okay, and to be expected, but I was decidedly uncomfortable when he asked about my relationships, especially with Henry Finkle sitting there grinning like an idiot. So I did my best to bob and weave. But in the end, when the name Harry Starke came up, I drew the line and informed him that my personal life was my own and that I wouldn't talk about it further.

I expected him to push the issue, but he didn't. Instead, he nodded, then asked, "Do you like your job, Catherine?"

Like my job? Catherine? Nobody calls me that. What the hell?

"Yes, Chief. I do. Why do you ask?"

He tilted his head sideways and looked me in the eyes.

"Why, exactly, do you like your job?"

What the hell kind of question is that? Am I about to get fired?

I thought for a minute, then said, "There's no good answer to that, Ch—"

Finkle sniggered, interrupting me. I cut him a sharp look. He grinned back at me, unperturbed. Johnston acted like he hadn't heard.

"As I was saying," I continued, trying hard not to roll my eyes. "There's no good answer to the question. I'm a cop, a good one, and I enjoy it. It's what I do. Always will."

He nodded. "Good enough... So, I have something special, something new, I'd like to try. It has your name written all over it. Do you want it?"

When the chief asks a question like that, there's really only one way to answer. But what the hell, it was time to buck the system.

I held his gaze and said, "That depends on what it is."

I thought he was going to explode.

Finkle sniggered again.

"That's enough, Henry," Johnston said, almost too quietly for me to hear. Finkle nodded and smiled at me like my demise was imminent.

The chief stared sternly at me for a long moment then, to my surprise, he shook his head and chuckled. I was completely taken aback.

"That's my Kate," he said. "All right, Lieutenant, I'll tell you. I've decided to create a new department, a cold case squad if you will, and you're it—you and your partner."

He glanced at Lonnie, then looked back at me and continued. "And when I say, 'you're it,' I mean exactly that, just the two of you. You will, of course, have access to any of our resources you may need, including forensics. I'll consider requests for extra manpower, of course, but those must go through Assistant Chief Finkle. Now, are you up for it?"

"Well...yes, I suppose, but why me?"

"As you said yourself, Lieutenant: you're a good cop. You're an even better detective, one of my best. Your talents are wasted chasing down drive-bys and domestics. We have a backlog of unsolved homicides that goes back decades. I'd like to see some progress on those, and I'd like for you to begin with these."

He leaned forward and pushed a pile of file folders across the desk toward me.

"There are plenty more where they came from, hundreds more. The one on top, the Sullivan case, I'd like you to make a priority. It's... well, let's put it this way, I knew Rhonda Sullivan. No, she wasn't a friend, just someone I knew. It's a strange case, as you'll see when you get into the file—no, don't look at it now, later.

"You should also know that I've scheduled an official launch for the squad, a party... Well, a reception at the Chattanoogan on Wednesday evening at seven o'clock. The mayor has agreed to attend, so will I, along with several senior officers and, of course, so will the press, and so will you and Sergeant Guest. The reception will also be open to the general public."

Oh hell, that sounds like it will be a blast.

The Chattanoogan is an upscale, downtown resort hotel. I'd been to several functions there, so I was quite familiar with it.

I glanced at Lonnie and inwardly shook my head at the supercilious look on his face. I think he was flattered to be included. *Give him time,* I thought. *Give him time.*

I looked at Finkle. He'd not said a word. His face was now expressionless.

"Yes, sir, but I have a question. I have a full caseload—"

"Yes, of course you do," Johnston interrupted. "Henry and I have already discussed it, and he's agreed to take care of it. Please have everything turned over to him by close of day. Well, that's it, I think. Thank you, Lieutenant. I'll see you at the reception. That will be all."

I looked at my watch. The meeting had gone on a lot longer than I thought it had. *Damn, it's already three o'clock.*

"Yes, sir. Thank you, sir!" I said, rising to my feet.

He nodded, looked up at me and said, "Don't let me down, Kate."

"No, sir. I won't."

I gathered up the files, handed them off to Lonnie, and we left. I could feel Finkle's eyes on my ass as I walked to the door and pulled it open. I turned my head and cut him a look I fervently hoped would shrivel his...

BACK IN MY OFFICE, I HAD LONNIE DUMP THE FILES ON MY credenza and then go fetch us some coffee while I cleared the open homicide cases off my desk. He was back in a matter of minutes before I'd even made a start. He shouldered through the door bearing two large mugs of what we laughingly called coffee.

"You need some help?" he asked as he plonked himself down in front of my desk, making it clear that he hoped I didn't.

"No, Lonnie. Just sit there, drink your coffee, and watch while I do all the work." The sarcasm was lost on him.

I took a sip of my coffee and looked at my watch. *Less than two hours.*

End of day for Henry Finkle meant five o'clock, and I knew I could expect him to be right on time. *Damn it all to hell! I wanted to at least be able to glance through the chief's file.*

I got busy. I tidied and closed three of the open files I'd been working on that morning and set them to one side. The reports within were up-to-date so I felt good about handing them off as they were. The rest of my workload, more than a dozen open cases, I organized into some sort of order and then shoved them into two plastic postal-style totes. It was all straightforward enough.

Oh, don't run away with the idea that I was done with any of it. That's not the way things happen. I would have to bring the individual detectives who received them up to speed on each case as they assimilated them into their own caseloads, and I'd be on call to answer questions from said detectives for at least a couple of weeks.

"So, what are you thinking?" Lonnie asked as I dumped the last three files into the tote and closed the lid.

As I looked down at my empty desktop that afternoon, I suddenly realized it was a sight I hadn't seen in the more than five years since I'd been promoted back in 2010. *Wow!*

"About what?" I asked as I retrieved the cold case files from the credenza and dropped them in the middle of the desk.

"Come on, LT. You know what. Cold Case Squad? What kinda bull is that? What's the old man thinkin' of?"

"Well, it's been done before, with some success, I believe, especially now with the advances in forensic science."

"Yeah, but—"

"Lonnie," I said as I slapped my hand down on the top of the pile. "These are all homicides, unsolved. That means there are people—families, mothers, fathers, sons, daughters—out there who want answers, justice, not to mention the killers that are roaming around out there, killers that could do it again. Some of them may already have."

I stared thoughtfully down at the pile of manila folders, then looked up at him and said, quietly, "You want out, Lonnie? I can arrange that." I said it with a smile, but he took it literally and bestowed a hurt look on me.

"No. 'Course not. I was just sayin'."

"Yeah, I know," I said as I sat down behind my desk. "Let's just enjoy the moment, okay. I have a feeling our new department will be like a donkey's gallop: soon over. As I said, it's not the first time, and it probably won't be the last. So, let's make a start."

I picked up the folder at the top of the pile, the Sullivan Case, and then the one beneath it. "Here," I said, handing it to him. "Take a look at this one." It was a slim, faded folder, less than a half-inch thick. The name and date *John Doe 367: January 11, 2001* typed on the label. "See what you can make of it."

He nodded, took it from me, sat down facing me across the desk, opened it, and began flipping through its contents.

Me? I picked up the Sullivan file, of course. The one Johnston had made clear was to be my priority. I flipped through the pages: the autopsy report, the detectives' reports, evidence lists, a DVD, and a stack of photographs. Then I set everything aside except for the DVD.

"Hey," I said. "Stick this in the player, would you please?" I handed him the jewel case.

As he did so, I sorted through the clutter in my desk drawer, found the remote, turned on the player, and settled down to watch. Lonnie turned his chair so that he could watch too.

The video was quite short, a little more than fifteen minutes, and was shot entirely inside the victim's apartment. Other than several minutes of footage of the victim lying face down on her bed, there was little of interest. The videographer had, with the exception of the body and the bedroom, shot only overall views of the two-bedroom apartment. The place was pristine: the bathroom clean, spotless. The personal items on the vanity were tidy and unremarkable. Her clothes were hung neatly in her closet. The interiors of the dresser, nightstand, and bathroom drawers were tidy. Everything was neatly arranged. *Maybe too neat. Was she OCD, I wonder?*

The kitchen was the same. It looked as if it had never been used and likewise the second bedroom. It was also spotless and tidy. The one anomaly was the body in the victim's bedroom.

The victim, as I said, was lying face down, and I do mean *face down,* at an angle across her bed. She was wearing a floral dress that appeared to be undisturbed. *Sexual abuse? Doesn't look like it.* I checked the autopsy report—*Nope.*

Her face was hidden in the bed linen, her arms stretched straight down alongside her. Her hands, palms down, were touching her hips, fingers curled, not quite fists. *Looks staged.*

Her feet were bare and sticking out maybe twelve inches off the bed, toes down, and from those alone it was easy to see that she'd been dead for quite some time: from the mid-soles to the tips of her toes, they were almost black. Lividity was fully set. *So, at least eight hours, then.* Again, I checked the autopsy report. *Twenty to twenty-four hours. Time of death on Sunday, sometime between nine PM and midnight.* That according to Doc Sheddon, who attended the crime scene and did the autopsy.

I ran the video several times, hoping something would catch my eye, but there was nothing, not a damn thing. Even her hair looked tidy. I froze the video at a point where we had a good shot of the body.

I stared at it for a moment, then sighed and looked quizzically at Lonnie.

"What d'you make of it?" I asked.

He cocked his head. "Looks staged to me. Someone laid her out like a board, but why would they do that? It makes no sense. It doesn't look natural."

Yeah, that's it, like a board.

"To hide something, maybe?" I said.

"Like what? A weapon? Hardly."

I pushed the file to one side and spread out the stack of eight-by-ten color photographs.

"Come and look," I said as I gazed at the array of images.

He came around the desk and stood behind me.

Most of the images were wide-angle shots taken inside the apartment; several of them were of the body, taken from various angles. Some were taken during the autopsy. One shot, in particular, caught my eye. It was a close-up of the inner fold of her elbow. Now I knew why the arms had been positioned the way they were. The entire underside of the arm was dark purple: lividity, but right in the center of the elbow crease, it was just possible to see a tiny bruise, which was obviously the subject of the photo. What it was, I had no idea.

All except nine of the photos, including those taken at the

autopsy, were signed on the back and dated 10/9/2006; the others were taken a day later on Tuesday, October 10.

One was of a detective, whom I didn't recognize, standing inside a dumpster and holding up what appeared to be a large, white plastic bag with red drawstrings. The second photo was a closeup of the bag itself. It was lying on the floor beside the dumpster and appeared to be about three-fourths full. There was another photo of the same bag —open this time with its contents in a pile on the floor. Visible among those contents was a second, smaller plastic bag: a well-known supermarket grocery bag, the top of which had been twisted and tied in a knot. A fourth photograph was a closeup of the grocery bag and its contents.

I picked it up, handed it to Lonnie, and said, "The murder weapon, I think. Where did they find it, I wonder?"

He took it from me, and as I turned back to my desk, I happened to look at my watch. It was just a few minutes short of five o'clock. *No way. Damn. Tiny will be here in a minute. I should—*

"Here, gimme that," I said, snatching the photograph from his hand. "I have to get the rest of my stuff to Finkle. I'll have to continue this tomorrow," I said as I ejected the disk from the player, scooped up the reports and photos and returned everything to the file. But it was too late, the door burst open and in he sauntered.

"Oh, don't stop what you're doing on my account." He dropped his tight little ass into the seat Lonnie had just vacated, crossed his legs, folded his arms, and...yeah, he grinned the grin. Inwardly, I shuddered, but outwardly I smiled at him and said," We're all done, Chief. Just wrapping it up so that I could turn those over to you." I nodded toward the two totes in the corner.

He looked at his watch. "A little early, don't you think? You must have a hot date. Anyone I know?"

I ignored the question and said, "Lonnie, give the assistant chief a hand with those two totes. They're probably more than he can handle by himself."

The grin now had teeth and was fixed.

"Now, gentlemen," I said, lightly. "I have some calls to make, work-related of course." That was only partly true, but what the hell?

Somewhat reluctantly, I thought, Finkle stood and waited for Lonnie, who rounded my desk and grabbed one of the totes.

"Where to, Chief?" he asked.

"My office, of course. I'll talk to you later, Lieutenant."

He waited until Lonnie left my office. "You should know, Lieutenant, that I advised Johnston not to give you this assignment. I don't think you're up to it." He glared at me then stepped over to the corner and lifted the remaining tote, one-handed. *The man has something to prove, methinks.*

"Don't think I won't be watching you," he said. "Screw it up and..." He didn't finish his thought. Instead he walked out the door, the tote swinging from his right hand almost dragging on the floor.

I WAITED UNTIL HE CLOSED THE DOOR BEHIND HIM, THEN called Harry Starke.

Back then, Harry and I had what one might call a semi-serious relationship ever since he'd left the police department more than three years earlier, even longer than that if the truth be told. Serious? Hah, for me more than him, I think. He'd finally crossed the line a few months earlier, during the Harper investigation. He had one little fling too many, so we split up, sort of. I tried to distance myself from him, but he was a tough habit to break.

We were supposed to have a date that evening; I wanted to confirm.

Harry was an ex-cop turned private detective, and he was a good one. He ran a private investigation agency in Chattanooga. He was also something of an anomaly: he was extremely wealthy although, by looking at him then, you'd never have known it. Most of the time he was dressed down: jeans, tee, leather jacket, that sort of thing. When he did bother to dress up, it was rarely anything more than dress pants and a golf shirt. He was extremely tough, and back in the day, my day, he had his weaknesses, especially where women were concerned. Oh, he didn't chase after them, well, rarely, but he had a tough time saying no when they chased after him. He was, after all, single, and he'd made no promises to me, though I'd assumed... Okay, I'm rambling again, so that's enough of that. Let's just say that when all this happened, we were still something of an item.

"Hey, Harry," I said when he answered my call.

"Hey, Kate. What's up?"

"We still on for this evening?"

"Of course. Why d'you ask? I made a reservation at the club. Is that okay? I can cancel it if it's not."

"No reason. I was confirming. The club's fine. Meet you at your place about seven?"

"I can pick you up if you like."

"No, I can't stay over. I need an early night. So, seven?"

"Why's that?"

"Umm...well, I have a new job. Look, I can't talk about it now. I'll tell you about it tonight, okay? So, seven?"

"Seven it is." And he hung up before I could say more.

A couple of times Harry had helped out as a sort of unpaid consultant, to good effect—the Harper case had made him famous. But I caught all sorts of crap for it, both from the chief and Finkle, especially from Finkle. Then the chief's daughter went missing and he, the chief, for reasons he never explained, would let nobody near it but Harry. Harry, however, insisted that the chief turn me loose to work with him which, under protest, he did. Funny how things work out.

So, that night, I wanted to run the Sullivan thing by Harry, to see if he'd heard anything.

I looked thoughtfully at the now black screen of my iPhone, and then placed it face down on my desk, reached for the office phone, called Doc Sheddon, and made an appointment to see him the following afternoon at two o'clock.

3

Harry's condo was situated on the north side of the river, on Lakeshore Lane. It must have cost him a small fortune, and another one to decorate and furnish it. His place was comfortable, elegant, with a stunning view of the Tennessee River and, in the distance, the Thrasher Bridge. At night, the panoramic view from the huge picture window in his living room was stunning... I loved that condo almost as much as I did Harry.

Knowing where I was going that evening, and with whom, and even though it was only Thursday, I'd dressed with some care. I have a thing for black. I think it complements my hair, but that's just me. I'm not into fashion... Well, not so much. Anyway, I decided to wear a version of the quintessential "little black dress," crimson pumps with four-inch heels, and to carry an envelope clutch that matched the shoes. For jewelry, I wore a slim gold chain with a tiny cross around my neck and my grandmother's antique gold wristwatch. Makeup? I never wear much, usually just some lipstick, mascara, and a little blush.

Advantage to me, Harry, I remember thinking as I did a final check in front of the mirror. *The heels make me six-three, an inch taller than you.* Yeah, I felt good. The more so when I saw his face as I walked into his living room that evening. Yes, I still had a key to his condo.

He was standing in front of the great window with a drink in his hand, looking out over the river. And he looked good: black golf slacks and shirt and black loafers.

He turned and watched as I walked toward him; he was smiling.

"Wow," was all he said. He would probably have said more, but I stopped him with a kiss, just a peck on the lips.

He set the glass down on the coffee table and kissed me properly. I closed my eyes and let my emotions take over, but not for long. Such things had a habit of getting out of hand, and I'm not just talking about Harry. Let's just say I enjoyed the long moment and then pushed him away.

He didn't resist. Above all things, Harry Starke was a gentleman. He did, however, unconsciously lick his lips. I couldn't help but smile.

"Drink?" he asked.

"Of course, but just one. I have to drive home."

"No, you don't," he said. "You can stay here. You always do...did."

"Yes, well not tonight. I have a big day tomorrow." I took the half-glass of red from him and sipped appreciatively. Harry loves fine wine, old scotch whiskey, and strong coffee: the red was glorious, and I suddenly had the feeling that I might be staying over after all.

He looked at his watch.

"It's time we left," he said. "Unless..."

"Uh, *no!*" I said. "I'm hungry. I intend to murder a ten-ounce filet, so?"

He nodded, set his glass down and put his hands on my shoulders.

"Wait," I said, and put my glass down beside his. Then I wrapped my arms around his neck, pulled him to me, and once again let my emotions take over: the filet had to wait.

It was almost nine o'clock when we finally sat down at Harry's favorite table at the club, in the bay window overlooking the ninth green.

The steak was amazing, the wine superb, and I was totally at ease, my hunger—not only for food—satisfied completely.

While we ate, I filled Harry in on the events of the day: I told him about my new assignment. He didn't seem particularly impressed. I asked him why.

"Kate, it's been done so many times before. Rarely does it ever end well for the officer in charge. Most cold cases are cold for a reason —lack of evidence. Most of them are unsolvable, and that makes for soul-destroying work. I don't envy you. I hope it goes well."

He gave me a sly smile before continuing. "By the way. When are you going to take me up on my offer and come work for me?"

"Not going to happen, Harry. Being friends is one thing, coworkers would be quite another."

It wasn't the first time he'd asked the question; he always asked. The answer I gave him was always the same.

"Friends?" he asked. "Is that all we are?"

"You know it is," I said, cutting him a look and quickly changing the subject.

"Harry, do you remember the Sullivan case?"

He sighed, shook his head, sorrowfully, thought for a minute, then said, "Yes...vaguely? In oh-six, I think. As I recall there wasn't much to it. I believe there was a suspect, though, a nurse? They were never able to tag him with it though. Wells, I think was the lead investigator; Steve Wells. He retired years ago. So, you caught that one, huh? Again, I don't envy you."

I often wonder how he does it. I think he must have an eidetic memory. He says he doesn't, but he never forgets even the smallest thing.

"There was a suspect?" I asked. I hadn't gotten that far into the reports, but I had noticed the three headshots among the photos, besides that of the victim.

"Yes, a male nurse. That's about all I remember. I had nothing to do with it. You'll need to talk to Wells if he's still alive. Last I heard, he was pretty sick."

"So, you can't help me, then?"

"Nope, and I'm betting no one else can. Wells was a good detective, one of the best. If he couldn't close it, I very much doubt anyone can. You'll find it's a dead end."

"Gee, Harry. Thanks for the vote of confidence."

He shook his head. "It is what it is. Go see Wells."

And, try as I might, I could drag nothing further out of him, at least about the Sullivan case.

All in all though, it was a lovely evening; evenings with Harry always were. I had no hesitation when he suggested we go back to his place: I agreed.

4

Needless to say, I was late into work the following morning and who should be waiting for me in my office? Assistant Chief Henry Finkle of course. *Damn,* I thought. *Any other day...*

"It's almost nine o'clock, Lieutenant," he said, sneering at me without getting up, looking me up and down. "Anything I should know about?" The question was filled with innuendo.

"No, I don't think so," I said as I sat down behind my desk. "Should there be?"

"Why are you late? Another wild night with Starke?"

"That, Chief, is none of your damn business. I'm late because there's a wreck on Amnicola, as Sergeant Mayfield in Traffic will confirm." It wasn't the whole truth, but true enough. "Now, is there anything else I can help you with? If not, I have a busy day."

"What are you going to do about the Sullivan case? Chief Johnston asked me to keep an eye on it—"

"Oh, he did?" I interrupted him. "I wonder why. Let's see, shall we?" I reached for my phone.

"There's no need for that," he said, quickly, rising from his seat. "Just make sure you keep me informed. Understood?"

I nodded, smirking at him, and he left my office, slamming the door behind him.

I buzzed Lonnie.

"Hey, come on back. Let's talk," I said when he picked up. "Oh, and bring the Doe file with you."

I wanted to get on with the Sullivan case, but I needed to clear the decks first. To do that, I needed to sort through the rest of the cold files, and to do that I needed help.

Detective Sergeant Lonnie Guest is an enigma. Back then, in the early days of our partnership, I had it in my head that he was something of an idiot; he could act really stupid. Later, much later, I realized that he wasn't stupid at all. It was a persona he actively cultivated. He was the latest in a growing list of partners I'd had foisted on me, mostly because no one else could work with them. Lonnie was dumped on me right out of uniform while I was working the Congressman Gordon Harper case.

Anyway, as I said, Lonnie's not quite as stupid as he would have you believe. In fact, at times, he can be positively brilliant. Physically, he's a big man... No, damn it—at the risk of being non-PC—back then he was fat. He needed to lose sixty or seventy pounds.

You know, on thinking about it, though, I guess the extra weight was a big part of his problem. For sure, he could be a real ass: obnoxious, arrogant. But underneath it all there was a softer side to Lonnie Guest, and you know what? Even then, I kinda liked him, felt comfortable with him.

So, we spent the next hour that morning sorting through the files. There were nine of them; all more than five years cold. The Sullivan case, even after what I'd learned from Harry the night before, I had no option but to deal with right away. The other eight—well, okay, I'm one of those orderly people that like to deal with my projects one at a time, though that's rarely ever possible in a busy department such as ours... Look, if I'm rambling, you'll have to forgive me, but I have to set the stage.

Anyway, that's what I intended to do with the Sullivan case as soon as I cleared my desk. I set it aside, along with the John Doe file—Lonnie had already made a start on that—and together we skimmed through the other seven files.

We discussed each in turn, briefly, making notes along the way and, finally, prioritizing them as best we could. That done, I turned the whole lot of them over to Lonnie with instructions to go through them all again, in detail, and report back to me with his thoughts.

With Lonnie out of the way, it was my intention to devote the next couple of hours to Sullivan, and I was itching to get at it. I checked the time; it was almost eleven-thirty. I went to get more coffee and, on the way back, put out the word that, unless someone died, I wasn't to be disturbed.

Back in my office, I set my coffee on my desk and picked up the somewhat dog-eared manila file folder labeled, *Rhonda Sullivan, October 9, 2006* which was the date the file was opened and the day after Rhonda died. The back of the folder had been signed by the detectives that had followed up on the case over the years: five of them. I added mine to the bottom of the list and dated it, and then opened the file.

First, I extracted the stack of photos and the DVD and set them aside. Then I made a copy of the autopsy report and set it aside also, returning the original to the folder. That done, I stood and taped the photos to my dry-erase board, the photo of Rhonda Sullivan at the top center. The three headshots—two male and one female—I added side-by-side just below Rhonda's. The names meant nothing to me, not then, but I added them to the board under their respective picture with a marker. *At least I know who's who.*

Finally, I taped the rest of the images to the board and stood back, staring at the three unsmiling faces.

I went back to my chair, leaned back, and stared intently at each of the twenty-six images in turn.

Not a damn thing! I thought. *Nothing... No trace, no prints, no blood, nothing but the grocery bag... It wasn't recovered until the next day. What's that about? I need to read the reports.* And I did, and that pretty much accounted for the next couple of hours, and then some, and I learned almost nothing.

Harry was right; it looked impossible. Rhonda Sullivan's body had been found by her friend, Lisa Marco, lying on her bed at around ten-fifteen on the morning of Monday, October 9, 2006, and she called 911. Detective Steve Wells had been first on the scene. Doc Sheddon, the ME, had arrived at five after eleven. He made a cursory examination of the body, then turned the scene over to Wells who, for some reason not mentioned in the report, didn't like what he saw. He in turn called in Lieutenant Mike Willis, our CSI commander, and his team.

CSI found almost nothing in the victim's apartment. The only physical evidence they recovered was an empty wine bottle and a glass found on the nightstand beside the body. They were dusted for fingerprints and tested for DNA. The only prints they found belonged to the victim; the same with DNA. If it hadn't been for the position of the body, all would have seemed perfectly normal.

It appeared that Sullivan must have been drinking alone when she died; she'd celebrated her twenty-sixth birthday only five days earlier.

It wasn't until the next morning when Wells received a call from Doc Sheddon urging him to go back to the scene that things took a turn for the better. At least that's how it seemed at the time.

Wells, having noted the empty trash can in the apartment kitchen, had decided to check the dumpster that served the small apartment complex. Inside it, he found a "tall" kitchen garbage bag that, from the examination of its contents, had obviously been removed from the trash can in the victim's apartment. The contents of the bag included the usual kitchen garbage, some wet and some—well, you get the idea, and a plastic grocery bag from a nearby super-market. It also contained several items personal to the victim, mostly bills—utilities and credit cards—along with their envelopes. All had her name and address on them, so it was thereby established beyond a doubt that the kitchen bag had come from the victim's apartment.

It was the contents of the supermarket grocery bag, however, that included the heart stopper, literally: two vials labeled KCL injectable potassium chloride. The grocery bag also contained a—*Oh yeah. Here we go*—hypodermic syringe and cap, and two swabs.

All of the items in the grocery bag were checked for fingerprints. None were found. Everything had been wiped clean; either that, or the killer had worn gloves. DNA recovered from the swabs and syringe was confirmed to be that of Rhonda Sullivan. No other DNA was present.

Okay, I thought. *Why would anyone throw evidence like this away, where it could be found? Why not get rid of it someplace else? On the other hand, who knows why killers do what they do? Arrogance, maybe? Overconfidence? Me? I would have taken the stuff with me and dumped it far, far away. Whoever the killer was didn't think it would be found, I suppose.*

But it was found. According to the autopsy report, Doc Sheddon, Hamilton County's Chief Medical Examiner, had found the injection site—the tiny bruise in the photo—during the post mortem, barely visible amid the lividity. *Surely the killer would have known that it would be found... Then again, it was almost ten years ago. Not so much CSI on TV back then. Still... But that indicates the killer knew all about lividity... Medical background? And why potassium chloride? Maybe the killer had easy access to the drug.* I glanced up at the photographs. *The nurse, Chad Pellman! Had to be.*

And so I continued digging through the case file.

Using the product serial numbers on the vials, Detective Wells had traced the potassium chloride to a local trauma center. Pellman, age twenty-seven, worked there in the emergency room, as did Sullivan's friend, Lisa Marco, who'd found the body; both were ICU nurses.

The two vials had been checked out of an automatic dispenser located inside the ER a week before the murder. And, according to the trauma center's records, it was Pellman who'd checked them out. *Surely, he couldn't have been that stupid.*

Apparently, users of the dispenser had to enter their employee number. The records showed that it was Pellman's employee number that had been used to check out the drug. He, of course, strongly denied it, insisting someone else must have used his number to access the dispenser. And from there the story got even more bizarre. It wasn't the first time that Pellman had been accused of reckless and unauthorized use of the dispenser; he'd done it before, and he'd been disciplined for it. *So why the hell would he do it again? He would have had to have known that the stuff would be traced back to him—if it was found, of course—which, if he did do it, he figured wouldn't happen. Whew.*

Wells narrowed the short list of suspects down to two: Chad Pellman and Sullivan's friend Lisa Marco. The fiancé Yates, the other male headshot, didn't have the medical background that would have been needed to administer the drug, so he was eliminated as a suspect.

Both suspects had alibis. Even so, Wells had managed to build a case, a somewhat weak, circumstantial case, against Pellman. His interview with the male nurse was also weak. Pellman insisted that it wasn't he that had stolen the drug that killed her, but her friend, Lisa Marco. Marco, however, at least as far as Wells could determine, had an alibi for the time of death. She was, however, on duty at the time the drugs were taken from the dispenser, but most important: she had no motive.

Not so Pellman. It was established that he knew the victim and that he had a crush on her, but she managed to keep him at arm's length. So, there you go, you'd think it was cut and dried, right? Detective Wells certainly did. He figured he had a pretty strong case against Pellman, but it was all circumstantial. His—Pellman's—finger-prints had not been found anywhere, not in the apartment, on the tall kitchen bag, the small grocery bag, the vials, syringe, nowhere. So

Wells couldn't physically link him to the crime scene, the murder weapon, the potassium chloride—anybody that knew his employee number could have gotten it. And there was even more. Pellman had a rock-solid alibi; he was out of town on October 8 when the murder took place. He was at his mother's home in Winchester, Tennessee.

Wells had asked him to take a polygraph which, on advice from his lawyer, he'd refused.

Eventually, Wells took the case to the District Attorney, but it was a lost cause: no charges were ever filed. What little evidence there was, wasn't strong enough. Pellman was never charged.

I read through the reports until finally I reached Wells' closing report. It was surprising in that it was so short, both on words and information. I got the distinct impression that he, Wells, was somewhat pissed. It was dated November 17, 2007, a little more than a year after the murder. Essentially, he'd given up and shelved the case.

Finally, I leaned back in my chair and stared up at the photographs of Yates, Pellman and Marco.

So, I thought, as I nibbled on a fingernail, *Pellman has an alibi, so does Marco. Yates didn't have the expertise to administer the drug. There's no physical evidence linking either Pellman or Marco to the scene or the weapon. Marco's fingerprints were found only on the doorknob, as you'd expect. No wonder the damn thing went cold... My money's on the male nurse. There are too many coincidences. One is okay, but two? Not likely, and I count at least five: he has a medical background; his code was used to check out the drugs; he knew the victim, had a crush on her, for Pete's sake; he'd been caught using the dispenser without authorization before, and he tried to frame Marco... Oh yeah; it's him, but how the hell am I supposed to prove it nine years after? Damn. I'll have to go back and start at the beginning, I suppose.*

Okay, I'm seeing Doc at two. Who else do I need to see?

I opened Notes on my iPad, and then my mind went blank. I stared at the empty screen, chewed gently on the tip of my thumbnail.

I started a numbered list, typed the word Doc, thought for a bit, looked up at the photos, then typed some more:

1. Doc
2. Chad Pellman – Nurse
3. Lisa Marco – Friend: Accused by Pellman. Alibi for TOD but not Dispenser.
4. Pellman's mother – Alibi?
5. Talk to co-workers
6. Lead detective, Steve Wells

I stared at the short list. *Is that all I've got? This is going to be a bitch... Pellman's co-workers...and what about that alibi? It's either fake, or he's not the killer. No one can be in two places at once. Hmmm... Time of death? No! Doc would not have gotten that wrong. Well maybe, I wouldn't dare ask him about it...but I have to.*

I shook my head, frustrated, then thought for a minute, and decided to move Wells up the list. Then I called him. His voice was breathless. I could barely understand him, but I was able to make an appointment to see him the following morning, Saturday. He seemed excited at the prospect.

And then I wrapped it up for the day, collected Lonnie, and went to keep my appointment with Doc Sheddon. After that...the dreaded reception.

5

Doc Sheddon was waiting for us in his office.

"Hello Kate, Lonnie," he said, standing up and reached across his desk to shake my hand. "It's nice to see you both. I was surprised to get your call. I'd almost forgotten the Sullivan case; had to read up on my notes."

Doc's a sweet little man, five-eightish, a little overweight, almost totally bald, with a round face and a jolly disposition.

"Take a seat." He waved me toward the single chair set in front of his desk. "Lonnie, drag that one over and sit down."

"So, Kate, I understand you've been assigned the case. That's good, but I hope you do better than those who've gone before you. They didn't do so well."

"Yes, I know, which is why the chief dumped it on me, I suppose."

"You do know we have a good idea who the killer was?" he asked. "We just can't prove it."

"Yes. I read the file and your report. You're talking about Chad Pellman, correct?"

He nodded, squinted at me over the top of his half-glasses, scratched the top of his bald head, and then reached for a slim file that was lying on top of his desk.

"He might have gotten away with it... Yes, yes, I know. He has gotten away with it, so far. But if I hadn't been the ME," he said, not at all modestly, "the potassium chloride might never have been found. The cause of death would probably have been recorded as natural causes due to a heart attack."

He smiled at me, leaned back in his chair, then continued. "There was absolutely nothing untoward about the body: no trauma, no bruises, no wounds, no bleeding. But I could see right away that there was something unusual about the position of the body. It didn't look natural. It looked as if it had been positioned very carefully, the arms in particular." He opened the file, extracted a photo and pushed it across the desk. I'd seen it before; it was on my board, but Lonnie and I looked at it anyway. Doc continued. "Why? I thought. But I already knew: lividity, young lady, lividity."

Young lady? That's funny.

Lividity, or livor mortis, in case you're unfamiliar with it, is the settling of the blood in a body after the heart stops pumping. Blood is a liquid, so it naturally flows to the lowest point; it's all about gravity. It generally becomes noticeable quite quickly and usually becomes fixed some eight to twelve hours after death.

Anyway, I nodded, agreeably. He waited for me to speak. I didn't. He looked at Lonnie; he didn't speak either.

"Lividity? You may ask," he said hopefully.

I didn't. Only smiled. I knew he would get there. He was simply making the most of his moment.

"Lividity," he said, impatiently. "Catherine, people do not lie face down with their arms stretched alongside them in that manner. It was damned unnatural. So that started me thinking that it must have been a homicide, and the killer must have positioned her that way to hide something. What it was I didn't know for sure, not at that moment. But I had a good idea, and I also knew that whoever had killed her knew how lividity works. Yes, I examined the arms while the body was still undisturbed, but I found nothing..."

He paused expectantly, grunted, and then continued. "I found nothing, but I knew damn well it had to be there, had to be, which is why I did the post-mortem examination first thing the next morning. And I found it. A tiny, tiny injection site here." He pointed to the crook of his left arm. "The slight amount of bruising caused by the insertion of the syringe was almost obscured by the *lividity*." He emphasized the word, almost shouted it, then folded his arms, and leaned back in his chair, grinning broadly.

Of course, I knew all that from reading the autopsy report, but hearing it from the master himself was—well, entertaining, to say the least.

"And?" I asked.

"And?" he asked. "And what? Oh, I see. Well, I sent old Wells right back out to see if he could find anything. I didn't know at the time what the injected substance might be, but I knew it had to be something, and I hoped that some indication of what it was would still be there, somewhere. And, well, well, well." He smiled widely at his terribly unfunny joke. "It was: two empty vials of potassium chloride, along with a hypodermic syringe. Potassium chloride is an extremely strong drug. It's used to treat patients with low levels of potassium in their blood. When injected, it's quickly metabolized into potassium and chloride, both of which are normally present in the body. An overdose, however—even a small one—can cause death very quickly, in a matter of seconds. It causes severe heart arrhythmias, and the heart spasms out of control and finally stops functioning. Essentially, the victim suffers a heart attack or SCD—sudden cardiac death."

"But it didn't show in the tox screen," Lonnie said. "Surely it—"

"No, it didn't, and it wouldn't, because as I mentioned a moment ago, potassium and chloride are normally present in the body. Yes, the levels would be elevated, but even that would normally go unnoticed, because a heart attack in and of itself will also produce elevated levels of potassium and chloride."

"So, for the killer to know all that he must have been a medical professional?" Lonnie asked.

Sheddon nodded. "To administer such a drug? I would say so."

"You were saying, Doc?" I asked.

"During the second search of Sullivan's apartment, Wells noticed that the trash can in the kitchen was empty; no bag, no trash. So he went and checked out the dumpster, and there it was. Boy, did we get lucky? The body was found on a Monday. If it had been found a day later, Tuesday, we would've missed it: the dumpster was scheduled to be emptied first thing Wednesday morning, always on Wednesdays, early, usually around seven. It was obviously a great find, Kate. Not just from an evidentiary point of view, but because I wouldn't normally screen for potassium chloride...but then again who knows?" He tilted his to one side, then said, "I might have."

"Okay," I said. "We have the murder weapon. We know where it came from. And we think we know who the killer is, but we can't prove it. We can't tie Pellman to either the crime scene or the weapon, and he has an alibi." I stared across the desk at Doc Sheddon.

I took a deep breath and took the plunge. "Doctor Sheddon," I said. He straightened in his chair, obviously made wary by the formality of the address. "Is there any chance, any chance at all that you might have gotten the time of death wrong?" Inwardly, I cringed, waiting for the explosion; it never came.

He simply nodded, and said, "I thought you might ask that. The answer, of course, is no. She died between the hours of nine o'clock in the evening and midnight, as it says in my report." He took it from the file and glanced at it. "I arrived at the scene shortly after eleven on the morning of the ninth. Lividity was fully fixed. The application of pressure had no effect; the color remained constant. That alone meant that she'd been dead for more than eight hours."

Again, he glanced at his report, then continued. "The body

temperature was eighty-one point two degrees. That indicates a time of death of at least twelve hours. Rigor Mortis? The body was stiff as a damn board... Shall I go on? There's more."

"No," I said. "I'm sorry, Doc, but I had to ask."

"I know. I understand."

I looked at him across the desk.

"You have a question?" he asked.

"Not really... Look, Pellman has a solid alibi. I'm pretty certain that he's our killer, but he couldn't have been in two places at once, so if you're absolutely certain of the time of death—"

He opened his mouth to speak, but I held up my hand and stopped him. "I know," I said. "I know. I'm not questioning you, but how the hell did he do it?"

"That, young lady, is your job. You're the detective."

I sighed, looked at Lonnie, shook my head and said, "Yeah, well. That's a whole lot easier said than done."

I looked up at the clock on the wall behind him. It was just after three o'clock; time for me to call it a day and go get ready for the reception that evening.

"Well," I said. "I guess that's it, then, at least for now. Unless..."

He smiled. "If I think of anything, I'll call you. In the meantime, if there's anything more I can do let me know."

There wasn't, and I never felt more helpless.

I stood. "Thanks, Doc. I'll let you know. Right now, I have a reception to attend."

"Good luck with that," he said as I turned to go.

I nodded, said goodbye, and we left.

Back in the cruiser at the rear of the forensic center, I turned the key, leaned my head back against the headrest and waited for the air to come on. After a couple of minutes of quiet, Lonnie said, "I think we caught us a piece o' crap, LT. That alibi's the kicker. If we can't break it, then he couldn't have done it. Where was he, by the way?"

I looked sideways at him and made a face. "He was with his mother, for Pete's sake."

"You've gotta be kiddin' me. Geez, I don't see it happening. She's not going to give him up, no matter what."

Reluctantly, I had to admit to myself that he was probably right. Pellman's mother wasn't likely to give him up. I could see no way, short of a confession, of solving the case.

"Something will come up," I said, shifting into drive. "In the meantime, we start over. We re-interview everyone, starting with Detective Wells tomorrow morning. We'll get to Pellman soon enough. In the meantime, you need to go home and get ready for the reception tonight. I'll drop you back at the office and then head home myself."

"Oh hell," he said. "I'd forgotten about that. What a great way to spend an evening. Hey, I don't suppose—"

"Don't even think about it. If I have to go, you have to go."

"*Damn!*"

6
———————

FRIDAY, MAY 8 – COLD CASE RECEPTION

I arrived home that afternoon at a little after four-thirty. It had been a long and tiring day and was about to get even longer. I needed to relax, so the first thing I did when I walked into my kitchen was grab a half-bottle of red from the refrigerator and pour myself a glass. Then I sat down in my ratty old recliner—it was comfortable if not stylish—and leaned back, closed my eyes, and sipped slowly and steadily until the glass was empty.

I was still in the chair, half asleep, when my phone buzzed on the coffee table. I picked it up and looked at the lock screen: *Harry.* I accepted the call and leaned back in the chair.

"What?" I said.

"Now is that any way to greet your best buddy, especially after last night?"

I got his drift, but I was in no mood for banter.

"I'm tired, Harry. It's been a very long day, but yes, I had a lovely time. The steak was delicious."

"Only the steak? I thought—"

I interrupted him.

"Harry, I don't have time to chat. I have to be at the reception at seven, and I haven't even begun to get ready. What is it you want?"

"You're still mad at me, aren't you? No, don't answer that; I already know. I was just checking in to see how it went with the Sullivan case today. From your tone, I'm guessing it didn't go well."

I sighed. "You're right. It didn't. You were also right last night when you told me it was a dead end. Unless I can break the nurse's alibi or get him to confess...well... Look, I have to go. Thanks for calling."

"Hey, hang on. When am I going to see you again?"

"We'll see. I'll call you. Bye, Harry."

I disconnected, put the soft rubber case of the iPhone to my lips and nibbled on it gently, thoughtfully. *Damn you, Harry Starke!*

After a few minutes, I finally managed to shake my black mood and headed for the bathroom. I showered, dried myself off, all the while running the details of the Sullivan case around in my mind. Anything was better than agonizing over Harry.

Then I debated long and hard with myself about what I should wear that evening. I decided that to avoid any negative connotations, I would wear my uniform, my dress blues.

I spent the next thirty minutes dressing and styling my hair in a bun. That done, I checked the mirror one last time: *Oh shit! I look like a security guard. I can't go looking like this.*

And so I changed into a pair of skinny jeans, a tan leather jacket over a white blouse, and shoes that made my legs look even longer. I also took my tawny blond hair down and tied it back in a ponytail. I checked the mirror: *Better!*

It was fifteen till seven when I arrived at the reception. The chief was there—he'd also dressed down, thank the Lord—and so was Assistant Chief Henry Finkle, resplendent in his dress blues. *Ha ha, he looks like he's just escaped from Disney World.*

I walked across the huge room to join them.

"Hey, wait for me," came a voice from behind me.

I looked back toward the door, Lonnie was hurrying after me, puffing like an old steam train. I waited until he caught up, and then we made our way through the crowd... Crowd? Not so much: maybe a couple of dozen civilians, many of them relatives of victims hoping for answers; several uniformed cops, including Mike Willis; and representatives from all four TV stations. The event could have been held in the chief's office.

"Good evening, Lieutenant, Sergeant Guest. You had a good day, I hope." Johnston stuck out his hand for me to shake, which I did; Finkle didn't offer his. He didn't speak at all, not then.

"Yes, sir," I replied. "I had a good day. How about you?"

"Good enough, Catherine, good enough. Now, how about we get this show on the road. Join me at the podium, both of you, please. No, Henry. Not you. Just the lieutenant and Sergeant Guest."

Finkle's face was a delight to see: his lips tightened into two white lines; his eyes narrowed to mere slits; the hatred in them was palpable. Me? I managed to keep a straight face; I didn't dare look at Lonnie as we joined the chief on the stage and turned to face the gathering.

The next ten minutes were among the most boring I'd ever endured—and the most embarrassing. The chief explained his plans for the new squad and then proceeded to praise my career and qualifications. Oh yes, it was flattering, but by the time he'd finished I was blushing like a schoolgirl, and then he handed the mike over to me to "say a few words."

I stood for a moment looking out across the room, wondering what the hell to say, and kicking myself, because I should have known I'd be expected to speak.

In the end, I simply thanked the chief for his confidence in me, and for the opportunity, assured the eyes staring up at me that I would do my best to provide the victim's families with some answers, and then I handed the mike back to the chief. It was a disaster, and Finkle lost no time telling me so.

As soon as I stepped down from the stage, he grabbed me by the arm, pulled me out of earshot, and said through clenched teeth,

"What the hell was that, Lieutenant? My chihuahua could have done better. You're an embarrassment to the chief and the department."

I snatched my arm away from him and spun on my heel to face him. "Don't you ever lay a finger on me again," I said in a tone that warned him not to mess with me. "If you do, I'll file a sexual harassment complaint against you. Now get the hell away from me."

"One of these days, Gazzara..." He didn't finish. He turned and walked quickly away and out of the room. At that moment, I figured my future looked kind of bleak, and then I brightened up and smiled to myself. *So what's new?* Then I felt something touch my arm, and I flinched.

"Oh dear," the woman said. "I didn't mean to startle you, Lieutenant Gazzara. I was just—well, I was hoping I might have a word with you."

She was about five feet six, nice figure, probably in her mid-forties but somehow looked older. The light gray dress she was wearing looked good on her but had obviously seen better days. Her auburn hair was cropped, pageboy style. Her brown eyes had a hollow look about them.

"You didn't," I said, smiling. "I don't think I know you—do I?"

"No, of course not. My name is Alice Booker. I was hoping I could talk to you about my sister. She disappeared, and nobody seems to care. Nobody's doing anything to find her."

And so it begins!

I looked at her, and then at my watch, considering my options.

"Oh, I'm sorry," she said. "Am I bothering you?" She sounded— not exactly angry—bitter.

"No, no. Of course not. It's just that you're talking about a missing person. I'm a homicide—" I'd seen the expression on her face; she looked pathetic. "I'm sorry," I said. "Would you give me just a minute, please? I'll get my partner."

I looked around the room, searching for Lonnie. He was out of the way in a far corner of the room, talking to Mike Willis. I caught his attention and waved for him to join us.

"Alice Booker, this is my partner, Sergeant Guest. Lonnie Guest, Alice Booker," I said, making the introduction. "She has a...problem she'd like to talk to us about."

They shook hands while I quickly thought about how I was going to handle the situation. Fortunately, I didn't have to. Lonnie took over.

"Mrs. Booker," he said. "I remember you. I was the desk sergeant when you filed a missing person report. It must have been...what, a couple of years ago?"

"Oh my, so you are. You were so nice. Thank you. No, it was three years ago last month. My sister, Jennifer Lewis." The tears welled up in her eyes.

"Yes, I remember," Lonnie said. "So, they didn't find her?"

"No, and they've given up looking. I haven't heard anything from Detective Tracy in more than six months. And he won't return my calls."

Tracy? No way. What the hell?

John Tracy—his nickname was Dick, for obvious reasons—was my ex-partner. He'd been foisted on me back when Harry left the PD in 2008. Apart from being a smartass and a misogynist, he was arrogant and lazy. He was also buddy-buddy with Henry Finkle. *Shit! Why can't I ever catch a break?*

"She's dead, Lieutenant," Mrs. Booker said, breaking into my thoughts. "I've always known it. We talked every day; never missed. If not in person, then on the phone. I haven't heard a word from her in more than three years. She...she's...dead." She looked up at me, tears rolling down her face. *"Can you help me, please?"* she whispered.

I looked at Lonnie. He was standing slightly behind and to her left. He nodded, slightly, though she couldn't see him.

I also nodded. "We can talk about it, but I can't promise anything. If Missing Persons still has it..."

She stared defiantly at me, slowly shaking her head. "They've done nothing in three years. Someone has to do something. Jennifer has two children..." The tears streamed down her cheeks.

"Okay," I said. "I'd like you to come to my office on Monday morning, about ten. Can you do that?"

She nodded. "Yes, I live in Farragut, south of Knoxville, but I'm staying here in town, at the Quality Inn on Shallowford Road. I can be there at ten."

"All right then. For now, I suggest you go back to your hotel and relax and try to have a nice weekend, and we'll talk on Monday."

Again, she nodded, and then, without even saying goodbye, she turned and left.

I looked at Lonnie. "What d'you think?"

"I don't know. I just took the report. I thought no more about it until just a few minutes ago. What are *you* thinking?"

"I'm thinking Tracy is a waste of skin. Other than that, I'm not thinking anything, nor will I until I've heard her story." I glanced around the room, looking for...not a damn thing.

"Geez," I said, finally. "I wish this thing would end and we could get out of here. These people are friggin' depressing."

He grinned at me. "Oh come on, LT. You love it. You know you do."

"The hell I do. And if that creepy little bastard keeps on staring at me..."

Lonnie looked around. As soon as he did, Finkle turned away, smiling. Suddenly, I felt self-conscious, out of place.

"I'm outa here, Lonnie. Go give the chief my apologies. Tell him I suddenly got sick to my stomach, which is not a friggin' lie. I'll see you at the office tomorrow morning."

And I left him standing there, grinning like the idiot he pretended to be.

7

SATURDAY, MAY 9 – SULLIVAN CASE

I was a little early when I arrived at the tiny duplex in the assisted living complex Detective Wells called home, but I thumbed the bell push anyway, and I waited. I was just about to ring the bell again when a disembodied voice emanating from a speaker hidden somewhere above the doorframe asked who the hell I was.

I had to smile. *Typical ex-cop: guns and gadgets, and possibly paranoid.*

"It's Lieutenant Gazzara, sir. We have an appointment."

"You're early, damn it. Eh, come on in."

There was a buzz and then a click. I tried the door knob. It turned, and I pushed the door open and went inside.

Steven Wells had retired from the Chattanooga PD in 2009, which made him seventy-two years old when I met with him for the first time that day. Unfortunately, the years had not treated him well: he looked ninety.

A life-long smoker, he was confined to an electric wheelchair, sucking oxygen from a tank attached to the rear of it. I'd checked his personnel file before I left the office that morning. The man had a distinguished career: he was a closer. *So why did he let this one get away?*

He was single—divorced twice—and entirely dependent upon his caregivers for his daily bread: a small, white-haired old man made even smaller by the chair he rode around in. He wasn't the only retired cop I knew that had seen better days, and I felt for him; I felt for all of them. They devoted their lives to protecting and serving and then... *Oh shit. There but for the grace of God.*

"Don't look at me like that, Lieutenant. I don't want, nor do I need your pity. I enjoyed every cigarette, every drag; no regrets. If I could, I'd still smoke. Now, d'you want to talk about Pellman or not?"

I hadn't been aware that I was staring at him, but I apologized anyway and told him I did.

"Sit yourself down then. I can't sit here lookin' up at you: makes m'neck ache."

I sat down on the sofa under the window. He rolled the chair up so that he was sitting in front of me, and then he stared at me, nodding slowly.

"Good, good," he said. "I've heard a lot about you Lieutenant; you're good, like a dog with a bone. You don't give up. If anyone has a shot at pulling this thing off, it's probably you. Now listen to me: Pellman's your perp. The son of a bitch killed Rhonda Sullivan and tried to tag the friend for it. But there's no doubt about it; it was Pellman. Lot's o' proof, all circumstantial, but he had a rock-solid alibi. All you have to do is break his damned alibi."

"And how would you propose I do that, Detective? You couldn't."

"You're right. I couldn't. And, to be honest, I don't think you will either. He was supposedly with his mother. I met with her a half-dozen times. She's as daffy as that damned cartoon duck, but I couldn't break her. She has a way of looking you straight in the eye and flat out lying to you, and she doesn't seem to care that you know she's lying. I guess she loves that piece o' shit son of hers—"

He sucked air in loudly, gulped, coughed, shook his head. "Freakin' hell," he gasped, then continued. "He even had a backup for his alibi, only I couldn't confirm that either. He also said he went to Walmart in Winchester early that same evening and, sure enough, his mother had a receipt, time-stamped at seven-fifty-four. It's all in my report."

I nodded. "I read that, but as you noted, it's also circumstantial. She's not handicapped so she could have gone there herself."

"Yeah, well. That's true, and I checked it out. Spoke to everyone who'd been working there that Sunday. No one remembered him or her; why would they? It's a Walmart for god's sake."

I thought for a minute, then said, "The time of death was established as being sometime between nine and midnight. It's what, seventy-five miles, give or take, from Winchester to Sullivan's apartment so it's, say; an hour and a half, in traffic or bad weather. He had time to take the groceries home to his mother and drive back to Chattanooga with at least a two-hour window."

He shook his head, slowly. "True, but two things: one, you're forgetting the time change. It was eight-fifty-four here, so by the time he dropped off the groceries... Eh, it still wouldn't have been impossible, I suppose. But there was still the mother. She's adamant that he spent the night up there, and there's no proof that he didn't." He sucked in a deep breath. "Eeeech," he wheezed, then gasped, coughed, and wiped his eyes on a tissue.

"I'm sorry, Lieutenant," he said, with some difficulty. "I wish I could give you something you don't already know, but I can't. The Sullivan case is my nemesis. I'm just hoping you can do what I couldn't, then maybe I can die in peace."

I didn't know what to say to him. I was as stumped as he was.

"Maybe I could get him to confess," I mused, out loud.

"Not a chance, short of waterboarding or puttin' a plastic bag over his head, or hers for that matter. I take it you haven't met him yet."

"No."

"He's one cold son of a bitch. You'll see."

He closed his eyes, breathed raggedly, the air rattling the back of his throat.

I stood, held out my hand. He looked up at me, his eyes watering, and he took it in both hands and squeezed. His grip was strong, the last, lingering clue to what once had been the man.

He turned me loose, but continued to look up at me, expecting... what? I had no idea.

I placed my hand on his shoulder. "Can I come and see you again, Steve?"

"Why the hell would you?"

I smiled down at him. "Because I want to."

He nodded, surprised. "Sure. Anytime. You're a sweetheart. If I was—"

I laughed. "You might not be much, Steve, but you're still a man. Tell you what: why don't I come by one evening and cook dinner for you?"

His eyes opened wide. "You'd do that?"

"I would. I'll give you a call, okay?"

He nodded. "Yeah, okay. I'll look forward to it, and good luck."

"Okay then. I'll see you soon. Take it easy, Steve." I squeezed his shoulder and then left him sitting there, staring at the sofa.

8

MONDAY, MAY 11 – LEWIS CASE

I spent the rest of the weekend taking it easy. Harry called a couple of times, but I let the calls go to voicemail. I still had a lot of thinking to do... I never did really explain that situation, between Harry and me, did I?

Back in January that year, 2015, Harry and I worked a case together, unofficially, which in itself was okay. It was the first case we'd been on together since he left the police department back in 2008. Anyway, Harry and I had been involved in a steady relationship almost since I was a rookie cop. I'd been his partner when he was with the department, and the relationship continued afterward until...

Look, I never had any illusions about Harry. I always knew he had a wandering eye, and I was willing to put up with it. At least I thought I was, until the Harper case, a particularly nasty affair that covered three murders. The case also involved a lady United States senator and a local congressman, Gordon Harper. Damn, he was one corrupt SOB. During the course of the investigation, Harry "interviewed" one of the murder victims—before she was a victim—Olivia Hansen, a rich bitch with a weird sex life. It turned out that Harry went a little beyond interviewing her. His DNA was recovered... Oh hell, you get the idea. He had the gall to claim it was "research," for Pete's sake. Anyway, since then, our relationship has never quite been the same. *Damn, the more I think about it, the more I want to strangle him.*

So, as I said. I ignored his calls that weekend and, instead, I spent some quiet time with the Sullivan file, a good book, and several bottles of a rather nice red wine.

The first thing I did when I got to work that following Monday morning was go find Detective Tracy.

"Well, well," he greeted me from the cubicle he called home on the first floor. He swiveled his chair around to face me. "If it ain't my old partner Lieutenant Tight-Ass Gazzara. What can I do for you, Kate?"

Old partner? Yep, that's yet another story, one I don't even want to think about.

I ignored the taunt. "What are you doing about the Lewis case?"

"The what case?" He looked puzzled.

"Don't act like an idiot, John. The Lewis case; Jennifer Lewis. She was reported missing three years ago by her sister, Alice Booker. It's your case. What's the status?"

"May I ask what business it is of yours?"

"Booker came to me at the reception on Friday and asked me to look into it...so?"

"Ah yes, the reception." He said it like he had a nasty taste in his mouth. "I heard about that. I also heard you pissed off the assistant chief. That right?"

"John, you're so far up Henry Finkle's ass it's pathetic. So, tell me, the Lewis case."

He shrugged. "There's not much to tell. According to her husband, she ran off with another guy; happens all the time."

I waited, but he simply sat there, staring up at me.

"That's it?" I asked, finally. "That's all you've got: she ran off with another guy? You didn't investigate?"

Again, he shrugged. "The husband seems like a nice guy. He said she walked out on him about a month earlier. She had an apartment off Bonny Oaks, in one of those extended stay hotels. I checked. She didn't leave a forwarding address. She worked at the Country Skillet on Shallowford. I talked to some of her co-workers. Sure enough, she'd been having an affair. So yeah, she ran off with another guy."

I stared down at him, breathed deeply. It was all I could do to be civil.

"I'd like to take a look at the file, please?"

He sucked in through his teeth. "Oooh, I dunno about that. I'm still working it."

"Bullshit! You haven't returned Booker's calls in more than a year. I want to see it, *now!*"

"I don't have it. It's down in Records, filed away under 'I don't give a shit.' You want it, you go get it. Oh, and be sure to sign for it."

He swiveled back around to face his computer screen, and I lost it. I grabbed the back of his chair, spun him around, grabbed him by the balls and squeezed. He grabbed the arms of the chair and squeaked like a mouse in a trap; eyes almost popping out of his head.

"This is how we first met, John. Remember?"

His face was a mask of pain, but he managed to nod.

"That's good, John," I said, twisting them a little. His backside rose six inches off the seat. "Now, here's how it's going to be. As soon as I turn you loose, you're going to get up and go fetch the file. Then you're going to deliver it to me in my office, understand?"

He nodded, and I let him down again, but I didn't let go of his package.

Instead, I leaned in close and whispered in his ear, "Don't screw with me, Detective. If you do, you'll regret it. Ten minutes. No more. You hear?"

He nodded, his eyes shut tight. I turned him loose, spun on my heel, and walked quickly away without a backward glance, back to my office.

Less than ten minutes later, the door burst open and Tracy stormed in and flung the file down on my desk in front of me.

"Thank you, John," I called after him as he stormed out again. "If I have any questions—" but the door slammed shut and he was gone. *Son of a bitch!*

Two minutes later, there was a knock on my door, and it opened.

"You okay?" Lonnie asked as he poked his head inside. "What was that all about?"

"Oh yeah. I'm fine. Come on in and take a seat. Dick's pissed at me. I had to put the screws to him, literally. He didn't seem to want me to have this." I picked the thin file up and then dropped it again. "I wonder why?" I said, more to myself than to Lonnie.

"Can I see?" He held out his hand.

"Sure." I handed it to him.

He flipped through it quickly. "Geez, I know why. Here, you take a look."

I barely had time to glance through the file before I received a call informing me that Alice Booker was at the front desk, but I knew what he meant. I shook my head and closed the file.

"She's here. Stay here while I go get her."

He nodded, crossed his legs and pushed back in his chair.

Alice Booker looked a little better than she had on Friday evening, but not much. I showed her into my office and asked her to sit.

Lonnie stood, said hello, and pulled up a chair for her, and she sat down beside him.

"So," I said, as I opened my iPad, "did you have a good weekend, Alice? Is it okay for me to call you Alice?"

"Oh yes, of course. No, Lieutenant, I didn't have a good weekend. I can't remember the last time I did. It's..." She lapsed into silence.

I nodded. "I understand. So, let's get on with it. I have the missing person file." I lifted the top cover and let it drop again. "But I haven't yet had time to look at it in detail. Why don't you tell me your story? Begin at the beginning. Umm. Alice, I'm going to record what you say," I said, as I set my digital recorder on the desk in front of her and turned it on.

"Yes. That's fine."

She lowered her head, looked down at her hands clasped together in her lap, thought for a minute, then looked up at me.

"Well, as I told you on Friday, Jennifer and I talked almost every day, sometimes more than once, especially toward the end... She was having problems."

I tapped notes into my iPad as she talked.

"Problems?" I asked. "What problems?

"She'd left her husband, John, about a month earlier. She was going to divorce him."

"Okay. Go on."

"So, the last time I talked to her was on Saturday, April 14, 2012. The first time quite early, around eight in the morning, and then again around five that same afternoon. She seemed fine. She said she was going out to eat and would be back home by nine, and she'd call me to let me know that she'd gotten home okay. She did, and that's the last I heard from her."

Alice adjusted her position in the chair and pulled a tissue from her purse.

"She didn't call me on Sunday, but I didn't think too much of it until I called her that evening. That was around eight. She didn't answer, so I left her a voicemail. I called her again at nine-thirty, and at ten, and again at eleven. I still wasn't too worried. I thought she might have been on a date. She was seeing someone, not seriously, of course—"

"Do you know who that was?" I asked, interrupting her.

"Yes, his name was Jeff Tobin but, as I said, it was just a casual thing. Anyway, I called her husband, John. I didn't really think she'd be there, but I knew he talked to her all the time. He told me he hadn't seen her or heard from her and didn't know where she was. So, I called Jeff. He said he hadn't seen her either and hadn't talked to her for several days. I also called her best friend, Amber—that's Amber Watts. She told me they'd had dinner together at Provino's on Saturday evening and that Jennifer had driven home just after eight-thirty. She'd heard nothing from her since...and neither had I."

I could see she wasn't really talking to me, or Lonnie. She was staring down at her hands, thinking out loud. I let her get on with it and continued making my own notes.

"I didn't know what to do," she continued. Finally, at around eleven that Monday morning. I drove to her apartment. She wasn't there, but all her belongings were: her clothes, shoes, everything. I spoke to her neighbors. No one had seen Jennifer for at least a couple of days. I knew she hadn't gone off somewhere. She would have told me; she told me everything. So, I came here and reported her missing, at around two o'clock, I think it was."

She glanced sideways at Lonnie; he nodded confirmation.

"And you've heard nothing from her since?" I asked.

She looked at me like I was an idiot, and no wonder. *What the hell am I thinking? Of course, she hasn't.*

She shook her head. I'm not sure if it was in frustration because of the stupid question or simply her way of saying no. Whatever, I didn't follow up on it. Instead, I asked about Jennifer's breakup with her husband, and then I picked up the file and flipped through it while she talked.

"She left him on Friday," she continued, "March twenty-third, after a terrible argument. She said she'd told him she wanted a divorce, and he went absolutely crazy. He hit her; gave her a black eye. They'd been arguing ever since... I never liked him. He's a mean man, drinks, and he went with other women." She looked up at me.

I didn't have to ask. I knew what she was thinking. *Maybe she's right. More often than not, it's the husband, or wife, whichever...*

That male chauvinist Tracy, I thought, as I contemplated the file and its sparse contents: the original missing person report, a single photograph of Jennifer Lewis, several single sheets of paper, each with hand-written notes. One was a report dated April 20, detailing the results of his search of Jennifer's apartment. In it, Detective Tracy stated that he'd found nothing out of the ordinary. On one of the sheets, he'd made notes of an interview he'd conducted with the husband, John Lewis; it was dated April 21. *He didn't record it?*

Another sheet also had notes he'd made while interviewing Jennifer's best friend Amber Watts; it too was dated April 21. And on another sheet also dated the 21st, he'd written a couple of sentences about an interview with Jeff Tobin. On the final sheet of paper, dated April 23, he'd outlined his own conclusions, namely that Jennifer had gone away with an unnamed man with whom she'd been having an affair for several months, that according to his interview with the husband. That was it. There was nothing more in the file. Just the missing person report, one photo, and five sheets of handwritten notes.

What the hell kind of investigation was this? He didn't record any of the interviews. He didn't go to the apartment until the 20th? That's three full days after the report was filed, and he didn't talk to anyone until the day after that. I leaned back in my seat, holding the file in front of me, staring at it. *And that's all there is? He didn't talk to anyone else? If he did, there's nothing here. What the hell was he doing... More to the point, what the hell was he thinking? I don't know, but I'm going to find out.*

I shuddered to think of the amount of work that now needed to be done because of his, Tracy's, lack of effort over the past three years. As far as I was concerned, the poor woman might as well have been reported missing only yesterday. If I were to agree to take it on... No, if I were to be allowed to take it on, I'd have to start from scratch.

I leaned forward, closed the file and handed it to Lonnie. I looked sharply at him, a warning not to say anything. He got the hint and nodded, discreetly.

"Alice," I said. "Detective Tracy," the words tasted nasty in my mouth, "is of the opinion that Jennifer simply ran off with another man. Who that man was, he doesn't say."

"She didn't!" Alice snapped. "She wouldn't, and even if she did, she would've stayed in touch with me. You're not going to help me, are you?"

"I didn't say that. Alice, I'm going to do what I can, but it's not going to be easy... Look, I happen to know a private investigator." I glanced at Lonnie. He had that idiotic smile on his face. I ignored him and continued. "I can have a word with him."

She started to shake her head. "I can't afford that kind of money."

"Don't worry about the money," I said, crossing my fingers. "We'll figure something out. For now, I want you to go home and leave it to me. Would you do that for me?"

For a long moment, she looked into my eyes—hers were watering —then, slowly, she nodded, rose to her feet, and said, "I'll stay in town for a few more days. You might need to talk to me."

Lonnie and I both stood. I smiled at her, and said, "If you're sure. I think that sounds like a plan."

"I am. I'll be at the hotel if you need me. Goodbye, and thank you for listening, Lieutenant, and you too, Sergeant. I'll look forward to hearing from you."

I waited until the door closed behind her before I let out a deep breath and sat down.

"Oh boy," Lonnie said, as he resumed his seat. "What the hell are you thinking, LT?"

He dropped the file he'd still been holding back on my desk.

"That's a friggin' joke," he continued, referring to the file. "There's nothin' in it. And what was that about Harry Starke? Are you out of your mind?"

I ignored the question about Harry, and said, "You're right. She's right. Tracy barely went through the motions, but I'll get to him later. Right now, I need to talk to the chief."

I picked up the office phone and punched in the number.

"Cathy," I said when his secretary answered. "I need to see the chief, right now if possible."

"One moment, Lieutenant."

The phone went to some annoying music as she put me on hold, and I waited.

"He'll see you now. Don't keep him waiting."

9

MONDAY, MAY 11 – CHIEF JOHNSTON'S OFFICE

As usual, Chief Johnston was seated like some medieval king behind his desk. Unfortunately, his chief jester Henry Finkle was in the seat beside the desk, his thin face an expressionless mask.

"Good morning, Chief," I said. "Thank you for seeing me."

"Good morning, Lieutenant. Please sit down. I hope you have good news for me."

"The Sullivan case?" I asked, sitting down in front of his desk. "No, sir. Not yet, I'm afraid."

I swear I heard Finkle snigger.

Johnston narrowed his eyes and leaned forward; the huge white eyebrows met in the middle and became one. *How does he do that?*

"Why not?" he asked. "I don't understand. It's clear that the nurse is the perpetrator. Why have you not arrested him yet?"

"Yes, I agree, but I can't prove that he did it. What evidence there is, is all circumstantial. I'm working on it, sir, but unless something breaks... Well, we'll see, but it's going to take time."

He leaned back in his chair, frowned even deeper, folded his arms across his chest. "That's not good enough, Lieutenant. I assigned the case to you because I thought you'd be able to close it out, and quickly."

"Sir—" Finkle turned in his chair toward the chief.

"Not now, Henry," the chief interrupted him.

Finkle turned back to face me. He looked like a hungry rat.

"So why are you here?" Johnston asked.

"I have something else I'd like to look into, but I thought I'd better run it by you first, sir."

He glared at me across the desk. Finkle's face lit up with a huge grin.

"I told you, Lieutenant," Johnston said with a fist slamming on the desk for emphasis. "I want the Sullivan case closed. I want that son of a bitch Pellman arrested."

"Chief," Finkle said. "If I might suggest. I'm not sure the lieutenant is capable—"

"Damn it, Henry," Johnston interrupted him again. "I said, not now, so shut the hell up."

Finkle's mouth clamped shut, his eyes narrowed and sparkled with anger.

Well, now I know Henry has my back, I thought. Yes, I was being sardonic.

"Tell me," Johnston said, "and it had better be good."

"Before I do, I'd like you to take a look at this, please, sir." I handed him Tracy's file on the Lewis case.

"What is it?" he asked, taking it from me and opening it.

I didn't answer. I let him look through it. It took him less than thirty seconds. He flipped through it again, his lips tightening as he did so. Then, finally, he looked up at me, his face stern, his eyes narrowed.

"What the hell is this, Lieutenant? Is it a joke? I've never seen anything like it."

"It's no joke, sir. It's a missing person file."

"*I can see that, damn it!*" His voice was raised louder than I'd ever heard. "It's more than three years old. There's nothing in it but a couple of reports and a few sheets of paper. It has Detective Tracy's name on it."

Now it was his turn: he twisted in his chair to face Finkle. "Go fetch that son of a bitch in here."

"Err, I'd rather you didn't, sir," I said, as Finkle stood.

"Why the hell not, Lieutenant? This is the worst piece of policing I've seen in all my years on the force."

He threw the file down on his desk.

"How the hell was he allowed to get away with this, Henry? And sit the hell down, will you?"

He didn't wait for Finkle to answer.

He leaned forward in his chair, folded his arms on the top of his desk, and glared at me. "So tell me, Catherine. Why don't you want me to tear Tracy a new one?" His voice was so low and menacing it reminded me of a wolf readying itself for the kill.

"For a couple of reasons that probably make no sense. Yes, I agree with you. It's pretty bad, but I know Tracy, and I think there must be a reason why the investigation is as cursory as it is. Second, I need to talk to him, and that means I also need him to cooperate."

He nodded, leaned back in his chair and looked at me, thoughtfully.

"There's one thing more."

He raised his eyebrows but continued to look me in the eye. "Go on."

I hesitated, then said, "I want to run it by Harry Starke."

Finkle snorted, derisively.

"You want to run it by him?" Johnston asked, quietly. "What exactly does that mean, and why would you want to do that?"

"She's screwing him, is why," Finkle snarled.

"Shut up, Henry," Johnston said. "Catherine?"

"I'm not asking permission to get him involved... well, not exactly, but that," I nodded at the file, "it's not just cold, it's dead. The woman is missing. We don't know if she's alive or dead. I'm betting she's dead, but if so, where's the body? And if she did run away, with whom, and why hasn't she contacted her sister? To get any answers at all, we need to find her. You know how Starke's mind works. Nobody I know thinks like he does."

Again, the derisive snort from Finkle. Johnston cut him a warning look.

"But it's not just that. I want access to his team," I said. "In particular Tim Clarke. He's a wizard at finding people. He's the best there is. If he can't find her, nobody can. I want access to him."

Johnston nodded, thoughtfully, then said, "Starke was a good detective, I must admit. All right, Lieutenant, but I'm not giving you carte blanche. He's no longer one of us, so tread very carefully." He thought for a moment, then continued. "I'll have the case reassigned to you. Keep me in the loop. And *do not* forget the Sullivan case. I want that one closed out soonest. That will be all."

I stood, picked up the file, thanked him, ignored Finkle, and turned to leave.

"You heard what the chief said, Lieutenant?" Finkle said. I turned my head to look at him.

"I heard everything the chief said. What are you talking about?"

"He told you to tread carefully. I reiterate. I'll be watching you."

"You always are, Finkle, especially my tits and ass, so what's new?"

Out of the corner of my eye, I could see that the chief was smiling. I left them to it.

———————

So, it was done. The Lewis case was now officially mine, and I had permission from the top to ask Harry for help—that is if I could persuade him to agree. He was kinda funny about working for free, especially when his employees were involved; he liked to get paid.

I returned to my office, sat down, and swiped the lock screen on my phone and called his cell. He answered on the third ring.

"Hey, Kate. What's up?"

"I need to talk to you, Harry. I need a favor. Can we meet for lunch, my treat?"

"Uh oh! What d'you want? Is this about the Sullivan case?"

"I can't talk about it now. So, how about it, lunch?"

I heard him sigh, which made me smile. *Gotcha!*

"Okay. Where? When?"

I looked at my watch. "Soon? Say thirty minutes? At the Boathouse?"

"Noon, then. Grab a table, on the terrace if you can. I'll meet you there." And he disconnected.

Okay, then, I thought, smiling to myself. *That's the first step.*

10

MONDAY, MAY 11, LUNCH – LEWIS CASE

It was already after eleven-thirty when I left for lunch with Harry that morning. I left Lonnie with instructions to track down Lisa Marco and, if he could, talk to her that afternoon about Rhonda Sullivan. I'd liked to have talked to her myself, but, in deference to the chief's wishes, I didn't want to put it off. Besides, no matter what other people might think of him, I knew I could trust my partner to do a thorough job and get the information we needed. So, I grabbed the Lewis file and headed out the door.

Harry still hadn't arrived when I walked into the Boathouse and, yes, I did manage to grab a table out on the terrace overlooking the river. It was a beautiful, warm day: fluffy white clouds drifted slowly on a startlingly blue sky with just the hint of a breeze blowing in off the water. It had all the makings of a romantic moment, only that wasn't why I was there, nor did I even feel like such a moment. *My, how times do change.*

I ordered a glass of iced tea, placed the file on the table in front of me, and waited for him to arrive. My head was a jumble of disconnected thoughts and questions, to which I was almost certain there were no answers.

I was sitting, drink in hand, staring out across the river when Harry pulled out the chair opposite me across the table and sat down.

"Oh, hi," I said. "You look nice." Yeah, I said it without thinking, but he did. He looked gorgeous: deeply tanned, three days of stubble on his chin, white polo shirt that contrasted nicely with the tan, and dark blue, lightweight pants. Yes, gorgeous, and I didn't like the feelings beginning to stir inside of me. Somehow, though, I managed to push them aside, at least for the moment.

"Thanks, so d'you. Have you ordered yet?"

"No. I was waiting for you."

"Why? You know what I like to eat here." He looked around and attracted the waiter's attention.

"You'll take the Veggie Panini?" he asked me, and he was right, that's exactly what I'd have ordered if he hadn't suggested it.

He's still taking me for granted.

"No," I said. "Can I see the menu, please?"

He smiled, shrugged, then ordered his usual, a Smoked Pork Sandwich with a Blue Moon beer, draft in a glass, no orange slice.

Me? I ordered a Grilled Chicken Salad and a refill for my glass of tea.

"So, what's this all about, Kate? And what's that?" he asked, pointing at the file on the table as the waiter walked away with our order.

"Can we eat first and talk later?"

"Sure, but you've piqued my curiosity. I hear nothing from you for days, then here we are. I hope this relationship is not going to turn into something... Well, if you're just using me..."

Damn, does he ever have a way of figuring things out?

"Oh, come on, Harry. Okay, yes. I need your help, but I'm not using you. Okay, yes I am, but it's not what you think."

"Oh, and what do I think?"

"I don't know, Harry. Who the hell ever knows what you're

thinking? I just thought—" And it was at that moment that rescue arrived in the form of our lunch. I looked gratefully up at the waiter and Harry smiled: enigmatic as always.

We ate for the most-part in silence until finally Harry pushed away his plate, signaled the waiter, ordered another beer, and waited until I too laid down my fork.

"So," he said, as the waiter left us, "how exactly d'you intend to use me?"

Oh hell! Here we go.

I picked up the Lewis file and, without saying a word, handed it to him. He opened it, glanced through it, looked at me over the top of it, then closed it and laid it down. After cocking his head to one side he said, "Okay. What is it you want?"

He smiled at me; mocking me.

He's making it tough.

"Harry, I need your help," I said, quietly, sincerely, I hoped. *"Please?"*

He picked the file up again, opened it, shook his head, then said, "Not one of Dick's best efforts, is it?"

"No, it's not!"

He sighed, set the file down again, and said, "You know I'll help if I can. There's nothing here. I—"

I interrupted him, saying, "Which is exactly why I need you. If it was simple, I wouldn't. I thought maybe Tim..." I let it tail off and waited, and waited, while he stared off into space until finally:

"Kate, I don't have time to get involved... Wait, now. Hear me out. I don't have time to get involved personally, but," he picked up the file again, "I can run it by Tim. I'll help if I can, when I can, but I don't intend to get sucked into another long, drawn-out investigation for which I'll never get paid. Understood?"

It wasn't exactly what I was hoping for, but I nodded anyway and told him thank you.

"Let me have the file," I said, reaching across the table. "I'll have copies made and send it over."

"Don't send it," he said. "Bring it over yourself. Look, Kate, I know I screwed up, and I'm so sorry."

"Don't sweat it," I said. "I'm over it, as well, you know."

He nodded. He leaned forward, folded his arms on the table and said, "You know how I feel about you. Can we...can we start over?"

Oh how I wanted to say yes, but the right words wouldn't come. Instead, I looked down at the table, shook my head, and said, "I'm sorry, Harry. I'm just not ready, not yet." I looked up, looked him right in the eye, and said, "What you did was—well, let's just wait and see."

He pursed his lips, gave me a wry smile, nodded, then said, "What was the other night, then? I thought..."

So did I, but the following morning...

"It was nice. It's always nice, but there's more to a relationship than just that, a lot more. Harry, I need to be able to trust you, and I don't. So let's just give it some time, please?"

He stood up, grabbed the check from the table, looked down at me smiling and said, "I understand, and it's better than I deserve but, please, bring the file over yourself. I'll take you to dinner; no strings, okay?"

Well, what the hell would you have said? I said okay, and he left, taking with him the check I'd promised to pay. I stayed for a moment, enjoying the moment, the quiet beauty of the great river, and an unexpected feeling of calm. *I think I love the river almost as much as Harry does. What am I going to do about him?*

Finally, after receiving a call from Lonnie wanting to know where the hell I was, I went back to the office; it was almost two o'clock.

"Yeah," I said, as I walked past his desk. "Give me a few minutes to get this copied." I waved the file at him. "Then come to my office. I need to know what you've been doing while I've been out."

11

MONDAY, MAY 11, AFTERNOON – SULLIVAN CASE

What he'd been doing was tracking down and interviewing Lisa Marco.

"Okay," I said. "Talk to me. Where are we?"

"I found her easy enough. She was at work... So, by the way, was Pellman, but I managed to steer clear of him. Anyway, she had little to add that we didn't already know. She did confirm that Pellman knew Sullivan and that they'd been friends, sort of, for quite a while. She also said Pellman had been trying to get her to go out with him, but she'd turned him down, several times. There was one more thing of interest she added that wasn't in the file... At least, I don't think it was. She said that Sullivan suffered from migraines, and that's maybe why she let Pellman shoot her up with the drug."

"You know," I said, "that drug, when injected, has to be administered by a qualified medical practitioner so, Pellman, then."

Lonnie nodded. "Or Marco. She would have been qualified to administer it, and she was on duty when the drugs were stolen, but she has an alibi. She was with her girlfriend all evening... That's all evening. Get my drift? So I don't see it. Then again, there's nothing so strange as people. Pellman said she did it, but he would, right?"

"So maybe we should talk to her again?"

He shrugged, made a face. "Couldn't hurt, I suppose. I'd say we need to interview Pellman and his mother first, though. Yates? I think we can cross him off the list. He works at Volkswagen—has since he graduated—so he couldn't have done it. He wouldn't have the medical know-how."

We both stared up at the board. After a moment of silence, I sighed and shook my head.

"So, Pellman or his mother?" I said. "Which one first? Pellman, I think." I answered my own question.

"When? Where?" Lonnie asked.

"Tomorrow afternoon, at his place of work. Let's put a little pressure on him to see if anything breaks."

"Why not now? He's there."

"I have other things on my mind. By the way, we have the Lewis case, officially. Johnston turned it over to me this morning."

"No shit? How cool is that?"

"I'm not so sure. It's more than three years cold. That reminds me, I need to make a call... No, no. Stay put. I want you in on this."

I picked up the office phone and buzzed Detective Tracy.

"John," I said when he picked up. "We need to talk, so please come to my office, now."

I put the phone down before he could make any excuses. Lonnie looked at me, nodding, a slight smile on his lips.

"Tracy?" he asked, and without waiting for an answer, continued. "Oh yeah," he said. "I wanna be here for this."

12

Monday, May 11, 3 PM – Lewis Case

Detective Tracy took his time. I waited exactly fifteen minutes before I picked up the phone to call him again; I didn't have to. There was a sharp knock on my door, it opened, and he walked in. I could see right away, from the thunderous look on his face, that the interview wasn't going to go well.

"What's this all about, Lieutenant? I don't work for you, so why'd you drag me up here? I'm busy. So—"

I interrupted him. "Take a seat, John." I pointed to the chair next to Lonnie.

"If this is about the Lewis case," he said as he sat down. "You have the file. There's nothing more I can tell you."

I leaned back in my chair and stared at him.

"You don't change much, do you, Detective?" I asked.

"What the hell's that supposed to mean?"

"Bad attitude," I said. "You have a bad attitude; always have."

He stood, looked down at me, angrily. "I don't have to take this kinda crap from you, Gazzara."

"Sit down," I said, quietly.

Slowly he lowered himself back onto the chair.

I picked up the file—I'd placed it on my desk right after I'd called him—and waved it in front of him. "What the hell is this, John?" I asked, not raising my voice.

"You're a detective, so they tell me," he said, sneering. "What does it look like?"

I dropped the file back on the desk. "It looks like a half-assed excuse for an investigation. It looks like you didn't give a shit, like you said this morning. What the hell were you thinking?"

"I don't know what you're talking about."

"Yes, you do," I said. "Even back when you worked with me, you were better than this. What the hell happened to you?"

"When I worked with you?" he said, his lip curling into a sneer. "That was a real boost to my career. I haven't recovered from it yet. You really screwed me over."

"I didn't screw you, John. You screwed yourself. As I said, you had a bad attitude then, and you do now, especially where women are concerned. And you haven't changed at all. So, I ask you again. What the hell is this?" I tapped on the file with the back of my hand.

"You're right, *Lieutenant.*" The word dripped with sarcasm. "I didn't give a shit, not when I found out what she was..." He let the words tail off, then continued. "Okay, that's not true. Of course, I gave a shit. Look, she was having an affair. She ran off with some guy; end of story."

"So, what was she, Detective?" I asked.

He stared at me across the desk, then said, "She was a freakin' hooker, is what she was."

"And you know that because? There's nothing about that in your file."

"Yeah, well, I left that out in deference to her husband."

"You did *what?*" I was dumbfounded.

"He was a nice guy; didn't deserve the slut, or the shit he would get if it came out. I cut him a break; so what?"

Why the hell would you do that?

"You cut him a break?" I asked. "She's been missing for three years. She's not been heard of in all that time, and you cut him a break? Why would you do that? What about her family? Don't they deserve answers?"

"You talking about Alice Booker? I stayed in touch with her."

"The hell you did, not for the last two years anyway."

"Geez," he said, shaking his head. "What's with you, Gazzara? She was just a freakin' hooker. The world's better off without her." He paused, shook his head. "And you, and you—you're no freakin' better. Geez! Freakin' women! I hate 'em!"

"What the f—" Lonnie exploded, almost said it, then continued. "Who the hell d'you think you're talking to? Show a little respect, you worthless piece of shit."

"Oh yeah, and what are you going to do about it, Fat Ass?"

Lonnie moved faster than I ever thought possible. He stood, spun around and, quick as a striking snake, his hand streaked out and grabbed Tracy by the throat and squeezed. Tracy came out of his seat choking.

Lonnie relaxed his grip a little and snarled. "I'll tell you what I'm gonna do about it, you smart-ass little shit. Step outa line again and I'll rip the tongue right outa your foul mouth. Get it?" he asked as he tightened his grip.

Tracy's face had gone red, his mouth was wide open, his eyes popping.

I stood, quickly. "Let him go, Sergeant. *Now!*"

I thought for a minute he was going to ignore me but, slowly, he lowered Tracy back to his seat and turned him loose.

"You—you crazy bastard," he whispered, hoarsely, massaging his neck. "I'm gonna turn you in for that—"

I interrupted him. "Turn him in for what, Detective?"

"For—oh, I get it. Well screw you, Gazzara."

Lonnie took a half-step forward, but this time Tracy leaped up, staggered a half-step backward, knocking over the chair, then turned and ran for the door, slamming it shut behind him; Lonnie sat down, grinning.

"Thanks," I said, "but you shouldn't have laid hands on him. If it gets back to Finkle..."

"It won't. He doesn't have the balls. And he sure as hell wouldn't want it to get out that I was able to..." He didn't finish, the smile was gone, and suddenly he looked very tired, and miserable.

"What's wrong, Lonnie? It's okay. I have your back. Hey, partner, you look like you just lost a hundred-dollar bill."

"I wish to hell that's all it was." He paused, looked at me.

"Come on," I said. "Out with it. What's bothering you?"

He sighed a deep sigh, looked down at his feet, then said, "You heard what that piece o' crap called me: Fat Ass."

"Yes, well..."

"No, not 'yeah, well.' I've had it with all that. I've been called it, and worse, all my life. High school was a nightmare, so was UT, so was the Academy. I've always been overweight... No, not overweight, fat, and I can't deal with it anymore. I gotta lose some weight, a lot o' weight. The trouble is, I've tried every diet there is; they all work for a while. I lose a few pounds, then it goes right back on again, and each time it's a little more. I don't know what to do anymore."

I sat back in my seat. "Do you know *why* you put the weight back on?"

"Oh yeah: lack of willpower, partly, but dieting just doesn't seem to work in the long run. Hell, I even tried one of them TV diets, where they supply the food. That worked better'n most, but in the end..." He trailed off, stared down at the floor. Then he looked up at me. "I've had it, Kate. I'd be better off out of it, doing something else."

"*What?*" I couldn't believe what I was hearing. "You can't be serious?"

"As a friggin' heart attack," he said. "I'm sick of the assholes we have around here, the looks I get, the fat jokes, the derisive remarks, the name calling behind my back, and the lack of respect. I'm a good cop, Kate, at least I try to be; not like that piece o' crap Tracy."

"So you're going to give up, take your toys and go home? I thought you were better than that. Lonnie, the people that matter do treat you with respect; I do, the chief does."

"What about your boyfriend, Starke? He treats me like shit."

"You can hardly blame—no, no, Lonnie. Hear me out. You can hardly blame him for the way he treats you. I've heard the way you go after him, every chance you get. I've lost count of the number of times you've wanted to arrest him—"

"Not without cause," he interrupted me. "He has no respect for the law, Kate. He treats the rules as if they weren't meant for him. You let him get away with more crap than you ever would me. And he hates my guts. Always has, ever since we were at the Academy together. Now you're letting him loose on us again, and I don't like it."

I sighed, made a wry face, and shook my head. I was in no mood for this kind of self-deprecating crap. I had to shut him down.

"Gotcha," I said, quietly. "You're fat, and because you're fat no one likes you, and it's everyone else's fault but yours. Lonnie, I'm going to tell you something, and you're not going to like it. It's not them, it's you; you're the problem. You can be arrogant, intolerant, and a pain the ass. If you want to quit, go ahead. But I suggest you take stock, grow yourself a pair, and do something about it—the fat, I mean."

He looked at me as if I'd slapped his face, then he stood, turned and walked out of my office.

I stared at the closed door, sighed, and checked my watch. It was almost five and I needed to take the file copy to Harry's office, which I did.

———

DINNER WITH HARRY THAT EVENING WAS NICE, AND PROBABLY would have been even nicer, had I allowed it to be, but I didn't. Instead, we arranged that I should meet him and Tim at his offices the following morning at ten, and he dropped me off at my car, which was safely locked away in his office parking lot.

He opened my car door for me, leaned in close and kissed me, and I let him, and then I pushed him away. He smiled at me, nodded, and went to his car and waited until I'd driven out of the lot.

I drove home that night. How I made it from one place to the other, I'll never know. No, I wasn't drunk; in fact, I'd had nothing to drink at all. Maybe it was because I had a lot on my mind, and not all of it about Harry: Lonnie was a big part of it, and so was Dick Tracy.

By the time I arrived home, I'd made a couple of decisions. One: no matter how much I tried, I couldn't figure out Tracy. Two: I was going to have to do something about Lonnie. Fortunately, I didn't have to.

13

Lonnie was waiting for me when I arrived at my office the following morning. He looked different, somehow; more upbeat. *That's m'boy!*

"You're in a good mood," I said. "Come on in. Sit down."

"I want to apologize for yesterday," he said, as he sat down in front of my desk. "You were right. I was being childish."

I nodded. "Yup, you were. No apology needed. I'd already forgotten about it," I lied.

"Yeah, right. Anyway, I've decided to do something about it. I'm going to have a lap band fitted."

I opened my eyes wide. "Wow! No kidding?"

He nodded. "I called the clinic already this morning and...well, I have an appointment at eleven, if that's okay with you."

"Yes, of course it is, but—"

"Don't go there, LT. There's nothing to discuss. I made up my mind."

"Okay. Well, what can I say? I'm proud of you, Lonnie. If there's anything I can do...well, you know."

"Do?" a male voice, not Lonnie's, said.

I looked up, startled. Finkle was standing just outside the open door. How long he'd been listening, I didn't know. *Long enough, I should think.*

"Do about what, Lieutenant? You *were* talking about the Sullivan case, I hope."

"No, Chief," I said, lightly. "I wasn't, but I can if you think it's important."

"Leave us, Sergeant," Finkle said, to Lonnie.

Lonnie started to get to his feet.

"Stay where you are, Sergeant," I said, never taking my eyes off Finkle's.

"*What?*" Finkle was dumbfounded. "You just countermanded my direct order. Are you mad, Lieutenant?"

"No, sir, far from it. As a female officer, it's my right to have a witness present. Anything you want to say to me, you can say in front of Sergeant Guest."

He stared hard at me, obviously lost for words. Inwardly, I smiled: *Gotcha!*

Finally, he smiled... No, it was more snarl than smile, and he sat down next to Lonnie.

"I've been talking to Detective Tracy," he said, conversationally, "and I didn't like what I heard."

Oh hell, here we go.

"If you think I'm going to let you run with this Lewis thing, you're mistaken. And if you think that I'm going to allow that—that shyster who poses as a private investigator, Harry Starke, back into this building, you're even more stupid than you appear to be. You are to concentrate on the Sullivan case until it's either closed or shelved. Is that understood, Lieutenant?"

I leaned back in my chair, folded my arms across my stomach, looked at Lonnie, who rewarded me with a wink, and I smiled at him, Finkle.

"Well?" he asked. "D'you understand?"

I shrugged. "Yes, I understand, Chief, but tell me, did you go to Tracy..." I paused for a split second, "or did he come to you?"

"That's none of your damn business. What the hell difference does it make?"

"Oh, it makes a difference. You know it does."

He didn't answer. Instead, he stood and went to the door, hesitated, then turned to look at me and said, "Sullivan!" And then he left.

"Geez, LT," Lonnie said. "That was intense. What was that about Tracy? What difference does it make, who went to who?"

"Not much. Mostly, I was rattling his cage, watching his eyes. Tracy went to him, which is not good."

"How d'you know?"

"You ever play poker, Lonnie? It's a rare player that doesn't have a tell. Finkle does. His eyes left mine, just a flicker, when I asked him, 'Did he come to you?' And if Tracy is reporting everything to him, we could have a problem."

"He didn't tell him about me, though," Lonnie said. "I told you he'd keep it to himself. Chicken shit!"

"That you nearly strangled him? We don't know what Tracy told him. Just be careful, okay?"

He nodded. "So, the Lewis case; it's off?"

"Not hardly. I have Chief Johnston's okay to go ahead with it, and to consult with Harry, in a limited way, of course." I winked at him. "Finkle can go play with himself... if he can find it. Look, I have to go in a few minutes. I have an appointment with Harry and Tim Clarke at ten and I don't want to be late. Good luck with your lap band interview. This afternoon, if you're back, we'll go talk to Pellman. Let's meet back here at one-thirty. Now, I'd like a minute, please."

Lonnie left, and I spent the next ten minutes thinking about what had just happened, searching for answers that didn't come. Unless... *Well, it's a possibility. Nah, couldn't be...could it?*

14

It was already ten o'clock when I arrived at Harry's offices on Georgia Avenue that morning. I parked in the lot and entered through the side door. Jacque rose from her seat and stepped around her desk to greet me: a kiss on the cheek and a quick hug.

"Hi, Kate," she said. "I'll tell him you're here."

"How is he this morning?" I asked.

"Like he always is. Dat man is an enigma, you know; you never can tell what he's t'inkin'."

Jacque is Jamaican, though she rarely drops into character; only when she's joking, or angry. She's been with Harry since he first opened his doors for business more than ten years ago, even before she graduated university. She has a master's in business administration and a bachelor's in criminology. Back then, in 2015, she was his PA. Today, along with Bob Ryan, she's a full partner in the company. I love her dearly.

"Hey you," Harry said. "Come on through. Jacque, have Tim come to my office, please."

I won't bore you by describing Harry's office, his "inner sanctum." Let's just say, turn of the century luxury would be an understatement.

"Take a load off," he said, leading the way to the coffee table flanked by two elegant sofas. We sat facing each other. "Can I get you some coffee."

"No, thank you."

The door opened and Tim Clarke—well, he almost fell into the room. His arms and hands were, as usual, loaded: a laptop, iPad, a cell phone, the copy of my file under his arm, and a brimming cup of coffee in his hand.

"Whoops," he said, grinning self-consciously. "Hiya, Kate. Can I sit here?" he asked as he began to dump his tech on the end of the coffee table. Harry watched him, smiling indulgently.

Tim is one of those rare people that nothing ever fazes. I've never seen him without a smile on his face. He lives, most of the time, in a weird world all his own. An IT expert, computer geek, hacker, he looks after the tech side of Harry's business. He's worked for him since before he dropped out of college when he was seventeen. Harry found him in an Internet café in North Chattanooga, just one small step ahead of the law. He's twenty-seven years old, looks sixteen; he's tall, skinny, wears glasses that he constantly fiddles with, and...he's a genius. Harry pays him an outrageous salary and treats him like a wayward puppy, which seems to suit both just fine.

"So, I read the file. It's a bit slim, right? What can I do for you?" he asked as he sat down beside me on the sofa and reached for his coffee, which he managed to slop all over the table.

"I need to know all there is to know about these four people."

I handed him the list:

1. Jennifer Lewis
2. John Lewis
3. Jeffery Tobin
4. Amber Watts

He looked at it, sipped on the coffee, set it down again, tilted his head to one side, looked sideways at me. "Okay. No problem—"

"Wait," I said, interrupting him. "Let me have that back, please."

He handed it to me. I took a pen from my inside jacket pocket and added two more names, then I handed it back to him.

He looked at it. His eyes opened wide. He looked at Harry, then at me.

"Are you kidding?" he asked as he shoved his glasses up the bridge of his nose with a forefinger.

Slowly, I shook my head.

"Let me see that," Harry said, reaching across the table.

He read; he smiled; he looked at me. "This could get you into a lot of trouble," he said and handed it back to Tim.

"No more than I'm already in," I said.

"Tracy I can understand," Harry said. "But why Finkle?"

"I think there's something going on that they don't want me to know about. Ostensibly, Jennifer Lewis is just another missing person, a runaway wife. It happens all the time. You know that, Harry." He nodded.

"The case is three years cold. Nobody cares about it, except Jennifer's sister. So why then is Tracy so sensitive about it, and why did Finkle warn me off it this morning? And he sure as hell doesn't want you involved."

"I don't know," Harry said. "Let's see what Tim can come up with." He thought for a moment, then said, "Tread carefully around Finkle and Tracy, Tim. We wouldn't want them to know what we're doing."

Tim gave him an, "are you kidding me," look, and said, "Hmm." He nibbled on his thumbnail. "These four...it depends on how deep you want me to dig."

"I want to know all there is to know."

He nodded. "You got it. Finkle and Tracy," he smiled, "shouldn't be any trouble...say, Friday? For the others, though, who knows where they are or how deep I'll have to dig. I may need a little extra time, Kate."

"That's fine," I said. "The gruesome twosome will do for a start."

He grinned as he got up, gathered up his stuff, and left the room muttering to himself. I couldn't help but smile.

"So," Harry said after Tim had closed the door behind him. "What now?"

"As far as the Lewis case is concerned?" I thought for a second, then said, "I have nothing to work with, not yet. Not until I hear from Tim. So I guess I'll concentrate on Sullivan for a few days. I'm planning to interview Pellman this afternoon. I'll see how that goes, then head up to Winchester either tomorrow or Thursday to interview his mother. That should be a boatload of fun."

"Is there anything I can do to help? I can let you have Bob for a couple of days if you like?"

I shook my head. "Thanks, but no thanks; not yet anyway. That would be like taking a sledgehammer to a thumbtack."

He smiled. "Well, you only have to ask... Would you like to get together this weekend?"

I tilted my head, frowned, narrowed my eyes, pursed my lips, then said, "We'll see. Right now, I have to go. Listen, Harry, you do know how grateful I am for everything you do, don't you?"

Now it was his turn: he smiled and said, "We'll see."

I laughed, stood, leaned over and pecked him on the cheek. He reached for me, but I managed to dodge him.

"Not today, Buster," I said, dodging away toward the door.

"Kate, you want to go get some lunch, then?"

"I said, not today. I'll talk to you later, okay?" He nodded, obviously disappointed. I left him still sitting on the sofa, and I headed back to the PD.

15

TUESDAY, MAY 12, 2 PM – SULLIVAN CASE

"Hey, you made it back." I slapped Lonnie on the shoulder as I walked by his cubicle. "Come on back to my office. You can tell me all about it. Then we'll go mess with Pellman's head."

"So," I said, as I sat down behind my desk. "How did it go?"

He sat down opposite me and said, "I made an appointment for Monday, June first—if that's okay."

"Of course."

"Good. I have to be at the clinic in Dalton at seven in the morning. Surgery is scheduled for nine, so I should be out of there by one or two." He paused. "I'll be off work for a week."

"That's fine, Lonnie. I'll manage. Will you need a ride?"

He shook his head. "No, I have that covered."

"Great! Well, I wish you luck, partner. Now, how about we go talk to Pellman?"

PELLMAN WAS WORKING IN THE ICU WHEN WE ARRIVED AT THE Trauma Center.

"I'm afraid he might be a while," the nurse acting as the receptionist said.

I flashed her my badge and told her that unless he was assisting with an emergency, I needed to see him right away and that if I had to, I'd go get him.

She made the call, told me he was finishing up and would be no more than ten minutes, then showed me to a waiting room. Twenty minutes later he came bursting into the room, his face bright red with anger.

Great start! I thought. *At least I don't have to wind him up.*

"Who the hell are you?" he began. "And why in God's name have you dragged me out of the ICU?"

I stood. Lonnie stood. We showed him our badges, and as we did so, I said, "We're police officers, Mr. Pellman. My name is Lieutenant Catherine Gazzara, and this is Sergeant Guest. We want to talk to you about the death of Rhonda Sullivan. Now, if there's somewhere quiet—"

He interrupted me. "Damn it all to hell. I thought that was over and done with. I have nothing to say to—"

"Shut the hell up." Lonnie took a step forward. "Either sit down or do as the Lieutenant asked and take us somewhere we can talk without being interrupted."

"Or we can take you to the police department," I said. "Your choice."

He glared at me, then at Lonnie, then seemed to calm down, a little.

He nodded, took a step back, looked at his watch and said, "Okay, there's an office we can use. I can give you five minutes."

Lonnie chuckled. "You'll give us as long as it damn takes," he said. "Let's go."

It was a small, bare office, just a desk, three chairs, and a credenza set against the wall behind the desk. I took the seat behind the desk—no point in giving him any sense of authority. Pellman sat down opposite me, and Lonnie dragged the other chair to one side, set it against the wall slightly in front of and facing our suspect. Then the large cop sat down, folded his arms, shoved his feet out in front of him, crossed his legs at the ankles, lowered his chin, and stared at him. Pellman squirmed uneasily on the seat but said nothing.

He was a nondescript individual, maybe five-ten tall, a hundred and eighty pounds, straight hair parted on the left and swept across his forehead. He was dressed in green scrubs; a surgical mask hung from his neck. He wore glasses and a gold ring with a snake head on his right pinky.

I glanced across the desk at him, opened my iPad and set it on the desk in front of me. Then I made a show of turning on my digital recorder and setting it down on the desktop in front of him.

"So," I said finally, looking him right in the eye. "Tell me about Rhonda Sullivan. How did you pull it off?"

"You've gotta be kiddin' me," he said, shaking his head. "After all this time—"

Lonnie interrupted him. "There's no statute of limitations on murder, asshole."

I shot Lonnie a warning look, then said to Pellman, "He's right. Look, Chad, we know you killed her. Your employee number was used to draw the potassium chloride from the dispenser. You knew her; you were even friendly with her. And we know you had a crush on her—more than a crush, I think. Anyway, she rejected you. So, you had the means, and you had a motive." *I only wish you'd had the opportunity. We'd be done with this!*

"You've gotten it all wrong, Lieutenant," he said, in a calm voice. "As I told Detective Wells, several times: it wasn't me that took the KCL, it was Lisa, Lisa Marco."

"So you did, but she was her friend, her best friend, and she didn't have a motive; you did."

"I was her friend, too. I'm not crazy, Lieutenant. If I was going to kill her, d'you think I'd be stupid enough to check out the drug using my own code? Give me a break, *please*."

"But you'd done it before, hadn't you?"

His eyes narrowed, questioning. "Done what before?" he asked.

"Misappropriated drugs from the dispenser."

"*That?* Are you kidding me? I have a bad back; nerve damage. My prescription for Tramadol had run out, so I took a few pills to tide me over. So what? Everyone does it."

I looked at the notes on my iPad, then up at him and said, "You refused to take a polygraph. Why was that, if you had nothing to hide?"

"I did as I was advised by my attorney. I always do. Why pay for one if you're not going to do as she says." *Damn! Good answer.*

I shrugged. "What d'you think, Sergeant Guest?" I asked, never taking my eyes off Pellman's. "Is he really that stupid, or does he think we are?"

"If he expects us to fall for that old ploy, he is. How many times have we heard that one, Lieutenant? 'D'you think I'd be so stupid' and so on, and so on."

"Yeah, I think he's stupid; stupid, and arrogant, but then, aren't they all? Killers, I mean."

Pellman straightened up in his chair, stared right back at me, and said, "I'm not a killer. I was in North Carolina when Rhonda was murdered, seventy-five miles away in Winchester, with my mother. Detective Wells checked. He interviewed her several times. You can check. Now, I'm not going to say anything more. I want my attorney."

"No, you don't," I said. "You're not under arrest. Is there anyone other than your mother that can corroborate you being in Winchester that evening? Did you go out to eat, to a bar, convenience store, go anywhere at all, Mr. Pellman?"

"Yes, I did. I went to Walmart for Mom. I told Detective Wells. She even kept the receipt."

"She did, and Wells checked. He spoke to every sales clerk and manager that was on duty that evening and, guess what... No one remembered seeing you there. So, let's face it. She could have gone to the store herself."

"She could have, but she didn't. I did, and you can't prove otherwise. I was there all night, at my mother's. I didn't leave until after eight-thirty in the morning, when I went home and got ready for work. My shift started at noon."

"I didn't do it," he said. "Now either arrest me and let me call my attorney, or let me go back to work."

I let him go back to work.

"So much for putting pressure on him," Lonnie said, as he slammed the cruiser door.

"Yup," I said. "And I didn't see any indications that he was lying. Wells said he was tough. I wonder how tough his mother is? I guess we'll find out."

16

We traveled to the Pellman residence in Winchester early the following morning, and we timed how long it took: one hour seventeen minutes in very light traffic.

No, we didn't call ahead, which could have been a disastrous mistake if she hadn't been home. But in fact, she was still in bed.

"Come in," she said, resignedly, when she came to the door. "I've been expecting you."

Elizabeth Pellman led the way through to the kitchen.

"Sit," she said, waving a hand at the round, white breakfast table and four chairs.

Hmmm, I thought, *a woman of few words.*

"Coffee?" she asked, opening a cupboard and taking down a jar.

"No, no thank you," I said.

Lonnie looked plaintively at me. I shook my head at him.

"Well, suit yourselves. I've got to have some."

I watched as she set the machine going, trying to size her up. I already knew that she was fifty-two years old. She didn't look it though. I also knew that she'd been divorced from her husband for some eighteen years.

The white, slightly oversized pajamas gaped open at the front, revealing a cleavage that bordered on the spectacular. *Boob job? If it is, it's one of the best I've ever seen.*

Her dark brown hair was close-cropped, almost like a man's. Her eyes were enormous and made even more striking by the eyeliner she'd neglected to remove before going to bed.

She grabbed a large mug and filled it almost to the brim, sat down at the table, cradled it in both hands, placed her elbows on the table, and sipped with her eyes closed.

"Oh wow, that's good," she said and opened her eyes.

"So," she said. "You want to talk to me about Chad?"

She didn't wait for an answer. Instead, she set her mug down on the table and continued. "I don't know why the hell you would. Nothing's changed in the last three years. He was here with me all night. He was here when I went to bed, and he was still here when I got up at six o'clock. Case closed."

She leaned forward slightly, the fingers of both hands lightly stroking the sides of the hot mug; the pajama top gaped even more. I could see her right nipple. I heard Lonnie moving slightly in the chair next to me. *Damn! Those can't be real.*

"Mrs. Pellman," I said, quietly. "Would you please cover yourself up? My partner's about to have a heart attack."

I smiled to myself when I heard Lonnie suck in his breath.

"Oops, sorry," she said, quickly fastening one more button, which still left little to the imagination. "You'll have to forgive me; I'm so used to living alone."

"How did you know we were coming?" I asked.

"Duh! My son called last night. Look, I've been through it all a half-dozen times. My son was here with me from around two on Sunday afternoon, October 8, until eight-thirty the following morning. I know it was nine years ago, but nothing's changed. You're wasting your time."

Okay, so let's give it to her straight.

"Listen to me carefully, Mrs. Pellman."

She smiled indulgently at me.

"I know, and you know, that what you just told me isn't true." I watched her eyes, they narrowed just the tiniest bit; the smile remained but hardened considerably.

"You're calling me a liar," she stated, quietly. "I think you'd better leave, now!"

Lonnie leaned forward, rested his arms on the table, looked her in the eye and said, "No matter what you say, or how often you say it, we know Chad murdered Rhonda Sullivan, in cold blood. He calmly and deliberately injected a lethal dose of potassium chloride into her, enough to kill a *friggin' horse! Your son is an evil piece of garbage, and he'll fry for it!*" he shouted, startling Mrs. Pellman so much she reared back in her chair.

She recovered quickly. "My son didn't kill her. He's not evil. He's a good boy. He'd never hurt anyone, especially Rhonda. He loved her."

"She rejected him," I said, grasping Lonnie's arm and pulling him back. "He made up his mind: If he couldn't have her, no one could. So, he injected her with a lethal drug and watched her die. Doesn't that upset you just a little bit?"

"No, it doesn't because he didn't do it. He was here with me that night, and nothing you can say will change that because it's the truth."

"What time did you go to bed that night, Mrs. Pellman?"

"It was just before eleven." She looked away, then back at me. "I know because I had to take my pills before I went to bed. I checked the time."

She's lying!

"Are you absolutely sure?" I watched her eyes. They narrowed, hardened. There was just the hint of a smile on her lips. She nodded slowly.

"He wasn't here, was he?"

She sighed and stood up. "I've nothing more to say to you. It's time for you to leave."

She walked to the door, opened it, and waited.

I nodded, stood, walked to the door, then paused in front of her, looked her in the eye, and said, "Your son's a sadistic killer, Mrs. Pellman, and I'm going to get him; sooner or later, bet on it."

She didn't answer. I turned and walked out into the morning sunshine. There was a slight breeze blowing across the hillside. *An ill wind, I think.*

"Well, what d'you think?" Lonnie asked when we were back in the car and driving along River Avenue toward Highway 64.

"I think we need to time the ride back to Rhonda Sullivan's old apartment."

"I know that. That's not what I meant. I meant: what d'you think about her?"

I knew that. "I think she was lying."

"Duh, yeah, she was, whenever her freakin' lips were moving. And the titty show; that was a diversion, right?"

I nodded as I swung the big car onto 64. "It was. Did you like that?"

"What's not to like? She's a good-looking woman, a little mature, maybe, but—"

"Yeah, yeah," I said, interrupting his enthusiastic flow.

"Yes," I said, concentrating on the traffic. "She was lying, but most obviously when I asked her what time she went to bed... Hey, I'm hungry. You want to eat?"

"No, I'm trying to watch my intake, especially now that...well, you know."

"Okay, coffee it is then. I think there's a Hardee's down the road a piece." There wasn't. There wasn't one, or anything like it, until we reached Kimball, by which time I thought I was going to die. But I digress.

"Did you notice how she looked away to the left when I asked her?" I said, knowing damn well that he didn't; he had eyes for only one thing...well, two.

"It was a classic tell: when someone looks left like that, they are usually fabricating the answer. If they look to the right, it's likely they are checking their memory. She lied, for sure, but we can't prove it."

I paused, thinking, then said, "I'll tell you this, though: I think she knows he did it... Eleven? That's when she said she went to bed. She knows how long it takes to drive from her house to Chattanooga.

I pulled into the Hardee's at Kimball, checked my watch and said, "Hell, if he was still there when she went to bed, if he was ever there at all, there's no way he could have made this drive back in time. We've been on the road forty-four minutes already and we're still at least another thirty-five minutes from Sullivan's apartment, if we get a clear run through the city. So an hour and a half, or slightly better..."

I pulled up to the drive-through. "Two large coffees, please, black."

"Ninety minutes?" I said as I pulled up to the window. "So, if he left at eleven when she said she went to bed, that would put him at her apartment at around half past midnight, but only if he left right at eleven. That's outside the window for time of death. Which means..." I handed over the cash, grabbed the tray, thanked her, handed the tray to Lonnie, and continued. "Which means—"

"Yeah, I got it," Lonnie interrupted me, impatiently. "We're screwed, and that she was lying, but we already knew that, and we have nothing new. So now what do we do?"

The short answer was that I didn't know. We didn't have a crime scene, not anymore, and I'd already asked Mike Willis to recheck what little physical evidence there was. He'd found nothing new. I was fresh out of ideas; I was stumped.

We were back in the office by two o'clock that afternoon. I left Lonnie at his desk and went to my office. I had a report to write, and I wasn't looking forward to it.

By five o'clock, I'd finished. It wasn't a long report, and I wasn't proud of it, but it would have to do. I'd simply laid out the facts as I saw them.

There was nothing new to report. There had been no progress, and there wasn't likely to be unless a miracle was to happen. I was certain that Pellman had killed her, but I couldn't prove it. We'd re-interviewed Lisa Marco, Pellman, and his mother, to no good result. That there was no point in talking to Sullivan's fiancé, Mark Yates. He had no access to potassium chloride or the medical knowledge to have administered the drug. Lisa Marco had nothing new to add to her previous statements. Pellman insisted he didn't do it—that it was Marco who took the drugs from the dispenser, but there was no way to prove that either. Mrs. Pellman insisted her son was with her when Sullivan died, and neither Sergeant Guest or I could break her. And that was it.

I sighed, shook my head, picked up the office phone and punched in the chief's number.

"Chief Johnston's office. This is Cathy."

"Hey, Cathy. I need to see the chief. It's important."

"Hold for me, Kate."

The line played that annoying music again, but she was back almost immediately. "He wants to know why you want to see him."

"Tell him it's about the Sullivan case."

She was back a few seconds later. "Okay, come on, but I warn you, he's not in a good mood."

Oh crap, that's all I need.

"Okay, thanks, Cathy."

She was right, and she was wrong: he was in a terrible mood.... And who do you think was sitting at his right hand...well to the right of his desk? You got it: Henry Finkle.

"Sit down, Lieutenant," he said. "You're not bearing good news, I assume."

I nodded as I sat down. Finkle was literally beside himself with glee.

"I'm sorry, Chief. The Sullivan case is dead." I placed the file on his desk and handed him my report. He snatched it away from me and proceeded to read it through. His face was like stone, but I could see the anger glittering in his eyes.

"So, you've quit on it," he said, finally, looking up at me.

"No, sir."

"Well, what else would you call it?"

"Sir," Finkle said, "if I may suggest—"

"No, Henry, you may not suggest anything. In fact, you may leave, now."

He looked crushed, stood and glared at me as he walked to the door. I waited for the door to slam. It didn't. He closed it gently behind him.

"So, Kate," Johnston said, his face softening a little. "What's this all about? I figured if anyone could get the son of a bitch, you could."

"That's what I thought too. Without his mother's alibi, I would have. But then, so would Detective Wells have nine years ago, and we wouldn't be here now. She's lying, sir. I know she is. But there's no way to prove that she is. I can't see wasting any more money investigating this thing further. Maybe, sometime in the future we'll catch a break."

I felt horrible letting the chief down. He looked across the desk at me, nodding slowly.

He picked up my report, tore it in half, dropped it in the wastebasket beside him, then pushed the file toward me.

"You're right, Kate. Maybe something will come up. Hang onto it for a while. It's better in your office than it would be in the morgue." He was talking about the basement room where the cold cases were stored.

"Thank you, Chief."

I stood, picked up the file and walked to the door.

"One thing more, Lieutenant."

I turned, my hand on the doorknob.

"Stay out of Henry's way. He means you no good."

"Yes, sir, and thank you." *If you only knew...*

17

I woke early on Friday morning...real early. I'd had Finkle and Tracy on my mind for most of the night. Finally, around five, I gave up trying to sleep and crawled out of bed, put on some running gear, and drove to the Greenway. By five-thirty, I was running at a good clip along the concrete path. Along the way, I passed several more like-minded fitness freaks—no, I'm not one of those—but I didn't really notice or acknowledge them. I still had Dick and Tiny foremost in my thoughts, and I wasn't sure why; intuition?

Did either of them have personal reasons for not wanting the Lewis investigation to go forward? If so, which one and why? Finkle? Maybe. He didn't seem to tire of trying to get into my pants. He's married but likes to play around. Maybe he knew Jennifer Lewis. If so, he could have told Tracy to go easy. Tracy? He's quirky as hell...

And so it went on, question after question but no answers, other than I was beginning to think Finkle looked good for it... No, no. Ass that he is, I didn't think he had anything to do with Jennifer's disappearance. If he did have anything to hide, it would be something purely selfish. *Maybe Tim will have found something. He said Friday, and I need to talk with Harry, too.*

I completed the five-mile run and was home by six-thirty. By seven, I'd showered, dressed, and was on my second cup of coffee. I scrambled two eggs, burned some toast, and was on my way to the office by eight. There, I made a couple of calls, had a few words with Lonnie, and headed out of the office to Harry Starke's downtown offices; it was eight-thirty.

"Good morning, Jacque," I greeted her as I entered through the side door. "He told you I was coming, right?"

"He did. Tim's with him, but you can go on in. I'll bring you some coffee."

I knocked on his office door and pushed it open. Harry was seated behind his huge desk; Tim was seated opposite him. They looked like high school principal and geeky student. Ah, but looks can deceive. Aside from Jacque and Bob Ryan, Harry thought more of Tim than anyone else on his team. He respected his expertise and never doubted a word he said.

They looked at me when I entered, and they both stood up.

"Hey you," Harry said. "Where've you been? We started without you. Grab a seat; sit down."

"Hello, Kate." Tim smiled self-consciously, looked down at the floor, then up again. "He's pullin' your chain. We haven't started; not yet."

He leaned over the desk, snatched a tissue from a box by the phone, took off his glasses, sat down, and busily went about polishing the lenses.

"So, Kate," Harry said, then paused as the door opened and Jacque handed me a cup of coffee.

"So, Kate," he said again. "Talk to me."

I thought for a moment, sipped my coffee—it was steaming hot—then said, "Tim said he'd have something for me by today. Do you, Tim?"

"He does, but let me go first."

He opened his iPad, flipped through several screens and found the one he wanted. "Henry Finkle was a patrolman back in '97 when I joined the force," Harry said. "So he'd already been on the job for a couple of years. I didn't know him, but I did know of him. He had something of a reputation for crossing the line. Apparently, he'd do just about anything to get ahead.

"Anyway, I contacted some of my old police buddies, and I learned a couple of things: One, he's definitely a lady's man—"

I tried to stifle a laugh, but it snuck out.

He looked up. "What?"

"I could have told you that."

"Yeah, well, I also learned that our boy liked to frequent certain, unsavory bars...and ladies; he'd been known to pay for his delights. He also liked to play rough." He paused, glanced up at me, then continued.

"I, myself, remember hearing a story that an official complaint had been made against him by a lady..." He consulted his iPad. "An escort, one Tina Gonzales. That was, supposedly, sometime in late 2004. Henry was a captain at the time. She claimed—and I got this from two different sources—that he assaulted and injured her; just how or how badly, nobody seems to know." He closed the cover of his iPad, then said, "I asked Tim to check it out. Unfortunately, he was unable to find any reference to that particular incident, so it was either just a rumor or someone went to great lengths to hide it. Which, knowing him as we do, is entirely possible. He's a violent man, is our Henry."

He looked at Tim, and said, "You did find two separate reports accusing him of excessive use of force, though, in 1998 and in 2000, both while he was still a uniformed sergeant. Internal Affairs investigated both, and he was cleared both times. No action was taken in either case."

I looked at Tim; I was in awe. He smiled brightly at me.

"You hacked his personnel file?" I asked.

He nodded, cheerfully, and said, "I did, and Tracy's too."

I shook my head in wonder. I always knew the boy was good, but...

"And?" I asked.

He consulted his laptop, then said, "I'll give you the short version. Detective John Tracy is forty-one years old, joined the force in 1998; he was then twenty-four. He spent his first three years in uniform, and the next seven in Narcotics, undercover." He paused, looked up at me and grinned.

Oh yeah, I knew all about that; that's when Chief Johnston dumped him on me.

"So, in 2008, he was assigned to the then Sergeant Gazzara as her partner." He grinned sideways at me, did the thing with his glasses, and then continued. "That lasted only for a couple of months when for some unknown reason," again, he made with the grin, "he was transferred back to Narcotics." He paused, looked at me, squinted, scratched at the back of his ear, and said, "And this is where it gets interesting. On April 17, 2012, he was transferred to Missing Persons, where he remains to this day."

What the hell?

"April 17, 2012?" I asked, stunned. "Are you sure?"

"Uh, yeah!"

"But...that's the day after Jennifer Lewis was reported missing."

"Again, yeah. And, according to the paperwork in the file, he was assigned the case on...the same day, the 17th."

I looked at Harry, my mouth hanging open.

"That can't be a coincidence," I said. "Who signed off on the transfer?"

"Chief Johnston did," Tim said.

I shook my head, my thoughts whirling. *That can't be right.*

"Okay," I said. "I'm going to need to talk to Johnston. Somebody must have recommended Tracy for that job, and I'm betting it was Finkle. And if it was, he did it for a reason... Who assigned the case to Tracy?"

"There's no signature—"

I interrupted him. "Oh, m'god, you don't suppose..."

"Take it easy, Kate," Harry said. "You're going too fast. You need to slow down, and you sure as hell don't need to poke the bear before you think it through. Johnston will eat your lunch."

I sat back in my chair and stared at the artwork on the wall behind Harry. *Wow! Finkle! And Tracy. What the hell have they done? What, to, do? What, to, do?*

Finally—it could only have been a few seconds—I knew how I was going to handle it. Oh yeah, very carefully.

I looked at Tim.

"Add Tina Gonzales to your list, please."

"Will do." He tapped on his iPad then looked at me and nodded.

"Great! Thank you. What else do you have for me?" I asked.

"That's it, for now. I'm still working on the others. It shouldn't take too long, but I do have other stuff to do."

He cocked his head and pushed the glasses higher on the bridge of his nose. He reminded me of a skinny owl. Somehow, though, I was sure he was a whole lot wiser, well smarter, than any owl.

"Take your time," I said. "The Sullivan case is already nine years cold. A few days is not going to make much difference now."

Tim nodded, closed his laptop, grabbed his phone, stood, and said, "I'll email everything to you. You should have it when you get back to your office. If I find anything I think you should know about, I'll call you. Talk to you later, Kate." And with that, he left us.

"So someone made sure Tracy covered it up," I said, thoughtfully. "But who? I can't believe it's Chief Johnston. The man's a tough SOB, but he's squeaky clean... Had to be Finkle. What d'you think, Harry?"

"I think you're on dangerous ground. I also think Finkle is a nasty piece of work and won't hesitate to discredit—or hurt you—in every way he can. You want me to have him watched?"

I laughed out loud at that. "No, Harry. You keep Ryan away from him. I can handle Finkle, and Tracy, and that's just what I intend to do."

"I believe you," he said with a smile. "Now, what about us? It's Friday. You want to go out tonight?"

I looked him in the eye as he smiled back at me, his eyebrows raised, blue eyes sparkled and...I melted.

"Sure. Why not?"

"Great, I'll cook."

"*Cook?* You said out."

"Out for you; in for me, I hope."

Well...what would you have done?

18

It was late morning when I arrived back at my office. Lonnie was out somewhere doing something. What, I didn't know, nor did I care. I had some serious thinking to do so I needed to be on my own.

I had my calls forwarded to voicemail, hung my home-made "Do Not Disturb" sign on my office door, which I then closed and locked. Next, I closed the blinds and sat down behind my desk, leaned my chair back against the wall, closed my eyes and began to try to unscramble my aching head. One thing I did know: Harry was right. I needed to think things through before I began to stir the swamp.

I lost all track of time. I might even have dozed, a little—can't remember when that happened before, or since—because it was almost one o'clock when I was startled by a loud and insistent knocking at my office door.

I stood, rubbed my eyes, then walked around my desk and unlocked the door.

"What the hell is this?" Finkle asked, waving the do not disturb sign in my face. "Have you gone mad, Lieutenant? This is a police department, not a freaking hotel. What were you doing?"

"I was working, Chief. What d'you think I was doing? Oh no; don't you dare go there."

He grinned, his teeth bared. He reminded me of an angry wolf.

"What were you working on that required you to lock yourself away with the window shuttered? Not the Sullivan case? I thought you'd closed that out."

"Yes, Chief, the Sullivan case," I lied. "Chief Johnston persuaded me to give it another try, so that's what I'm doing. Now, what can I do for you?"

"It's Friday. I need to know what the hell you're up to."

Damn, I'm glad you don't.

"I'm trying to figure out what my next move is going to be." *That was not a lie. It was exactly what I was doing, but not concerning the Sullivan case.*

"Now, will you leave me alone so that I can get on with it?"

He rewarded me with a snarly smile and backed out of the door. "Keep me informed, Lieutenant. In fact, you can put your intentions on paper and have them on my desk no later than..." he checked his watch, "shall we say, five o'clock today?"

Oh hell. That's screwed it!

I closed the door and went back to my desk, opened my laptop and began to type. Ten minutes later I was done. I hit enter and sent the report to the printer. I grabbed the sheet of paper, read it through, and shook my head. It wasn't going to win me any awards, but it was all I had.

I checked the time—it was almost three—then headed out and down the elevator to the first floor where Finkle's office was located, right next door to Chief Johnston's suite of offices. I knocked, walked in and dropped the single sheet of paper on the desk in front of him.

He didn't ask me to sit, so I crossed my arms and stared down at him.

He picked up the report and read the three short paragraphs, then looked up at me and said, "What the hell is this? There's nothing here, other than you intend to re-interview the suspect and his mother and spend more of the tax payer's money on re-examining the physical evidence."

Yeah, I know. It was all BS I'd made up just to keep him happy. What the hell else was I to do?

"Right, that's the plan," I said, staring him in the eye.

He nodded, his eyes glittering, thought for a moment, then he looked away and said, offhandedly, "And the other thing, the Lewis case?"

"What about it?" I shifted my weight from one foot to the other. "You told me, as did the chief, that Sullivan is the priority and that I was to concentrate on it, and that's exactly what I've done, am doing." It wasn't entirely true, but true enough.

"Hmm. Well then, that will be all, Lieutenant. Keep me informed...about the Sullivan case."

What's he up to?

I left Finkle's office and closed the door behind me. I stood for a moment, looking at Chief Johnston's door, hesitating, then I took a deep breath, knocked once and walked inside. Cathy looked up at me, surprised.

"Lieutenant Gazzara. I didn't know you had an appointment."

"I don't. I was wondering if maybe he could spare me a few minutes, in private."

She tilted her head, stared at me for a moment, then nodded and picked up the phone.

"Chief, Lieutenant Gazzara's here. She'd like a private word." She listened, nodded, and then set the phone back in its cradle.

"He'll see you. Go on in."

"Come on in, Catherine. Sit down. This is...irregular. So, before we begin, I'm going to ask Cathy to join us."

"Of course, sir. If that's what you prefer..."

"It is. I make it a rule never to interview a female officer without a witness present."

That didn't seem to bother you when you kicked Finkle out yesterday.

He picked up the phone. "Cathy, join us, please."

"Don't worry," he said, returning the phone to its cradle. "She's discreet. Whatever you have to say, you can say in front of her."

Cathy entered the room and took the seat usually occupied by Assistant Chief Finkle, which was fine with me, but then she placed a small digital recorder on the desk in front of her, and that *was* a little disconcerting.

"Now, Lieutenant, I know this is not about the Sullivan case, so what is it I can do for you?"

"Sir, I'm not so sure we need to record what I have to say."

He nodded at Cathy. She picked up the recorder and turned it off.

"Be very careful, Lieutenant. Now, talk to me."

I nodded, took a deep breath, and began.

"This is about the Lewis case, Chief."

He leaned back in his chair and folded his arms. "Go on."

"You saw the file, sir. It's...incomplete to say the least." I took another breath. "And there are some troubling anomalies."

I looked at him. He said nothing.

I looked at Cathy. She looked back at me, a slight smile on her lips.

"Sir, you authorized Detective Tracy's transfer to Missing Persons on April 17, 2012. I'd like to know who recommended that transfer."

"And why do you want to know that?"

"Please, sir. Humor me. Who was it?"

"You'd better have one hell of a good reason for this. It was Assistant Chief Finkle," he said.

My heart leaped.

"Did you know, Chief," I said, "that the 17th was the day after Jennifer Lewis was reported missing, and there's no record of who assigned the case to Tracy?"

He stared at me. I felt decidedly uncomfortable. I looked at Cathy; her face was a mask.

"What are you saying, Lieutenant?" he asked, quietly.

Okay, here we go.

"Sir, I'd like to question both Detective Tracy and Chief Finkle—"

"*STOP!* Are you saying that you suspect one or both of those officers had something to do with Lewis' disappearance? If so...by God you'd better be able to back it up."

"Unfortunately, sir, I can't. What I have is circumstantial at best, coincidences, mostly, especially Tracy's transfer and assignment to the case."

He waited. I continued. I laid out everything I had, everything Harry had said, leaving out only Tim's hacking of the PD's computers. How did I manage that? Well, I put it all down to the grapevine and rumors.

"You're right, Lieutenant," he said when I was done. "You have nothing. Nothing concrete. I can, however, confirm the two cases of excessive use of force by the then Sergeant Finkle. The rumors and the allegations about Miss Gonzales well..."

He stared right into my eyes. There was something about that look. *Damn it! He knows. Harry was right.*

He caught my reaction; his lips twitched, slightly. *Was that a smile?*

"I can't confirm any of that, of course," he said. "Nor can I officially sanction what you propose. However, you may talk to the two officers concerned, but," again, he made with the stare, "be very careful, Lieutenant. Henry Finkle is not a man you may wish to cross. I have your back but, for your own protection, keep me informed. You may go now."

"Thank you, sir."

He nodded, and I left the room, my heart beating like I'd just sprinted five miles.

19

FRIDAY, MAY 15, WEEKEND

To say I was excited when I left the chief's office that Friday afternoon would be an understatement: I was both exhilarated and daunted at the enormity of the task I was about to undertake. Was I on the brink of professional suicide? I was about to take on an extremely savvy senior police officer, and equally devious detective. Compared to Finkle, though, Detective Tracy was inconsequential. Even so, I knew from experience that he was a clever, vengeful individual with the survival instincts of a cornered rat: the man didn't spend seven years undercover among Chattanooga's drug community without learning how to stay alive. Together, the two would pose a formidable threat and, try as I might, I couldn't clear my head of the wandering thoughts and questions that I knew would dog me throughout the weekend.

Harry did indeed cook dinner that Friday evening and, not for the first time in my life was I grateful for the diversion...and the sounding board.

I didn't arrive at his condo on Lakeshore Lane until almost eight o'clock. He was outside, on the patio, with a glass of scotch in his hand.

"I'll have one of those, please," I said, dropping into the seat next to him.

"Whoa, that's not you. Hard day?"

"You have no idea."

He poured a large one for me, dropped a single cube of ice into it, handed it to me, and said, "Well, are you going to tell me about it?"

So I did, and he listened thoughtfully without interrupting me until I was finished. And still he said nothing. He just stared out across the river, seemingly lost in thought.

"*Well*," I said, impatiently. "What d'you think?"

He raised his eyebrows, made a wry face, then said, "I think it's possible you've bitten off more than you can chew, and there's little I can do to help. Johnston might have sanctioned my limited involvement, but he's not going to allow me to interrogate one of his senior officers, or even Tracy for that matter."

"Thanks, buddy," I said, "for the vote of confidence. That's not the kind of help I was looking for. I was looking more for moral support and advice. I can handle the interviews."

"I'm sure you can. I'm sorry, Kate. That's not what I meant."

"Just what did you mean, then?"

"Finkle will block you at every turn. He's an experienced interrogator, vastly outranks you, and he'll do his damnedest to discredit you. He and Tracy will collaborate to bring you down. You think today was tough; you have no idea." He looked at his watch, then stood and said. "It's past time we ate, and I still have to grill the steaks. Let's continue this after dinner, okay?"

"Yes, okay. If you don't mind, though, I'll stay out here and relax, until it's ready." I held out my glass. "Hit me again, please."

Dinner was delicious: some sort of fancy salad, Greek, I think, and a filet mignon the size of a house, cooked to perfection and served with a loaded baked potato. But that's about all I remember of it. I do remember that my head was in a whirl, already living the interviews yet to come, and I was, in Harry's own words, "in dreamland."

Finally, he cleared the table, and we settled down on the sofa in front of the expansive picture window. It was almost dark and beginning to rain. The water was still, motionless except for the needle-like splashes of the raindrops that scattered the reflections of the lights on the Thrasher Bridge. It was, as always, spectacular and, yes, romantic, and any other time... But, as you might guess, I was in no mood for that, at least not then. I needed to talk, and Harry knew that I did.

"So," he said, closing one eye and holding his glass of Laphroaig up so that one of the lights on the far side of the river shone through it. "I imagine you'll want to get this started first thing on Monday morning?"

He stated it in the form of a question, and it was so simple I hadn't even thought about it.

"Well, yes," I said, hesitantly, "of course."

He nodded. "And how, exactly, will you approach it? More to the point: who will you approach first?"

I hadn't thought about that either. Up until then, all I'd thought about was how I was going to handle Finkle, and I was still trying to figure that out.

"I think...Finkle."

"Why?"

"Because I think he's the reason Tracy did such a lousy job of the investigation. I think Tracy's covering up for him, and that could only be because Finkle was involved with Lewis. What else could it be?"

"You're thinking that because of Finkle's history with women?"

"That, and the way he treats me."

He slowly shook his head. "You'd better be well prepared, Kate. If you're not, he'll eat your lunch. You need a list of specific questions you want him to answer, and it had better be complete. You may not get a second chance."

Hmmm, I mused, staring, unseeing out across the river. The rain had increased, and the surface of the water was a roiling black mass streaked with orange and white reflections. *Food for thought.*

"Okay," he broke into my thoughts. "You'll start with Finkle. He's going to use his rank to try to intimidate you. You'll need to nullify that right at the beginning. Where d'you plan to interview him? His office, or yours? Before you answer that, I suggest you do neither. Treat him just as you would any other suspect; you pick the battleground. Use an interview room. Have Lonnie there, stick to the rules, and record and take video of everything."

Interview room? I thought, inwardly shaking my head. *I don't think so. He wouldn't go for it.* Harry's "full speed ahead and damn the torpedoes" approach might work for him, but it wouldn't work for me; that I knew for sure. No, mine would have to be a much softer, subtler approach, but I wasn't going to tell Harry that.

I sighed. "Harry, I'm an experienced interrogator. I know all that. I can handle it. Don't worry. He will *not* intimidate me."

"So you say, but this is going to be different from anything you've ever dealt with before."

"I know, and I appreciate your concern."

"Okay, can I make one suggestion before you go half-cocked? Talk to Tim first. See what he's come up with."

I sighed. "I can't put it off, Harry. I don't want Finkle forewarned. And I'm stressed enough already, and tired, and I can't even think straight anymore." I let out an exasperated sigh. "Oh hell, you're right, as always. Okay, but I need to talk to him soon."

"Let me call him." He stood, stepped up to the window, and hit his speed dial.

I watched and tried to listen as Harry talked to Tim, but I managed to get only one side of the conversation: "Yes. Yes. I know. That's good. Yes. Okay, I'll tell her." He disconnected and sat down again.

"He says to tell you he has a couple more avenues to explore and then he'll be finished. So, eight o'clock Monday morning in my office, will that work?"

I heaved a sigh of relief, and said, "That will work. Now, can we drop it, at least for tonight?"

He nodded. "Sure we can. Are you planning on going home or…"

"Oh come on, Harry. You know better than that. I've had two glasses of that stuff you love to drink and two glasses of wine. I'm not fit to drive…and hell, I want another drink, please?"

And that, as you might imagine, wasn't all I got that night. In fact, I had an amazing weekend.

20

MONDAY, MAY 18, 8 AM

I left Harry early on Sunday morning, not something I would normally have done, but I was antsy and wanted to prepare for what was to come the following morning.

I spent most of the day and evening with a yellow legal pad and pencil—the salient points I transcribed onto my iPad. Old fashioned? Yes, I know, but so easy, and totally visual. By nine o'clock that evening, I'd done all I could; all that was left was to talk to Tim.

My last act that Sunday night before I went to bed was to call Lonnie and ask him to meet me at Harry's offices no later than eight o'clock the following morning.

Typical Lonnie; when I arrived, he was already there waiting for me, outside in the parking lot. Me? I arrived a little before eight and, wouldn't you know it? I was the last one to get there.

Harry and Tim were already in the conference room, heads together, discussing...me, I supposed.

"Ah, there you are," Harry said, getting to his feet. "Hey, Lonnie. Good to see you. Why don't you two grab some coffee and let's get started? I have a nine-thirty appointment."

Good to see you? Wow, that's a first. I thought they hated each other's guts?

Lonnie grudgingly acknowledged Harry's greeting and went to the breakroom to get the coffees.

I dumped my stuff on the table and sat down opposite Tim. Jacque joined us a minute or two later, and Lonnie returned with the coffee a couple of minutes after her.

"Okay, we all ready?" Harry asked when everyone was settled a few minutes later. "Good. Tim, you have the floor. Go!"

"Oh... Er, yeah, yes, okay." He clicked his mouse, stared at his laptop, then cleared his throat and said, "I'll begin with Tina Gonzalez." He looked around the table, quizzically.

I smiled at him, nodded, opened my yellow pad, flipped through it to a blank page, and picked up my pen. They all stared at me. I smiled, tilted my head a little, and raised my eyebrows.

"Wow," Tim said, staring at the pad and shaking his head. "I didn't know they still made those. Okay! Tina Gonzalez; originally from Conyers, Georgia. You had her on the list because of her association with Henry Finkle. She's thirty-nine. She works as a stripper at the Starburst on East Sycamore and has done so since she arrived in Chattanooga at the age of eighteen in 1998. She's been arrested two times for prostitution, and once for public drunkenness. All three arrests resulted in fines; no jail time. I found an ad for her services on the Dark Web as, and I quote, 'a beautiful, sophisticated companion,' and then the ad goes on to list her services. Apparently, she's available for dates, travel, conventions, and so on. Sex is not mentioned. Her last arrest was in 2006, for prostitution, which means she's managed to stay out of trouble for the last nine years, which also indicates that she's either very savvy or someone is looking after her. She has good credit; not great, but okay. She has two bank accounts, checking and savings. There's nothing unusual about the size of the checking account; the savings account, however, is questionable. It seems she's managed to put aside a nice little nest-egg, slightly more than $81,000. Again, that indicates she's savvy and maybe, she's...selling her wares?"

He waited for a reaction, but got none, so he continued, a slightly wounded look on his face. "I could find no references in 2003, 2004 or 2005, to the alleged assault by the then Captain Finkle. If it happened, the records have been thoroughly cleaned." He looked up, and said, "And that's about it... Oh, here's a photo of her."

He handed each of us a glossy eight-by-ten print.

She was indeed lovely, though I wondered how much of it was due to Photoshop. I was the last to lay my copy down.

"You want me to continue?" Tim asked.

"Keep going, Tim," Harry said.

"Jennifer Lewis," Tim said, "missing since April 16, 2012, was born in Dalton, Georgia, in 1974 where she grew up with her older sister Alice. She graduated high school in 1992 and, etcetera, etcetera. I won't go any deeper into her life story other than that she worked for a while in the carpet industry and moved to Chattanooga in 2000; she was then twenty-six. She had several jobs, including a thirteen-month stint at Dillard's as a sales clerk, and two years at J.C. Penney, also as a sales clerk. From October 2003 until she was reported missing, she worked at the Country Skillet on Shallowford Road. Now, this is where it gets interesting. She also worked part-time at the Starburst, for a period of five weeks, from March 12, 2012, until she vanished...as what, I can't say. Maybe as a waitress; maybe as a stripper. Either way, she'd be required to take her clothes off. Well, not all of them if she was a waitress. Only if she was—"

"Yes, yes," Harry interrupted him. "We get the idea. Get *on* with it, Tim."

"Yes...yes, I will. Okay, there's no evidence that she was...a prostitute, but... Okay, she worked at the Country Skillet on April 14 and was supposed to work that evening at the Starburst, but she never arrived. That means," he said, triumphantly, "that we can almost pinpoint the moment when she was abducted, if she was abducted, or maybe she did run away..."

He caught Harry's warning look and hurriedly continued. "Anyway, I couldn't find out when or where she met John Lewis, but the two were married in 2008; she was then thirty-four and he forty-six and, from reading the reports," he looked at me, "it seems she left him on March 2, 2012, and went to work at the Starburst ten days later. What happened to her from then until she was reported missing...I don't know. Her cell phone stopped working at two-thirty-seven in the afternoon of April 15, and it hasn't worked since. None of her credit cards have been used since April 13 when she went through the drive-thru at Taco Bell on Shallowford Road at three-seventeen that afternoon. I ran her social security number. She's received no benefits, no unemployment, and she hasn't ever filed taxes on her own; the last time was in March 2012 when she filed jointly with her husband, John Lewis. She seems to have vanished from the face of the earth. Questions?" He looked at each of us in turn; we shook our heads.

"All righty then," he said, taking off his glasses and holding them up to the light. He shook his head, muttered something unintelligible, and grabbed a tissue from the box on the table. He huffed on and polished each lens in turn, then jammed them back onto his nose, shoved them higher with a forefinger, and then turned his attention back to his laptop.

"John Lewis is an interesting character," he said. "He's fifty-three and comes from Highton, a small town in Walker County, West Virginia, to the south of Wheeling. He has a younger brother, Michael. Their parents died when John was three. The two children were brought up by their grandparents on the mother's side, Peter and Martha Howlette. Both brothers attended high school in Highton; both graduated, neither of them went to college. John's been married two times—"

"Whoa, whoa," I interrupted him. "Wait a minute. That's not right. Jennifer Lewis' sister said that Jennifer was his first wife."

Tim's face betrayed a moment of hurt that I was questioning his intel. "Be that as it may, John Lewis married Sapphire Williams on June 6, 1981. He was nineteen; she was eighteen."

Wow, I thought. *That's weird, puts a whole new perspective on things.*

"That marriage didn't last very long. Sapphire left him in August 1982 and divorced him three months later, in November the same year." He paused, clicked his mouse a couple of times, then continued. "So anyway." He paused again, sniffed, tugged at his earlobe, then said, "After the divorce, it seems John moved back in with his grandparents and younger brother, and lived with them until he left Highton sometime in early 1983 when he moved to Louisville, Kentucky and went to work at one of the small whiskey distilleries. He stayed there until early October 1987 when he moved again; this time to Denver... Okay, look: he moved again, several more times in fact, before he finally arrived in Chattanooga in 2007. He's now in real estate. It's all in my report. I can print it or email it to you; whichever you prefer."

"Why don't you do both, please, Tim?" I asked. "But you have more, right?"

He nodded. "I do. John Lewis married Jennifer Tullett on June 14, 2008. He was forty-six, she was thirty-four. He's now a realtor. Does quite well, according to his tax returns—"

"Oh my God, Tim. You hacked the IRS? You can't tell me stuff like that. I'm a cop for Pete's sake."

He grinned at me. "No, Kate. I didn't, but he has his taxes prepared at—oh, well, never mind. You don't need to know. Anyway, his taxable income last year was a little less than $130,000. His credit score is 781, and he hasn't been late on a payment in more than ten years. He keeps his nose pretty clean, I guess."

"Okay, so what about," I checked my notes, "Sapphire Williams Lewis? What about her? And where is she?"

"Uh, I'm still working on that. I'm also still trying to track down John Lewis's brother, Michael. I'm going to need a little more time."

"That's okay, Tim," I said. "You've done great. Thank you. So, maybe tomorrow, d'you think?"

He cocked his head and scrunched his face, causing his glasses to move up his nose. "Maybe. It all depends...well, on a lot of things. I have work to do for Harry, and Bob and Jacque, and—"

"Okay." I held up a hand and stopped him. "I get the idea. Whenever you can. There's no great rush. I have what I need for today, I think. I hope."

"Cool," he said, closing his laptop. "How about I email it to you as I get it? That way you don't have to keep coming back here, okay?" He raised his eyebrows.

"That, Tim, sounds like a plan."

He nodded, gathered up his belongings, and left.

"Jacque, thank you for sitting in on this and for taking notes, too. Harry, I really do appreciate all you do, but we need to go. I want to meet with Finkle as soon as possible, but before I do, I need to call Alice Booker. Talk to you later?"

"Oh yeah," he said, rising to his feet. "I'll be waiting to hear from you. I hope all goes well." He checked his watch. "I have to go too. Talk t'you later. Good luck, Kate. You too, Lonnie."

IT WAS ALMOST NINE-THIRTY WHEN WE ARRIVED AT THE PD. WE went straight up to my office where I called Alice Booker.

"Mrs. Booker. How are you this morning? Good. Do you have a minute? I have a couple of things I need to clear up. Good, thank you. Alice, I think you told me that Jennifer was John Lewis' first wife. Is that correct?"

"Yes, that's right. Why do you ask? Oh my god; he's been married before."

"That's what our research has turned up. It looks like he was married back in 1982, to someone named Sapphire Williams. Have you ever heard that name before?"

"No. This is the first time I've heard it. I—I don't know what to say... Lieutenant Gazzara, that was more than thirty years ago. He must have still been a kid."

"Thirty-three years ago, to be precise and, yes, he was nineteen at the time. Apparently, the marriage didn't last long, just a few months—"

"Where is she, this Williams woman? I want to talk to her," she interrupted me.

"We're still working on that. In the meantime, I'll talk to John Lewis myself. Is there anything more you can tell me about him that I should know before I do?"

She thought for a few minutes, then said, "We never liked him much. He was very quiet. Not talkative at all. There was just something odd about him. He told us that he was an only child and that his mother and father had been killed in an accident—never would talk about that—and that he'd been raised by his grandparents. But they had both passed several years ago, and he had no other family. And he also told us he'd never been married before. That's all I know, I'm afraid. Oh my God, that sounds so ridiculous. He was married to my sister for four years, but I know nothing about him." I heard her sob.

"Well, if that's what he told you, he was certainly lying. He *was* raised by his grandparents, but he was married before, at least once, that we know of, and he also has a brother, Michael. We're still trying to track him down too... No, Alice, it's still early days yet... No, I don't know any more than I've told you... Thank you... Okay, that's good... So, look, if you don't have anything else, I need to let you go... Yes... Yes, of course. As soon as I know something, I'll be in touch. In the meantime, if I have questions, I'll call you. Thank you, Alice."

I stared at the screen of my iPhone for several seconds after she'd disconnected. John Lewis, I now knew, was indeed a liar, but was he also something else? Was he a killer?

I shook my head, looked at Lonnie, and said, "It's time we talked to Finkle."

He smiled, nodded, and slowly got to his feet. "You sure you're ready for that?"

"Oh yes, as ready as I'll ever be." And I was; I was also looking forward to the impending confrontation with some trepidation and a whole lot of excitement, which I hoped didn't show.

21

Finkle's movements were always erratic on Monday mornings, but I hoped he was in his office. Yes, I know, I could have called him, but I didn't want to forewarn him. My plan was to beard the lion in his den, so to speak. I smiled at the thought. *He might be able to have me thrown out, but he sure as hell won't be able to walk out on me.*

Instead, I called Chief Johnston's secretary, Cathy, and asked her if Finkle was in his office: he wasn't, so I asked her to give me a buzz when he arrived. Then Lonnie and I settled down to wait, during which time I filled him in on what I planned. He heard me out, his smile growing wider by the minute. When I was done, he just shook his head and said, "Good luck with that!"

The call came at five after ten. At fifteen after ten, I knocked on his door and, without waiting for an invitation, walked right on in, with Lonnie close behind.

I stood aside to let Lonnie by, and then I closed the door and turned to face the desk.

Finkle's office was, in deference to his rank, much larger than mine. Its furniture included, not only the usual office accoutrements, but also a mid-sized round table with six chairs; a small conference table, if you will.

I noted that Finkle was seated behind his desk, but I didn't acknowledge him. Instead I dumped my stuff—the Lewis file, laptop, phone, and iPad—on the table, then turned and smiled at him.

He was staring, slack-jawed at me.

"Good morning, Chief," I said, brightly.

"What the hell is the meaning of this?" He began to rise from his seat, both hands on the desk.

"Why are you barging into my office...and why is Sergeant Guest with you?"

"Chief," I said, taking a seat at the table and arranging my stuff in front of me. "We need to talk."

"So, make an appointment, damn it."

"I thought about doing just that, but I didn't think you'd go for it. We really do need to talk, Chief, and right now. So, would you please join us? The sergeant is here because I'm here; you know the policy about men and women alone together in the same office. Lonnie, sit down."

Lonnie sat down next to me. Finkle remained standing behind his desk.

"Have you gone mad, Lieutenant? This is not happening. Now gather up that crap and get the hell out of my office, or I'll have you removed."

"Well now," I said easily. "I can do that, but we'd still have to talk. We could, of course, if you prefer, go to one of the interview r—"

He interrupted me. "What the hell are you talking about?"

There was no easy way to do it, so I took a deep breath and dove right in.

"As you know, Chief, I'm working on the Lewis case, and I need a little help." *Hah, well, I did say I was going to try the soft approach.* "Your help. So, if you wouldn't mind..." I pointed to the seat across the table from me.

"Lieutenant Gazzara, you can't just barge into my office and—"

"Yes, I know, Henry, and I apologize...but it really is necessary that we get it done now. Can we get on with it, please?"

He came around the desk, slowly. For the first time since I'd known him, he looked unsure of himself and, inwardly, I allowed myself a tiny smile. *So far, so good.*

He sat down opposite me. The scowl was intimidating. He clasped his hands on the table in front of him.

"You have five minutes, Lieutenant. Now, what's this about?"

I nodded, made a show of turning on my digital recorder and placing it in the center of the table.

"Please turn that off, Lieutenant."

"No, sir. I can't do that. I need to record this meeting for the record." And then I continued to state for the record the date, time, and those present. That done, I opened my laptop and then my iPad and flipped through the screens until I found my notes.

"Chief Finkle," I began, "as you know, I've taken over the investigation into the disappearance of Jennifer Lewis who was reported missing on Monday, April 16, 2012. You're familiar with the case, correct?"

He nodded.

"Please answer for the record, Chief."

"Yes," he growled. "I'm familiar with it."

For the next several minutes, I led him through the essential details of the case culminating with it being assigned to Detective Tracy. He listened quietly, answering my questions, for the most part, in monosyllables.

Finally, I sat back in my seat, folded my arms, and looked him in the eye. "Assistant Chief Finkle, within hours of Lewis being reported missing, instead of following protocol and allowing the case to be handled in the normal way by the commander of the Missing Persons unit, you took matters into your own hands and *personally* transferred Detective Tracy to the MPU and then assigned the case to him. That's an extraordinary breach of protocol, wouldn't you agree? And I was wondering, why did you do that?"

"How...did, you know that?"

"That's irrelevant, Chief. I ask again: Why did you breach standard procedure and transfer Detective Tracy to the Missing Persons unit and then personally assign the Lewis case to him?"

"I—I." He grabbed the recorder and turned it off.

"What the hell are you doing?" he hissed.

"I'm just trying to find out what your reasoning was. Now, please turn the recorder back on and answer the question. If not, then we'll have to adjourn to an interview room and videotape the interview, that will place it into the official records. Is that what you want, Chief? I think not."

"I don't answer to you, Gazzara. I suggest you think very carefully about what you're doing." He paused, then said, "Does the chief know you're about this?"

I nodded. "He does, and he's sanctioned the interview. Now, will you please turn on the recorder and answer the question?"

He looked down at the recorder still in his hands, contemplated it for a moment, then turned it on and slowly set it down.

He hesitated, then cleared his throat and said, "He was the best man for..." He paused for a second or two and then continued. "He's a good man. He deserved a break. He never recovered from the way you screwed him over when he was your partner. I gave him a helping hand, that's all."

I ignored the comment.

"Do you know Jennifer Lewis, Chief?" I asked.

"I do not."

I nodded. "You're sure?"

"I just said, I don't know her...but it's possible, I suppose, that I might have met her at some time."

Good play, Chief.

Again, I nodded. "Chief Finkle, when I interviewed Detective Tracy on Monday last, I asked him why he didn't properly investigate Jennifer Lewis' disappearance. The reason he gave was, in part, and I quote, "she's a freakin' hooker.' I looked him in the eye and asked, "What do you make of that, sir?"

He hesitated for a moment, then said, "I'm not sure what Detective Tracy was thinking when—if, he said that, but of course I do not condone it. I will question him myself and, if what you say is true, I'll see that he's disciplined and reassigned."

Yes, I'm sure you will.

"Chief Finkle. Are you familiar with a—I'm going to call it a nightclub, but that might be a little too kind. Are you familiar with an establishment," I made a show of consulting my notes, "called The Sorbonne?"

"You well know," he replied, "that, as a police officer, I'm very familiar with that establishment. Where are you going with this, Lieutenant?"

I ignored the question and said, "Have you ever visited The Sorbonne, Chief?"

"In the line of duty, yes. You know I have."

"You've been a police officer for more than twenty years, since 1995 in fact. Chief Finkle, have you ever, during your twenty years as a police officer, visited the Sorbonne socially, outside of the line of duty?"

His face was white. "I—I. Yes, I have."

"Is The Sorbonne, would you say, an appropriate establishment for a senior police officer to visit...socially?"

"This is ridiculous. I enjoy a drink now and then, as do we all. I go to lots of places. I like to keep an eye on the city's underworld, as I know do you, Lieutenant."

"How many times have you visited the Sorbonne socially, would you say?"

"I have no idea."

I thought for a moment, *Okay, now's the time to give it to him. Be careful how you word it, Kate.*

I breathed deeply, then said, "Would it surprise you, Chief, if I were to tell you that the owners of The Sorbonne have identified you as a frequent visitor there?"

"Frequent visitor? Yes, it would. I haven't been inside the place in months." There was an edge to his voice.

Ooh dear, Benny. I fear I may have dealt you a bad hand. Benny Hinkle is the owner of the Sorbonne, and a good friend of mine, and Harry's.

"But in the past...well, never mind. Chief, would it also surprise you if I were to tell you that several witnesses would also confirm that you *are* a regular visitor to The Sorbonne and that you actively solicit prostitutes there?"

I watched his eyes, looking for...well, I didn't see it. What I did see were his eyes bulging with indignation. It did indeed, surprise him. *It would surprise me too.*

"It would indeed." He ground his teeth in anger. *"Because it would be a damned lie."* He almost shouted it. He was so angry I was glad there was a table between us.

"This is outrageous!" The veins in his neck stood out like purple cords. "I am deeply offended by this line of questioning, so I ask you again, Lieutenant: where the hell are you going with this?"

For a moment, I didn't answer. Instead, I looked down at my iPad, pretending to consult my notes, then asked, quietly, "Chief Finkle, do you know a...Tina Gonzalez?"

Slowly and deliberately, he stood, reached out, grabbed the recorder, and turned it off.

"That's enough," he growled. "I know what you're doing, Gazzara. This is all about..." He hesitated, then said, "Well, you can forget it. If you want to continue this bizarre interrogation; this, this blatant attempt to tarnish my character and good name, I demand to have my attorney present."

I looked up at him and smiled.

"Okay, Henry," I said. "No, it's not what you think. I'm just trying to do my job. There's something hinky about this whole Lewis case, and I need to find out what it is. Now please sit down. It's best for both of us that I get truthful answers to my questions, now rather than later. You'd agree with that, right?" I didn't expect an answer, nor did I get one, so I continued. "Tell you what," I said, trying to calm him down. "We can continue this here, off the record, informally if you like, but I should warn you: I will be taking notes."

Reluctantly he sat down again and nodded his consent. He did, however, keep possession of the recorder.

I leaned back in my chair and glanced at Lonnie. He winked at me.

"Chief," I said. "I know all about the Tina Gonzalez incident. I also know that you were cleared of any wrongdoing. My problem is this: Gonzales is a known prostitute. She works at a strip club, the Starburst which, in and of itself, is not a surprise. What is a surprise, is that the Starburst is the same strip club where Lewis worked. They must have known each other. How well, I don't yet know, but I'll find out. Detective Tracy has stated that Lewis is—was—a prostitute. I, that is we, don't know that. She's never been arrested, for anything.

"I'm sorry, Chief, but all that makes me wonder if Tracy's sudden transfer to the MPU, his assignment to the case assigned him, *and* his lack of investigative effort thereof, are not an attempt to cover up your...possible association with Ms. Gonzalez and Ms. Lewis. Well, you've got to admit, it all looks a bit...coincidental?" I held my breath and waited for the explosion. It didn't come.

He stared at me, seething, then seemed to calm down a little. "Before I address all that, Lieutenant, would you mind answering a question for me?"

"Of course, if I can."

"How did you find out about Ms. Gonzales' accusations? Did Harry Starke's geek hack the police department's records?"

My heart leaped as he looked me in the eye, but I kept it together, held his gaze and didn't hesitate. "I'm sorry, Chief. I can't reveal my confidential source. You know that's not what we do. But you also know, I'm sure, that there is no official record of the Gonzalez incident, at least none that I'm aware of. Is that not so?"

He didn't answer the question. Instead, he said, "I did *not* know Jennifer Lewis. There was no association between Jennifer Lewis and myself. I do *not* consort with prostitutes. The facts you have laid out are nothing more than unfortunate coincidences." He paused, then continued, "They say no good deed goes unpunished, Lieutenant. My providing Detective Tracy with an opportunity to better himself—to leave undercover work—is such a deed." He stood and laid the recorder on the table. "This interview is over. In the interests of professional courtesy and harmony within the department, I'll not hold this interview against you. I would, however, say this: be very careful how you proceed with this investigation. If any of what's been said here today is leaked, either within the department or to the press, I will see to it that—well, I'm sure you understand. Now, I have nothing more to say. Please leave my office."

I nodded. "Very well, Chief. I appreciate your candor. I do, however, reserve the right to question you again, should the need arise."

"I don't think so. Get out, Lieutenant."

<hr />

Lonnie and I didn't speak to each other until we were back in my office and behind closed doors.

I flung the file down on my desk and set the rest of my stuff down beside it.

I flopped into my desk chair, swiveled around, and stared out through the open blinds into the incident room.

"That was intense," Lonnie said, breaking into my thoughts. "You gonna talk to me, or what?"

I swiveled back around, looked at him and said, "I noticed you kept your mouth shut in there. You're smarter than you look. You heard what he had to say. What did you think?"

He grinned at me. "Yeah, I did, didn't I? What did I think? I think he's a lying sack o' shit, is what I think. He knew Lewis, I'm certain of it. And what the hell was all that stuff you brought up about the Sorbonne? That was the first I'd heard of any of it."

I smirked, leaning back and clasping my hands behind my head as I recalled the conversation. "I was just jerking his chain. I wanted to get his reactions. I did. He seemed sincere... Look, if Tracy had done his job three years ago, he would have followed up on his premise that Lewis was a hooker. He didn't. We will, though where that will lead us, God only knows. In the meantime, I'm prepared to give Tiny the benefit of the doubt. Maybe that's all there was to it, that he gave Tracy a break... But was there a little quid pro quo involved? I don't know." I thought for a moment, then continued. "I'm not sure we did the right thing: interviewing Finkle first. If he gets to Tracy before we do, well..." I brought my hands down and shrugged.

"I don't think it would have made much difference, either way," Lonnie said. "Tracy would have run straight to Finkle and warned him. No, you did right, LT."

"I sure as hell hope so."

"You haven't yet told me what you think," he said.

"Something's not right. Did you see his reaction when I brought up Gonzalez?"

He nodded.

"I think he knows her. Whether or not he's had relations with her is another matter. Well, she's going to say it happened, but unless she has witnesses, it's all he said, she said. I don't know... What I do know is, I don't believe in multiple coincidences. It just doesn't happen. Was there an ulterior motive behind Tracy's transfer? I think so. I think Finkle knew Jennifer Lewis. How well he knew her, we'll probably never know."

"So where do we go next?"

"Tracy, of course, and we need to talk to John Lewis, but first I need to know what Tim was able to find out about Sapphire Lewis and John's brother, Michael. We also need to talk to the so-called boyfriend, Jeff Tobin, and Amber Watts, but not before I have all the information."

I checked the time. It was almost noon.

I stood. "Let's go get some lunch. I need coffee, in the worst way. We'll do Tracy this afternoon, then I'll give Tim a call."

"Do?" he asked, with a grin.

"Get your mind up out of the gutter, Sergeant. Where d'you want to eat?"

"Arby's would be good. I can get a salad."

"Arby's it is then."

22

I've mentioned before that John Tracy was, some ten years ago, my partner. It lasted only for a few weeks. I couldn't stand the man. He was a nasty little shit: arrogant, lazy, sloppy, and a smartass. He'd been a cop for more than twenty years, yet he'd never climbed higher in the ranks than detective.

His unimposing build was only a little over five-eight—yes, they made a good pair, him and Henry Finkle—and thin, skinny even, with brown hair that he wore almost to his shoulders.

Having told you all that, you'll understand why the interview with Detective Tracy that afternoon did not begin well.

"Well, if it ain't Boris and Natasha," he said, with a sneer, when we arrived at his cubicle on the first floor. "I've been expecting you. Chief Finkle mentioned that you might drop by and that I should cooperate. You want to do this here, or shall we go somewhere more comfortable?"

"That's up to you, shithead," Lonnie snarled. "You want the rest of the squad to hear how you screwed up an inv—"

I placed a hand on Lonnie's arm, interrupting him.

"I think it would be best if we didn't do this here, Detective. My office or an interview room. Either way, I'm going to record you, so it's your choice. What's it to be?"

"Your place, I think."

There was no mistaking the innuendo, or the salacious grin. I still had my hand on Lonnie's arm; I felt him tense up. I squeezed, to let him know it was okay.

"My place it is, then. Let's go."

THE LEWIS FILE WAS STILL ON MY DESK. LONNIE TOOK A SEAT slightly behind and to Tracy's left.

"Before you begin... Is that thing on? If it is—" he asked, looking at the recorder in front of him.

"It is," I said, interrupting him, and then, for the record, I stated the time, place, and so on. Then I asked him, "You were saying, Detective?"

He flipped the lock screen on his iPad, then said, "I was about to say that I have nothing to add to what I told you last Monday. Jennifer Lewis was having an affair with some guy, name unknown, and she ran off with him. End of story. I interviewed her co-workers and found nothing to indicate otherwise. She had been seeing a Jeff Tobin, and I did interview him, but he said he'd met someone else and had stopped seeing her a couple of weeks earlier. He said he didn't know if she was seeing someone else or not. John Lewis was a nice guy, at least I thought he was. I believed him. That's it."

I'd let him ramble on without interruption because I was looking for anomalies, but he'd stuck strictly to the script. He seemed to know it by heart, which I found incredible for someone who hadn't even looked at the file in more than two years.

"Can I see that, please?" I asked, holding out my hand.

"Why? Wha' for?"

"Just hand it over, John."

He did, reluctantly, and I read through his notes. He'd recited them almost word for word. *He friggin' rehearsed it.*

That troubled me, but I let it go and handed the iPad back to him.

"Why did Chief Finkle transfer you to the MPU?" I asked.

He cocked his head, made a face, looked puzzled at me. "Because I asked him to?"

"I don't know, John. Did you?"

"Yes, I freakin' did. I'd had a gutful of Narcotics." He sighed. "And my freakin' cover was blown."

"How well do you know the assistant chief?" I asked.

Again, he made with the puzzled face. "About as well as anybody, I suppose. He's not so bad. He always treated me well enough, like when he transferred me to Missing Persons."

"What did he tell you when he handed you the Lewis file? Did he give you any special instructions?"

He shrugged. "No, nothing. He told me it had just come in and to get on with it."

"Did he ask you to...how shall I put it?"

"To cover it up?" He finished it for me. "Hell, no he didn't, and I wouldn't have if he had. Are you out of your freakin' mind, Lieutenant?"

"Hey," Lonnie said. "Tone it down."

"Screw you, Guest," he snarled.

"What the hell's going on here, Lieutenant?" Tracy asked. "Am I a suspect, or something? Is the chief?"

Lonnie looked like he was about to say something, probably something he shouldn't, so I raised a hand and shook my head at him. He relaxed a little.

"Do you know Tina Gonzalez?" I asked.

"No," he answered, quickly.

Too quickly I thought. I also didn't believe him.

"Oh come on, John. You spent god only knows how many years in Narcotics, and you never met a known prostitute?"

His face reddened. "Well, I might have, but if I did, I don't remember it. I certainly don't *know* her."

"How about Jennifer Lewis?" I asked. "Did you know her?"

"No, I freakin' did not," he yelled, indignantly. "And I know damned well I never met her."

That one, I believed.

"To your knowledge, Detective, did Assistant Chief Finkle know Jennifer Lewis?"

"Oh, my, God." He was incredulous. "You think it was him she was having an affair with?" He burst out laughing.

No, I didn't think that, but now that you mention it.

"As far as I know," he said, "he never even met her. How the hell would he—"

"You said she was a hooker," I interrupted him.

He just sat there, staring at me, slowly shaking his head. "That's what her husband said. You can't be serious, Lieutenant. You're suggesting that Henry Finkle... Nah, I don't believe it."

"It's been said, John. You've heard the rumors."

"Yes, but that's all malicious bull. You're— You're freakin' crazy."

"Okay, let's talk about something else. You waited four days before you checked her apartment. Why?"

He frowned, looked away to the left, then back again, and said, "As I recall, I was busy, very busy. I'd just been transferred out of Narcotics. I still had a lot of loose ends to deal with there."

You're lying, John.

I nodded. "And when you did finally check it out, you found she'd left all her belongings behind. The only things missing were her cell phone and pocketbook." I looked up at him and frowned. "That didn't seem unusual to you?"

"No. It didn't. Those are the things she *would* have taken with her, so I figured she'd just decided to start over, make a clean break."

I shook my head in disbelief. "I don't believe you, John. I think you were doing just enough to be able to write a report and then shelve the case. How well d'you know John Lewis?"

"I don't know him, well, other than to interview him. As I said, he seemed okay. I had no reason not to believe him. You're not saying he had anything to do with—"

"I'm not saying anything. I'm looking for answers, and you don't seem to have any."

He shrugged. "Whatever!"

"John," I said, looking him right in the eye, "I hope you're clean, because if you're not..." I didn't bother to finish the comment.

"I'd look to your own self, if I were you," he said, his narrow slits glinted with anger. "You're making some powerful enemies, and I'm not just talking about the assistant chief."

"What the hell's that supposed to mean?" Lonnie, said, leaning forward and grasping the back of Tracy's chair.

Tracy jumped up and spun around to face him. "What d'you think it means, Fat Boy? Stay the hell away from me."

He turned his head toward me, still keeping an eye on Lonnie. "You done with me, Lieutenant?"

I nodded, slowly, staring up at him. "Yes, you can go, for now."

He circled around Lonnie, gifted me with a sneer, then closed the door behind him.

"He's right, you know," Lonnie said, sitting down. "Finkle's a nasty little bastard, but he has connections, and not just in the department. So does Tracy. Better be real careful from now on, LT."

"You may be right," I said. "I think we hit a raw nerve; two raw nerves, in fact. Did you believe him?"

"Not for a second."

I nodded. "Me neither. His answers were just a little too pat. He as good as told us that Finkle had warned him, which is exactly what I was afraid of. He's covering something up; they both are. I'm sure of it. We need to interview Gonzales, and quickly. Let's hope they haven't gotten to her."

I leaned forward, my elbows on the desk and chin in my hands as I thought.

"Lonnie, you do realize what this could mean, right?"

"Oh yeah: a cover-up, corruption, and who the hell knows what else. As I said, watch your back."

I leaned back in my chair and stared up at the ceiling. *What the hell's happening to me?*

Three days later, I found out. Lonnie was right: I should have been watching my back.

23

MONDAY, MAY 18, EVENING – LEWIS CASE

I was late getting home that evening. I did my usual thing: showered, a little yoga to calm my jangling nerves, got into my pajamas,
and then I made myself a sandwich—cheese, lettuce and tomato.
That done, I poured myself a large glass of a cheap red wine I'd
gotten from the supermarket. Then I settled down with the recorder
and pad to listen to the recordings I'd made that day, make notes, and
plan my strategy.

It was close to eight o'clock when my cell phone buzzed. I looked
at the screen and smiled.

"Hey, Tim. I bet you have some news for me?"

"I do. I'll give you a quick rundown of the main points, then email
the report, okay?"

"Good plan. Let's hear it."

"Okay! Sapphire Williams Lewis. As I told you before, she
married John Lewis in 1981 and left him fourteen months later in
August of 1982. Now get this: she then went to work at a strip club in
Wheeling. Crazy stuff, huh?"

Wow, more coincidences? "Okay, so where is she now?"

"I don't know, she turned up for work on the evening of Friday, December 10, 1982, worked a full shift, and left the club at one o'clock on Saturday morning. She didn't turn up for work on Saturday evening. From what little I could find out, she's not been seen since."

"How d'you know all this?" I asked.

"I had to do a lot of digging. The Kitty Kitty Club went out of business in February 1985. It was closed down by the sheriff's office, so that was a dead end. However, Sapphire has a brother, Ryan, eight years older. They grew up in Highton and went to high school there. Ryan lives in Boston now, has since he got out of the army in 1980. I called him. He told me he used to talk to Sapphire at least once a week, usually on Fridays. He talked to her that morning, the tenth. He said she was in an unusually good mood but didn't tell him why. He called her as usual on the seventeenth, but she didn't answer the phone. He said he wasn't worried, not then, not until he called her on Friday, December 24, Christmas Eve and she didn't answer. He called her again on Christmas Day, three times, and then again on the 26th; still no answer. Finally, he called her ex-husband, John Lewis. Lewis told Ryan he didn't know where she was, but that she'd probably gone off with one of her boyfriends. That's all I have."

What the hell! That's the same line Lewis is using about Jennifer's disappearance.

"Why wasn't she reported missing?"

"She was, by her brother, on January 4, 1983, in Wheeling, but nothing came of it."

"Who handled the missing person case, d'you know?"

"It was a detective... Wait, I have it here somewhere... Ah, okay, it was Detective Ellis Benton. Unfortunately, he died in 2016; he was seventy-seven. Old age, I guess. That's all I have on Sapphire, Kate."

"How about Ryan Williams, d'you have his number?"

"Of course."

I wrote the number on my yellow pad intending to call Ryan the following morning.

"Okay, Tim." I heaved a sigh. I was tired, and just about done in. "What else d'you have for me?"

"I also did a little more digging into John Lewis' past, but I didn't find much. I did get hold of some names of high school friends, but I didn't call any of them. I didn't have time. You'll find the list—there are six names—in the email I'm going to send you. As to John's younger brother, Michael, he's a mail carrier. He still lives in Highton with his wife in the old Lewis family home. He has two children, both grown up and moved away. I didn't talk to him either, because I didn't want to step on your toes, say the wrong thing. I do have his number, though. You want it?"

I wrote that down too.

"It appears John Lewis left Highton sometime early in January 1983. I couldn't pin it down exactly, but he started work at the distillery in Louisville on Monday, January 24. As far as I could tell, he's not been seen in Highton since then."

I heard some clicking, and I swear I heard Tim push the glasses up higher on the bridge of his nose. Then he continued.

"Okay, that's all I have for you right now. I'm still trying to track down Tobin and Watts, but I'm really busy with other stuff for Harry and Bob. Don't worry, though. I'll stay with it and get back to you as soon as I have something."

"Thanks, Tim. You're the best. I gotta go. I need to get some sleep. Bye."

And I hung up before he had a chance to digress into one of his long and boring diatribes.

But I wasn't lying. I was exhausted. I turned off my phone, set the alarm for six o'clock, and went to bed. I don't even remember my head hitting the pillow. What I do remember are the dreams. One of them featured me looking up into a bright light with Doc Sheddon looking down at me through a transparent face shield. That one, I'll never forget.

24

I was more than glad to wake up that Tuesday morning, the day after my interviews of Finkle and Tracy. The nightmares were like none I'd ever experienced before. And the final one? Was I really on Doc's autopsy table? I shuddered at the thought and hoped to hell it wasn't a portent of things to come.

Anyway, I arrived at the office in a mood to brook no crap from anyone, but who d'you think was waiting for me by the elevator when I arrived? You got it, Henry Finkle.

"Good morning, Chief," I greeted him brightly, though inwardly I was seething. I didn't need a confrontation with him, not then. "What can I do for you?"

"I was wondering if there had been any progress on the Sullivan case? We're not going to let it go; you do know that?"

Hah, he's fishing.

"I do, but that's not why you're here, is it? You've been talking to Tracy."

I could tell by the look on his face I was right.

He nodded. "Yes, he told me what you're thinking." He hesitated for a moment, and I kept my mouth shut and waited.

Finally, he said, "You're way off the mark, Lieutenant, and you're going to get yourself into a great deal of trouble if you continue with this line of inquiry."

He waited for me to answer; I didn't.

"Very well, then. Carry on. But remember: I'll be watching you."

He turned on his heel and walked back to his office.

I punched the elevator button and rode up to the second floor, shouldered through the door into the situation room, and tapped Lonnie on the shoulder as I walked past his desk. He rose to his feet and followed me to my office.

"Close the door and sit down," I said. "I was just confronted by Finkle. The little creep is on me like a duck on a June bug. He's been talking to Tracy, and he was fishing. I didn't bite, and then he as good as warned me off again."

"That's not good, LT. What're you going to do about it? Maybe you should talk to Chief Johnston?"

"Oh yes," I said. "That would look really good. No, I can't do that. I can't go crying to him every time I hit a bump. I have to handle it myself. Right now, though, I want to talk to Tina Gonzalez. You ready to go?"

He nodded. "Yeah, but can I finish off what I was doing? It will only take a minute."

"Yes, and if I see that game on your screen again... Just get rid of it, all right?"

I didn't tell him about my dreams. I figured I was being paranoid, so I shrugged off my feelings of impending doom, gathered up my gear. Ten minutes later, we were out of the building and heading east on Amnicola in an unmarked cruiser; Lonnie was at the wheel.

As he drove, I filled him in on the intel Tim had shared last night.

Tina Gonzalez lived in one of those apartments off Shallowford Road, just a few blocks from Highway 153.

As per my usual modus, I didn't call ahead. I didn't want to warn her and, knowing that she was a working girl, I was pretty sure she would be home when we arrived at a few minutes to nine that morning, and I was right. She was, in fact, still in bed.

"Oh shit!" she said when she came to the door. "Cops, right?"

"Tina Gonzalez?"

"Yeah. What do ya want?"

"I'm Lieutenant Catherine Ga—"

She shook her head and sighed in exaggerated frustration.

"I know who you are, Detective," she interrupted me, "and I have nothing to say to you. Now piss off and let me go back to bed."

She started to close the door. I took a step forward. She glared at me. "You're not going to leave, are you?"

"Not until you answer my questions."

"Well, I guess you'd better come in, then."

She opened the door wide, stood back, wrapped her robe more tightly around her, and then turned and walked off into the apartment. We followed her into her kitchen.

Even though she was pushing forty, she really was a striking woman: tall, almost as tall as me, nice figure, bright red hair and lips that must need a lot of maintenance.

She hit the button on the coffee maker and said, "You want coffee? No? Well, I do. Sit down, will you?"

She grabbed the mug of coffee and sat down at the kitchen table opposite us.

"So talk to me," she said after taking a careful sip.

"You said you know who we are. How?" I asked.

"That's an easy one. You have 'cop' stamped all over you. And," she grinned at me over the rim of her mug, "you have a badge on your belt."

I knew that wasn't it. She'd been warned we were coming, and she knew that I knew it, but she didn't seem bothered.

"Nobody warned you that we were coming?"

She shook her head, staring at me defiantly.

She put the mug down on the table and said, "Lieutenant—what did you say your name was?"

"I didn't. You didn't give me a chance. It's Gazzara."

"Lieutenant Gazzara. If this is about my work, I'm not going to talk to you."

"It's not about you being an escort, well, not specifically, but I do have some questions. So, if you don't mind..."

She picked up her mug, frowned, but nodded.

"Do you, or have you ever, worked at the Starburst—"

"*Damn,*" she interrupted me. "What did I just tell you?"

"Calm down, Tina. I'm just establishing the parameters."

She pursed her lips, then nodded.

"So, the Starburst?"

"You know damn well that I do."

"How long have you worked there, Tina?"

She shrugged. "I dunno...sixteen, seventeen years, I suppose. I've never worked anywhere else."

"What do you do there?"

"I strip, for God's sake. You know that."

"Are you a prostitute? Do you work as an escort, Tina?"

"Go screw yourself, Lieutenant."

"I'll take that as a yes."

"Take it how the hell you want. I told you I wouldn't talk about my work."

"So you did... Okay, let's move on. Do you know a Jennifer Lewis?"

She frowned, looked perplexed, then brightened a little and said, "Yeah, I knew her, but I haven't seen her in years. What's she done?"

Boy, is she good, or what?

"She's missing, that's what," Lonnie said, impatiently.

"Wow. I wondered what'd happened to her."

"When was the last time you saw her?" I asked.

"How the hell should I know? I told you, it was years ago."

I nodded, then looked at her and said, "Do you know Assistant Police Chief Henry Finkle?"

She was ready for it. She slammed the mug down on the table and said, "I'm not going to answer that."

"You don't have to, Tina. I already know that you do, and I know your history with the assistant chief."

She glared at me but kept her mouth shut tight.

"You claimed he assaulted you."

Her mouth tightened even further.

"Did you have an affair with him?"

Still no response; her face could have been made of stone.

"Okay, let me ask you this: do you know Detective John Tracy?"

"I'm not going to answer that either."

"I'll take that as a yes, too."

"And you can take that however the hell you want, too. I'm still not answering."

I looked her right in the eye and said, "Fine. I get it. So I'll ask you just one more question, and then you can go back to bed. Think very carefully before you answer." I paused, waited a second, then said, "To your knowledge, did Assistant Chief Finkle know Jennifer Lewis?"

And there it was, barely a blink, but it was enough. She knew.

"I have no idea, Lieutenant. As I recall, she only worked at the Starburst for a few weeks. I didn't know her, not well anyway. Just to say 'Hi' in passing, that's all. Now," she said as she stood up. "I'll show you out."

"There's no need," I said. "We can find our way to the front door. Thank you, Tina. You've been most helpful. I'll be sure to let Chief Finkle know just how helpful."

Her eyes narrowed, and the frown lines deepened. "Get the hell out."

"THAT WAS SHORT AND SWEET," LONNIE SAID AS HE SLAMMED the car door. "I hope you got more out of it than I did."

"I got enough. In fact, I got more than enough." I started counting on my fingers. "One, she knew we were coming. Two, she'd been coached. Three, she as good as confirmed that Finkle knew Jennifer, and that's what I really wanted to know. Four, she sure as hell knows Tracy, too. Five, she also knew Jennifer, though how well, we'll probably never know."

"Geez. How do you do that?" He nodded, thoughtfully, then said, "So, where do we go from here?"

"Right now? Back to the office. I have some thinking to do... By the way, when did you say you're scheduled for the surgery?"

"Monday, June first, why?"

"Well, it's just that I was thinking that maybe I might travel to Wheeling...or Boston."

"That's not happenin', Kate." He turned his head and grinned at me. "Johnston's not going to turn that kind of money loose, not with what little we've got."

I sighed. He was right, of course.

25

TUESDAY/WEDNESDAY, MAY 19 & 20 – ON CALL

Unfortunately, I didn't get to work much more on the Lewis case that day or, indeed, the next several days. Cold Case Squad notwithstanding, I was still attached to the Major Crimes Unit and as such, still a member of the Homicide Division. As a result, I was expected to take my turn "on call." Lonnie too.

Oh, don't get the wrong idea, I didn't have an assigned caseload per se, but I *was* obliged to work the first forty-eight hours of any cases I caught while on call before I could hand them off. If you watch any TV at all, you'll know that after that, the case becomes more and more difficult. If you can't find a lead within the first forty-eight hours, the chances of solving the case decrease dramatically. The first forty-eight are when witnesses' memories are still fresh; when you have the opportunity to find clues and follow them from one to the next, and then the next. As time goes by, evidence gets contaminated, witnesses disappear, and surveillance video gets copied over.

Well, wouldn't you know it? We caught two homicides that day, one after the other: a gas station robbery gone bad, and a drug deal, also gone bad. Both were simple enough, but time-consuming all the same.

The first was a "shots fired" call that came in over the radio as we were driving back to the office. We were the closest unit, so we had to respond and were directed to a small white house in Highland Park. Thus, I became the first detective at the scene. That's a sure-fire way to end up with the investigation.

When we arrived, there were two blue and white cruisers already on site, and a dead, black male aged about nineteen lying on the kitchen floor in a pool of blood. He'd been shot several times. There were dollar bills—mostly small denominations—scattered all over the kitchen table and floor. Two large caliber handguns lay on the floor, and there was an open brick of marijuana on the table.

I recognized the boy as one I'd dealt with several times in the past. He was...well, he was a product of the environment, and seeing him lying there, I couldn't help but feel sorry for him. I already had a couple of ideas as to who might have shot him, and I was right. I arrested the young man early that same evening; he hadn't even bothered to change his pants, upon which the blood spatter was easy to see. When I pointed it out to him, he simply shrugged and held out his hands to receive the cuffs. I wish they were all that easy.

And later that same evening—well, it was actually early the following morning: one-twenty-three, to be precise—we were called out to a convenience store in the East Lake area. The owner decided he wasn't going to hand over the contents of his cash register and had died for it. Fortunately, he had good security cameras. Unfortunately, the robber knew about them and managed to keep his head down.

But most gas station robbers are usually pretty dumb, and this one was no exception: he made his getaway on a Suzuki motorcycle. He parked it behind the convenience store on a side road, where it was dark, but didn't notice the camera on the back of the building. No, he didn't turn his lights on, but he did hit the brakes and that lit up the license plate, providing the camera with a good image of the number.

No, it wasn't quite that easy. We tracked down the owner of the bike, who claimed it had been stolen, and that he had an alibi. It turned out that it was stolen, and that his alibi was good. It took some time, but we questioned his friends and, eventually, we found one who fit the description: an eighteen-year-old with an attitude. He was, well, antsy during questioning, but he did give us his permission to search the house where he lived. I guess he didn't think we'd find the bike hidden in a ditch *behind* his house. He looked quite outraged when we charged him. They always do.

All of that took us through Wednesday. By the time we got through, it was almost seven o'clock, and I was exhausted. John Lewis would have to wait until morning.

26

I wasn't surprised to get a call from Chief Johnston when I arrived at the office that Thursday morning. In fact, I'd been expecting it.

"Sit down, Lieutenant," he said as Cathy ushered me into his office. "You too," he said to her.

He assumed his usual position—leaned back in his chair, folded his arms, and stared at me across the desk.

"Just what do you think you're doing?" he asked me. "I haven't talked to Tracy yet, but I have spoken to Chief Finkle. He is..." He shook his head, seemingly lost for words. "He's furious. It was all I could do to dissuade him from filing a formal complaint against you. Kate, your interview with the assistant chief crossed the line. I warned you—"

"Yes, sir, you did," I interrupted him. "And I was mindful of that, but I had to push him. I had to know if either one of them, or both, was involved in some sort of cover-up."

He rocked his chair slowly back and forth, his chin down, looking at me through hooded eyes.

"And?" he asked, so quietly I could barely hear him.

I closed my eyes and shook my head. "I'm not sure."

For a long moment, he stared at me across the desk, then said, "I hate to hear that, Catherine. It presents me with something of a problem, as I'm sure you must realize. Assistant Chief Finkle is insisting that I put a stop to whatever it is you're doing and, unless you can provide me with a good reason why I shouldn't, I'm inclined to acquiesce."

"Chief, you really need to let me run with this."

He leaned forward, placed his folded arms on the desktop, and waited.

"I talked to both of them," I said, "and I do think they're trying to cover something up, but what it is—I don't know, not for sure. Chief, I'm almost certain that Chief Finkle knew Jennifer Lewis, but how well, I don't know that either. I really don't think he had anything to do with her disappearance. I think it's something else. I think that he may have—that maybe he... Look, sir, Tracy told me that Lewis was a hooker. I don't know if she was or not. If she was, and if the assistant chief... Oh shit, sir. You know what I'm getting at. It wouldn't look good if it got out." I shut up and waited.

Johnston leaned back, steepled his fingers, and stared at me over them. I glanced at Cathy; she was looking down at her hands.

Finally, he nodded, and said, "Very well, you may continue, but finish it, quickly, Lieutenant. That will be all, for now."

"Er...sir?"

"What?"

"I may need to go to Boston...and Wheeling."

"Don't push it, Catherine. Cathy will see you out."

"Wow, you've got nerve, I'll give you that," Cathy said after she'd closed the door behind us.

I grinned at her. "You noticed he didn't say no, right?"

She rolled her eyes. "Good luck with that!"

JOHN LEWIS HAD A SMALL REAL ESTATE BUSINESS LOCATED IN A strip mall on Bonny Oaks Drive. It was just after ten o'clock that morning when Lonnie and I arrived there. A pretty young woman seated behind a desk in the front office greeted us with a smile.

"Good morning. Welcome to Lewis Realty. What can I do for you?"

I made the introductions and told her I would like a word with her boss. She frowned, hesitated for a moment, stood, asked us to please wait, and then she disappeared.

"Let me do the talking, okay?" I whispered to Lonnie.

He nodded.

She was gone only for a moment.

"He said he'll see you. I'll show you the way."

She led us through a door and along a long, narrow corridor with doors equally spaced on either side: small offices, I assumed.

She knocked once on the closed door at the end of the corridor and pushed it open. Lewis was seated behind a desk at the far side of a fairly spacious office; not huge, but bigger than mine.

"Please, come in," he said as he stood up behind the desk. "Lucy said you're with the police. Please sit down. What can I do for you?"

"I'm Lieutenant Gazzara," I said as we sat down. "This is Sergeant Guest. We'd like to talk to you about your wife."

"Jennifer? Have—have you found her?" He sounded concerned, even hopeful, but he also looked agitated.

That doesn't sound natural. Damned if he isn't faking it. I made a show of opening my iPad as I watched him in my peripheral vision.

"I was handed the case only a couple of days ago, Mr. Lewis," I said. "I'm just getting started, so no, not yet. I do have some questions, though, if you wouldn't mind."

"Of course. Anything."

I reached into my jacket pocket and took out my digital recorder.

"I'm going to record our conversation," I said, as I turned it on and set it down on the desk between us. "It's routine; just for the record. Do you have any objections?"

He looked at the little machine, frowned, but shook his head.

"Out loud, if you don't mind, Mr. Lewis."

"No, I have no objections, but what's this all about? I haven't—"

"One moment please, sir," I said, interrupting him. Then I spoke into the machine adding the date, time, and pertinent details. That done, I settled against the backrest.

"I'm sorry this is taking so long," I said as I picked up my iPad. "Just one more minute, and I'll be ready."

He didn't answer.

I swiped the iPad screen and brought up an old, faded photograph of him—and Sapphire? I studied him over the top of the device. The years had been kind to him. In the photo he was slim, thin-featured with what they used to call a "bowl" haircut. Still do, I suppose. Anyway, he looked like a geek, but thirty-odd years later, though he was now fifty-three—he still retained something of his youth. His hair had thinned a little and was receding. His face had filled out; he must have been at least thirty pounds heavier, but he looked fit and healthy. But there was something about his eyes. They were light gray; most unusual.

He moved slightly in his seat as if he was uncomfortable under my scrutiny, but he smiled at me, a set smile that had no humor in it, or his eyes.

"Yes," I said, lowering the iPad a little and repeating what I'd said so the recorder could pick it up. "It's about Jennifer and, no, we haven't found her, not yet."

"You think she's dead, don't you?"

"I don't know," I said. "Do you?"

He shook his head. "No...but it's possible, I suppose. I haven't heard from her in more than two years."

"*Two years?*" I said. "She was reported missing in May 2012. That's three years."

"Yes. I know. She called me. She wanted money."

"*What?*"

He shrugged, then said, "She called me," he tapped the keyboard of his computer "in February 2013. She was in some kind of trouble. I asked her what. She wouldn't tell me." He shrugged.

"You didn't send the money?"

"Hell no. She left me in a mess. I was glad to see her gone. If I'd have sent her money, she'd have asked for more. I wasn't gonna start that mess."

"Where was she?" Lonnie asked.

"I don't know."

"You didn't ask her?" Lonnie asked, skeptically.

"No."

"No? Weren't you at least a little bit curious?" I asked.

"No! I didn't give a damn."

"Your wife had been gone for more than a year—and you didn't give a damn?" Lonnie asked. "I don't believe you."

"Believe what the hell you like. I didn't care then, and I don't care now. Are we done, here? I have work to do."

I ignored the question and said, "When exactly did she call you?"

He glanced at the computer screen. "February 19, in the evening sometime."

"What time?"

"I didn't make a note of it."

"How about the number?"

"I didn't make a note of that either."

"No problem, I'll check your phone records. I'll need the phone number please."

He grabbed a pad of sticky notes, scribbled down the number and handed it to me. "Go ahead," he said smirking. "Knock yourselves out."

The son of a bitch. He planned it. He set it up. "And you never tried to call her back?"

"No."

"Why didn't you report that call to Missing Persons? They would have followed up on it."

He shrugged, looked away and said, "I don't know. It didn't seem important, at the time. I told you, she went away with some guy. I simply assumed..." He didn't finish his thought.

"What did you assume?"

"To be honest, I was worried that she might have left him and wanted to come home. *That*, I didn't want."

I nodded, thought for a minute, then said, "Was Jennifer your first wife, Mr. Lewis?"

He looked startled, hesitated, just for a split second, then said, "No. I was married before, briefly, in 1981. I was nineteen. Why d'you ask?"

"Mr. Lewis, you told Jennifer and her family that you were a bachelor, that you'd never been married before. Why did you do that?"

"That's not true. I told Jennifer I'd been married when I was a kid. I didn't tell anyone else. It was none of their business."

"So, you're telling me that Jennifer knew about your first wife and that she didn't tell anyone else?"

"If she did, she didn't tell me."

"You also told Alice Booker you came from Indiana, but that's not true. You're from Highton, in West Virginia. Why did you lie to her?"

"I didn't tell her that."

"You also told her you were from a dysfunctional family."

"So?"

"Well, are you?" I asked.

"Depends what you call dysfunctional."

"What do *you* call dysfunctional?"

"My parents died when I was three years old. I was brought up by my grandparents. I'd call that dysfunctional. Wouldn't you?"

"No. That's not at all unusual."

Again, he shrugged.

"Did they provide you and your brother with a good home?"

"My brother? I don't—" He paused, narrowed his eyes, hesitated, then said, "How d'you know about him?"

I dodged the question. "You told Alice Booker that you were an only child."

He shook his head. "That's not true either. Look, me and Alice Booker didn't get along, okay? She's an interfering bitch. She doesn't like me, and I don't like her. When Jennifer ran off, she accused me of every kind of abuse, mental and physical, you can think of. None of it was true."

"During your interview with Detective Tracy, you stated that Jennifer was having an affair, and that she had," I looked down at my iPad, "run away with the guy. What was his name?"

"I don't know."

"You were pretty angry when Jennifer told you that she was going to divorce you," Lonnie said. "Isn't that right, Mr. Lewis?"

"Yeah, I was *freakin'* angry. Wouldn't you be?"

He closed his eyes, shook his head, and muttered something I couldn't understand.

"What was that, Mr. Lewis?"

"Nothing. Look, this shit has got to stop. I've told you everything I know—"

I interrupted him, and said, "Did you know that Jennifer worked as a stripper, and possibly as a prostitute as well?"

He laughed. "You've got to be kidding me. That's crap. You're talking about those few weeks she spent working part-time at that club, the Starlight, or some such. She worked there as a waitress, that's all. Look, she met this guy there a couple of weeks before she ran away with him. That's the end of it. Now, if we're done..." He was becoming annoyed.

"No, we're not done, Mr. Lewis. Did you ever visit the Starburst? That's the name of the club by the way."

"Occasionally."

"How often is occasionally?"

He adjusted in his seat. "I don't know—three, maybe four times?"

"Why?"

"Why what?"

"Don't be stupid, Mr. Lewis," I said. "It's a simple question. Why did you visit the Starburst?"

Oh, that pissed him off, as I intended.

"I'm *not* freaking stupid, Lieutenant. Yes, I have. I like to go out occasionally. Who doesn't? I visit several clubs, *occasionally*. I like a drink; I like women, and I'm single for God's sake."

"No, you're not. You're still married to Jennifer, at least you were last time I checked."

"Yeah, right!" He made a wry expression, rolled his eyes, and shook his head.

"Were you there because you knew Jennifer would be there?" I asked.

"No."

"But she was there, correct?"

His eyelids flickered. "Yes."

I nodded and changed the subject. "Do you associate with prostitutes, Mr. Lewis?" I asked.

"*What?* Hell no. What the hell has all this got to do with anything?" His face was flush with color, his voice rising.

Lonnie leaned forward, placed his elbows on his knees, clasped his hands together, and glared at him. Lewis got the point and seemed to calm down, some.

I flipped through several screens, found what I was looking for, then showed it to him.

"Do you know this man?" I asked.

He took the device from me and looked closely at the photograph of Henry Finkle.

"Yes, well, maybe. I think I've seen him around."

"At the Starburst?"

"Yes. Maybe. I don't know."

"More than once?"

"*I, don't, know!* Eh, a couple of times, I suppose."

"Who was he with?" Lonnie asked.

Again, his eyelids flickered as he glanced away to the left.

"Some girl. I didn't take any notice."

"Was it Jennifer?" Lonnie asked.

The eyelids flickered again. He shook his head, then said, "No."

"Were you stalking Jennifer, Mr. Lewis?" I asked.

"No! *Hell no!*"

"Then why were you at the Starburst, watching her?"

"I wasn't, damn it, watching her. I was—I wasn't watching her... Okay, I was. She was my wife, for God's sake. I saw her with a guy; yeah, I watched her. That's all. Wouldn't you?" That last question he directed at Lonnie.

Lonnie simply smiled at him.

I nodded, took the iPad back, flipped screens, and said, "How about him? Did you ever see him in the Starburst?"

He took a quick look at the photo of Detective Tracy, looked at me stupefied, then said, "Are you out of your freaking mind? That's Detective Tracy. He interviewed me three years ago. No, I've not seen him anywhere since. He's not even contacted me."

Oh hell, don't remind me.

"Your first wife's name was Sapphire, I believe."

He nodded but said nothing.

I looked him in the eye. "You know what bothers me, Mr. Lewis?"

Again, he didn't answer.

"Coincidence. That's what bothers me."

Again, I waited for him to answer, but he didn't. He simply stared at me, almost unblinking, so I continued.

"We know that Sapphire also worked at a strip club, in Wheeling. So, that means you have two wives both of whom worked in strip clubs. That's a bit of a coincidence, don't you think?"

No answer; no reaction.

"Sapphire has a brother, Ryan, but you knew that."

I watched his eyes: no reaction.

"Several days ago, one of my associates interviewed Ryan. Did you know he hasn't seen his sister since 1982?"

He sat rigid in his chair, hands clasped together on the desk in front of him.

"Would you like to know what else Ryan told my associate?"

"Quite frankly, my dear," he ground the famous quote out through his clenched teeth.

"No? Well, I'll tell you anyway. Ryan told my associate that he called you the day after Christmas 1982, two weeks after he last talked to Sapphire. He asked you if you knew where she was. Do you remember what you told him, Mr. Lewis?"

He didn't answer. He just sat with his hands clasped together on the desk in front of him and stared at me.

"You don't?" I asked. "Well, I'll remind you." I looked at my iPad —the image of John Tracy stared right back at me. I looked up at Lewis, and continued, "You said, and I quote, 'I don't know where she is. She's probably gone off with one of her boyfriends,' end quote."

I watched his eyes; I've seen warmer eyes on a dead fish.

"Sound familiar, Mr. Lewis? You see what I mean about coincidence?"

His lips were two thin white lines. The muscles in his jaw were tight, bulging.

"Where the hell are they, John? Where are Jennifer and Sapphire?"

His lips twitched slightly and then, suddenly, his mood changed, and the gray eyes seemed to be laughing at me.

"Well," he said, brightly, as he stood up and offered me his hand across the desk. "If that's all, Lieutenant. I really do have work to do. So, if you'll excuse me, I'll get on with it."

"Sit the hell down—"

I put a hand on Lonnie's arm, interrupting him.

"It's all right, Sergeant," I said, also rising to my feet.

I ignored Lewis' hand, picked up my recorder, turned it off, looked him in the eye, and said, "You're one cool, sick son of a bitch,

Mr. Lewis. I know you killed them, and what's worse, you know I know. Don't you?"

He cocked his head to one side, smiled, then said, "I have no idea what you're talking about, Lieutenant. You really should be very, *very* careful though," he paused. The menace in his voice was palpable, chilling, and then, with an obvious lack of concern in his voice, he continued. "You should be very careful what you accuse people of, especially when you have no proof. It could...well, get you into serious trouble. Now, are we done?"

"Is that a threat, Mr. Lewis?" I asked.

He didn't answer, but the evil smile he gifted me with told me all I needed to know.

"GET US OUT OF HERE, NOW," I SNARLED AT LONNIE AS I slammed the car door. Oh, I was pissed, and I wanted to get as far away from Lewis as I could get.

He reversed out onto Bonny Oaks, put the big car in drive and, with a whole lot more restraint than I would have been capable of, drove west toward Highway 153.

"That, LT," he said, as he exited the on-ramp and eased into the traffic, "was intense. Did you lose it in there, or did you really mean to accuse him?"

"No, I didn't lose it, but I wouldn't have done it... I wouldn't have done it but for the patronizing look he gave me. That smart-ass piece of shit was laughing at us, well me."

"You really think he done it?"

"You heard what I said about coincidences. This case—and the Sullivan case—is one great basketful of coincidences. Yes, I think he killed both of them. Maybe others too. He's one cold bastard. Did you notice he was about to deny that he had a brother, then thought better of it? Oh yes, he's smart—and careful. I already know there's not one damn incriminating syllable on the tape. John Lewis just became my prime suspect. We need to get back to the office. I want to run his phone records."

And we did, and sure enough, Lewis had received a call on February 19 at seven-nineteen PM that lasted for almost nine minutes. *Son of a bitch. How the hell did he pull that off?*

There was only one way I knew of to find out: I called Tim Clarke and asked him to run the number for me. Guess what? He couldn't.

"The call originated from a fake phone number," he said when he called me back. "I'm fairly certain it was obtained from an app, such as NoTrace."

"What are you talking about, Tim? You're telling me that the call was made from a burner phone?"

"No. I mean yes, but not really; better than that. Whoever made the call downloaded the number from an app. It's done all the time in dating circles. The app provides the user with a temporary phone number that essentially turns the phone—any phone—into a burner. Except that you don't have to burn it, throw it away, the phone I mean, when you're done. Instead, you simply delete the number from your phone, and it can't be traced back to you. It does, however, leave the number in the recipients call log and, of course, the phone company's records. Neat, huh?"

"Oh my god. Are you kidding me? Burners are out, apps are in?"

"Essentially, yes. You got it. Burner apps have been around for a couple of years, since early 2014."

"So where did the call come from?" I asked.

"We'll never know. It could have originated in Alaska or right here in Chattanooga."

"You're saying he could have placed that call himself?"

"Yup. All he needed was a second phone and the app. They could have been right next to each other... Okay, let me give you an example. Did you ever get a call from a local cell phone number, a number you didn't recognize, but you answered it anyway because you saw it was a local number, only to find it was a computerized sales call? That's how they did it. They used an app like the one I just described."

"Oh wow, what will they think of next. No, no, no; don't tell me. I don't have time to listen. I have to go. Thanks, Tim. I'll talk to you later. Tell Harry hello for me."

Damn, damn, damn, I thought, after I'd hung up. *Lewis is one sneaky son of a bitch. I need to talk to the brother, Michael Lewis, and not on the phone. I need to check flights to Wheeling. The big guy isn't going to like it, but what the hell?*

I was right, Johnston didn't like the idea of my flying to West Virginia, not one bit. But after he heard my pitch and listened to some of my interview with Lewis, and knowing the drive would take a couple of days and cost almost as much as the airfare, he grudgingly okayed it.

I didn't want Michael Lewis to know that I was coming because I didn't want him to call his brother. But I needed to be sure he would be home. I figured that the weekend would give me my best shot, so I decided to go the following Saturday morning. Even so, I still couldn't be absolutely sure. So what to do? I couldn't call him. Hell, I couldn't even hang-up call him—caller ID is a bitch, sometimes.

In the end, I decided I needed some local help, so I called the local sheriff, Ben Jacobson. It was a call I had to make anyway: I was going to be in his patch, so protocol dictated that I let him know. I did that, and then I asked the favor, which caused him to laugh. At first I was taken aback, a little, but it turned out that he wasn't laughing at me.

Highton is a small country town, one of those sleepy little places —much like Mayberry—where everybody knows everybody; the sheriff knew Michael Lewis. Now that was one coincidence I was happy about.

Anyway, it turned out that Lewis and a bunch of his friends ate breakfast every morning at the local diner; so did Sheriff Jacobson. He claimed that Lewis hadn't missed a Saturday morning in more than ten years. *Hah, with my luck, this one will be the first.*

27

FRIDAY, MAY 22, MORNING – LEWIS CASE

I spent most of Friday morning going over my interview with John Lewis. The more I listened to it, the more convinced I became that he had done away with both of his wives. He'd been careful in what he said, but in my mind's eye, I remembered each one of the little giveaways that told me when he was lying: the facial tics, the flickering eyelids, slight dilation of his pupils, the sideways glances, the hesitations. He was good, though. I never would have seen them had I not been looking for them.

And then there were the coincidences. There were way too many of them, but the one that stood out above all the others, at least to me, was his story—stories—that both women had run off with lovers unknown never to be heard from again.

The frustrating thing about the case, though, was that I knew that somewhere out there were two bodies, and unless we could find either one of them, he was in the clear: no body, no murder, no evidence of foul play. They were just missing persons.

And the morning dragged on, interminably until I was jerked out of my reverie by the buzzing of my iPhone.

I looked at the screen, swiped it and said, "Hey, Tim. How are you?"

"I'm good, Kate, very good. So, I have a little more information for you, but you're not going to like it."

I sighed. That was all I needed, more bad news.

"Go ahead, Tim. Make my day."

"You asked me to find Amber Watts and Jeffery Tobin and run backgrounds on them."

"Yes, for the Lewis case. Watts is the friend and Tobin a supposed boyfriend."

"I did... Well, sort of... Tobin, yes, but—"

Oh, come on, Tim. I don't have the patience for this today.

"Yes, Tim," I said, hoping my frustration wasn't too obvious. If it was, he didn't seem to notice.

"Kate, I couldn't find any reference to Amber Watts after Saturday, May 5, 2012. That was the last time she used her debit card. And believe me, I looked. That's not all, though. The last call she made on her cell phone was also on May 5. Her bank account is still open and shows a balance of nineteen thousand, three hundred and fifty-one dollars and seventeen cents, but there's been no activity on the account since Friday, May 4, 2012, when she deposited seven hundred dollars, in cash. I found out where she lived. She doesn't live there...not now... Anyway, so I called her former landlord. It seems someone cleaned out her apartment and paid the remaining balance on the lease, also in cash, on Monday, May 7. The landlord can't remember if it was a woman or a man."

"Are you serious?" I asked, dumbfounded. Amber Watts had disappeared only a couple weeks after Jennifer Lewis.

"Oh yeah, very serious, and—"

"Hold on, Tim. I need to make a quick call."

I grabbed the desk phone and buzzed through to Missing Persons.

"Hey, Laura," I said. "I need a favor, a quickie, please. Okay, great. I need you to look up a missing person report on an Amber Watts. It would have been sometime in 2012, after May first. I gotta go. I have someone waiting on another line. You'll call me, right?"

She said she would, and I dropped the handset back in its cradle.

"Okay, Tim. I'm back. I was just checking with Missing Persons. Laura's going to call me back."

"There's no need for that. I already checked. She won't find anything."

"Oh shit, Tim. You hacked the computers again? Please stop doing that. If you get caught—"

"Oh yeah, as if—"

"Okay, okay," I interrupted him. "Amber Watts; there's more, right?"

"There is. She has no relatives, at least none that I could find, not without going very deep. She's a product of the foster care system. She aged out of the system sixteen years ago. I also called her last foster parent, a Mrs. Judy Brownlee. She hasn't heard from Amber since she moved out... Kate, you're gonna love this: Amber Watts worked at the Starburst."

"No frickin' way!" I swear I heard him laugh.

"I assure you she did, but she hasn't been seen there either. Her last day was Thursday, May 3. She was supposed to work Friday, but she never showed. That's it, Kate. That's all I have, on her anyway."

The desk phone buzzed.

"Hold on, Tim."

I picked up the handset. "Gazzara. Hey, Laura... There isn't? Well, okay. Thanks for looking... No, not right now. I'll talk to you later. Thanks again."

"That, Tim," I said, "was Missing Persons. You're right. She has not been reported missing, ever."

"That's what I told you. Now, Jeffery Tobin. Nothing bad; nothing good. He's a sales manager at one of the nicer used car dealers. He's thirty-six, has fair credit—his score is 710—divorced twice, no outstanding warrants. Lives in Hixson with his girlfriend, Tonya Wix. He's clean. Do you want his number?"

I made a note of the number, told him thank you and goodbye, and then I hung up.

I spent the next half-hour lost in thought. The Amber Watts thing had thrown me. I now had three missing women. And I was certain all three were tied together and that John Lewis was the one who'd tied the knot, maybe literally.

I badly wanted to talk to him again, but the more I thought about it, the more convinced I became that I needed to wait. The extra knowledge gave me a certain advantage, and the Lord knew I needed all of that I could get.

Finally, I buzzed Lonnie and had him join me, and then spent another half-hour filling him in on what I'd learned and discussing the ramifications of the new information.

I say half an hour, but the arrival of Assistant Chief Henry Finkle cut it short.

As usual, he burst into my office without knocking, but then why would he? To my certain knowledge, the only door on which he ever did bother to knock was the chief's.

"Good Morning, Chief," I said, as he parked his butt in the chair next to Lonnie. "Is there something I can do for you?"

"It's Friday, Lieutenant. I haven't heard a word from you since our little talk on Monday. I was hoping you'd keep me updated. What's the status of the Sullivan case?"

Hah! That's not what you're after, and playing Mr. Nice doesn't impress me...at all.

"Chief," I said, weariness in my voice. "If I'd had any news you would have been the first to know. I turned Sullivan back in, you know that, but the chief asked me to keep at it for a while. D'you want to look at it?"

"That won't be necessary... What about the other thing, the Lewis case?"

Ah ha! Here we go.

"Lonnie," I said. "I need a private minute with the chief, please."

He grinned at me, caught the look on Finkle's face, wiped off the smile, and stood up.

"Look, Chief," I said after Lonnie had closed the door behind him. It was time to ingratiate myself a little. "I'm sorry about Monday, but it had to be done; you know that, right?"

He looked warily at me but made no response.

I sighed and shook my head. "Okay, this is what I have so far..." And there went another fifteen minutes as I brought him up to date on the case, leaving out only the parts that affected him and ending with what I just learned about Amber Watts.

"Now," I said, finally, "you know as much as I do. I'm going to try to talk to Tobin this afternoon and Michael Lewis tomorrow."

"So you think John Lewis is a serial killer, then?"

"I don't know, Chief, and if that gets leaked to the press, I never will know. So please, keep everything I've told you to yourself." I had no doubt that he would. It wouldn't have been in his best interests to do otherwise.

He stared thoughtfully at me. Strangely, there was no animosity in the look and, for a moment, I was tempted to think I was maybe dealing with a softer, kinder Henry Finkle. It was but a fleeting moment. I knew the man too well.

Finally, he nodded and said, "I understand."

You do? Wow!

"Good work, Lieutenant. Keep it up. Come see me on Monday and let me know how it goes in Wheeling."

Then he stood, smiled benignly, and left me sitting there with my mouth wide open.

I buzzed Lonnie.

"What was that about?" he asked.

"You really don't want to know. Let's go find Jeff Tobin."

We found him in his office at Skyler's Auto Brokers; brokers being an upscale definition of what was essentially a used car lot.

I was expecting a version of the caricature used car salesman; he wasn't. He was smartly dressed, clean-shaven, trim and obviously fit.

"Hey," he said brightly as he came around his desk. "You looking for a nice clean ride? If so—"

"No, Mr. Tobin," I said, interrupting his flow. "I'm Lieutenant Gazzara, Chattanooga Police, and this is Sergeant Guest. I need a word, please."

"Sure, sit down. What's this all about? I'm not in any trouble, am I?"

"I don't know," I said as we sat. "Are you?" I said it with a smile, but he looked uncomfortable.

"No. *No!* Of course not. How can I help you?"

"I want to talk to you about Jennifer Lewis," I said.

"Whew, you do? Wow. I haven't thought about her in years. Has she turned up, then?"

"You knew her when she worked at the Starburst?" I said.

"That's right. She was a nice kid."

Kid? She's about the same age as you. "You had an affair with her," I said.

"*Affair?* Not hardly. I had a bit of a fling with her. I went out with her a few times, but that's all there was to it. It wasn't an *affair*. Look, the Starburst; it's a strange place, but you know that, right? She was waiting tables there, maybe more. I don't know. She wasn't exactly the sort of—look, I wasn't sure if maybe she was an escort, or not. If she was, I didn't want..." He shook his head, frustrated, then continued. "Maybe she was, maybe she wasn't. She never asked me for money. We just went out a few times. That's all. I told that detective." And somehow, I believed him.

"We've been led to understand that she was having an affair with someone. You say it wasn't you. Do you know who it was?"

He was slowly shaking his head. "No. If she was seeing someone else, she kept it to herself."

"When did you last see her, Mr. Tobin?" I asked.

"Oh Lord, I don't know. I can't even remember what month it was. Just before she left, maybe a week, or so."

I changed the subject, flipped through several screens on my iPad, found the photo I was looking for, and said, "How about this woman? She worked at the Starburst at the same time as Jennifer Lewis." I turned the iPad and showed him the photo of Amber Watts.

He looked at the photo and shook his head. "No, I don't think so. She's lovely. I would have remembered."

I nodded, flipped through several more screens, then turned the device toward him again.

"How about him?" I asked as I showed him a photo of Henry Finkle.

He nodded. "Yes, in the Starburst, among other places. Who is he?"

I ignored the question, and asked, "When Jennifer Lewis worked there?"

He shrugged. "I suppose. He's often in there. Likes the ladies."

"He is? Oh. How often?" No, I didn't really care, but hell, I was curious.

"A couple of times a month, I suppose."

Sheesh, Henry. You need to be more careful. "Did you ever see him with Jennifer Lewis?"

He hesitated. "No, I don't think so, but he does look familiar. Who is he?"

Again, I ignored the question. My problem now was how to get out of there without arousing his curiosity any more than it already was. If he figured out who Finkle was...

"So, when you took Jennifer out, did you ever notice anything unusual? Were you ever followed? Anything at all?"

"You mean that creep of a husband?" he asked, leaning back in his chair and smiling. "Yeah. In fact, he threatened me. I'd just dropped her off at her apartment. I was about to get into my car when he crept up behind me and pushed my car door shut. The son of a bitch grabbed me by the shirt and said if I ever went near her again, he'd break my legs. And, by god, I believed him. That was the last time I saw her."

"Why didn't you mention that before?" I asked.

"I did. I told that other detective. I don't think he believed me."

Oh, John. That's something else you left out of your report.

I stared at Tobin. He held my gaze. I believed the man. I was ready to get out of there, but I asked him several more questions, mainly to make sure he'd forgotten about Finkle. Then I stood, thanked him, gave him my card, and we left.

"HE'S TELLING THE TRUTH," I SAID TO LONNIE AS HE DROVE OUT of the car lot. "John Tracy really screwed this one up. I'm not sure what to do about him."

"Yeah, I thought that too, that he was telling the truth. Hey, did you see that Beamer in the lot? I wonder what they're asking for it. I could see me in that sucker."

"That's it?" I asked. "That's all you're good for, a frickin' used BMW? I want to know what you're thinking about the case, damn it."

"Sorry, LT. You gotta admit, though: it's sweet."

"Damn," I whispered, shaking my head. "Lonnie, where the hell is your head? Did you listen to any of the conversation at all?"

"I did, and I agree with you: he's telling the truth. My question is, though: where does Finkle fit into all this? And what the hell were you two talking about this morning, by the way?"

I smiled, and said, "You're right, Lonnie. That Beamer is a sweet-looking ride."

"Right!" he said. "Okay, so don't tell me."

28

SATURDAY, MAY 23, MORNING – LEWIS CASE

When I landed at Wheeling that following Saturday morning, Ben Jacobson was waiting for me and, even before we'd had time to properly introduce ourselves, I knew he was my kind of sheriff.

He had a caustic sense of humor, an infectious laugh, a never-ending smile, and blue eyes that twinkled whenever he spoke, which was often, and not always appropriately. He was a fun kind of guy; even so, there was a serious side to him too, as I found out when I filled him in.

By the time I'd finished, the smile was gone, and he was shaking his head in disbelief.

"I was at high school with John Lewis," he said. "He's a crazy son of a bitch, and Sapphire was all it took to set him off. I remember her too. We were a year ahead of her. She loved to push his buttons, always flirting and fooling around."

"Fooling around?" I asked.

"Not what you think. She was a happy little thing, a flirt, as I said, liked to joke around a lot. But as far as I know, she never stepped out on John, although he always claimed she did."

He continued to fill me in as we drove to the Lewis family home, obviously enjoying reminiscing about the past. By the time we got there, I knew everything he knew, which was, in fact, not a whole lot.

He parked the cruiser in front of the house, and together we mounted the steps to the porch. I stood back while he thumbed the bell push.

"Hey, Mike," he said when the door opened.

I found myself looking at a mirror image of his brother, only younger, but older...if you get what I mean. He had a hollow look about his eyes, sported a beer belly, and his hair was almost white. *He's what, forty-five? What's that all about, I wonder?*

"Ben?" he said. "What? Who's that with you?"

Jacobson introduced me, and I flashed my badge.

"I need to ask you a few questions, Michael, if you don't mind."

"But, you're from Chattanooga. I've never been there. What d'you want with me?"

"I'd like to talk to you about your brother John."

"Oh. *Oh!* Well, I haven't seen him years... You'd—I guess you'd better come in then."

He stood aside, and we entered and followed him into the kitchen.

"Where's Amy?" Jacobson asked. "She not here?"

"No. She went to Wheeling, shopping. She'll be back this afternoon. Can I get you anything, coffee, water, anything? No? Well...okay. Sit, please."

Wow, the guy's nervous. "I need to tell you that I'm going to record this interview, Mr. Lewis," I said as I turned the tiny machine on.

"Why? What for? I don't know how I can help you. John left here more than thirty years ago. We haven't really stayed in touch." He looked at Jacobson, frowning. "Ben? D'you know what this is all about?"

"It's okay, Mike," Jacobson said. "The tape is mostly for your protection. Just answer the lieutenant's questions truthfully, okay?"

He nodded, and said "okay," but I could tell he wasn't happy about it. His face had lost all color.

We talked for several minutes about things long since passed. The man's memory wasn't too good, but maybe that was just a put-on. I tried to take him back through the months leading up to Sapphire's disappearance, but it was uphill going. I had to drag it out of him syllable by syllable. It wasn't until I asked him what had happened after the divorce that he began to open up, a little.

"I understand that after he divorced Sapphire, he moved back in with you and your grandparents, here, correct?"

He nodded. "Yes, ma'am."

"When would that have been, exactly?"

"Exactly? I don't know. As I told you, it was more than thirty years ago. November '82, maybe?"

"And you two got along okay?"

"Yeah, for the most part, I suppose."

"What does that mean?" I asked.

"Well, he kept to himself. Stayed in his room, mostly. Look, John and me...we never was what you'd call friends. Tell the truth, he was a miserable brother. I was glad when he left."

"When did he leave?"

"We knew he was planning on going, but he went kinda sudden-like, on a Sunday. January 16, I think. He just packed his things, loaded 'em into his truck, and drove. Didn't even tell us goodbye."

Hmm, that was a full week before he started work. Why the hurry? Where did he go, I wonder?

"You knew he was planning to leave? Did he say why?"

"Yeah. He'd gotten himself a good job in Louisville. He told me about it a week or so earlier, then he dropped it on me that Sunday afternoon that he was leaving that day. I was kinda shocked because I knew he wasn't supposed to start his new job for another week. Anyway, I told Grandpa. He was shocked too and said he wanted to talk to him. We found him in the garage packing his stuff. He was stuffing clothes into a big old wood box."

My heart started to race. "What kind of box?"

"A wood box. I helped him make it a few days earlier. He said he was going to use it to store some of Sapphire's clothes, in case she came back for them. He took it away with him when he left. We thought no more about it."

That doesn't make any sense.

"Mike," I said, "you said he made the box to store her clothes in case she came back for them, so why would he take them with him?"

He stuck out his bottom lip and frowned, obviously thinking about it.

"I dunno," he said. "I never thought about it."

"And you didn't see him again for what, four years?"

"Almost five."

"How so?"

"Well, one day, I got a call from Hank Tully—he's the guy who runs the Triple A storage units in town. He told me that John hadn't paid the rent on his unit in a couple of months and he couldn't get hold of him. I didn't even know he had a unit."

He shrugged, and then continued. "Anyway, I figured I better go pay the rent...for John, so I did. It wasn't much back then, just seven dollars a month. I gave Hank twenty-one dollars, that's three months' rent, includin' the past due, and then..." He hesitated, coughed, then said, "Then I called John and asked him to send me the money—"

There's something going on here. He can't look me in the eye.

"Just a minute, Michael," I interrupted him. "Did you enter the unit?"

He hesitated, then looked at me and said, "Yeah, I did. Tully had a spare key."

"And?"

"There was a lot of old stuff in there."

"What old stuff?"

Again, he hesitated, then said, "You know: furniture, an old bike, stuff we played with when we were kids...bags of old clothes. Paint cans. Tools, an old file cabinet. Several wooden boxes—"

"Wooden boxes? Was one of them the box you saw him putting Sapphire's clothes into in your grandparents' garage?"

He nodded.

"Did you open it?"

"I—no. No. I didn't?"

"I don't believe you, Michael. You were curious, right? You *had* to open it. What was in it?"

"I didn't open it, I tell you. That was the first thing John asked when I told him I'd paid the rent on the unit. Look, Lieutenant, you don't screw with John. He's—he's freakin' crazy. He scares the shit outa me. I watched him almost kill a guy one night, just for looking at Sapphire wrong, and they was already divorced then. He beat him half to death with a tire iron. If they hadn't stopped him...well, you don't mess with him, is all. Hell no. I didn't open the box."

"You told him you saw the box? Why would you do that? It was just one of a number of stored items. Why did you mention that particular one to him?"

"I didn't. He asked me. It was the first thing he said after I told him I'd paid the rent: 'Did you open any of the boxes?' I told him no."

"But you did, didn't you?"

"No!" He looked away, wouldn't look at me.

I glanced at Ben Jacobson. He was shaking his head.

"Okay," I said, "then what?"

"He came and got the box."

"*What?* When?"

"That same damned night. He drove straight over from Louisville; three hundred and fifty miles. It must've took him five or six hours. He was here just before ten. I helped him load the box into the back of his pickup. Then he drove away. He wasn't here but a few minutes. He told me to keep m'mouth shut or else."

"Okay, Michael," I said. "I need to know exactly when this happened."

He thought for a minute, shook his head, sucked air in through his teeth, then said, "Geez, it was so long ago. I know it was on a

Monday in 1987 that Hank called me, but what month it was...I can't remember... Wait...wait a minute. I do remember. It was Labor Day. I know 'cause it was a holiday and I had the day off."

I looked at Jacobson. He shrugged.

"Labor Day, 1987," I said, more to myself than Lewis and Jacobson. "Okay. So, it would have been around ten o'clock that same night when he arrived here, yes?"

"Yes, the same night. He told me he was leaving right away and that I wasn't to touch anything."

"What about the other boxes? Did he take them too?"

He shook his head. "No. Just the one. We loaded it into the back of his truck, then he slammed down the storage unit door and asked me for the key. I gave it to him and he locked up. Then he left."

"What about the unit? Does he still have it?"

"No. A couple of months or so later, I got another call from Hank Tully. The rent was overdue, again. I told him, 'tough,' and I gave him John's number. He called back an hour later and told me the number was disconnected. He told me if I'd pay the past due rent, I could take the stuff out of the unit. If not, he was going to get rid of it. I told him to do just that, and I never heard from him again."

"When did you hear from John again, after he left that night?"

"I didn't. I called him a couple of days later, to see if he got home okay, but Hank was right. The phone was disconnected. That was it for me. It must have been a couple of years later that I heard from him again. Since then I've talked to him maybe a half-dozen times, basically just to say hello how are ya."

"When did you last hear from him?"

He looked quickly away, then said, quietly, almost in a whisper, "Four days ago."

No shit? Why am I not surprised?

"What did he want?"

"He said—he said I'd be hearing from the police."

"And?"

"And I was to keep my mouth shut about the box. If I didn't... He killed her, didn't he? Sapphire. He said he would, that night when he beat that guy. He called her a slut that didn't deserve to live... Lieutenant, John is family, but I haven't been able to sleep since he carted that damned box away. That's why I told you about it. I have nightmares about the frickin' thing. No, ma'am. I swear to God I didn't open it, but I sure as hell had a good idea what was in it. It was her, wasn't it?"

Now I believe you.

"I don't know, Michael. I surely don't know, but I'm going to find out. If he calls you, be careful what you tell him."

"Are you kiddin' me? He calls, I ain't even gonna talk to 'im."

"SO WHAT THE HELL HAPPENED TO THE BOX?" JACOBSON ASKED as he drove me to the airport. "And what was in it?"

"I don't know what happened to it, but I think we can guess what was in it...or should I say who?"

"You think John Lewis killed Sapphire?"

I stared straight ahead through the windshield, nodding. "Yes, and maybe others too. His second wife has been missing since April 2012, which is why I'm here."

"No kidding? You didn't tell me about that. Well, as I said, he was one crazy son of a bitch. Double murder though? Wow! Well, he wouldn't be the first."

We drove the rest of the way to the airport for the most part in silence. I had a lot on my mind and so, it seemed, did he.

"Listen, Kate... It's okay if I call you that, right?"

"Sure. Everyone does."

"Good. So if you ever need anything, anything at all...follow-up interviews, whatever. You only have to give me a call. I'll help if I can."

I thanked him, said goodbye, and passed quickly through security to my gate. I was back in Chattanooga and walking up the steps to my apartment by nine o'clock that evening, tired out and ready for bed, but, as I put the key in the lock, I suddenly had the darnedest feeling I was being watched.

29

Sunday, May 24 – Lewis Case

The rest of the weekend passed quietly enough. On Sunday I had lunch with Harry and his father at the Club. That could have turned into an all-day thing, but I had my head full of what I'd learned in West Virginia about Sapphire Williams Lewis. And, of course, I was on call. So I spent Sunday afternoon and evening alone in my apartment with pencil, paper, iPad, and laptop computer.

Where the hell is that box, and what was in it?

I knew that without the answers to those two questions, my investigation of John Lewis was going nowhere. I considered calling Ryan Williams, Sapphire's brother, but then I figured it would be a waste of my time. Tim had already talked to him and he, Tim, was nothing if he wasn't thorough. No, I'd learn nothing Tim hadn't already learned.

I thought about my interview with Michael Lewis. I listened to the recording, two times, and one thing I became certain of; the mysterious wood box contained the remains of Sapphire Williams Lewis. I was also pretty sure that Lewis would have been in one hell of a hurry to dispose of the box. After all, he'd been in one hell of a hurry to retrieve it when he learned that his brother had found it. And, let's face it: if it contained Sapphire's body, he sure as hell wouldn't want to get caught with it. He would have wanted to get it as far away from Highton as possible, but he would also have been desperate to get it out of the truck ASAP. That being so, I figured I knew approximately when—probably after midnight, but while it was still dark, on the Tuesday after Labor Day, 1987.

Probably closer to midnight than dawn, I thought. *Say two to three hours after he left Highton. So that would have been early hours of the morning on September 8... But where? Somewhere say four hours tops... He wouldn't have taken the Interstate—too many cops; couldn't risk getting stopped. And he wouldn't have driven over the speed limit, for the same reason. So somewhere within a two-hundred-mile radius of Highton.*

I pulled up Google Maps on my laptop.

So, he'd be wanting to get back to Louisville as soon as he could, maybe... I would... So, West Virginia? No, I don't think so. He'd want to get it out of the state, but I can't rule it out. Ohio, then, and Kentucky... Maybe even western Pennsylvania. Indiana? Don't think so. Virginia? Nah! Couldn't hurt to include either one, or both... Six states? Wow, that's a lot of territory.

And so it went on. By the time I called it a night, my phone showed nearly eleven o'clock. I was bushed; the traveling and long hours were beginning to catch up with me. But I went to bed happy in the knowledge that I was getting close, and that I had a plan. Not much of a plan, but better than I had forty-eight hours earlier.

30

MONDAY, MAY 25 THRU JUNE 1 – LEWIS CASE

The first thing I did when I arrived at the office the following morning was grab Lonnie and have him come to my office.

I filled him in on the events of the weekend and all that I'd learned from Michael Lewis. Then I had him send an email to every sheriff's office and police department in the six states, the gist of which was this:

I wanted to know if anyone had a record of finding a hand-made, wooden box sometime after Labor Day 1987. If so, would they please contact me. Yeah, I know: it was one hell of a long shot, a twenty-five-year-old long shot, but it was all I had. That done, there was nothing left to do but wait. That's the worst part of what we do. It can take months before a multi-state query bears fruit. In the meantime, I had six more files I was working on and plenty more where they came from.

Five of the six were solved quite quickly. We ran DNA harvested from the victims through CODIS—the Combined DNA Index System—and were rewarded with three matches. Of the remaining three cases, we were not so lucky. Then, when we reran the latent fingerprints found at the crime scenes through the constantly updated AFIS—the Automated Fingerprint Identification System— we nailed two more bad guys. So, five down and one to go.

The last case was a bummer. It should have been a simple solve. The naked body of a woman aged about twenty-six had been found in a storm drain. She'd been raped and stabbed eleven times. We had the body, possibly the killer's DNA, and his fingerprints; we even had the murder weapon, a skinning knife. None of it was helpful because we were missing the single most vital clue to solving the case, any case: the identity of the corpse. Without that...well, we were screwed, as were the detectives more than a decade ago. The investigation had stalled then and gone cold and, even with the advances in technology...nothing we did could breathe new life into it.

I had no option but to send the file back where it came from. We called that place the morgue, the storage room in the basement where it would be revisited, officially once a year. Too bad, that because of the shortage of manpower, it might be another decade before it again saw daylight.

I wondered if Amber Watts was in a file down in the morgue. An unidentified body never claimed.

By June first when Lonnie was scheduled for surgery, I'd had no hits on the email search for the wooden box, and I was becoming decidedly discouraged. I was convinced I had a killer, but unlike the case I'd just consigned to the depths, I had no bodies. I needed a body: no body, no murder.

And that wasn't my only concern: I still had the Sullivan folder on my credenza. Like a sore tooth, the daily sight of it niggled away at me, until finally, I grabbed the thing and flung it into my desk drawer: out of sight, out of mind...not!

31

Monday, June 1, Late Morning – Sullivan Case

It was just after eleven-thirty on the morning of June first when my cell phone rang. I looked at the screen and was surprised when I saw the number. *Lonnie? What the hell? He can't be out of surgery already.*

"Hey Lonnie. I wasn't expecting to hear—"

"Kate, listen to me," he interrupted. "I had to call. Something's happened—" He sounded breathless.

"What do you mean, something happened?" I interrupted *him*. "What's wrong. Are you all right? Did something go wrong with your procedure?"

"No, no, no, nothing like that. It went fine. I'm in recovery. I would have called you earlier, but the nurses wouldn't let me have my phone. Listen, Kate, this is important."

And then he proceeded to tell me.

I listened to him without interrupting for what seemed like a very long time; it wasn't, but what he said stunned me.

"Wow!" I said when he'd finished. "I've got it. Lonnie, that's one hell of a stretch, and something I never would have thought of, but it's sure as hell worth a try. Well done. I'll get right on it... Hey, are you sure you're okay? Would you like for me to come and get you?"

He declined the offer, said he was okay. He was tired and feeling a little woozy, but he had a ride home and would call me later that evening. Then he hung up.

I sat back in my chair, put my hands together behind my neck, stared up at the ceiling, then closed my eyes and whispered a prayer.

I sat like that for several minutes, mulling over the crazy idea Lonnie had just described to me. The weirdest thing about it was that he was able to back it up with experience. My brain was in turmoil. Surely it couldn't be that simple, could it? What Lonnie had described was entirely viable; hell, I'd even seen it myself. I still couldn't believe we could get that lucky, but I hoped. Oh, how I hoped.

Finally, I opened my eyes, picked up the phone and punched Mike Willis' button.

"Hey, Mike. You got a minute?"

"Sure. What d'you need?"

"Mike, it's the Sullivan case. I need a favor."

"Okay, if I can."

"You remember I asked you to recheck the DNA on the two swabs and the syringe?"

"Of course, and I did. I told you, and it's in my report. It was Rhonda Sullivan's. Nothing's changed."

I took a deep breath, then said, "Right! Okay, this is what I want you to do..."

"No freakin' way," he said when I'd finished.

He sounded skeptical, and I wasn't surprised. I didn't believe it myself.

"How long, Mike?"

"Five days...six at the most."

"Great," I said. "Soon as you can."

And there I was again, playing the waiting game.

32

MONDAY, JUNE 8, AM – SULLIVAN CASE

When Lonnie called me from the recovery room the morning he had his lap band fitted, he'd had something of an epiphany.

He'd been lying on his bed in pre-op waiting to be taken into surgery when the nurse came in to administer a sedative. As he watched, he noted that she removed the syringe cap with her teeth. Apparently, it didn't register immediately what she'd done. He was already getting the anesthesia and counting down from one hundred when he realized the significance of what he'd seen, but by then it was too late; he was already in la-la land.

It must have had one heck of an impact on him, though, because it was the first thing he remembered when he came to in recovery. He figured that whoever had injected the potassium chloride into Rhonda Sullivan might have done the same. I knew when he told me exactly what he was talking about. I'd seen it done myself, several times when I'd had blood work done. Most nurses will take off the syringe cap and lay it down, but some are in the habit of using one hand to steady the injection site and the other to hold the syringe: in which case, the only way to remove the cap is to use their teeth.

And that meant what? Well, if that's what had happened, there would be DNA on the cap. And in the Sullivan case, the DNA would belong to Pellman.

When Mike Willis called me on Monday morning a week later, I had no real hopes of hearing anything good. As I told Lonnie more than a week earlier, it was one hell of a stretch. Even so, sometimes you catch a break, right?

"Hey Mike," I said. "I need some good news, my friend."

"Well, I'm sorry, Kate," he said, and my heart sank.

"I have bad news and some not so bad news," he said.

"The DNA doesn't match, right?"

"Right. Well—no and yes—"

"What the hell's that supposed to mean?" I asked, interrupting him.

"It's not Pellman's saliva."

Shit, shit, shit!

"That's the bad news," he said. "But here's the thing: while it's not a match for Pellman himself, it does belong to a *close* member of his family. A female."

"You're kidding me?" I was stunned. "You're sure?"

"No doubt about it. It's impossible to pin it down to a single person, but when the DNA test came back negative for Pellman, they ran a mitochondrial test. They kind of reverse engineered it, traced it backward. The saliva belongs to a female member of Pellman's family. A sister, maybe?"

"But he doesn't have any sisters... Oh, my god. Mike. You, you, you frickin' angel. So what are the odds?"

"Better than one-in-thirty...million." I could almost see him smiling.

"Oh, my, god. Thanks, Mike. Thanks. I gotta go."

I hung up and pumped my fist. "*Yes!*"

I picked up the desk phone, punched in the number, and when he picked up, I said, "Lonnie, get your ass in here, *now*."

"No fricking way," he said after I'd given him the news. "You're frickin' kidding me?"

"The hell I am."

"But if the DNA is not Pellman's, it's...?"

"It's his mother's," I finished for him.

"Yeah...yeah...hell *yeah!* But how? Why? *How?*"

"The why is easy. He's an only child; his mother is besotted with him. Sullivan rejected him, and then she humiliated him. Overprotective mommy couldn't allow that to go unpunished. So she killed Sullivan. The how is going to be the problem. She also has an alibi—Pellman. Kind of ironic, isn't it?"

"Ya think?"

"Pellman always maintained that he was out of town during the time-of-death window, at his mother's home in Winchester, Tennessee. That works for her too, unless..." I thought for a minute, shook my head, exasperated.

"I wonder how many female relatives she has?" I said it out loud, but I was really talking to myself. "We need to know."

I grabbed my cell phone and called Tim Clarke.

"Hey, Tim. It's Kate. You got a minute?"

"Sure, Kate. What's up?" Tim asked.

"You ran a full background check on Elizabeth Pellman, right?" I held my breath.

"No. You didn't ask for one."

Shit! "I'm sorry, Tim. I should have. This is time sensitive. How long will it take you to run one?"

"Not long... Well, I say not long, but it depends on how deep you want me to dig. If all you want is—"

"The works, Tim. I need to know all her family secrets, job history, social media—everything. I want to know what makes the woman tick."

"Wow! Okay, I'll get right on it. I'll call you later today."

"Tim, wait—" But I was too late. He was gone. *Damn it, Tim. I don't know how Harry puts up with you. Ugh, maybe I'd better call him too.* My stomach knotted. *Maybe later.*

It was a couple of hours later when Tim called back. Harry should pay him more.

"You ready?" he asked.

I said I was, and he began to reel off Mother Pellman's background information. There wasn't a whole lot that interested me about her childhood, but then it got interesting.

"She spent the early, formative years of her life in the army; well, I guess they were formative. Anyway, she graduated high school in 1982, went to community college for two years, and then enlisted in the army. She was honorably discharged in July 1988 with the rank of E4, or specialist, after serving a term of four years." He paused, took a breath.

"She married Harvey Pellman a month later, and Chad was born seven months after that. The marriage lasted roughly nine years. She divorced Harvey in February 1997, citing abuse and infidelity—"

I interrupted him. "What does her work history after discharge look like?"

"Well, she was already pregnant, so she didn't go to work until January 1990, and then only part-time at Sears in the Hamilton Place Mall. After her divorce, she went full time but injured her back. She's been on disability ever since."

"So she doesn't work, then?"

"No, not according to her tax returns."

"Hmm. Do you know if she has any close female relatives?"

"Only one that I could find, her mother Mrs. Elsie Billingham. She's seventy-seven, lives in Florida, at The Villages. Why d'you want to know about her relatives? Is there something I can do?"

"I don't know. Maybe I'd better explain."

I told him about the partial DNA match and its implications. For once, he listened without interruption, almost.

"So," I said, finally, "what I need to know is—"

"It wasn't her mother," he interrupted me. "Couldn't have been. She's in an assisted living facility. I doubt she's able to travel."

Well, that rules that out, I guess. Damn! I still don't have what I need. What I need is a live sample of Elizabeth Pellman's DNA. Even then... Oh hell, I don't know.

Then I had a thought.

"Tim, what did she do when she was in the army?"

"She was a 68W."

"Oh-kay, and what, exactly, is a 68W?"

"She was a healthcare specialist, a medic. These days she would be called a combat medic."

"Ah-hah!"

And there it was, the medical expertise to administer the drug and know about the technicalities of death: rigor mortis, lividity, and so on. I had another key to the puzzle.

"What?" Lonnie mouthed at me.

I held up a hand. "One minute, Lonnie."

"What?" Tim asked.

"I don't know, Tim. I need to think about what you just told me. Thank you so much for all this. Listen, tell Harry hello for me, and that I'll call him later. Tell him I said I owe him dinner." And I hung up and smiled broadly across the desk at Lonnie.

"She was a freaking army nurse, Lonnie, a medic."

He grinned and said, "No shit? That's fantastic. Now we have means and motive."

"We do, but opportunity is going to be tough. As I said, what worked for Chad also works for her."

"But the DNA? One in thirty million? Surely that's conclusive, right? What is it Harry always says? 'When you've eliminated the impossible, whoever's left is who done it,' right?"

I had to smile at that. "Not quite, Lonnie, but you have the right idea. And it wasn't Harry, it was Sherlock Holmes. The correct quote is 'When you have eliminated the impossible, whatever remains, however improbable, must be the truth.'"

"Whatever! We got her, right?"

I sighed. "That, Lonnie, depends on the DA. Maybe I should give Larry Spruce a call."

Hell, what can it hurt?

I picked up my iPhone, scanned through my contact list, and called him. Lonnie leaned back in his chair, frowning.

It rang once, then, "Mr. Spruce's office."

"This is Lieutenant Gazzara, Chattanooga PD. I'd like to have a quick word with him if I can."

"Hold please."

It wasn't but a minute when I heard a click and then, "Hey Kate. I haven't heard from you in a while. How the hell are you?"

"I'm good, Larry. How about yourself?"

"Me, I just keep on keepin' on, but you didn't call me to make small talk. What can I do for you, Kate?"

"I'd like my partner, Lonnie Guest, to hear this, so if it's okay with you, I'm going to put you on speaker."

"Sure. Go ahead."

I took a deep breath, and then I laid it all out for him finally asking the DNA question.

"So," I said, "is the partial match, on its own, and considering her alibi, enough for you to charge her with murder?"

"Hmm, good question. So, all you really have is some odds and ends of circumstantial evidence and a mitochondrial DNA match to one or more of your prime suspect's relatives—"

"No, not relatives," I interrupted him. "One relative; there *is* only one: his mother."

"Ye-es," he sounded like he was thinking. "Thirty million to one... Those are good odds, and juries are very tech savvy these days, thanks to the TV. I'd need to look at all of the evidence in context but, considering... Hmm. Yes, I think it could work, but I'd feel a whole lot more comfortable if you could get a confession."

"I'm thinking that's probably not going to happen," I said.

"You'll never know, Kate. Not unless you try. Now, I have to go.

Let me know. If you decide to charge her, I'll back you, but you'd better get it right." And then he disconnected.

I stared for a moment at the phone, then up at Lonnie.

"You heard all that. What do you think?"

"I think you're right. She ain't gonna confess. D'you think we have enough to charge her, then? And if you do, what about him, the son?"

As it turned out, the answers to those questions didn't matter...not then.

33

"So," Lonnie said, "are we just going to question her, or are we going to arrest her?

"Question her, for sure, but I'm thinking we'll do better if we bring her in and interrogate her here. The problem is, Lonnie, we can't just go breezing into Franklin County and arrest her. We have no jurisdiction there."

"So what do we do? Not the TBI, surely?"

"No, not them. Not if I can help it."

I thought about it for a minute, then said, "I think what we'll do is arrest Chad."

He grinned at me and raised his eyebrows. "*Chad? Pellman?* There's nothing that would tickle me more, but what the hell?"

I didn't answer. I tilted my head a little to one side and grinned back at him.

He continued smiling, then said, "What? Let me think. Well, he is in our jurisdiction. Oh, I gotcha." Then he frowned and said, "I think. Ah, maybe not."

"Who loves Chad more than anything else in the world?" I asked. "Who loves him enough to kill for him?"

"Well, his mom." He stopped frowning. "But how does that help us get her?" He squinted at me quizzically.

"Come on, Lonnie, it's simple enough. We arrest Chad Pellman and give him his phone call. Who d'you think he'll call?"

"His attorney?"

I rolled my eyes. "No, he's a momma's boy. He'll call his mo-ther."

"Okay, maybe, maybe not, but even if he does..." And then his eyebrows raised. "She hightails it in here? And we have her; she's in our jurisdiction. Nah, it can't be that easy, can it?"

"Why don't we give it a shot and see? You want to go get him? Take a couple of uniforms with you. Let me know when you get back."

He was right, it wasn't that easy. Lonnie called an hour later and informed me that Pellman wasn't at work—he had the day off—and he wasn't at home either. I told him to come on back.

"So what now?" he asked as he sat down. "Do we call him, find out where he is?"

"Can't. I don't want him to know we're after him. When will he be back at work?"

"Tomorrow."

"Shoot! The minute he walks in the door he'll know; someone will tell him."

"So what, then?"

I shook my head. "There's no telling where he is or when he'll be back. There's only one thing we can do: you'll have to go sit outside his apartment."

"Oh, hell. Are you serious?"

I made a face and nodded. "Yep! Off you go. Stay in touch."

And wouldn't you know it? Pellman didn't arrive home until fifteen after ten that evening.

"You want me to go ahead and haul his ass in, LT?" he asked when he called it in.

I was at home, still dressed, and could have gone back out again. But by the time we would have gotten him comfortably settled in an interrogation room, it would have been after eleven. And by the time Mrs. Pellman arrived, I was thinking well after midnight. So I hesitated.

I was standing by the window, gazing out across the wasteland toward East Brainerd Road about two hundred and fifty yards away to the north, thinking.

"No, I don't think so. It's late. Go home, Lonnie. Get some sleep. You can grab him first thing tomorrow morning."

"You got it. See you tomorrow."

He disconnected. I glanced at the screen, thinking, not really seeing it. Lost in thought, I raised the iPhone to my lips and nibbled the edge of the soft, neoprene case, staring out into the darkness... And then something off in the distance caught my eye. It wasn't much, just a tiny glitter of light that came and went as the seconds passed.

What the hell is that? Looks like... Shit. It's in the parking lot of the gift shop. Someone's freakin' watching someone... Me? And then I realized it wasn't the first time. *Oh my god, that could be a scope—a rifle. Take it easy, Kate. No sudden moves.*

I turned and moved away from the window, out of the line of sight. I thought about turning the light off but decided against it. Instead, I grabbed my Glock, racked one into the chamber, and headed out the door, making sure I couldn't be seen through the window.

I crept out through the front door and ran, keeping as low as I could, the few yards to where my car was parked. I hit the button on my key fob and... *Damn, damn, damn...* The lights flashed, and the interior light came on as the doors unlocked. *Why the hell didn't I think of that?*

And right then I knew it was a lost cause. No matter, I had to check it out. I drove up to the automatic gates and waited for them to open, cursing myself for my stupidity, and then I drove out and onto the access road. A minute later I swung the unmarked cruiser into the gift shop lot and hit the brakes.

There was nothing there. I got out of the car and walked the lot, my Glock in my hand at my side: nothing. I looked out toward East Brainerd Road: all was quiet. Even so, I had that god-awful tickling feeling that I wasn't alone.

Finally, I went back to my car and drove back to my apartment.

I turned off the lights and went to the window: nothing, just the street lights and the occasional headlights on Brainerd. *Maybe I was wrong. Must be getting paranoid.*

I made some hot cider in the coffee machine and went to bed.

Sleep...did not come easy that night.

34

TUESDAY, JUNE 9, MORNING – THE PRECINCT

Sleep did come, eventually, but it was a rocky night full of dreams and nightmares. As you might imagine, I rose early that Tuesday morning.

A long, hot shower washed away the night terrors, and when I arrived at the police department, I said nothing of the events of the night before. Lonnie already had Chad Pellman stewing in an interview room.

Lonnie and I stood side by side watching Pellman through the one-way glass. He was seated at the steel table, dressed in green scrubs, staring down at his hands. They were in his lap, and he was twisting the snakehead ring around and around on his finger. He looked nervous. *He's had a haircut since I last saw him.*

"Are we going to talk to him?" Lonnie asked, without taking his eyes off his prey.

"Of course, but we'll let him stew a little longer, say an hour."

Lonnie looked at me, smiling. "You know you can be a wicked bi—"

"Don't say it," I said, interrupting him. "Let's go get some coffee."

As it turned out, we kept him waiting way more than an hour, because while we were in my office going over our notes, I received a phone call.

"Gazzara," I said.

"You have a call from a Sheriff Gene Drake," the receptionist said. "You want me to put him through?"

"Gene Drake?" I asked.

"That's what he said."

I don't know any Gene Drake.

"Okay, put him through."

The phone clicked. "This is Lieutenant Gazzara. How can I help you, Sheriff?"

"Hello, Lieutenant. This is Gene Drake. I'm Sheriff of Bolton County, Ohio. I don't know if you can help me or not, maybe you can, maybe I can help you."

"O-kay."

"I received an email from you a couple of weeks ago... Yeah, I know. Sorry. I didn't recognize the sender, so I didn't open it right away. Lucky I didn't trash it. Anyway—"

By then I knew what he was calling about, and I was tingling with anticipation.

"Sheriff Drake," I said, interrupting him. "Hold on while I put you on speaker. I need for my partner to hear this. Okay, Sergeant Guest, say hello to Sheriff Gene Drake."

They greeted each other, and then Drake told us his story.

He told us that a state trooper had found a weird-looking wooden box on a county road. It contained, among other things, a dismembered, skeletonized body of a young woman. Drake, then a deputy, as one of only two county detectives had caught the case.

"So," he said, "when I opened your email and read that you were hunting a box, I remembered my box. So I checked the dates and all the other details, and I figured, hey, I think that's the one. So here we are."

"Hold on, Gene... It's all right for me to call you Gene? Okay, good. I need to pull up a map. Where exactly is Bolton County?"

I opened Google maps and found the tiny county some one hundred and sixty miles southwest of Highton, West Virginia, via State Route 7—a three-hour drive, maybe a little more. *Oh shit*, I thought, barely able to believe it. *This is it. This is freakin' it. If he left Highton at ten, as his brother said, that would put him at the dumpsite around one in the morning. Yes!*

"Okay, I got it," I said, barely able to contain my excitement. "You found the box. I need the exact date."

"It was Tuesday, September 8, 1987, the day after Labor Day."

"At what time, exactly?"

"Now that, I ain't sure, but in the morning, early-ish, say around ten."

"Were you able to determine exactly when the box was dumped?" I asked, my fingers crossed.

"It hadn't been there long. Old man Cackleton—he was the coroner back then. He's dead now, of course—well, he reckoned from the condition of the grass under the box that it hadn't been there but a few hours. Strange thing is though, the vic' had been dead for years: five, maybe six: strangled."

It's her. It has to be. Everything fits.

"Did you get her DNA?" Lonnie asked.

"In 1987? Are you kidding? Listen, I'd forgotten about her until I received your email. We, that is me, I worked the case for almost eighteen months before I gave up on it. We buried her bones in the churchyard... Well, not all of them. I kept the skull."

"*You what?*" I asked, stunned.

"I kept the skull. She had nice teeth; good dental work, and well, you know... I figured if ever anyone came looking for her, and we needed to do a dental comparison, we wouldn't have to dig her up.

Like I said, she's in the churchyard, here in Raglan. The pastor was kind enough to donate the plot."

"O-kay. You kept the skull. What about the box, and the stuff she was wrapped in?"

"Yeah, we kept all that too. Hey, how'd you know about that, the clothes and the blanket?"

"It's a long story, Gene. Can we keep it for another day when I have more time?"

"Sure. Everything is in the basement. So, d'you think she's what you're looking for?"

"Could be. Gene, I need all that stuff, including the skull. Would you, could you..."

"Sure. I'll have it packed up and FedEx it to you. I'm gonna have to bill you the shipping charges, though. So, are you gonna tell me who she is?"

"Gene, I would, but the truth is, I don't know, not for sure, which is why I need it all. As soon as I know, you'll know. Is that okay?"

"Yup, but how about the rest of her. We buried her in a child-sized casket. You want me to dig her up and send that too?"

"No, not right now, but if it's who we think she is, we'll need it for the family."

"Sounds good. Glad I can help. You can expect the package next couple of days. Give me a call and let me know it arrived safely. Bye for now, and good luck, Lieutenant. You too, Sergeant."

He hung up. I tapped the button on the desk unit to end the call.

"So what d'you think of that?" I asked Lonnie.

"Sounds too damn good to be true, if you ask me."

"I agree," I said, "but we deserve a break, for Pete's sake. This could be it. It's gotta be it, Lonnie. Everything fits. It's her. It's Sapphire. I know it is."

He nodded. "Sure does sound like it. So what about Pellman?"

"Oh shit. I'd forgotten about him. Let's go."

35

TUESDAY, JUNE 9, 10 AM – SULLIVAN CASE

"At frickin' last," he said when I walked into the interrogation room. "What the hell am I doing here? Why did you leave me here? It's been more than two frickin' hours."

"Hello, Chad," I said, amiably. Yes, I was feeling pre-tty good. "Can I get you some coffee?"

"Hell no. You can let me outa here, is what you can do. And when you do, I'm calling my frickin' attorney. I'm pissed off with you keeping on harassing me, and I'm not having any more of it."

"Let you go?" I said, smiling at him. "Oh, I don't think so."

I nodded at Lonnie. "Turn on the camera and recorder, please, Sergeant."

"So. Chad," I said, brightly, after I'd stated the time, place and all the usual details for the record. "I know, and you know, that you killed Rhonda Sullivan. So how about you tell me all about it?"

"Screw you," he snarled. "I didn't. I—I loved her I, frickin', didn't, kill, her. You can't prove I did."

"Oh, I don't know."

I smiled a big smile at him. He didn't like that. In fact, he looked decidedly disconcerted.

"Are you going to charge me? Because if you are, I need to call my attorney."

And right then, I knew I'd screwed up. *Damn, damn, damn it!*

My feeling of euphoria generated by the call from Gene Drake had caused me to forget the goal. I wanted him to call his mother, not his attorney. *Now what?*

I stared at him, no longer smiling, and he noticed and smiled right back at me. *He's confident; too damn confident. I need to smack him down.*

"No, Chad, that's not why you're here. I just have a few questions. Do you mind?"

He shrugged and rolled his eyes.

"Is that a yes?" I asked.

He sighed, loudly, then said, "Yes, go ahead. Ask your questions. It won't do you any good."

"You're going to stick with your alibi, that you were in Winchester, with your mother?"

"Of course, because it's true."

I nodded and said, "Okay, so let's say that what you say is true, that you were in Winchester that Sunday. What about your mother? Where was she when Rhonda was murdered?"

His mouth dropped open. His eyes widened in disbelief.

"What? What the fri—"

I interrupted him. "Now you can make your phone call; your *one* phone call." I stood up, picked up the phone from the nook in the wall and slammed it down in front of him.

"Let's give him a little privacy, Sergeant." I walked out of the room, followed by Lonnie.

I looked through the glass, and I had to smile. He was sitting at the table staring at the phone like it was a rattlesnake readying itself to strike. Now all we had to do was watch and wait. If he made the call, we'd know who to: it would be on speaker and recorded.

Attorney or mother? I needed him to lure her into town. Either way, I'd have to let him go... *Eventually!* I smiled at the thought.

"What're you smiling about?" Lonnie asked.

"Myself, mostly. Is he going to make a call, or what?"

He must have sat there ten minutes before he made a move. When he did, he reached slowly, picked up the handset, and dialed. It rang three times before it was answered.

"Yes? Who is this?"

I slapped Lonnie on the shoulder and whispered, "*Yes!*"

"It's me, Mom. They arrested me."

"*What?* They arrested you? Who arrested you? Where are you?"

"I'm at the police department in Chattanooga. That bitch lieutenant sent some fat ass sergeant, and he grabbed me as I left for work. You have to come and get me, Mom."

"Did you call our attorney? Did you call Kelly Roberts?"

"No. I only get one call. I wanted to talk to you. I figured you'd call her."

"I will. I'll call her right now. You sit tight. Don't say a word until she gets there. I'm on my way. I'll be there as soon as I can. You say *nothing.* You understand?"

"Yeah, okay. Thanks. Listen, Mom, I think they know you—"

Holy shit. That, I wasn't expecting.

"*Shut up,* you—you stupid..." she spluttered, interrupting him. Then she got hold of herself and said, "Honey, just remember what I said: keep your mouth shut. Don't say another word unless Kelly tells you to. I'll be there soon, sweetie."

Click! She'd hung up the phone.

"Oh, my god," I grabbed Lonnie's arm. "Got her!" I was jubilant.

"Yeah, but I don't think we can use it. Her attorney will get that call thrown out."

"Doesn't matter. Larry Spruce can deal with that. The call's not enough on its own anyway. She'll just make something up to explain it away, but now we know; now we freakin' know. I'll hold him until his mother gets here, then we'll grab her."

36

TUESDAY, JUNE 9, 1 PM – SULLIVAN CASE

Kelly Roberts, the Pellman's attorney, arrived first and insisted that we either charge her client or turn him loose. I told her that I would do neither. I was holding him for questioning and would begin doing so as soon as possible, and she was welcome to wait with him or by herself in a waiting room. She chose neither. Instead she kept on insisting that I had no right to hold him. It was a debatable point, and one I chose to ignore.

To say that she was annoyed would be something of an understatement; she was pissed. I couldn't get the woman to shut up. Eventually, I decided I'd had enough and walked out, leaving her with her client in the interrogation room.

By that time it was twelve-thirty in the afternoon, and I was famished, but I couldn't go to lunch. I had to wait for Elizabeth Pellman to arrive. I settled for a tall mug of paint stripper—PD coffee —and a Snickers bar from the machine.

I was in my office when I was notified that Elizabeth Pellman was in the lobby. I downed what was left of my coffee, grabbed my iPad and briefcase, and headed for the elevator. On my way through the incident room, I circled by Lonnie's cubicle, tapped him on the shoulder, and signaled for him to follow me.

On the ground floor, the elevator is located just beyond the lobby, reception area. As we stepped out into the corridor, I could see her through the glass door; she was pacing back and forth like an angry tiger in its cage at the zoo.

I smiled to myself, nudged Lonnie, then nodded to the receptionist to buzz the door. She did, and I pushed it open.

"Good afternoon, Mrs. Pellman," I said, brightly. "It's so nice to see you. You can come on through."

"Where the hell is he?" she asked as she stormed through the doorway. "Where's my boy? You had no right to arrest him."

"Calm down please, Mrs. Pellman," I said, soothingly. "I haven't arrested him. I just brought him in to answer a few questions. If you'll follow me, please."

She followed me, chattering all the way like an angry gibbon. Lonnie followed behind, grinning like an idiot.

"In here, Mrs. Pellman," I said, standing to one side to allow her to enter the vacant interrogation room.

She walked through the door, stopped, turned around and said, "Where the hell is he?"

"Please sit down, Mrs. Pellman," I said, backing out of the door. "I'll be just a minute." I closed the door behind me, clapped Lonnie on the back, smiled at him and said, "This should be fun. Let's go relocate Chad."

"Cool," he replied, grinning widely.

"Yeah, cool," I said, rolling my eyes. "Here's what I want you to do."

I opened the door to the room where Chad and his attorney were still seated together at the table and strode inside.

"Okay, Chad," I said, smiling brightly. "Let's go. Sergeant Guest will show you the way."

"But my mother should be here soon."

"Really," I said, frowning. "Well, you can't wait here. Please show him where he can wait, Sergeant."

They both stood, then walked out together into the corridor.

"Oh, just a moment, counselor. I'd like a word, if I may."

They both stopped.

"Just you, Ms. Roberts."

I waited until Lonnie and Chad had rounded the corner and were out of sight. Lonnie was taking him to a holding cell.

"Please step this way, Ms. Roberts," I said, opening the door to the room where we were holding Mrs. Pellman.

"Kelly," Mrs. Pellman said, rising to her feet. "What are you—where's Chad?"

"Oh," I said. "He's waiting for you. I need to ask you some questions, then you can see him. Please sit down, both of you."

"What questions?" Mrs. Pellman asked as they sat.

I ignored the question and made a show of opening my iPad and briefcase, and then I signaled through the glass for the camera to be turned on.

"Before we begin," I said. "I must inform you that everything that's said in this room will be recorded, audio and video. Do you understand, Mrs. Pellman?"

They both stared at me, like a couple of owls, across the steel table.

"*What* are you doing, Lieutenant?" Roberts asked. She sounded outraged.

"My job. Oh, there you are," I said as Lonnie entered the room. "Sit down Sergeant. You both know Sergeant Guest, so we'll dispense with introductions."

I stared across the desk at them for a couple of seconds, and then I began.

"Elizabeth Pellman, I'm arresting you for the murder of Rhonda Sullivan—"

"*What?*" she screamed and jumped to her feet. "What the hell are you doing? Kelly, say something."

"Please sit down," I said, quietly.

She did, slowly, and I started over. "Elizabeth Pellman, I'm arresting you for the murder of Rhonda Sullivan. You have the right to remain silent. Anything you say can and will be used against you in a court of law. You have the right to an attorney," I looked at Kelly Roberts. She stared back at me, her eyes narrowed. "If you cannot afford an attorney," I continued, "one will be appointed for you. Do you understand these rights, Mrs. Pellman?"

She slowly shook her head, then said, "You're frickin' crazy. Kelly, for god's sake, say something, do something."

I held up my hand and stopped Roberts before she could speak.

"I'll ask you again: Do you understand your rights as I have read them to you, or would you like me to read them again?"

"Screw you, you crazy bitch."

"I think you'd better answer her," Roberts said, quietly.

"Screw her."

I nodded. "In that case, there's nothing more to be said. Sergeant Guest, please take Mrs. Pellman away and lock her in a cell."

"*What?*" Mrs. Pellman screamed as Lonnie stood and walked around the table. "No. *No! Wait!* Okay, okay, I understand. Now stop."

I nodded to Lonnie. He came back around and sat down again.

"Now," I said. "Is this person sitting next to you—Ms. Kelly Roberts—your attorney, and do you wish for her to be present during this interview?"

She looked wildly around at Roberts, who nodded.

Pellman looked at me and nodded.

"Out loud, please."

"Yes, for god's sake, *yes*. But you can't charge me with murder. I didn't do it. You have no proof."

"Oh, but I do. I have everything I need: motive, opportunity, and means. And I *can* prove it."

"Don't say anything, Beth," Roberts said.

She didn't listen. "You can prove I murdered her? That's crazy. You're crazy. Why would I do that? How would I do that?"

"If you give me a minute, I'll tell you. Oh, and I should also tell you that I'll be charging your son as an accessory."

They both stared at me, seemingly not comprehending what I was saying.

"Mrs. Pellman, is it not correct that you spent four years in the United States Army?"

"Yes—"

"I told you not to answer any questions," Roberts interrupted her.

"Shut up, Kelly."

"And you received an honorable discharge with the rank of E4?"

"Yes."

"What, exactly, were your duties during the time you were in the army?"

"I was a medic."

"Yes, you were," I said, quietly.

I reached into my briefcase and took out a photograph of the contents of the grocery bag Detective Wells had found in the dumpster.

"Do you recognize these items?" I asked, knowing full well that she'd deny it.

"No," she said, staring me right in the eye.

"Do you know what the items are?"

She glanced down at the photo, then said, "Looks like two vials of something, a syringe, and some swabs."

I nodded. "That's right. The vials contain, no, they contained potassium chloride. As a medic, you'd know what that is, correct?"

"Yes. So what?"

"And this—you know what that is?"

"Yes, it's a syringe."

"Not that, Mrs. Pellman. This," I picked up the photo, held it up for both of them to see, and pointed to the syringe cap.

"Yes, it's the syr—" She stopped talking. Her face had drained of its color.

I nodded. "Of course you do. Do you remember how you removed it from the syringe?"

"I—I didn't," she stuttered, looked at Roberts, then said, "I'm not saying anything else."

"That's all right, Mrs. Pellman. I have everything I need, so let me tell you how it went down. Your son was in love with Rhonda Sullivan, and he told her he was. Unfortunately, she didn't love him, and she told him. And that would probably have been the end of it, but she told her friends. She also told them that Chad was a stupid idiot that reminded her of Dopey, the big-eared dwarf in Disney's Snow White. And guess what? One of her friends told Chad what she'd said, and it upset him, badly. It upset him so much that he told you too, which in turn upset you. You love your son very much, Mrs. Pellman. We know that, and we know that you're very protective of him. You hated her for what she'd done, which is why you decided to punish her. How am I doing so far?"

She didn't answer. She just stared at me, wide-eyed and white-faced.

"Not good, right? Because you didn't decide to punish her, did you? You decided to kill her, but how? That was the easy part, wasn't it? Being an ex-nurse—okay, a medic—you figured you'd inject her with potassium chloride. That way her death would look like a heart attack.

"You knew that Chad had access to the drug, so you had him steal some, which means, Mrs. Pellman, that *Chad knew what you did.* And he told you on the phone that we knew. We recorded that call. That makes him an accessory. I can charge you both with first-degree murder."

"You, can't, prove, any, of, that," she said.

I nodded, then said, "As I understand it, Mrs. Pellman, you have no living female relatives other than your mother, is that not correct?"

She nodded. "Ye-es. Why d'you want to know that?"

"Well, you see this?" I tapped the image of the syringe cap in the photo. She stared down at it, mesmerized. "When you removed it from the syringe, you used your teeth, remember?"

She looked up at me, shaking her head, but she didn't answer.

"So, here's the thing," I continued, softly. "We always figured it was Chad that injected the drug into Rhonda. But then we sent that cap away for DNA testing and, well, there was no match, at least not for Chad." I paused and looked her right in the eye.

"Do you know what mitochondrial DNA is, Mrs. Pellman?"

She stared back at me, uncomprehending. And then she got it.

"You frickin' bitch," she said, jumping up and swinging her fist at me across the table.

She took me totally by surprise, Lonnie too. Her fist clipped the side of my jaw and knocked me sideways out of my chair, and then she was over the top of the table grabbing for me. Fortunately for me, Lonnie recovered before I did, and he grabbed her and threw her to the floor.

I struggled to my knees, my jaw hurting like nothing I'd felt before.

Slowly I rose to my feet, shaking my head. I put my hand to my jaw, feeling it already beginning to swell.

I stood upright, took a step back. By then, Lonnie had the cuffs on her and was dragging her toward the door.

"Wait," I gasped. "Sit the hell back down. I'm not finished yet."

Lonnie had her by the arm, he swung her around and marched her back to her seat and sat her down.

"Damn it, Beth," I said, massaging my jaw. "What the hell did you do that for? By the way, glad to see your back is feeling better." My voice was heavy with sarcasm. And I couldn't resist rolling my eyes.

"Screw you, bitch."

"Okay," I said. "I get it. Now, where was I? Oh yes, mitochondrial DNA. As I said, the DNA results came back no match for Chad, but when the lab got that result, they decided to go a step further: they decided to do an mtDNA scan. That one did deliver a match, not for Chad, but for a close female member of his family. The odds against a mistake are one in thirty million." I watched her; she didn't flinch. *Boy is she a cold one.*

"And that, Beth," I said, "means that either you or your mother removed that cap from the syringe and pumped the drug into Rhonda's arm. And I don't think it was your mother," I said, still trying to regain some of my composure.

"How did you do it, Beth?" I asked.

"Do not say a word," Roberts said, putting a hand on her arm.

Pellman calmed down, some, looked at me through slitted eyes, smiled, then said, "What about Chad? He had nothing to do with anything."

I shook my head. "He knew what you did and covered up for you. That makes him an accessory. He'll probably be charged with first-degree murder along with you."

"Screw that, Lieutenant. Chad goes free. That's it. If not, you'll not get another word out of me."

I thought about it for a minute. I doubted Larry Spruce would charge him with anything more than manslaughter, and I could have told her that, but I needed a full confession.

I stood up, and said, "I need to make a phone call. I'll be back in a minute." I left the room.

I returned a couple of minutes later, resumed my seat, and said, "I just talked to the district attorney. He's prepared to offer you a deal—confess, admit to what you did, and he won't bring charges for murder against Chad."

That wasn't exactly what Larry said. He said he'd reduce the charges against Chad to manslaughter, but what the hell. I needed to dig it out of her. But she was smarter than I gave her credit for.

"That's not good enough. He goes free, or you can go to hell."

I smiled, shook my head, then said, "The best the DA's office would go for was involuntary manslaughter: twelve months prison, suspended, and five years of supervised release. Yes, he'll go free, but he'll have to stay out of trouble."

She turned and looked at her attorney. Roberts nodded.

"You can guarantee that?" Roberts asked.

I shrugged. "That's what Assistant District Attorney Spruce said. You can call him."

"It's acceptable," she said. "Beth, be careful what you say. Lieutenant, I will stop her if I need to."

"Go ahead, Beth," I said.

She glared at me for a moment, then shrugged nonchalantly and said, "Frickin' bitch deserved all she got. I hope she went straight to hell."

Suddenly, the pain was gone. Adrenaline? Maybe, I don't know.

"It was so frickin' easy," she continued. "I knew Chad was treating her for potassium deficiency. She had no medical insurance, and couldn't afford to go to a doctor, so he'd been dosing her with a diluted solution of KCL, potassium chloride. She called him that night. 'Oh, Chad, I feel awful. I'm hurting really bad. Can you come over?'" She mimicked a little girl's voice.

"Chad, the stupid fool," she continued, "said he'd be right there. I told him not to go, but he insisted, so I said I'd go with him. He introduced me to her, told her I was a nurse. That impressed her, so I asked if she'd like me to administer the drug. Poor little bitch was in a lot of pain. Her legs were cramping like hell. She told me she would... I injected thirty milligrams of undiluted KCL into her arm." She shrugged, looked down at the photograph still on the table. "It stopped her heart. She was gone in seconds," she said more to herself than to us.

All three of us were stunned, even Kelly Roberts. I stared into Mrs. Pellman's cold, unblinking eyes and, I couldn't help myself; I shuddered. She smiled.

I shook off the feeling of utter repulsion and said, "And then you laid her out, hoping lividity would hide the injection site... You cold, wicked bitch."

"Yeah, I didn't think it would be found; should have known better. Eh, it is what it is. I got my revenge... We done now?"

We were, and I couldn't get out of there fast enough: my jaw was aching, and I was totally disgusted by what I'd heard. I needed coffee and some ibuprofen, fast.

"Have her make a written statement, Sergeant, then make her comfortable and come find me." *Make her comfortable. Sadly, we no longer use the electric chair.*

37

TUESDAY, JUNE 9, 3 PM

The first thing I did when I got back to my office was call Chief Johnston and tell him the good news, that we had Rhonda Sullivan's killer.

Weirdly, so I thought, he didn't seem overly impressed by it, but then he rarely ever was impressed by much. His attitude being that it was our job to solve cases: it's what we were paid for. What he was interested in, though, was the Lewis case. *What's that about?*

"I'm making progress," I said. "You want me to come by your office, Chief, and bring you up to speed?"

"That won't be necessary, Lieutenant. Please tell me it's not going to take much longer."

"I think not, but you know how these things go. Right now, I'm waiting for FedEx to deliver a package from Bolton County, Ohio."

"A package?"

"Yes, sir. The sheriff has the remains of Lewis' first wife, Sapphire. He's sending...well, he's sending some artifacts—"

"I see," he interrupted me. "Let me know how it goes." And he hung up. *Damn! No, thank you, Kate, you did a great job. Not even a*

*goodbye when he hung up. Maybe I should reconsider Harry's offer...
Nah!*

I took my cell phone from my jacket pocket and tapped the speed
dial.

"Hello, Kate," Harry said when he picked up. "How the heck are
you?"

"I'm good. You?"

"Good. You sound tense. What's up?"

"Well, one, I owe you dinner...and two, I solved the Sullivan
case."

"You *did*? Congratulations. Want to tell me about it?"

"Not now. I don't have time. Tomorrow night, though, over
dinner?"

"Geez, Kate. You're going to make me wait. That's just plain
mean."

I couldn't help but smile at that. He sounded like a spoiled
little boy.

I'M GOING TO SKIP OVER THE NEXT PART OF THE STORY. IT'S KIND
of personal and well... Oh, just use your imagination. Suffice it to say
that the following night, Wednesday, Harry and I had a nice meal at
St. John's and then we went to the club for a nightcap. By ten-thirty, I
was done, tired and ready for bed; so was Harry, but not to sleep. Any
other night—well, you get the idea.

Anyway, I decided not to stay at Harry's that night. He drove me
back to his apartment where I'd left my car, and I kissed him goodnight and left; it was just after eleven.

The drive from Harry's apartment on Lakeshore Lane to my own
apartment took about fifteen minutes. I remember little of the drive
home. I was on automatic, my head full of the events of the past
couple of days: one case closed and a second well on the way, I
hoped.

I was almost home and about to turn into my apartment complex when I noticed the lights of another vehicle close behind me. Then they followed me down the drive to the gates. I stopped the car, punched in my number while the other vehicle waited behind me. *Must belong to another resident.*

The gates opened and, sure enough, the vehicle followed me through. I pulled into my parking space and turned off the engine, but I didn't get out, not right away.

I watched as the driver of the other car pulled into a space two stalls away and turned off their lights. I thought no more about it. I took a moment to gather my things from the passenger seat. Needless to say, I looked around before I turned my attention to my belongings. With my trusty leather bag in one hand and my keys in the other, I exited the car and walked the few yards to my front door. I was about to put my key into the door lock when something hard slammed into the back of my head. There was a blinding flash of white light, pain searing through my head, and then...nothing.

38

WEDNESDAY, JUNE 10, MIDNIGHT

When I came to, it was dark, and I was lying spread-eagled on a bed, a bare mattress, my hands and feet fastened to the bedframe and...I was naked, and oh so cold. My mouth was dry. I tried to lick my lips. I couldn't. My mouth was taped shut. My head was aching. I could move it, but I couldn't see much. Just enough light emanated from the small, darkened windows high up in the wall to my right, for me to realize that I was in some sort of small basement room.

I hadn't been awake more than a couple of minutes when the door opened. The overhead light flickered and then came on, momentarily blinding me.

"Ah, you're awake. Good."

John Lewis!

He came to the side of the bed and looked down at me. He was holding what looked like a large fileting knife: the long, thin blade glinted under the fluorescent light.

"Nice tits."

I guess you'll believe me when I say I didn't take it as a compliment.

He leaned over me. *Oh shit, what—*

But all he did was rip the tape from my mouth.

"That better?" he asked.

I licked my lips, swallowed noisily, and nodded, and then screwed my eyes tight shut as the movement caused pain to sear through my brain.

"Thirsty?" he asked as he reached for a bottle of purified water on a small table set against the wall.

He put the bottle to my lips and I drank greedily, my eyes locked on his. They twinkled, full of mirth. *The son of a bitch is laughing at me.*

"What the hell have you done, John?" I asked, my voice cracking. "You won't get away with it. I'm a police officer. They'll know it's you. They'll hunt you down."

"Oh, come on, Kate. It's okay if I call you that, isn't it?"

"You're sick, John. You need help. Just let me go and—"

"Sick? *I'm sick?* Yeah, I'm frickin' sick. Sick of... You have no idea how much I hate women. They lead you on, all sweetness, big eyes and promises. And then they get their claws into you, and they suck, and they suck, and they suck...the frickin' life out of you."

He paused, stared at my breasts, licked his lips... *Oh hell. He's going to kill me.*

"Let me go, John... *Please?*"

"Hah, as if. You were about to spoil everything," he said, never for a moment taking his eyes off my breasts. "Everything I've worked for all these years. I couldn't have that, now could I? I have to stop you."

He pulled up a chair and sat down.

"This is not going to stop it, John," I said, quietly. "They'll have the box with Sapphire's remains tomorrow. When they do, they'll identify her, and they'll come for you."

"It won't matter," he said, gently trailing the tip of the knife down my chest between my breasts. "I'll be gone by then. There's a little place I have picked out...but that's enough of that," he said as he started to get up. *Oh shit. I have to keep him talking.*

"How did you know we were onto you, John?"

He looked down at me, then slowly lowered himself back onto the seat.

"Typical for a woman. You all think you're so damn smart, so clever. I was way ahead of you. You remember your visit to my brother, Mikey? I'm sure you do. Well, he played you like a fish on the hook. Right after you left him, he called me and filled me in on what you two had discussed... Yes, Kate. I know what he told you: that he wouldn't call me, or even talk to me. He always was a frickin' little liar. He tells me *everything*. He hates women almost as much as I do. You do realize he's whacko, right?"

And you're not? Damn!

"Loves to play mind games, he does. I'd told him to expect you. He was supposed to find out what you know, not spill his guts. He called me the minute you left him."

He paused, stood, walked around the bed, staring down at me, whistling almost soundlessly.

"Damn, Kate. You're a good-lookin' woman," he whispered, almost as if he was talking to himself.

"Sapphire," he said, thoughtfully, "was... She was white trailer trash, screwing anybody she could get her hands on. Then the little bitch decided she was going to divorce me. Well, what would you do?"

"What would I do? Are you serious, John?"

"Anyway," he continued, "I knew back in '87 that they'd found that box. It was on the news the next morning. It couldn't be helped, though. My brother, Mikey, found it in the lock-up unit, so I had to get rid of it." He paused, obviously experiencing some sort of flashback.

"See, Mikey knew she was inside it. Yeah, yeah, I know, he told you he didn't look. Hah, and you believed him. The little prick couldn't help himself. Anyway, after he found it, the box, he called me. Told me he'd found it, and that he knew what was in it. I had to go get it." He lapsed into silence once more, then continued.

"Kate, you have no idea what that drive from Highton with that box in the back of my truck was like that night. I was scared shitless I'd be discovered, all the damn way, till I could stand it no longer. I had to get rid of it. So, finally, I pulled over and dumped the thing among the trees at the side of the road. I had no idea where I was. Then I hauled ass outa there. Next day, it was on the news that they'd found it. They never did trace the damn thing back to me though... Not until you turned up."

By now he was standing at the foot of the bed, staring at me, at my crotch. *Oh shit, he's going to rape me before he kills me! I have to keep him talking.*

"What about Jennifer, John? Why did you kill her?"

He smiled. "That bitch..." He paused, stared down at me, his eyes unblinking. Maybe he was remembering.

"She was like all the rest," he said. "Loved only me one minute, putting it around to anyone and everyone the next. Typical woman."

"So you killed her!"

He shrugged but didn't answer.

"What about Amber? Did you kill her too?"

"Freakin' little busybody had her nose stuck in where it didn't belong. Got it chopped off, didn't she?"

"What did you do with the bodies, John?"

His eyes glittered in the low light. He laughed, then he said, "Gone, but not forgotten. Isn't that what they say, Kate?"

I stared up at him and shuddered. I knew what was coming next, but I was only half right.

"See the box over there, Kate?" He pointed with the tip of the knife. It was on a table, on the dark side of the room to my left.

"That will be your final resting place, but not before—"

He was interrupted by a loud crash as the door burst open and someone—I wasn't able to see who—stumbled headlong into the room.

Lewis was taken completely by surprise. He spun around, the knife high in the air, then BAM, BAM, BAM. He shuddered under the impact of the bullets, fell sideways, and landed on top of me, crushing the breath from my lungs.

I couldn't move; I couldn't breathe. Then someone was pulling Lewis off me. I looked up and saw a grinning face, one I knew well. One I never thought I'd be happy to see.

What the hell? Detective Tracy? How?

"Surprise!" my former partner said as he dropped the body. There was a dull thud as it landed on the concrete floor. "Hold on, Kate," he said, flipping open a pocket knife. "Backup's on the way. I'll cut you loose."

I felt first my right hand drop onto the mattress, then my right leg, and I immediately tried to roll onto my left side in a vain attempt to hide my naked body.

"Hey, hey, take it easy. I'm not looking at you. Here," he said as he cut the final cable tie, the one holding my left wrist, and handed me my clothes. "Get dressed, I'll wait." And he turned his back to me while I put them on, which in itself was an ordeal. I was aching all over, and my head... *Shit, I think that son of a bitch Lewis has cracked my skull.*

"What are you doing here?" I asked. "How the hell did you find me?"

"You're welcome, Kate," he said, grinning. "No need to thank me... Truth is, I've been following you for weeks, and him too, but not for as long. I chanced on him watching your apartment a couple of Saturdays ago. First chance I got, I slipped a GPS tracker under his rear fender. I've had one on your car too, since day one. Shit, that boy owns a lot of properties. Anyway, I was sitting in my car on East Brainerd. I already knew where you were, more or less. I'd followed you to Harry Starke's place—"

I interrupted him. "Wait a minute. Day one? You sneaky son of a bitch. You put a tracker on my car?"

"Ain'tcha glad I did? Hehehe, Kate. That piece o'shit might have gotten you preg—"

"Oh, for god's sake, John. Stop trying to screw with my head. Get on with it."

"Okay, so when you left Starke's place, I headed back toward your apartment. I parked on Brainerd and watched your blip, and you came right past me. I knew you were heading home, so I figured I'd go home too. I was heading back toward I-75 when for some reason—curiosity, I suppose—I flipped screens to see what Lewis was doing, and damned if his blip didn't pass right by me going the other way. It took me by surprise, and it didn't really register for a couple of minutes. Then I figured he was following you, so I turned around. But by the time I got there, he was gone. I parked, climbed the fence, and found these on your step." He handed me my keys. "The lights were out in your apartment, so I told myself, 'screw it,' and hammered on your door: nothing. So I ran back to my car and chased after him. That's it. End of story."

"The hell it is," I said, angrily. "If you knew where I was, what the hell took you so long? Where are we, anyway?"

"Ah, well, I didn't...know, where you were, well, not exactly where. I knew where his car was: here, on Dodson Ave, in the parking lot of an old church. I knew you had to be in here somewhere, but there's a hell of a lot of it, the complex, outbuildings, and such. And I had to wait for backup, and then I had to find you... It was frickin' dark, everywhere, Kate. All I had was this." He held up his iPhone. "I couldn't see a damn thing. And, well, when I did...find you, I listened at the door for a couple of minutes. Hey, how long d'you think it was, anyway? It couldn't have been much more'n thirty minutes, well, forty-five at most."

I looked at him, aghast. I thought it had been hours. Then I realized I couldn't have been unconscious many minutes.

"You son of a bitch. You listened at the door. Why would you do that? He could have killed me."

"Are you kiddin'? I heard what he said. I'm your witness. You have what you need to close the case. Look, he wasn't going to kill you, not right then, anyway." He grinned at me, I looked away. I knew just what he was thinking. But he insisted on telling me anyway.

"He wanted to play with you first, Kate. Then kill you. Can't say's I blame him either—wanting to play with you, that is—I mean... Oh shit. I'm sorry."

"Yeah," I said, disgusted with him. "I know what you mean, you sick... And anyway, why in god's name were you following me in the first place?"

"Ah," he grinned. "You have Big Brother Henry Finkle to thank for that."

He noted my astonishment, grinned, and said, "You didn't think for one minute that he was going to stand by and let you screw with his career, did you? He's had me watching you since you interviewed him three weeks ago."

That was a serious waste of department money, and Finkle probably could have been fired for it, but he'd gotten lucky, and I made no complaints. In fact, I was damn grateful.

Tracy helped me to my feet, and then out to his car. I leaned against the passenger side door, my arms resting on the car roof, and looked around. The place was alive with flashing blue and red lights; dozens of cops were standing around everywhere. I felt terrible: my head was aching, my wrists were sore, and my pride had taken a direct hit. I'd been beyond stupid to allow myself to get taken like that and, well, I knew what Tracy would be thinking every time he looked at me from now on.

I looked to the building where I'd been held captive. I knew exactly where I was. The old church, long time vacant, had once been beautiful. Now, I couldn't help but wonder why they hadn't torn it down.

"You do get yourself into some scrapes, don't you, Lieutenant," a voice from behind me said.

I turned and was confronted by Henry Finkle.

"Hello, Chief," I said. "Fancy seeing you here." The sarcasm was lost on him.

"Yes, Detective Tracy called me. It seems he solved your case for you."

I was absolutely stunned.

"The hell he did. He saved my life, but I solved the case."

"Yes, of course you did," he replied. His sarcasm wasn't lost on me.

I grabbed his arm and pulled him to one side.

"I think you and I need to talk, Chief. We need to clear up a few things, not the least of which is you having Tracy follow me around for the last three weeks."

"I like that idea, Kate. How about I take you out to dinner one evening next week?"

I stared at him, open-mouthed, and shook my head in repulsion at his temerity. The nerve after what I'd just been through.

"Not one chance in hell," I said. "Damn it, Henry. Will you never change?"

He smiled benignly up at me. "Not one chance in hell, Kate; not one chance in hell. Seriously though, Lieutenant, you look like hell. How are you feeling?"

"Oh, I feel wonderful. How the hell d'you think I feel? I feel like shit."

He nodded. "Yes, I'm sure you do." He looked around, then said, "I see the ambulance is waiting. I suggest you go get checked out. Lewis is dead, so Detective Tracy is on automatic suspension while the shooting is being investigated. Internal Affairs is handling that. I'm sure they'll want to talk to you too. There's no hurry, though. I'll run interference for you until you're feeling better...and after you and I have talked on Monday. So, when you've finished at the hospital, I suggest you take the rest of the week off to recuperate." And then the son of a bitch turned and walked away.

Damn you, Henry Finkle!

I checked the time: it was just after one in the morning. *An hour.* I thought. *Only an hour... Seems like a lifetime.*

39

No matter what Finkle said, there was no way I was going to take that much time off. I did, however, take his advice and let the doctors check me over. Apart from a few bruises, a raging headache—no, my skull wasn't cracked—and my badly wounded pride, I was none the worse for my final encounter with John Lewis. But what galled me most was that I knew I had both John Tracy, and yes, Henry Finkle to thank for that. Had it not been for them...well, let's not go there.

When I was done with the doctors, I called Lonnie to come and get me; bless him, he was already there, in the ER waiting room.

Lonnie is a strange cat. I found him in the waiting area leaning on the information desk; he looked like I felt.

He turned, spotted me, walked quickly to me and, without saying a word, wrapped his arms around me, squeezed, and didn't let go.

"Oh shit, Kate," he whispered in my ear. "I'm so frickin' sorry. I should have been there. I should have known that crazy son of a bitch would do something. I should have been watching you."

"Hey, *hey*," I said, gently pushing him away. "You couldn't have known; I didn't."

His eyes were watering.

"Stop it, Lonnie," I said. "I'm fine, well, except for a screaming headache."

He grabbed my hands, hesitated, then said, "He didn't..."

"No, Lonnie, he didn't, thanks to Tracy's timely arrival. Hey, look. I don't want to talk about it, okay? You want to get some breakfast? I need something in my stomach to calm it down. And about two gallons of coffee. Oh, but wait, I should call Harry."

"I already did," Lonnie said. "I told him what went down, and that you're okay. He went ballistic. Wow, was he upset. I guess you'd better call him. He's waiting to hear from you... Yeah, breakfast would be good."

I nodded. "Okay, just give me a minute."

And I made the call. I should have known better. Harry was—as Lonnie had said—upset. Upset? The word didn't even come close to describing it.

"*Where the hell are you?*" he shouted. "What the hell happened? Are you all right? Freakin' hell, Kate—"

"*Hey!* Stop it. I'm fine. I'm just leaving the ER with Lonnie. We're going to get breakfast."

"Lonnie? The hell you are. Stay where you are, I'm on my way." And before I could answer, he hung up; I called him right back.

"*What?*"

"I told you, I'm fine. There's no need for you—" He hung up again.

I looked at Lonnie.

"It's okay," he said. "Go have breakfast with Harry. I'll see you later." Then he grabbed my arms, leaned in close, pecked me on the cheek, and left me standing there.

I was mad as hell. *Damn you, Harry Starke!*

So I sat down and waited, and the longer I waited, the more pissed off I became.

I was seated there, twiddling my fingers, for fifteen minutes before he finally arrived, and I was ready to tear him a new one. But when he walked through the door...well, it was good to see him. And then he made an ass of himself.

The first thing he did was walk up to me, grab my face in both hands and kiss me, hard. Then he took a step back and proceeded to give me all kinds of hell.

"I should kick your fickin' backside," he said.

"Hello to you too, Harry. I'm fine thanks. Can we get out of here? I need coffee, and my gut aches."

And we did. Without bothering to ask me, he took me to his condo and, with the mood he was in, I knew better than to argue. The ride to Lakeshore Lane was a nightmare: he drove too fast and didn't stop nagging me until he parked the car. Then he stopped talking; I mean he didn't say another word until we were seated together at his kitchen table, coffee in hand and toasted bagels on the table.

"So, are you going to tell me about it?" he asked, finally calm.

Harry has a temper, but it's like a firework: it blazes hot for a short while, then fizzles away to nothing.

I really didn't want to talk about it, but I knew he wouldn't quit nagging me until I did, so I told him. He listened without speaking until I was done. Then he stood, grabbed my cup and his own, and made refills.

"Do you have any idea how lucky you are?" he asked as he sat down again.

I stared at him over the rim of the cup, the steam from the hot coffee shimmering in front of my eyes.

"Yes, Harry. I do."

He stared at me, shook his head, exasperated, then said as he stared into his coffee, "Frickin' hell, Kate. You should be dead, *right, frickin', now!* How could you do it? How could you let yourself get into such a frickin' mess? We, none of us, not even Lonnie, had any idea."

"Damn it, Harry. D'you think I did, for god's sake? I didn't know he was freakin' psycho. If I had—"

"You frickin' should have known. You've been a police officer for how many years, thirteen? You should have seen the signs. They were all there, for god's sake... Two missing wives? And you knew for sure he killed his first wife. You also knew he cut her up and put her into storage. That's a psycho, Kate. Sheesh!"

"You're right, Harry. I should have, but I didn't. I'm not you. He, he seemed harmless."

Harry opened his mouth to speak, but I stopped him.

"Yeah, yeah, I know. They're all harmless, until... Oh, screw it. I don't want to talk about it anymore. And I don't want to sleep with you, either, and probably not for a long time to come. I'll use the spare room."

I stood, left him sitting at the table, went to the guestroom in the basement, slammed the door behind me, stood for a moment with my back against it, my eyes closed, then collapsed on the bed and burst into tears.

And suddenly, Harry was there, holding me, rocking me...

40

THURSDAY THRU FRIDAY, JUNE 11 & 12

I DON'T KNOW WHEN HARRY LEFT ME. I DO KNOW IT WAS VERY early in the morning, and that I slept right on through until three in the afternoon. When I finally awoke, Harry wasn't there, but he'd left a note on the kitchen table. There was a frittata in the refrigerator and a bottle of Cabernet in the cooler.

I ate half the frittata but drank two cups of black coffee instead of the wine. Then, after a long hot shower, I put on a jogging suit—yes, I still kept a change of clothes there—and went for a short walk, much shorter than I intended. My mind was too full of the events of the past several days for me to even remember the walk, let alone enjoy it... And then there was Harry. He sure as hell hadn't made my life any easier when he called last night, or Lonnie's for that matter. The more I thought about it, the more I knew I had to do something, but what?

The answer was, of course, obvious, so I went back to the condo and spent the next half-hour packing my things. I stuffed everything that belonged to me in one of Harry's suitcases, called Uber, and went home, feeling better about myself than I had in a very long time.

I didn't speak to Harry again for several days, not until after I'd finally put the Lewis case to bed. Oh, he called me, several times, but I let the calls go to voicemail. I knew I had to end my on again, off again relationship with him once and for all. But I needed time, time to get over the trauma of the last twenty-four hours, and almost getting killed...

Look, Harry and I always had a special, but different kind of friendship, and I knew he loved me in his own way, but that way wasn't good for me.

THE NEXT DAY I WENT BACK TO WORK. IT WAS FRIDAY, JUNE 12. Yeah, I know, I'd been told not to go in to work until Monday, but the hell with that. John Lewis might be dead, but I still had to wrap things up. Writing up the case notes took all day. Between writing about my ordeal, what I'd learned from Lewis, and the seemingly endless parade of people stopping by to gawk at the Lieutenant who'd managed to get herself kidnapped, I was drained. And then, to top it all, Chief Johnston insisted I speak with a counselor, so there was that too.

LONNIE STOPPED BY TO CHECK ON ME OVER THE WEEKEND. I WAS pleased to see him, of course, but then he insisted that I needed to get out of the house. I really didn't feel like it, but he wouldn't give up so, reluctantly, I agreed to let him take me out to dinner that Saturday evening. We went to Blue Orleans downtown and, much to my surprise, I enjoyed it; even more surprising, so did Lonnie. The Shrimp Etouffee was to die for. The conversation...was a little strained, at first.

Right out of the gate he asked, "How are you doing, really doing, Kate?"

"Look, Lonnie..."

"It's okay," he said, soothingly when I couldn't continue. "I know what you've been through. What the hell it must have been like... Well, I dunno, but it might help if you were to talk about it."

I shook my head, laid down my fork, looked at him, and said, "No! Look, I'm fine." I picked up my fork, took a bite of my meal, and tears sprang to my eyes. I swallowed and looked at Lonnie. "I'm not fine. I do want to talk. But I just want you to listen, Lonnie. This isn't a problem that needs solving, all right?"

He nodded, looked relieved, and said, "Sure. Okay."

By the end of the evening, I had talked about it, and it did help. Lonnie had listened without interrupting or blaming. That's what partners do. They help each other.

Sheriff Drake's package arrived the following Monday morning. Sapphire's skull had been carefully and lovingly wrapped. *What a nice person you are, Gene Drake.*

I unwrapped the skull and compared it to Sapphire's photograph. It didn't help. In fact, I was suddenly overwhelmed with...first sadness and then with an all-consuming rage.

I rewrapped it and handed everything over to Mike Willis for analysis.

Henry Finkle called me into his office as promised for our "talk." The man is slippery. There's no doubt in my mind that he was consorting with—well, I'll just call them "professionals." He certainly stepped way over the line when he had me followed, but he got away with it because it saved my life. He was all sweetness and light. He claimed that, knowing what a "reckless cop" I was, he only had me followed for my own protection. When I asked him what prompted it, he simply smiled and said, "That will be all, Lieutenant."

There was still work to do. We hadn't yet found the bodies of Jennifer Lewis or Amber Watts. It was then that, for one fleeting moment, I regretted that Tracy had killed John Lewis. Although Lewis had confessed to the murders, he hadn't given away the location of their remains. Now, maybe we'd never know what happened to them. Still, I had to try.

On Tuesday, Lonnie and I were in my office trying to make sense of what we'd learned about John Lewis and his past. My thinking was that maybe if we talked it through, we'd come up with a fresh approach.

"What about his brother?" Lonnie asked. "He's an accomplice, right?"

"Yes, but we'd never be able to prove it. I recorded my interview with him and never once did he say anything to indicate he had anything to do with anything. I only have John's word for that, and he's dead."

"Maybe we should interview him again, then?"

I made a wry face and shook my head. "We could, but I don't think it would do any good. He knew exactly what he was doing when he spun that yarn for me. John Lewis said he was crazy. I think he is, crazy-smart."

"So what, then?"

I leaned back in my chair and stared up at the ceiling. In my head, I retraced the timeline from 1982 until the present... And then I had an idea.

"He had a storage unit in Highton," I said. "D'you suppose he had one here too?"

He stared at me, then jumped to his feet and said, "I'm on it. I'll make some calls." I smiled as he all but ran from my office.

He returned less than an hour later, grinning from ear to ear.

"I got one," he said. "It's not in his name though. It's under his company name, Lewis Realty."

"Okay. We need a warrant."

"I already arranged that. We can pick it up in thirty minutes."

"Great," I said, grabbing my phone. "Let's go."

The storage facility was located off Bonny Oaks Drive, some five blocks from Lewis' office.

Lonnie cut the hasp of the padlock with a pair of bolt cutters and hauled up the overhead door.

The first look inside was disappointing. The little room was packed with four-drawer file cabinets, all locked, some dated and labeled, some not. It was in one of the unlabeled cabinets that we found what we were looking for. Well, not exactly. There were no bodies stored in the unit, which was both a disappointment and also something of a relief.

What we did find, in one of the cabinet drawers, was a briefcase. It contained some papers, a Ziploc bag of what looked like several bone fragments, and some photographs. The photos included a very old one of Sapphire and John together; two old photographs, both of unidentified young women; a fairly recent photo of Jennifer Lewis; one of Amber Watts; and finally, one of...me. *Shit, that's one hell of a club to be a member of.*

I had Lonnie hand the Ziploc bag of bone fragments off to Mike Willis for analysis and send the two photos of the unidentified women to every law enforcement community in the United States. John Lewis was a serial killer, that much we now knew for certain, but what he'd done with the bodies...I had a horrible feeling we'd never know.

MIKE WILLIS CALLED ON FRIDAY. WE HAD AN ID: THE SKULL did indeed belong to Sapphire Williams Lewis.

With deep sadness, I called Ryan Williams and told him we had the location of his sister's remains. He took it well, better than I thought he would, but then again, she'd been gone a very long time. He thanked me and said he'd have her returned to Highton where she could rest in peace with her mother and father. Oh, how I hate making those phone calls.

Unfortunately, it wouldn't be the last such call I would make regarding the Lewis case. My call to Alice Booker was, if anything, more depressing than the one I made to Ryan Williams. I told her that Lewis had admitted that he'd killed Jennifer. She didn't take it so well. I could hear her sobbing. I felt like shit... *Well, at least she can stop searching.*

The bone fragments we found in the briefcase? Yes, they were human; small pieces of skull. They were also quite old, ranging from between at least ten years and as much as twenty, and they belonged to four different women; none of them Sapphire Lewis, Jennifer Lewis or Amber Watts.

WHAT DO I THINK HAPPENED TO THE SIX MISSING BODIES? I think Lewis learned from his experience of 1987, that nothing stays hidden forever, at least not in storage lockers. I think that at one time or another, years ago, he probably did have four bodies in storage, maybe more. And after his earlier debacle ending in Bolton County, he decided to get rid of them. But like all serial killers, he just had to hang on to something to remind him of "the good times," so he kept the bone fragments.

Finding Sapphire and finally putting her to rest was bittersweet.

Solving the Sullivan case, thanks to Lonnie's innovation, was very sweet. If you're wondering why Chief Johnston was so interested in solving that one, I can tell you, because I asked him. Rhonda Sullivan was the daughter of Georgia state senator Laughton J. Sullivan, Johnston's roommate at the University of Georgia.

And so it was over, all but for one final detail: I had a promise to keep. I'd promised to cook dinner for Detective Steve Wells. I was excited to surprise him with the news about closing the Sullivan case, one that he'd opened so many years earlier. And so, a week after we had the Lewis and Sullivan cases wrapped up, I called him, but he didn't answer. *Strange.*

I called him again thirty minutes later, still no answer, so I called the complex's admin office and was informed that Wells had passed away two days earlier. His funeral was to be held the following day, Saturday. I was devastated. I should have called him sooner, but with all that had happened over the—oh hell, there was no excuse. I...forgot...and I'll never forgive myself. He died, and I'd cheated him out of closure on the Sullivan case.

I thought of all the cold cases still in the morgue. The unsolved crimes, the unidentified bodies... Those victims and their families deserved closure, too. And that, I *could* do something about. So I pulled myself together, sat up straighter in my chair, and grabbed the next case file off my credenza.

VICTORIA: CASE FIVE

A LT. KATE GAZZARA NOVEL

BOOK 5

BY

BLAIR HOWARD

1

OCTOBER **2018**

"HONEY, I'M DRIVING," MARCIE COX SAID AS SHE CLENCHED her phone between her shoulder and her ear. "Well, we'll see if Alex can stay overnight on Friday. I'll check with his mom. Later, okay? I've got to go. Yes, you can have the last blueberry bagel. I love you, too."

She quickly took her phone in her left hand and hit the tiny red circle to disconnect. Of course her twelve-year-old son Gary had to call while she was trying to get to work, especially when she'd told him to call only if it were an emergency. Such an emergency would, of course, include him wanting to know if Alex could spend the night on Friday.

She took a deep breath and dropped the phone on the empty passenger seat. Normally, she wouldn't be so aggravated, but an accident, a jack-knifed semi on I-75, had caused a traffic backup almost to Ooltewah, well, Bonny Oaks, anyway.

"Mrs. Randolph," Marcie said to herself, out loud, rehearsing her excuse, "I'm sorry I'm a little late, but there was an accident on I-75. It was sooo bad, you wouldn't believe it. I'm sure if you turn on the radio, you'll hear all about it."

Victoria Randolph was the worst of her clients. Anyone else would say that being fifteen minutes late due to a traffic accident was not a big deal. Especially when it rarely happened inside the city limits. Maybe in the winter when the streets were covered with black ice, or if a springtime rainstorm hit early in the morning, would Marcie run a little late. Oh yeah, normal people would understand, but not the Randolphs.

Marcie shook her head as she turned north onto Shallowford Road, heading in the opposite direction of her destination in order to avoid the train of cars. Marcie decided to take the roundabout route and so, of course, did everyone else in the southbound lanes.

At North Terrace she rejoined the interstate, I-25, at Market Street, and from there to Scenic Highway and Lookout Mountain.

"If she starts anything with you, Marcie, just quit. Tell her to shove it," she said to herself, ignoring the stunning views to her left. "Just quit, okay? And find another client or two to replace her."

That was easier said than done. The Randolph family was her wealthiest client. What Marcie made cleaning their home alone paid for her son's tennis lessons. Tennis lessons were expensive. But Gary was exceptionally good at it; his coach said so.

And Marcie also knew it burned Victoria Randolph that her son got private lessons from the same coach to whom she sent her two daughters. It wasn't very Christian, but Marcie didn't think the Lord would banish her to the fiery pit for this one small indulgence. Besides, He knew what kind of woman Victoria Randolph was.

"Where does your son go to school?" Victoria had asked when she interviewed Marcie for the weekly housekeeping job.

"He attends Whitewater Preparatory School," Marcie had replied proudly.

"I see," Victoria had said, wrinkling her nose slightly. "How nice. And what does your husband do?"

Marcie had cleared her throat. "He's in construction."

She hadn't liked the line of questioning, but she needed the job. One job on Lookout Mountain might lead to more if she could impress the Randolphs. Little did she know that nothing impressed Victoria Randolph.

"Construction? Oh how nice." She didn't actually roll her eyes, but she might as well have with that condescending tone she used. Oh well!

Marcie shivered at the recollection of that interview. At the time, she'd wanted to work for the Randolph family, confident that her happy personality and reliability might crack through their hard shell. She'd never been so wrong, and every Thursday she found herself considering the same thing. Quitting.

The thought of quitting the Randolph family was a tempting one. But Victoria was well-connected. For a woman who had come from even more humble beginnings than Marcie did, she had climbed the social ladder with impressive speed. Of course, being tall with an hourglass figure and long blond hair hadn't hurt.

Marcie looked in the rearview mirror, smoothing her plain brown hair that she'd pulled back into a ponytail. She was wearing black yoga pants and a white T-shirt—her standard uniform when she arrived to clean a client's home.

"Just remember the money, Marcie," she muttered to herself as she pulled into the long cobblestone driveway.

When she'd interviewed with Victoria and her husband Darby, Marcie remembered thinking how the trickling, natural stone fountain in the front yard was the most beautiful thing she'd ever seen. Now, it made her insides recoil as she dreaded setting foot inside the house.

Victoria, after seeing that Marcie drove an old Dodge Neon, had her park behind the guest house and walk to the back entrance. Normally, that wouldn't bother her. But on days when it was raining or cold, or when she was running late, it added another five minutes to her trek just to get inside the house. She'd been going through this routine for six months now. It wasn't getting any easier.

"Lord, keep one hand on my shoulder and the other over my mouth," she muttered as she parked, grabbed her caddy of cleaning supplies, and locked up her car before heading to the main house.

Marcie knew that as soon as Victoria realized she was there, she'd give her that look. Her lips would be pinched together, and she'd look at Marcie as if she had shown up on a day she wasn't scheduled. She'd have something sarcastic to say like "Oh, you *are* working today then," or "Oh, I see you managed to make it after all."

She felt like Sisyphus, but instead of pushing a boulder up a hill only to have it roll back down, she was carrying cleaning supplies that kept getting heavier and heavier with every step. She was sure that Victoria didn't know who Sisyphus was. A woman didn't have to be smart if she looked like Victoria did.

As she reached the back door and pulled out her keys, Marcie seriously thought about turning around and leaving. But she didn't. She opened the door, steeled her nerves and went inside, locking the door behind her. Normally, there would be the pounding of footsteps as Victoria came running down the stairs to confront her. But this time, as Marcie stood there listening and holding her breath, she didn't hear anything. She let her breath out slowly... relieved.

"I better buy a lottery ticket because today might just be my lucky day." She smiled as she headed across the mudroom and up the stairs to the middle level of the house.

Not quite convinced that this wasn't some kind of setup, a new game Victoria might be playing, Marcie entered the kitchen slowly and carefully and looked around.

The girls were at school already, she knew, and by then Darby would have left for the office. He thought he was a big-shot lawyer, but everyone knew he rode on his grandfather's coattails.

Hmm, Marcie thought, *Victoria must have a social engagement, or maybe something's going on at the church... No, she would have left a note.*

That was something else that always agitated Marcie. Victoria had wrangled herself a part-time job at the church. You'd think that Jesus Christ Himself had come down in all His glory and pointed to Victoria anointing her as His holy secretary.

"I don't *need* to work," Victoria had made sure to tell Marcie. "But I just feel like I'm being called. And Pastor Ed was kind enough to offer me a position in the church office." She then followed it up with a lecture on how Marcie would be responsible for her duties at times when Victoria wasn't there to check up on her.

Marcie had not had a single complaint from any of her clients in her more than a decade-long career as a housekeeper. She enjoyed the work. She knew how to do it. And without being too prideful, she had to admit she was good at it. But if she was fired from this job, she could kiss goodbye any future employment possibilities at the residences of the movers and shakers on Lookout Mountain. Her goal was to find one more client in the neighborhood and then drop the Randolph family.

"Pastor Ed has no idea what he's getting himself into," Marcie mumbled to herself, shaking her head as she began her chores.

In the old Southern tradition, Victoria designated Thursday as silver polishing day for Marcie, in addition to her regular duties of changing the sheets and pillowcases, mopping the kitchen floor and counters, clearing cobwebs from the corners of the ceiling, and the weekly laundry that included ironing. That was what she decided to do first. While the laundry tumbled in the machine in the basement, she'd polish the silver. By the time all the laundry was washed and dried, the silver would be spotless and sparkling. Well, that was the plan.

The laundry basket was in a closet upstairs, on the same level as the four bedrooms. She climbed the hardwood stairs, dragged the basket out into the hallway, then went to the girls' room to grab whatever they'd left lying around. Of course the room was pink with their names, Taylor and Courtney, emblazoned on the walls in giant letters. The bedroom was as big as Marcie's living room. She shook her head at the extravagance of it all: luxury on a scale she'd never know, and that was just the kids' room.

She picked up the stray socks and T-shirts that were on the floor, opened the hamper in the corner of the room, and grabbed the rest of their laundry. She stood for a moment and looked around the room. Every flat surface was covered with girlie things: nail polish, dozens of hair ribbons and barrettes, teen magazines and popular books for young adults. Marcie sighed, looked at the unmade beds and shook her head. She'd strip them and make them up with clean sheets and pillowcases after she'd finished doing the laundry.

She dumped the kids' dirties into the basket and went to the master bedroom. For the umpteenth time, she admired the beautiful décor, the California king four-poster bed, antique dresser, chairs, hope chest, and a down comforter that would have made Scarlett O'Hara pea green with envy, as it did her.

She finished grabbing laundry upstairs, grasped the heavy laundry basket, and headed downstairs to the basement. Her arms aching from the weight of the basket, she had to set it down on the kitchen counter for a moment. With any luck she'd be done and out of the house by three o'clock, just in time to welcome Gary home from school.

"Okay, let's get this done as quickly as possible," Marcie said to herself as she hoisted the heavy basket onto her shoulder. Carefully, she negotiated the stairs to the basement, the mudroom, turned right and with her foot pushed open the door to the laundry room. To the left of the laundry room was a beautifully furnished basement—an apartment with a kitchen, full bathroom, and guestroom. It was rarely used so Marcie had no reason to go in there.

Her usual routine was to walk into the laundry room, set the basket on the washing machine, then turn and flip on the light. Today was no different. When the light came on, she blinked and rubbed her eyes. She turned to the laundry basket, grabbed it, and then banged it down on the long table set against the far wall.

She dumped its contents on the table, picked up a piece of

clothing and... something not quite right, something out of place caught her eye.

Victoria Randolph was very particular about there being a place for everything and everything being in its place, which is why she noticed it.

What on earth? she thought. *Who dumped that there, I wonder? And what's with all the red paint on the wall?* Those were the thoughts that went through Marcie's mind as she looked toward what looked like a heap of clothing flung into the corner of the room. Her eyes saw the body, but Marcie's brain didn't register what her eyes were seeing.

Must be a trick of the light, she thought. *A pile of clothing, that's what it is. Nothing more.* Her mind was racing, trying to find a rational explanation for what she was seeing. *But the paint... it's not... paint. It's blood.*

Marcie stood stock still, staring into the corner, and she began to tremble. With one of Darby's button-down shirts clenched tightly in both hands against her chest, she stepped slowly away from the table toward the heap. What she'd thought to be a pile of clothes morphed into a crumpled-up body. What she'd thought was a shadow on the floor next to the body was blood, darker in places where it had pooled in the folds of skin and fabric. One leg was extended, the other twisted unnaturally beneath the body. A woman's body.

"Oh, my God! Victoria?" Marcie whispered, and jumped at the sound of her own voice. Not that the thing on the floor was going to answer her, because the entire left side of what had been her face was shattered, unrecognizable.

From where she was standing, Marcie had the incongruous thought that someone had taken a pound of ground sirloin and slapped it on her boss's pretty face, leaving it to hang and drip there. If only that was true, but it wasn't. Victoria's face had been smashed, mangled, almost beyond recognition. But that wasn't all. Her body had been beaten bloody.

And then Marcie had a horrible thought, *Oh, my God... Somebody killed her. I'm here all by myself. What if the murderer is still in the house?*

She put her hands, still clutching Darby's shirt, to her mouth, staggered backward against the table, still staring at what once had been her employer, looked wildly toward the door, then dropped the shirt and ran to the door, out and up the stairs to the kitchen, grabbed the phone from its cradle, ran outside, down the steps, and didn't stop until she was at the end of the driveway where, shaking uncontrollably, she dialed 911.

It was less than five minutes later when the first police cruiser screeched to a stop beside Marcie Cox, now calm, but red-eyed and cooperative. Had they arrived only one minute earlier, they would have seen her violently retching into the hydrangeas.

2

I HATED GOING INTO McDONALD'S FOR A COFFEE TO GO. IT WAS just across the street from the Police Services Center on Amnicola, and that meant every cop in the building was in there at one time or another throughout the day. Yes, I know, I could go through the drive-through, but that was an even worse nightmare. No matter the time of day, the line was always all the way out to the street. It was quicker to run inside and... well, I'm sure you've done it yourself.

Anyway, unfortunately, that also meant the likelihood of me running into someone I know and getting sidetracked was more than a possibility. Talking shop in a fast-foody wasn't really a break; it was an off-sight meeting.

There were days when I didn't mind such meetings, but that day I just didn't want to talk at all. I was waiting on results from the lab, hoping for a match on some DNA. The case was over three months old, and it was the one thread I had that I hoped would sew it up for me. It was a bit of a Hail Mary, but stranger things had happened. But I'd learned the hard way, a long time ago, that when all your eggs are in just one basket, rarely does it turn out the way you want it to.

So, instead of McDonald's, I decided to drive to Hamilton Place and stand in line at Starbucks, ready to fork over too much money for a black large. So there I was, drink already ordered, waiting, happily dreaming about nothing at all when my cell phone rang. *Tracy*, I thought when I looked at the screen. *Damn!*

"Look, Tracy," I grumbled into the phone, "you begged me for this one, and I was happy to hand it over. Now you want me to help you with it? If you think I want to be up to my eyeballs in semen and spit, you're crazy."

As the words left my mouth, I happened to glance at a barista on the other side of the counter from me. He had a beard, was wearing a knit cap, his forearms were covered with tattoos, and he stared at me wide-eyed as I continued to speak.

"Yes," I said into the phone. "Yes... No... Okay, go check with Collins. I think he has a CI over there. If so, he—or she—might be able to help. But don't tell him I told you. And I can't promise anything will come of it, but it's what I would do. Now, can I get back to work?"

Detective John Tracy was not my favorite person. Not by a long shot, but boy did I ever owe him.

To his face we called him either John or Tracy. Behind his back he was Dick Tracy, or just Dick, which he was, and is.

Back in the day, for just a few weeks, he was my partner. It didn't work out and I... well, we won't go into that. It's a long story and not a pretty one. It was ironic then, that not too long ago, the man saved my life—literally. And I have to say that for a vice cop, at that moment when I was sure I was going to become the next day's headlines, he came through like a pro.

But for me... well, there was no way I could repay him for saving my ass, so I handed him a juicy case that had all the makings of a Quentin Tarantino movie. Drugs, sex, a seedy gambling house: it was like his birthday, Christmas, and New Year's Eve at five to midnight all wrapped up in one neat package.

I won't lie. I would have loved to have kept the case for myself, but Tracy played the puppy-dog-eyes ploy and like I said, I owed him.

"You think? Well, okay. Good luck, John," I said before tapping the red button on my phone to disconnect the call.

"Kate! Black grande!" a different barista shouted at the other end of the counter. What a production. I grabbed the paper cup, made sure that it was my name scribbled on the side, with a smiley face, and I left the coffee shop.

I'm Lieutenant Catherine Gazzara, by the way; Kate to my friends and just about everyone else, so it seems, even my superiors. I'm a homicide detective assigned to the Major Crimes Unit of the Chattanooga PD. I'm thirty-six years old, and I've been a cop since I graduated from college in 2002. For six years I was partnered with Harry Starke—you've heard of him, right? If you haven't, you're not living on this planet. Anyway, he quit the force in 2008 and I became a lead detective, which is when Henry Finkle foisted Tracy on me as my partner.

Harry? He and I had been something more than just partners. There was a time when I thought we'd be even more still. But, never mind about that. Harry went into business for himself: Harry Starke Investigations. He... Oh hell, I don't know why I'm telling you all this. It's not really relevant to this story—not at this point anyway.

So I grabbed my coffee and left the coffee shop—the hairy barista unashamedly watching my ass. Of course, the stuff was too hot to drink so, as I walked back to my car with my purse hooked over my shoulder and my phone still in my right hand, I checked the time. The lab didn't like getting calls before eleven o'clock; it was ten thirty-three. Damn!

And then my phone rang again.

"I don't like getting calls before eleven o'clock either, but that doesn't stop anyone," I muttered before answering it.

"Hey, LT." It was the very chipper, newly appointed Detective Janet Toliver. My new partner of just ten days when Lonnie Guest retired, much to my dismay. "I got some news for you this morning. You ready?"

"Lay it on me." I shook my head as I took a sip of coffee, knowing it was hot but unwilling to wait any longer.

"First, I was called detective this morning by one of the uniforms," she said.

I waited for the rest like they'd catcalled or maybe made some derogatory remark.

"And?"

"And? Isn't that great? They all know I'm Detective Toliver now."

I could almost hear her smiling like a lunatic on the other end of the phone and couldn't help joining her. I remember how I felt the first time I was called detective. There is something about it, that first time. Like when the first rays of sun come up after a girl's wedding night. Everything has changed.

"It is. What is the second, Toliver?"

"Ah, yes. We got a call. A homicide at 400 Laurel Lane, Lookout Mountain. Female. Found by the housekeeper. We're to get up there ASAP."

"Lookout Mountain?" I yawned. "They've got their own police chief. I think he's also the fire chief."

Lookout Mountain is a small but very exclusive community set high atop the mountain of the same name. It's where the elite of Chattanooga live. Just the address bestows a level of prestige that most of us peons would never know. Harry and Mrs. Starke live up there on East Brow Road. *It doesn't come more prestigious than that.* I thought. *Good for you, Harry.*

"Yeah," Janet said, "Chief Wilbur. He responded to Miss Cox's call. The situation requires they bring in the big guns, I guess."

I smiled at that. Janet was enjoying her new status, perhaps a little too much. Maybe I should take her down a little? Nah. She's fun. Can't dampen that youthful enthusiasm.

"If we are the big guns, that's kind of pitiful." I chuckled. "Okay, Janet, talk to me. Is it a residence or business?"

"Residence."

"I'll meet you at Amnicola in..." I checked my watch. "Let's say fifteen minutes. Call Mike Willis and tell him I said to stand by."

"You got it, LT."

"Fifteen minutes," I said. "Be at the door, Janet. We'll leave right away."

"Yes, ma'am," she replied and hung up.

Ma'am? What am I, the queen? Geez.

I took another gulp of the hot coffee that was just the perfect temperature now, climbed into my unmarked cruiser, turned on the blue lights and the siren, and swung the big vehicle out of the Starbucks lot. I weaved my way through the traffic onto Shallowford, swerved left onto I-75 then right onto Highway 153 to Amnicola Highway and the police department; I made it in thirteen minutes.

Janet, bless her heart, was standing out front. She saw me and ran out to meet me, jumped into the passenger side, and away we went.

I glanced sideways as Janet took out her little notepad and smiled to myself when I saw the CPD sticker she'd applied to the front cover. She flipped it open and began to fill me in on the few details she had already gathered. Her handwriting was loopy and neat, and I wouldn't have been surprised to see she dotted her "I's" with tiny hearts or smiley faces, but she didn't.

"Okay," she said. "The address is 400 Laurel Lane. The initial call to LMPD came in from the family's housekeeper, a Marcie Cox. She's worked for the family for several months. Chief Wilbur said that the woman is in shock. It sounded like he was, too."

"I can't say that I blame him," I said.

"Wow. Do you believe these houses?" Janet asked as we drove through the Lookout Mountain neighborhood. "The lawns look like they are covered in carpet, not grass."

I nodded but didn't say anything. The houses were beautiful. Added together, I'd say the inhabitants of Lookout Mountain here in Tennessee had some of the oldest money in the country. I doubt a new family had moved into this part of town since Lincoln was president. Okay, that might be an exaggeration. But to some people, marrying into the right families was more important than being in love, not that I was an expert in such things.

I parked on the street outside the home, noting the brass plaque that informed me and any other interested party that we had arrived at the Randolph Estate, Established 1854. There was one black-and-white cruiser and an ambulance already there. We exited the vehicle, and I immediately spotted a woman who was sitting with a blanket around her in the back of the ambulance staring at the wall, unblinking, with the EMT taking her blood pressure.

"That must be the housekeeper who found the body," I said to Janet. "Go talk to her. I'll see what's happening inside. Be gentle, okay?"

Janet nodded, strutted the few steps toward the ambulance, her badge in one hand and her notebook in the other. I saw her extend her hand to the woman who was looking terribly shaken up. *The girl will make a good detective once the green has worn off.*

Me? I strolled along the short driveway to the house. The rear door was open. I entered, flashed my badge at the uniformed officer, told him who I was, and he showed me to the door that led to the basement. I thanked him, watched him go back to his post at the rear entrance, then I turned in the opposite direction and walked into what I took to be the living room. I wanted to get a feel for the place before I did anything else.

The house was even more beautiful on the inside than it was on the outside. It was an extravagant world of fancy crown moldings against high ceilings, stark white walls with hardwood accents, banisters, doors, and trim. I'm no interior designer, but I know expensive when I see it. The Randolph residence was top-notch, spotless, a place for everything and... you get the idea. The furniture looked new, untouched by human hand or butt. It was an old-world parlor intended for only entertaining and pre-dinner cocktails; no television and, as far as I could tell, no signs of a struggle.

There were family photos on the mantle over the natural stone fireplace, and on the bookcases, and on the... Is that a harpsichord, for

Pete's sake? Victoria Randolph was featured in almost every one of them. I was especially surprised to see the wedding pictures. Umm, not the pictures exactly, but the wedding dress.

It was crystal clear that it was not the image of a blushing Southern bride she was going for. I'd never had a problem with a well-endowed woman using the gifts the good Lord had bestowed upon her, but among Tennessee's high society you didn't show 'em off at church, and you sure as hell didn't display them for all to see at your own church wedding.

Wow, and I thought I was lucky in that area, not so much, I thought gazing at her stunning figure. *No wonder Darby Randolph is smiling,* I thought, as I moved on out of there.

The kitchen was all white, everything, walls, countertops, cupboards, even the floors. I wondered if she hired Jo and Chip to design the interior. It sure looked like it. Not that I spent much time watching HGTV, but enough to recognize the style. My kitchenette was beige, an easy-on-the-eye baby-poop beige I found almost impossible to keep clean. Bubbling spaghetti sauce is not conducive to clean walls, or floor, or backsplash or anything and, try as I might, I couldn't imagine cooking anything at all in an all-white kitchen. *Who am I kidding? They probably have a cook as well as the housekeeper.* Even so—

"Detective?"

Startled, I turned quickly and was relieved to recognize Chief Wilbur, who I assumed had just come up from the basement. Poor guy. He didn't look at all well... No, he looked like he'd just come up from below decks on a boat heading out of a perfect storm.

"Chief Wilbur," I said, holding out my hand to greet him. "Lieutenant Gazzara, Homicide." I flashed my badge and creds.

He shook my hand, weakly, and I continued, "By the look on your face, I have a feeling I'm not ready for this."

He nodded and wiped his brow with the back of his hand.

"That bad, huh?" I asked, still making a mental note that there were no signs of a forced entry and, so far as I could tell, nothing in the kitchen seemed to have been disturbed.

"Detective Gazzara," he said in a low voice. "Thank you for helping us out. Yes, it's bad. More than we can handle, that's for sure."

Chief Wilbur was, to put it politely, a robust man who hadn't had to chase a suspect on foot in many a long year, if ever. He was about five-ten, an inch shorter than me in bare feet, gray, balding, impeccably dressed in a fitted blue uniform with two stars on each collar. He wore a gold band on his left ring finger and... well, it was a smart look spoiled by the cheap, gold-plated watch on his right wrist: the plating was worn to the point where dull gray metal showed through.

"I understand," I said.

"You'll need to get your ME up here," he said. "And forensic team. We don't have anyone to assist and no place to put her, what's left of her." Wilbur looked down at the glistening floor, shook his head, and said, "Frankly, Detective, I don't mind passing this one off. I've got two years left until I retire. I've seen enough. When I took this job here in Lookout Mountain, I was sure I'd be able to skate through with nothing worse than a burglary to handle, the occasional domestic, but nothing like this."

"You should know better than that, Chief." I smiled at him, sympathetically. "When did police work ever go without a hitch? It's like, well, expecting a politician to be honest."

"You've got me there, Lieutenant. Listen, I've got to get some air. Go on down and take a look. It's a freakin' abattoir down there, a hell hole. We'll talk when... when you come up for air." He stepped past me and headed outside.

I pulled out my phone and called Mike Willis and asked him to get moving, and then I called Doc Sheddon. It went to voice mail.

I sighed, silently to myself, then left him a message, "Doc, when you get this message call me back. Need your help on Lookout Mountain. Thanks."

Doc Sheddon, Hamilton County's chief medical examiner, knew

my voice even if he didn't know my number by heart. We'd worked on lots of cases together. I'd hear from him soon.

As I carefully made my way down the stairs to the basement, I had a bad feeling in my gut. I'd seen some horrific crime scenes during years as a homicide detective, but very few that were so bad I could sense it before I even saw the body. This... was one of those occasions.

3

I reached the bottom of the steps to find the entire floor flooded with bright sunlight from the floor-to-ceiling windows, something I wasn't expecting because, from the street view, the house had only two stories.

At first glance, the white tiled floor appeared to be spotless. It wasn't. I spotted what looked like two small bloody smudges on the wall and two scuff marks on the floor.

"A white mudroom? That's just over-the-top," I muttered, trying to imagine what it would look like after a midwinter rainstorm.

I shook my head and made my way across the mudroom and turned right into a short passageway. A uniformed officer stood outside the door to what I assumed must be the laundry room.

I held up my badge.

He nodded, stepped to one side, grabbed the doorknob, pushed open the door and, without turning to look inside, said, "She's in there." Like Chief Wilbur, the officer was visibly shaken.

"Thank you, Officer... Quinn," I said, squinting at his name tag, then taking a pair of latex gloves and a pair of Tyvek shoe covers from my jacket pocket, put them on and entered the room, closing the door behind me.

"Holy cow," I muttered to myself when I saw what was left of her head. "Whose cat did you kick?"

The left side of her head from just above the ear to the jaw was practically caved in. She was wearing a burgundy skirt with a white blouse. I stood beside the body, not wanting to disturb anything, and observed some anomalous blood stains. At first, I thought they were tears in the fabric of the blouse. I crouched down and inspected them closely, and I realized they were stab wounds, but unlike any I'd ever seen before. The fabric had been rammed deep into the flesh.

I shook my head, leaned in closely. "How in the world?"

From what little I could see without moving her, I could tell that Mrs. Randolph hadn't put up much of a fight. There were no defensive wounds.

I stood up, took a step back, looked around the room once more, then turned and walked to the door, opened it, and stepped out into the passageway.

"Do you know if the rest of the house has been searched?" I asked the officer.

"I don't think so, well, just the basics, Detective. Chief Wilbur said to leave it to the experts."

"Who was in the house when you all arrived?"

"Just the housekeeper. Except, really, she wasn't in the house. She was outside. She was the only one here. The two girls had left for school, and Mr. Randolph had left for work, so the housekeeper said."

I nodded. "Stay here. Don't come in," I said as I turned and went back inside the laundry room, leaving the door open.

"So that doesn't leave a lot of time," I said, loud enough for the officer to hear. "Yet the place is almost spotless."

I took out my iPhone, turned on the flashlight and shined it across the spatter on the white cement wall and then on the tiled floor. Other than the small amount of spatter, there wasn't much else, just a few tiny smudges, including those I'd spotted when I first entered the room.

I turned to face the officer who was standing at the door watching me.

"The place had been cleaned," I said.

He shook his head and said, "I don't see how. There wasn't no one here except the housekeeper. We didn't find no signs of forced entry. No signs of a struggle. Nothing missing as far as we can tell. The Chief called the husband, told him there was a problem but didn't tell him what it was. He's on his way here now."

"How did you get his number?" I asked.

"Darby Randolph? Wasn't hard. The guy's known all over Chattanooga, Detective," the officer offered.

"He is?" I asked.

"Yeah. He's the grandson of Alexander Randolph." Quinn must have seen the stupor on my face. "Governor Randolph?"

"Oh, I remember; the guy who had the Little League scandal a few years ago?"

"That's the guy," Quinn replied. He didn't look at me when he spoke. Instead, he turned his head like I was changing my clothes and he was trying to be a gentleman.

Many years ago—I don't remember exactly how many—the then Governor Randolph had been accused of taking kickbacks... free luxury vacations, to be precise. Nothing was ever proved and the investigation, if it could be called that, was eventually dropped and, with time, all was forgotten. Ha, not really. It still comes up now and again, as it did then.

"Great," I said, rolling my eyes. "A politician's grandson. Please tell me you've been able to keep a lid on things. The press will be salivating all over every little detail as soon as this gets out."

Quinn shrugged, then said, "As far as I know, the only call that went out was to you."

I nodded, walked across the laundry room still shining my flashlight. Compared to the rest of the house, this room was like a dungeon. There was only one small window that was at ground level with the yard and it was glazed with glass block, the kind you can't see through.

"Okay," I said. "Nobody in; nobody out until Doc Sheddon or Lieutenant Mike Willis and his CSI team get here. Got it?"

"Got it," Quinn said.

I walked to the door and turned again to look back into the room. I didn't feel good about it. There was... something. I shook my head. I was frustrated, but there was little I could do but wait.

"I have a feeling we are overlooking something, Quinn," I said. "It's just too clean."

"I thought the same thing," he said, "and the chief commented on it, too."

I sighed and headed back upstairs just in time for the ruckus.

"Victoria? Victoria!" a male voice shouted, obviously that of Mr. Darby Randolph. He was in the kitchen. As soon as he saw me, he charged at me.

"Whoa!" I said loudly and put my left hand up and my right hand on my pepper spray. "Mr. Randolph—"

"Where's my wife!" he shouted, interrupting me.

"Mr. Randolph, you need to calm down," I said, holding up my badge. "I'm Lieutenant Catherine Gazzara, and I need you to take a step back. Now, sir!"

And he did exactly that. He stopped dead in his tracks, then took a single step back.

"Where is she? Where's Victoria?"

"I'm afraid your wife has suffered a severe injury to the head. Mr. Randolph, your wife is dead, sir."

Yes, I know. It was cold of me to lay it on him like that, but the man was hysterical. I couldn't let him go charging down to the basement to be confronted by Quinn, who wouldn't hesitate to restrain him by any means necessary. Fortunately, it didn't come to that.

"What?" he whispered.

I saw the color drain from his face.

"I'm sorry, Mr. Randolph," I said quietly. "Your wife... is dead."

He stared at me, his mouth wide open, slowly shaking his head.

"No," he said. "Nooooo."

Darby Randolph was a tall man, impeccably dressed in a dark blue business suit, white shirt, light blue tie, and tan Oxford shoes. I looked at his hands. There were no cuts or scratches that I could see, no blood on his hands, clothes, or shoes.

"Are you all right, Mr. Randolph?" I asked, taking a step toward him.

He looked like he was about to fall.

"She's dead?" He blinked then shook his head. "She can't be. You're wrong. She was here this morning. She was sleeping when I left for work. I had to go to the office early. I had work to do; important work... I had to get some work done that I should have done yesterday." He was almost babbling. The enormity of it was slowly sinking in. He swayed.

"Please, Mr. Randolph. Sit down." I motioned for him to take a seat on one of the stools at the kitchen island. Before I could ask any questions, my phone rang. It was Doc Sheddon's number.

I told Randolph that I had to take the call and that I'd be just a minute, then I went out into the living room and took the call.

"Hey, Doc."

"We're starting rather early this morning, aren't we Detective?"

"Sorry, Doc. We have a bad one. I need you, ASAP."

I heard him sigh. "You'll be the death of me, young lady. Fine. Tell me where."

I smirked and gave him the address.

"Lookout Mountain? Hmm, most peculiar. All right. I'll be there shortly."

I returned to the kitchen and Darby Randolph.

4

MIKE WILLIS AND HIS TEAM ARRIVED JUST AS I WAS ENDING MY call with Doc Sheddon, and they quickly locked down the crime scene. There was no room for me down there, but I knew Mike would come and get me if he needed to, so I continued my conversation with Darby Randolph.

I opened my iPad, tapped the icon to activate the record app, informed him I'd be recording the conversation, and then, as gently as I could, I gave him a very limited version of what I thought might have happened, leaving out the gory details.

"Can I see her?" he asked, subdued. "Oh, Lord, please let me see her."

"Not yet, Mr. Randolph," I replied. "Lieutenant Willis has secured the scene, and Dr. Sheddon, the medical examiner, is on his way. You really don't want to see her just now."

I watched his reaction as I said it. His face was pale, his look stoic. He'd slipped into that weird state of calm that people in his situation often do as the magnitude of what has happened sinks in. It isn't acceptance or understanding. It is usually the calm before the storm.

"Mr. Randolph, I'd like you to tell me about the events of this morning."

Darby stared at the kitchen counter, then at his hands. They were meticulously clean, the fingernails impeccably manicured and... clear-polished.

"I..." he began hesitantly. "I had billing to do. It has to be done by the fifteenth of every month. Today's the seventeenth. I was late because I had depositions all day for the past two days." He folded his hands in front of him and looked up at the ceiling. "If I'd stayed late on Monday and did my work like I was supposed to, maybe—"

"But you didn't," I said, interrupting him. "And you left this morning before the rest of the family arose? What time would that have been?"

"No, the girls were already up, ready for school. I gave them cereal for breakfast, and we left the house at around seven. I dropped the girls off at school, and from there I went to the office. Victoria was still in bed, asleep. She's not... wasn't an early riser."

"Can you think of anyone who might want to hurt your wife, anyone who might have a grudge?"

"No!" He looked sharply at me, then continued, "My wife was an angel, a saint, Detective, a living saint. Oh, I know what you're thinking. Everyone says that about their loved one."

I tilted my head to the right and stared at him, quizzically.

"But it's true," he continued. "You can ask anyone who knows her." He paused for a second or two, then continued, staring down at his hands. "My wife came from very humble beginnings," he said very quietly. "She never forgot that. She never forgot her roots."

He sat up straight and cleared his throat. "She was a wonderful wife, thought only of helping others. She volunteered at the food pantry at our church. In fact, Pastor Ed at our church just hired her as his new assistant. She was a friend to everyone she met. And our daughters, she..." And then he lost it, he broke down, tears streaming down his cheeks. He lowered his head into his hands, and he sobbed, blubbered. "How am I going to tell our daughters? What will they do without their mother? And what am I going to do without her?"

"Excuse me, Detective?"

Was I ever grateful for the interruption. I twisted around in my seat.

"Yes, Chief Wilbur?" I said as I rose and joined him just inside the kitchen door

"Doctor Sheddon's here. He's gone around the back. Coming in the same way the housekeeper did. By the way, I had my officers do a search of the outside of the house. They found no sign of a break in; nothing appeared to be disturbed, but I... I dunno, Detective, something doesn't seem right." He shrugged.

"Okay, and thank you, Chief, but I imagine Mike Willis will want to search the grounds in detail," I said. "How's the housekeeper doing?"

"Still talking with Detective Toliver."

I nodded and decided I needed some air before I went downstairs to join Doc and Mike, but just as I was about to head downstairs, Janet appeared in the kitchen doorway. For such a young woman, her poker face was perfection.

"Chief," I said quietly. "Would you mind asking one of your officers to watch Mr. Randolph? The last thing I need is for him to go charging downstairs. He's in shock, and I think a familiar face might help."

"Sure, Detective. Just give me a holler if you need anything else."

He tapped his radio and asked officer Quinn to join him. Randolph was still seated beside the kitchen island, his head in his hands, weeping silently.

I put a hand to Janet's elbow and steered her out of the kitchen.

"What did you find?" I asked her quietly.

She consulted her notebook.

I really must get the girl an iPad.

"The housekeeper's name is Marcie Cox," she began. "She's worked here for six months, well a week shy of six months, actually."

I couldn't help but roll my eyes; thankfully, she didn't catch it.

"She's not a shy woman. Didn't hesitate to inform me that it's the worst job on her route," Janet said quietly, her lips barely moving as she looked up and around the foyer in which we were standing, probably trying to gauge the cost of the furnishings, just as I had.

"Really?" I said.

She nodded. "That's what she said. She also said she'd never pray for harm to come to anyone but, and I quote, "That Mrs. Randolph is not a nice lady. Mean-spirited, always bragging, nothing is ever right for her."

Hmm, I thought. *That doesn't quite gel with what her husband just told me.*

"Okay, Janet. Right now, I need to go talk to Doc. So we'll talk later, in the car."

I turned and peered into the kitchen at Randolph. He had his arms crossed on top of the island, his face hidden in the crook of his elbow. His shoulders were shaking; the man was still crying... *If he's faking it, he's one hell of an actor.*

I turned again to Janet and said, "Why don't you look around upstairs while I go check in with Doc. I'll come and find you when I'm done down there, okay?"

Janet nodded before slowly and carefully going up the winding staircase to the upper level. She pulled out her flashlight even though the entire house was bright and, dare I say, cheery? She shined it along the floorboards and in the corners. I smiled: for a rookie, she was doing just fine.

I descended the stairs to the basement and the laundry room with Marcie Cox's words echoing in my head: "Worst job on her route." *What did that mean?* I wondered. *Hardest? Most boring? Worst pay?*

I needed answers, but I didn't want to ask Darby, give him the heads-up that the "angelic" Victoria Randolph might not be quite the saint he thought she was. Darby was her husband and that, by definition, made him my prime suspect. That was a given, and it also meant he was about to come into serious, in-depth scrutiny.

Will his alibi hold up, or did he simply drop off the kids then come on back home and beat his wife to death? Did anyone see him at his office, I wonder? If not...

Even without any physical evidence, in situations like this, the spouse is always at the top of the list of suspects.

I stepped off the stairs into the mudroom. Mike Willis and his team were working in the basement apartment. If I could, if he could make time, I'd talk to him a little later, when I'd consulted with the medical examiner.

5

"Hey, Doc," I said, taking a tentative step into the laundry room.

He was down on one knee beside the body, head covered, a surgical mask over his mouth and nose, latex gloves on his hands.

"Hello, Kate. Give me just one moment, will you, please, and I'll be with you," he said, without looking up as he delicately touched Victoria's head.

Doctor Richard Sheddon was a small man in his late fifties, five-eight, overweight, almost totally bald, with a round face that usually sported a jovial expression, but not today.

Finally, he turned his head, looked up at me, and stood. "You were right, Kate. This is a bad one; one of the worst I've seen in quite a while."

"Indeed," I said. "I hope I didn't ruin your breakfast."

Doc's incongruously large black bag was open, close at hand, but his hands were empty.

"Ah, my dear Kate. It would take a lot more than this to ruin my breakfast." He glanced down at the body.

"We have something of an anomaly," he said thoughtfully. "She's been dead for a while."

"What do you mean for a while?"

"Since last night. Judging by the liver temperature, the state of rigor, at least ten hours, give or take an hour. I'd say she died sometime around midnight. Here, take a look."

I stepped closer.

"Closer, young lady," he said and crouched down again beside the body. "See... come closer, look here."

Victoria was lying partially on her left hip, facing us, her legs one atop the other; her torso flat on its back, her head twisted to the right. He pointed round to the back of her thighs. I had to lean right over her to see what he was pointing at. The bluish gray of her skin at the backs of her legs was interrupted by the dark purple of livor mortis; the blood had pooled beneath the skin.

"That means whoever did this had to be in the house, which explains why there were no signs of a break-in."

I looked up at the ceiling, below the kitchen, thinking about Darby Randolph's response to the news of his wife's death. My training told me he was our man; he was the only person in the house that could have done it. Not the kids, that's for sure. Marcie Cox? Nah. So I knew it had to be Randolph... But my gut was telling me, *not so fast.*

"Actually, it means the body's been moved, rolled over onto its side. But yes, someone in the house, and it's personal. Whoever did this to this poor woman was extremely upset," Doc said, pointing at the strange punctures I observed earlier. "Look at these stab wounds."

"Upset? Ya think?" I paused, staring at the ragged holes, then said, "I was right, then. The punctures are stab wounds. She was stabbed as well as bludgeoned. So the cause of death?"

"Oh please, Catherine, you know better than that. I won't be able to tell you that until I've completed the autopsy. I will say this, though. What we have here is a textbook case of overkill," Doc said.

"I'll need to get her under the lights to find out what else was done to her."

"Sexual assault?" I asked.

"Again, I won't know until I've finished the autopsy, but somehow I doubt it. Her clothes don't seem to have been disturbed."

"Well, that's something, I suppose. When will you do the autopsy?"

He stood up; so did I.

"I'll try to get it done later today. I already have a client, a six-year-old girl—"

"Whoa, Doc. That's enough. More bad news I can't handle. Just give me a little notice, okay?"

He nodded. "I'll call you when I'm ready, but it could be late?" He raised his eyebrows, questioningly.

"Sounds like a plan," I said. "You know how I love our late nights together, Doc." I winked and patted his arm.

He chuckled softly. "Do me a favor, Kate, if you wouldn't mind. Send the boys down here with the gurney?"

"Has the scene been photographed and videoed?" I asked.

"Yes, Mike did it himself, just before I arrived, so she's good to go. Then he can get back in here and work his magic. And I do hope he can conjure up a little physical evidence." He laughed at his own joke, though I could see little humor in it, but that's Doc for you.

It was then that I realized I'd missed something. *Didn't Darby say that he'd seen her this morning? I need to talk to him, right now.*

I ran up the stairs to the kitchen and found Randolph still sitting at the island with his head in his hands. Officer Quinn was standing stoically beside the kitchen door, chest out, hands locked together behind his back. He nodded at me as I entered the room.

"Mr. Randolph," I said as I sat down at the island opposite him and opened my iPad. "There are a couple of things I need to clarify, if you don't mind."

He looked up at me, his head still in hands. He nodded, his finger pushing his cheeks this way and that; it would have been funny in any other situation.

"You said that you left your wife in bed, asleep, when you left to take the children to school," I said gently.

He nodded again.

"But that's not true, is it?"

He sat upright with a jolt, grasped the edge of the worktop, and stuttered, "I... But... No, yes, it is true. Her door was closed. She was asleep."

"What you're telling me is that you didn't sleep with your wife last night?"

He stared at me for a long moment, then resignedly shook his head and said, "No, I don't sleep with her anymore; haven't for... well, more than a year. She says... said I snore. I use the guest room at the end of the hall."

"So when did you last see her?"

"I'm not sure. I'm usually in bed by nine. I was last night. I get up early you see, and..." He trailed off, staring down at the pattern in the granite top.

"So you last saw her where? Doing what?"

"Downstairs. Watching TV, but she was also looking at Pinterest on her iPhone."

I nodded. "And the girls?"

"They were in their room when I went up. I looked in on them, said goodnight, and I went to my own room."

"And you didn't go down into the basement?"

"No. Why do you ask?"

That wasn't a question I wanted to answer, not then anyway, so I changed the subject. "Why didn't you tell me all of this when we talked earlier?"

He shrugged. "I didn't think it was important. No, that's not true. I didn't think of it at all. All I could think about was my wife. When can I see her?"

That one I was ready for. "I'll talk to Doc Sheddon and let you know." But I didn't.

I stood and headed toward the basement stairs. I told Quinn to keep an eye on Randolph. He nodded.

So, I thought as I made my way down the stairs, *if Darby didn't go down there, he couldn't have moved her. So who the hell did?*

By the time I reached the basement, Victoria Randolph was already on the gurney.

It didn't take them long to load her into the back of Doc's converted Chevy Suburban. Unfortunately, they weren't quite quick enough. Just as he closed the vehicle's rear doors, a crazed Darby Randolph came running out of the mudroom door.

"Where are you taking her?" he shouted, his eyes red and wild.

"Damn it, Chief," I shouted as Wilbur and Quinn came running out after him. "How did he get down here?"

"I want to see her!" Randolph yelled as Quinn grabbed him from behind. "Let me see my wife!"

The two officers hung onto him as he struggled like a fish on the end of a line.

"Let me see my wife!" he wailed, his voice echoing across the yard.

I was taught a long time ago to be prepared for such situations and to subdue the crazy quickly, before he could hurt anyone, or himself.

Randolph was indeed crazy, out of his mind.

"Mr. Randolph. You are not helping her right now," I shouted. "Please, sir, I need you to calm down."

"Don't tell me to calm down," he screeched. "You come in here and tell me my wife, the mother of my daughters is dead. And then you tell me I should calm down! What the hell is wrong with you, woman? Let me see my wife!"

Smack! "Calm DOWN, young man."

Doc Sheddon said with emphasis as he smacked him across his cheek, leaving a deep red handprint.

Darby froze, stood still, stiff from head to toe, shocked. Chief Wilbur and Officer Quinn stood like a pair of bookends holding his arms.

And then it happened, Darby's legs gave way and he sank to his knees, hanging by his arms as the two police officers tried unsuccessfully to hold him upright. And then he began to wail again, long shuddering howls.

I shook my head. I'd had enough. I could take no more. I turned away, left them to it, and headed back into the house. I could still hear him as I climbed the stairs.

I met Janet in the kitchen. She was sitting at the island paging through her notebook.

"Well," I said, somewhat impatiently and immediately regretting it. "Did you find anything?"

"This house is amazing. What does a girl have to do to get a set-up like this?"

"Marry an ex-governor's grandson," I replied almost bitterly. "So, did you? Find anything?"

She shook her head and said, "No. I didn't see anything out of place, anywhere. Even the girls' room was all neat and tidy, and you know how they are... worse than boys. The victim must have been a neat freak."

"What about the guest rooms? No, forget it. I need to see for myself," I said. "Let's do it again. No, dang it. Mike Willis will probably have the place locked down for a week. I hope Darby and the kids have somewhere they can go. Why don't you go and ask him? Just to make sure." You've no idea how glad I was to pass that buck.

Finally, maybe thirty minutes later, we left, drove away down Scenic Highway back to Amnicola and sanity... Yah think? Not hardly!

It was not quite noon and my head was pounding, so I made Janet drive. She eased the big car onto the road, and I swear I could still hear Darby Randolph's pitiful cries as we drove away. *Yeah, if he's faking it, he's one hell of an actor.*

6

"So, what's Marcie Cox's story?" I said as Janet merged with the traffic on Highway 41.

"Well, she didn't hold back, that's for sure," Janet said. "She didn't like the Randolphs, not one bit. She liked their money, though, but she said that Victoria Randolph was a rabid snob. And she didn't know how a woman who claimed to have a direct line to Jesus in Heaven could be so uppity and conceited."

"Okay," I said, "so our Vicky is not the saint her husband claims she was. So what?"

I reached for the Starbucks cup in my cupholder, happy I hadn't thrown out my morning coffee. It was cold, but it was wet, and bitter, and surely better than nothing.

"Right," Janet nodded, staring ahead at the traffic on Broad. "Anyway, Marcie said she was at home all night, with her husband, Michael, and kid, Gary who's twelve. They also had a neighbor over. Apparently, the neighbor's kid plays with Gary. I have her name, the neighbor, so I can talk to her, check the alibi. Anyway, Marcie was in a state of shock, I suppose. She kept rabbiting on about quitting the Randolphs. She said she did that every Tuesday night, dreading that she had to go the next day but, like always, the money talked: she had to pay for her son's tennis lessons."

I opened my mouth to speak, but Janet was on a roll.

"She was late getting to work this morning, due to that wreck on I-75. So even that worked for her, because Gary, her son, called her this morning while she was driving to the Randolph's place. Wanted to get her permission for the other kid to sleep over, on Friday, I think. Cell towers can verify that easy enough."

"Yeah, I heard about that truck accident," I said, thankful for the opportunity to break up Janet's enthusiastic diatribe. Yes, I know; I'd asked for it. I took another sip of coffee, and then she was off again.

"Mrs. Cox is a straight shooter, LT. She didn't hold anything back. She said she only hated working for the Randolphs because of Victoria. Said she normally wouldn't speak ill of the dead and would pray for the woman's soul, but she really didn't like her."

"That's interesting," I said. "Victoria's husband called her a saint. Kind to everyone. Loved by all."

"Yes, that *is* interesting," Janet said. "He doesn't know her very well, does he?"

I didn't answer, so she continued.

"Mrs. Cox said she didn't see anyone or hear anything when she got to work. She assumed that Victoria was either at some coffee klatch or at her new part-time job at the Church of the Savior. According to Mrs. Cox, Victoria never tired of telling her that she didn't need to work but that she was called to work. That she was the preacher's right hand."

"So Victoria saw herself as a saint, too?"

"Sounds like it, doesn't it?" Janet said, merging with traffic on Riverside Drive. "I asked Mrs. Cox if Victoria had any enemies, or if she and Darby got along. But Marcie said she didn't know about any of that. Claimed that as far as she could tell, Victoria had Darby wrapped around her finger, and he seemed to like it that way, and that's about all I could get out of her."

"Huh! That's a blast. Doesn't give us much to go on. Nothing, in fact." I chewed my lower lip, and then my phone rang.

"Where are you, Lieutenant?"

Oh hell; it's Finkle.

"On Riverside. We just left the Randolph residence. It's definitely a homicide. Toliver and I were just—"

"Well, you need to quit screwing around and get back to the office, *now!*"

I clenched my teeth. Although Assistant Chief Henry Finkle and I had come to an understanding about where my boundaries lay, it didn't stop him from being a misogynistic, rude little turd. But he was still my boss.

"We'll be there in—" I started to say, but he'd already hung up.

The creep was an expert at playing head games, and now he had me wondering what the hell he wanted. I'd tried to get along with him, treat him with respect. Not that he deserved it. The guy was married, but that didn't stop him trying to get into my pants. *As if I'd ever be that desperate.* It reached a point where I had to do something about it, so I played him. I agreed to have a drink with him at a bar called the Sorbonne.

I plied him with drinks and an unspoken promise... Hey, it was a harmless prank. Just a couple of drinks and a few selfies, although no one can tell who is in the selfies except Finkle... with pants around his ankles. No one knows about it except for Laura and Bennie who run the Sorbonne. It was my little secret, a little security to keep him off my back, and it worked, so far anyway. I couldn't keep his eyes off my chest and ass, or his crass remarks, but I had stopped the constant innuendos.

So, I was diligent in my efforts to keep our relationship professional, but Finkle was having none of it. He was out to get me. If I made a mistake, he couldn't be reasoned with. He'd get revenge eventually. There wasn't going to be an explosion or huge temper tantrum. He was more subtle than that. He'd get back at me. I just didn't know when or where. So, in the meantime, I was going to do my job.

"Here we are," Janet said, easing the big car into my parking space.

"Yeah, here we are," I said dispiritedly. "So, I need you to do a background check on Victoria Randolph, Darby Randolph and, oh hell, you may as well go ahead and get the information on Marcie Cox, too. We'll need to cross her off the list sooner rather than later."

"You got it, LT."

"Let me know what you find," I said to Janet as she headed off to her desk.

I walked past my previous partner Lonnie Guest's old cubicle. He'd been gone for a couple of months, and his desk was still unassigned. Not gone as in dead. Gone retired. The SOB became a barber; opened a little shop in Harrison, would you believe? So, the Chief, in his wisdom, assigned Janet Toliver to be my new partner and promoted her to detective, the youngest on the force.

It wasn't that Janet wasn't a good detective. She really was. But I wasn't all that comfortable with her. Not yet. She'd spent her formative years in Chief Johnston's office where she'd been little more than a file clerk. She earned her stripes on our last case together, but that didn't change the fact that she had been in close quarters with the chief for almost two years. I'm not saying she was a mole or anything. But you never know, do you?

Yes, Finkle had me going again, just like always. I couldn't imagine what the flap could be about, and I wasn't going to go out of my way to find out. I'd already had my clock cleaned by Internal Affairs, and I couldn't imagine that there'd been another complaint; I'd been a model police officer ever since... not. Okay, so I could be tough; I was trained to be. But that wasn't it. It had been my language and tone that had gotten me in trouble. Can you believe that?

So when I got to my office, I closed the door, flopped down behind my desk, sipped my cold coffee, and stared up at the ceiling, trying to organize my thoughts.

The message light on my desk was blinking. *Screw 'em.* I opened my laptop. *Emails, oh how I hate thee.* There were more than I could count... Okay, maybe twenty, and half of them had those annoying little red tags that flagged them as "urgent." *Urgent my rear end. I've played that silly game myself. Still, I'd better... Nah, I'll look at 'em later.*

There was also a stack of files on my desk, but only a half dozen of them that I hadn't updated to my lord and master, the aforementioned Henry "Tiny" Finkle, assistant chief, responsible only to the mighty Wayne Johnston, the Dark Lord of Amnicola. Anyway, those half dozen cases were in a state of limbo, awaiting lab reports or witness interviews, so I couldn't see them being the issue. But hey, what did I know about how the man's mind worked? Then again, maybe it didn't... work, that is. I always figured him for a dumbass.

I went back to the emails and tapped the first of the day that had arrived in my inbox at five-oh-three that morning. *Who the hell's at work that early in the morning?* It was a request for some info on an old case I'd solved years ago. Some dude in prison had claimed he was responsible for the crime, and my guy was trying for a new trial. Those guys sitting out their lives at the Riverbend Maximum Security Institute in Nashville would cop to anything if it provided them with a diversion, or a thrill, while they waited for the inevitable.

As crazy as it seemed, once I got started, I managed to knock out all the flagged emails, put out a couple fires, make a few deals, and before I knew, it was almost four o'clock.

I just had one small errand to run, to pick up some paperwork from the County Clerk's office, before heading home for the day. That being so, I was just about to head out when there was a knock on the door. It opened and a shock of red hair appeared.

"I got something, LT. Got a minute?" Janet asked.

I waved her in, and she sat down in front of my desk. Little did I know that what she was about to tell me would keep us there until almost seven o'clock... and my nemesis Finkle made nary an appearance.

7

—————

"It's quite a story," Janet said, smiling and shaking her head as she dumped a pile of paperwork and notes, "so you might want to grab some popcorn."

I sat back in my chair, laced my fingers together in front of me and stared at her. I didn't find it at all funny. I wanted out of there, and from the size of the pile of crap she had in front of her, I knew that wasn't going to happen.

Come on, Kate. Go easy on the kid. She's thorough, and she's just trying to please. She can't help it that Lonnie retired.

She stopped smiling, looked a little chastened, and said, "Okay, ready?"

I nodded.

"Darby Randolph is the grandson of Alexander Randolph. I'm sure you've heard of him." She looked up at me.

I nodded again.

"Darby met Victoria Tate at a frat party his senior year at UTC— he'd applied for several of the Ivy League schools but wasn't accepted. It was love at first sight. She graduated from Francis M. Paul High School, but she didn't go to college."

"Really?" I asked politely, not at all intrigued.

"Yep. They were married six weeks later, just before he gradu-ated. It was a small affair, considering Darby's family, just fifty guests according to the Times Free Press, which is really weird. The Randolphs are high society. You would think the wedding would have been a blockbuster; it wasn't. And that leads me to believe that the wedding might not have been blessed by certain members of his family. For the honeymoon, they spent a month in St. Kitts and Nevis, in the Caribbean."

She was right. Darby's parents' wedding is still talked about today... at least by those who care about such things. *Maybe Victoria wasn't the family's first choice.*

"What about *her* family?"

"She doesn't have one. Victoria's an only child. Her mother passed away when she was three. She didn't know her father; he disappeared before she was born. But her stepfather, Harvey Tate, appears to have been a steady influence in her life; he adopted her shortly after he married her mother. Harvey had a couple of minor brushes with the law. Driving under the influence. Public intoxica-tion. He died a couple years ago. If he was abusive, it was never reported. He gave her away, and he's in some of the wedding photos. So, I think they must have gotten along okay."

"He's in some of the wedding photos?" I said, a little surprised. "I didn't see any at the house with him in them, and there were plenty. Plenty of Victoria by herself and with Darby and his family, but not with anyone that looked like a father of the bride. Where did you see them?"

"I pulled up the Times Free Press coverage of the wedding during my research. See?" She handed me several print outs.

I looked at them, one after the other. Tate was a good-looking man.

"So," I said, laying the printouts down on my desk, "A girl from the wrong side of the tracks, so to speak, makes good by marrying into a prominent family. Happens all the time." I'd heard it all before, many times. Totally bored, I sipped the last drops of my cold coffee.

"It does. But most don't end up dead." Janet looked down at her notes. "So, Victoria and Darby married. They had two girls. They were living the dream until all this. She had recently been hired at the Church of the Savior as the pastor's personal assistant."

"Hah, living the dream, you say?" I said. "If that's the way the Real Housewives of Lookout Mountain live the dream, I'll pass. It all sounds rather boring to me... Any financial issues? What about insurance?"

"Nothing out of the ordinary there, either." Janet flipped a couple of pages in her notebook. "Darby's doing very well for a dumb—" She didn't finish the sentence. "He's a senior partner in the prestigious law practice of Hirsch, O'Shea and Randolph which, considering that he was no better than an average student in college, would ordinarily be unthinkable, but... Well, I think we know how he landed that gig. It's not what you know, or don't know—it's who granddaddy knows, right?"

I nodded and made a circling motion with my forefinger, indicating for her to get on with it. I was getting antsy, impatient.

"She did have an insurance policy for just a couple hundred thousand dollars, but so did he. Both of them signed the forms. To me it doesn't look like their relationship was anything out of the ordinary." She shrugged.

"So, no financial issues?" I said. "How about visits to the doctor, plastic surgeon, Botox, tucks? Lavish hotel and restaurant charges? Shopping sprees? Rumors of affairs? Alcohol? Drugs? Rehab? Anything at all that you would consider out of the ordinary?"

"Nope."

I took a deep breath and folded my arms behind my head, closed my eyes and tried to think.

Someone undoubtedly had a real problem with Victoria. The level of violence inflicted upon her indicated rage out of control, and in my experience, only one thing ever caused such rage: jealousy.

And that meant she must have pissed someone off big time: either her husband or a boyfriend which, as far as we know, she didn't have.

So that brings us back to Darby. But I've had enough. I wanna go home, take a nice hot bath and enjoy a large glass of red... Huh, not hardly. God only knows when Doc will call.

"I've had it, Janet," I said. "I don't think we can do much more tonight. I'm going home to wait for Doc to call. I'd suggest you do the same. We'll get an early start in the morning, okay?"

"Sounds good, LT. You got any big plans for this evening?"

"After I get finished with Doc Sheddon, yeah. A bottle of wine and a hot bath," I said. "See you tomorrow."

Janet nodded, rose to her feet, gathered up her papers, and left the office.

After she'd gone, I thought maybe I'd been a little rude to her. I didn't mean to be. It niggled at me all the way home. I decided I'd apologize to her the next day.

By nine o'clock, I'd had enough of the waiting, and I called Doc. He told me to stand down. Seems he'd developed a headache and had decided to go home. *Gee, thanks for letting me know.*

I hung up, poured myself a glass of the good stuff, took a shower, and went to bed only to be awaked at three o'clock by the sweet sounds of my phone. Reluctantly, I dragged myself out of one of those peaceful, but heavy dreams; you know what I mean, right?

"Gazzara," I grumbled as I fought to stay awake and out of dreamland.

"It's me, LT," Janet said breathlessly. "We've got another one."

8

"WHAT?" I SQUEAKED, SUDDENLY WIDE AWAKE.

"Yeah, another one," Janet said. "The address is 612 Lincoln Avenue. Lookout Mountain."

I closed my eyes, trying to figure out exactly where it was.

"That's just a mile south from where the Randolph's live," I said as I dragged myself out of bed. "612, you said?" *Better put that in my phone right now before I forget.* "Okay. I'll meet you there as soon as I can. Make sure the scene is secured. Have you called Mike Willis? No? Okay, do it now! And call Doc Sheddon. Good, that was smart. You go on up there. I'll be there soon."

I staggered into the kitchen, punched the button on the coffee maker, and headed for the bathroom. I took a quick, scalding-hot shower, then back to the bedroom where I quickly dressed in jeans, white blouse, and a black leather jacket, twisting my hair into a pony-tail. Then I grabbed a tumbler of coffee and ran out of the apartment to where my car was parked on the road, slopping the coffee as I ran down the steps. *I'll need to get one that's spill-proof if this keeps up.* I all but fell into the driver's seat, set the coffee in the cupholder, and then lay my head back against the rest, closed my eyes, and breathed deeply for several minutes.

Finally, somewhat more relaxed than I'd thought possible, I inserted the key and started the car.

When I pulled up in front of the home on Lincoln Avenue, all was quiet, just a single cruiser—its lights flashing red and blue—and Janet's car, no gawkers, no one on the sidewalk. Janet and Chief Wilbur were standing together on the porch. Next to them sat a man on the steps with his elbows on his knees and his head in his hands.

I sighed, shook my head, and exited the car, just as Doc Sheddon's black Suburban pulled up behind me.

"Morning, Kate," he said as he climbed down from the big vehicle. "I was just about to call you when Janet called. I don't think we've had a homicide up here in more than ten years. Now we have two in less than 24 hours. What the hell's going on?"

I watched as he circled around the front of the SUV and then dragged his big black bag out from the passenger side and placed it on the ground beside him.

"It's a full moon, Doc," I said then yawned.

"Isn't it always?" he replied.

"You were going to call me? I wouldn't have answered, not at four o'clock in the morning."

He grinned at me. "Yes, you would. You can't help yourself. Meet you inside."

I nodded and headed up to the house where Janet was waiting for me.

"Hey, Chief," I said. "Janet, Mister…"

The man looked up at me and said, "Dilly, Connor Dilly." His eyes were red. He let his head sink back into his hands.

Wilbur looked tired. No, he looked worn out.

"It's good to see you, Lieutenant," he said wearily. "What can I do to help?"

"Right now, I need you to secure the scene. Have you been inside? Are you all there is?"

"Yes, unfortunately, I've been inside, and I wish to hell I hadn't. Don't even ask. I'll let you see for yourself. And no, I'm not all there is. Quinn and Jones are on their way. I had to get 'em out of bed. Should be here anytime now. I'll get them on it as soon as they arrive. I'll go wait for them. Can you take care of..." He pointed down at Dilly and mouthed silently, "Him?"

I rolled my eyes and nodded, then said, "Where is she, Chief?"

"Living room. First on the right. You can't miss it." He walked down the steps and headed down the drive to the road.

"I'll be with you shortly, Mr. Dilly. I'm sorry for your loss. Are you okay?"

He mumbled something through his fingers I took to be in the affirmative. I turned to Janet, took her arm, and steered her to the far end of the porch.

"Talk to me," I said.

Janet consulted her pocket notebook. "I haven't been inside yet. I just got here. But Chief Wilbur—he was first on the scene as you can see—said they got a 911 call from the husband, Mr. Connor Dilly. Mr. Dilly told the dispatcher that he'd arrived home from a business trip and had found his wife dead."

"How did he know she was dead? Did he touch her? Did he touch anything?"

"Oh she's dead all right, but no, I don't think he touched anything, but I haven't talked to him yet."

"What do you mean by that, that she's dead all right?"

I looked back along the porch at Dilly. He hadn't moved.

"According to Chief Wilbur," Janet said, "she was killed in exactly the same way as Victoria Randolph. And—you're gonna hate this—she's been dead for days. Well, at least two." Janet wrinkled her nose.

"What?"

"That's right. She was killed before Victoria Randolph."

"Sheesh, is this a bad day or what?" I said under my breath as I checked my watch. "It's only frickin' four o'clock," I grumbled. "Come on. We have a lot to do."

I walked back to Dilly; Janet followed me like a puppy that had lost its mother.

"Mr. Dilly," I said. "I'm sorry, sir, but I need to check the—" I was going to say body, but thought better of it and said instead, "I need to secure the scene. I'd like to talk to you when I'm finished so please, I'd like you to stay here. I'll be but a few minutes. Is that okay?"

"Where am I going to go?" he whispered, without looking up.

At that, Janet and I stepped inside the house, into a large open foyer. It took just a couple of seconds to figure out which was the living room. We could have simply followed our noses. The smell of a corpse that has been left out in the open for thirty-six hours, or more, is one that will never leave you: a thick, sweet smell that settles over everything and can't be scrubbed away.

I pulled a pair of Tyvek shoe covers out of my bag and put them on. Janet looked at me like a kid who hadn't brought a pencil to class, so I handed her a pair too. *I'll have to remind her to get some of those from supply.*

Doc Sheddon was already at work when we stepped into the living room.

"Ah, Kate, Janet," he said, looking up at us. "Do come in. I'm almost done. Another nasty one, I'm afraid. I don't envy you, Kate. I'd say this poor woman died sometime around mid to late afternoon on Tuesday. Come take a look."

And we did, at least I did. Janet stayed two steps back and put her hand over her nose. *I'll have to remind her to get some face masks from supply also.*

I joined him, crouched down opposite him on the left side of the body. He was correct, it was indeed a nasty one. The left side of the victim's head had literally been crushed. Even I could see that the left side of the skull, including most of the eye socket, had been smashed, caved in, by several heavy blows: five, maybe six. Obviously, I didn't know for sure, but judging by the shape of the indentations, the weapon was similar to the one used to kill Victoria Randolph.

"Looks like the same weapon," I said. "Cause of death?"

"Really, Catherine?" he said, smiling. "One, you know I can't say for sure. Two, ain't it freaking obvious? Blunt force trauma."

"Silly question," I said. "Sorry, force of habit."

He nodded, smiling; he always was, smiling. Nothing ever seemed to faze him. Wish I was like that.

The body was fully dressed in jeans and a button-down shirt, lying flat on its back, arms and legs spread wide, head turned to the right. And yes, there were puncture wounds through the clothing.

"Are those what I think they are, Doc?"

He nodded. "Looks like it. Can't say for sure, not yet."

I sighed, stood up, and looked around. *Holy shit! What a frickin' mess.*

There was blood spatter everywhere: on the carpet, the furniture, the ceiling and when I took out my iPhone and shone the flashlight on the wall, I could easily make out the droplets there, too.

How the hell hard did he hit her to send it that far?

"Doc," I said, "I'm going to have to leave you to it. I have the victim's husband on the porch and need to talk to him. You'll call me, right?"

"I will. Please answer the phone when I do."

"I promise. I will."

The house was huge—five to six thousand square feet, maybe more, and it screamed wealth: white walls and dark furniture, paintings—original oils—that depicted the Antebellum South. They depicted pre-Civil War Southern living in all its glory, and I was certain they must have cost a pretty penny; there was dried blood on at least two of them.

"Check the upstairs, Janet. I'm going to talk to the husband."

Janet nodded and left, still covering her nose.

I took another quick glance around the living room, taking in the family photographs on bookshelves. Mrs. Dilly wasn't anything like

Victoria Randolph. She was a rather plain-looking woman, not exactly pretty, but somehow attractive. In most of the photos, she was wearing casual clothes, jeans, sweaters, laughing with a wide, toothy smile, making faces with her children. Had I seen her at the grocery store, I'd never have guessed she lived as she did on Lookout Mountain.

The epitome of the modern Southern lady, I thought. *What a waste; what a damn shame!*

"Later, Doc," I said, finally.

"Later," he replied. "Wait, I need to move the body. Where's Willis?"

"On his way, as far as I know."

"I can't wait for him. I'll photograph the body for him. Tell him to call me when he has a minute."

I nodded, stepped carefully backward out of the room, and headed toward the front porch.

9

I STEPPED OUT ONTO THE PORCH AND BREATHED IN DEEPLY THE sweet, clean, early morning mountain air. *Wow, did I ever need that?*

Connor Dilly was seated on the porch swing staring into space, his hands on either side of him grasping the edge of the seat.

"Mr. Dilly?" I said.

He nodded and sniffled, stood quickly, and extended his hand to me. "Connor Dilly, ma'am."

I shook his hand and said, "I'm Lieutenant Catherine Gazzara. I know how difficult this must be, sir, but I do need to talk to you. Can you please tell me why she was here by herself and... how you found her?" I was trying to be gentle with him, but how the hell could I?

"I was out of town, at my other office in Memphis. I go twice a month. I left early on Tuesday morning. I don't usually stay more than two or three days. My return flight was delayed. I called my wife at about seven last night, to let her know, but she didn't answer. I thought nothing of it. It was after midnight when I arrived back in Chattanooga. I drove home and... I found her."

"You drove home? I didn't see your car."

"It's in the garage."

I nodded.

"When did you last talk to your wife?" I asked.

"That was on Tuesday morning," he said, his eyes filling with tears.

"It didn't worry you that your wife didn't answer last night?" I asked, shifting from one foot to the other.

"Please, Detective. Let's sit down. The swing will hold both of us."

We sat down together, and I repeated my question.

Connor Dilly slowly shook his head. "We're not that kind of couple. We don't worry about each other, where we are, what we're doing. We love each other, trust each other. Meryl was my whole life. The good Lord saw fit to bring us together. Let no man put asunder. I just assumed she was busy, in the shower, perhaps."

"Mr. Dilly, can you think of anyone who would want to hurt your wife... or you?"

I watched his reaction. His eyes were red, bruised where he'd been rubbing them. He shrugged, and I prepared myself for another diatribe such as Mr. Randolph had given me about his wife being a saint, walking on water, working for world peace, climate change, helping orphans and puppies, but that's not what I got.

"My wife wasn't perfect," he said. "She was a plain-speaker, pulled no punches. Whatever she said, no matter who to, she always told the truth, sometimes to her detriment. Some people don't like hearin' the truth," he said, working his jaw. "But no, I can't think of anyone who'd want to hurt her. This is the work of the devil. Plain and simple... Oh, my beautiful Meryl. What will I do without you?"

Behind me, I could hear the rattling sound of the ME's gurney.

"Mr. Dilly," I said, trying to divert his attention, "did your wife ever mention seeing anyone suspicious loitering around the house, or the neighborhood, currently or in the past?"

He shook his head, leaned forward, put his head in his hands. His shoulders were shaking. I gave it up, told him I'd talk to him later and to call me if he thought of anything. He was a suspect, of course, but his grief seemed genuine.

I stood, placed a business card on a small side table, and was about to leave when he looked up and reached for the card. He stared at it, then said, "Lord, please give me the strength to deliver this news to my children."

Dilly looked at me. "Our son Joseph just moved to Virginia. Landed a government job. My daughter, Elsie, is finishing college at Alabama... Yes, Detective, I'll call you."

"I'm very sorry, Mr. Dilly."

"The Lord will see me through this. I'll weather this storm with His hand to steady me." He stood, stiff and proud, obviously holding himself together.

I suddenly felt unnaturally sad, something that didn't happen to me very often. I wished I could offer him some words of comfort, but I couldn't. I'd long ago learned to keep my distance. If I didn't, I'd lose my mind. Yet, there was no denying that this was a bad one.

Who the hell could have done this? I thought. *What kind of animal hammers a woman's head to a pulp? Why? Why did he do it? What was his motive? Two harmless, defenseless women. There has to be a connection. What the hell is it?*

Back in the living room, I watched as they carefully lifted Meryl Dilly onto the gurney, covered her with a fresh white sheet, and rolled her out to Doc's SUV. I was about to take a look around the area where the body had been when Janet appeared at the door.

"Anything?" I asked as I waved a hand goodbye to Doc Sheddon.

She looked around as if to make sure no one could hear her, and then jerked her head toward an empty, dark hallway that led to the family room and the back of the house.

"There was no sign of a break-in," she said," just like at the Randolph house." She put her hands on her hips and continued, "Other than the religious pictures and statues in every room, the place is unremarkable, clean, tidy, lived-in. I peeked in some of the drawers and closets, nothing; no fancy underwear, just the opposite in fact." She shrugged.

I nodded, not really listening to her; my mind was elsewhere. "Where the hell is Mike Willis?" I muttered. "You did call him, didn't you?"

"Yes, of course. He said to make sure Chief Wilbur keeps the scene secure and he'd be here as soon as he could. His team is still working the Randolph place. He said he had all eight of his techs there, and that he'd have to split them into two teams."

"Geez, good thing Doc had the foresight to photograph the body before he took it."

Janet scrunched up her face.

She's probably remembering the sight and smell of the body. I was like that too, the first time, I remembered.

I continued, "Well, it looks like we're getting to the office early today. Oh, I was going to ask: did you find out anything more about the Randolphs?"

"Yeah. I was going to bring you up to speed when we got back to Amnicola. LT, I know I don't have much experience, but it seems to me that we... that we..." She paused, looking helpless.

"Come on, Janet, spit it out."

She pinched her lips together and shook her head, obviously frustrated. I could see her mind working to put the pieces together. *That's what I like to see.*

"It's just that we don't seem to have anything to work with... I can't see how either Mr. Randolph or Mr. Dilly could have done this, and so far, we have nothing—"

"You're right," I said, interrupting her. "We don't, but we will. I promise. You just have to be patient, Janet. It's here, we have to find it. Mike's the best. He'll find something for us to work with."

My new partner stood looking at me, soaking up my words.

"Janet, the one certainty about a murder is that the killer always leaves something at the crime scene, and always takes something away from it. So, for the moment, all we can do is leave the searching to Mike and his team while we talk to people, dig into the past, ask questions, find the inconsistencies. Look, I'm almost done here. Why don't you head on back to the office and run the Dillys through the wringer? I'll pick up coffee and bagels. Then we can talk over breakfast. I'll buzz you when I get in."

Janet smiled at me, sheepishly, nodded and left. Me? I hung around for a while longer and roamed the house looking, for what I don't know. I would have been grateful to find anything right then, but Janet was right: the place was pristine, virtually undisturbed, except for the bloody mess in the living room.

There was a basement, mostly devoted to a home gym and a family room—no bar, of course.

At the far end of the family room, I found what I assumed was Connor Dilly's office. Beautiful, something I'd always wanted for myself: floor to ceiling bookshelves filled with books, and two desks, pushed together facing each other.

"His and hers," I mumbled out loud.

Janet was right about the religious iconography. Religious paintings adorned every wall. I peeked at the papers on the desk: nothing there that grabbed my attention, just a bunch of bills, all marked paid, two church magazines, and several pamphlets for The Church of the Savior beneath a paperweight that read "Jesus is my Lord and Savior."

That's where the lovely Mrs. Randolph was working, I mused, not getting overly excited about it. *Hmm, they both belonged to the same church. Well, they would, wouldn't they?*

The Church of the Savior wasn't the only church on Lookout Mountain, but it was well attended; I knew that from what little research I'd already done. Pastor Ed packed the seats every Sunday and on Wednesday evenings.

Okay, so I've got nothing else, I thought as I picked up one of the flyers, folded it, and stuffed it in my pocket.

I returned to the living room and took one last careful look around the spot where the body had been... and I saw something I hadn't noticed before. There were two bloody indentations in the carpet like it had been pierced. Whoever killed Mrs. Dilly stabbed her so hard, the weapon went right through her body and into the carpet. I took out my iPhone and photographed the indentations. Yes, I knew Mike would do it, but I wanted copies of my own to study.

"This kind of rage can't easily be hidden," I mumbled to myself.

"What's that, Detective?" Chief Wilbur asked.

"Nothing. I'm just talking to myself."

"You know what they say about people that talk to themselves?" He smirked.

I tilted my head and smirked back.

"Yeah. That it's the only way to have an intelligent conversation."

Chief Wilbur chuckled, nodding. "A neighbor dropped by, a Mrs. Courtland, attracted by the lights. She's sitting with Mr. Dilly. I don't know what to say about all this, Detective. I've never seen anything like it before. I'm not trying to sound like a jackass, but things like this don't happen on Lookout Mountain. That's why people live here."

"Mrs. Courtland, you say?" I asked as I made a note of the name. "Yes, I hear you about the neighborhood, but you know, Chief, that's why criminals eventually come here," I said. "They know how lax homeowner security in a community like this can be. But we aren't dealing with your average criminal, are we? What can you tell me about the Dillys? How well do you know them?"

"I know them pretty well. Like the Randolphs, they're in church every Sunday. I see them there myself." He cleared his throat and hitched up his pants. "They're close with the pastor and half the congregation. Darby Randolph, coming from the family he does, has to maintain a good rapport with the community, you know."

"Politics, right?" I asked.

"Right! Connor Dilly runs a successful carpet business, here and with outlets in Nashville, Memphis, and Birmingham. He donates generously to the church, and the school. He's a member of the Fairy-land Club, and the golf club, as is Randolph. I mean, the guy gives back, Detective. He didn't deserve this. Neither did Meryl."

"No one deserves it," I replied. "You say you all go to the same church?"

"Yeah, everyone here on Lookout Mountain goes to one church or the other. Savior is a little highbrow for me personally, but my wife happens to like Pastor Ed. He's good people, right enough but... well, she'll be the first to tell you that as far as the Church of the Savior is concerned, I'm a square peg in a round hole."

I chuckled and nodded my head. "I hear you, Chief."

"How can you joke?" Connor Dilly shouted at us from the doorway. "My wife is dead and all you're doing is standing around joking? What's wrong with you? Don't you have any sense of compassion?"

"You've got it wrong, Mr. Dilly. I can assure you."

"I know your name, Detective," Dilly shouted, pointing at me. "I'll file an official complaint. You bet I will! And you, too." He pointed at the uniformed Chief. "I have donned the armor of God. I shall fight to my last breath to find who did this! Even if you don't." He continued to rant, calling upon Jesus to give him strength and assuring us that the good Lord would smite his enemies down.

"I think it's time for me to go, Chief," I said. "I don't need another official complaint on my record."

Wilbur smiled and told me not to worry, that he'd handle Dilly.

And then, just at the right moment, Mike Willis arrived with his CSI team. I told Dilly that we had the situation in hand and asked him if he had anywhere to go while the forensics team was at work in the house. He said he didn't, but that he would get a hotel room.

That's awful, I thought. *All alone in a hotel room after this. I feel for the guy, I really do.*

He disappeared into the house, I assumed to pack a few things. Willis checked in with me and also headed into the house, followed by four members of his team.

Lord, I hope we don't get another one. Willis is already stretched to the limit.

I turned again to Wilbur and said, "If we don't get something soon, and Dilly carries through on his threat, his accusations will stick, even if they aren't true. I'm sure you know how IA can be."

"That I do," he concurred. "That's why we do what we have to do, in order to stay safe and sane."

I nodded, somewhat dejected. "As I said, Chief, it's time for me to go." I clapped him on the back and headed to my car.

As I drove down the mountain into the city, I thought about the similarities between the two murdered women. Or lack thereof. They were as different as chalk and cheese. As far as I could tell, the only thing they had in common was they both went to the same church.

So much rage. So much violence. Whatever could they have done to generate so much hate?

So far, I had only two suspects, and neither of them seemed likely. And now I had to go face my nemesis, Henry Frickin' Finkle. Just thinking about it gave me a headache.

10

When I walked into our reception area at the Police Services Center on Amnicola that morning, I was more than a little surprised to be told by the duty officer that someone was waiting to talk to me.

I checked my watch. It was six-fifteen. *What the hell? Who would be here at this hour? Hah, I might have known.*

"Clemont Rhodes," I said, not offering my hand, walking straight past him to the elevators, "of the Chattanooga Gurgle." Yes, I was pulling his chain. It's the Bugle, not Gurgle.

He smiled a row of perfectly even teeth that must have cost the equivalent of a year of my salary: they almost blinded me with their whiteness.

"Nice to see you too, Lieutenant."

"Oh, yes, and why would that be, and what the hell are you doing here at this time in the morning?" I said, not waiting to hear the answer. I hated reporters.

I reached for the elevator button, but what he said next made me stop and turn to look at him.

"What can you tell me about the murder on Lookout Mountain, Kate?"

He blinked and continued to grin. It was creeping me out.

"What murder?" I asked. "And don't call me Kate."

"Please, *Lieutenant* Gazzara. I know that Mrs. Victoria Randolph was found dead in the family home early yesterday morning, murdered. Do you have any leads? Is the husband, Darby Randolph, cooperating with the investigation? Is he a suspect?"

"I don't know what you're talking about," I replied.

"Come now, Detective, the people of Chattanooga have a right to know. Victoria Randolph is a mother and wife, an active member of her church, a saint, so I hear. A regular Mother Teresa. What are you doing to bring her killer to a swift and final justice? Do you have any persons of interest?"

Geez, 'a swift and final justice'? What the hell has he been reading?

When I heard the word "saint," I squinted at the reporter.

"Who have you been talking to?" I asked. Stupid question. I already knew the answer.

"You know I can't reveal my sources, Detective," he sneered.

"What can you tell me, Detective? Or do you intend to keep secrets, as usual? If there's a killer on the loose, the people of this city need to be aware of the danger."

"Piss off, Clemont. I have no comment for the press. If you're looking for a juicy story, go talk to Detective John Tracy. He's about to break open something big. But take a little advice, don't just show up on his doorstep like you did to me." I cleared my throat. "He's Vice, and he has some nasty habits. Then again, if you play nice, he might have something for you."

"I'm not sure I'm interested in a drug case," Rhodes said. "Not when there's murder afoot on Lookout Mountain. Hmm, I like the sound of that," he said, more to himself than to me. "And you know," he continued, "how much the people love to hear about scandals among the rich and famous, how they love to see the elite one-percent get their comeuppance."

"Comeuppance?" I rolled my eyes. "Wow, where did that come from, Clemmo? And since when is a snoopy son of a bitch like you not interested in a story about drugs? Drugs mean sex, right?" I looked him up and down. "And you *do* look like a guy who enjoys—what should we call it—the seedy side of life. Didn't I see you out at Summit a couple of weeks ago, poking around the... Oh, never mind. I don't have time for this crap. Go talk to Tracy."

I reached for the elevator button.

"You can't rattle me, Detective, with your... innuendo."

"Wow, another big word. Who are you trying to impress, Clemmy?"

I looked behind him.

"I can't rattle you?" I smirked. "Maybe not, but she can."

I jerked my head at Janet, who was standing behind the reporter with a notebook in her hand. To her credit, she instantly slipped into character.

"You're a reporter?" she squawked, loud enough to gain the attention of every uniform on the floor as well as several secretaries. "Y'all know who this is, right? He's the media. Who the hell invited him in here anyway? Get him the hell out of here. We've got work to do!"

The press is never kind to any police department and, over the past several years, Rhodes had been particularly vocal in his criticisms of our department and of several unfortunate individuals. So, as soon as they realized who and what he was, a half-dozen uniforms advanced on him like zombies on a fat man. One had a Taser in his hand. It was almost comical to watch the cocky smirk fall from Rhodes' face.

"What the hell?" he howled at Janet. "Why did you do that? If I get hurt, you're gonna..." He didn't finish the sentence. Instead, he turned and hurried toward the exit.

"That was fun," Janet said as we rode the elevator. "Should we go and make sure he leaves?" Janet asked, her face morphing from angry scowl to cute young lady.

"No," I said. "Let him go. He was here because someone leaked the Randolph killing to him, and I want to know who it was."

"Wha-at?" Janet said. "That's not possible... is it? Unless it was Chief Wilbur, and I just don't see that. One of his officers, do you think, maybe? I hear tell that some of those reporters will pay big bucks for an exclusive."

I shook my head. "I don't think so... I need to think. Let's both go to my office."

I hung my jacket on the back of a chair beside my desk, flopped into my seat, set my phone and iPad on the desk, and opened my laptop, and that's as far as I got. I heaved a sigh, leaned back in my chair, closed my eyes, and nothing. I guess I'd been awake far too long, and then I realized I needed coffee, real coffee, not the paint-stripper from the incident room. Then I remembered something; I was supposed to get bagels on the way back to the precinct. I'd promised Janet.

I opened my eyes, looked at Janet and said, "Hey, I forgot the coffee. I can't drink the crap from the incident room. You want to run over to McDonald's and get us some decent coffee and bagels? My treat."

She grinned at me and literally jumped to her feet. "No," she said. "*My* treat," and off she went.

Wow, where the hell does she get her energy?

Then I got to thinking again, *No. I don't think any of Wilbur's guys are responsible for the leak. It's a small department in a high-value community. They get paid well enough... No, I think I know who it was that tipped Rhodes off.*

I must have sat there daydreaming for some fifteen minutes, or so, until Janet returned loaded up with a tray of four large coffees—two each—and a paper sack with four sausage and egg bagels therein—two each. *Good thinking, sister.*

She dumped the lot on my desk and sat down across from me.

"Did you figure it out?" she asked, grabbing a bagel. "Who's the leaker?"

"Maybe," I said, taking a sip of the strong, dark, life-restoring liquid. "But first things first. Tell me about Meryl Dilly."

She wriggled her backside in the chair, got comfortable, and began flipping through the pages of her first notepad; oh yes, she was now on her third. *I really must get the kid an iPad.*

"This is rather sad, LT—" Janet began.

"Hold that thought," I said, interrupting her and reaching for my desk phone.

"Hey, Jimmy," I said when the quartermaster picked up. "How are you, buddy? Great, that's good to hear... Yes, not bad, busy, but that's better than the alternative, right? Jimmy, I need a favor. My new partner, Detective Janet Toliver, needs an iPad. She's still scribbling in paper notebooks... You do? Oh yeah, used is good... An iPad Pro. Yes, sir. That will do fine. Thanks, Jimmy."

"You didn't need to do that," Janet said reproachfully. "I like my notebook."

"Tough," I said. "I need for you to get with the program. You can't record an interview with a friggin' notebook, and you can't share your notes, read and send emails, Google stuff. It's the way we do things, Janet."

"Well, okay, then. If you insist." She really did seem a little put out, but she'd get over it.

I nodded and said, "Meryl Dilly?"

"Yes, of course. Well, it seems that Mrs. Dilly is a cancer survivor —ovarian. She went into remission about nine months ago, after radical surgery."

"Lots of doctor bills?" I asked.

"Yes, but they had insurance. They're all paid up. Nothing in default. Not much debt, either. He makes good money. The company is sound, making a profit, and they're wealthy, as you might imagine, and that huge house is paid for—no mortgage. They'll be good to go when they retire."

"Well, *he* will be," I said after clearing my throat. "She's awaiting the good offices of Dr. Richard Sheddon."

Janet's face lost a little of its color. I figured she must have been contemplating her first autopsy, and I didn't blame her.

"So there's nothing out of the ordinary in their financials?" I asked.

"No, they're clean."

"That's about what I expected," I grumbled.

"But I did find something," she said. "It's not much, but it is, well, interesting."

She flipped the page of her notebook and looked at me from the corner of her eye.

"I like interesting," I replied.

"The two families, they both belong to the same church, the big one, the one where Marcie Cox said Victoria was working, the Church of the Savior."

"Yes," I said, "I know. Chief Wilbur goes there too. I think just about everyone on the Mountain belongs to that church."

"Right, but what you don't know is that Darby Randolph is listed as the church's attorney, and that both victims worked there, and that Connor Dilly donated the floor coverings. That must have cost him a fortune. Have you ever been inside that church?"

I shook my head.

"Well, I have. I went to a wedding up there last year. Would you believe the sanctuary can seat fifteen hundred people? Carpeting that space would have been a huge donation. And there's more: it seems like there might have been a little quid pro quo, because less than a week after the carpet was installed, Meryl Dilly was appointed the church's hospitality coordinator. What kind of a BS made-up job is that?" She looked at me. "Seems to me that both Mrs. Randolph and Mrs. Dilly were... well, I dunno. Bit of a coincidence, don't you think?"

"You mean maybe we need to talk to some of the congregation?" I said, smiling. "Is that what you're hinting at?"

It wasn't much of a lead, but hell, any lead is a good lead when you have nothing else.

"Yes, exactly," she said enthusiastically. "People who attend church talk to each other, open up to their friends, their pastor." She leaned forward in her seat. "Maybe someone knows something." And then she ran out of steam and slumped back in her seat.

"Yes, they might at that," I said thoughtfully.

11

I STOOD UP, YAWNED, STRETCHED, WALKED OVER TO THE WINDOW and looked out. The sun was up, and for a short while there were blue patches in an otherwise overcast sky, but it didn't last long. The blue soon disappeared, engulfed in a roiling mass of dark clouds that matched my mood perfectly. I was tired, cranky, and having a hard time staying focused. And, of course, it was at that moment that Assistant Chief Henry Finkle barged into my office, without knocking, as always.

"You," he said, pointing at Janet. "Out!"

She jumped to her feet, startled, and was gone before I had time to blink.

"What the hell—" I said, turning away from the window.

"Shut up and sit down," he snarled, interrupting me.

"And good morning to you too, Chief," I snapped. "I'll stand, thank you," I said, as I stepped forward, knowing that my extra four inches in height intimidated the hell out of him. It was a mistake, as I found out less than a minute later.

"Have it your way. You've been talking to the press, Lieutenant. Explain."

He stood there looking at me, smirking, staring at my chest. I was instantly embarrassed. I was wearing only a T-shirt, and I was sure he was checking to see if I was wearing a bra.

"Yes, I spoke to a reporter, Clemont Rhodes. I think you two know each other," I said snidely. "I told him to leave, and I had a couple uniforms escort him out of the building. Why? Has he made a complaint? Did they rough him up? If they did, he provoked them."

"Rough him up?" he replied, just as snidely. "From what I remember that's your forte, Lieutenant, at least according to Internal Affairs."

I rolled my eyes and said, "I've never laid a hand on anyone, ever, and you know it."

It wasn't the first time he'd provoked me by referring to my one run-in with Internal Affairs, and it wouldn't be the last; of that I was sure.

Some months ago, I arrested a creepy little shit with a record that filled a file folder six inches thick. He lodged a formal complaint against me, claimed that he didn't like "my tone," and that I'd used excessive force and verbally abused him. It wasn't true, and I denied it, of course, but it earned me an IA investigation which came down to my word against his. I lost, and it earned me a mandatory week off and a black mark on my permanent record, much to Finkle's delight.

"I'm disappointed in you, Lieutenant. Even a raw rookie knows not to talk to the press. He's another one you're sleeping with, I suppose. How many more are there... besides Starke? By the way, does his wife know you're screwing him?"

Finkle sniffled, put his hands on his hips, and straightened himself up, all five-feet-nine-inches of him.

"Perhaps someone should let her know..."

That did it. I felt my blood boil. How the hell I didn't slap his stupid face, I don't know. Good thing I didn't, because it would have totally screwed up what I was about to do next.

"Screw you, Henry," I said, not backing down this time. "I've taken all of the bullshit from you I can stand. You know damn well I didn't talk to that reporter. It was Victoria Randolph's husband, Darby, that tipped him off. No, I'm not sleeping with him, and I'm not sleeping with Harry Starke either—"

"That's enough, Lieutenant," he snapped, interrupting me.

"Damn right, it is," I said, picking up the desk phone.

"What are you doing? Put that phone down."

I ignored him, punched in the number and waited, staring at him, defiantly.

"Cathy, it's me, Kate Gazzara. I need to make an appointment to see Chief Johnston. Yes... No... As soon as possible."

I saw the color drain from Finkle's face. He turned and strode out of the office, slamming the door behind him.

"Three o'clock this afternoon is fine, Cathy, and thank you."

I ended the call and slowly returned the phone to its cradle, thinking, wondering... *Okay, Kate. You just crossed the line. You better have your damn ducks in a row.*

I smiled at the thought, nodded to myself, closed my eyes, and enjoyed the moment; it had been coming a long time.

12

"Yikes," Janet said when she returned to my office after my meeting with Finkle. "What was that all about?"

"That, Janet, was a typical review of my caseload." I yawned. "You ready to go take a peek at The Church of the Savior?"

"You betcha," she said enthusiastically.

Inwardly, I shook my head. The kid was as perky as a parrot. *Was I ever that excited about this job? I think I was... I must have been... when I was a rookie and partners with Harry. Before "Tiny" Finkle started bothering me.*

"Good. You drive."

We arrived at The Church of the Savior, an imposing structure, typical of the Southern Evangelical movement, half ancient Greek temple, half modern American courthouse. Think Supreme Court of the United States, but with a tall spire with a gleaming white cross at the tip. Huge windows lined the building, not the delicate stained-glass variety one associates with most Catholic churches, but crystal clear, sparkling behemoths, that on a sunny day, must have bathed the inside of the church with sunlight.

A pair of vast oak doors with a massive cross carved into the surface graced the front entrance. Not quite a cathedral, but it was indeed a church in the grand manner. I decided whoever designed the church wanted to be sure that both God and man took notice.

To the side, a two-story building attached to the main structure housed, I assumed, the church offices. A second building, as indicated by the sign out front, housed the primary school run by the church.

Janet parked the car, and we ascended the steps to the church doors. I grabbed one of the handles and tugged, then tugged again, but they were locked.

"Are they only open on Sunday, then?" Janet asked.

"I guess so, let's check around the back. Come on."

At the bottom of the steps, I noticed a tiny sign pointing the way to the church offices where we were confronted by a video doorbell. I thumbed the push and a tinny female voice I could barely hear asked how she could help us.

I introduced myself. Less than a minute later, an imposing woman, with an amazing bust that seemed to be at odds with the sweatshirt she was wearing, opened the door and smiled condescendingly at us.

"The po-lice?" she said, drawing the word out for emphasis. "And how may I help you?"

"We are hoping to talk to the pastor. Is he available?"

The woman stepped back, looked us up and down, then drew the door open for us to enter.

"This is about Victoria Randolph, isn't it?" she asked.

She was unremarkable yet kind of attractive, with a round face, tan complexion, and wire-rimmed glasses that made her look older than she really was. I estimated she was about forty years old, tall, almost as tall as me, and looked to be in good physical shape. Her heart-shaped face was accentuated by a pair of rosy cheeks surrounded by a wreath of lustrous brown hair that hung in gentle waves to her shoulders.

"What do you know about Victoria Randolph, Miss..." I asked.

"Karen Silver. Call me Karen, please. Miss Silver sounds so...

formal, don't you think? I'm the church administrator. Mr. Randolph called yesterday and told us the terrible news. Pastor Ed was devastated. He rushed right over, of course. I made the family a casserole. Who could possibly cook after such a traumatic event?"

Or eat? I thought but didn't say.

"Is the pastor available?" I asked. "We have a few questions."

"He is. If you'll wait here, I'll announce you."

The waiting area looked more like the lobby of a law firm than a church office.

"Look at these seats," Janet said. "They're leather."

She ran her hand over the loveseat and then the side chair.

"You sure they aren't fake?" I asked skeptically.

"I'm sure. My sister-in-law loves leather furniture," Janet said as she pressed the cushion of a seat with her index finger. "See how it wrinkles? That indentation will stay there. That's one way to tell if it's real leather." She leaned down and sniffed the armrest. "Yup. You can tell by the smell."

"I didn't know you had a brother," I said, wrinkling my nose as I watched her inspect the material. "Is he older or younger?"

"He's three years older than me," Janet said as she continued taking mental pictures. "He and Sarah have been married for almost five years. They live in Memphis."

I nodded, not really listening to her, and stepped out into a reception area even more luxurious than the waiting area. A pair of double doors stood wide open, so inviting to an inquisitive mind like mine, so I stepped into what was obviously the main office. Lined with shelves stocked with enough office supplies to keep the Pentagon in business for a month, I had to wonder what it was all used for. Filing cabinets flanked the bookshelves. Paintings of Jesus in various poses hung wherever there was a space: some of them traditional depictions that reminded me of Catholic school when I was young, others were more modern: bolder colors and geometric shapes reminiscent of works by Picasso.

There were two desks. One was covered with stacks of papers

and a laptop adorned with colored sticky notes, and three framed photographs of the same two cats: a tabby and one with black and white fur. That desk, no doubt, was where the erstwhile Ms. Silver served her masters, one in his office, the other in Heaven.

The other desk was vacant, the fifteen-inch MacBook Pro laptop thereon was closed.

"Hmm, that's an expensive piece," I mumbled to myself. *I wonder if that's where Mrs. Randolph worked?*

I turned around slowly, taking in the furnishings and the expensive books.

"No expense spared, is there?" Janet asked.

Before I could answer, Karen came hurrying in.

"Ah, there you are," she said, smiling brightly. "Taking in the sights, were you? Lovely, isn't it, the church? I do so enjoy working here."

She stretched out her hand, touched the empty desktop with the tips of her fingers.

"This is where Vicky worked. I put everything away when I heard... well, you know." She stared pensively at the MacBook, then said, "So, if you'd like to follow me, Pastor Ed is waiting for you. Can I get you anything: coffee, tea, bottled water perhaps?"

We both declined and thanked her.

She guided us along a wide, expensively furnished corridor to another huge oak door whereupon was a large brass plaque with the words "Pastor Edward Pieczeck" engraved in ornate letters.

Karen knocked three times, opened the door, and announced us as if we were entering His Majesty's royal chamber.

"Lieutenant Catherine Gazzara and Sergeant Janet Toliver."

I half expected her to complete the introduction with the words, "My Lord."

Pastor Ed rose to his feet beaming, his arms open wide, welcoming us into his sanctuary as if he was the Pope himself, only I was sure the Pope's office, if he had one, was nowhere as luxurious.

"Ladies, do come in. I'm Pastor Ed. What can I do for you?"

His voice was deep, resonant, and I could imagine him in the pulpit, pounding the podium with his fists, shouting halleluiahs and about hellfire and the Lord's wrath. He was around forty, fit—ripped, I think, would properly describe him. The cuff of his short-sleeved shirt hugged his biceps and stretched snuggly across his chest. He wasn't exactly in Arnold's league, but I mean, the man obviously worked out.

"Thank you for seeing us, Pastor. We'd like to ask you a few questions about—"

"About Victoria. Such a terrible thing, poor, poor woman," Pastor Ed interrupted.

"About Victoria Randolph and Meryl Dilly," I said, and watched as the color drained from his face.

"Meryl Dilly?" He swallowed and licked his lips. "What about her?"

"She's dead, murdered. Her husband found her early this morning," I said as I pulled my iPad from my bag. "Do you mind, Pastor? I'd like to record our conversation," I said while holding up the device and tapping the green icon to start it recording.

I smiled to myself as, out of the corner of my eye, I saw Janet opening her notebook.

"Yes, yes, of course, please do," he said, "and please... sit down."

We did, and I watched as he sank slowly back into the leather monstrosity that could only have been called a throne. *Hell, even Harry's chair is not that big,* I thought.

Harry? I hadn't seen him since that altercation, if you could call it that, with Nick Christmas and his private army. My hearing will never be what it was... But that's another story.

"Pastor, what can you tell me about Victoria Randolph? I understand you recently hired her to work in your office, is that right?"

The pastor sat, his hands clasped together on top of the desk, stared at me, said nothing, then seemed to come together with a start.

"I'm sorry, Detective." He blinked. "I had no idea about Meryl

Dilly. Oh dear, what is this world coming to? I have a feeling we're quickly approaching the end of days."

He took a deep breath and looked up at the ceiling, mumbling something I couldn't understand: a prayer maybe, whispering in tongues? Who knows?

"And yes. Victoria Randolph expressed an interest in working part-time in the office. She came in twice a week."

"What was her job?" I asked.

"She would just do a few things to help Karen. Filing. Stuffing envelopes or maintaining my schedule, that sort of thing. The congregation has grown so much over the past few years, thank the Lord, Karen needed the help."

"Was Victoria happy? Did she ever mention any problems at home?" I asked.

"Oh yes, she was very happy, and no, she never mentioned any problems at all. She was a devoted wife and mother." He placed his hands flat on the desk and spread his fingers. "She really was salt of the earth."

I was feeling myself cringe as the pastor said that. Everyone said it except the housekeeper.

"Would she come to you if she were having a problem?"

"Yes... well, I would hope so," Pastor Ed replied. "But now that you mention it, there was something I noticed when she first started working here. I don't think it means anything but..."

He spoke so quietly I had to lean forward to hear him.

"Victoria Randolph was a beautiful woman," he continued. "Some of the ladies in the congregation were envious of her."

"Really?" I looked at Janet who was listening and scribbling in her notebook.

"You know how women can be, Detective. You're a *beautiful* woman, yourself."

Are you freaking hitting on me?

He continued, "You no doubt have experienced the judgmental gaze from women who wonder how you attained the position you now hold. There is a reason the serpent approached the woman in the garden first." He gave me a sad expression like "Oh, you poor woman."

Holy shit! What the hell?

"No, pastor, I didn't sleep with the chief, if that's what you're implying. I earned my promotion by working hard and closing cases," I replied quickly.

"Oh, please, Lieutenant. I wasn't implying anything. I wasn't suggesting that at all. Please forgive me if I've offended you. I certainly didn't mean to."

I looked hard at him. He stared right back at me. There was something about that stare that was unnerving.

"Who was it that had a problem with Victoria?"

"Oh, I don't want to name names." He smiled sheepishly. "Gossip is one of the devil's favorite tools."

"You brought it up, Pastor. I need the names, please."

"I'm sorry, Lieutenant. In all confidence I...well, I can't."

"You do realize we are investigating the homicides of two members of your church?" Janet interrupted. "Murder is one of the devil's tools, too."

"Yes, Detective, that's so true." He'd recovered his composure, leaned back in his chair and steepled his fingers together.

"The Randolph family," he said, smiling benignly, "has been an important part of this congregation since our inception. Victoria, however, joined us only after she married Darby. It was only recently that she approached me, stating that she was looking for a way to serve. I suggested she come work in the office, and she seemed happy with the idea. For the short while we had her, she was an absolute joy."

"Salt of the earth, yes," I said dryly, "so I've heard, many times over the last forty-eight hours. You said it yourself." I cleared my throat. "Tell me about the Randolph family, Pastor. Did they accept Victoria?"

Pastor Ed took a deep breath and laid his palms flat on the desk again. "Eventually, yes, I do believe they accepted her, although it was rather rough sailing at first."

"How so?"

"Well, Victoria wasn't from around here, you know. She didn't come from—well, let's just say her family wasn't as affluent as was the Randolph family."

He smiled, showing his teeth, and then I got it: his smile reminded me of a prominent politician.

"You know how these Southern families are, Detective." He grinned innocently. "Lineage is very important. The Randolph family is proud of theirs."

"So you don't think they were pleased that Darby married Victoria then?" I asked.

"I think they believed she was after the family name and... the money," he admitted. "But you know, I can't say I ever saw anything in Victoria that wasn't absolutely genuine. Unfortunately, jealousy and envy can cloud a person's judgment. And I do believe that several members of the Randolph family, and indeed some of my flock, are victims of the green-eyed monster. It's really a shame."

"Did you ever see anything strange while she was working at the office? Any strangers dropping her off or picking her up. Anyone you didn't recognize lurking around? You know how a pretty girl can become the object of unwanted attention." I smirked.

"As I'm sure you well know," he said slyly. "But no, not that I know of. Well," he said, rising to his feet, "I believe I've answered all of your questions."

"Not yet, Pastor. What can you tell me about Meryl Dilly? She was also a member of your church."

I watched Pastor Ed as he appeared to re-center himself. He took a quiet, deep breath, squared his shoulders and sank slowly back onto his throne.

"Meryl was a very fine woman. I am so sorry to hear of her passing. She was a lovely woman... and had been the hospitality coordinator here at the church for years." He swallowed hard, and his eyes darted around the top of his desk like he was searching for something.

"Are you all right, Pastor?" I asked.

"I'm afraid I have to close this interview," he said. "This is all so very shocking. I feel I must consult with the Lord. He will show me the way, guide me, and Mr. Dilly must need me now."

"Of course," I replied, somewhat taken aback. "But you will make yourself available, I'm assuming. Either Sergeant Toliver or I will be in touch. Or perhaps it would be easier for you to come down to the Police Service Center on Amnicola to talk to us?"

"Whatever is easiest," Pastor Ed stuttered. "I really must ask you to leave now. I will be happy to answer any questions you may have, but not now. Not now."

He rose again, looked first at Janet, then me, and then the door. As if on cue, it opened to reveal Karen Silver. She looked happy and accommodating. But I have to admit that the hairs on the back of my neck stood up.

How the hell did he do that? There must be a button under his desk.

I grabbed my iPad, closed the cover, stood, and said, "Thank you for your time, Pastor. We'll talk again soon."

I extended my hand. He took it, weakly. The power was completely gone from his grip; his hand was moist with sweat.

We stepped out of the office, and Karen pulled the door closed behind us.

"This is such a terrible turn of events," Karen said in a whisper. "I don't know if this is any help to you. I'm sure Pastor Ed didn't mention it, but we've been having a problem with our groundskeeper."

"No. He didn't," I replied, looking at Janet.

She quickly retrieved her notebook and began to write.

Karen led us to the front door, looking over her shoulder at Pastor Ed's closed office door.

"God forgive me for breaking the pastor's trust, but Marty Butterworth, he's been our groundskeeper for several years," Karen said quietly, conspiratorially. "He does good work when he's sober, but the Lord sees fit to test him. And he really doesn't always cope well, and there's been some talk. He watches... the ladies."

I stared at her, inwardly shaking my head. "This Mr. Butterworth, did he know Victoria?" I asked, skeptically.

"He knew her husband, and he knew Mr. and Mrs. Dilly, but..." Again, she turned her head and looked back toward the office. "I can't say anymore. I really can't. I need this job. I live alone, you see. But I thought you should know." She pulled the front door open and held it for us. "God bless you both and keep you safe."

"Thank you, Karen." I handed her one of my business cards. "If you think of anything else that might help us, please give me a call."

She nodded but looked down at the ground as she shut the door behind us. We headed back to the car and climbed in.

"That was one weird interview," Janet said. "Did you notice how the pastor acted when you brought up Meryl Dilly? That was a strange response."

"Yes, I noticed, and it was, especially since he seemed so comfortable talking about Victoria... You know," I continued thoughtfully, "there was a moment when I had a feeling he was hitting on me."

"You did? Well he did get a little personal about how you got your job, but hitting on you? Can't say I noticed."

I buckled my seat belt, and Janet pulled the cruiser out of the parking lot. Thoughts swirled in my head about the case and my upcoming meeting.

"We need to head back to Amnicola. I have an appointment with Chief Johnston at three, and I need to prepare." I looked at her, "Aren't you tired? We've been up almost the entire night. I'm frickin' exhausted. How come you have so much energy?"

She laughed. "I don't know. I'm excited, I guess. I'm sure I'll fall over as soon as I get home tonight. Okay, so when we get back to

Amnicola, I'll run a background on Marty Butterworth and see what I can find out. And I have a funny feeling about... well, I thought I might run one on the pastor too. What do you think?"

"You read my mind." I yawned and closed my eyes.

13

It didn't take long for me to gather together what I needed for my interview with Chief Johnston. I was done and ready an hour after we arrived back at Amnicola, a little after one o'clock that afternoon.

Janet went to lunch and then to work on her background checks. Me? I didn't want another run-in with Finkle before my meeting, so I left the building and spent a pleasant forty-five minutes on the deck of the Boathouse, drinking coffee, enjoying the view, and thinking... and that was a mistake. Suddenly, I was filled with doubt and the enormity of what I was about to do... and I almost didn't, do it. But the more I thought about it, the more I knew I had to.

So, reluctantly, I went ahead with the next part of the plan. I called Sheriff White. He'd mentioned more than once that he'd love to have me on his team. That was the back-up plan if what I was about to do went wrong and I had to walk away from the Chattanooga PD. That done, I drank what was left of my coffee and drove back to the Police Service Center.

It was ten minutes to three when I parked my car at the rear of the building. I grabbed my laptop from the seat beside me and walked confidently, so I thought, into the building. The Chief's suite of offices was two doors down the corridor and on the left. I opened the outer door and walked inside.

"Good afternoon, Cathy."

She had the phone to her ear, but she nodded, smiled, and pointed to a chair. I sat down, feeling like a schoolgirl awaiting an interview with the school principal which, in a way, I suppose I was.

Cathy finished her call, disconnected, tapped a button on her console, and said, "Lieutenant Gazzara is here, Chief."

She nodded, though of course the Chief couldn't see her, and set the phone back in its cradle.

"He's waiting for you, Kate. You can go on in."

I'd known Police Chief Wesley Johnston for many years. I can't say he was a friend, or even a sympathetic boss, but he was a fair administrator. I knew he would listen to what I had to say. Yes, he would listen; how much good it would do me I wasn't sure. Well, I was prepared for the worst, hence my call to Sheriff White.

Johnston was seated at his desk but stood when I entered.

"Please sit down, Lieutenant," he said, indicating a chair in front of his desk. "Now, tell me, what can I do for you?"

He was in uniform: the blue shirt pressed to perfection, the four silver stars in each of his collar tabs glinting under the artificial lighting. He was a big man... No, he was larger than life with a large head, bald, shaved, polished. The Hulk Hogan mustache was pure white and perfectly trimmed, and the man had an air about him, not quite arrogance... no, he was confident, supremely confident. I never, ever felt really comfortable in his presence, something I think he actively cultivated.

So I sat down, my laptop on my knee, and I took a deep breath and began.

By then, he was seated too, leaning back in his chair, elbows on the armrests.

"I wish to lodge a formal complaint against Assistant Chief Henry Finkle."

I paused, looked at him. He didn't even blink, just looked stoically back at me.

"Go on," he said.

This is not going to be easy, I thought. *Ah, screw it.*

And, quite suddenly, the heavy weight lifted, and I relaxed.

"I've had it, Chief. I can't take his crap anymore. I don't deserve it, and I won't stand for it. I'm done. Either you get me out from under him, or you can have my gun and my badge, right now."

"Take it easy, Kate. Keep your weapon and badge. I don't want them. Talk to me."

"Sir, I'll let Finkle talk for me," I said.

I placed my laptop on the edge of his desk, opened it, took a thumb drive from my jacket pocket, inserted it, opened the file, and tapped play. Henry Finkle's voice sounded from my computer.

"I'm disappointed in you, Lieutenant. Even a raw rookie knows not to talk to the press. He's another one you're sleeping with, I suppose. How many more are there... besides Starke? By the way, does his wife know you're screwing him? Perhaps someone should let her know."

I tapped the icon and halted the recording.

"That, sir, is just the latest. I have more, many more, going back more than a year. The man has been trying to get me into bed with him even longer than that. I have it all recorded." I had to struggle to stop myself from tearing up.

"So, finally," I continued, "I... It's... over. Either he goes or I do. And I suppose that will be me. He is, after all, an assistant chief—"

"Stop it, Kate, before you say something you'll regret. How did you get those recordings?"

I looked down at my wrist, shrugged, took off my watch, and laid it on his desk.

"I tried the usual methods—iPhone, iPad, laptop, but he was too smart. Made me turn them off, so I used that." I nodded at the rather plain-looking man's watch lying on the desktop.

"It belongs to Harry Starke, a gift from the Secret Service. I borrowed it from him, more than a year ago. The recording equipment is in the trunk of my car."

"It was that bad, huh?" He looked at me.

Is that sympathy I see in his eyes?

He picked up the desk phone, tapped an icon on the screen and said, "Henry. Come in here, will you?"

Two minutes later, the door opened and Finkle sauntered in.

"Yes, Chief. What can I do for you?'

"You can sit down. No, not there," Chief Johnston said as Finkle moved toward the couch by the wall, "There." He indicated the seat next to me, in front of the desk.

That's a first, I thought.

The Chief tapped another icon on the console and said, "Chief Finkle, I must inform you that this conversation is being recorded. Lieutenant Catherine Gazzara has indicated that she wishes to lodge a formal complaint of sexual and workplace harassment against you. Do you have anything to say before I accept her complaint?"

"Say? Hell, yes, I have something to say. It's bullshit. She's a lunatic. I've never—"

"*Stop!*" Johnston said loudly. "Lieutenant, please play for the assistant chief what you just played for me."

I tapped the play icon.

"I'm disappointed in you, Lieutenant..." Finkle's voice seemed to echo around the room, at least to me it did.

I turned my head to look at him. His face was white, the muscles of his jaw rigid. I didn't know if he was angry or scared and, frankly, I didn't care.

"That's... that's just..."

"Just the tip of the iceberg," Johnston finished the sentence for him. "She has more, Henry, much more, going back many months."

He swung around in his seat. "How, did, you—"

"That doesn't matter," the Chief interrupted him. "It's what you did that matters. What do you have to say for yourself?"

"I want my FOP representative present before I say another word."

Johnston nodded. "That, of course, is your right." He leaned forward and placed his hands on the edge of his desk, then reached out and tapped the off icon on the console, and said, "But before we do that, I should warn you that if you turn this into a formal IA inquiry, and should the outcome not be in your favor, it will result in your dismissal from this department for cause. And I can assure you, from what I've heard, that's exactly how it will end. She's got you by the balls, Henry, so is that really what you want?"

He tapped the on icon and started recording again.

"We can handle this situation one of two ways, Chief Finkle," Johnston continued. "Lieutenant Gazzara no longer wishes to work for you, and I can't say I blame her. I, personally, no longer have confidence in you as a leader in this department. That being so, I offer two options. You can either take a demotion or early retirement. Which is it to be? I suggest you leave now. Go home and think about it. I'll see you in this office at nine o'clock sharp tomorrow morning."

Holy crap! That, I didn't expect.

Finkle sat still, stiff, his jaw working, eyes blinking. Then he stood, turned on his heel, and walked out the door, slamming it behind him.

"That work for you, Kate?"

I didn't know what to say, so I didn't say anything.

He smiled benignly at me and said, "Do you think I didn't know what was going on? I did. Let's just say there's someone else in the department that's got your back, kept me up to speed. The problem was, there was little I could do about it, other than chew Henry's ass, not until you made a complaint, gave me something to work with." He chuckled, then said, "Go on, get out of here, Kate. Go back to work. I need results on the Lookout Mountain cases."

And I did.

14

"ARE YOU ALL RIGHT?" JANET SAID AS WE TOOK THE ELEVATOR down to the ground floor. "You look really tired. Would you like me to drive you home?"

"No. I'll be fine. Go get some rest. I'll see you tomorrow."

"How did your interview with the Chief go?"

"Fine," I said, not wanting to talk about it. "He said he needed results, and quickly." It wasn't a lie, and I wasn't prepared to talk about what had just happened—with Janet, or anyone else. In fact, I was still overwhelmed by the outcome. My problem was solved... or was it?

Surely, he wouldn't accept a demotion... Oh, dear God, I hope not.

Janet left and, as I watched her go, I half regretted not taking her up on her offer; I could barely keep my eyes open. So I sat behind the wheel of my car for several minutes, the engine running, wondering if I shouldn't get one of the uniforms to drive me home.

Nope, right now the only company I need is my own.

I rubbed my eyes, rolled down all the windows, turned on the AC, and pulled out of the lot onto Amnicola.

Ten minutes later, I was parked out front of my apartment

wondering how the hell I'd managed to get from point A to point B. Have you driven from one place to another and when you arrived, had literally no memory of the drive? That was me that evening. I sat in my car, freaked out because I didn't remember a damn thing.

Wow, Kate, that's freakin' scary.

"Hey, baby," I said as I opened the door to my apartment and scooped Sadie Mae into my arms. "Were you waiting for me?"

The little chocolate-colored wiener dog was my attempt at having a semblance of a normal life. And who doesn't appreciate some unconditional love when you arrive home? I certainly didn't have time for a man in my life, even though that would be nice, someday.

Sadie Mae came to live with me after her owner ended up in jail, put there by me. At the time, we both needed a new friend. Believe it or not, the little dog was instrumental in putting away a sadistic murderer and his accomplice. You may remember the Saffron Brooks case...but that's another story.

Sadie Mae? She came home with me. I still have her. I managed to cure her of her addiction—nicotine: she loved to chew cigarette butts—and she is now the sweetest little friend I ever had, other than Harry Starke, of course.

"But we don't talk about that, do we, Sadie Mae?" I said as I picked her up and set her on my lap.

She licked my chin and struggled to climb higher up my chest. "Okay, okay. That's enough." I put her down, scratched her behind the ears. She seemed happy with that and trotted off to a square of early evening sun shining in through one of the living room windows. She circled the chosen spot two times then flopped down, stared soulfully at me, and closed her eyes.

I was ready to do the same. I changed her drinking water, added a half-cup of kibble to her empty bowl, and headed to the bedroom. I stripped off the sweaty T-shirt and jeans, showered, and crawled into bed, naked as nature intended. I stretch luxuriously between the cold sheets and... that's the last thing I knew.

It was a little after one a.m. when I woke to find Sadie Mae curled up next to me on the bed. That was a big no-no, but I let it slide. I stroked the soft fur on her back. She grunted, rolled over, little legs sticking up, and I rubbed her tummy. I looked at the bedside clock: I'd been asleep for almost seven straight hours; good enough. I was wide awake and going to stay that way.

I showered again. I stood under the scalding water, hoping it would wash away the trauma of what happened in the Chief's office. It didn't, and much as I tried, I felt no sympathy for Henry Finkle. He pushed me to the edge, but I turned on him and tossed him over into the abyss.

Screw him. He brought it on himself. What will he do, I wonder? He's too proud to take a demotion, isn't he? I wouldn't, and if he does? What a disaster... that doesn't bear thinking about.

I got out of the shower, toweled myself off, and pulled on sweats. Then I slipped Sadie Mae's harness over her head, attached the leash, grabbed my Baby Glock and slipped it into my pants pocket. Two minutes later, we were outside and enjoying the quiet of the night. The air was cool. I could see my breath. I would have liked to run, but that was out of the question. Sadie Mae's little legs had to work hard enough as it was just to keep up when walking.

I lived in an apartment in a gated community, so it was safe enough to be out alone in the middle of the night, and besides, I had my Glock, so I was able to let it all go, relax under the stars, and think. I thought about Finkle—I couldn't help it—and I thought about the case, and how wonderful it was going to be without him breathing down my neck, and I smiled. I also thought about the two victims and wondered why I hadn't had a call from Doc Sheddon.

I didn't check my messages yet. Maybe he did call. I put my hand in my pocket, feeling for my iPhone. *Crap! I've left the damn thing at home. I'd better head back.*

As soon we were back inside, I grabbed my phone and, sure

enough, there were several messages, one of them from Doc Sheddon's number.

"Kate. It's Doc. Call me when you get this message, please."

I looked at the clock. It was two in the morning. Doc's message was timed at five after eleven that evening. I didn't hear the phone ping; must have been dead to the world.

I thought for a minute, wondering if I should call at that hour in the morning. I shook my head. If he called that late, he needed me. I dialed his number; he answered almost right away, and I felt guilty when I heard his croaky voice. I'd woken him up.

"Sorry, Doc," I said. "My sleep schedule is all off track. I thought I'd better return your call." I winced as I spoke, expecting him to grumble. I know I would have had I been awakened at that time of night.

"No, Kate. I'm glad you called. I knew I was going to have to do double duty with your homicides. Finished up with my young friend and then went home to await your call. Can you meet me at the office? Mrs. Randolph and Mrs. Dilly are waiting for us."

"I can. I'll be there in twenty."

"What about your young side-kick?" Doc asked.

"I'll let Janet sleep in," I said. "She put in a lot of hours yesterday. And I don't know how well she'd handle her first autopsy at three in the morning."

We hung up, and I headed for the bathroom. I washed my face in cold water, brushed my teeth, found a clean pair of jeans, a brand-new white blouse I didn't really want to wear, and put my hair back in a ponytail. Finally, I settled Sadie Mae down in her own bed, refilled her water bowl, left a note for my dog sitter, grabbed my Glock 17, badge, and wallet, and headed again out into the night.

15

THE HAMILTON COUNTY MEDICAL EXAMINER'S OFFICE WAS AN unimposing, anonymous building set on Amnicola Highway just a couple of blocks from the police department. I'd lost count of the number of times I'd stood across from Doc and watched as he violated the one-time home of some poor soul sent too early to meet his, or her, maker.

I parked at the rear next to Doc's BMW. The doors were locked so I had to knock. I knocked. I rang the bell. I knocked some more.

Come on, Doc, damn it.

"Cool your jets, girl!" I heard Doc shout from inside as he came to let me in. "You'll wake my guests," he said as he opened the door.

"Sorry, Doc... Would you like to tell me why we're doing this in the middle of the night?" I asked.

He sighed. "We've got a busy night ahead of us. They brought in a student early last night, a girl, pretty young thing. Opioid overdose coupled with alcohol. Our Mrs. Randolph and Dilly will take us well into mid-morning, and I must get the young lady done as well. It's not like we haven't done this before, Kate, you and I. I think we work quite well together, don't you?" he said.

He led me back along the corridor to the examination rooms. There were just two of them: one on the left and one on the right: two autopsy tables in each room.

Doc swiped his badge in front of a black pad on the wall, a security protocol for opening the door on the left. A little light turned green, and a loud click echoed down the corridor. We entered the anteroom and suited up.

"Let's start in the order of introductions. First, Mrs. Victoria Randolph," Doc said, picking up the clipboard that dangled at the end of the autopsy table.

He pulled the sheet down to expose Victoria's dead naked body. I have to admit it: I winced when I saw the damage.

The skin was a bluish-gray color. As far as I could see, the poor woman didn't have so much as a pimple anywhere on her body, nor any cellulite.

I snapped on a pair of blue latex gloves and parked my ass on a tall metal stool on the opposite side of the table to Doc, close to Victoria's head. Since I was there merely to observe, there was no reason for me to stay on my feet.

"Female," he began, speaking for the overhead mike that was recording the procedure. "Caucasian. Age thirty-one." He used his thumb to pull open an eyelid. "Blue eyes. Blond hair." He looked down at the measure fixed to the edge of the table. "Five-feet-eight and one-half-inches tall. He glanced at the readout from the scale beneath the table. "One hundred and nineteen pounds three ounces."

He inspected the fingernails, collected scrapings and clippings, then examined the body for trace evidence of which he found none, at first.

"No tears in or around the vagina; no signs of trauma. But... hmmm..."

"What have you found?" I asked, rising to my feet as he grabbed a pair of tweezers from the tray at the side of the table.

"Maybe nothing. Victoria's husband has dark hair. But, we'll know soon enough," he said as he carefully lifted a single hair from her pubic area.

I sat down again, already bored to distraction by the droning of his voice and the slow pace of the work.

"Victoria Randolph died of blunt force trauma to the head several minutes, I should say, before she was stabbed. The stab wounds were inflicted postmortem... Six times, she was stabbed. What with I have no idea. I've not seen their like before. Anyway, they certainly aren't what killed her, although any one of them certainly would have, had they been administered before the killer deemed it fit to beat the living daylights out of her head. Such... unnecessary violence. One blow would have been quite sufficient."

Some people found Doc's morgue-ish sense of humor to be insensitive. But you only had to spend five minutes with the man, and you'd know that wasn't the case. He offered the kind of comic relief only a brother ME or a cop could understand. He didn't make light of the tragedy in front of us because he was cold-hearted; quite the opposite, in fact. So, if you can, try to imagine being in the morgue with not one, but two murder victims. A little levity can help a lot in such circumstances. I've seen strong men, Detective Tracy included, turn away and throw up at the first incision.

"I had a hunch that might be the case," I said. "There was so little blood.

"Ye-es," he mused, his face mask close to her head. "If you look here, you can see the indentation of the blunt instrument." He took a set of calipers from the tray along with a small metal ruler and set about measuring the wounds, scribbling notes as he spoke.

"I believe this to be the first blow. It came from behind and her left. It is the largest. Deepest. She didn't know what hit her, literally."

I looked carefully where Doc was pointing. It was obvious Victoria's skull had been cracked open. It was misshapen, and even I could see the indentation.

"If I had to guess she was struck with a crowbar, or possibly a nail bar, the kind roofers use. You see this arched indentation?" he said as he pointed his finger to a dark blue swirl on the side of her head. "One of her lesser injuries. It looks like the curved end of a crowbar to me." He adjusted the light from his visor to better illuminate the bruising.

"If you say so," I replied.

"The assailant hit her on the back of the head, killing her, but as her body fell, he kept on hitting her, and continued to do so until she landed on her back. But that wasn't enough. He drove the pointed end of the crowbar, or nail bar I would think more likely, into her chest." He pointed to the multiple stab wounds.

"I count five distinct blows to the head," he continued with about as much emotion as the local weatherman. "With multiple secondary blows overlapping. No less than seven. There are six stab wounds to the chest. The good news—as if there is such a thing in a case like this —is she was already dead before she received the second blow to the head. After that, she didn't feel a thing, poor girl."

"What kind of person could do something like this, Doc?"

"Unfortunately, dear Kate, there are many, always have been, always will be.

"So the answer is," I said, smiling, "you don't know."

"Right. I don't speculate about such things because it is a futile exercise to which there is no definitive answer. Now, please allow me to continue. I don't want to be all night." He consulted the wall clock and said, "Oh dear, it seems I already have been."

I smiled and said, "You saw the crime scene, Doc. There was very little blood in that laundry room. That, I don't understand. It should have... well, it would have looked like the Dilly's living room."

"You are absolutely right, Kate. She was indeed moved after the attack. That laundry room wasn't where she died. We were able to find some trace evidence. Not a lot. I haven't gotten anything back from the lab yet. It's still too early," he said dryly.

"Time of death?" I asked.

"Sometime between the hours of ten and midnight on the sixteenth, probably closer to midnight."

"That's a pretty tight window," I said. "Could be helpful."

"It could indeed."

"I wonder if Mike Willis found anything?" I said. "Though he would have called me if he'd turned up anything significant. Still, I'd better check in with him first thing when I get to the office. What else, Doc?"

And so it went, for another ninety horrifying minutes as he delved into what once had been Victoria Randolph's vital organs

Finally, he covered her with the sheet, stepped away, and said, "Carol will close her up in the morning."

Carol Oates being his assistant.

"So," he said, rubbing his still gloved hands together. "A quick cup of coffee, I think, then on to round two, Meryl Dilly. Ready?"

"No, I don't think so, Doc. One is more than enough, unless you can't do without me."

"I understand completely, my dear." He looked again at the clock. "Carol will be in soon, in about thirty minutes in fact. Let's have some coffee, and then off you go... You know, I hate being alone in this godforsaken place."

Now that did surprise me. I looked at the clock. It was almost seven. *My, how time flies when you're having fun.*

"Well, okay then," I said, "but I need to use the restroom first."

"Very good," he said. "I'll meet you in five."

He pulled off his gloves and tossed them into the hazmat container. I did the same and then stepped into the yellow lights in the hallway.

When I exited the ladies' room, Doc was already waiting for me at the far end of the hallway holding two large porcelain mugs.

"When I'm here at this hour, I brew the good stuff. No Folgers for us this morning, Kate. This is Dunkin' Donuts house blend," he said, handing one to me as I approached.

"Doc, if you weren't married, I'd whisk you away to paradise."

"Ah, Kate, my love, I don't think I could handle that kind of paradise, but answer me this," he said as he led the way into the tiny reception area. "Black or cream and sugar?"

"Black, of course."

"Then our love can never be. I have to have cream and sugar."

He held the door open for me. I chuckled and sat down.

16

It was almost eight o'clock that morning when Carol arrived. I stayed with Doc until she did, and then I headed home to clean up, and by that, I mean to shower and change for the fourth time in twenty-four hours. That being so, it was just before nine-thirty back at the Police Service Center when I closed my office door behind me; a fat lot of good that did. Barely had I sat down than there was a knock at the door.

"Got a minute?" Mike Willis asked as he stuck his head inside.

"I was just about to call you," I said. "Yes, come on in. Take a seat. You have good news, I hope."

"Nope, not really, but we're not finished yet," he said dejectedly. "There's a lot of trace evidence but, except for two small fibers we found in the laundry room at the Randolph scene, and four more on the section of hardwood floor at the Dilly scene, none of it is foreign to the crime scenes. Same with latents; plenty of them, but none that can't be accounted for."

I leaned forward in my chair to ask a question, but Mike answered it before I had a chance.

"And before you ask, yes, we did print the housekeeper and the two husbands to eliminate them... or not, as the case may be. We're still working both scenes, but so far, we've not found a single fingerprint that shouldn't be there, including the Randolph's house-keeper's. The blood at both scenes appears to belong to the victims; no anomalous drops or smears; that according to preliminary typing. I'll know for sure when we get the DNA results back. Sorry... By the way, I understand Doc found a pubic hair on the first victim's body. Let's hope it's not the husband's. We could do with a break."

"Yes, me too," I said. "What about the fibers, any footprints?"

"I'm thinking they're carpet fibers. But I wouldn't get your hopes up. Even if they are, they probably came from somewhere in the home, homes. I'll let you know exactly what they are when I've completed a mass spectrometry analysis. I'm having Arty Moor gather samples of the carpeting in both houses for comparisons." He paused, then continued.

"Footprints? None at the Randolph scene. The Dilly scene seems promising but, as I said, we're not yet done with either scene, so I'll let you know."

I leaned back in my chair. This wasn't what I was hoping to hear.

"So, once again, I have two major crimes, obviously connected. Well, I won't know that for sure until I hear from Doc. And I have nothing to go on. Darn." I picked up the phone, buzzed Janet, and asked her to join me.

"Okay, Mike. Thank you. Call me if you need me."

He nodded, rose to his feet, and stepped to the door, stood for a moment, then looked at me, hesitated, then said, "What's this I hear about Chief Finkle?"

My heart skipped a beat, I looked up at him, startled. "What about him?"

"He's been demoted to captain and moved over to Narcotics. You didn't know?"

"No, I didn't know," I replied, truthfully, my stomach doing cartwheels.

"What the hell happened, I wonder?" Mike said. "He was your boss. You wouldn't happen to—"

"I've no idea," I lied, cutting him off.

I was just about to dig my hole a little deeper when Janet tapped on the door and came in.

Whew, that was a close one. Demoted? Narcotics? I can't imagine he's happy with that... Not quite what I'd hoped for, but at least he's out of my way... I hope. What the hell was he thinking taking the demotion?

"Hey, Janet," Willis said. "How are you? All good, I hope."

She nodded, held the door for him.

"Later, Kate," he said.

Janet closed the door behind him.

"Sit down, Janet," I said.

And she did, in the seat Mike Willis had just vacated.

"Well," I said, leaning back in my chair and lacing my fingers together behind my neck, "we're off to a grand start: two friggin' murders and nothing concrete to go on."

I was interrupted by my iPhone buzzing and vibrating across the top of my desk. I grabbed it before it could fall over the edge, looked at the screen, and smiled hopefully.

"Hello, Doc," I said. "Long time no see. Hold on a sec. I'll put you on speaker so Janet can hear."

"Ah, Janet," the tiny voice said. "My very favorite detective. Well, except for you, of course, Catherine."

"That's enough schmoozing, Doc," I said. "What do you have for me?"

"Ah, but you're a cold-hearted woman, Detective. Well, first, you might be surprised to learn that Meryl Dilly was extremely fit for a woman in her late forties. You might want to check gym memberships in the city."

That was something worth looking into.

"I don't recall Victoria Randolph being particularly ripped," I said.

"Oh but she is, was, though it's not so easy to see. Mrs. Randolph was a rather... I want to say voluptuous, but she wasn't at all fat... well-endowed, shall we say."

"Yes, I assumed they were real," I said.

"They are indeed, Kate, as are Mrs. Dilly's though she is not quite so well blessed... Let's get on with it, shall we?"

"Please," I said. Making a mental note to have Janet check out the local gyms.

"I found seminal fluid in Mrs. Dilly's vagina so she engaged in intercourse within twenty-four hours of her death, which means it could very well be her husband's so let's not get too excited yet."

Or maybe not, I thought.

"As to her wounds, we have three primary blows to the head. Victoria only had one. I'd say that means the unfortunate Mrs. Dilly saw it coming. That could explain why the assailant had to use more force.

"Now we come to the wounds on her chest and torso. There are five stab wounds to the chest and abdomen. One shattered the sternum, a second fractured the fourth rib on the left side and penetrated the left lung, the third fractured ribs five and six on the right side of her chest. The two wounds to the abdomen are horrific. So much force..."

I noticed Janet going paler by the second.

"The assailant must have used both hands to drive the weapon completely through the soft tissue of the abdomen into the carpet. The entry and exit wounds are roughly one inch in diameter, consistent with a crowbar."

"That's intense," I muttered.

"Indeed," Doc said. "Rage, fury. Whoever did this to our two ladies was more than a little ticked off."

"So nothing new then?" I asked. *Stupid question!*

"Other than the seminal fluid, no."

I shivered, felt kind of lost. Then I shook the feeling off. *Get a grip, Kate. This is what you do.* I told myself. *It's just another murder case. There will be clues. There will be someone somewhere who has a hunch or was a witness to something out of the ordinary. Someone will eventually remember something. And I will find those clues, those individuals.*

At least, that's what I told myself. But there was something niggling at the back of my subconscious, something I couldn't get a grip on. There was a sinister twist to it all that I just couldn't put my finger on.

"I can tell you that the assailant was right-handed," Doc said, interrupting my thoughts. "And by the way the blows sliced across Meryl's face, the attacker got sloppy; maybe he was in a hurry," Doc said.

"You keep saying he," I said. "Could it have been a woman?"

"It's possible, I suppose, but..."

"I understand," I said. "It would have taken a lot of strength to inflict those head wounds: even more to drive what is essentially a blunt instrument through to the floor. But Meryl Dilly fought back, right?"

"She did. There are defensive bruises on her forearms. One of the blows shattered the radius and cracked the ulna in her left arm; she must have been trying to protect her face."

"Meryl Dilly was killed first," I said. "Her body had been there for how long?"

"Yes, about two and a half days ago, judging by the livor mortis and rigor," Doc said. "And there is already signs of insect activity. The little devils find dead meat quickly. So sometime in the late afternoon of Tuesday the sixteenth, about eight to ten hours before Mrs. Randolph."

"Little devils," I muttered, to myself.

"How's that?" Doc asked.

"Nothing. I spoke with the pastor of The Church of the Savior and, well, he had some things to say about the devil, too."

"I'll bet he did." He chuckled, but not loudly.

"DNA?"

"Just the fluid. I'll let you know what the lab says as soon as I hear from them."

"I'd appreciate that." I cleared my throat. "Mr. Dilly was away, said he left early Tuesday morning, so the semen is probably his. If it's someone else's... well, I should get so lucky. Anyway, I'll have Janet check it out." I looked at Janet and nodded.

She nodded back, scribbled a note.

I started to think out loud. "If it's his, and he left home when he said he did, he's in the clear. If not..."

"I don't envy you, my dear," Doc said.

"Neither do I, Doc. Neither do I."

"I have no doubt the same weapon was used on both women," he said. "Other than that, what the connection is, well, I'll leave that to you, the experts."

"There's no such thing as experts in this job, Doc," I said as I flipped absently through my files. "There are just people like me, too stupid to stop digging even when the dirt keeps falling back in on 'em. But you know what? We get there in the end, and I'm damned if I'll let this one beat me."

I paused, then said, "I need to let you go, Doc. You'll send me a copy of the files tomorrow? And would you please put a rush on those lab submissions?"

"Oh, of course. You know how they jump whenever I ask them to hurry."

I felt the sarcasm even over the phone.

"You're a peach, Doc. Call me when you have the results." I disconnected, set the phone down on my desk, and leaned back in my chair and closed my eyes.

Truthfully, I was disgusted. I had a lot of information, but without something to connect it to, it was useless. I sighed, checked my watch—it was almost eleven.

"Janet," I said, "I've been up since three. I need a little me time."

"Since three? Why didn't you call me?" She caught the look I was giving her and said, "Oh, okay. I'll go check out Mr. Butterworth, the airlines, and the gyms."

I waited until she'd closed the door, then transferred all of the photographs I'd taken of the two crime scenes from my iPhone to my laptop. Then I spent the next two hours going through them, sending those I thought might be useful to the printer. With the pictures in hand, and having heard from Mike and Doc, I began to set up my incident board.

The Meryl Dilly crime scene was a bloodbath. Even so, as far as I could see, there were no footprints or handprints. Instead, there were tracks in the blood across the carpet. Whoever did this, he made sure to smear the gory mess, and any possible footprints. I smiled.

Nice try, asshole, I thought. *Somehow, somewhere between the body and your vehicle, you left either a bloody footprint or handprint, and Mike is a genius... If you did, he'll find it.*

I gave up, went across the road to Mickey Dee's for coffee and a burger. It was while I was there, stuck away in a corner, hopefully out of sight from any other member of the department who'd had the same idea as I'd had, when thoughts of Henry Finkle popped into my head.

Narcotics? What's up with that? Why the hell didn't the Chief just get rid of him? The thorn may no longer be in my side, but it's still around, waiting for a chance to stab me in the back.

Then I had another thought, something the Chief had said: *Let's just say there's someone else in the department that's got your back... But who could that be? And why didn't he come to me?*

It was a puzzlement.

I finished up, went back to my office, worked on my board some more, handled a couple of routine tasks, returned several calls, and then headed home. It was still not quite three in the afternoon, but what the hell? My bed was calling me for a nap. Saying I was beat from my haphazard schedule the last few days would be an understatement. I needed some rest, not to mention I was more than a little frustrated at the lack of progress in the murder cases.

A long weekend of mulling over the details stretched before me. I knew I was going to drive myself crazy if I spent it at home with just the dog. So, being the resourceful problem-solver that I am, I called Lonnie Guest and invited him to dinner.

He'd been my partner on the force for years. Who better to discuss the cases with? We'd made a good team, and I missed our coffee sessions going over the details and connecting the clues. At one point we'd tried dating. Although we hadn't worked out as a couple long-term, we were comfortable together, could be ourselves and relax, and still had great physical chemistry.

As a bonus, he's a great cook and... when he left just before six the following morning, I was, in every way, feeling more like my old self again.

17

I'D BEEN IN MY OFFICE NO MORE THAN A COUPLE OF MINUTES when Janet arrived with her arms full of files, notebooks, and printouts.

"Morning, LT," she said brightly, looking fresh as always. Her red hair swept back into a ponytail added color to her freckled face. She was wearing skinny jeans, a white tee and white tennies. If it hadn't been for the Glock and badge on her belt, she'd have looked like a teenager heading to class. "Hope you had a nice weekend. Did you get some rest?"

"Good morning, Janet and yes and yes. How about you? You look happy. What have you got for me?"

"Me too, but I worked on Saturday, and I have some good news. I almost called you. Hold on a sec'."

She sat down in front of my desk, shuffled through some papers and extracted a printout from the criminal database and handed it to me. I didn't recognize the mug shot at the top left, but I did recognize the name.

"Okay," Janet said, having sorted her pile into neat little stacks. "Martin "Marty" Butterworth age thirty-nine. Seems he has quite a history," Janet said, raising her eyebrows and leaning forward slightly. "Two years in the county jail for aggravated assault in 2007. He beat up a girl who turned him down for a date. In May 2010, he was arrested for assault, but the victim refused to press charges. He hit the guy upside the head with a pool stick; they were playing eight ball, so it seems, and our Marty doesn't like to lose. And he has three drunk and disorderlies, including one resisting arrest."

"Nice. What a charmer."

"But here's the kicker," Janet said, wiggling in her seat. "Also in 2012 he killed a dog, beat it to death with an iron pipe. He told the arresting officers that it had rabies, but they could smell the booze on him and didn't buy the story." Janet leaned back in her seat.

"And he's working at the church?" I shook my head.

"To be fair, all of these charges happened six or more years ago, when he was in his twenties. Alcoholic. I could, if I were a compassionate person, say it might have been the ignorance of youth."

"And how old are you, Janet?" I asked, finding the irony in her last statement.

"I'll be twenty-five in January, but I'm not stupid," she replied defensively.

"Never said you were." I smiled. "You got an address for him."

"Yup." Janet sat up straight. "Oh, and you'll like this: he has a connection to both Victoria Randolph and Meryl Dilly."

As you can imagine, my eyes widened, it was music to my ears.

"Oh, really. Do tell."

"Turns out that Mrs. Dilly had a couple of encounters with Butterworth. Seems he was a tad bit, let's say, inappropriate." Janet held up her thumb and forefinger about an inch. "Must have grabbed her ass or something. Anyway, it turned out that Darby Randolph was doing some pro bono work for the church, and he offered Mrs. Dilly some legal advice and Dilly filed for a restraining order against Butterworth. A temporary order was granted, and he was to stay at least one hundred feet away from Mrs. Dilly at all times. The temporary order, however, was not made permanent. Apparently, Meryl didn't turn up for the court date."

"Good work, Janet. Hmm, so we have motives for both murders then. Butterworth has an ax to grind with Randolph and Dilly. What about Connor Dilly's alibi?"

"It's good. He was on the seven-fifteen flight to Memphis out of Lovell Field on Tuesday morning."

"Did you check the gyms?"

"Yup. Both Meryl Dilly and Victoria Randolph were members of the Fit for Life gym on East Brainerd Road. I haven't been down there yet. I quit on Saturday at four-thirty, and well, I took Sunday off. I was bushed. Sorry, LT."

"Don't apologize. I don't blame you. We both needed a break. I'm surprised you worked at all. Thank you for that. At least now we have something to work with. How about we go pay Marty Butterworth a visit? Oh, and by the way: no more of those damn notebooks. Use this from now on." I handed her the iPad Pro that Jimmy had, sometime after I left on Friday afternoon, left on my desk with a note, "For Detective Toliver. User and password are..."

She took it, opened the case, looked at it, sighed and said, "I already have one, at home, but thank you. This is a better one."

IT WAS A LITTLE AFTER EIGHT-THIRTY THAT MORNING WHEN WE headed out to Marty Butterworth's home. He lived alone in a small split-level in North Chattanooga. There were iron bars over the basement windows and the front screen door. The gravel driveway was dotted with weeds growing up through the stones, though the grass in front of the house was neatly trimmed and the house itself was freshly painted and seemed to be in good shape. The address was spray painted in white on the black mailbox, and there was a beat-up, red Chevy 1500 pick-up truck in the driveway. I pulled up behind it and shut off the engine.

"Ready?" Janet asked.

I nodded before she pounded on the bars of the security door. From inside the house, we heard some shuffling around. But for several seconds, no one came to the door. Janet knocked again.

"Marty Butterworth?" she called out. "Chattanooga police. Come on and open up."

"Ah, shit," a male voice growled.

After a little stumbling around, the sound of glasses or dishes being collected and moved, the sound of a security chain and dead-bolt being unlocked, the front door opened and an unseen pall of cigarette smoke mingled with a hint of marijuana billowed out and enveloped me.

Gross, and he's living in this? It's enough to kill him.

"Yeah? What?"

Marty Butterworth struck me as a man who was not living up to his potential. He appeared to have slept in his clothes. He was maybe six feet tall, very fit and muscular, wearing a pair of khaki pants and a white T-shirt. They weren't dirty, but he did look disheveled: his hair was messy but without even a hint of gray, prominent cheekbones from good bone structure, soulful brown eyes, and he had a five o'clock shadow that might or might not have been worn intentionally.

Wow! Put this man in a suit and tie and he'd be a knockout, handsome.

"Mr. Butterworth," I said, making sure he could see the badge on my belt. "I'm Lieutenant Gazzara. This is Sergeant Toliver. We need to talk to you. Can we come in?"

"Well, I uh," he stuttered, looking over his shoulder. "The house-keeper didn't show up on her usual day."

"That's okay," I said. "We need to talk to you about your job at The Church of the Savior. A... Ms. Karen Silver suggested the we talk to you."

"Karen?" he said. He took a deep breath, smiled slightly, then nodded, stepped forward, unlocked the barred door, and held it open for us to enter.

I was surprised at how neat the inside of the house actually was. Furniture was old and worn, but good quality. The couch where Marty routinely sat had obviously seen better days, but the floor was clean and uncluttered and, aside from the cigarette butts and crumbs on the coffee table in front of the couch, all of the flat surfaces were also free of clutter and dirt. A solitary picture of Jesus adorned the wall behind the couch, and a sixty-inch TV on an antique sideboard faced it. The only anomaly was the two longnecks half hidden behind the chair next to the couch.

Janet, with her hand on her weapon, walked through to the rear of the home.

"Shall we sit down?" I asked as I took my iPad from my shoulder bag.

"What the hell is she doing?" he asked. "What's this about?"

"As I said, we need to talk to you about your job at the church."

He shrugged, muttered something I couldn't hear, nodded, waved his hand in the general direction of the couch, sat down in a recliner next to it, and grabbed a pack of cigarettes from the coffee table.

Janet joined me on the couch. I informed Marty Butterworth that I would be recording the interview and entered the usual date, time, and so on for the record, and then I began.

"Is there anyone else in the house, Mr. Butterworth?" I asked.

"No. Just me." He coughed the cough of someone who smoked... a lot.

"Mr. Butterworth, I understand that you are the handyman at The Church of the Savior. Is that correct?" I said.

"That's right. I'm also the gardener. I've been there for about six years." He took a long drag on his cigarette.

"Then you must know the people who attend the church?"

"Some of them. Some of them speak to me, say hello, that kind of stuff. Others don't. I'm not in their social league," he replied. "Look, are you going to tell me what this is about or not? Because if you're not, I don't want to talk to you."

"Mr. Butterworth, we are investigating the suspicious deaths of two members of the church," I said, closely watching his eyes.

He frowned, and said, "Oh yeah, and what's that got to do with me?"

"Do you know Victoria Randolph?"

"Everyone knows her. Hell, how could you not? She's hard to miss."

He took another drag then tilted his head back and blew out a long stream of smoke. I could only imagine the dirty movie scrolling through his mind at the thought of Victoria Randolph.

"Did you know her well enough to talk to?"

"Nope. I'm way out of her league. She never speaks to me. I'm just the hired help." He looked at me like a thirsty man eyeballing an icy cold glass of water.

"Does that upset you, make you angry?" I asked.

Marty chuckled. "Nope. I'm not her type. She likes the tall, dark, controllable types, and rich."

"What makes you say that?"

Marty rolled his eyes. "You've met her husband? That guy wouldn't wipe his ass without asking the Little Wife for permission. I heard that he almost lost his family fortune when he married her. But, you know what they say: what lies between those thighs..." He chuckled again, looked at me and said, "Why? Why the interest in Lookout Mountain's Barbie Doll?"

"She's dead, Mr. Butterworth. Murdered, last Wednesday."

"Last Wednesday? You're kiddin', right? How come there's been nothing on TV about it?"

I kept my eye on his body language and facial expressions. Did he already know?

"It's been kept out of the press, for obvious reasons." I looked directly at him, trying to keep my expression neutral, and continued, "How do you know Darby's family didn't want him to marry Victoria?"

He sucked hard on the cigarette, held it up in front of his face, contemplated it, then smiled and said, "That's the thing about a guy like me in a place like that. No one pays any attention to me. I was at the frickin' wedding. Who do you think cleaned up before and after them? Did you ever see rich people playing in someone else's yard? They leave a mess." Another drag on the cigarette as his eyes squinted for a moment.

"Anyway, I heard the mother of the groom, Mrs. Randolph, cursing Victoria's name to anyone who'd listen. She was sure Victoria was going to drain Darby's bank account and ruin the family name. 'White trash,' she said. 'Ruin the Randolph's stellar reputation,' she said. She forgot her own father-in-law was a crook, I guess." He winked at me before taking another long drag then leaning forward and scrubbing out the cigarette in an over-filled ashtray.

I leaned forward in my seat. "What about Meryl Dilly? Did you know her?"

"Meryl Dilly's dead too?" Marty asked, quietly, his expression deadpan.

Hmm... That's not the reaction I was expecting.

I nodded. Out of the corner of my eye, I saw Janet tap something into her iPad. *Good, she caught it too.*

Marty chuckled again. "Well now, ain't that something. Maybe now they'll get some decent music in that place."

"You think it's funny, Mr. Butterworth?"

"I don't know if it's funny or not, and you know what? I didn't give a rat's ass for either of 'em, but if you think I had something to do with the deaths of these women, you're barking up the wrong tree."

"It's funny you'd say that, Marty—it is okay if I call you that, right? Both women were beaten to death with some sort of blunt instrument. Didn't you, Marty, beat a dog to death with a piece of steel pipe?" I watched for the tell.

The smirk disappeared from his face. He narrowed his eyes, frowned at me, tilted his head slightly.

"That was a long time ago," he replied, so quietly I could barely hear him. "When I used to drink."

"You don't drink anymore?" I squinted back at him, quizzically. "These bottles," I leaned over the edge of the couch and picked one up. "They're not yours? Did someone plant them here?"

"So I drink a beer once in a while. So what? I barely drink at all, not since I started working for Pastor Ed."

His eyebrows nearly met in the middle casting a shadow over his eyes; it was a look of pure malevolence, and I almost shuddered.

"Wow," I said. "So you've been almost clean for six years," I needled, placing the bottle on the coffee table. "You've never fallen off the wagon, not once? You must be the hero at your AA meetings. You do go to AA? Lord grant me the serenity..."

He chewed his lower lip; I think I'd struck a nerve.

"Marty," Janet said then paused, stared at him for a couple of seconds, then continued, "There's an empty vodka bottle in your kitchen trash can. Let me guess, you had a buddy over, and it's his."

"That's right," he snapped.

"So," she said. "Let me ask you this: how much have you had to drink the past few days?"

I looked him in the eye, then at the bottle on the coffee table.

"That's none of your frickin' business. I answer to no one but Pastor Ed." He reached for the pack of cigarettes, flipped one into his mouth, his hands shaking slightly as he lit it.

"When two women at the place where you work turn up dead, beaten to a pulp, and you have a history of deadly violence, albeit just a dog, well, you can see how I might connect the dots," I said. "Were you drinking, Mr. Butterworth, during the past five days?"

"Yeah. I had a couple beers. So what? I don't drink on the job. I do my work, and I collect my check, and what I do with my money is none of your business." He took an angry drag and blew the smoke out his nostrils like a bull in a Bugs Bunny cartoon.

"You want to know what I think, Marty?" I said. "I think that on Tuesday afternoon—yes, I know you weren't at work that afternoon—I think you had 'a couple of drinks,' probably a whole lot more than a couple, got drunk, went to the Dilly's home, and you beat Mrs.

Dilly to death. She had a restraining order against you, so you had motive."

He stared at me, then said, "You know what, I don't have to take this shit from you. You're fishing, Lieutenant. You've got nothing. I'm not saying any more to you. You can go get screwed," he hissed.

"Where were you that afternoon, Marty?"

"Between two o'clock and six on the afternoon of the sixteenth," Janet added.

"I was mowin' the lawns at the Craven House. I do it every week, you can check. Now, I'm not answering any more questions. You've got the wrong guy. I know it's not like the cops to actually do their job, but do a little more digging, and you might find the guy who's really responsible."

"And who would that be, Mr. Butterworth?" Janet asked without looking up from her iPad. "What else did you observe while you were roaming the church grounds unnoticed?"

"Look," he hesitated, "there are tons of people coming and going, in and out of that place all the time. Not to mention the house calls Pastor Ed makes. More than any doctor ever would."

"Is that so?" I asked. "You're insinuating that the only person who ever gave you a chance; the guy who, even though you have a police record and a history of drinking, gave you a job, is a murderer?" I looked at Janet. "Can you believe this?"

She shook her head. "He is what he is."

"Screw you, both of you. Typical shoddy police work. I got a record, so I must have done it. Like I said, screw you. Now either arrest me or get the hell off my property."

"Is that what you think?" Janet chuckled. "You watch too much television, Marty."

"Get out of my house," he said through clenched teeth.

"What about Victoria Randolph?" I asked. "Did you kill her because you couldn't have her, or because her husband helped Meryl Dilly get a restraining order against you?"

I stood up.

"You're trying to make me angry," he said, smiling. "You think I'm that frickin' stupid? That maybe I'd take a swing at you with your partner over there just waiting to make a name for herself? She looks like she's still pedaling a freakin' bike with training wheels on it," Marty hissed, but remained seated.

Janet, to her credit, didn't bite. Instead, she stood up, put her hand on her weapon, smiled, and watched Marty fidget. She remained calm, and I couldn't help but think how Lonnie would have acted in this situation. *By now,* I thought, smiling to myself, *he'd have Marty by the scruff of his neck, politely suggesting that he apologize.*

"Mr. Butterworth, can you tell me where you were four nights ago? Did you see Meryl Dilly?" I pushed.

"I ain't going to tell you again, no more freakin' questions. Now push off."

"Stop it, Marty. Just tell us where you were and we'll leave you alone," I said quietly.

"And I said, get the hell out of my house. You did say you were recording this right? That works in my favor too, right?" He leered.

He was right. It did. So I picked up my iPad from the coffee table, tapped the off button, tucked it into my bag, and headed toward the door.

"We'll be in touch, Marty," I said as I opened the door.

Janet watched him carefully but said nothing. I was glad about that. She was a smart cop for as young as she was.

"I'll look forward to it," he sneered. "Have a great day, Lieutenant. You too, Annie."

Don't do it, Janet. Don't give him the pleasure.

"Annie?" She looked puzzled. "My name's—"

"Little Orphan Annie," he finished for her.

She looked confused for a second, touched her red hair, and then rolled her eyes.

18

"Wow," Janet said as she pulled the driver's side door shut. "What a creep." She sucked in a deep breath and shook her head as I fired up the engine and backed out onto the street. "I was sure I was going to have to go all John Wick on him. He was wound as tight as anyone I've ever seen."

"Yes, I think we may have something there, but a hunch and a couple of coincidences aren't going to get us an arrest. He's slick. Did you notice how he wouldn't tell us where he was? Either he doesn't have an alibi, or he's pulling our chain. He has motive for both killings, and if you add in the alcohol factor, it becomes a whole lot more viable. We still need means and opportunity and, as yet, we can't tie him to either scene. We're going to have to dig deeper."

"Do you think there was anything to what he was saying about the pastor?" Janet asked.

"Not really. He's probably just throwing it out there. Why, do you?"

"Well, he's close to both families, perhaps too close. And he couldn't wait to go visit... Oh, I dunno."

"Come on, Janet. That's what pastors do: offer comfort and support in times of need and loss. Sounds pretty normal to me."

"Okay," she said. "So here's another thought: why did Darby Randolph get in touch with the press? Was that his idea or was it Pastor Ed's? Did he tell Wonder Woman at the church to drop Butterworth's name in front of us, hoping that if the press lit a fire under us, we'd grab the first obvious suspect, Marty, and call it case closed?"

Geez, I thought, *who did you say has been watching too much television?*

"Wow, you do have a fertile imagination, Janet. I bet you think there was more than one shooter on the grassy knoll too?" I said, smiling as I concentrated on making the turn onto Hixson Pike.

"What? What shooter? What grassy knoll?"

"Forget it, Janet. I was just teasing."

"I'm just saying," she said, "that since our evidence against Butterworth is circumstantial, and we can't put him at either of the scenes, we might want to take a look at who is pointing us in his direction. I'm not saying Pastor Ed is a criminal mastermind, but—"

"I don't think it's Pastor Ed, Janet."

"And you know this because?"

"One, it's too easy, and two, my gut tells me it isn't."

"Huh," she said as she folded her arms. "I've heard that somewhere before."

"Always trust your gut, Janet. You'll find it's your best friend when you're in need. And, for what it's worth, mine has rarely let me down... well, once or twice, maybe," I smiled as I thought about it. *You're kidding, right?*

19

I parked my car at the rear of the Police Service Center, and we entered through the back door.

"Hey, Lieutenant," Reggie Green, the duty sergeant said as we walked past his desk. "There's a reporter, Clemont Rhodes, waiting to talk to you."

"Get rid of him, Sergeant," I said.

"Er... I can't. He said he had an appointment, so I figured you'd be on your way back, and I had Trask escort him up to your office. Sorry. Oh, and when you are done with him, Chief Johnston wants to see you."

I stared at him, dumbfounded. "You did what?"

He shrugged. "He had an appointment, LT, at ten."

"He most certainly did not. Next time, you call me before you allow a stranger into the building, much less my office."

"Yes, ma'am," he said. "I—"

"Oh, forget it, Reggie. I'll handle it. Come on, Janet. Let's see what's crawled out of the newspaper."

I walked silently to my open office door. Clemont Rhodes was sitting comfortably in front of my desk, his legs crossed, checking his iPhone. I eyeballed my files and my computer, but nothing looked out of place.

"What are you doing here, and where's Officer Trask?" I said quietly.

His head spun around quickly, startled.

"I... I told him he didn't need to stay on my behalf, that I had some emails to answer while I was waiting for you."

"So help me, Rhodes, if you touched any of my files, I'll lock your ass up and throw away the key," I said through clenched teeth.

"No! No. Detective, I swear. It isn't like that." He stood, turned to face me, put up his hands, still holding his phone, and smiled that broad, blinding smile at me. "I haven't touched anything. I was waiting to talk to you. That's all."

"You lied to the duty sergeant, so get the hell out

of my office, or I'll arrest you for trespassing on government property."

"Okay, okay. Look, you've got it all wrong. Just hear me out, please?"

I didn't answer. I just stared at him.

"Okay, so have you been watching the media over the past few days?" he asked. "You saw nothing, right? Nothing... nothing about the murder of Victoria Randolph. I'm playing ball with you, Lieutenant. I've sat on it but can't for much longer. Right now it's still under lock and key, up here." He tapped the side of his head with a finger.

I walked past him, sat down, swiveled my chair, and stared up at him. He'd had a haircut, wasn't bad looking, except for that slimy sheen of self-effacing journalistic integrity he exuded.

Ah, what the hell? Can't hurt to listen to the greasy son of a...

I looked at Janet and told her to give me a few minutes, then turned to Rhodes and said, "And why would you do that?"

"Can I sit down?"

I nodded.

"Well, there are two reasons..."

I circled my hand in the air for him to hurry and get to the point.

"First, I wasn't really sure that my source was telling the truth about everything."

"Why do you say that?"

"Have you ever looked at a person and thought they were trying to get you to do their dirty work? Like you are being used?"

"Uh, yeah. All the time."

"Look," he said. "I'll admit... Okay, I was excited when I got the call and, from what I heard, I was at first convinced the CPD was screwing up this case from the get-go. But after talking further with my source, I realized I was dealing with someone who, shall we say, has more than a passing interest in the outcome and was, well, trying to use me to put pressure on the PD."

I sighed and said, "What exactly do you mean?"

"I mean, I think my source might be a little too eager to point the finger away from him or herself. Does that make sense?"

"Mr. Rhodes—" I said.

"Please. Call me Clemont," he interrupted me.

"Mr. Rhodes, is your source a member of the Randolph family?"

"You know there's no way I can answer that. Look, I'll say this much: he was a big man yesterday, still is, even though he's retired."

"Holy shit. You're talking about Governor Randolph?" I almost whispered.

Clemont Rhodes didn't move, nor did he nod or shake his head, hell, he didn't even blink, just sat there rigid, frozen to the seat. I'd nailed it. And I was even more sure when I remember him referring to Victoria Randolph as a regular saint. Mother Theresa to be exact.

"Relax, Clement. I got it. So, what do you want for this little nugget of information? As if I don't already know."

He let out his breath and said, "What do all reporters want, Detective? Exclusive rights to the story."

He looked behind him toward my open office door, then scooted his backside forward to the edge of his seat and leaned his elbows on his knees. He couldn't get any closer to me without banging his head on the edge of my desk.

"See, here's the thing," he said quietly, conspiratorially. "I thought that maybe, if I was straight-up with you, we might be able to establish a foundation for future endeavors."

"Is that what you thought? And how, exactly, might that work?"

"Look, Lieutenant." He straightened up, folded his hands together, and placed them on my desk as if he was about to say a prayer. "I'm not like those others. I've got a moral compass."

I couldn't help it. I chuckled.

"I know, I know. You don't believe me." He fidgeted again. "But I know what it's like to be the outsider. Believe me when I tell you, I've got my eyes and ears on the street all the time; I know a lot of people, contacts, sources, who know... everything. You understand, right? They're none of them exactly monuments to society, if you catch my meaning, but..."

My right eyebrow shot up.

"Lieutenant, I've worked hard to develop my sources. I can be an asset to you. I can."

"And you are willing to share this fruitful world of limitless information with me for an exclusive?" I shook my head and shrugged.

"Not for just one exclusive. Look, I'll be honest with you, Lieutenant. I also write crime novels. My pen name is Jasper Crabb, and I'm pretty damn successful." He paused, looked me directly in the eye, and said, "I need more than just an exclusive; I need access to you, and the PD. I need authenticity."

Now I laughed out loud. "You've got to be kidding me. Do you think I am going to fall for a line like that? You almost had me, Rhodes. Almost. You've been watching too much TV."

Hah, where have I heard that line before? A freakin' crime novelist? Is he kidding me? Jasper fricking Crabb? I need to Google him.

"It's true," he said and sat back in the chair and folded his arms.

"I'll tell you what, Rhodes. No promises. I'll check out your lead.

If it pans out, we might have a one-time deal." I stood indicating that our little chat was over.

"That's all I ask." He extended his hand, but I folded my arms in front of me and nodded toward the door.

After he left, I was wondering if I wasn't walking into some kind of trap. *Time will tell, Kate. Time will tell.*

20

THERE WAS NO GETTING AROUND THE MEETING WITH CHIEF Johnston, so I gathered up my courage and went to meet my doom. Well, that's what it felt like.

Cathy, his secretary, wasn't at her desk so I knocked on his door and waited.

"Come."

I took a deep breath, opened the door, poked my head inside, and said, "Am I interrupting?"

"No, Lieutenant. Come on in and take a seat."

Hmm, he doesn't sound too bad. Maybe...

I closed the door behind me and sat down in front of his desk, crossed my legs at the ankles, folded my arms, and waited.

"I understand you had a visitor this morning, a reporter, and this isn't the first time he's come to see you. What's going on?"

"That's right, sir. Clemont Rhodes. Someone in the Randolph family tipped him off. I think I know who, but still, I need to do some digging."

"The Randolphs aren't your average family, Catherine. They're affluent, and well-connected, all the way up to and including the

White House. Members of that family sit on every board and committee in the tri-state area. We have to be very careful how we proceed."

"I understand that, sir, and you don't have to worry. I'll handle them gently—*the hell I will*—but I will handle the investigation diligently, just as I would with any other homicide case."

He assumed his signature pose, fingers of both hands steepled together at his lips, and stared at me.

"Chief," I said, "you can rest assured that I'm doing everything I can to get to the bottom of the two homicides as quickly as possible. They are linked: same killer, same MO. Doc Sheddon is convinced of it, and so am I, and we have a person of interest." I paused, took a breath, and then continued.

"Sergeant Toliver and I have just returned from interviewing a Mr. Marty Butterworth, the groundskeeper at the Church of the Savior. Both the Randolphs and the Dillys are members of that church. Butterworth has a beef with both victims, so he has motive. It's also possible that he doesn't have an alibi, but as yet, we can't place him at either crime scene. It's not much, I know, but it's a promising lead, and I intend to follow up on it."

And there I stopped talking. By the look on the Chief's face, I could tell he wasn't going to allow me to question the one-time governor of Tennessee, not without cause anyway.

"You need to mollify the Randolph family, reassure them that you're doing all you can to close the case quickly. Keep the lines of communication open, but do what you have to do, Kate."

The Chief looked at me across the table: there was a hidden message in those eyes, and I couldn't help but feel a wave of relief wash over me. He was practically giving me permission to interview the family.

"I understand, sir, and I'll do my utmost. You have my word on it."

"Good." The stare intensified. "You'll report directly to me. No one else. Understood?"

"Absolutely. Yes, sir."

"You can go, but be careful how you handle that reporter. I want no leaks, *none*."

I stood and turned to go.

"Lieutenant... I'll call you when I have more time," he said quietly.

I turned again and looked at him. He looked back at me, nodded, and then looked at the door. Again, I got the message, and I couldn't help myself. My eyes rolled on their own. I swear they did.

I went straight back to my office. I didn't even have time to sit down when Janet entered.

"Everything okay?" she asked. "When you left, you looked awful. What did the Chief have to say?"

"Everything is fine. He just wanted an update," I said. "You up for another road trip?"

"Absolutely. Where are we going?"

"We're going to talk to former Governor Alexander Randolph," I said, "but if anyone asks, we're going to the morgue."

"Stealth mode. I got it. I'll go get my jacket."

"Don't forget your iPad," I said dryly.

21

I rolled down the car window and told the guard at the security booth that I wanted to see the governor.

"You got an appointment?" he asked.

"Chattanooga PD," I said. "I don't need one."

I offered him my badge and ID. He grabbed them, waggled his hand at Janet, took her creds too, and studied them. He checked our badges and IDs like we were about to enter the Pentagon. He looked back and forth from the photos to our faces, lingering much longer on Janet. I couldn't blame him for that. She did, after all, look more like a kid than a cop.

Finally, satisfied we were who we said we were, he reentered the guard booth. I watched as he made the call.

"He ain't here," he said, leaning around the door jamb.

"Oh, yeah? How about we go see for ourselves?" I yelled back at him.

He talked into the phone some more then exited the booth, came to the car window, leaned down, handed us our creds, and said, "Drive on, go straight to the front steps of the house where you'll be met. Do not stop along the way."

Then he stood back, pressed a button just inside the door to the booth, and the huge iron gates swung slowly open. He waved us through and, in the rearview mirror, I saw him step into the middle of the driveway and make a note of our license plate.

"Wow," Janet said. "That guy was really serious. Better safe than sorry, I suppose... Holy crap, would you just look at that."

Holy crap indeed. I'd always known that Lookout Mountain was *the* high-status area in Chattanooga, but I had no idea just how high.

We followed the perfectly paved road through the woodland for maybe a quarter mile. Every tree along the way was lush and green.

"Will you look at that fricking house?" I said as the dazzling white mansion came into view.

It stood atop a slight rise. A traditional, Antebellum structure with two-story windows, each flanked by heavy black shutters. Gigantic white colonnades guarded the front of the home, supporting the roof over a vast front porch.

Holy cow, I thought. *Talk about Gone with the Wind. All we need now is Scarlett O'Hara and Rhett Butler.*

"I feel like I should have gotten dressed up for this one," Janet joked, looking down at her skinny jeans and white tee.

"You look fine," I said. "Ah, there's our chaperone, just like the man said."

I parked the car almost at his feet and we stepped out into the sunshine.

"Can I help you?" he said in a deep, resonant voice.

"You can." I smiled as I held up my badge and introduced us both. "We'd like to talk to Governor Randolph."

"I'm afraid Governor Randolph is not in residence." The man stood like a fricking statue.

Not in residence? What kind of talk is that?

"I take it you mean he's not in?"

"Exactly so, Lieutenant."

"Okay, then would you be so kind as to tell us where we can find him?" I said, still smiling.

"The Governor is at his club golfing. He left about two hours ago."

"Was anyone with him?" I asked.

He didn't answer.

"What's your name and function, Mister..."

"My name is Oliver, ma'am, and I'm the butler."

I stared at him, not believing what I was hearing. I looked at Janet. She didn't exactly roll her eyes, but I could tell she'd come close.

"Oliver? Okay, Oliver. We're investigating the murder of the governor's granddaughter-in-law, Victoria Randolph. Perhaps you could answer a few questions for me?"

He frowned, shook his head, then said, "I really can't."

"Oh, come on, Jeeves," I said, impatiently. "It's for the family for Pete's sake."

"The name is Oliver, ma'am and... Oh, very well then. Ask your questions."

"Can we go inside?"

"Follow me," he said, and with that, he turned and strode purposefully up a flight of stone steps too many for me to bother to count.

We followed him into the foyer and from there to a small parlor, where he invited us to sit and offered us a beverage. We sat, thanked him, but refused the offer.

"Now, ma'am. If I can be of assistance, please ask your questions. I'll answer them if I can."

"I'd like to get a little background on Victoria Randolph. What kind of person was she?"

He almost shrugged. I saw his shoulders begin to rise, but he caught himself and the shrug died almost immediately. *Interesting!*

"She was... a very attractive lady," he replied.

Very diplomatic. I can see where this is going, and it's not going to work. I need to give him a kick, jerk him out of butler mode.

I nodded. "I'm sure she was, and I understand your desire to be loyal to the family, but loyalty is not going to help me find Victoria's killer. I need to know what kind of woman she was, who liked her, who didn't, who hated her, how many people did she piss off and their names. Got it?"

He nodded, smiled, sort of, then said, "I have indeed. Victoria Randolph was a bitch, but on some levels quite likable. She had a wonderful sense of humor but didn't know when to keep her mouth shut and... well, she didn't hide her feelings. Told it like it was is the phrase, I think."

So, the house cleaner Marcie was right then.

"Did she have any enemies?" Janet asked.

"No, none that I know of. Well, none who would want to kill her. She did try to fit in and, for the most part, she did. In fact, I think she was quite popular among some of the members of the church. She worked hard at it, perhaps too hard."

"And you?" I asked. "What did you think of her?"

He thought about it, then said, "Mrs. Randolph and I didn't always see eye to eye. She... was not one to mingle with the staff."

"How about the family?" I asked, remembering what Marty Butterworth had told us. "Did she get along with them?

"Quite honestly, I don't think the Governor or his wife or anyone else with the name Randolph cared much for Victoria, with the exception of Mr. Darby, of course. He was quite besotted with her."

"Why didn't they care for her?" I asked.

This time he did shrug. "You must have heard the expression, 'You can put lipstick on a pig, but it's still a pig?'"

"Yes." I smiled. "I think I understand." I stood. So did Janet and Oliver. "I think I'll go and find the governor."

"That, Lieutenant, is not a good idea. He does not like to be disturbed when he's golfing."

"Well, never mind. We're in the neighborhood now, so we'll give it a shot."

THE VALLEY VIEW GOLF AND COUNTRY CLUB IS ONE OF THE most exclusive in the Tri-State area, if not all of Tennessee. It's not a huge facility; quite small as such places go, but what it lacks in size it more than makes up for in luxury. The golf course, designed by none other than Alister MacKenzie, has nine double greens and eighteen tees. The clubhouse is low profile, but luxurious. I heard membership was by invitation only and limited to one hundred fifty of Tennessee's most influential movers and shakers. The fees were a closely held secret, but I happen to know it's presently set at one-hundred-and-thirty-thousand dollars. I know that because August Starke, Harry's famous dad, told me; he just happens to be a member.

"That was helpful," Janet said as we drove back to the highway.

"Yes, and I'm beginning to see a pattern: Victoria didn't like the hired help," I mused.

"Well, if she comes from the wrong side of the tracks, that kinda makes sense," Janet said. "She was obviously sensitive about her roots."

"I suppose," I said, and we drove the rest of the way in silence.

Once past the electronic gates at the perimeter of the club property, we had to show our IDs at two more checkpoints. When we arrived at the main entrance, a young man offered to park the car for me, but I insisted on parking it myself, as close to the entrance as I could get.

"The last thing I want is to get thrown out of the place and then have to wait for the valet," I muttered, more to myself than to Janet.

"Do you plan on getting us thrown out of here then?" she asked.

"You never know, Janet; you never know."

"I'll tell you what, LT. I'd bet my pension that there are more than a couple members here who literally have skeletons buried in their backyards. I mean real ones, skeletons, bodies. It's what rich people do."

"That's a little prejudiced, isn't it? Not to mention morbid."

"Not really. It's just the law of averages. They get away with things because they can: one law for them, another for the hoi polloi," she said as we strolled up to the entrance.

"Hoi polloi? Where the hell did that come from?" I asked as we exited the car.

"Dunno. College, I think."

I shook my head. "Janet, you never cease to amaze me."

We were met at the door by the club vice president, a Mr. Humbert, and a security guard.

"I know who you are," the VP said, nervously. "And I must say that this is highly irregular, if not downright offensive, for you to come to a peaceful place of leisure for our members in order to harass them."

"We are not here to harass anyone, Mr. Humbert. I am pronouncing your name correctly?"

He nodded his gray head. He was a handsome older man. His tailored suit fit him perfectly, and his shoes were spit-shined. I liked him at first glance. There was something about him that made me think he was a savvy old cuss and could be trusted.

"We need to speak to Governor Randolph."

"Governor Randolph is out on the course, I'm afraid. You'll have to come back when he's finished his game."

I sighed and shook my head. "Can't do it," I said. "We're investigating a homicide. It is imperative that we speak to him... *now*."

I didn't say any more and my hunch about Humbert proved to be true; he got it, and within seconds, he had a young man running through the clubhouse and out of sight.

"Would you and the detective sergeant care to wait in the bar?"

"That might be a little less obtrusive. Yes, thank you, Mr. Humbert."

We might have been visiting royalty the way Humbert escorted us to two seats at the bar and informed the bartender that our drinks were on the house.

"Two iced teas comin' right up."

"This is some kind of swanky," Janet said, sipping her tea and looking around.

"Isn't it just?" I replied and smiled casually at the bartender.

"I haven't seen you ladies here before."

He took my smile as an invitation to talk. *Don't they always?*

Janet held her badge up, and I introduced us.

"Is there a problem?" he asked.

"No. Not at all," I said casually. "We're just here to talk to one of the members, Governor Randolph."

I watched the bartender's reaction. He bounced his eyebrows, smirked slightly, looked down, grabbed a lime and began to slice it.

"That was a strange look," Janet said. "Do you know him?"

"Oh yeah, I know him all right. I know all of the members." He continued to slice the lime.

"Anything you'd like to tell us about him?" I watched as he grabbed another lime and started in on it.

"Are you kiddin'? You tryin' to get me fired?"

I nodded. "Gotcha. So..." I looked at his name tag. "James, how about you just answer a few yes or no questions for me? Does Governor Randolph ever come in the bar?" I took a sip of my iced tea and watched the bartender's reaction.

"Yes."

"Does he ever talk about his family?"

"Yes."

"Has he ever mentioned his grandson's wife, Victoria?"

The bartender looked up at me, then across the room to see if anyone was paying any attention to him. He was also attractive, like his boss, Humbert, except that he was about twenty years younger. Tattoos peeked out from beneath the white cuffs of his shirt and there was a hole in his left earlobe but no earring.

"I think everyone in the clubhouse knows about Victoria. She's been here a few times," he said quietly.

"Hold on," he said. "I'll be right back."

He turned away and went to the other end of the bar to grab a bottle of something and chat for a second with one of the members. Then he was back in front of Janet and me.

"So," I said, "does he speak well of her?"

The bartender chuckled. "No."

"Really?" I asked. "Why do you say that?"

"He... She isn't exactly... Oh hell, he called her trailer trash. He even said it in front of Darby. Darby is his grandson."

I nodded, not really surprised, as he picked up another lime and began to slice it.

"What was Darby's reaction when he heard that?" I asked.

"He didn't like it, obviously, but he didn't say anything. He wouldn't, would he? The governor is a real badass, if you get my meanin'. You don't argue with him."

He topped up our glasses with more tea.

"Of course," he continued, "he never spoke like that in front of her. Uh-oh, here comes the boss."

"Excuse me, detectives," Humbert said. "Governor Randolph is waiting for you in the sitting room. Follow me, please."

I took a twenty from my shoulder bag and tossed it on the bar with a wink to the bartender. He took the money, graciously said thank you, and dropped it in the tip jar.

We followed Humbert through the bar with all eyes on us. I didn't feel particularly out of place—I'd spent a lot of time at Harry Starke's club, and it's also upscale, and if you've seen one country club, you've seen them all—but it was obvious we didn't belong at Valley View.

There was no doubt that within minutes of our arrival half the staff and most of the members knew that two detectives were on the premises. It wouldn't take but a few more minutes for someone to deduce we were there to see Governor Alexander Randolph.

Humbert knocked on a door, opened it, and led us into a small, comfortably furnished sitting room. Governor Randolph was standing at the window, his hands clasped behind his back, looking out over the golf course.

"Lieutenant Gazzara and Sergeant Toliver, sir."

Randolph nodded but continued staring out of the window. Humbert left, closing the door behind him.

As soon as the door closed, Randolph whirled around, his eyes angry and his fists clenched.

"What the hell do you think you are doing coming to my club?" he spat.

"Hello, Governor Randolph," I said reasonably.

It felt kind of funny calling him that, considering the old man hadn't set foot in the Governor's mansion in more than two decades.

"A little bird told me you didn't think the police were moving fast enough to catch your granddaughter-in-law's killer," I continued. "So we are doing everything we can to do just that. We have a couple of questions for you."

Janet introduced us as I got my iPad out, turned it on, and told him I'd be recording the conversation. That really pissed him off, especially when he saw Janet open her iPad too.

"I... You..." he spluttered, and then, with great effort, he seemed to get a grip on himself and slowly began to calm down. The angry, red flush on his face cooled to pale pink.

"I apologize, Lieutenant. Perhaps I was a little hasty. This... this... debacle has disrupted my entire family," he said. "Please, do sit down."

Randolph was in his early seventies, but still an imposing figure used to getting his own way. Tall, fit, strong, back straight, glittering blue eyes, aquiline nose, pure white hair receding slightly at the front... and, I'm sure, an intimidating SOB, to some, but not to me. I'd met his type before, and I'd never taken any crap from any of them; this one would be no different.

We sat in a semi-circle around a coffee table that, had it been taller, could have done duty as a small dining table: Randolph to my left, Janet to my right.

I set my iPad down, recorded the date, time, etc., and then I had a thought.

"Does playing golf clear your head?" I asked conversationally.

"Why, yes," he responded, sounding surprised, "it does. Ah, I see. You're wondering how I can play golf when my grandson's wife has just been murdered? What the hell else do you expect me to do, Detective, sit at home and mope? That's not who I am, young lady."

"I don't know, Governor," I said nodding. "I'm not sure how I'd handle such a situation myself. So, let me ask you this: how and when did you find out about Victoria's death?"

"I didn't want Victoria working at that church," he said, out of the blue. "She didn't need to work. It was just another way for her to manipulate Darby, get him to do what she wanted... He's weak, a weak man," he said quietly, almost as if to himself.

"Why do you say that?" I asked. The conversation seemed to have made a left turn, but far be it from me to interrupt the bird when it's singing.

"She wanted Darby to buy a building in Memphis, a rental property for God's sake. She had it in her head that she wanted to be a landlord; ridiculous. The girl was a complete moron, no business acumen at all. She was a gold digger, plain and simple, and no great loss to this family."

"Did you call her that, a gold digger, to her face?" Janet asked, her eyes wide with disbelief at what she was hearing.

"I did. Of course, I did. Darby is my eldest grandson. I expected great things of him. I expected... Well, unfortunately, he is, as I said, a weak man, and he fell under the spell of a pair of long legs and a pair of tits that... I'm sorry, please excuse my coarse language."

"We've heard worse, Governor. Go on," I replied.

"I told Darby he was not to buy that property. Being a landlord is a tough and thankless business. I told him to make Victoria focus on their home, and being his wife, have more children," he paused, shook his head, then continued.

"Not two days after that conversation, I get the news that Victoria is going to work at the church to earn money of her own." He nearly choked.

"Why would you disapprove of that?" Janet said. "A job, her own money, that would prove she wasn't a gold digger, wouldn't it?"

"Of course it wouldn't," the Governor spat. "That was *not* her motive. All she wanted to do was put pressure on Darby to buy her that damn rental property. Not only that, the woman was promiscuous and working at the church would have provided her with the opportunity to... well, let's just say she would have had access to the wealthiest men in the community."

"Promiscuous?" I asked. "You're saying she had an affair?"

He shrugged. "You'll have to ask Darby."

"No, Governor. You brought it up. I'm asking you. Who was she having an affair with?"

"I don't know that she was. I do know she was an outrageous flirt, and that she dressed like a damn floozy."

"That doesn't make her promiscuous, Governor," I said. "Aren't you being a little unfair?"

He sighed, then said, "Maybe I am... maybe I am. I don't know, Lieutenant. This whole business, it's unsettling. All I know is that if Darby got it into his head that she was playing around... Well, my grandson, being the weak, simple soul that he is, would capitulate and offer her the sky, moon, and stars just to keep her in line. She'd get her money pit."

"But that's your grandson's business and not yours?" Janet said.

"You're wrong," he said. "You have to understand. It was my money. Darby would have nothing if he was left to his own devices. My son, Michael, Darby's father, and my two daughters married well. They brought success and pride to the Randolph name. I have two grandsons and three granddaughters. One of the girls is married to a fine man, the son of a Texas oilman. The other is married to a doctor. My other grandson is at West Point. Darby, however, is an anomaly. He managed to find himself a piece of local trash to bring into the family."

His eyes were wide, icy blue, with not a hint of fatigue in them.

Oh yes, I thought, *he could have killed Victoria. He has motive. I bet he'd do anything to protect his family and reputation. And he's strong enough... But then there's Meryl Dilly. Why would he want to kill her?*

"I know what you're thinking," he said, jerking me back to reality.

He pulled his lips back in a sly grin. I've seen friendlier smiles on a shark.

"You think I'm a snob, a rich old man whose shit doesn't stink. Well, you're wrong. I'm just an old man who worked for every penny I have, and I don't see anything wrong with protecting my legacy and reputation. Victoria's gone, and I feel sorry about what happened to her, but I can't say that I'm sorry... she's no longer a problem."

Wow, what a cold-hearted son of a bitch. If that's what money does to you, you can keep it. Hmm, time to change the subject, I think.

"Pastor Ed told us that he visited your grandson shortly after Victoria's body was found. Did you, by any chance, see him there?"

The Governor wrinkled his nose, and said, "That man is too involved with his flock. He should stay where he belongs, in the pulpit. I don't like his church, and I don't like the way everyone's in everyone else's business and... well, never mind; it's not natural. I, myself, do not attend."

"But everyone who is anyone on Lookout Mountain is a member of the church," Janet said. "Why would you cut yourself off like that?"

He smiled. "I'm not running for office anymore, Detective."

"You were the Governor of Tennessee, a public servant all your life," I said. "You must have made a lot of money and a lot of friends over the years... good friends, friends who owe you favors."

"That's true. I did. What? Are you implying that I... Damn it, Lieutenant, that's outrageous. I resent your insinuation."

He swallowed hard, then said, "Yes, I wanted Victoria out of my family, but I would never have harmed her. Do you have any idea how this has affected my grandson? Do you? He's suicidal. I'd give every penny I have to bring her back to him, but I can't. I can't even give him closure. Only you and your people can do that. And it seems to me that you don't know what the hell you're doing. Whatever it is, it's not much. And you sit there and accuse me... *ME!* How dare you?"

"I didn't accuse you of anything," I said, easily. "I'm just doing my job and—"

"And nothing," he interrupted me. "You're doing nothing."

I looked him in the eye, thought for a moment, then said, "You know, Governor, I can understand your frustration, but I don't believe you when you say you're not running for office anymore. You're not so old. What are you, seventy-two, seventy-three? Not even as old as the president. You're the consummate politician, Governor. You can't help yourself."

He glared at me but didn't answer, which told me all I wanted to know.

"Your call to Clemont Rhodes, your attempt to put the squeeze on the Police Department wasn't a smart idea." I leaned forward and moved my iPad a little closer to the Governor.

"What's that phrase you politicians are so fond of?" I asked. "Oh, I remember: Never let a good crisis go to waste?"

The Governor scowled, clenched his teeth, and then said, "Is that what you think? If so, then you're mistaken. All I want is for you to find Victoria's killer."

"What do you think we are here for, Governor? A reference?" I chuckled. "I've heard that you aren't the only member of the Randolph family that disapproved of Darby's choice in women. How does your wife feel about it? Darby's father and mother? Have they asked for your help recently?"

"You obviously don't know who you are talking to. Detective Gazzara. I may no longer be governor of this great state, but I still have, as you so rightly noted, a great many influential friends. I will be calling Chief Johnston to inform him of this exchange. You really are something, Lieutenant. While a crazed lunatic is getting away with killing my granddaughter, you're wasting valuable time harassing me. What's that saying you have in law enforcement? Something about the first forty-eight hours, as I recall. I'm sure you're quite familiar with it."

He stood up. "We're finished here, I think. If you have anything else to say to me, you'll have to contact my lawyer... Oh, and one more thing," he said, taking an iPhone from his pocket. "I too recorded this interview. Good day to you both."

And with that, Governor Alexander Randolph turned and stomped out of the room, leaving Janet and me sitting there, staring at the door, then at each other. I couldn't help it, I burst out laughing.

I tapped the off icon on my iPad and sat back in my chair.

"Oh, my Lord," Janet said. "That was, like, *intense*. What do you think?"

"I think... that the chief is going to have a lot to say to me when I get back." I paused, then continued, "But, you know, I'm not convinced that the ex-governor didn't have something to do with Victoria's death. Think about it, if he is running for office, Victoria would have been one hell of a liability. Maybe he did call in a favor. But then, there's Meryl Dilly... Unless..." I scratched my head.

"Unless what?" Janet asked.

"Unless she was somehow collateral damage?" I asked as well as stated. "Or that she was killed to make it look like... Oh hell, now who's been watching too much TV? I must be losing it. That kind of crap just doesn't happen in real life." I looked at my watch and grunted.

"I guess we'll have to see ourselves out."

"LT," Janet said, "do you think he'll make good on his threat to call the Chief?"

"Oh, yes. Just as sure as I am that he's a lousy golfer and an even lousier governor. He's probably on the phone with him right now. People like Randolph never pass up an opportunity to toss their weight around."

I stood, tucked my iPad into my shoulder bag, and we walked out of the door and out of the country club.

I have to admit, I don't scare easily, but I had knots in my stomach when we walked into the PD that afternoon.

I guess he must have tasked the duty sergeant to call him when I returned, for no sooner had I entered the building when my phone rang.

"Gazzara! My office. Now!"

22

It was six-thirty that evening when I pulled into the parking lot of my apartment building. I was wiped out, and not just from lack of sleep; two hours in front of Chief Johnston will do that to you. Governor Randolph did indeed make good on his threat and called the chief. During my session in the chief's office, however, I got the distinct impression that the call had not gone all the Governor's way; Chief Johnston managed to get him to admit that he had, indeed, called Clemont Rhodes.

I thought long and hard about that meeting with the Chief and let me tell you, it was intense. No, I'm not going to go into detail... I can't. I promised myself I'd forget it, put it behind me, and that's what I've done. Let's just say that the old tyrant gave me a hard time for what he called "stepping over the line" during my interview with the former governor, and then assured me of his unwavering support, so long as I kept him in the loop, and leave it at that. So yes, when I pulled into that parking lot that Tuesday evening, all I wanted to do was take a shower, grab a bottle of red, and hide my sorry ass.

I found a half a bottle of Cabernet gathering dust on the kitchen counter and three slices of two-day-old pizza in the fridge.

"That will have to do it," I muttered to Sadie Mae as I scratched her behind the ears.

I didn't want to think about work for the next eight hours. Sadie Mae certainly didn't want to hear about my day, I was sure, so I showered, warmed the pizza in the microwave, poured the entire half bottle of wine into a pint mug, and we settled down on the couch. I ate pizza and drank wine; Sadie Mae just ate pizza.

I turned on the TV, flipped through a hundred offerings on Netflix before deciding to binge watch Alias. I love Jennifer Garner; she kinda reminds me of me... *Hah, don't I just wish?* The series was kind of out there, more fantasy than reality, but it captured our attention enough that Sadie Mae and I nestled together under a blanket for the next four hours. It was just what I needed, to escape from the rigors of life and the job. It was wonderful. *She really does remind me of me!*

I'd dumped my gun, badge, and phone on the coffee table in front of the couch next to the pizza and mug of wine. I wanted reminders of work out of my sight, but I also wanted them close at hand: force of habit. Police work is like a freakin' drug. Once you have a taste of it, you're hooked for life, and you can never fully let it go. You can slip away for a couple hours, fall into a deep sleep in front of the TV; no bad dreams, no mutilated women, no mangled bodies on silver tables in the morgue, just blackness... but then you're jerked back to reality wondering where the hell you are and how you got there.

So, when my phone rang at just after five-thirty that following morning, my eyes snapped open and I sat upright with a jerk and put my hands to my head.

Oh shit, my head.

I looked at the empty mug, shook my head—big mistake—and let the call go to voicemail.

I sat still for a moment, took a deep breath, scratched Sadie Mae's tummy, then stood up and went to the window: the sky was just beginning to lighten a little.

I turned my head and looked at my phone. The frickin' thing was a magnet. I couldn't help myself. I went to the table, grabbed the damn thing, swiped the screen, tapped in my code and put the phone to my ear.

"Hello, Lieutenant Gazzara," the male voice sounded so tired I could barely hear it. "This is Chief Wilbur. You don't know how sorry I am to have to disturb you at this time in the morning, but you need to call me. We've got another one."

Holy shit, no!

My mouth went dry. This was not happening. I dropped back down onto the couch and, in a daze, I called him back. He started to tell me, but I stopped him; there was no point. I took down the address and told him I'd meet him there as soon as I could.

I called Janet, gave her the news, the address, and instructions to meet me at the scene. And, for good measure, I contacted Chief Johnston.

"Thank you, Catherine," he said, not sounding the least bit sleepy. "Go to it. Be sure to keep me in the loop."

"Got it, Chief," I muttered and hung up.

I tapped the button on the coffee machine, took Sadie Mae outside for a few minutes, let her do her business, then gave her breakfast. Next, I took a two-minute cold shower, climbed into a fresh pair of jeans, tee, and leather jacket, grabbed my Glock, badge, and shoulder bag, wrote a quick note for my dog walker and dropped it onto the kitchen counter. I left my little girl sleeping comfortably on a blanket on the couch and, twenty minutes after receiving the call from Chief Wilbur, I was in my car, coffee in hand, driving west toward Lookout Mountain.

23

THE HOME I WAS HEADED TO WAS ON THE OPPOSITE SIDE OF Lookout Mountain from where the other two bodies were found. The victim, a Lucille Benedict, was a wealthy widow just forty-two years old.

As I drove, I called Doc Sheddon and asked him to meet me at the address Chief Wilbur had given me.

"We've got to stop meeting like this, Kate," Doc said. "My wife is already beginning to wonder about us," he joked.

"Tell me about it," I replied. "I'll see you in a bit." Then I called Mike Willis.

The house on Fern Lane was beautiful, of course. A faux, rustic, farmhouse built no earlier than 2000, it must have cost its owner a mint of money. The bright blooms of red roses and petunias were a breathtaking complement to the Confederate Gray color of the house. Old Glory waved proudly above the Tennessee state flag from a tall pole in the middle of the front lawn. The front door was flanked by miner's lanterns, old tin buckets and milk pails, all filled with more red flowers.

Chief Wilbur's cruiser and a second one were there, and an

officer I'd not seen before was standing guard at the entrance to the driveway. I flashed my badge and told him that my partner, the ME, and CSI were all on their way, and he waved me through.

When I arrived at the house, Wilbur was standing on the front porch talking with a man in shorts and a T-shirt. His feet were bare, but he was wearing a bizarre, incongruously large Aussie-type bush hat.

"Detective." Wilbur shook his head as he stepped down off the porch and came to greet me.

"Chief Wilbur," I said, offering him my hand. "For Pete's sake, tell me something good."

He shook his head. "The door's unlocked, but I haven't been inside yet, nobody has. I looked in through the window. From what I could see, it looks just like the others. Kyle Baker, there, found her." He turned his head to look at him.

"He's her neighbor. He was out early walking his dog when he noticed that the lights were on and decided to check on her. He knocked, got no answer so he peeked in the window, saw her lying there, and that's about it. He called us. I took the call and called you."

I heard a car approaching on the driveway. It was Janet. She parked behind my car, and I waved her over, gave her a quick rundown of what we had, and then asked her to interview Baker. The man was still standing on the porch looking like he'd just lost his best friend, which he may well have done. Wilbur and I donned Tyvek booties and latex gloves and we went inside.

The interior of the home was carefully and tastefully decorated. Every piece of furniture, every picture frame, every accent, even the covers over the heating vents, had all been chosen with care and deliberation. And there, center stage in the living room, lay the mangled body of Lucille Benedict, the right-side rear of her head caved in, cracked like a coconut, brain matter and blood pooled around her head and body. Even at first look, I could see she'd also been stabbed several times. Unlike the other victims though, her blouse was torn exposing a rather risqué black bra.

Now why, I wonder, would a widow be wearing something like that? Then again, she's not that old.

"I... er... I don't need this. I'll leave you to it, Detective," Wilbur said, backing out of the door.

I nodded absently, looked around the room, the crime scene, and was surprised that there were no photos. I shrugged, backed out of the room myself and began to wander around the house. As far as I could tell, nothing, other than the crime scene, had been disturbed. I trolled through the house until, finally, I found myself in what I assumed must have been the victim's office or den.

A large walnut desk was set against a wall under a window, upon which were several small stacks of papers, mostly bills from the likes of the electric company and the cable company, and an open check-book. Now that did give a surprise: Lucille Benedict had just over one-hundred and two thousand dollars in her checking account.

Who has that kind of money in checking? I thought. *Motive maybe?*

"Of course, it could, but it ain't likely," I muttered to myself as I looked over the rest of her desk but found nothing else that interested me... except for a small monthly planner and a single framed photo of five people standing together with their arms around each other's shoulders, all of them very attractive, and all of them except one well known to me: Lucille Benedict, Meryl Dilly, Pastor Ed, Victoria Randolph and another young woman I didn't recognize.

Pastor Ed? Hmm, I wonder... Church function? Who's the other woman? Everyone in this town is a member of that church. It's only natural that this guy's face would pop up here and there. Nope, three out of four of those women are dead. That's no coincidence. We need to find out who that fourth woman is, and quickly.

I picked up the planner, opened it, flipped through the pages, found the one I was looking for, and saw something that made my heart leap.

Nope! That's just too frickin' easy.

I flipped slowly backwards through the pages.

Geez, Mrs. Benedict had one busy social life.

"See anything, LT?" Janet said as she walked into the room, her iPad open in the crook of her arm.

"Maybe." I looked up at her. "Probably nothing. What about you? Anything from Kyle Baker?"

"He's a nice guy, a bit of an insomniac. Lives with his wife and mother-in-law—she's an invalid, the mother-in-law—in the house next door. He's a registered nurse, but stays home and looks after her, and he does most of the homemaking while his wife goes to work; she's an attorney."

She looked at her notes but didn't really need them.

"Anyway, as I said," she continued, "he doesn't sleep much and he's in the habit of taking his dog for long walks in the middle of the night. So that's what he was doing last night. He went out at around ten after four and he noticed her lights were on. He was gone for more than an hour, and when he came back, the lights were still on. He thought that was strange because he'd never seen them on at that time in the morning before, so he decided to check on her."

She paused, checked her notes again, and looked at me, quizzically.

"And?" I asked, a little more impatiently than I intended.

"Well, he knocked on the door, and when no one answered, he peeked in the window and saw her. Then he called the police... You think I should go talk to the mother-in-law?"

"Yes. Go ahead. I'll wait for Doc Sheddon." I looked at my watch. "But when we get done here, we'll go talk to Pastor Ed. According to an entry in the victim's day planner, he was supposed to pay Mrs. Benedict a visit yesterday... at six-thirty in the evening."

"Could it be that easy?" she asked, her eyes lighting up.

"No! It never is. But, check this out."

I showed her the photograph of the four women and Pastor Ed.

"Three of those women are dead. He sure as hell is beginning to look like a person of interest," I said.

Her mouth opened as if to speak, but she didn't. She just looked up at me in disbelief.

I smiled at her and said, "Don't get too excited, Janet. Nothing is ever what it seems. Go talk to the mother-in-law." And she did, just as Doc Sheddon had arrived.

"You look tired, Kate," he said as he ambled into the room, already dressed from head to toe in white Tyvek. "Another nasty one, I see. Let's take a quick look, then you can get out of here and go do something useful."

And so it began... again. I closed my eyes and threw back my head. I'd seen so many I'd lost count.

"No signs of a struggle; no defensive wounds on her arms or hands," he said as he rose to his feet and stepped away from the body.

"Time of death?" I asked, holding my breath.

He looked at his watch. "It's now almost seven o'clock," he said, taking a digital thermometer from his bag.

She was lying partially on her back, her right leg crossed over the left, exposing her lower back. He tugged her blouse out of her waistband and inserted the probe through the skin into her lower back.

He waited a moment then said, without any hesitation, "She's been dead about thirteen hours, so between five and seven yesterday evening."

Holy shit! Got 'im.

"You sure, Doc?" I said, biting my tongue as I caught my mistake.

He gifted me with one of his reproachful looks and said, "Yes, Catherine. I'm sure. The liver temperature is seventy-nine-point-four degrees, a loss of about nineteen degrees, give or take. The normal body temperature is ninety-eight-point-six. The body cools at a rate of about one and a half degrees per hour, so she's been dead roughly thirteen hours. I'll pinpoint it more arcuately when I do the postmortem.

"It looks like our assailant is pretty well set in his ways," he continued. "The same method of attack on each of the three victims, that we know of, and I'd say the same weapon too. They are all

women of a certain age, weight, height, and they're all attractive."
Doc pouted his lips as he pondered.

"What about this." I pointed to the torn blouse exposing the scandalous black bra beneath. "None of the other women had torn clothes. This rip looks like it was done on purpose."

"Yes, I'm not sure what to think about that," Doc said, looking down at the body, his left hand supporting his right elbow, right hand stroking his chin, still pondering. "But I'm almost certain the same person is responsible for all three crimes.... And the violence is escalating.

"This one didn't see it coming. I wonder why? She was attacked from behind by a right-handed assailant. See, the right rear of her skull is shattered, but look at her face. The killer tried to destroy it. Fortunately, if I can use such a word in these circumstances, she didn't feel a thing; the blow to the back of the head killed her instantly... The injuries to her face were inflicted postmortem, as were the stab wounds: same weapon, same MO... more rage. What on earth could have caused such blind anger?"

"I'm going to catch this guy, Doc," I said in barely a whisper. "I think I know who it is, and as soon as Detective Toliver gets back, we're going to go talk to him."

"I do so hope he's your man, whomever it is," Doc said. "This is all too much. Oh, and by the way, I probably should have started our conversation by telling you that we did find something odd with the lab results. I was afraid that there might have been a mix-up so I sent them back for a redo."

"A mix-up in the lab? That's my worst nightmare, Doc," I replied and stepped closer so Doc's report wouldn't be overheard.

"Yes, mine too. They were able to identify Victoria Randolph's blood and Meryl Dilly's blood. And, as you know, there was seminal fluid present in Meryl Dilly. But the DNA to that sample doesn't match that of the husband... so either she was having an affair, or it belongs to the killer. However, that makes no sense, because there was no DNA material present inside Victoria Randolph and, by the look of her state of dress, this one wasn't raped," Doc said, scraping the tips of his fingers up and down the stubble on the right side of his chin. "And that begs the question, why Dilly and not Randolph? If I find evidence of sexual activity here... well, we don't know yet. Do you see what I mean, Kate?"

I did.

I looked down at Lucille Benedict's body and let out a deep sigh.

"So," I said, "we have foreign DNA present in one victim and not the other. Dilly wasn't raped, so it must have been consensual... No, I have no idea what that means, Doc."

And then Janet showed up looking as discouraged as I felt.

"Hi, Doc." She gave him half a wave and half a smile.

If the two of them were to walk down the street together, they could easily be taken for grandfather and granddaughter, instead of the Chief Medical Examiner and the youngest homicide detective on the Chattanooga police force.

"Detective Toliver," he said. "How nice to see you again. I only wish it were under better circumstances. You have good news for us, I hope."

"No, not hardly." She sighed. "Kyle's mother-in-law is Shelby Winterborn. She's seventy-seven years young. She was in a diving accident about ten years ago that left her paralyzed from the neck down—such a nice woman—such a shame." She paused, shook her head, and then continued. "Anyway, since then her son-in-law has been taking care of her pretty much full-time. She's got all her faculties. His story checks out."

"Okay, well, that's good for him," I replied.

"Oh, and just as I was leaving, Kyle mentioned seeing a car, parked here in the driveway late yesterday afternoon, around six-thirty, he thought it was. I asked him the make and color. He didn't know the make, but he thought it was an expensive model, either white or silver, he's not sure which, but he seemed to want to err on the side of white. He didn't think to get a plate number or the make of the car since he knew that Mrs. Benedict had a lot of visitors, almost every day, in fact. It may or may not mean anything." Janet swallowed.

I sighed, nodded, patted her encouragingly on the shoulder, and said, "Good job." Then I turned to the ME and said, "Doc, I'm going to leave you to tend to Mrs. Benedict. Mike Willis should be here shortly. See you soon, I'm sure."

"Sure, Kate. Meet me at my place later. We can enjoy a quiet dinner by candlelight." He winked.

"That's the best offer I've had in months, but what would your good wife say?"

"She would welcome you with open arms, my dear. You know that. She cooks a mean lamb chop, you know. You really are welcome to join us; you too, Janet."

I laughed. "I'll think about it," I replied, but I knew I wouldn't, my nerves were jangling. I was itching to get to the Church of the Savior and talk to Pastor Ed, officially. A simple mouth swab would answer most of my questions.

I looked sideways at Janet, nudged her with my elbow, and said, "You ready to go talk to Pastor Ed?" She was.

24

Janet followed me as I drove across the top of the mountain to the Church of the Savior and then parked behind me just outside the entrance to the offices. We exited the cars, but before we approached the door, I grabbed her arm and told her about the appointment I'd found in Lucille Benedict's day planner.

"If Pastor Ed has an alibi for Benedict's time of death," I said, "we're screwed, even if the DNA Doc found in Meryl Dilly is his. It could have been inside her for up to seventy-two hours. She was found in the early hours of Thursday the eighteenth, so that means the DNA could have been deposited as far back as Sunday evening the fifteenth; it's circumstantial. Ed could have been screwing her anytime during those three days."

"So the DNA is no good to us then?"

"Not unless we can put him at the Dilly residence between the hours of five and seven on the day she was killed, and even then... Well, according to her day planner, she's been seeing quite a lot of our dear Pastor, among others, over the last six months or so."

I thought for a minute, then said, "Do me a favor, Janet, go check the cars in the parking lot. White or silver is what we're looking for. Then come on in and join me."

"You don't really think he did it, do you?" she asked. "The guy is, like, as creepy and weird as all get-out... but a murderer? He's a man of God for goodness' sake."

"I hear you, but he's the only common thread that runs throughout the cases."

Janet left, and I stepped up to the door and rang the bell. Karen Silver opened the door almost immediately. This time, though, she was an entirely different person. She looked tired, harassed, and cross. She was obviously working at tasks other than secretarial because she was wearing coveralls, rubber boots and yellow rubber cleaning gloves.

"Good morning, Ms. Silver," I said breezily. "Is the pastor in? We have a few routine follow-up questions for him."

"I'm afraid Pastor Ed isn't here. He didn't come in this morning, and he didn't let me know. If you'd like to try again tomorrow you are welcome to do so," she said and began to close the door.

"One second, Ms. Silver, if you don't mind. The tip you gave us about Marty Butterfield was very helpful," I said as Janet joined me.

"Yes, well, at great risk to myself. Why haven't you arrested him yet? I haven't seen anything in the news."

"It's not quite that easy," Janet said. "We need proof. We can't just arrest him on your say so."

"Proof? He's a convicted felon. What more proof do you want? He's a nasty, nasty man with a very shady past. Furthermore, he's not shown Edward the least bit of gratitude for all the help he's given him. On the contrary, he's repaid him with scandal." Karen folded her arms and stared at me, defiantly.

I nodded. "I understand, and thanks to you," I said, ingratiatingly, "we've interviewed Mr. Butterworth and are actively investigating him as a person of interest."

She softened a little, nodded, and said, "I should think so too. So what do you intend to do about it?"

"Well, as I said, we have some questions we think only Pastor Ed can answer. Would you mind giving us his home address, please?"

"Um... er... Oh... I'm on my own here today, Detective, and very busy, as you can see." She waved a yellow-gloved hand in the air.

"I know, and I'm sorry. We can, of course, get it from the police department, but that means a phone call, choosing options, getting put on hold... You know how it is, so I was hoping that you'd help us out... please?"

She stood stock still, staring at us.

"Please?" I said again.

"Oh, very well," she said impatiently. "It's the Cloisters on Colonial Park Drive. It's about ten minutes from here. You can't miss it; there's a gravel driveway to the left. Now, if you'll excuse me. I have work to do."

The door closed with a bang.

"What's she so mad about, I wonder?" Janet asked.

"There's no telling. The pastor didn't let her know he wasn't coming in and, from the look of those coveralls and gloves, she could be cleaning the toilets, on her own. And, if the church does indeed hold fifteen hundred people, there would be a lot of them. That would piss anybody off. Let's go see if we can find Pastor Edward."

"You caught that, too?" Janet said, smiling. "By the way, there was only one car in the office parking lot," Janet whispered, "and it wasn't silver or white; it was a black Honda Civic."

"Must be hers," I said. "Okay, you have the address. Meet me there."

25

Karen Silver hadn't lied when she said the house was just about ten minutes away, but it wasn't as easy to find as she said. If I hadn't been using my dashboard mapping system, I would have driven right past the hidden driveway. It looked like nothing more than a gravel turn-around, but it was, in fact, the unmarked entrance to The Cloisters.

The driveway was little more than a well-worn dirt road through a forest of trees and dense undergrowth; it was deceiving. One hundred yards or so in, we reached a gate with an intercom.

I pulled up and pressed the intercom button, then took out my badge and identification and held them for the camera.

"Hello?"

The voice was female.

"I'm Lieutenant Gazzara, Chattanooga Police," I said, hanging out of the car window. "I'm here to talk to Pastor Ed."

There was a buzz and the gate opened slowly. I drove on through and the driveway transformed into a gray cobblestone pathway that led up to a large, contemporary, somewhat ugly home with very few windows.

"This guy is a preacher?" Janet asked as she joined me beside my car. "He owns all of this property? Must be a couple of hundred acres of prime real estate." Her eyes wide, mouth hung open. "Man, am I ever in the wrong profession?"

"I say that to myself all the time," I replied, smiling.

She just shook her head and said, "He's a preacher, for goodness' sake."

"Yes, another huckster of holiness, I shouldn't wonder. When I was a kid, the pastor at my church lived in a two-bedroom ranch house. To live in something like this would, in his mind, have been... sinful." I smiled at the memory.

"Okay, then," I said brightly. "So this should be interesting."

Janet thumbed the doorbell and an attractive blond lady answered the door, one I'd seen before. *Holy... It's number four.* And it was; it was the fourth woman in the photograph on Lucille Benedict's desk.

"Detective Gazzara, I'm sorry you made the trip all the way up here, but my husband isn't home."

"You're Mrs. Pieczeck?" I asked.

"I am," she said, rather tight-lipped. "He's been at a retreat since yesterday."

"A retreat," I said.

"Yes. It's his monthly Shepherd's Walk Men's Retreat." She swallowed. "It's to help the men of our community to remain faithful to God's calling."

"Can you tell me what time he went to the retreat?" I asked.

"He left early this morning, around seven."

"And what kind of car does he drive?" I pushed.

"An Audi S4. Why? Is he in some kind of trouble, Detective?"

"No, ma'am." I smiled. "What color is his car?"

"Metallic silver," she said frowning. "But—"

"And you, Mrs. Pieczeck? What do you drive?"

"I... have one too, but—"

"And is your car also silver?" I asked.

"Yes, but—"

Hmm. "I'm sorry to keep interrupting you, but I'm sure you've heard by now of the deaths of two members of your church."

"Yes, my husband told me about it, but I didn't know the women," she said rather quickly... too quickly.

"Really?" I said. "You didn't know them? From what Pastor Ed told us, they were both members of the church and had been for several years."

I was getting that familiar tingling sensation up my spine. This was suddenly becoming a very interesting interview.

"The church is my husband's job, Detective. I attend on Sundays, but that is all. It is no different from having a doctor or a lawyer as a husband. I wouldn't interfere with, or insert myself in, his job. I can't do what he does. Only he can. He... is called. And he can't do what I do here at home. You see?" She smiled at me like she'd somehow successfully explained the cause and effect of the Vietnam War in less than two minutes and so the issue was resolved.

I took out my iPhone, brought up the picture of the four women and the pastor, and showed it to her.

"How do you explain this, then?"

"Oh my," she said, not looking at all surprised. "I'd completely forgotten about that. Where did you get it?"

"I'm sorry," I said. "I can't tell you that, but that's you, right there on the end, correct?"

"Yes, of course it's me. That was taken about two years ago at another of Edward's retreats. We had photos made with all of the women that attended."

Oh, yes. Sure, you did, but I bet the others, if there are others, aren't all dead.

I nodded, seemingly satisfied with her explanation, and said, "I see. So when do you expect him home?"

"He's at the retreat center until Thursday evening," she replied before looking over her shoulder into the house.

"And where is this retreat center?" I asked.

"I do hope you're not planning to go there," she snapped, frowning. "The retreats are for men only, and any disruption could have a serious effect on those in attendance."

"I'm sorry," I said sweetly, "but I'm investigating multiple homicides. I promise we'll be discreet."

Reluctantly, she gave us the address. It was more than two hours away.

"I'm not happy about this. Not one bit," she said, folding her arms across her chest and shifting from one foot to the other. "In fact, I'm going to call him... wait, I can't. He doesn't allow phones at the retreat."

I couldn't help myself, I smiled. "I understand how you feel, Mrs. Pieczeck, but—"

She interrupted me, "Why aren't you out there hunting down the killer? Why are you bothering my husband? He's a man of the Lord. He loves his flock and... and... everyone." She choked on those last words. Her eyes began to water; she wiped them with the back of her hand.

"Just one more question and I won't take up any more of your time. How often does your husband usually visit the members of his church, Mrs. Pieczeck?" I asked quietly. "Once a year, once a month, weekly... what?"

"Whenever they need him."

Again, she replied quickly, too quickly. There was something there. Something she wasn't going to share with me. I could tell by the narrowed eyes and the sudden tilt of her head to the left. I could also tell that the conversation was just about at an end. I wrapped it up quickly, thanked her for her time, and gave her one of my cards.

"If you think of anything, Mrs. Pieczeck, anything at all that might help us, please give me a call. Even if it seems unimportant. Many times families of murder victims receive closure because someone remembered something: an unimportant detail..." I watched her eyes, but they didn't waver from mine.

She took my card, looked at it, spun it around in her fingers, obviously thinking about something, but she simply nodded, stepped back inside the house, and slammed the door.

I stared at the closed door, shaking my head, then turned to Janet and said, "She is not all she would have us believe, nor did she tell us the truth about the photo, and she's hiding something."

"Yeah, I sort of got that... But why, do you think, Karen Silver didn't tell us he'd gone to a retreat and save us the trip over here?" Janet asked.

"Maybe she didn't know?" I said. "Maybe he didn't bother to mention it to her because it's below her pay grade. Maybe she did know and didn't think it was any of our damn business. Who knows?"

Janet nodded and said, "Yeah, right, but it wasn't a wasted journey, was it? We now know our man drives an expensive silver car. So what's the plan now, LT?"

"A road trip, of course," I said. "Tomorrow morning, early. Let's go back to the office. There are things I need to do."

26

It was just after two-thirty that afternoon when we arrived back in my office. I sent Janet across the street to McDonald's to get coffee, dumped my bag on my desk, turned to look at my incident board, grabbed a dry erase marker, and began to add names and dates to it.

I hadn't been at it many minutes when I heard someone clear their throat. I turned my head, looked over my shoulder and, who should be standing there, leaning casually against the door frame, arms folded, legs crossed at the ankles, but Henry Finkle... The two stars on his collar tabs were gone, replaced by captain's bars, and he was smiling.

"You really do have a nice ass, Kate," he said quietly. "Ah, I see you're not wearing your fancy watch today."

"What do you want, Henry?" I asked, looking around for my phone. I found it and turned on the recording app, then waggled it in his face.

He actually laughed.

"There's no need for that, Lieutenant. Actually, I just stopped by to thank you for my new opportunity you made possible."

He sounded bright and cheery, but he wasn't. His eyes were chips of ice, and he was no longer smiling.

"I'd been asking the Chief for a field job for months, but he wouldn't hear of it. Now, thanks to you... Well, I really must thank you properly one of these days. I hope you have a nice rest of the day, Lieutenant." Then he stood upright, turned on his heel, and walked quickly away through the incident room.

You sneaky little SOB, I thought as I watched him go. *"I really must thank you properly one of these days." Oh yeah, Tiny, I understand. That was a threat. You intend to get me back. Well good luck, you little...*

I saw Janet exit the elevator holding two cups of coffee and stand to one side to allow Finkle to enter. He didn't stop, and he didn't look at her. She did stop. She turned and stared at him as he punched the elevator button. Even from where I was, I could see his shark-like smile as the doors closed.

"Hey, guess who I just saw?" Janet said as she placed the coffees on my desk. "*Captain* Henry Finkle... Oh, no, he didn't come to see you, did he?"

I smiled at her. "Sure did. He wanted to thank me would you believe?" And then I told her the rest of the story.

"Okay," I said. "So now you know. Let's get to work. What the—"

"Hi Lieutenant," Detective John Tracy said as he knocked on my still open door. "You got a minute, a private minute?"

I was about to tell him to get lost, but then my curiosity got the better of me. I gave Janet the nod, she nodded back, grabbed her coffee, and Tracy took a step back to let her pass. Then he stepped inside and sat down on the seat Janet had just vacated.

"I'm done with it, John," I said, grabbing my coffee. "You wanted the Barone case. I let you have it, and I've helped you all I could. That's it. I don't have time to fool with you. Now tell me what you want, then get out and let me get on with my work."

He leaned back in his seat, smiled at me, folded his arms, and said, "That ain't what I'm here for, Kate."

"Don't call me that, Sergeant. Only my friends call me that, and you're not one of them. So, what do you want?"

"Well, first I want to congratulate you. How the hell did you manage to pull it off?"

I screwed up my eyes, stared at him, then said, "Pull what off?"

"Oh, come on, K—" he started to say. "Sorry, LT. I heard Johnston is promoting you to captain, and that you're to head up the homicide division."

I almost dropped my coffee. I did let my mouth fall open, and I know my eyes almost popped out of my head.

"*Shut. Up!*" I finally managed to blurt out. "Where did you hear that? It's not true."

"Oh, I think it is. A little bird told me, a very special little bird."

I couldn't help it. I fell back in my seat and stared across my desk at him, open-mouthed.

"Get the hell out of here, John."

"No, ma'am. Not before I tell you why I came. If you're promoted to captain, and I know you will be, there will be a lieutenant's spot open in Homicide. Yours, and with you running the division, and with me up for promotion too, well, I thought that maybe you could put in a good word for me... After all, *Kate*, I did save your life. Let me know, okay?"

And before I could answer him, he stood and walked out the door, leaving me at my desk staring after him, not daring to believe what I'd just heard, but vowing to find out, and frickin' quickly.

Almost fearfully, I picked up my desk phone, punched in the Chief's extension, and waited. It rang only once.

"Chief Johnston's Office. How may I direct your call?" Cathy's voice was bright and cheerful.

"It's me, Cathy. I need a quick word with him."

"Putting you through now. Lieutenant Gazzara for you, Chief."

"Yes, Catherine. What can I do for you?"

"I just heard a rumor that you're promoting me. Is it true?"

There was a long moment of silence, and then he said, "Who told you, Kate?"

"So it's true, then?"

Again, the silence, then he said, "I told you when you left my office last Monday that I was going to call you when I had the time. This is not the time."

"Chief, you can't do this to me. How am I supposed to do my job with something like this hanging over my head? Talk to me. Tell me... something."

I heard him sigh, then he said, "Yes, Lieutenant, it's true. I do intend to promote you to captain, but not before you've cleaned up the mess on Lookout Mountain. How close are you to solving it, by the way?"

I was so taken aback I could barely get my breath, much less speak.

I... Umm. Geez, Chief, gimme a minute, will you?"

"Take your time, Lieutenant."

I took several deep breaths, shook myself mentally, *Freaking captain. Me? Holy cow. I'm not even time qualified yet.*

"Okay, Chief," I said, hoping I sounded suitably professional. "I have a person of interest. Well, he's more than that. Right now he's my prime suspect."

"And who might that be?" he asked.

"Not yet, sir. Not until I'm certain. If I'm wrong, and it gets out—"

"I understand," he said, interrupting me. "Keep me in the loop. I want to know as soon as you're prepared to make an arrest. In the meantime, I expect you to keep your pending promotion to yourself. No one is to know until I announce it. Understood?"

"Yes, Chief. Understood."

I dropped the handset into its cradle and leaned back in my chair, grinning like an idiot. *Fricking hell. Captain Gazzara... I like the sound of that. I sure as hell do. Yay me!*

"Oh, my God," Janet said. "What on earth is that look on your face?"

"Nothing, absolutely nothing," I said, jumping to my feet and grabbing my now cold coffee. "Come on. We have work to do."

Captain frickin' Gazzara... Wow!

27

"You look chipper this morning, LT," Janet said when she walked into my office the following morning, Wednesday. Dressed in jeans, a pink blouse, and white tennies, her red hair tied back in a ponytail, if it hadn't been for the Glock 17 and badge at her waist, she would easily have passed for a high school senior on her way to school.

"Yes, well," I said, "I had a good night's sleep for a change. That's usually all it takes... That and Tiny Finkle gone from my life. I only wish it was for good." I glanced up at her from the pile of paperwork I was trying to sort through. "How about you? You ready to go beard the Lion of God in his own den?"

She laughed, then said, patting her Glock, "Locked and loaded."

"Good, give me just a few minutes to clear away this pile on my desk and then we'll go."

"You want coffee? I can run over to Mickey D's while you're doing that."

"That would be lovely, but don't take too long. It's a two-hour drive to the retreat, and I don't want to get there just as they're breaking for lunch."

Divine Springs Camp and Family Retreat Center was a few miles west of Spencer off Highway 285, near Telula, at the border of Fall Creek Falls State Park.

We turned off 285 and followed a narrow winding road for several miles until finally, we found the retreat tucked away on top of a bald overlooking the rolling hills of the Cumberland Plateau and Caney Creek.

I didn't count them, but there must have been at least thirty cars, SUVs, and pick-ups parked in the lot at the front of the vast log cabin style structure. I parked discreetly in the back row hoping to blend my somewhat beat-up, unmarked Crown Vic' in among the array of high-value vehicles, not one of which could have cost less than forty grand.

Yeah, Janet's right; we're in the wrong profession.

"That looks like the entrance," Janet said as she climbed out of the car and pointed to a mile-long—joking—stretch of glass doors at the front of the building.

Our arrival hadn't gone unnoticed. Even before we made it across the parking lot, much less to the glass doors, a woman, smartly dressed in a pearl gray business suit, clipboard in hand, bustled out of the building and came to greet us.

"Hello," she said, with not even a hint of a smile. "Can I help you?"

I guessed her to be in her late forties, early fifties. Her hair was natural with gray streaks, and she wore no makeup: she had the beady eyes of an eagle.

"Yes, you can," I said, looking around. "Boy, but this is a beautiful place." I showed her my badge and ID.

"My name is Lieutenant Gazzara. I'm with the Chattanooga Police Department. This is Sergeant Toliver. You are?"

"I'm Barbara Loomis, director of the Divine Springs Camp and

Family Retreat Center," she said proudly. "How can I help you, Lieutenant?"

"Mrs. Loomis, we're here to talk to Pastor Edward Pieczeck," Janet said.

"It's Ms. Loomis, and I'm afraid that won't be possible," she said, drawing herself up to her full height, asserting her ample bosom. "The pastor is conducting his monthly retreat. You'll have to come back at another time," she said to Janet as if she was speaking to a smart-mouthed teenager.

It was probably something Janet was well used to. Her youthful appearance might work to her advantage with the opposite sex. But as a cop, it had to be something of a handicap... well, at times.

"It's not a request, Ms. Loomis," I said. "I'm investigating the homicides of three members of his congregation." I narrowed my eyes as I smiled. "So please tell him we're here."

"Oh, my." She put her hand to her throat. "Yes, of course. I'm sorry, I didn't know, please, follow me."

She turned quickly and led us into the building where we were greeted by the heady scent of sandalwood, the pleasant sound of trickling water, and the haunting tones of bamboo flutes. I was reminded of the music used for relaxation at spas, yoga studios, and new age shops—and I wanted to stay and soak it up.

"Please wait here. I'll return directly," Loomis said, waving a hand at several of what I knew to be zero gravity chairs, and then she hurried away across the lobby and disappeared down a hallway.

"How would you like to spend a couple days here every month?" Janet asked.

"Uh, I'd love it. Wouldn't you?"

"Yeah, but I don't get it. When did church become such a cushy lifestyle?"

"When they took God out of it," I muttered.

"Do you believe Pastor Ed is some kind of flimflam artist?" Janet asked.

"Flimflam artist? You've been watching those old gangster movies again, with Humphrey Bogart and James Cagney, haven't you?"

Janet blushed and shook her head. "Maybe."

"You know," I said thoughtfully. "I read a book once, some time ago, about a televangelist and his wife —can't remember their names —who made millions of dollars from their TV show. People were sending them their life savings, hoping it would help them get into heaven. That televangelist lived like royalty; didn't steal a dime. His congregation gave it all to him."

I shrugged and then continued, "But he still went to jail for it, and his wife divorced him. That was a long time ago. He's dead now, so is his wife, I think, but there are more just like him, many more: smarter, savvier, and a whole lot more careful than he was, but hucksters just the same. Beats me just how gullible the public can be."

"Yeah, I know," Janet said. "You think this is the same kind of scam then?"

"Doesn't matter if it is. We're here investigating three murders, not Pastor Ed to find out if he's using the church collections to furnish his summer home."

"I don't know. I find it all a little creepy," Janet said. "Jesus didn't say 'follow me and get filthy-stinkin' rich,' did he? It was something like, 'Give up thy worldly goods and...' Oh, I don't know. Maybe I'm just too old-school," Janet said.

I chuckled. "You're old-school? At the age of twenty-four?"

"Will I get in trouble if I tell my Lieutenant to shut up?" Janet asked.

"No, Old School. Not this time anyway." I laughed.

Before she could say anything more, Loomis reappeared with Pastor Ed following behind, and he didn't look happy.

"Detective Gazzara, this is quite a surprise," he snapped.

"I know, and I'm sorry. I hate to bother you, Pastor Ed. Is there somewhere where we can talk privately?" I said looking at Loomis.

"Of course," she said.

She kneaded her hands as she looked to Pastor Ed for direction. I had the impression he'd scolded her for interrupting his ministry.

She led us down another hallway and opened the door to a small conference room, with a round table in the center surrounded by four chairs. The exterior wall was wall-to-wall, floor-to-ceiling windows that overlooked a vast panorama of lush gardens, tall grass, wildflowers, and old-growth trees.

Loomis left us alone, closing the door behind her.

"Please sit down, Pastor," I said as I took my iPad from my shoulder bag.

He did so, and I informed him I was going to record the interview.

"Am I under arrest?" he asked as he slowly sat down.

"Should you be?" I asked.

"Good Lord, no."

I smiled at him. "No, sir. You're not under arrest, but I do have some follow-up questions. I'm sure Ms. Loomis informed you that we've found another body, Mrs. Lucille Benedict," I said slowly as I watched the pastor's reaction.

"Lucille?" he gasped. "Oh God, no. Loomis didn't tell me... But I just saw her."

Wow, give the man an Oscar!

"When was that?" I asked.

"Just yesterday, around five-thirty in the afternoon. She asked me to stop by. I... I can't believe it," he stuttered.

"Why did she ask you to stop by?"

"She knew I was going to be gone for a couple days with the retreat. She just wanted... to talk and to visit... ohhhh."

"Just to visit and talk? What about?" I arched my eyebrows.

"What transpires between a pastor and a member of his congregation is private. I can assure you that it was harmless." He cleared his throat and fidgeted in his seat.

"What are you talking about? You mean confession?" Janet asked. "That's a Catholic thing, not a Baptist thing."

"No, I'm talking about the conversation we had together. It was between Lucille and I. There was nothing insidious about it," he stuttered. "I feel insulted that you would insinuate that I would be improper. In fact, I don't think I want to discuss it with you anymore. I'm extremely busy with the retreat. If I'm not under arrest, I'm not going to answer any more of your questions."

Pastor Ed folded his arms, just as his wife had done, and pressed his lips together.

"Pastor, Lucille Benedict is dead. Victoria Randolph and Meryl Dilly are dead. They were all beaten and stabbed. They were members of your church. I have to find the killer. Your feelings don't come into it. I need answers, and I need them now."

I watched as his gaze flitted here and there, everywhere but in my direction. He pressed his lips tighter together.

"Even our dear Lord suffered wrongful accusations," he said finally, quietly.

"Our dear Lord wasn't the last person to see three women who were bludgeoned to death," I snapped.

He looked balefully at me, then said, "I really can't do this now. I need to get back to the members."

"Very well," I said, "we'll continue this in Chattanooga. Before you go, however, I need a DNA swab from you."

"What?" he shouted.

"The medical examiner found seminal fluid and blood on the victims. I need a sample so that we can eliminate you as a suspect." I smiled sweetly at him.

"No... No, I... don't have time for this. You... you need a court order. Please leave now."

"No time for a simple swab? My, you are a busy man, aren't you, Edward? You're right, if you won't cooperate, I do need a court order. I'll have one waiting when you return."

I picked up my iPad and shut it off. Janet got up and walked to the door. She opened it and stepped outside. Pastor Ed also stood and followed me to the door.

"Tell you what, Pastor," I said, turning and staring him in the eye. "How about you come down to the police department when you return to Chattanooga? We can wait a couple of days. The victims aren't going anywhere."

I could see his body start to tremble. So I upped the heat even more.

"Oh, and by the way, that's not a request. I'll call you."

The hell I will. I'll drag your sorry ass down there in handcuffs.

Without another word, he stomped out of the conference room and disappeared in the opposite direction from where we'd come. I joined Janet in the hallway.

"That's it then," Janet said as we walked toward the exit. "He won't cooperate. We're screwed. Why didn't you arrest him?"

I sighed. "Come on, Janet. You know why: no probable cause. Just because the man drives a silver Audi and was probably screwing one of the victims, doesn't mean he killed them. We can't ride roughshod over his rights."

"But he admitted he was with Benedict the evening she was killed."

"So he did, and that means what?" I asked.

She thought for a minute, then said, "It means we can place him at the scene and that he had opportunity."

"Good one, Janet, but what else do we need?"

She sighed. "Motive and the murder weapon."

"And physical proof," I said. "Fingerprints on the weapon would be ideal. What we have right now isn't much, and it's circumstantial. I told you before, the DNA, even if it's his, doesn't mean very much. The silver Audi, his admission to being at the scene during the window of opportunity... It doesn't mean a whole lot either.

"His refusal to give us a sample though, that's something else. Why would he do that?" I pondered. "He knows we'll get a court order and that he'll have to comply, eventually. Nope, we need more, much more, and I think I know how to get it. Come on. Let's get out of here."

"So what's the plan now, LT?"

"I need to make a phone call."

28

"A stakeout?" Chief Johnston asked. "Surveillance? Of one of the wealthiest, most popular pastors in the entire city? You'd better be sure of what you're doing, Lieutenant."

"Chief, I know, and I am. I've got a feeling that Pastor Ed is hiding something, and his wife is privy to it."

I swallowed hard. "Victoria Randolph is the only victim who was killed somewhere else. I need to find that crime scene. The pastor is my prime suspect, for several reasons I can't go into over the phone. If he did it, sir, and I'm thinking he did, he and his wife are hiding something, and it's not that they're dipping their fingers into the collection plate. I just want to watch their comings and goings for twenty-four hours. Forty-eight at the most."

"Forty-eight at the most? Hmm. I'm not entirely opposed to it, Lieutenant, but I can't spare the manpower. If you do it, you must do it by yourself. Do *not* involve Detective Toliver. Understood?"

I sighed, promotion or not, Finkle or not, things hadn't changed a whole lot.

"Yes, Chief. I understand."

I had him on speaker. I looked at Janet in the seat beside me; she'd heard it all. She just shrugged and looked as if someone had stolen her last piece of candy.

I DROPPED JANET OFF AT THE PD THEN WENT HOME, SHOWERED, changed clothes, took Sadie Mae out for a few minutes, and then called Lonnie and asked him to come get the dog and look after her for a couple of nights. Next, I grabbed a few bottles of water and headed back to the retreat center, only this time I didn't park in the lot. I found a secluded spot among the trees, parked there, checked the time—it was almost five-thirty in the afternoon—grabbed my binoculars from the glove box, got out of the car, locked it, and headed west about a hundred yards to the tree line. There I settled down to watch... and then the first mosquito found me.

Damn! I forgot to bring bug spray.

As it happened, it didn't matter... well, not much. I hadn't been there more than thirty minutes when I spotted Pastor Ed hurrying out the front doors of the retreat center, dragging a roll-on suitcase, shuffling clumsily toward a silver Audi S4. It was spotless, shiny, and rather sporty for a guy with a wife at home. He flung the suitcase into the trunk, almost ran around to the driver's side doors, jumped in, and peeled out of the parking lot as if the devil himself were chasing him. Little did he know it wasn't the devil. It was me.

What the hell's going on? I thought. *The retreat doesn't finish until tomorrow night. What's he up to? Oh shit. He's running... but where to?*

I figured it would be one of two destinations: the Chattanooga Metropolitan Airport or Texas and the Mexican border.

He drove like a freaking maniac: sixty, seventy, even as high as eighty on those narrow back roads, forcing me to do the same, risking my life to keep up with the crazy SOB. Luckily, my Interceptor had more than enough oomph in her to keep up.

The silver Audi turned south on Route 111 and increased speed, which could mean trouble, for both of us. I considered radioing a request for mutual aid, but didn't; I wanted to know what he was doing, not arrest the stupid SOB for speeding.

He turned south again onto US 127 and scorched through Soddy-Daisy and then inexplicably slowed as he entered Red Bank.

Sheesh, he's not running, he's headed home. So why the urgency? Talk to his wife about me showing up at his retreat? And risk your damn life? That's frickin' crazy. What the hell is wrong with you?

But that wasn't it, not at all. I continued to follow him into Red Bank and from there into a secluded new subdivision of mid-level bungalows. He then drove straight to a corner unit and pulled onto the short driveway.

Things were about to get tricky. If he spotted me, I'd ruin my chance of finding out what he was up to. I parked on the street two houses back, and I waited, watching.

He sat in his car for almost fifteen minutes; I couldn't figure it out. I could see through my binoculars that he wasn't on the phone. He was just sitting there.

He's waiting for someone? Oh well, time to check out the neighborhood.

I didn't need to get out of the car, just a quick glance around told me the development wasn't quite as new as I first thought it was. The houses had that lived-in look, the one Ed was parked outside more so than most of the others.

Surveillance can be one of the most rewarding police tactics, but you have to have patience, and that I had aplenty. So, I pushed my seat back as far as it would go and reclined it so my head was barely visible, and I continued to watch.

The minutes ticked by, but Pastor Ed stayed right where he was until finally, I saw him put his phone to his ear. He talked for only a few seconds before throwing his phone onto the passenger seat. He sat for a moment more, his hands to his forehead—thinking or crying, I couldn't tell. Then he exited the car and stomped—*angrily*, I thought—to the front door of the home, pulled keys from his pocket, unlocked the door, stepped inside and slammed it shut behind him.

Oh, now that's interesting, I thought. *A man with a house in Lookout Mountain has a second home just twenty-five minutes away. There's something weird going on. It's more likely they'd have a cottage in the Berkshires or maybe a condo in Miami. Not a crappy bungalow on the other side of town.*

I settled down to wait again. *It looks like I could be here all freakin' night. Oh well...* And then I was struck by a truly demoralizing thought. I had no coffee. *Oh dear Lord, this is going to be the longest and most miserable stakeout ev-er. What is he doing in there, I wonder?*

Fortunately, I didn't have long to wait at all. Some twenty minutes later, the pastor stepped out onto the front porch, looked warily around, then walked unsteadily to his car and drove away, leaving me there looking at the house and wondering what to do next: chase him some more or...

"No search warrant, Kate," I muttered as I contemplated the question. "Ah, screw it. What've I got to lose?"

Your frickin' promotion, and possibly your job, stupid!

It was almost eight-thirty and growing dark when I exited the car. I looked up and down the street. It was deserted, so I took a deep breath and walked up the front steps and looked around. Where the doorbell was supposed to be was just an empty hole in the doorframe. I knocked; no answer. I tried to look in through the windows. It wasn't happening: the curtains were heavy, drawn tightly closed.

Damn it!

I scratched my head and decided to check around back.

The ground was dry. The grass, primarily the crab variety intermingled with weeds, hadn't been cut for at least a couple of weeks.

If I stood on tiptoe, I could've seen over the sills of the side windows, but I could see the thick curtains would've blocked any view I might have had of the inside there, too.

Maybe he's decided to go into real estate and this is a piece of prop-

erty he bought to flip. Yeah, right, that would make perfect sense, I thought sarcastically. *Would a guy like Pastor Ed with the world and Heaven at his feet, really dirty his hands on a place like this? Not hardly, I think.*

I stepped up to the back porch and gently pulled on the screen door handle and was thrilled when it opened. I went inside the screened-in porch and tried the back door; it was locked. I went to one of the windows. It was covered only by a lace curtain, dirty but transparent enough for me to see through it into a kitchen that looked like it had never been used. There were no dishes, no tea towels, none of the niceties you'd expect to find in any kitchen.

I knocked on the door: nothing. I knocked again, harder, pressed my ear to the doorframe, listening for anything that might indicate someone was inside, but I heard nothing.

It was an impossible long shot, but I felt along the top of the door frame for a key anyway. My fingers encountered nothing but dust and dead bugs. *Ew!* I flipped the doormat and...

Holy shit, a freakin' key. Who does this anymore? I should buy a lottery ticket. It must be my lucky day.

The key slid smoothly into the doorknob, and with a gentle twist, I pushed the door open. I held my breath and listened, pulled my Glock, and stepped inside.

The light in the kitchen was enough to look around, but down the hallway, toward the front of the house, it was nearly pitch black.

I took a deep breath, said a quick prayer, hoped that no one was home, and stepped forward into the dark nether world that was the hallway and, at the same time, I also stepped way over the line. Internal Affairs would salivate over this one, if ever they found out.

The floor creaked as I made my way slowly along the hallway. I paused, took out my iPhone, turned on the flashlight, and the darkness became a weird, shadowy half-light; not great, but at least I could see that there were four doors, two on either side, all of them closed but one.

Again, I listened for movement, but heard nothing but my own heartbeat pounding in my ears.

The entire house smelled of cheap incense, the sort you could pick up at a gas station, fifty sticks for two bucks.

The open door gave entrance to a bathroom. The glass window was frosted, a dark rectangle faintly illuminated by the orange light of a nearby streetlamp. I stepped inside. There was a medicine cabinet over the vanity. I opened it, shone my flashlight into it, and stared at the contents.

Wow, would you just look at that?

I counted six boxes of condoms—one of them open—and a half-dozen tubes of a well-known lubricant. I smiled as I picked up a bottle of those famous little blue pills and read the label: the prescription was for... *Edward freakin' Pieczeck! Holy cow!*

I replaced the bottle exactly as I'd found it, closed the cabinet door, stepped back into the hallway and listened: nothing. By then, I was sure there was no one in the house but me. Yeah, that; I was alone, but that didn't make what I was doing any the less nerve-racking. I opened the door to one of the other rooms and looked inside. It was as bare as a baboon's butt, no furniture, nothing, unused. The same with the next one.

I closed that door and opened the last one. The beam of light from my phone cut through the darkness and... I'd prepared myself for another body, or a naked prisoner bound and gagged, so I kind of giggled to myself when the reality of what I did find sank in.

I felt along the wall for the light switch and flipped it on. *Geez!* I shook my head in amusement. Four red fluorescent lights set high on each of the four walls flickered then popped on, bathing the room in an eerie red glow.

There was a bed set against the far wall. Next to it, on a cheap nightstand, were a variety of sex toys, some of them so bizarre I didn't know what they were. On the walls, belts and straps of different sizes and thicknesses, chains, handcuffs, and shackles dangled from hooks.

Holy shit! Is that a fricking sex swing? Hahaha, our dear pastor is Lord of the Swings?

To top it all off, a high-end digital video camera was positioned on a tripod in the corner of the room.

I stepped into the room, turned it on, and hit the play button... pushed rewind, then play again... and there I found the answers to several of my questions... sort of.

29

"You did what?" Lonnie asked.

"Well I had to see what was going on inside the house, now didn't I?" I asked as I drove to his house.

Lonnie and I had been through a lot together, and I could talk to him like I could no one else... except Harry Starke, and that wasn't an option, not with Amanda the way she was... but that's another story. And Lonnie watched Sadie Mae for me when I had to put in long hours. That little dog absolutely loved him. He had a yard for her to run around in, which I didn't, and Lonnie took her to his barber shop where she got more attention than a newborn baby. Little minx.

"I can't believe you did that, Kate. It was a huge risk. What if you'd gotten caught? You'd have lost your freakin' badge."

"Yeah, but now at least I have some answers, something to squeeze him with. The pastor of the wealthiest church in the Tri-State area, on film, doing the nasty... and a whole lot of weird kinky stuff with a member of his church, now dead, murdered, beaten to death... Hey, I'm pulling in your driveway now."

I heard Lonnie shut off his phone as I drove up the short gravel driveway and stopped in front of the garage.

The front door opened and Lonnie appeared with a beer in his hand, and Sadie Mae galloped out between his legs. I gathered her up, and she covered my face in kisses.

I really don't like beer that much, but what the hell. I was parched, so I set the dog down and happily accepted the beer.

I stretched out in my usual spot on the corner of the couch. Lonnie, mineral water in hand, dropped into his throne, a worn-out leather recliner. Sadie Mae leaped up into his lap, flopped down and stared sleepy-eyed and content at me.

Lonnie glared at me over the top of his bottle.

"Don't even say it," I said. "I had to do it; you would have done it too... You know you would. So would Harry. He wouldn't even have thought about it; Bob Ryan would have kicked the damn door in. I had to go into the house, right? I know he did it, the pastor, but I can't prove it, not even with this." I showed him the memory card from the video camera.

"You sure as hell can't now that you stole the frickin' thing. Why did you do that? You could have gotten a warrant. That thing is not admissible now. More than that, it could get you arrested."

I shook my head. "You don't understand, Lonnie. He was acting suspiciously. He could have been in there destroying evidence. And anyway, I can still get a warrant to search the place. I'll make a copy of the card and put it back where I found it." I was looking for his approval, but all I got was a shrug.

"So now you have this information, but you can't use it, and if IA finds out you committed a B&E, you're screwed. Unless..." Lonnie looked down at the dog and stroked her head.

"Unless what?" I smirked. "And it wasn't B&E. I used a key."

"Unlawful entry, then. Come on, Kate," Lonnie said, frustrated. "You're a senior police officer. You know you can't do that: unlawful search and seizure. It's cop school 101. Yeah, you've got to put it back where you got it, but first, maybe, just maybe, you can put the screws to the pastor and get him to admit to... I dunno, something... He sure as hell isn't going to confess to murder; kinky sex, maybe, but not murder," Lonnie replied like he was apologizing for standing me up on a date.

I took a long, deep gulp of my beer. It tasted good. The bitter flavor brought back memories of hot summers, hotter nights, and a more carefree time when... At least for me, it was.

"Yeah. I know. And I've got to get to it sooner rather than later."

I gulped down the last of my beer, put the bottle on the side table, and mentally prepared myself to get up and go. I would have given just about anything to stay there and talk strategies, but I was bushed. I needed sleep, in the worst way, because, as Scarlett O'Hara said, tomorrow is another day.

And then, wouldn't you know it? My phone rang.

"Gazzara," I answered.

"Kate. It's Doc. You busy?"

"No, Doc." I looked at my watch. It was almost eleven-thirty. "I was just about to call you," I said, a little more sarcastically than I intended, but he didn't seem to notice.

"Yes, well that's good, because I just finished with my swimming accident postmortem, and my wife has gone to visit her sister in Atlanta, so I thought I'd get started on Lucille Benedict. But that's not what I'm calling about. I received the reports back from the lab. This is a second round, remember?"

"Yes, I remember."

"We have the same result. They identified the victim's blood, but there are two other unidentified DNA profiles: the seminal fluid and the blood.

"So, I could be looking for two killers, not one."

My heart sank to the pit of my stomach. The pastor was my only viable lead, and I was ready to bet my job that the semen would be a match for his DNA profile.

Then, I lightened up and snapped my fingers. "That's great news, Doc." I looked at Lonnie and winked.

"I'm glad you think so," Doc replied.

Oh yeah, I bet you do, I thought, *and there goes any thoughts I had of sleep.*

"I'll be there in a jiffy. You can tell me all about it."

I said goodbye and hung up.

"Sorry, partner," I said to Lonnie. "Duty calls. I have a date with Doctor Death, so I'll take a rain check on the next round, if you don't mind."

I stood. Lonnie was about to do the same, but I stopped him.

"You'll disturb the baby," I said, nodding at the sleeping dog. "Thanks again for watching her. You're a good egg, Lonnie."

"Good egg? You've been watching too many old movies," Lonnie replied as I kissed the top of his head.

"Very funny," I said, remembering I'd said almost the same thing to Janet. "I'll let you know when I can pick up the dog."

"Take your time, Detective. You know where to find us," Lonnie called out as I shut the screen door behind me and hurried to my car.

I missed having Lonnie as a partner. But, it was how things usually worked at the Chattanooga Police Department, and probably everywhere else. Give it a couple more months and who knows, maybe Janet would be gone too.

I reversed out onto the street, turned on my emergency lights and siren, and hit the gas; I didn't intend to waste time driving to Doc's lair.

30

This time Doc was waiting for me. The door opened as I walked across the parking lot.

"You hungry?" he asked as he pulled the door closed behind me and snapped the deadbolt in place. "I have some goulash left; I made it yesterday."

"Sounds great," I said, not really that sure that it did... sound great.

I couldn't remember the last time I'd eaten, but left-over goulash? *I dunno!*

"I worked up an appetite on the way over here," I lied.

"Fine. Let me get the files and we'll take them into the kitchen," Doc said.

The kitchen was a sterile, much smaller clone of his autopsy room: all stainless steel and white plastic. A large pot was simmering on the stove. He opened a cabinet, grabbed two stainless steel bowls, and spooned the hot food into them: chunks of beef, potatoes, carrots, and speckles of fresh parsley sprinkled throughout.

"This smells fantastic," I said, "but steel bowls and plastic spoons?" I smiled. "Doggy bowls, Doc?"

"Not exactly, my dear, but they're all I have. Ah me... if only I had some red wine," he said, opening the refrigerator door and extracting a three-liter bottle of Orange Crush. "Then we'd really be in business."

Orange Crush? Gross!

We ate in silence for several minutes, then we put our bowls aside, and Doc spread the three files across the table and opened them.

Each file contained photographs of the crime scene, the bodies, the stages of the autopsy procedures, and copies of his reports.

"Here you go, my dear," Doc said as he handed me three sets of reports each stapled together. "I printed these out for you, and I emailed the photographs."

"Just give me the Reader's Digest version, Doc," I said, setting them aside.

"I spoke to Mike Willis earlier this afternoon. As I mentioned earlier, he was following up on a semen sample, pubic hairs, and blood samples. The semen sample on Meryl Dilly is not her husband's," he said. "Neither are the two pubic hairs."

He looked at me and raised his eyebrows.

"I'm not surprised," I said.

He continued, "It appears the attack on her was so violent that the assailant cut himself, thus providing us with an additional DNA profile. Several of the blood spots Mike found on her clothing didn't match Mrs. Dilly's profile, nor that of Connor Dilly, or that of the seminal fluid, I'm sorry to say."

Doc paused and took a sip of his soda.

"So, one must conclude that Mrs. Dilly had sexual intercourse with someone other than her husband, and then after that, either someone else killed her on their own, or there were two people present when she was killed, one of them the person she had sex with."

"How about the semen and the hairs?" I asked. "Are they a match?"

"They are indeed."

"Well, that's something, I guess."

I stared at the crime scene photos, lost in thought. *Wow, that's not good. So if the pastor was screwing her, and I'm sure he was... But if he wasn't, and someone else was... That means there's a third person out there somewhere with whom she was having an affair... So who the hell does the blood belong to? Geez... geez... geez.*

"I dunno, Doc. I checked Connor Dilly's hands at the scene, Darby Randolph's too. Neither one had any cuts or scratches on their hands." *And neither did Pastor Ed.*

I thought about Pastor Ed's video. Unfortunately, due to the camera angle, and the fact that the woman was blindfolded, I couldn't be absolutely positive that it was Meryl Dilly he was doing disgusting things to, and never once did I see him actually penetrate her. He could have, but again the camera angle made it difficult to see.

"Are you ready to get started?" Doc asked, breaking into my thoughts.

I looked at my watch. It was just after midnight. I looked at him and said, "No, not really, but let's do it." And we did.

Back under the lights, I took my seat on the opposite side of the table and watched Doc work his magic.

There was little difference between the state of poor Lucille's body and those of the other two victims. The cause of death was a single blow to the left side of her head that split her parietal bone almost in half—*another single killing blow*—indicating a right-handed assailant. Her face had been beaten almost to a pulp. From the shape of the wounds, Doc surmised the killer had used the same weapon as was used to kill Victoria Randolph and Meryl Dilly, probably a crowbar. And, just like the other two victims, she'd also been stabbed... twelve times, three of them through and through.

No, I thought. *I can't do this, not now. I need to get out of here and catch the SOB when he's not expecting it.*

"Doc," I said, "it's been one hell of a long day. I'm about to fall over. Do you mind if I head out?"

"No, no, of course I don't, my dear. Run along home. I'll call you when and if I find something."

"Thanks," I said. "You know, I feel like we are on the edge. Just one stiff breeze and we might be able to topple it over."

He nodded, the plastic face shield banging his chest, and gave me a casual wave with his bloody, purple-latex-covered gloved hand, scalpel glistening with blood in the artificial light.

"Until next time, my dear. Be careful out there."

31

It was well past midnight, and I was bone tired. It really had been a long day, but I wasn't ready to quit, not yet. I hit the gas and headed to Pastor Ed's home on Lookout Mountain.

I know it probably makes me sound like a real jerk, but the idea of busting into his house at that hour of the night gave me a thrill.

I drove up to the gate with my bright lights on and the grill-mounted blue and red emergency lights flashing, just to make my point.

I pressed the intercom button, and pressed again and again, like I was tapping out a message in Morse code.

"Who is it? Do you have any idea what time it is?" Pastor Ed shouted, his voice crackling with distortion through the speaker.

"It's Lieutenant Gazzara. Open the gate. I need to speak to you, *now*."

"Uh, er, I'm sorry, Lieutenant, but my wife and I have retired for the evening. I'll meet you at the Police Service Center tomorrow morning."

"I said, open the gate, Pastor. If I have to call for backup, you'll be headed down there tonight, in handcuffs, and I know you don't want that. So do as I ask and open the gate."

Several minutes went by, but the gate didn't open, and I was beginning to get nervous. Sometimes when suspects realize they're cornered, they react in a bad way. I pressed the intercom again.

"Pastor Ed? Can you hear me?"

Nothing.

"Pastor Ed? Mrs. Pieczeck?"

I continued pressing the button. The last thing any cop wants is some kind of standoff or a murder-suicide. Hell, for all I knew, he and his wife could have been card-carrying members of the NRA with an arsenal of firearms in there.

I pressed the buzzer again.

Finally, after what felt like an eternity, the lock on the gate clicked and it slowly began to open. I let out a deep sigh of relief, licked my lips with my dry tongue, and rolled slowly through the gate.

As I drove to the house under the canopy of the trees, with the window rolled down, I was sure I could smell rain in the air. The crickets were having a grand time making their sweet music for each other.

PASTOR ED WAS WAITING FOR ME AT THE FRONT DOOR. HE WAS wearing a robe tied at his waist. It revealed the top of a hairy chest, well-defined pectoral muscles, sculpted calves, and bare feet. The man was in great shape for a pastor.

"What's this all about, Lieutenant?" he hissed as I exited the car.

"It has been a really long day, Pastor. Mind if I come in? My backside could use a break from the rough seat of my car." I smiled. I wasn't joking: police Interceptors are not built for comfort.

He took a deep breath and when he exhaled, his whole body

slumped. He stepped aside for me to enter. I did and was immediately taken aback by the breathtaking beauty of the interior.

It was a truly amazing home. As I stepped inside, just to the right of the foyer was a life-sized wooden cross. There was no Savior nailed to it. No symbol of the risen Lord. It was just a big cross.

He motioned for me to step into the living room, a vast chamber with high ceilings, white walls, and gold trim. The furniture, the picture frames, the knick-knacks all were white, some with gold trim. The room was absolutely spotless.

"Please, sit," he said distractedly.

I took a seat on the white sofa, opened my iPad, tapped the record icon, crossed my legs and leaned back, and informed him I would be recording the interview.

"Do I need my attorney present?"

"I don't know. Do you?"

He didn't answer. He just stood there staring down at me. I probably should have been wary that he might attack me, but for some reason, I wasn't.

"Oh, this is nice," I said, rubbing the smooth white fabric. "What is this? Silk?"

"Please," he said plaintively. "What is this all about, Detective?"

"Oh, right, we're hurrying this right along. By the way, will your wife be joining us?"

"No. She's asleep."

I nodded. "Yes. Well, why don't you tell me about your little... shall we call it, retreat, in Red Bank. And please, tell me the truth. It kinda hurts my feelings when someone tries to bullshit me."

The man's face didn't just pale, it turned ashen. It was as if he died standing up but couldn't quit breathing. I have to admit, I felt kind of sorry for him. "Maybe you should sit down before you fall down, Pastor," I said firmly.

He looked over his shoulder toward the open hallway. The lights were off, and it was dark and, as far as I could tell, Mrs. Pieczeck wasn't out there listening.

Pastor Ed nodded, sat down opposite me, and wiped his top lip with the back of his hand.

"She... she can't know about that," he stuttered, his voice hushed.

"I really don't care what your wife does or doesn't know," I said. "What I want to know is why you didn't tell me about it?" I folded my arms and stared at him.

The pastor chuckled nervously, his lip twitching on the right side. He didn't answer.

"Let me ask you this, how do you think Mrs. Pieczeck will react when she finds out that you have a secret hideaway where you take the lady members of your church for kinky sex games?" I tilted my head to the right, opened my eyes wide, and smiled at him.

His demeanor changed. "I don't know what you're talking about," he said defiantly.

I took the memory card from my jacket pocket and held it up between finger and thumb for him to see. "This isn't you in the video? It sure looks like you..."

His lip twitched again.

"Yes," I said, teasing him. "It is you, and oh, my Lord if that isn't Meryl Dilly swinging there while you... well, you know, don't you, *Pastor?*"

I sat still and watched him. It was like watching a building collapsing in slow motion.

"I didn't kill her," he said finally. He closed his eyes and let his chin drop to his chest.

"I didn't... kill her. We had a mutual arrangement." His eyes started to glisten. "Oh God. Oh God."

"Oh God is right, but He can't help you. Only you can do that. You, Pastor Edward Pieczeck, are my prime suspect for the murders of Victoria Randolph, Meryl Dilly, and Lucille Benedict. What have you got to say for yourself?"

"Oh God! No. You can't be serious. It was nothing like that. She was home alone, Meryl. She said her husband was preoccupied with his business. She was lonely. She came to me for help, and things just happened." He stood up and started to pace.

"What about Victoria Randolph? Did you make videos of her, too?"

"No. We were only alone together once, and we didn't have sex. There was a lot of heavy petting, but she never let it get any further than that," he confessed.

"Is that why she was working for you? So you could push the issue with her, too? She was very beautiful, very sexy."

Pastor Ed swallowed hard, almost as if he was remembering. He looked toward the hallway and then back at me. He ran his hand through his hair, sat down again and leaned toward me, his elbows on his knees, kneading his hands.

"Yes, I wanted her, but she was a tease, Victoria. She liked to play the game but wasn't ready to go all in." He looked down at his hands.

"Is that why you killed her?"

"I didn't kill her. I wanted her, yes. I wanted to share my visions with her. We were getting closer, and I knew she'd soon see how I felt about her," he stuttered. "But I didn't kill her."

"Your visions? What are those, exactly?"

He cleared his throat as his eyes darted all around the room.

"I enjoy domination. Every woman I've ever been with understands that and has willingly accepted the submissive role. Every one of them. They all agreed to being videotaped in addition to... everything else, except for Victoria." He pointed to the floor for dramatic effect.

Holy cow. The man's a raving perv. Fricking hell, who would have thought it? He's freakin' nuts.

"So, what happened with Meryl, Pastor? Did something go wrong? Perhaps you didn't catch her safety word? Things got a little out of hand and oops... Goodnight Meryl." I shrugged. "So you covered it up by beating her almost beyond recognition."

And then something just popped into my head. "Or did your wife do that? She couldn't let word get out that her pastor husband is a pervert, now could she?" *Oh, wow, that could be it. Why didn't I think of it before? She drives a silver car too, a twin to Ed's.*

"No. That didn't happen; none of it. I'm telling you the truth. As God is my witness, I did not—"

"I hate to think of what God witnessed in that house on Baker Avenue. What about Lucille Benedict? Was she one of your willing participants, too?"

"Yes, yes. She was. Unbelievable... Oh, God. I'm sick. Do you hear me? I'm sick. I need help, I've got a beautiful wife who adores me, and I've strayed from the paths of righteousness."

He stood, threw his head back, folded his hands in front of his chest, and looked pitifully up at the ceiling.

"Please, dear God, forgive me."

"Stop praying, Pastor. You'll have plenty of time for that later. Look at me."

He did, his arms still crossed over his chest.

"You were the last person to see Meryl Dilly alive. You were the last person to see Lucille Benedict alive, right?" I shook my head. I was almost becoming as overwhelmed by it all as he was.

"Lucille was leaving to visit her son in Atlanta," he whispered. "She wanted to see me before she left. I went to her house. We had sex, sweet, sweet sex, and then I left." He sat down again, panting, as if he'd just run a marathon. "Oh, God. Please forgive me."

"Unprotected sex?" I asked.

He nodded.

"Out loud, please, Pastor.

"Yes, unprotected."

So that could account for the semen in Meryl Dilly.

"And then you killed her?" I asked quietly.

"I didn't kill anyone!" he wailed quietly, his eyes rimmed with red, his teeth clenched. "I swear to you. It was only sex. I didn't kill these women."

"You know what I think, Eddy? I think you're a team, you and Mrs. Pieczeck. Oh, look at you! I just don't believe that she doesn't know, about the house, the deviant sex... Does she participate? Maybe we should get her in here."

He stared at me in horror. "You... you can't. She doesn't know about the house. She doesn't know about what I do. Please, please, don't tell her."

I sat there looking at him for a full minute before I decided it was time to go. I had what I'd come for, in part. No murder confession, but boy would Clemont Rhodes like to get his hands on what I had?

Thankfully, getting the pastor to admit to the house, the videos, and withholding information made things a little easier for me. How I'd gone about getting him to admit his sins wasn't ethical, not by any means. But then, when dealing with multiple homicides, lines tend to become blurry, sometimes almost invisible.

"Pastor Ed, I need to look inside the Red Bank house. I have what I need to get a search warrant, but if you want to keep it quiet, and I'm not promising I can, I need your permission." I stood up. "Let's see if we can avoid unnecessary publicity, shall we? Do I have your permission to enter the home at 221 Baker Avenue in Red Bank, and will you agree to accompany me?"

He nodded, looked miserable, then shrugged.

"Out loud for the recording, please, Pastor."

"Yes, you have my permission. You can do that. I will do that." Pastor Ed nodded slowly. "Just please, don't tell my wife. That's all I ask."

"I won't say a word unless I absolutely have to. That I promise, but I can't promise that the story won't get out, develop a life of its own." I put my hands on my hips.

"Can we please go to the house tomorrow?" he pleaded. "That way, my wife won't become suspicious?"

"Does she know I'm here now?"

He shook his head. "No, we have separate bedrooms."

"I understand. I'll meet you there at ten tomorrow morning, not a minute before, not a minute after. Understood?"

"Yes, I understand," he mumbled.

"I should warn you that the house is being watched," I said sternly. "So don't get any ideas about cleaning the place up before I get there. If you tamper, I'll arrest you on the spot for obstruction of justice. Do you understand, Pastor Pieczeck?"

Pastor Ed swallowed hard and nodded.

I turned and walked to the door.

"Ten o'clock, Pastor. Not a minute later." And then I turned back again. "Just one more thing before I go. I need that swab, please."

This time there was no argument. He simply opened his mouth and let me take it.

I let myself out and was happy to be out of the house. It was a beautiful home, but after hearing all that I had from the pastor, it had become little more than a mirage, all a huge fake, and I wanted to get away from it. His sex bungalow in Red Bank was more real than his expensive monument to modern architecture. It was seedy, sickening, true. But it was real, and I could deal with real. The smoke and mirrors that was the home of the Pieczecks I could deal with if I had to, but... I'd said it before, and I was right. Pastor Ed Pieczeck was just another huckster of holiness.

Sheesh, and this guy is supposed to be helping people.

I got in my car and drove home. It was almost two o'clock in the morning. I texted Janet and told her to call me at six-thirty in the morning, then I set the alarm for six o'clock, stripped off my clothes, and fell naked into bed.

32

THE FOLLOWING MORNING, I LEFT MY APARTMENT FRESH, enthusiastic, and ready to do battle on behalf of my three murder victims. I drove to Red Bank, stopping at Hardee's along the way to get coffee and two sausage and egg biscuits to go. Thus, it was just after eight o'clock when I arrived at the subdivision and parked on the street directly in front of Pastor Ed's hidey-hole.

Janet had called earlier as I'd requested, and I'd given her the address and told her to meet me there at nine-thirty, thirty minutes before the pastor was supposed to meet me. She agreed.

So why was I there so early? I was just covering the bases. If our erstwhile pastor arrived early, I wanted to be there.

I took a couple sips of the steaming hot coffee, unwrapped a biscuit, rolled down the window, reclined the seat slightly, and settled down to watch the house.

The ninety minutes passed uneventfully. Janet arrived at nine-thirty. She parked behind me and then clambered into the passenger seat of my car with two large coffees and a dozen donuts.

A dozen? Are you kidding me? It would take me two weeks to burn off the extra calories.

True to his word, Pastor Ed arrived at ten o'clock sharp. The black bags beneath his eyes were telling: the guy probably hadn't slept all night. I so wanted to ask him if and what he'd told his wife, but I bit my tongue. It wasn't important. It wasn't my business, and it wasn't relevant to the case.

"Here, put these on," I said, handing Janet latex gloves and Tyvek booties.

"Good morning," he muttered, without looking at us as we joined him on the front porch. He unlocked the front door, pushed it open, and stepped aside for Janet and me to enter.

I asked him to stay out on the front porch while we cleared the house. In the harsh light of day, with the drapes not open, it was beyond depressing.

My first stop was pastor Ed's inner sanctum. I stood for a moment, looked around, then I looked sideways at Janet. She was wide-eyed, smiling. She looked at me and rolled her eyes. I smiled, shook my head and went to the camera, pretended to look through it, and slipped the memory card back into its socket, smiling as I did at the thought that I'd made a copy of it before I left home that morning.

The other bedrooms were also unfurnished and unused except for a spider that had taken up residence in the corner of the ceiling. The kitchen, the last stop on the tour, was also bare, except for a half-dozen bottles of water in the fridge. I turned to go back to Ed on the front porch when I noticed a door partially hidden by the open kitchen door.

No wonder I missed it last night.

I opened the door to find a rickety flight of wooden steps that led down into almost total darkness. I flipped the light switch on the wall and descended the steps into a windowless basement. But for a couple of ancient dining chairs and a rickety kitchen table, it was bare, unused... At least that's what I thought at first glance, but then I spotted a large, discolored patch in the otherwise uniform gray color of the concrete floor. And then I noticed another patch on the back wall. Above that, and on the ceiling, I could see what I was sure was blood spatter. I'd found what I believed to be my crime scene, where Victoria Randolph had spent the last few terrifying minutes of life.

Oh, my Lord...

"Janet, come down here," I called up the stairs.

"Look at this," I said when she arrived, pointing to the patch on the floor. "And this, and this. Look at the ceiling."

"It's blood, isn't it?" she asked. "Someone's tried to clean it up, but it's blood. Is this where Mrs. Randolph was killed, do you think?"

"I don't know," I said despondently. "Not for sure, but probably. Go get the field kit from my car and test it. I'm going to go talk to that frickin' freak of a pastor. Let me know the results as soon as you know."

She ran up the stairs. I followed and went out onto the porch to talk to Pastor Ed. He was sitting on the steps with his head in his hands, crying.

"Pastor Ed," I said gently. "Does anyone else have a key to this place?"

"I have a key, and I leave another under the mat on the back porch." His breath hitched in his throat. "It's sometimes necessary for some of the games we play. That's it, just the two keys."

"Who knows about the key under the mat?"

"Just my... friends."

Oh geez, what a creep.

"What about the basement?" I asked, watching for the tell. "What do you use it for?"

He frowned, shrugged, then said, "Nothing. I've only been down there once..." and then he shuddered.

It could have been one of those involuntary things that happens every now and then—we all know about those, right? Or it could have been that he was reliving the demise of Victoria Randolph.

Janet appeared in the doorway, her face white. She looked like she was about to throw up.

"Do you have a minute, LT?"

I nodded and stepped back inside.

"You're right; it turned pink. There's blood all over the place, everywhere. Oh, that poor woman. Someone tried to clean it up. We should call Mike Willis, ASAP. If we had a Luma-lite, I think the basement would light up like a Christmas tree."

I nodded. "Call him, now. Tell him what we found and to get here ASAP."

And she did.

I ran my tongue over my lips, turned and looked toward the front door, then pulled my cuffs from my belt and walked back out onto the porch.

"Edward Pieczeck," I said. "I need you to stand up for me please."

He turned his head to the right, attempting to look over his shoulder.

"Excuse me?"

"I need you to stand up and put your hands behind your back."

"What for?" he asked as he slowly started to stand.

Janet was now behind me, her hand on her weapon.

"I'm arresting you for the murder of Victoria Randolph," I replied.

"But I didn't kill her. I swear to you." He started to back off the porch with his hands up.

"Don't try it, Ed," I said quietly. "Don't make me take you down. Just turn around, put your hands behind your back, and we'll get you to Detective Toliver's car and then to the PD as quietly as possible."

"Quietly? Are you out of your mind? My wife is going to find out. She's going to find out about everything. She's going to think I'm a murderer." He began to sob. "Please. Don't do this. I swear by the Almighty God that I didn't kill anyone!"

"You have the right to remain silent," I began.

I carefully took hold of his right hand and drew it gently behind his back. The man was as limp as a piece of tissue paper left out in the rain.

I continued with the Miranda Rights up to the point where I had to ask, "Edward Pieczeck, do you understand these rights as I've just read them to you?"

"No. I don't understand them. I don't understand anything. Why are you doing this to me? I've done nothing wrong."

He cried, his cheeks wet with tears, his eyes wide and wild, as the cuffs tightened around his wrists. He began to twist in my hands, as if, even with the handcuffs on, he could somehow get away from me and take off running.

"Please, stay calm, sir," Janet ordered as she walked to her car and opened the back door.

I helped him into the back seat of the car... and stood for a minute, and then closed the car door. I would have stayed with him and left the door open if he hadn't started to cry and shake like a baby. It was too much for me to handle. I hated to see a grown man cry even under the most tolerable of circumstances: His mom dies. His dog dies. But this... It was pathetic, and God knows he had money enough for the best attorneys.

Hell, if anyone should be crying, it should be me. I'm the one who has to make a case out of the mess. I just arrested a man for murder and, as yet, I'm not even sure he did it. I don't know whose blood is in the basement; I'm betting it's Victoria's, but it could be anybody's.

I watched as Janet stretched the yellow tape across the front of the driveway, and then I heard the sound of sirens wailing off in the distance. Minutes later, there were blue and white cruisers lined up along the street and more on the way: Baker Avenue was about to become a very active place.

"Janet," I said, "get the pastor out of here. Have one of the uniforms take him to Amnicola and make sure he understands that he's to put the pastor in an interview room, *not* the tank."

"I understand, LT. An interview room; not the tank."

I posted two officers at the entrance to the driveway, one with a visitor log, and went back inside the house. It's always the same. You make the call and everybody and his uncle arrives on the scene. *Talk about overkill.*

As I mounted the porch steps, I heard one of the neighbors, a black woman, talking to one of the cops I just posted at the driveway.

"It's about time," I heard her say.

I turned and joined her at the roadside, interrupting her discourse with the officer.

"Excuse me?" I said, "I'm Lieutenant Gazzara. Can I help you?"

I looked hard at the woman. She was an older lady, heavy-set, thin red hair, and she wore a lot of makeup. She looked like a tough one. I could tell she was not only not intimidated by me, but eager to talk to someone.

"Help me? I was just..." she said, drawing herself up to full height.

I had to smile, tongue in cheek.

"Yes, I heard you," I said. "What did you mean, 'it's about time'?"

"Well, it is. Look at the place, girl. It's a disgrace to the neighborhood, and I gotta live next door to it. And the comin's and goin's... It's disgraceful. Why are you here? What have they been doin' in there?"

"Care to tell me about it?" I asked, ignoring her question and handing her one of my business cards.

"I've seen that man you just put in the back of the police car. He's been bringin' women here, different women, two or three days a week. They stay an hour or two, and then they leave. I seen 'em. Pretty women," she replied. "Otherwise, the place is like it's vacant, the grass never mowed, weeds growin' everywhere... Is it a crack house I got next to mine? I'm retired. I'm not movin' until they plant my fat ass in the ground at St. Josephine's Cemetery over on Lincoln. The last thing I want is problems with the neighbors."

"What is your name, ma'am?" I asked, taking out my iPad and opening the Note app.

"My name is Lorretta Friedman. I've lived here for more'n ten years. I was happy when they finally sold this house." She pointed a bony finger at Pastor Ed's place. "I thought they'd fix it up." She shook her head and frowned. "But they didn't, did they? So what's been goin' on in there?"

"I'm going to ask you to make an official statement, Miss Friedman. I'll record it and have it printed out, then you can read it and sign it. Can you do that for me, please?"

"Well, I suppose," she huffed and folded her arms.

I took her up onto the porch and we sat down, side by side, on the steps. I turned on the recording app, entered the relevant details, and then guided her through what she'd already told me.

"So what else can you tell me?" I asked.

"Well," she said earnestly. "Sometimes there's no one in the house for days and days. And then suddenly, at around eleven or twelve o'clock at night, you hear people goin' in there. An' it's just the voices I hear. Then there are... the other things." She wrinkled her nose as if the thought of it caused an insufferable smell.

"What other things, Miss Friedman?" I prompted her.

She moved closer to me. "The whippin' sounds. The groaning. The yellin'. It was disgustin'. I may be old, but I'm not dead. I know what those sounds were. They was doin' the nasty, an' a whole lot more, if you ask me. And that man they just took away... he was always here when it was going on."

"So you could hear people having sex inside the house?" I asked.

She chuckled, then said, "It weren't the kind of sex I know about, but yes, I guess it was. How his wife could go along with this, I have no idea."

"His wife?" I asked as a cold shiver ran down my back.

So she is in on it. Lying little SOB. He was so desperate that his wife must not find out about his deviant second life. Did he lie to protect her? Was she part of this scene, too?

"I'm assumin' it was his wife. I saw her come to the house without him sometimes, and sometimes they came together. I just thought that maybe she came to clean the place, or check on it. I don't know... You know, I think there's a family of raccoons taken up residence up there in the attic." She pointed at a couple of torn shingles on the roof.

"Can you describe her for me?" I asked.

"I don't really remember much about her. She usually came in the evening. She was dressed nice, like. She had hair to her shoulders. More of a healthy athletic build than one of those too-skinny types. But I never got a close look at her face."

"You didn't happen to see what kind of car she was driving, did you?"

She nodded. "Not the model, but it was silver. That's all I know." She pointed to a nearby streetlamp. "And the only reason I know it was silver is because one time she parked under that light."

Out of the corner of my eye, I saw Mike Willis's CSI Command Unit pull up two houses back. He couldn't get closer because of the police cars; the count was up to nine, along with two fire trucks and an ambulance.

"Thank you, Miss Friedman. I'll get all this transcribed and then have you read and sign it, okay?"

"I suppose," she said.

"And I may be back to ask you a few more questions, would that be okay? I'll call you first, of course."

She shrugged. "Okay," she said as she pulled her sweater tighter around her.

I thanked her, told her goodbye, then went to meet Mike.

33

"Frea-ky," Mike said when he looked inside the pastor's bondage room. He was dressed from head to toe in white Tyvek complete with a face mask and latex gloves.

He was right, it was freakish. I know a lot of people will say live-and-let-live and who am I to judge and all that mumbo-jumbo. But we do judge, don't we? And the playroom at 221 Baker Avenue was, by any standards, just plain weird.

You know, I've seen some horrible things during my years as a homicide detective, and maybe it's because of that, the idea of bringing it home and into my kitchen or the bedroom is beyond me. I can't wrap my head around it.

I thought back to those first couple of days after they made me Harry's partner. I remember he showed me some crime scene photos. This is what? Ten years ago...

Anyway, there was this old couple, both in their mid-seventies. What he did to piss her off, I've no idea, but she beat him to death with a ball-peen hammer. She hit him with that thing so many times, well, they had to stop counting at eighty-one. The rest of the blows were unidentifiable, so was the old guy; it was hard to tell he was even a human. Can you imagine? I can still see those photographs. Terrible... but it's what I do, right?

"This stuff can wait, or maybe you can put your techs on it," I said, taking Mike's arm and pulling him away from the torture chamber. "Where I need you is downstairs."

I pointed him toward the basement and then followed him down the rickety steps.

"Oh boy," he said, placing his case on the floor at the bottom of the steps. "Someone's been hard at work."

"What's that?" I asked as we descended the steps into the basement.

"Don't you smell it? Bleach."

It hadn't registered with me since so many homes have washing machines in the basement. When I came down the first time, I didn't even think about it. Why wouldn't the basement smell like bleach or any other cleaning fluid? But as I looked around, I was ashamed to admit I didn't even notice that there was no washing machine or dryer... And, it was a frickin' big basement.

"No problem, though," Mike said. "Turn off the lights will you please, Lieutenant."

He popped open his box of goodies... Well, I thought it was a forensic kit, but it wasn't. It was a Foster+Freeman Crime-lite. He removed the device from its case along with two sets of what looked like one-piece welding goggles; one of which he handed to me. I remembered the department had ordered him one from the UK, but I'd never seen it. Now I got to do so up close and personal.

We donned the goggles, and he turned on the Crime-lite and integrated video camera. The entire south side of the room was illuminated, almost from our feet to a point on the ceiling just in front of us. I'd never seen anything like it...

And oh, my, God! There was no doubt now of what happened in that basement. It had been a blood bath. It was everywhere— all over the south wall and floor and what do you know: there were footprints, one full, the other a partial.

"I'll take it from here, Kate," Willis said thoughtfully. "I'll gather samples and get them to the lab immediately. The photographer will get the footprints. Have you any idea what happened, or to who?"

"Oh, I have ideas... I'm thinking that this is where Victoria Randolph died. She was the only one not killed at home," I replied, shaking my head. "And I think I know who killed her, but the footprints don't look right."

The partial was smaller than I would have expected. Pastor Ed was tall and worked out. I hadn't checked his shoe size. He could, I suppose, have small feet. I took my iPhone from my pocket and snapped a couple of quick photos of the glowing footprints for myself.

Two people? Could he and his wife... She's looking more and more like a person of interest.

"Okay, Mike," I sighed. "I'm out of here. I have a suspect to question. Keep me up to speed, will you please?"

"You got it, Kate. Take care."

As I ascended the steps, I felt a weird twisting in my gut. It wasn't the delicious nervous state of anticipation I usually experienced when I was about to interview a suspected killer. Nope. This was something else. A piece of the puzzle wasn't fitting, and no matter how hard I tried to force it, it wasn't going to.

Janet was waiting for me outside. She'd already stripped off her gloves and booties; I did the same.

Pastor Ed had been transferred to a blue and white and was already on his way to the station.

"What's the matter, LT?" Janet asked.

"Something isn't right. Mike's magic light revealed a blood bath and a couple of footprints. So someone walked in the blood, possibly two people... or not. I dunno. We'll have to wait and see,

"Maybe they're Victoria's footprints," Janet said.

"Well, that's a thought. I don't think so. What the hell was she doing down there in the first place?"

"Well," Janet said, "the footprints could only belong to one of three people, right? The victim, the killer, or an accomplice, or both, and I'm liking Pastor Ed. You should have seen him when I transferred him to the blue and white. It won't take much for him to crack and spill his guts. Especially when he finds out we're going to call his wife."

"Did you tell him that?"

"Not yet... Hey, there were originally sixty blue pills in that prescription. Is that for just one month, do you think? One a day, two, three? Who has that kind of stamina?"

I had to smile to myself when I thought about that. I did actually know someone... *Hmm, those were the days. And he didn't need any frickin' pills to keep him going.*

"Hey, LT, what are you smiling at?"

I didn't know I was, smiling.

"No one can," I said. "That's why they take the little blue pills," I muttered. "Come on. I'll meet you at the station. You want to play bad cop?"

"Ooh yeah. Don't I always?" Janet nodded enthusiastically.

I had to laugh because she looked like a sweet young kid, but she did have a knack for the bad cop routine. Though I didn't mind; it made a change for me to be the good cop, kind of refreshing.

34

For some reason traffic was light that day, and we made it to Amnicola quite quickly.

The first thing I did when we arrived was send Janet to check on Pastor Ed. He was secured in interrogation room C. A and B were occupied by a woman who'd been caught shoplifting at a convenience store and a guy Traffic had picked up walking on the hard shoulder of I-75 in torn jeans, a ratty shirt and with more than three-thousand dollars in his pocket along with a bag of heroin. It takes all sorts.

The second thing I did was call the Chief.

"I hear you've made an arrest, Lieutenant, Pastor Edward Pieczeck. That makes me very nervous. I hope you have it locked down tight."

Sheesh, so do I, I thought, and that thought made me nervous too.

I quickly brought the Chief up to speed, and then continued, "He never told us about the house. Mike Willis and his team are there now. Someone died in that basement, Chief and I'm convinced it was Victoria Randolph. He owns the house, and he's lied to us consistently. I have his DNA, but we still have to send it to the lab for processing. He's admitted a lot, but not to the homicides. I'm going to interrogate him now. I don't think it will take much to get him to talk."

"I hope you're right, Catherine; I hope you're right."

So do I, Chief, so do I.

"There are some anomalies, though, Chief. Lieutenant Willis found some bloody footprints at the scene, and I'm thinking there's something not quite right about them. It could be that Pieczeck had an accomplice. We'll have to wait and see on that."

"Are you going for a confession?"

"I think I have to. There's plenty of evidence to suggest that the pastor is the perp, but it's all circumstantial and fairly easily explained away. A good attorney would have him out of here in minutes, but the guy is a wreck. I might be able to get him to cop a plea."

"I'm afraid a plea will not be good enough, Catherine. I have half the movers and shakers on the Mountain breathing down my neck, especially Governor Randolph. You need a confession, free and clear."

"I'll do my best. He may be a wreck, but he's got everything to lose."

"Well, get in there. Let's see if you can work your magic. Good luck, Kate." And he hung up.

Again, as I headed down to the interview room, I could feel that twisting feeling churning away in my stomach.

I stood for a couple minutes with Janet, watching Pastor Ed through the one-way glass. She'd already gotten him a bottle of water. It stood unopened on the table next to his right hand. He was still wearing the cuffs, his hands clasped together on the tabletop; his eyes were red, puffed, his hair mussed.

"Has he said anything?" I asked, finally.

"No. He just cries and then stops and then cries some more." Janet shook her head. "It's pitiful," she added, taking a sip of coffee then looking down at her watch.

"Janet, you want to start?" I asked.

"No. Lieutenant, you start," Chief Johnston said, almost making me leap out of my skin.

I hadn't heard him come in and neither had Janet.

"Geez, Chief," I said. "Don't do that. You'll give me a heart attack."

He smiled, a rare occurrence in itself, then said, "You're only going to get one shot at this, Catherine. If he lawyers up... You did Mirandize him, I assume?"

"That I did, Chief, and I recorded it, just to be sure."

He nodded and smiled again.

Wow, two in a row.

"Okay, Janet," I said. "Let me have the file, please."

She handed me not one file, but three. I laid them on the table, opened the Randolph file and flipped through the images, again noting the minimal amount of blood found around the body. I nodded to myself, gathered my thoughts, and then the three files, stepped into the small room and sat down opposite the pastor.

He looked up at me. His eyes were wet, his bottom lip trembling; it was freaking pitiful.

"Detective, this is all a mistake. I didn't kill anyone—"

"Stop," I said, interrupting him.

He looked startled.

"Edward Pieczeck," I said quietly. "I must inform you that this interview is being recorded. Do you understand?"

He nodded, then whispered, "Yes, I understand."

I then read the date, time, etc., for the record and, read him his rights again, and asked him if he wanted his attorney present. He hesitated, then declined, and I had to wonder why. He was in more trouble than he knew. I glanced up at the one-way glass and shrugged.

"So you think this is all a mistake?" I said.

He nodded vigorously, then said, "I had extra-marital affairs, yes. To that sin I humbly confess. I did, but that's not a crime. As God is my witness, I did not commit murder. I should not be here, like this." He held up his cuffed wrists.

I stood, took them off him, then sat down again.

He was drenched in sweat. His shirt, a pink button-down, once stiff with starch, was a wrinkled rag. Dark circles of sweat had formed under his armpits.

"Do you own the property at 221 Baker Avenue in Red Bank?" I asked.

"Yes. Yes. I bought it when the neighborhood was starting to change. It was a foreclosure. I got a real deal on it and was able to pay cash. I just wanted a place to get away... and..." he stuttered.

"You wanted a place where you could play your games, and... kill?"

"*No!*" he yelled. "I'm telling you I didn't kill anyone!" He looked down at his hands.

"Pastor," I said, "we found blood evidence in your basement. Someone died horribly down there."

I opened the file and laid out the pictures of Victoria, Meryl Dilly, and Lucille Benedict.

"Oh, my God," Pastor Ed muttered.

"These women had families, Pastor. Friends. Neighbors and people who cared about them. Now they are gone. They must have suffered terribly, all of them. How did you feel, Pastor, as you smashed their heads and faces, over and over and—"

"*I didn't hit anyone!*" he shouted, rising to his feet, his hands curled into fists on the tabletop, supporting his weight. "I didn't do this! I could never do this!"

He stood upright, then leaned forward over the table. I didn't move, not an inch. His hands were trembling as he pushed the pictures away, and then he sat down again, looked down at the table, took several deep breaths then looked up at me.

"I was having an affair with Meryl, yes," he said quietly. "It had been going on for almost two years."

He paused then continued, "Lucille, may God bless and keep

her, we had the same tastes, the same desires. Both of them were willing participants. They signed their contracts. It was just sex. That was all."

Contracts? I thought. *What the hell is that about?*

But I didn't interrupt him. Now that the door was open, even if was only a crack, I wanted to keep him talking.

"And what about Victoria?" I said. "That's her blood in your basement, isn't it?" I took a deep breath and folded my hands in front of me.

"No, it can't be. She hadn't signed a contract," he stuttered.

"Contract?" I leaned forward.

"A dominant-submissive contract. All my partners signed a contract. It was part of the game. Part of the role-playing. Victoria hadn't signed hers yet. She wanted something in exchange, and I was working on it," he blubbered. "Oh, God."

"What was that? What did she want?"

"She wanted to buy a piece of property in Memphis. I told her I'd front her the money, but then she'd owe me. We were negotiating the terms." His cheeks burned red.

"Is that what you were doing when you killed her?" I asked. "Negotiating the terms?"

He sighed, his shoulders drooped, his chin dropped to his chest, and he whispered, "No. I didn't kill her. You've got to believe me."

"I'm sorry, Pastor, but that's not going to happen. You see, we have your video camera and the memory card. There are recordings on it of you engaging in sexual acts with Meryl Dilly in your house at 221 Baker Avenue. One is time-stamped between twelve-twenty-three and two-twelve on Tuesday afternoon. She died less than two hours later. Her husband was away on business. You were the last person to see her alive. What do you have to say about that, Pastor?"

He just shook his head and said, "I didn't kill her. I didn't kill anyone."

"By your own admission, you were also the last person to see Lucille Benedict alive. Look, Pastor Ed," I said gently, pleading with him. "Just tell me what happened. If the sex got too rough and there was an accident, we can work it out. Believe me, it wouldn't be the first time that something like that has happened. You got excited; she tried to stop you, but... If it was an accident, it's better to admit it now, while you still can."

Holy cow. What am I thinking? How the hell can you accidentally beat three people to death with a crowbar? Oh well, it was worth a shot... And where the hell is that crowbar?

"No, no no!" he yelled, interrupting the thought.

"Fine," I snapped. "So, you beat them to death to cover up a sexual act gone wrong."

"NO!" He began to sob.

"Then if you didn't kill them, who did? Who else has access to that house, Pastor? Who else could have lured Victoria there and then killed her?"

I watched his expression change. The man was a chameleon. He sat a little more upright, put his shoulders back, wiped his eyes on his shirt sleeves, narrowed them, thought for a minute.

"No one. I told you, I have the only key, except for the one under the mat." His voice was quiet, controlled.

It was then I had a sudden thought, one I should have had much earlier.

"What about Martin Butterworth? Did he know about the house?"

"Well, yes. He did some work on it when I purchased it, but—"

"Did he know about the key?" I asked.

"I... I don't think so. I don't know how he could."

"Did he know why you purchased the house?"

He slowly shook his head, then said, "No, I kept that to myself, but..."

"But what, Pastor?"

"He could have followed me, I suppose."

That, I would have to look into. I changed course.

"So who is the woman your neighbor saw coming and going late at night?" I asked.

He looked up at me and shrugged.

"I don't know." His demeanor changed yet again. He began to cry and howl, "I don't know, I don't know," over and over again.

"Pastor, if you are covering for your wife, we'll find out. You have to tell us, and it would be better for you if you did so now. You're not helping anybody by covering for her."

Another change, he became self-righteous. "Shelly knows nothing about it. I made sure of that," he snapped.

It was like he expected some kind of approval for keeping his kinky affairs secret from his wife.

"How many women from your church *have* you been sleeping with?" I was almost afraid to hear the answer.

"Over the past few years, just the women you..."

"Just the women who are dead?" I said. "I don't believe you."

"And... Karen Silver," he muttered.

Now, I had to admit, I didn't see that one coming.

His chin was on his chest again. I turned and looked toward the mirror, my eyebrows raised in surprise.

"Karen Silver? And how long has that been going on?"

"Years, five, six, a long time." He looked at the palms of his hands. His breath hitched in his throat as he choked the sobs back. "I think I want my lawyer now, please."

I knew what was happening to him. I'd seen it so many times before. The initial shock was wearing off, and he'd just realized he was out of his depth and in it for the long haul. It had suddenly come home to Pastor Edward Pieczeck that he was in big trouble and he wasn't equipped to handle it. This was real. He could pray and make deals with the Almighty all he wanted, but that wasn't going to help him one bit here in the real world. He needed a good attorney.

"All right, Pastor," I said, rising to my feet. "You get one phone call." I grabbed the files and left the room.

I entered the observation room to find Janet staring at me with her mouth wide open.

"Close that," I said, "before something nasty flies in."

"Oh, my God," she said, drawing out the words. "Karen Silver? I wouldn't have guessed that.""That's exactly what I thought. I think we need to go talk to her again. She was very insistent that we focus on Marty Butterworth. She obviously knows more than she's letting on..." and suddenly, an image of those two bloody footprints popped into my head.

What size did Mike say they were? Nine-and-a-half? I tried to remember what size shoes Karen Silver had been wearing when we interviewed her, but I hadn't taken that much notice. *Still, judging by the size of her, that sounds about right.*

I looked at Chief Johnston and raised my eyebrows quizzically.

"Fine," he said. "You can hold Pieczeck for forty-eight hours, and then you have to charge him with something or let him go. Do what you have to, but I need a result, and quickly." He turned to go, then changed his mind, turned again and said, "Before you go, Lieutenant, I need to talk to you. In my office, in say, ten minutes."

It was said in a casual manner, but I thought there might be an underlying menace rippling away beneath it.

35

"What is it, Chief?" I asked warily as I took my seat in front of his desk

"That reporter, Clemont Rhodes showed up again. He was asking for you, but I had him brought here, to my office," he said as he steepled his forefingers and placed them on the tip of his chin.

"I haven't spoken to him or anyone else," I said firmly.

"I didn't say you did. But he told me something very disturbing. Did you know he's been following your every move for the last week? No, I can tell by the look on your face that you didn't. Be that as it may, he observed you entering the house on Baker Avenue on Wednesday evening, illegally. He's insisting that he gets an exclusive or he's going to run with the story... Catherine, we can't have that."

"Sir, I had probable cause."

"You didn't have probable cause until after you went into his house."

"It was a house he failed to mention when I initially interviewed him," I said. "I had him under surveillance, as we agreed. He led me to the house. I thought it must be the Randolph crime scene. I was also concerned that he might be holding someone hostage in there, another victim. So I entered the property. I was right, the basement was a bloodbath and probably where Victoria Randolph died."

I thought it sounded like a solid defense. But I knew I didn't have a damn leg to stand on; if the Chief decided to throw the book at me, well, I'd be screwed.He put the forefingers to his lips and looked at me, contemplating me and the situation, I was sure.

"Hmm... That's extremely thin, Catherine. Still, it seems you were right so, as I've said before, I'll back your play. Talk to that reporter. Tell him you'll give him what he wants. Now get out of here. Go catch me a killer. I really don't think it's the pastor, do you?"

Inwardly, I shook my head. *The old bastard really does have my back. Wow!*

"Perhaps not," I said. "Thank you, sir. I will."

He smiled at me—it was kind of scary; he never smiles, ever—and said, "I know you will."

So, in a daze, and with a mental sigh of relief, I thanked him for his support and left his office, and almost ran to my own.

I buzzed Janet and asked her to join me.

"You okay, LT?" she asked as she came into my office.

"Yes, why, what's up?"

"Pastor Ed called his lawyer. They took him to holding. He'll have a few hours to sit and stew there," Janet replied.

"He'll have exactly forty-eight hours, unless we can gather enough evidence to charge him with something... He didn't call his wife?"

"Nope." She shook her head. "What did the Chief want? Anything I can help with?"

"He just wanted an update, and yes, there is something you can do: find out all you can about Karen Silver. That relationship is one hell of a poke in the ribs. I *wasn't* expecting it. Maybe I should have seen it, but I didn't."

I pulled my hair back from my face. "And get the property info on Pastor Ed's love shack. I'm going to head home for the day. My body has run out of gas. I need to sleep. We'll talk to Ms. Silver in the morning when we know a little more about her."

"You got it. I'll have everything on your desk first thing tomorrow." She nodded. "Anything else?"

"Yes, actually. Find out what you can about a local reporter named Clemont Rhodes, but keep it under your hat. Okay?" I winked. "Oh, and if he should show up here, or calls, tell him I'll talk to him tomorrow... On second thought, let's head him off at the pass. Here's his card." I dug in my desk drawer, found it, and handed it to her. "Give him a call now and tell him I'll be in touch and that I'll have something for him soon."

"Sure thing," Janet said with a devilish glint in her eyes.

"Thank you, Janet. You're doing a great job," I said. And I meant it.

She blushed. "Thanks, LT. I appreciate it." And she left.

I stayed at my desk for a few more minutes, then shut everything down and left my office, taking with me a short list of phone calls I could make once I got home. I pulled into my parking space in front of my apartment, got out of the car, and then, via my peripheral vision, I spotted a silver Kia sitting in a fire zone in front of a store at the Minnie Mall just across the greenway on East Brainerd Road, and my paranoia kicked in. I could see there was a woman behind the wheel, and it looked like she was talking on the phone.

I shook my head.

Silver cars. I'm seeing them everywhere. Pastor Ed drives a silver Audi. His wife, Shelly, drives its twin. Some unknown woman, maybe the pastor's wife, or maybe Karen Silver, has been visiting the playhouse in a silver car. No, Ms. Silver's car is a black Honda... or is it? And now there's a woman parked in a towaway zone in a silver car across the street.

I looked around my own parking lot and noticed there was a silver Jeep, a silver Honda CRV, a silver E-class Mercedes, and a gray Volkswagen.

"Geez, Kate," I muttered as I inserted the key in my front door, "get over it... Gray doesn't count."

I opened the door and stepped inside, slipped the key ring over my finger, and closed the door. I set the deadbolt and the security chain, then I dropped my shoulder bag on the kitchen table, took my badge and Glock from my belt and laid them down next to it, poured myself a glass of wine, eased down on the couch, and began to mull over the events of the day... and then I fell asleep, glass in hand; fortunately, it was already empty.

IT WAS JUST AFTER TEN O'CLOCK THAT NIGHT WHEN DOC called.

"Damn it, Doc. If I were married, my husband would think we were having an affair. Can't you ever call during normal business hours?" I grumbled.

"What are those?" he asked with a chuckle. "Look, I don't have time to talk endlessly, but your hunch was right. The blood spatter in the basement does indeed belong to Victoria Randolph. She was killed at the pastor's house." He cleared his throat. "We need a swab from him to match it with the DNA found on Meryl Dilly, as soon as you can please, Kate."

"Damn it, Doc. I forgot. I already have one. It's in my bag. I'll drop it by on my way into the office in the morning. How did you get the DNA report back so quickly? It's only been a few hours."

"I didn't. I matched her blood type. She's A-negative. It's rare, but it's not definitive; it's close enough, though, and would have been enough to convict back in the good old days before DNA. I'll have the profiles expedited, which means they should be available... when they are available." He chuckled.

"Pastor Ed already confessed to having affairs with Meryl and Lucille," I said. "He hadn't gotten around to Victoria yet, not sexually, anyway, but he was working on it." I yawned.

Doc continued, "We need a match for the foreign blood on Meryl Dilly. If it isn't his, the killer is still out there."

"True," I said, "and maybe not just one killer."

I told him about the bloody footprints.

"I think I have enough to get a warrant," I said. "I'll grab his personal and work computers. These sexual predators like to share their experiences online. Maybe Mike's people will find something there."

"Good luck, Detective. We'll talk again soon."

"Good night, Doc. I'll not forget to drop off the swab."

I checked my watch. It was just after ten-thirty, way too late to request a warrant. Even I wouldn't dare call a judge at that time of night, not even my good friend, Henry Strange. It would have to wait until morning, even if it was a Saturday.

36

The following morning I woke up before the sun, slipped into a pair of sweats, tied my hair back in a ponytail, grabbed my keys and my pocket mace and headed out for a run, a big no-no, and I'd made the mistake before, much to my regret. I was supposed to go armed, always, but the damn Glock weighed a ton. The mace would have to do, not that I expected to have to use it.

I checked the towaway zone. The silver car was no longer there, not that I really expected it to be, but paranoia is a strange bedfellow and one I never chose to ignore.

Without Sadie Mae to slow me down, I was able to push myself a little harder than usual, and it felt good to feel my lungs burning, my thighs tightening with each stride. I was hot and sweaty by the time I got back to my apartment.

The sun was up, just over the horizon when I caught sight of a cardinal flitting through the trees. My mom always said if you saw a cardinal, it meant there were angels close by. Whether it was the angels that made me turn and check the towaway zone once more, or just blind luck, I can't say, but the silver car was back.

I didn't hesitate; I leaped over the fence and ran flat out across the greenway... and she saw me. I heard her start the engine and then she reversed out of the parking spot and peeled away.

I swear I broke the record for the sixty-yard dash. I knew there was no way I could catch her, but I wanted her plate number. Fortunately, the early morning traffic on East Brainerd Road was heavier than usual, and she had to wait for a gap. I ran across the parking lot and was just in time to catch a glimpse of the plate. Unfortunately, I managed to get only the first three digits of the number before she disappeared at high speed heading toward Gunbarrel Road.

The three digits were LS8.

THE FIRST THING I DID WHEN I ARRIVED AT THE PD THAT Saturday morning was buzz Janet and ask her to do a DMV search for a silver Kia with LS8 as the first three digits of the registration. Then I called Chief Johnston.

"Chief, I just wanted to let you know I'm going to get a warrant for the Pieczecks' computers. His wife has access to both. Guys like Pastor Ed like to share their experiences, and I suspect that she might be involved somehow, and she might pull a Hillary on us and BleachBit the drives."

"That's what I like about you, Catherine," he said. "You think of everything."

"Err, not hardly," I said, thinking about the damn swab I still hadn't dropped off at the forensic center.

"What else do you need, Lieutenant?"

"Nothing, sir, that I can think of right now."

"Good. Call me when you have something."

He hung up the phone, and I made the call to Judge Isaac Walker, whom I knew was on duty that weekend, and asked for search warrants for the Pieczeck home and the Church of the Savior.

Probable cause wasn't a problem as we already had the pastor in custody. The judge told me he'd prepare the warrants, and I could pick them up whenever I was ready. I told him I'd be by within the hour.

37

"Good morning, LT," Janet said, bright and breezy as she bopped into my office, her red hair was pulled back in a ponytail, two large Mickey D's coffees in hand.

Wow, did I ever have that kind of energy, and if I did, where the hell did it go?

"You're not going to believe what I have to tell you," she said, with a giggle, as she set the coffees down on the desk and sat down.

"I probably should have called you, but I knew you were tired, and I didn't want to disturb you. Anyway, about twenty minutes after you left yesterday, Mrs. Pieczeck arrived downstairs. She asked to talk to her husband, so I escorted her to an interview room, and she and the good Pastor had a long talk."

Janet looked down for a moment before lifting her head and meeting my eyes. "I... well, I couldn't help myself. I watched, and I recorded the conversation... Yes, I know we can't use it, but I thought maybe you'd like to see it. He, like, spilled his guts, LT. He told her everything, about his affairs, his perversions, the little house in Red Bank, everything, but he insisted he didn't kill anyone. He cried, too... like, a lot."

Oh, how I would have liked to have watched it with her.

"So," I said. "What did she say?"

"Just what you might expect?" She smirked and raised her eyebrows. "She told him goodbye."

I sat back in my chair, sipped my coffee, thinking, then said, "You know, Janet, you did good, recording that conversation. I'll look at it later, but right now, I'm thinking that if she didn't know about the pastor's secret life, it rules her out as the killer's accomplice."

"Killer?" she asked. "So you don't think it's the pastor?"

I shook my head.

"Wow! If it's not him, then who is it?"

"I have an idea who it might be, but I'm not quite sure."

She smiled, looked slyly at me, and said, "Yes, you are, and I think I know who it is."

"Oh, you think so? Do tell."

"Karen Silver! It has to be."

"Go on," I said, smiling indulgently at her.

"It might take a while."

"We have time."

"Well, you had me run a background on her," she said, flipping through the screens on her iPad. "The lady has quite a past."

She glanced up at me. I sipped my coffee, said nothing.

"Karen Lyn Silver," she continued. "She's forty-two years old. Divorced. Graduated from Columbia College in Chicago with a degree in Communications. Got a job with the Diocese of Chicago where she worked for almost ten years... until she was let go."

Janet looked at me, smiling. "She was having an affair with the spiritual director at the diocese home office, a guy named Marcus Burkowski. Seems they both were members at the same gym and worked out a lot... together."

She paused, looked at me, sipped her coffee, then continued.

"Anyway, they had an affair and it went bad. He dumped her, and she must have gotten totally pissed off, wouldn't accept it, because she was served with not just one, but two restraining orders by Burkowski and the Diocese of Chicago. Apparently, she began stalking him, kept showing up outside his home, at the gym, at the church on Sunday. She even threw a rock through his office window."

"So she's got a temper, then?" I felt a knot growing in the pit of my stomach.

"Uh, yeah, but I'm not done yet."

"Curiouser and curiouser," I said. "Please continue, my little mouse."

"*What?*" she screwed up her whole face as if totally confused.

"Nothing," I said. "I was just quoting *Alice in Wonderland*. Go on. Tell me more."

"Well," she said, a little less enthusiastically, "she moved to Chattanooga about ten years ago and got the job at the Church of the Savior. Since then she's been a good girl: her record is clean... Oh, but you're gonna love this: she owns a silver Kia, registration number LS8 6RP."

I nodded grimly. "She's stalking me," I said thoughtfully.

"*What?*"

"That car was parked near my apartment last night, and again this morning. I ran after it, but she was too quick, but I did get those first three digits. That's why I had you do the search. I didn't know it was her, but now I'm not surprised," I said. "Seeing as how she has a history of obsessive behavior. And I have, after all, taken Karen Silver's lover away from her."

"But you didn't say anything about it?" she said.

I shrugged. "There was nothing to say, not until we knew. Look, Pastor Ed admitted to having an affair with her, and Meryl Dilly and Lucille Benedict—"

"But not with Victoria," Janet interrupted me.

"No, but he was working on it," I said, thinking out loud. "And the more lovers Pastor Ed added to his harem, the less time he'd have for Karen, right? She wouldn't like that, would she? And if she has OCD—obsessive compulsive disorder—and we know she does, I wonder if she decided to remedy the situation?"

Janet nodded enthusiastically. "Yeah, that, and plus, she works out, a lot, as does Pastor Ed. They are both members of the Fit for Life gym. How convenient it must have been for them to meet up there, get sweaty, and then slip on over to the little playhouse on Baker Avenue for some S&M... G-ross!"

"So—" I didn't get the rest of the thought out because she interrupted me.

"Oh, my God," she yelled. "They were all members of Fit for Life: Ed, Karen, Meryl Dilly, Lucille Benedict, and Victoria Randolph."

I already knew that, but now it took on a much greater significance.

"She killed those three women," I said thoughtfully. "But the question is, did she kill them because Pastor Ed told her to, or did she do it of her own volition?"

And then I had another thought. "But if she killed Victoria Randolph in that basement, who helped her move the body? Fit and strong she might be, but she sure as hell didn't move that body on her own."

"C'mon." I stood up, grabbed my iPad and car keys, and headed out the door.

Janet, taken totally by surprise, jumped up, flipped the cover of her iPad closed, and followed me.

"Hey," she said, hurrying to keep up with me. "What's the hurry? Where are we going?"

"First to drop off a swab. Then to get the warrants and then to the church. Call Chief Wilbur and have him meet us there with backup."

"You're going to arrest her?" she asked, dumbfounded. "Do we have enough?"

"We will when I'm done with her," I said, a little more confidently than I felt.

38

CHIEF WILBUR ARRIVED AT THE CHURCH OF THE SAVIOR JUST A minute or two before we did. I drove around back and... the parking lot was empty: no other cars, either in the front or the back. Nada.

I sat for a moment, thinking, *Where the hell is she? She must know by now that we've arrested the pastor. Where would she run to... She wouldn't. She'd want to finish the job... If there was another... And if he's in custody... Then he couldn't... But who?*

I closed my eyes, mentally scanned through the crime scene photos... *Oh, my God! Got it: number four.*

I hopped out of the car and briefed Chief Wilbur on what I planned to do. I had a warrant for the Pieczeck home. So that would be my first option.

The second part of my plan was for Wilbur to find Karen Silver.

It was all a bit of a Hail Mary, but what the hell. If I was right, we were dealing with an extremely dangerous woman and, somehow, we had to get her out of circulation before she killed again... because I had the creepiest feeling that I was next on her list... after Shelly Pieczeck, that is.

"I'm not liking this one bit, Chief," I said. "Janet and I will head on over to the Pieczeck home and serve the warrant. In the meantime, you need to try to locate Karen Silver. I'm thinking her house, the gym, or she's still stalking me and watching us right now."

Janet and Wilbur involuntarily glanced over their shoulders.

"Chief, if and when you or your men find her, you're to sit tight and call me. Do *not* approach her, is that understood?"

Wilbur nodded. "I'm to call you if I find her. Good enough, Lieutenant."

We talked for several more minutes then Wilbur went to meet with his crew, gave them their instructions, then got into his car and drove away, presumably to Silver's home.

Janet and I headed to the Pieczeck home where I hoped to find Shelly Pieczeck still in one piece... and alive, hiding out, ashamed to show her face in public after her husband's arrest.

Or throwing his things in the trash, more likely, I thought.

I turned the cruiser off the highway, through the unmarked entrance to The Cloisters, onto the gravel driveway, and then on to the electronic gate... It was open, smashed, hanging askew. One of the hinges had been torn out of the brick post on the right side, and there were chunks of brickwork scattered on the driveway. As we drove past the gate, I glanced at Janet. Her face was white, a stark contrast against her red hair.

"This isn't good, LT," she said, shaking her head.

"Not good at all, Sergeant. Be prepared, okay? Check your weapon."

She did.

The cruiser's tires sang a tune on the cobblestone pathway as we continued driving toward the house. We rounded the corner and approached the ugly, block-shaped home from the east. At the south side, a silver Kia Optima with a badly damaged front end was parked out front next to a beat-up, red Chevy pick-up truck.

I parked at the west side of the house, in front of the garage, out of sight of the front door.

"I think we have ourselves a situation, Janet," I said as I looked sideways at her. "You okay?"

She gulped. "You don't think we should wait for backup, LT?"

I shook my head. "No. If Karen Silver's inside, Shelly Pieczeck's in big trouble. She's number four in that photo with Pastor Ed, remember?"

She nodded.

I grabbed my phone and called Wilbur. "She's here, at the Pieczeck home. We're going in. Come as quick as you can, Chief." And I hung up.

"Vests," I said.

We exited the vehicle and donned our body armor. I set my iPhone to record, stuffed it into one of my vest pockets, and then we drew our weapons and headed to the front door. I placed my hand on the hood of the Kia. *Still warm; maybe we aren't too late.*

Believing a crime to be in progress, I didn't bother to ring the doorbell. This wasn't a social visit.

Janet and I stood on either side of the door, backs to the wall, weapons drawn. I looked at her, took two steps forward, turned and nodded. She grabbed the knob, turned it, and I slammed the door open with a well-placed kick.

We burst into the room... Shelly Pieczeck was sitting on the center of the couch, her face ashen, her hands clasped in her lap as if praying. Karen Silver was sitting next to her.

"Lieutenant," Shelly Pieczeck said, half rising to her feet. "Oh, thank God you're here. I've been trying to convince Karen here that it's over between me and Edward, that I know all about what's been going on and that I've already instructed my attorney to file for divorce, but she doesn't believe me."

Karen Silver reached over and grabbed Shelly Pieczeck's wrist. "Shut up and sit still, bitch. I'll do the talking. Lieutenant, why don't you put those nasty guns away. You're scaring my friend."

Karen was a mess, dark bags under her eyes, hair unkempt, and she had several nasty-looking cuts on both hands.

I nodded to Janet, and we holstered our weapons. We had to try and get Karen away from Pieczeck before we could make a move.

I wonder where the hell Marty Butterworth is, and where the hell is Wilbur and his men; they'd better get here and damn soon.

"Karen, we'd like to talk to you," I said calmly.

Her eyes were glazed over. "Screw you, bitch... and your little girly friend. You think I don't know what you're here for? Not to talk, that's for sure. You're here to arrest me." Her voice was calm, her demeanor relaxed, her eyes mere slits that glinted in the artificial light.

I had a sudden feeling it was all about to go sideways. I shifted my weight onto my left foot and hooked my thumb in my belt, an inch in front of my Glock.

"No, Karen," I lied. "Why would you say that?"

It was now obvious to me that either she was on something or her mind had slipped and her brain was on the dark side of nowhere. *This isn't going to end well.*

"*You took him away from me,*" she screeched, so suddenly and so loudly I just about jumped out of my skin. "And now..." she said, all calm and serene again, "you've come for me too. You want to keep us apart, but you can't because I'm going to be his bride. It's destiny, don't you see?" she said dreamily. "You just have to understand, that's all, and then you'll see... you'll understand God's plan for Edward and me, *and it doesn't include you, you slut,*" she screamed in Shelly Pieczeck's ear.

"Understand what, Karen?"

"It's part of my job," she continued in the sing-song voice.

"Part of your job?" I asked gently. "What job? Was it your job to kill those women? Did Pastor Ed ask you to kill them?"

Shelly Pieczeck gasped.

Karen's eyes seemed to clear a little. She blinked rapidly. It was like she'd been daydreaming, but when she heard the word "kill," it was a trigger and brought her out of it.

"No, he didn't ask me to kill them. He had nothing to do with it.

How could he? He's a man of God. It was just... something I had to do."

"Why, Karen? What had they done to you?" I asked.

I glanced at Janet. She was standing rigid, transfixed by what she was hearing. I looked at Shelly Pieczeck; she was trembling.

Karen's eyes flickered rapidly, gazed here, there around the room, at me, at Janet, Shelly, as if she were searching for something. *Maybe she's looking for Marty.*

"I don't expect you to understand," she snarled. "I love him, you see. And he loves me too. He said he was my protector, my master, my God. And like our heavenly father, he would create me anew."

Holy cow. Are you serious?

"God tells us to love our enemies, as we love our friends," she said. "And I did, for a while; all of them, with all my heart, until I realized that they were just using him, taking advantage of him."

"Karen," I said ever so gently, trying not to spook her. "What happened to your hands? How did you get those cuts?"

She held her free hand out in front of her and admired it.

I'd known other detectives who talked about seeing the face of a killer shifting, darkening, transforming from a normal person into something abnormal like they were possessed. I'd never seen it myself. Not until that moment.

"Those women didn't have a real desire to serve Edward. We were his servants, his handmaidens. He was the master. We followed his commands inside the fortress and out. It was the way it had to be but... they weren't... doing... that," she said. Her eyes narrowed and she licked her lips.

Oh, my God. A forty-three-year-old handmaiden. It can't get any better than that.

"The fortress?"

"The house on Baker Avenue. You know what I'm talking about. I saw you there yesterday, talking to that nosey old skank next door. And you took Edward away from me," she said snarling.

Fortress? That nasty little two-bedroom property? Yuck!

"I had to, Karen. You know that, don't you? That house is where Victoria Randolph died, isn't it? Would you like to tell me about that?"

"Yes. Yes, yessss," she shouted, standing up and waving her arms like the sails on a windmill. "I killed her. Killed Meryl Dilly too, and Lucille. Meryl wanted Edward all for herself. That was against the rules. But then she started seeing Edward by herself. I saw the videos. Who did she think she was?"

"How did you see the videos?"

"I have a key. When I couldn't find Edward, when he wasn't answering his phone, I'd go to the fortress. No one was supposed to enter without his permission, but I did. I couldn't help myself. I'd park outside the house if I saw his car and wait for him and Meryl or Lucille to leave."

"Lucille went to the fortress, too?"

Karen looked at me as if I was stupid. "Edward would call, and we would come. It was the way of things."

"How come you had a key? Did Edward give it to you?"

"I..." she drew the word out, swept her arms out in front of her, "am his principal handmaiden. I know everything about him. I know where he is... always, every day and every night. I know his schedule, his finances, his likes and dislikes. I am the gatekeeper. I was the first one, the first of his handmaidens and... And I made a copy of the key under the mat, you silly bitch." She dropped her chin to her chest, her arms spread wide, "He was ready to replace me with... one of *them*."

She began to cry.

"It's okay, Karen," I said. "I'm here to help. You can tell me everything."

"I didn't mean for him to get the blame. He didn't know," she said as if I wasn't there. "I didn't think anyone would ever figure out what happened. I went to talk to Meryl at her home to try to convince her to stop seeing Edward. She was married, you know. She was committing adultery—a terrible sin—willingly and without remorse."

And killing her isn't? I tried not to let any negative emotion show on my face.

Karen continued, "I thought if I appealed to her woman to woman that she'd see what I was trying to say. She had a husband. I didn't. But she wouldn't listen to me. She laughed at me. She laughed while I cried."

"What did you hit her with, Karen?"

"I had a crowbar in my car." She smiled. "That was lucky. She told me to leave, that she was going to tell Edward. I almost did, leave. But the Lord intervened, spoke to me, showed me the way and the awesome power of his will." She said it with her eyes closed, arms held out slightly from her sides, palms out, like Christ welcoming his children, as if she was reliving a dream.

Her eyes snapped open. "I went to my car, took the crowbar from the trunk, and returned to the house. She hadn't bothered to lock the door. I walked right back in and..." She shrugged.

It was as if she had gotten caught stealing a second slice of chocolate cake when she was supposed to be on a diet. My mouth fell open.

"What about Victoria Randolph?" I asked her again. I had to force the words out.

Shelly Pieczeck tried to wiggle away, but Karen pointed at her and said, "Don't move. I'm not done with you yet."

Shelly whimpered.

Karen's face became serious and angry. "Victoria Randolph," her voice changed to a flinty rasp, "was not one of the chosen. She spurned Edward. For even the smallest shred of attention, Edward would gush over her. He became weak, gave her a job in the office so he could watch me suffer her barbs. He said jealousy is a sin, and that I was being punished for it, and that I needed to learn humility. So he planted that tease in front of me so I'd have to look at her."

She looked down at her hands, began to nervously pick at her fingers. She chewed her bottom lip as she stepped slightly away from the couch. I raised my hands so she would see I was not going to make any sudden moves.

"I was being punished for loving him. She was being rewarded for using him. I saw he had a contract drawn up for her that included the exchange of certain favors. He would give her money to buy an apartment building in Memphis or somewhere, and she would sit at his feet for an hour. Can you believe that? And he was willing to go for it. To have a woman like a Jezebel, sitting at his feet." Tears flooded her eyes. "He never did that for me. The things I did for him, the horrors I endured for him."

I didn't dare speak for fear of ending her rant.

"I told Victoria," she continued, "that Edward wanted her to meet him at the fortress. I told her that he had some paperwork for her to sign, that he was closing on a piece of property. Ha, the silly bitch ate it up. Poor Victoria, she had no clue what it was like to be told no. She found out soon enough."

"How did you get her to go down to the basement?"

"It was easy. I just left the lights on down there and the door open. The radio was on playing some nice music. Of course, she thought it was for her. And it was, in a way, but not in the way she thought... Oh, don't be so shocked, Detective."

Karen Silver rolled her eyes and then continued, "Victoria was willing to cheat on her husband. It was early in the morning, just after midnight. She crept out while Darby was still asleep—you see, I knew they slept in separate rooms. She told me so. She was always sitting at her desk," she said and waved a hand at an imaginary desk, "bragging to me about how she didn't have to screw Darby anymore, and how she didn't have to work, but couldn't say no to Edward when he offered her the position. She didn't think I knew about their plan. Bitch! She didn't know I was the gatekeeper and everything that Edward did had to go through me first."

"How did you get the body out of the basement, Karen?"

"Marty Butterworth helped me, naturally. Edward was the only person ever to do anything for him. He worshipped Edward. He would do anything to help Edward, to keep his secret from getting out... And, of course, for his reward." She put back her shoulders, pushed her ample bosom forward, and slid her hands down the curve of her hips.

I felt exhausted, from the endless tension, but I couldn't let my guard down. She began to pace back and forth, babbling on about her undying love for Edward and how she didn't mean for him to get hurt, be blamed for what she had to do.

"I'd never wanted anything bad to happen to him. He is my master, and I'm here to do his will."

That was when I saw it for what it really was. I couldn't help it; I rolled my eyes as I listened to her confess her undying love for a man who enjoyed abusing her, tormenting her not just physically but also mentally.

"Karen? Karen, you didn't tell me anything about Lucille Benedict. What happened to her?"

"Lucille? Oh, that little cheater. She was screwing Edward, too. I actually liked her," Karen admitted reluctantly. "But she was *so* needy."

"What?" I said, trying to control my sarcasm. "She was needy?"

"Yes. You see, she was always trying to change the rules. She succeeded in persuading Edward to go to her house. That was a strict no-no."

"Why is that?" I asked. I really didn't care, but I had to keep her talking.

"Because we were only supposed to be with Edward at the fortress. If it was at anyone's home, it was they who were in control, not the master."

Good grief, this woman has some screws loose.

"I followed Edward, you know," she said, distantly, staring down at some doodad on the side table. "I always followed him. One night he led me right to Lucille's doorstep *knowing* that they were breaking the rules, *his rules*," she snapped. "If the rules don't apply to all, then you have anarchy, don't you? She screwed him, many times, right there in her own house. I know she did. I could hear them. It made me so mad. I almost burst in on both of them and... Well, all I can say is that she deserved to die for her transgressions... and, she did." The woman actually smiled at me.

"So why are you here, Karen?" I asked. "Why his house?"

"To finish what I started, of course. When my master Edward gets out of jail—he didn't do anything wrong you know—he's going to need me, going to marry me. And his bitch wife here is in the way... of our happiness."

I'd heard enough. I turned my head, looked at Janet, and nodded. She drew her weapon.

"Karen Silver," I said, "I'm placing you under arrest. Please put your hands up where I can see them."

"Oh, no! Wait! You can't. You don't understand!" She began to sob as she backed up next to a side table. She had her hands up, but she wasn't complying. She was stalling.

"Karen, I'm not going to ask you again," I said gently. "We have the place surrounded. You won't get out of here."

"That's okay," Karen said.

Not a good sign.

"Turn around and put your hands behind your back. Now!" I shouted, taking my cuffs from my belt.

Karen looked at me, then at Janet, then at Mrs. Pieczeck, and then she turned slowly around to face the side table. But instead of putting her hands behind her back, she bent down and grabbed something on the floor beside the couch and spun around, grabbing Shelly's arm and yanking her up off the couch.

Karen was now standing behind Shelly holding one of the biggest crowbars I'd ever seen; it had to have been at least three feet long.

The murder weapon?

"Don't come near me!" she screamed, holding Shelly by the collar with one hand, and waving the crowbar over her head with the other. Her face contorted, her eyelids flickering wildly.

Shelly Pieczeck struggled frantically to get away.

"Karen, stop this!" I said, loudly. "We can work this out if you'll just put the crowbar down."

"You'll have to kill me." She was defiant.

"You don't want that any more than we do, Karen..." I hesitated for a second, then tried to mollify her.

"Look," I said, "love makes us do stupid things. You think you are the first woman to kill for her man?" I shook my head. "Do you think you're the first woman who had a man who didn't appreciate her love?"

She blinked, stopped waving the crowbar in the air, and stood still with it suspended over her head.

"Look, I've been there, too," I continued. "I had a guy, once. I was crazy about him. But I wasn't enough. He cheated on me."

"What did you do to her. How did you *punish* her?" Karen asked as her eyes filled with tears.

"I didn't do anything to her. It wasn't her fault." I took a deep breath. "Even if it had been her fault, what good would it have done? Then I'd look like the bad guy when I wasn't the one who cheated."

"But how else was she going to learn?"

She was on the edge, teetering. She'd lowered the crowbar a little, listening to my story. Just a few more seconds and this could all end peacefully.

"What about him? Did you punish him?" she asked.

"I broke up with him."

"You broke up with him? Then you didn't really love him. Not like I love my Edward." She shook her head. "When you love someone, you'll do anything to be with them," she said with fire in her eyes.

She let go of Shelly, grasped the crowbar in both hands, raised it over her head, and directed it at the back of Shelly Pieczeck's head.

I didn't see it coming. There was a flash of blue and white as Janet streaked by me, leaped into the air, and landed on top of Karen Silver. And then they were on the ground, struggling. Karen was without a doubt the stronger of the two, but Janet was the more limber. She managed to get her fingers onto Karen's carotid artery and apply pressure, and in seconds, it was over. The crowbar fell from her nerveless fingers, and she lapsed into unconsciousness.

I swooped in with my cuffs, snapped them onto her wrists, and just a few seconds later, she was awake again, groggy and submissive.

Shelly had retreated to a corner of the room, slid down to the floor, and sat there, her head in her hands, shaking and crying.

And then Chief Wilbur and his officers burst into the room, weapons drawn.

"Oh, I see," he said, holstering the gun. "You don't need me then? Shame. How about him?" he asked, gesturing toward one of his officers who was holding Marty Butterworth by his arm; Butterworth's hands were cuffed behind his back.

"My men found him downstairs, in the basement," Wilbur said.

What is it with these people and basements? I wondered.

"He was waiting at the bottom of the stairs with a tarp and rubber gloves."

"Geez, she *was* going to do her in then? Good job, Chief."

"Thank you, ma'am. I think Governor Randolph will be grateful..."

"Ha," I said and laughed. "I wouldn't count on it, but I wish you well anyway," I said with a wink and shook his hand. "You want to bring them to the PD on Amnicola so we can formally charge them both?"

He nodded. "You got it!"

"Thanks... and you might want to call for the EMTs. Mrs. Pieczeck looks like hell."

I shook his hand again and then walked with Janet back to my cruiser.

"Great work, Janet," I said as she opened the passenger side door. "That was one hell of a takedown. I was about to shoot the bitch."

"Thanks. It *was*, like, intense," she said. "Hey, was that true what you were telling her about a guy? It was Harry Starke, wasn't it?"

"No," I lied. "I made it up. Let's get out of here... rookie."

39

Janet put the call in to Amnicola about the arrest of Karen Silver and Martin Butterworth, and we arrived there just in time to see a very disheveled and wrinkled Pastor Edward Pieczeck being escorted out of the holding cells. He was carrying his tie, belt, and a large brown envelope containing his personal effects.

"Pastor Ed!" I shouted. "Don't go on any long vacations, and don't leave the country. I haven't finished with you yet."

He scowled at me, then saw Karen Silver and Marty Butterworth being escorted into the holding area, in handcuffs, by two Lookout Mountain officers.

Karen saw him and for a second, their eyes locked, until the pastor looked away.

"I didn't mean for it to happen!" Karen shouted. "You know I love you and that I'd never do anything to hurt you!"

He glanced back at her, his face deadpan, and then he did the worst thing he possibly could to a woman like Karen. He ignored her. He looked past her as if she wasn't there. She wilted, and I couldn't help but feel a little sorry for her.

She did love him, in her own twisted way, and so did he love her, maybe, but she was a victim, too. Not like Meryl Dilly or Lucille Benedict or the beautiful and manipulative Victoria Randolph, but Karen Silver was a victim. Pastor Edward Pieczeck was a sexual predator of the worst kind.

Oh, I know what you're thinking. You're thinking that she made her own choices, and you're right. She did, and they were bad choices, the worst, but that didn't make what had happened to her any the less sad. You think I'm soft, right? It's true. I do have a softer side, but I try to keep it well hidden.

I was just finishing my paperwork when Janet knocked on my office door and peered at me through the glass window. I waved her in.

"Hey, LT," she said. "You okay?"

"Yes, of course. Why wouldn't I be?"

"Just checking, I guess. Look, I didn't get a chance to tell you about that other guy you asked me to look into, the reporter, Clemont Rhodes," she said as she gingerly sat down on the edge of the seat in front of my desk.

"Oh, shit. I forgot all about him. What did you find out?" I sat back, stretched my arms up over my head as I yawned.

She took a piece of paper from her pocket.

"He does work for the Bugle but only as a sort of stringer. He's focused on the crime beat. And really blasts the CPD for not doing their job in his stories. Seems to me like he's trying to get the paper to hire him as a regular. I think he's looking to make a name for himself."

"Really?" I said. "Too bad I have to be the one to make it for him. I have to give him an exclusive, per Chief Johnston."

"Um, I hate to have to tell you this but," she said, hesitated, then took a deep breath and continued, "Clemont Rhodes is Captain Henry Finkle's brother-in-law." She winced as she said it.

I sat there staring at her for a moment, then said, "Okay, so you just made my frickin' day. That's just about the worst news I've had this frickin' year. Definitely the worst..."

Does Chief Johnston know that, I wonder? I bet he does: the old goat knows everything. I chewed my bottom lip. *That sneaky bastard Finkle set me up.*

I could feel my rage begin to bubble up deep in my gut. Thoughts of revenge whirled around inside my head. I was beginning to feel light-headed.

"Are you okay, LT?"

I snapped out of it, smiled at her, and nodded. "Yeah, I feel just great," I said sarcastically. "But do me a favor and keep it under your hat. I don't want Finkle to know I know, and I certainly don't want anyone to know that you know. Let's just forget we ever looked into it, okay? I'll give Rhodes a call and tell him to drop in for his exclusive on Monday. Go on home, Janet. Get some rest."

"Okay, that sounds fine, LT."

"Great," I said, smiling at her. "Look, you did an amazing job on this case. You should be proud of yourself. So, what are you going to do tonight to celebrate?"

"Well, I hadn't given it much thought, you know. I—"

"Sergeant Toliver!" Finkle shouted from my open doorway. "I just dropped by to congratulate you on your amazing work on the Randolph case. A couple of us are going out for a drink. You must come with us. We'll celebrate. You'll be the guest of honor."

"Well, Lieutenant Gazzara was the lead investigator," she said hesitantly.

"We all know what Lieutenant Gazzara's role was. But I don't think she'd deny that it couldn't have turned out the way it did if it wasn't for your contribution. Isn't that right, Gazzara?"

Finkle was loving this. He was no longer my boss, but he hadn't given up.

"That's right, *Captain.*" I looked at Janet. "Go on, Janet. Go and have a good time, you deserve it. Just make sure he keeps his hands to himself."

"What do you mean by that, Gazzara?" he snapped.

"Not a thing, Chief, whoops, I mean *Captain.*"

Finkle's posture stiffened.

"I know these cheapskates, Janet," I said. "You'd better grab the free drinks while you can because they won't buy you another round until you reach retirement."

Janet laughed out loud. "Okay, I will. Are you coming too?"

"Ohhhh, no." I shook my head. "I've got more work to get done. Then I'm calling it a night. You have fun... Oh, and by the way, there's a great place called the Sorbonne, a really fun joint. Maybe you should ask Henry to take you there. It's one of your favorites, isn't that right, Captain?"

The expression on his face was a joy to behold, a mixture of surprise, anger, and embarrassment.

"I think we'll stick a little closer to home," he growled.

"See you tomorrow, then, LT," Janet said.

"Nope. Tomorrow's Sunday, and I'm going to church."

I waited until they'd all left. Then I picked up the phone and dialed a number I knew by heart. Maybe it wasn't the best idea I'd ever had, but what the hell. What did I have to lose?

"Hello?"

"Case is closed. I'd like to get my dog back."

"Aww," Lonnie said. "And we just got comfortable in the recliner. Hey, there's a COPS marathon on TV. Come on over. There's plenty of room for you on the couch."

"You got a couple of cold ones for me?" I asked, unable to hide the smile in my voice.

"Sure do. I even have a nice bottle of Merlot. I bought it just for you."

"You did? Great. Give me an hour. I need to go home, take a shower, and change clothes."

"No rush, darlin'. Take your time. We'll be here when you're ready."

I disconnected the call.

Wait... did he just call me darlin'? What was that about... Oh no, that's not happenin', I thought as I headed to the shower. *No, no, no, I'm way too busy for that kind of... any kind of serious relationship...*

Hmm, Captain Gazzara... I like the sound of that...

GENEVIEVE: CASE SIX

A LT. KATE GAZZARA NOVEL

BOOK SIX

BY

BLAIR HOWARD

1

THE SOUND OF THE DOGS' TOENAILS ON THE CONCRETE walkway made a pleasant click-click-click-click as Cole Meredith walked his five "clients" on their favorite stroll along the Tennessee Riverwalk.

"I was barely able to get out of bed this morning, man," Cole grumbled into his Bluetooth. "That was, like, a blast last night. Did you get that girl's number? The one with the nose ring? She was hot."

The sun was rising into a cloudless sky as the dogs hauled Cole along the winding path. They were quite a diverse gang: two Chihuahuas, a Dalmatian, a boxer, and a pug, and they barked at any and every other person, dog, bird, or itinerant plastic bag that might flutter into their path.

"You didn't? Oh wow, man. Why not? She was hot. You missed out, bro. She, like, acted like she was interested, for sure," Cole said.

The group was approaching a sharp bend in the path flanked by a stand of trees and bushes, just west of the C.B. Robinson Bridge. Cole struggled to keep the alpha dog, the Dalmatian, in check as they rounded the bend.

"*No way,*" Cole said incredulously, dramatizing the nugget of information he'd just been given. "She had a boyfriend? No way, man. Did he see you? I mean, she wasn't acting shy when I saw you guys at the bar."

The previous evening, Cole had gone to a local hangout called Sid's, a staple in the neighborhood where local talent plays music every Friday night. And, even better, it was within walking distance from his place. The neighborhood, North Chattanooga, was popular among the young and twenty-somethings just out from under mom and dad's thumb. They could act wild, let it all hang out, connect, get drunk, get high, step outside the box, man, and have an adventure for a few hours.

That was what Cole had been looking for, to connect... with a girl —he didn't do drugs. And there was never a shortage of single girls to flirt with at Sid's. He liked the Sorbonne better, but that was too far to walk, and he liked to drink. And driving drunk wasn't cool.

Sometimes he'd bring a girl home, sometimes wake up at her place. But last night had been a bust. He'd been unlucky, arrived home around midnight, half wasted, fell into bed, and slept like one of his charges until the alarm shattered his dreamless slumber at five AM. He'd had just enough time to do the necessary, shower, and shave before picking up Lance, the pug, the first pooch on his route.

Cole had picked up the last of his charges, Rupert, the Dalmatian, at a little before six that morning and had then driven west along Amnicola to the Robinson Bridge entrance to the Riverpark. There, he'd parked in one of the designated lots just east of the great bridge, gathered together his gang of five—with no little difficulty—and had set off on his six-mile walk—three miles each way.

Life was good: the weather gorgeous, he worked only three hours a day, and all was right with the world. Why wouldn't it be? At fifteen bucks per hour per dog, the three-hour daily walk provided him with all the necessities of his simple, uncomplicated life: a roof over his head, nice clothes, a nice Jeep Wrangler, plenty to eat, and the wherewithal to show the ladies a good time, whenever the opportunity arose.

As he walked that morning early in May, he talked on the phone with his friend about the events of the previous evening, of which there were none... well, except for the girl with a ring in her nose. He stretched his neck and shoulders, then slipped his sunglasses over his nose while holding all the leashes in his right hand.

"Are you going to the gym today, bro?" he asked, as the Dalmatian hit the end of his leash and almost jerked all five leashes out of his hand.

"Yeah? Good. Me too. What time? Sure man, I'll meet you there," he said as he watched an attractive female jogger in tight black yoga pants and a bright yellow top trot past.

The girl's hair was in a ponytail that swung with her hips as she ran. He glanced back over his shoulder at her and caught her looking back, smiling at him. That was one of the best things about Cole's job. There was never a shortage of pretty girls to flirt with, and any girls who were out at that hour were totally into keeping in shape. He liked that.

The dogs began to tug harder at their leashes. All five of them were acting as if they suddenly had to go to the bathroom. As Cole listened to his friend talk, he clicked his tongue and pulled on the leashes to keep the little beasts under control.

Frickin' little monsters!

Of course it was Rupert, egged on by Lance who was the most aggressive, tugging and pulling on his leash, dragging them all into the dark shadows under the trees and the bushes, down the grassy bank that stretched all the way to the river.

"Yeah, okay, bro. I'll see you there. Hey, do you have any more of that protein powder you gave me? That stuff really made a difference, man. Yeah, I added it to my smoothies and I'm telling you, I had raw energy the whole day. I had—"

Cole stopped talking; something not quite right, something out of place, caught his eye. He froze. The dogs strained at their leashes, but

Cole remained still. His friend on the other end of the phone continued talking, but Cole didn't hear a thing he was saying. How many times had he traveled the route under the great bridge and beyond? Too many to count. It was embedded deep in his psyche. He could walk it blindfolded, both ways. But this time there was something different, something that didn't belong, and although he was sure he was seeing what he was seeing, his mind wouldn't accept it.

"Hey... bro, shut the hell up for a minute, okay? Oh wow, man! You... you're not going to believe this," Cole stuttered into the phone. "I think... I'm looking at a dead body. No. Uh-huh! For, for real."

Cole swallowed hard, crept closer, straining to hold the dogs in check, to keep them back from...

Holy crap!

The boxer started to whine. Lance sniffed the air, his flat mug trembling with tiny growls. The two Chihuahuas and Rupert the Dalmatian danced and barked and ran this way and that, braiding their leashes together.

As Cole crept even closer, he saw a woman's foot sticking out from among the bushes. She was lying on her side, crumpled up like she'd collapsed... *right there, on the frickin' spot.*

Nah, it can't be... but...

For a split-second Cole thought he might be wrong, hoped he was wrong, that she wasn't dead, just passed out, wasted. He could see she was a pretty girl with long black hair, expensive clothes, and a body that was made for better things than sleeping one off in the park. She sure as hell wasn't supposed to be found dead lying in the grass.

No.

"I don't know, man," Cole said into the phone. "This is *too* messed up."

But even as Cole's own mind tried to convince him the beauty wasn't dead, the cool flat hue of her skin told him otherwise. Her hair covered most of her face... all but for one milky eye that stared up at Cole, sending shivers down his spine.

Even the dogs had gone silent.

"Bro, I gotta call the cops," Cole stuttered. "This is so bad, man. She's just lying there in the bushes. Knock it off, Lance! Dude, I gotta go. Yeah, I'll call you back."

Cole tapped his ear to disconnect his Bluetooth and quickly pulled out his phone and tapped in 911.

He described the scene to the police dispatcher along with the location as the dogs nervously paced and yipped and snapped and tugged at their leashes, anxious to get on with their walk, but sensing, as dogs do, that something bad had happened.

While he waited, Cole got down on one knee and gently petted and scratched the dogs, trying to keep them calm.

A crowd was beginning to gather on the walkway, and with every passing minute another person joined him, stretching to see what he was looking at.

A man with long hair who looked like he had yet to sleep off the effects of the previous night joined the small group of gawkers. When he saw what everyone was looking at, he pulled out his phone.

"Yo, dude. Don't do that, man. That's frickin' disrespectful. You some kind of ghoul or what?" Cole heard himself say but hadn't even been aware he thought it.

"Screw you, pal," the long-haired man said, tugging clumsily at his T-shirt and stuffing his phone back in his pants.

"What did you say?" Cole took a step closer to the man.

"You heard me."

"Erase that photo, screw-head. That girl is dead. Don't you have any respect?"

"You gonna make me? Or maybe you ain't even as tough as those little bitches you're walking."

The man swayed with the breeze that had kicked up from the river. Had it blown just a little harder he might have tipped over and joined the dead woman on the grass, face down and motionless.

But before Cole could do anything, the wail of distant sirens that had been wavering in and out above the early morning sounds was now coming through loud and clear.

Cole wasn't alone when he told the drunk to leave. The small crowd of people also urged him along. By the time the police arrived, pulling their cruisers up onto the grass just feet from the concrete walkway, the drunken gawker had disappeared through the crowd only to collapse on a park bench a few yards from the crime scene.

2

"Gazzara," I snapped into my phone, angry at being disturbed on my precious day off.

It was six-thirty on Saturday morning and I'd planned on having a lazy day, but things never do work out the way you plan, do they? Mine certainly didn't, not that day.

"Captain," the dispatcher said, "we have a report of a female body on the Riverpark Walkway east of the CB Robinson bridge. Officers are on the scene. They have the area roped off, but the morning foot traffic is making things difficult. You're up, Captain," the dispatcher said, sounding more than a little gleeful.

Oh geez, I knew it was too good to last.

"Okay. I'll be there ASAP," I said, tipping my fresh cup of coffee into the sink. "Has the ME been called?"

"Yes, ma'am. Doc Sheddon has been notified. Officers on the scene contacted him immediately upon arrival."

"Good. Tell them I'm on my way." I clicked off the phone without saying goodbye.

I sat for a minute, staring out of the kitchen window, trying to gather my thoughts. I'd been about to leave my apartment for my morning run, so it was way too early to even begin to think about work.

I sat breathing deeply for several more minutes, then shook myself awake and headed for the shower.

Twenty minutes and a good scalding later, I was dressed in my work clothes, jeans, white top, and a tan leather jacket; I was ready for whatever the body on the riverbank had to say to me.

"Good morning, Captain." The Officer on the scene was a pleasant guy I'd dealt with many times before, Randy Tadwell. "Sorry to get you up so early."

"Yeah, who do I file a complaint with about that? What have we got, Randy?"

"We have a problem, Kate."

Randy's lips hadn't moved; he was smiling, nodding. I turned quickly, startled by the voice behind me. It was Doc Sheddon. He was covered from head to toe in white Tyvek coveralls and booties, his eyes looking up at me over his half-spectacles.

Doctor Richard Sheddon, a small man in his late fifties, at five-eight was a good five inches shorter than me, a little overweight, almost totally bald with a round face that usually sported a jovial expression, but not that day. And when he said we had a problem, I knew he was serious.

"What did you do, Doc? Beam over here?" I said as I held out my hand.

"No," he muttered as he handed me his large cup of Dunkin Donuts coffee. "Don't drink it all. Save some for me."

Gratefully, I took a sip, closed my eyes and thanked the coffee gods for DD. Doc held the yellow tape up for me to duck under.

"Come and take a look," he said. "Tell me what you see."

He led me to the body. It was lying close to the riverbank, half-hidden among the trees and bushes. The first thing I noticed was her shoes: high heels, little more than a series of metallic gold straps crisscrossing her feet and up her ankles. *Expensive!* I thought.

She was wearing skinny jeans, also expensive, and so tight they could have been a second skin, leaving little to the imagination. The silver lamé top had ridden up showing her midriff, but not so much that it indicated sexual assault, not to me anyway.

I took another thoughtful sip then handed Doc his coffee, pulled a pair of purple latex gloves from my purse, and snapped them on. Then, being careful where I stepped, I leaned over her and tried to study her face.

I looked up at the CSI photographer. "You done here?" I asked.

He nodded. I reached out and moved her hair a little.

"What a pretty girl," I muttered and knelt down beside her.

"Such a shame," I said, then turned my head to look up at Doc and said, "Did you see this?" I pointed to the woman's neck. A pair of purple and blue marks circled her throat.

He nodded.

Carefully, I lifted one of her eyelids and observed the telltale red spots and broken blood vessels—petechial hemorrhage—that indicated asphyxiation.

"I'm going to guess no sexual assault," I said. "No one could get her back into those jeans... and her bra seems to be undisturbed."

I twisted my head sideways and looked up at Officer Tadwell. "Did we get a statement from the witness who found her?"

"We did, but I asked him to hang around in case you needed to talk to him," Tadwell said.

He pointed to a nearby bench where a young man was seated hanging onto the leashes of the weirdest assortment of dogs I'd ever seen; five of them, and they were all sitting too. I nodded and thanked him, asked him to tell the witness I'd be with him shortly, and then turned my attention back to Doc and the body.

"So, we have us a ligature strangulation," I said. "From the looks of it, she must have been on her way home from a night out. I'm guessing, from the position of the body and the mud on her heels, that she was dragged over here and dumped."

I looked up at Doc. He was shaking his head, his arms folded across his chest.

"No? What did I miss?" I asked as I looked back down at the body. Then I saw it. "Aha. Looks like her jewelry was taken. At least her rings were. Tan lines."

I pointed to the lighter stripes of skin on her fingers.

"So where's her purse? She must have had one. She couldn't have gotten even a comb into the pockets of those jeans."

I looked around and found it. "There it is, underneath her left hip. You get this, Jimmy?" I asked the photographer.

He said he did but took several more shots of it anyway.

I took a deep breath and then gently eased the purse out from under her, hoping I wasn't disturbing any key evidence.

As I pulled, the silver lamé top rode up a little higher at the back, thus allowing me to see the top of a white thong and a tramp stamp tattoo... along with the initials EEC4. I had no ideas what that meant, but before I pointed it out to Doc, I looked at the purse, a black snake-skin envelope.

"Holy shit," I exclaimed. "It's a frickin' Gucci, cost at least eighteen hundred." Oh yeah, I know my purses. This one would have cost me a couple of weeks' pay, maybe more.

I looked up at Doc; he smirked, his arms folded across his chest. He looked like a snowman; only the top hat and pipe were missing.

I shook my head, opened the purse and looked inside. She was obviously careful about her sexual activity because there were four condoms tucked inside the small side pocket. There was also a tube of lip gloss, a tube of crimson Clé de Peau Beauté lipstick, a tin of Altoids and a wallet, another slim snakeskin envelope. There was no cash in the wallet, but there was a driver's license and three credit cards, one of them an American Express Black. *What the hell?* I shook my head in awe, then dragged myself back to reality and the job at hand.

"Okay, Doc," I said. "She was strangled. Other than that, and the fact that she must have been worth a dollar or two, I don't see anything unusual. So what's the problem?"

"She's worth a dollar or two all right. Don't you know who she is, Kate?" Doc asked, smirking down at me.

"Uh, yeah. It's Genevieve Chesterton. See?" I held up her driver's license so that he could see the picture.

"I know that, but I'll ask you again: Don't you know who Genevieve Chesterton is?"

"What? Yes... Okay, no, Doc. I don't know who she is. Who is she?" I stood up, took my phone from my pants pocket and photographed the driver's license.

"Genevieve Chesterton," he said dramatically, "is the grand-daughter-in-law to Edward Eaton Chesterton the Second."

He lifted his chin as if that should settle matters. I had to be driving him crazy because when I shrugged, he raised his hands in disgust and shook his head.

"She married into the third wealthiest family in Tennessee," he said, frustrated at my lack of knowledge. "A real Cinderella story, it was. The wedding was plastered all over the news last year. You don't remember?"

I shook my head, grimaced as if I might get a crack aside the head from Doc for not following.

"Do you live under a rock, or something, Kate?"

"I wish," I replied. "Then no one would bother me. Come on, Doc. Just give me the condensed version, okay?"

"Don't you remember? Of course you don't. It was about this time last year that the media was covering the upcoming wedding of Edward Eaton Chesterton the Fourth. He was considered Tennessee's most eligible bachelor."

"The fact you know so much about this wedding just shows me how much I really don't know about you, Doc. I think I'm a little frightened."

"Oh, tosh. Seriously, Kate, this is a real problem. It's going to be all over the news before lunchtime." Doc pointed to the crime scene photographer and ordered him to hurry. "The press covered everything about the wedding from her dress to how many bridesmaids she was going to have, to her china pattern and of course, the dream honeymoon to Australia and New Zealand. The paparazzi documented every movement the couple made, every store they shopped, every restaurant... They were an obsession."

"Well, if she married the hottest commodity in Tennessee, it shouldn't be too hard to find that missing wedding ring." I pointed to the line on her ring finger.

And that should be all I need to wrap it up, I thought.

At that moment I really did think it was going to be an open-and-shut case. We had a high-profile victim, out on the town, obviously screwing around on her marriage. All I needed was the jealous husband with means and opportunity—motive, he already had—and I knew I'd be meeting that husband very soon.

Okay, so I didn't really think the rich guy actually strangled her himself, but I did think—because of the missing cash and jewelry—that he probably hired somebody to do it for him. I also figured that "somebody" would probably want to grab a few extra bucks for her rings. That being so, a swift check around the local pawnshops would produce the killer, and a little pressure thereon would give me all I needed to hang said husband... Not literally, of course.

"What did you say her husband's name was?"

"Edward Eaton Chesterton the Fourth," Doc replied.

"Make sure you get close-ups," he said to the photographer as he pointed to the hands and toes of the victim.

"And those, please," I said, pointing out some drag marks in the dirt.

"EEC4," I said to Doc. "Well, in my book that's true love if she gets the man's initials tattooed on her lower back."

Doc was not amused, which was okay because I wasn't trying to be funny. But it is true that in some parts of the country, a woman can express no deeper love than to brand herself with some dude's name. It might not be how I would do it... *And thank the Lord I didn't!* But in some circles it's an acceptable expression of devotion... but then again, not exactly what you'd expect to find on the wife of a member of one of the wealthiest families in Tennessee.

Ah, who knows? Stranger things have happened.

I watched closely as the paramedics loaded the body onto the gurney. I wanted to get a better look at the girl's face.

Oh yes, now I remember, I think... She does look kind of familiar.

But that wasn't important. At that moment I wanted to focus on the marks around her neck. I placed a hand gently on her forehead and tried to move it to the left. It wasn't easy. She was stiffening quickly as rigor advanced.

"Looks like she was attacked from behind. What do you think made these, Doc?" I asked as I pointed to the two thin, deep bloody lines around her throat.

"I have no idea, nor will I have until I examine her."

I nodded, thoughtfully, then said, "So how long has she been dead, do you think?" I smiled innocently at him, knowing full well how he hated that question, and stuck out my hand for more coffee.

He looked at me, pursed his lips, shook his head, handed me the cup, and said, "You know better than to ask... Oh, what the hell. The liver temperature is ninety-one point two degrees. Normal body temperature is ninety-eight point six, so roughly five hours, say between two and three this morning, but I'll know for sure when I get her back to the lab. Meet me there, but for God's sake bring some coffee of your own."

He took the Styrofoam cup from me, sipped and gazed wide-eyed at me over the rim.

I thought for a minute, then said, "Can't, not for a few hours anyway. I have to inform the husband and go into the office and get the ball rolling first. I have responsibilities now." I looked at my watch. "Oh crap, look at the time. It's almost eight already. Maybe I can get to you at noon... twelve-thirty?" I asked, squinting quizzically at him. "Can you wait for me? Can I give you a call when I'm on my way?"

I just knew I was being more than a little optimistic; I was heading up a new division Chief Johnston, in his infinite wisdom, decided to call Special Projects, so I now had a team of officers and detectives—three—plus my partner Janet, to coordinate. With this being a high-profile case, there'd be a lot to get in motion before I could visit the husband or attend an autopsy. I had a lot to cram into one day, and I still had to talk to the witness who discovered the body.

"Sure can. All right boys load her up," Doc told the paramedics.

They loaded the gurney into the ambulance for transportation to Doc's little shop of horrors.

I thanked him and turned my attention to the guy with the five dogs. The puppies all sat up, paid attention, tails wagging as I approached. I just had to smile.

"I'm Captain Gazzara," I said as I flashed my badge and then realized I hadn't taken off my latex gloves.

"I'm Cole Meredith." He replied. "I—"

"Wait," I said, interrupting him. "Give me a minute, please." I peeled off the gloves and opened the recording app on my iPhone.

"Now, Mr. Meredith, would you please tell me how it was that you discovered the body?"

3

DOGGY MEREDITH WAS A GOOD WITNESS. HE HAD HIS FACTS IN order and told his story without much thought. I questioned him as to what he'd observed, and he told me that he'd driven off some drunken fool that had been snapping photos of the dead Mrs. Chesterton.

That raised alarm bells in my mind. Every cop is taught that sometimes a murderer will loiter at the scene and mingle with the gawkers. And taking pictures of his victim was also something a killer might do. That's what I had in mind when I approached the picture-taking man, who was sleeping it off on a bench, but I soon got that out of my head. This guy was totally wasted and no more capable of strangling the girl than was one of Meredith's Chihuahuas. I was pretty confident that this particular drunk was nothing more than that, a drunk.

He insisted on acting like an ass, waving his arms around in the air, rolling around on the bench, talking about his girlfriend—his ex-girlfriend—yacking on about what a bitch she was, and...

I got angry and... Hell, I stepped over the line. I did something that could have gotten me fired, but this guy had really pissed me off. He'd taken photos of the dead girl, not couth, not in my book.

So, I grabbed his phone from his coat pocket, deleted the photo—there was only one—and returned it to his pocket. He was so out of it he didn't even notice.

I shook my head, and beckoned Officer Tadwell.

"I'm sorry, Randy. I need you to take this... thing to Amnicola and make a deposit at the drunk tank for me. I'd do it myself, but I don't have the time to book him. D'you mind?"

"Not a problem, Captain. I'm heading that way anyhow."

I started to back away as I said, "I'm sorry, Randy. I really do have to run."

"See you around the playground, Captain." Randy waved and got behind the wheel of the cruiser and drove away, the drunk making menacing faces at me through the rear window.

I ran to my unmarked cruiser, and two minutes later I was driving back through the Riverpark toward Amnicola Highway. I used my phone's Bluetooth and called my partner, Detective Janet Toliver.

"Morning, Cap," she chirped into the phone.

"Hi, Janet. I'm just leaving a crime scene. Where are you? What are you doing?"

"I'm at home. It's Saturday. Remember? I, that is we, have the weekend off... Oh, I see, now we don't. Okay, what do you want me to do?"

Her voice was cheery, upbeat—just what I needed—and it matched her personality perfectly. She was a bubbly little thing. A rookie detective, only twenty-four years old, she looked like a school-girl: red hair, green eyes, upturned nose, freckles, you get the idea. When my partner, Lonnie, retired last year, I was on my own for a while, but Chief Johnston decided I needed a partner and—would you believe—he assigned his own PA to me.

Now, don't get me wrong, Janet and me, we hit it off right from the start. The kid's a natural and soon proved herself to be one hell of a good detective. I was glad to have her.

"Right, the weekend off," I said, dryly. "When did that ever happen? Come on in to the office. I'll meet you there. I was called out early this morning..." And I proceeded to give her a quick run-down of the events.

She arrived in my office thirty minutes later loaded with a tray of two cups of Starbuck's coffee. *Sometimes I could just squeeze that girl.*

I had a new office... Henry Finkle's old office. It was kind of strange to sit on the other side of his desk and see the room from his angle. I had a large, shiny wood desk instead of my old steel one, a really nice leather chair, a matching credenza, and a huge whiteboard on the east wall. I'd also had eight chairs brought into the room. They did little for the ambiance, but I was there to work, not enjoy the good life.

"Thanks, Janet," I said as I grabbed a cup of coffee and sat down. "Sit yourself down and listen up."

I took a sip of coffee, which gave her the opportunity to jump in.

"What about the rest of the team? You want me to have them come in?"

"No, not today. We'll let them have their weekend and bring them up to speed on Monday."

She nodded.

"Okay," I said, "take notes—"

"You want me to record?" she asked, interrupting my train of thought.

I scowled at her. "Whatever."

"Okay, I'll record." She smiled sweetly at me.

Inwardly I shook my head and grinned. *Geez, am I ever going to get used to this kid?*

"So," I continued, trying to look stern, but failing miserably, "we know Genevieve was out on the town last night, dressed to kill and with a pocketbook full of condoms. I want to know where she went and who she was with. The prime suspect is the husband, so I want you to dig up everything you can on the Chesterton family. Now look, you can bet the entire family is steeped in Tennessee folklore, so you'll probably have your hands full," I said.

"I've heard of these guys," Janet said. "We're talking *beaucoup* bucks," Janet replied.

"Right!" I said. "Dig up everything you can on the victim, her husband, her parents, his parents, the whole damn schmeer. I'm thinking the woman was a free spirit, in every sense of the word, and that would *not* go down too well with that family so, as I said, I'm liking the husband for it. Nine times out of ten it's the spouse, right? Clean off the incident board and make a start on it."

We both looked up at the images, notes, theories left over from the last case, then she looked at me and nodded.

"Okay, so that's where we begin. I have the feeling this will be an easy one. So let's get on with it and close it out."

I should have known nothing that appears easy ever is. You'd think after fifteen years on the force, I would have known that simple principle.

"Any questions?" I asked.

"Not right now, but I'm sure—"

"Good," I said, cutting her off.

"I have to go and notify the husband, so don't call him, or any other members of the family until I give you the all-clear, okay?"

"You haven't done that yet?" Janet asked.

"No. I haven't had time, damn it. I haven't even eaten yet."

I stood and walked around the desk. "Make a start, okay? I'll call you when I'm on my way back to the office."

I had the husband's address from Genevieve's driver's license. Surprisingly, it wasn't on Lookout Mountain where I thought all the elite of Chattanooga lived. Nope. Edward Eaton Chesterton IV and his wife lived in a luxury apartment in the heart of downtown. It would have been an easy jaunt to get there from the crime scene, but I had to take care of my responsibilities at the office first. I made it to the Edward Eaton Chesterton IV residence by eleven.

4

THE CHESTERTON APARTMENT WAS ON THE TOP FLOOR OF A luxury, downtown complex. To reach it, I had to walk through a lobby full of shops and boutique cafés: the heady aroma of dark coffee wafted over me like an intoxicating tsunami. I hesitated, almost caved, but I didn't dare waste any more time and neither did I dare turn up at a high-value residence with a Café Grande in my hand.

And I had something else to worry about: leaks. I hadn't had time to check the news outlets, and I hadn't heard any gossip around the department, but if there had been even a whisper across the media of the high-profile death, I might well find myself telling EEC4 what he already knew. *That...* wouldn't look good for me, a newly appointed senior police officer.

So I forewent my fix and took the elevator to the top floor, stepped out into the lobby, took a moment to compose myself, then knocked on the door and braced myself for the inevitable hysterical ranting of a distraught husband. Boy, was I ever in for a surprise.

"Yes, what is it?" A groggy, red-eyed Edward Eaton Chesterton the Fourth asked as he peeked at me over the security chain.

"My name is Captain Catherine Gazzara. I'm with the Chattanooga Police Department," I said, formally introducing myself.

I held up my badge for him to see and inwardly let out a sigh of relief. If the news had reached the press, my man hadn't gotten word of it yet.

"Mr. Chesterton, I need to speak to you about your wife," I said. "May I come in?"

He didn't answer. He shut the door, and I heard the chain slip out of the groove. The door opened, and he stood aside for me to enter. And I did.

I entered an apartment awash in sunlight. The entire east side was a wall of glass, a giant window affording a spectacular view of Lookout Mountain. The place smelled clean, looked spotless, everything in its place and, as far as I could tell, almost unlived in.

"Please, sit down," he said, waving a hand in the general direction of a gorgeous white sofa. "Can I get you a drink, or something?"

I remained standing. "No, thank you, Mr. Chesterton." I looked at my watch and raised my eyebrows; it was a little after eleven.

"Call me Eddie. My father is Mr. Chesterton."

"Eddie," I said, not at all comfortable speaking the name, "I think you had better sit down."

He was a tall, slender man, made even more so by the plush, voluminous white robe he was wearing. His feet were bare, his dark red hair was sticking up at odd angles, and he had a five o'clock shadow that I was sure was not intentional... *Not like... Oh, come on Kate. Stop it.*

He turned around to face me, blinked, rubbed his eyes with closed fists, then sat down on one of a pair of pale gray Chesterfields. He looked up at me, then leaned forward, his elbows on his knees, hands linked together in a single fist. I remained standing.

"So? You look very serious," he said. "Why are you here? What has Genevieve been up to this time?"

I looked down at him. He gazed up at me, a tight smile on his lips.

"Eddie, I'm sorry, but I have to tell you that your wife is... well, she's dead."

Sheesh, it never gets any easier.

I watched for his reaction, or lack thereof; there was no visible reaction other than a slight tightening of the already tight smile, so I continued, "Her body was discovered by a dog-walker on the River-walk near the CB Robinson Bridge at around six-thirty this morning."

His Adam's apple bounced as he swallowed. I waited for the outburst, but it never came. Instead, his lips parted and the smile became bitter, angry. He looked away from me, stared down at the floor between his feet for a moment, slowly shaking his head.

"So, he finally did it," Eddie said, so softly to the carpet beneath his feet that I could barely hear him. He looked up at me and said, "I didn't think he'd actually go through with it, but I guess the old bastard proved me wrong."

"What old... Who are you talking about?" I asked. "Do you mean your father?"

"Ha! My father wouldn't wipe his own ass without first asking permission from the old man. No. I'm talking about good old grand-dad, Edward Eaton Chesterton the Second, the man with all the money, the man who when he says jump, you ask how high."

Eddie, his face now devoid of color, stared at me, frowning, his eyes blue chips of ice, the knuckles of his double fist had turned white from the pressure he was applying. It wasn't what I was expecting, but it was a reaction.

"You're saying your grandfather killed your wife?" I asked, unable to keep the incredulity out of my voice. "Why would you think that? Wait, just a minute before you answer that, please."

I took my iPad from my purse and turned on the video recording app and held it so that the camera was pointing at his face.

"Edward Chesterton the Fourth, my name is Captain Catherine Gazzara and I must inform you that, for the record, and for your protection, I will now be recording the rest of this interview. Do you have any objections?"

He shook his head. "No! Do whatever the hell you want. I don't care."

"A moment ago, you mentioned that your grandfather, Edward Chesterton the Second, killed your wife. Would you please explain that for me?"

He nodded, somber, his hands still locked together in front of him, and said, "He hated Genevieve, hated that I married her. She wasn't good enough for me. No, scratch that, she wasn't good enough for him, not... cultured enough... Oh hell, let's just say it: he thinks... thought that she's a lowlife, trailer trash. Stupid old bastard."

He paused, looked at his hands, then up at me and chuckled.

"The truth is that, even in his wildest fantasies, he could never have dreamed up a woman like her and it was killing him."

"You think he was jealous of your marriage?" I asked.

Again, he chuckled, but it wasn't a nice sound, then he said, "He would have screwed her if he could... not sure he didn't, now I come to think about it. Would you believe that he tried to bribe her just after we became engaged?"

Eddie cleared his throat and continued, "He offered her half a million dollars to leave me." He shrugged, looked down at the floor, and whispered, "But she was smarter than that. She didn't take the bait."

"That must have made you feel good about her... proud," I said.

"Well yes, it did, at first, until it dawned on me after we were married that she stood to receive a lot more in a divorce settlement and alimony. But now that doesn't matter, does it? She's dead."

He sucked at his teeth as if his wife's death was no more than a minor detail in a much bigger story.

"So... you and Genevieve were talking about getting a divorce?" I asked.

"No. Not talking about it." He let out a deep breath.

As I studied his face, I saw tears fill his already red eyes.

"You see, she didn't think she was good enough for me either. I thought if I married her, she'd come to understand that she was, that she was just as good as the rest of our... so-called bluebloods. Hell, she was better than them. But you know what they say. You can take the girl out of the trailer park but you can't take the trailer park out of the girl."

"So you married a girl from the wrong side of the tracks, knowing it would upset your family?"

I watched for his reaction, hoping to see something that indicated deception, that it was all an act, but I didn't see it. He was distant, as if he was talking about someone he didn't know. My hunch that he killed his wife hadn't changed. What he was saying about his grandfather was typical of a guilty spouse trying to pass the blame. I wasn't impressed.

I did figure, however, that much of what he was telling me about his grandfather's feelings toward his wife was probably true. And so the point of the spear of doubt inserted itself into my theory. I had just been handed a possible second suspect and I began to feel that my open-and-shut case was slipping away from me. The more players involved, the hairier everything becomes.

"Dear old granddad runs this family like a corporation," Eddie mumbled. "He decides what everyone does. No one argues with him. No one dares to say boo to him." He growled, clenching his fist. "Not even me."

"And that's because?" I asked, probing for more information.

"Because he holds the purse strings, of course. Duh." Eddie smirked up at me. "You obviously don't come from money, do you? If you did, you wouldn't be a cop, that's for sure."

"That's probably true," I said, "but you obviously didn't take much notice of him, did you? You married someone below your station, someone your grandfather didn't approve of. That was a pretty bold move. You weren't worried he'd cut you out of his will... or something?"

"Ha! That'll be the day. You see, I am the only boy in my generation. He has twelve more grandchildren—I guess I'm unlucky number thirteen—and all of them girls. Can you believe it? Edward

Eaton Chesterton II isn't going to let his legacy be snuffed out. I'm the golden boy, no matter what I do. I have to carry the Chesterton family flag into the future."

He stood up, stepped over to a small wet bar, poured himself three fingers of some sort of amber liquid from a crystal decanter, and tossed it back in one huge gulp.

"But the silly old fool doesn't realize what he's done," he continued. "Genevieve would have provided him with great-grandsons, plenty of them. Not like my mother who just had me and then swore she'd never go through childbirth again."

He poured himself another drink and returned to his chair.

"What's your mother's name?" I asked.

"Regina Mae... Cottonwell-Chesterton," Eddie replied with a sloppy grin. "Oh, you'll just love her. You both have *so* much in common," he finished, sarcastically.

"What about your father? Edward Eaton Chesterton the Third?" I replied, ignoring his comments.

These damn names are getting to be a mouthful.

"His name should be Absentee Chesterton." Eddie laughed bitterly. "He's been in Europe for the past three weeks 'working.'" He made quotes with his fingers as he said it. Apparently, according to Eddie, his father was too busy jet-setting around the world to worry about the goings-on in his only son's life.

Eddie muttered something under his breath I couldn't hear then looked at me bleary-eyed. It was obvious to me that he'd been drinking heavily all morning. Whether his binge was the result of guilt—that he'd murdered his wife—prior knowledge of his loss—I didn't think so—or a general lack of purpose in his life, I couldn't say. But he was slowly checking out right in front of me.

"I'll need you to identify the body," I said.

"There's no need for that. You'll find my initials tattooed on her lower back." Eddie smiled. "She did that for me right before we got engaged. She could really be sweet when she wanted to."

I shook my head and said, "I'm sorry, Mr. Chesterton, I'll need you to formally identify the body."

He shrugged and said, "Whatever."

"Eddie, you never said where your wife was or who she was with last night. Do you know?" I watched him gulp down the rest of his drink and shake his head.

"No I don't. She was a... free spirit." He thought for a minute then continued, "Like I said, Detective. You can take the girl out of the trailer park..." He wiped his lips with the sleeve of his robe.

I decided to let him ramble a bit longer but to not ask any more questions. His answers at this point were less than helpful, and I could always interview him again later.

His face tightened up as he continued, "I will tell you this, though. My granddaddy is no dummy. He'll have an airtight alibi; he knows people. People in our family who would do just about anything for a buck. Just remember that when you go poking around among the skeletons. Rich people don't go to jail, Detective. Justice is... to my people, quite different than it is to the masses."

I wasn't sure if he was telling me that as a fact or as a slap in the face. Sure, justice could sometimes be slow when coming around to certain people, but it eventually came around. I had to believe that. Otherwise, my whole career was based on nothing.

"Why don't you ask him about the Frenchman?" he said.

"The Frenchman? Who's he?"

"Ask the old man; see if he'll tell you."

"No, Eddie. You tell me."

"The hell I will. Now please, go away."

I stared at him, then nodded and said, "One last thing, Eddie, before I go. Where were you last night?"

He smiled and shook his head, then said, "I was with a friend. We went to eat, then to several bars. We ended up at the Sorbonne and then someone, I have no idea who, brought me home. I think Alex and George must have. They were both here until a couple of hours ago."

Now that's a break, I thought. *If he was at the Sorbonne, it will be easy to check.*

"What time would that have been? And Genevieve wasn't home. Didn't that bother you?"

"Oh, come on. She was never home. Why d'you think I get wasted every night? She was a... she..." He looked up at me like a lost child, tears in his eyes, and said, "I loved her; I really loved her."

"What time did you get home?" I repeated the question, quietly.

"Late, after two, maybe, I don't know."

"How about your friends, would they know?"

He shrugged. "You'll have to ask them."

"Thank you, I will," I said. "Alex and George, I think you said. D'you mind telling me their last names?"

He didn't, and he did, and I stood up, closed out my recording app, put away my iPad, thanked him, and handed him my card.

"If you can think of anything, anything at all that might be helpful, please call me."

He took it, stared at it, looked up at me and told me he would.

"I'll also need you to come down to the Forensic Center and formally identify your wife. I'll have Carol Oats call you to make an appointment. Is that okay?"

He nodded. He was done talking. I had the feeling his binge was about to continue, and that once I was gone he was going to forget all about me. A couple more shots and a long nap would just about do it.

"Will you be all right?" I asked. "Can I call someone for you, someone to come and stay with you for a while."

"Oh, you needn't worry about that. As soon as she finds out, my mother will be all over me."

And so I left him to it. As I closed the door behind me, he was already back at the bar pouring himself another drink.

I took the elevator down to the main lobby, grabbed a cup of coffee, and called Janet to let her know I was on my way back.

"Chief Johnston wants to see you," she said quietly.

"I figured he would," I muttered. "Let him know I'm on my way and will come by his office as soon as I get there."

5

"Hey, Cap!"

I'd no sooner sat down at my desk when Janet opened my door and stuck her head inside.

"Come on in and sit down," I said.

"Did you see the chief?"

"Not yet. Why?"

"He was looking for you. I told him you were on your way, but all he did was nod and walk away."

She sat down on the edge of the seat in front of my desk and dumped her usual stack of notes topped by her iPad on my desk.

"I tried," I said, "but Cathy said he was out. He knows where I am. So," I said and looked up at the big board, "why don't you tell me what you've got?" I glanced at the stack on my desk and said, "From the looks of that, you have a lot."

I leaned back in my fancy chair and took a sip of the fancy coffee I'd gotten from the café in Eddie Chesterton's apartment building. At that moment, life was good. I closed my eyes and wondered how long it would last.

"The Chesterton family is like an octopus," she said, spreading the files and notes across the desk in front of her. "Just when you think you've seen it all, another tentacle emerges." She shook her head, making her red hair fall across her face. She brushed it aside quickly and began her lesson on the Chesterton lineage.

"According to the marriage license database, Genevieve Chesterton was Genevieve Bluford—"

"Hold on Janet," I said, leaning forward and placing my fancy cup on my fancy desk. "I'm not sure this is the best time for you to disseminate what looks to be an enormous amount of information. We'll need to do it all again on Monday for the rest of the team."

"That's so-oo true," she said. "So what now?"

I looked at the pile she'd placed on my desk and shook my head.

"You can go home. There's nothing more we can do today, it being Saturday. I'd better go find the chief and tell him what we're up to. Then I have to attend the autopsy. Doc's waiting for me. He's patient, but not that much, so... I'll see you here in my office with the others, bright and early on Monday, well, at eight o'clock. If by chance you should make it in earlier," I said, knowing full well that she would, "you can make a start on the board."

I glanced at the great white space knowing it would be filled to capacity by close of day on Monday.

"Go on, get out of here. You can leave all that where it is," I said, as she stood and moved to pick up the pile on my desk.

"See you Monday, then," she said, then turned and left me to it.

I sat for a moment luxuriating in my heavenly chair, then I got up and walked out into the corridor, closing the door behind me.

"Ah, there you are," Chief Johnston said as I bumped into him when I turned away from my office door.

"Chief, I am sorry. I was just on my way to find you to let you know—"

"Not here, Captain. My office, if you please." And he turned and walked the twenty yards or so to his own suite of offices, and I followed him, nodding at Cathy, his secretary as we passed through her office.

"Sit, please, Kate," he said as he rounded his desk and sat down.

I sat down in front of his desk and crossed my legs, placed my hands together in my lap, and waited.

Police Chief Wesley Johnston was an imposing figure of a man. Not over tall, but broad. He was, as always, impeccably dressed, his uniform pressed to perfection, his head shaved—it always seemed to me that he polished it too because it shined brightly in the sunlight streaming in through the window. He also wore an unusual mustache, one that Hulk Hogan himself would have been proud of, and it was just as white, which was, I'm sure, the reason for the shaved head. I couldn't imagine him with white hair. But he also had an air about him, more of confidence than of arrogance. If he had a sense of humor, I'd never seen it; hell, I don't think I'd ever seen him even smile.

"I've had a call from Edward Eaton Chesterton the Second," he began.

My heart sank. "Yes, Chief, I know. I got the call out this morning—"

He held up his hand, so I stopped talking, and he continued, "I received a call from Chesterton less than an hour ago. Apparently you've been to see his grandson, the husband of the deceased, is that right?"

"Yes, I—"

Again, he held up a hand.

"He is somewhat unhappy in the fact that no one bothered to inform him directly, that he had to find out from... let's say his slightly impaired grandson."

"Impaired?" I asked, outraged. "The man was wasted when I left him and still working on it. I'm surprised he was able to talk at all."

The chief nodded. "I assumed as much. However, Chesterton is an influential member of this community and—"

"Which one, Chief? There are three of them for Pete's sake." I was already regretting interrupting him, but he seemed to think nothing of it, much to my relief.

"All of them," he said, staring across the great expanse of walnut at me, unblinking.

"Tell me what you have, Kate, and we'll go from there."

And that's what I did. I also told him that my prime suspect was EEC4 with EEC2 as my second. As to EEC3, I'd not yet met him, but he was likely going to be on my list somewhere.

He listened carefully to all I had to say, nodding occasionally, asking the odd question for clarification, until I was done.

"I have to attend the autopsy in..." I said and looked at my watch, it was twelve-twenty-five, "five minutes. I'll familiarize my team first thing Monday morning. In the meantime, Detective Toliver has gathered a great deal of information, and I'll continue to familiarize myself with that, the victim, family, and friends over what's left of the weekend."

"You didn't think it might be prudent to bring your team in and begin your investigation today?"

"I did think about it, sir," I said, without hesitation, "but I didn't think you'd okay the overtime," and there it was, just the hint of a smile. "I did bring Toliver in and, of course, myself—"

I was interrupted by my phone buzzing in my pocket.

"If you'll excuse me, Chief," I said, taking the phone from my pocket.

He nodded. I checked the screen and answered it.

"Five minutes, Doc," I said, looking quizzically at Johnston who nodded his assent. "Yes, five minutes." I disconnected and stood up.

"I don't have to tell you how high profile this case is, Kate. Handle it with care. Handle the family with care. Don't hesitate to call on me for help. That's all, Captain. Tell Dr. Sheddon hello for me."

6

I LEFT THE GREAT MAN'S OFFICE, SAID 'BYE TO CATHY, AND called Doc back. Oh, was he ever PO'd? He was beside himself.

"Kate, don't ever do that to me again."

"Do what?" I asked, confused.

"Hang up on me."

"I couldn't talk, Doc. I was with the chief. What on earth is wrong?"

"I need you to get over here immediately, and I mean right now."

"Oh-kay. Is it to do with Genevieve Chesterton?" I asked somewhat tentatively.

"Yes, it is. Why the hell didn't you tell me she was black?"

My breath caught in my throat. "What?"

THE PD IS ONLY THREE BLOCKS FROM DOC'S FORENSIC CENTER, but to save him from having an aneurysm, I turned on my emergency lights and peeled out of the PD parking lot like the devil was chasing me.

I arrived at the Forensic Center just a couple of minutes later to find Doc pacing back and forth outside the rear doors.

"What took you so long?" he snapped. "Oh never mind, let's get to it. You did bring your own coffee, I hope?" and with that he turned his back on me and pushed through the doors.

"Actually, Doc, I've only had two cups of coffee all day. You have any in the pot?" I asked, hopefully.

He swiped his ID over the small pad on the wall. There was the flash of green, a loud click, and he turned the knob and held the door open for me.

"No. My intern, Mallory, forgot to get some, and she doesn't come in during the weekend."

My heart dropped. I let out a defeated sigh as I followed Doc into the anteroom where we suited up and then moved on into the autopsy room.

Genevieve Chesterton was lying on her back on the first of three stainless steel tables. She looked like a marble statue; the overhead lights made everything look sharp, surreal.

I'd never met Genevieve, of course, but as I looked down at her, I experienced a whole range of feelings, the first of which was that she was no longer a person but just a slab of meat. Cold, I know, but if you've ever been there... well, you'd know what I mean.

My second thought was to wonder what the future, the world, had missed by her sudden and untimely demise.

I looked up at Doc, wrinkled my nose, and squinted at him through my safety glasses. "What makes you think she's black?"

"Before I begin work on a body, I draw blood, so does Carol... Where the heck is she?"

"I'm here," Carol said as she stepped into the room. "I don't want to be here on Saturday afternoon any more than you do, Richard, so ease up, please. I've cleaned and vacuumed the body. She's ready for you. What else do you need?" she said impatiently. "Hi, Kate."

"Umm, hi, Carol," I said.

"Carol ran her blood," he said, totally ignoring her attitude.

"Thank you, Carol. Would you like to enlighten the good captain for me?"

She nodded and said, "I actually ran it three times, just to be sure. She has U-negative blood."

I frowned, wrinkled my nose again—*I need to stop doing that.* "I've never heard of that blood type," I replied.

"I doubt many people have," she said. "Only six percent of the black population across the globe have the U-negative blood type, and it's found only in black people. It has never been found in Whites, Asians, or any other race. Never."

"She is, legally, and in fact, a black woman," Doc said.

"But she looks... absolutely white," I said. "I mean, even her hair looks Caucasian. Are you sure?" I leaned over Genevieve's face and studied her features. There was nothing about her that would make me think she was black. And if there was nothing obvious to me, I wondered if her husband knew.

"Yes, of course I'm sure," Doc snapped. "And that isn't all; she was pregnant." He pinched the bridge of his nose beneath his glasses.

My heart sank. There are certain things cops never get used to, and one of the primary things is when a child dies, especially an unborn child.

"How far along was she?" I asked

"About seven weeks," Doc said.

"Eddie Chesterton didn't mention it," I said thoughtfully, "so I assume he doesn't know, unless he's one cold, calculating SOB."

I sat down on the metal stool at the head of the examining table, folded my arms and stared at the body.

"She'd obviously been out for a night on the town," I said. "How much had she had to drink, Doc?"

"Some. Not a lot. She may not have known she was pregnant, but I doubt it," Doc replied. "Young women are pretty savvy about such things these days."

"Drugs?" I asked.

"We won't know that until we get the tox screen back," Carol said.

I knew that, I thought. *Stupid question.*

I nodded.

"Do you have any more surprises for me?" I asked.

"Do you want some more?"

"Whew. Not really. I really don't think I can take anymore, Doc. But if you have anything, now's the time to lay it on me. If not, let's get on with it. We've been up since six o'clock, and it feels like I've crammed sixteen hours' worth of work and worry into eight hours."

Doc nodded and began his examination of the exterior of the body. I didn't bother to record it. It was already being done: voice and video, every word, every move, every nook and cranny.

Genevieve had a total of seven tattoos, including the tramp stamp: a bird, a swallow on her ankle; an infinity symbol on her left wrist; a heart on her upper right shoulder; the word Sexy on her right hip bone; a rose on her right buttock, and the word Forever with a date beneath it on her mons pubis, or mound of Venus.

Probably her wedding date, I thought. *Something I need to check. If it's not, what else could it be?* I made a mental note to check it out.

"Time of death?" I asked.

"I can now confirm that she did indeed die somewhere between two and three in the morning," Doc said. "Just after closing time for most clubs, I think."

"Cause of death, Doc?"

He sighed and shook his head, then said, "I can't tell you that yet, Catherine, not for sure. At first glance, though, I'd have to say ligature strangulation, but there's a long way yet to go."

I clicked my tongue, stood up, and stepped across the room to the table where Genevieve's clothing was laid out. Carol had had to cut the skinny jeans off her. Beside the silver lamé top and matching shoes lay a white lace bandeau bralette and a matching thong.

All were neatly folded and ready to be bagged. Everything had been vacuumed and treated with four-by-four clear lifting sheets to gather hairs and fibers. Small sections of cloth had been removed to be tested for fluids.

I had no doubt that the testing and documenting of what had been gathered from the clothing and the body would take days.

The woman had been partying—meeting people, dancing, hugging—and, whenever two objects meet—in this case Genevieve, multiple human beings, and her killer—something is always exchanged: hair, fiber, bodily fluids. And they could be exchanged by a simple kiss or even peck on the cheek. This young lady would, no doubt, yield a plethora of useful—and useless—information.

I touched nothing, sighed deeply, and returned to my stool.

"I don't believe she was sexually assaulted," Doc said. "I'll have Carol complete a rape kit." He glanced at her, then continued, "But I don't see signs of force," he said as he continued to examine her skin for anomalous markings, punctures, wounds or bruising.

By the time he reached her head, we were almost an hour into the examination, and I was beginning to see things that weren't there.

He began his scrutiny of the area around her throat. "Now this is very interesting," he said. "You see this?"

He pointed to the two deep, almost threadlike ligature marks that partially encircled her throat, one above the other, separated from each other by about a half an inch.

"I haven't seen this type of ligature mark for many years. It's consistent with people in jail who have hung themselves using their shoelaces."

"Is that so?" I mused and studied the markings even closer.

"It is, and that's why inmates are forced to wear flip-flops. Back in the day, though, I examined more than one inmate suicide all with very similar marks. These, however, are somewhat different. A typical hanging produces similar indentations—usually deeper, but certainly similar. Here's the difference, though. Look at these small bruises."

He pulled her hair aside and, at the nape of her neck, as I leaned in closer, I could see that the ligature marks did indeed end in a cluster of smaller bruises."

"Those were made by the killer's knuckles!" I stated, leaning back again.

"They were indeed," he said. "There's a similar pattern of bruises on the other side of her neck. Obviously, the ligature was quite short, forcing the attacker's fists into contact with her neck. Nasty, very nasty. I would say our perpetrator snuck up behind her, wrapped the shoelaces around her neck, and then twisted them tight using her own neck as a fulcrum, like this..." he held up his two hands clenched into tight fists and twisted them in opposite directions.

He stood back a little, contemplating his scenario, then stepped forward again, took a small penlight from his pocket and snapped it on.

"And see here: You can see the gouges in her skin where she clawed at the laces but couldn't get a finger beneath them because they were so tight."

I'd noticed the gouges earlier, at the crime scene, but under the harsh lights, and against the almost porcelain-white skin, they looked raw, red, turning the ligature wound into a gruesome necklace.

I sat back, hearing but not listening to Doc's words, staring unseeing at the wounds, lost in thought as I absorbed these new developments and wondered at the brutality, the viciousness of the attack.

Someone really hated this poor girl, I thought. *It's... so violent, up close, personal, full of hate, anger. What the hell did she do to piss off someone that much?*

My phone buzzed in my pocket, snapping me out of my trance. I glanced at the screen, expecting to see Janet's number or maybe even Chief Johnston's. But it was neither of them. It was a number I didn't know.

I stood, walked to the door, and accepted the call. "Gazzara."

"Is this Detective Catherine Gazzara?" The voice sounded sweet, feminine, but distressed.

"Yes, it is."

"Detective, my name is Regina Mae Cottonwell-Chesterton. I just received the most distressing call from my son. Is it true? Is my daughter-in-law dead?" The words sounded like they tumbled out of her mouth.

"Yes, ma'am. I'm afraid it is."

I heard the woman begin to sob. I listened for a few seconds, waiting for her to speak, but she didn't, so I took the initiative and dove right in, thinking that this was the perfect opportunity to start the investigation rolling.

"If I may, Mrs. Cottonwell-Chesterton"—*Geez, what a mouthful* —"I'd like to drop by and talk to you. Shall we say in thirty minutes?"

I would have preferred to talk to Granddad first, but since I had Regina Mae on the line...

"Of course, Detective. I'll see you then." Regina Mae sniffled and hung up the phone.

I looked at Doc. He and Carol were hovering over the body like a couple of great green vultures. Doc had a scalpel in his hand and was about to make his first cut.

"Are you done with me, Doc? I have an appointment," I said as I pulled off my latex gloves.

"Yes. I think so. I don't expect there will be any more surprises. I'll call you if I discover anything else. My report should be done by tomorrow if no one bothers me, that is," he said, looking up at me.

I got the message.

"I'll be sure to stay out of your hair, but if you could send it to me..." I replied, smiling sweetly at him as I tossed the gloves in the trash. "And you might want to have a talk with that intern about the importance of coffee."

"I think she drinks tea," Doc muttered with a frown.

"Ugh, and you hired her? Doc, I'm shocked," I teased. "Well, I don't care if you discover tentacles and an alien implant, I won't be back until there is coffee in the pot. No coffee? No Kate." I jerked my thumb at my chest.

"You can be sure I'll get right on that," Doc said without emotion as he stroked the scalpel through the flesh from shoulder to pubic bone. Then he looked up at me and winked.

Five minutes later, sans the Tyvek suit, cap, booties, mask and safety glasses, I closed the car door, pushed the starter button and glanced at the display and literally gasped; it was almost four-thirty. Where had the day gone? And I wasn't done yet. I'd talked myself into what could turn out to be another lengthy interview.

7

Regina Mae Cottonwood-Chesterton lived in a swanky penthouse at the other end of town, where I had to show a doorman my driver's license as well as my creds in order to pass through the lobby. I flashed my badge and was allowed to retain my license. The lobby was decorated with beautiful pieces of art in gold frames, but there was no café churning out steaming hot coffee. I liked her son's place better.

The doorman walked me to the private elevator and inserted a key to open the doors. There were only four buttons on the panel: one down to the garage, one to the lobby, a third to the second floor, and the fourth going directly to the penthouse. That one also required a key, and again the doorman obliged then stepped out as the doors closed.

My stomach jumped a little when the fast-moving elevator came to a sudden stop. The doors slid open, giving access to another, much smaller, lobby and a beautiful pair of walnut double doors. I exited the elevator and looked around, noting the black glass dome that housed the security cameras, a red emergency phone on the wall, and a door leading to a stairwell.

I raised my hand to knock, but before I could one of the heavy doors opened.

"Detective Gazzara?" the woman asked.

She couldn't have been much more than five feet tall. Her hair was cut very short and was unnaturally white. She was wearing a pale blue, off-one-shoulder sweater complemented by a slim gold chain with a pendant of an eagle claw grasping a tiger's eye gemstone that complemented her light brown eyes. I could easily see that she'd had some work done on her crow's feet and at the corners of her mouth. But she was still a strikingly beautiful woman with a lovely figure, highlighted by her skinny jeans and leopard-print shoes.

"Yes, ma'am. Are you Mrs. Cottonwell-Chesterton?"

"Oh, please, call me Regina Mae and come on in." The accent was pure Southern belle.

She extended her hand, palm down, as if she expected me to kiss it. I couldn't help but note the perfectly red manicured nails and several large rings. I glanced down at her left hand; the wedding set on her ring finger was big enough to choke a pig.

"Jonathan the doorman told me you'd arrived. Won't you come in?"

I gripped her fingers gently, then turned them loose—it was the weirdest handshake ever—and followed her inside to be greeted by the sweet smell of peaches.

Nah, she can't be baking, not dressed like that.

I quickly dismissed the thought when I saw the scented candle burning on the marble island in the kitchen. *Geez,* I thought, as I gazed around the massive open-plan complex. *So this, I guess, is how the one-percenters live.*

It wasn't a critical thought, more one of... not even envy; perhaps it was wishful thinking. I don't know.

The ceilings were high, the crown molding at least a foot deep. Everything was pristine... pure white: white leather couch and matching easy chairs, throw rugs... Unbelievable.

"My son called me just after you left. He's absolutely torn apart," she said as she walked ahead of me, her voice echoing off the hard-wood floors in the foyer.

"I'm so sorry for your loss. The Chattanooga PD wants to do everything possible to find the person responsible," I said, remembering the chief said to be extra careful how I handled the family.

She led me into a sitting room area where the afternoon sun was peeking in through vintage lace curtains.

"Please, sit down, Detective. Can I get you something to drink? Sweet tea or a glass of water, perhaps?"

"No, thank you, ma'am," I said as I sat down on one of the easy chairs. "I'd like to ask you a few questions if you don't mind, and I like to record my interviews if that's acceptable."

I watched Regina Mae's expression as she watched me set my iPad on the coffee table in front of me.

"By all means," she said and quickly sat down on the matching chair opposite me. She sat demurely, knees together, feet crossed at the ankles and positioned slightly to the left, her hands clasped together in her lap.

Her well-manicured fingers played with her rings. "I'm sorry. You'll have to forgive me. I'm just a basket of nerves. I cannot believe this has happened. Poor, poor, Genevieve. Can you tell me what happened?"

"I'm afraid I can't discuss the ongoing investigation, Mrs. Cot... Regina Mae. If you don't mind my asking, what was your relationship with your daughter-in-law like?" I watched as she twisted the large diamond around and around her ring finger.

"What did Eddie tell you?" she asked.

"I'd rather hear it from you, if you don't mind," I replied, smiling benignly at her.

"We weren't very close, I must admit. I always thought that Eddie made poor choices, especially when it came to women. Oh please, don't take that the wrong way. I want nothing but the best for my son, just as any mother would. You see, he's my *only* son and someday he will have big responsibilities; he has big shoes to fill, I'm afraid." She looked off to the side for a moment, before turning back to me.

"I do think he could have done better. There were plenty of girls from reputable families that..." She let the thought trail off. She blushed slightly, obviously embarrassed by what she'd said.

"Why didn't you think Genevieve was right for him?" I asked.

"Are you serious?" Regina Mae's voice was losing that Southern softness. "She had quite a reputation. She... Uh! When she began working for Grandfather at the company, it was common knowledge that she was looking for a free ride."

Geez, this is one cold... piece of work. Her daughter-in-law was murdered only hours ago and she talks about her as if...

"Other than your son," I said, "was she seeing anyone else that worked at the office?" I leaned a little closer.

"Was she having an affair, you mean? Not that I'm aware of, but you know how it is when you are part of the family that owns the business. You're the last to know anything. The rank and file... well, they stick together, don't they? Why do you ask?"

I decided it was time to bring the hammer down and said, "Did you know that Genevieve was pregnant?"

"*What?*" Regina Mae asked, stunned.

"The medical examiner took a sample of her blood. He said she was around seven weeks along. So, you didn't know?"

"I had no idea, but it doesn't surprise me. Her Hail Mary, I should think." She turned her head away, lifted her chin, sat up a little straighter in the chair, and continued. "That really does just take the cake, doesn't it? I mean, it is really too bad. It's too bad about Genevieve, I know... and now another innocent life has been taken." She paused for a moment, stared down at her hands.

"Genevieve was no angel, Detective," she continued. "Yes, I know, it's not right to speak ill of the dead, but it's true, and I do believe that Eddie was beginning to realize it."

"Do you believe that Eddie was the baby's father?" I asked.

She heaved a huge sigh, lowered her eyes, shook her head and said, "That, of course, is the question, isn't it, Detective?" She turned her head toward me and locked eyes with me. "I would hope so, but I'm a pragmatist. She was a maverick in every sense of the word. She carried on... If you'd seen how she dressed or how she... Well, we just can't be sure, can we? Let's just say I wouldn't be surprised if my son was not the father."

"Has Eddie ever confided in you that they were having problems? Did he ever mention them having arguments, physical altercations?"

I watched Regina Mae's eyes. She had a strange look on her face. Perhaps she was disappointed that I'd interrupted her rant about what a slut she thought her daughter-in-law was.

"No?" she said. It was more a question than a denial. She looked puzzled.

"You're not sure?"

"Eddie has never said anything to me, and... No!" she said suddenly very confident.

"Did Genevieve?"

"No... Well, yes, she did ask for my advice on occasion, but I tried to stay out of it. If she couldn't cope with Eddie, it was probably because she was out of her league. The Chesterton's are... not like other... Oh dear, how shall I put it? Ordinary people? No, that's not quite right, but I'm sure you understand, Detective. I, on the other hand, knew exactly the type of man I was marrying, and I knew what to expect and how to handle it. Edward and I moved in the same circles. I didn't have to pretend I was something I wasn't."

I watched as Regina Mae nodded her head while looking at me. *Who the hell is she trying to persuade?* I thought.

"Well, you know how it can be," she continued. "It isn't easy having a lot of money." She cleared her throat after realizing what she'd just said. "Please, I hope I don't sound snobbish."

I didn't answer. I waited for her to continue.

She looked down at her polished fingernails, adjusted all of her rings, then said defiantly, "I am *not* going to apologize for being wealthy."

"I'm not asking you to do that, Regina Mae," I replied. It was almost like I was talking to a small child.

"I'll tell you this," she said, the anger rising in her voice. "I did *not* care for my daughter-in-law. Genevieve did *not* belong in this family."

Wow, why don't you tell me what you really think?

Regina Mae stood up, walked around to the back of her chair, kneaded the soft leather of the back as if she was giving it a massage.

"And now you tell me there's a baby."

I swear she had tears in her eyes, and *that* I wasn't expecting.

"There was a baby," I clarified. "They are both dead."

"Well, maybe that's for the best," she said, in a whisper. "The child has been spared. Perhaps that's the silver lining in all of this." Regina Mae looked at me, shook her head, and then shrugged. "God does indeed work in mysterious ways."

I stared up at her. Wow! I was disgusted, and I'd had just about enough of her crap.

Time for the hammer again, I think.

"Mrs. Chesterton, did you know Genevieve was black?"

She looked down at me, her eyes wide, her mouth open.

"What did you say?"

"I said, did you know your daughter-in-law was black?"

Regina Mae chuckled. "You're joking?"

Hmm, either she's one hell of an actress or she really didn't know.

Slowly, I shook my head, maintained eye contact with her.

"No... You're wrong. She is as lily-white as I am. I don't believe it."

It took me only a few seconds to relay Doc's findings to her, and then I watched her as she stared at me. It was as if I'd suddenly grown antlers.

"Then I can say with all certainty," she replied, "that it *is* for the best that, that this *tragedy* occurred. What kind of life, do you think, would the poor child have had? It's unthinkable!" Regina Mae shrugged and rolled her eyes.

Wow, I thought. *What kind of person is she? Who talks like this?*

There wasn't a shred of compassion or concern in her voice, not for Genevieve or the baby... her grandchild. Even the concern she'd expressed for her son was absent.

"Regina Mae, where were you between two and three o'clock this morning?" I asked, trying to put my personal feelings for the woman aside.

She glared at me, seemingly stunned by the question, then said, "You can't be serious. You don't think for one moment that I had anything to do with it... *do you?*" She held up her hands, fingers spread, palms inward, as if her bright red nails were still wet. "Since when is it a crime to not like someone?"

"It's not a crime, ma'am. But I have to establish the whereabouts of everyone concerned, including you. Would you please tell me where you were and who you were with?" I bit my lower lip and raised my eyebrows.

"Where do you think I was, for goodness' sake?" she snapped. "I was here, at home, in bed."

"Can anyone verify that?" I asked, knowing that her husband was out of town.

"Yes," she said nastily, folding her arms defiantly. "Yes." The sweet Southern drawl had disappeared, along with her ladylike composure.

"And?" I asked.

"Tyrone and Baker Security Systems." She smirked. "This entire apartment is wired for sound and video... cameras. The feed goes directly to T&B's servers where they are archived. If you want to check *my alibi,* you can. I'll call them and give my permission for you to view the recordings."

"Thank you," I replied. "I'll need the address, please. I'll verify your *alibi* and eliminate you as a person of interest." I'm ashamed to admit I allowed a little sarcasm of my own to slip in.

"Oh, you will, will you? Fine."

She turned and stalked over to an antique desk set against the far wall, snatched open one of the drawers, sorted through the contents, slammed the drawer shut, and then walked stiffly back to me and handed me T&B's business card. I glanced at it, nodded, thanked her, and slipped it into my purse.

"You do understand, Mrs. Chesterton, that none of this is personal. I have a job to do, a murderer to catch."

She stepped away, turned again to face me, folded her arms, and glared down at me, but didn't answer.

"I appreciate your being so honest and forthcoming with me," I said, rising to my feet, thinking I'd just about had enough of the woman, and her attitude, and that she'd certainly had enough of me.

I would have loved to have given her a piece of my mind, but that would have been inappropriate. My job was to investigate, not judge. But what kind of woman—a so-called lady—talks about the murder of a mother and her unborn child that way, intimating that God had a hand in it? It was unsettling, to say the least, but it didn't mean she'd had anything to do with it.

No, it shows her up as the bitch she really is.

"I think I've answered enough of your questions, Detective," she said pompously. "So, if you'll excuse me, I have to go and meet with Grandfather Chesterton. I'm afraid we'll have much to discuss, sad things, so sad..."

And then, slap me if she didn't sniffle. I almost wanted to burst out laughing, but I didn't.

I picked up my iPad, looked unseeingly at the screen, lost in thought, and then I had an idea.

"You're going to see Edward Eaton Chesterton the Second?" I asked. "That reminds me of something your son said to me. Do you have any idea why Eddie would say that his grandfather had killed Genevieve?"

Regina Mae froze.

"I'm sure I don't know the answer to that," she hissed.

"Well, if you're going to visit him, I might as well tag along with you, if you don't mind. I need to talk to him, too." I had a hunch what her answer would be, and I was right.

"Yes, I do mind. I mind very much," she snapped.

"Well then," I said casually. "Perhaps you're right. Maybe it would be better if I had him brought to the police department."

Then, as if it was an afterthought, I said quietly, "You'd be surprised at how quickly the media gets to know of this sort of thing... who we're questioning, and why. They monitor us, you know. If they were to find out that Edward Eaton Chesterton the Second's grandson had accused him of murder... well, that's news. Especially when the accused is as... let's say as well-known as he is. That sells advertising."

Sure, it was petty to add that last tidbit, but it was true. The media vultures were always more interested in the wealthy than the lush in the drunk tank, unless it was a wealthy lush, of course. They'd be all over EEC2 in a second.

"If you think you can make a name for yourself by humiliating one of this country's most respected statesmen, you're greatly mistaken."

Regina Mae lifted her chin defiantly. "He's much too smart for the likes of you. He'll be three steps ahead of you all the way. I will tell you this, though. Eddie doesn't care for his grandfather. I had so hoped that it was just a phase he was going through, but my son is almost twenty-eight years old and nothing has changed."

"But to blame his grandfather for murder right off the bat," I said. "Why would he do that?"

"Look, Detective, I'm not the only one who didn't like Genevieve. Grandfather, Eddie's uncles, his cousins, everyone for heaven's sake. I don't think even the gardener liked the woman. Remember what that Palin woman said? If you put lipstick on a pig... Yes, well it's true. Grandfather may have been the most vocal in his distaste, but only in closed circles. It's no wonder then that Eddie is upset with him."

"Did you ever see Mr. Chesterton senior and Genevieve

exchange words? Were there ever any arguments, or threats of violence uttered by either one of them?"

I watched as Regina Mae became noticeably more agitated. I had the notion that Grandfather didn't just rub Eddie the wrong way, but Genevieve too. It was obvious the old man wielded a lot of power, even when he wasn't around. Hell, even I could feel his presence.

"No. Not to my knowledge. I myself have never seen a cross word pass between them." She smoothed her sweater and smiled sweetly. "Grandfather was very discreet. Now, I do believe I have been more than cordial, Detective. I am afraid I must ask you to leave. There are errands I must run."

"Just one last question," I said. "Do you think Edward Eaton Chesterton the Second murdered Genevieve?"

She stared daggers at me.

"I always knew it!" she snapped. "I knew that girl would poison my son against his own family! That a grandfather would murder his own granddaughter-in-law is the most ridiculous thing I've ever heard. He might be a lot of things but a murderer? No, absolutely not. You obviously don't know much about our family, Detective, or you wouldn't have displayed such blatant ignorance!

"My son is heartbroken and not thinking clearly. He'll accuse anyone and everyone who ever expressed any concern for him. Today it's his grandfather, tomorrow it will be his own father, or Uncle Sam Wheaton, or even me. Unfortunately, we spared the rod, and now we are reaping the consequences. Good day, Detective. Please show yourself out," she said, her voice trembling with emotion.

"Uncle Sam Wheaton?" I asked. "Who's he?"

"I said good day, Detective. Now please leave." Then she turned away and disappeared into the nether regions of the apartment.

And so I did as I was told. I left. I went home, exhausted, my mind in a whirl. *Open-and-shut case? Right, and if you'll believe that...*

8

"How did it go?" Janet asked.

I'd called her to touch base and had her on Bluetooth as I drove home; her voice echoed from the car's speakers. It had been one heck of a long day, and all I wanted was a hot shower, a couple glasses of wine and some mindless television.

"It was interesting to say the least," I replied. "You got your pad in front of you?"

"I do. I'm ready when you are."

I first brought her up to date with Doc's findings: Genevieve's ethnic background and her pregnancy. Her reaction was similar to mine.

"Oh dear," she said. "If that doesn't beat all. How sad."

I could see her shaking her head of red hair over the phone.

"Yes... sad isn't the word for it," I said. "But that's not all. I also interviewed Genevieve's mother-in-law, Regina Mae Cottonwell-Chesterton. Try saying that three times quickly. Anyway, she's a real piece of... well, this is not the time or place. I don't want to have to repeat everything for the rest of the team. You did get everybody organized for Monday morning, right?"

"The rest of the new team? Yes, they'll all be there."

"Good. I recorded her interview, and Eddie's. We'll have them transcribed on Monday. We should have the autopsy report by then, too. Okay, so look, it's been a tough day and I'm on my way home, but if you have time, I'd like for you to call Lenny Miller and have him dig into Genevieve's background; give us a bit of a head start for Monday. Ask him to put out a few feelers to the more unorthodox information outlets, if you catch my drift," I said.

"Got it."

"And while he's at it, I'd also like for him to check into a guy named Sam Wheaton. I need an address and the basics: criminal background, credit check, et cetera. You know the drill."

"On it."

Lenny Miller is one of the three members of my new team. He knows computers, so he's my go-to guy for in-depth research: background checks and the like. He's good, but he's no Tim Clarke.

"Good," I said. "It's been a heck of a day and I intend to take it easy the rest of the weekend, so don't call me unless it's urgent, okay?"

"Yes, ma'am. Take it easy. See you Monday," and she disconnected.

Me? I couldn't get home fast enough. Normally when I got home, I'd be greeted by Sadie Mae my chocolate Dachshund, her tail wagging happily. I'd adopted her from a couple I'd put away for murder some months ago. They don't allow lifers to have pets, so I took the little scamp.

I soon realized, however, that I was serving a life sentence of my own to the Chattanooga PD and that it wasn't fair to leave the little lovebug home alone all day, sometimes at night too, so I boarded her out with my ex-partner, Lonnie. I missed that little brown face and those big black eyes that seemed so full of love and affection... the dog, I mean, not Lonnie.

I dumped my Glock and badge on the kitchen counter, went to the fridge, grabbed an already opened bottle of Cabernet, poured myself a large glass and, with the bottle still in my hand, I closed my eyes and sipped: *oh, how heavenly!*

I took the bottle with me into the living room, flopped down on the couch, snapped on the television and flipped through the channels until I found a romantic comedy about a woman who was in love with two guys. It wasn't what I wanted, but I found myself watching it anyway. It was all stuff that never happens in real life, not to me anyway.

I'm young, right? I told myself. *Well, thirty-seven isn't old... is it? And I'm attractive, funny too, when I want to be, and feel like it. So why doesn't it ever happen to me? I can't find one dude let alone juggle two.*

The truth was, I couldn't find anyone who could live with what I do for a living: my hours, my bosses, my visits to the seedier parts of town, my need to keep my gun with me at all times, even on my nightstand.

Let's see some brainiac in Hollywood make a romantic comedy about that. I won't hold my breath.

I needed a shower, but I just couldn't be bothered, so I finished off my bottle of wine, made a start on another, and sat through the rest of the rom-com, not really seeing or listening to it; it was way above my paygrade, a fantasy but, crazy as it may seem, I was in a state of contentment. Maybe it was the wine.

And then I found myself thinking about Regina Mae Cottonwell-Chesterton. *That name is too much.*

I figured she must have high-tailed it over to Grandpappy's place and told him everything I'd said, and then some. She struck me as a woman on a mission, someone who would say and do just about anything to secure her share of the old man's estate. *C'est la vie.* At that moment, with the wine running through my head and the soft cushions on my couch, she could keep it. *I wouldn't trade places with any of those bluebloods, not for all the money in the world...* and at that point I must have fallen asleep, because I remember nothing more.

I woke early that Sunday morning, and I felt like... Well, you know what I felt like. I staggered to the window, opened the drapes, and looked out on to what was about to turn into a lovely day. It was the perfect morning for a run.

I went to the bathroom, stripped off my clothes from the day before, splashed cold water over my face, donned a pair of running shorts, sports bra and top, and headed out into the cool, early morning air.

9

It was just seven o'clock that following Monday morning when I parked my car in my assigned space at the rear of the PD; my batteries were fully charged and I was eager to get to work.

Five minutes later I was at my desk with my office door closed. I tackled my emails first, made a couple of quick phone calls, emailed the interview recordings to the department secretary for transcription, grabbed my first file and, just as I was about to open it, there was a knock on the door. It was Janet.

"Don't you ever go home?" I asked her.

She was carrying her usual stack of notebooks and files, and she smiled at me.

"I do. But I love this stuff so I don't like to be away for too long," she said, smiling. "The others are all here, by the way. They're in the incident room. You want me to have them come on in?"

"Yep, might as well get started," I said, looking at the expanse of shiny white that was the storyboard. "You didn't do much with it on Saturday, did you?"

"No, I didn't. Sorry, Captain." She shrugged. "I was going to but... I had to go to Home Depot."

"Don't worry about it," I said. "I took Sunday off too, remember."

Home Depot? I thought. What on earth?

She nodded, smiling sheepishly, and I knew that she knew what I was thinking, but she didn't explain. Instead, she picked up my desk phone and called Detective Hawkins and asked him and the rest of the team to join us.

They arrived together a few minutes later, laden with laptops, iPads, files, notebooks, coffee... and speaking of coffee.

"I'll go get you some," Janet said, reading my mind.

How does she do that?

While I was waiting for her to return, they, my three new team members, exchanged small talk about their goings-on over the weekend. I dug through my files and extracted several 8x10 photographs: Genevieve, EEC2, 3 and 4 and Regina Mae. I taped the photo of Genevieve to the big board at the top dead center—no pun intended—and the other four in a row, in order directly below. Then I wrote the names beneath each photo.

"Here you go, Cap," Janet said, setting the cup down on my desk. "Black, no sugar."

I grabbed the cup and sniffed the contents. *Not bad... not great, but not bad.*

"Where did you get this?" I asked. "It's not that crap from the incident room, is it?"

"No. I made it myself in Cathy's office."

I sipped. "Hmm... Okay, let's get on with it." I grabbed a twelve-inch plastic ruler from my desk drawer, tapped the topmost photo and began.

"Genevieve Chesterton was found strangled to death on the Riverwalk at six-thirty on Saturday morning. Time of death: between two and three o'clock that same morning. She was attacked from behind. This was not, I repeat, not, a sexual assault. Whoever did this had only one thing on his mind... to kill her. She is ethnically black, although to look at her you'd never know it, but I believe she's been passing herself off as white. She was also pregnant."

I paused, looked at each of the four faces one by one. Three of them, including Janet were taking notes. Hawkins, the oldest and most experienced of them was not.

Arthur "Hawk" Hawkins was sixty-four years old. He'd been a detective for twenty-nine years and had one year left to go before retirement. I think he'd been transferred to me so that he could work out the rest of his term in relative peace. He was a handsome man, five-ten, a little overweight at two hundred ten pounds, clean-shaven, with white hair, blue eyes, a sharp nose, sunburned face and arms, and was wearing suspenders with his shirt sleeves rolled up. He was seated at the back of the room with his arms folded, watching every move I made. To anyone else that might have been unnerving, but I'd known Hawk a long time. He was a tough old man with a big soft heart.

"Genevieve was married to this man." I tapped the photograph of EEC4. "Edward Eaton Chesterton the Fourth, the only grandson of one of the wealthiest men in Tennessee; this man, Edward Eaton Chesterton the Second... Yes, Anne," I said in answer to Anne Robar's raised hand.

"Did he... Edward Eaton Chesterton... Oh hell, we can't keep calling them all by that long, convoluted name—"

"Which one, Anne?"

"The young one, the husband."

I nodded. "Yes, you're right. From now on, the husband is Eddie, his father is Daddy, and the old man is... the old man," I said, adding the nicknames to the photographs. "So what's your question, Anne?"

I'd also known Anne Robar a long time. At forty-three, she was five years older than me with more than twenty years on the job. True she was no great beauty, but she was quite a striking woman: prematurely graying hair cropped very short, a round face, hazel eyes surrounded by crow's feet—the woman had spent far too long in the sun without protection and now her skin was suffering for it. She wasn't quite as tall as me, but she carried herself with more than a little attitude. In other words, she didn't take crap from anyone. She was also married with two teenage boys, both of them still in high school. She was a senior detective and a good one. Why she wasn't at least a sergeant was beyond me.

"Eddie," she said. "Did he know she was black?"

"Good question," I said. "Eddie, the husband, has to be our prime suspect, so the answer goes to motive. I don't know. I interviewed him yesterday morning—I'll have transcripts for you all later today—but I didn't know she was black myself, not then, or that she was pregnant, so I didn't ask him, which means a follow-up interview. I'll do that myself, later." I paused, turned to the board and picked up a marker.

"One more thing before I move on," I said, drawing a blank square on the board, "Eddie said I should ask the old man about the Frenchman. He wouldn't tell me more than that. We need to find out what, or who, he was talking about." I drew a large question mark beside the blank box. "Regina Mae mentioned a Sam Wheaton, more about that later," I said, and I drew a second empty box and question mark.

"Okay," I said, setting the marker down, "so moving right along, I also interviewed Regina Mae Cottonwell-Chesterton."

"Whew, what a fricking mouthful," Anne said. "What are we going to call her?"

"Regina, I think will do well enough," I said. "She's something else, this one, a real piece of high society, nose in the air, self-centered... Okay, she's a snob, and she didn't approve of Genevieve *at all!* Right at the end of the interview, she threw me a name—not sure if she intended to, but she did—someone named Sam Wheaton. I asked about him, but she ignored the question and ended the interview."

I looked at Lenny Miller.

"Come on, Lenny," I said, impatiently. "Don't keep me on tenterhooks. What did you find out?" I grabbed my own pad of paper and a pen.

He looked at me, puzzled, then said, "I'm afraid the verdict is still out on Genevieve Chesterton. I'm still working on it."

I nodded. "How about Sam Wheaton?

It was Janet who answered.

"Umm, I think I can shed a little light on him." She looked up at me, wide-eyed.

I said nothing. I waited for her to speak.

"Well, I wasn't able to get hold of Lenny until Sunday morning." She glanced at him, then continued, "and... well, I had nothing much to do, so I called my boyfriend. He's a corporate finance major at UTK and a bit of a computer whiz, so I thought he might have heard of him, Wheaton..."

Again she glanced sideways at Lenny. Lenny grinned at her, seemingly not the least bit bothered that Janet was encroaching into his domain.

"Anyway, Josh—that's my boyfriend—was at work at the Home Depot, and it was late on Saturday. I go there often. At that hour nothing is usually happening so I can learn how to use the power tools. They offer classes and dating one of the employees has its perks." She scooted in her seat.

I heaved a sigh, rolled my eyes and said, "I guess so. Okay, so you went to see your boyfriend at Home Depot, and..."

"I asked him if he could check into Uncle Sam Wheaton." She looked up at me and then to the side at Anne, then again at me and said, "I'm really not sure where to begin."

"Just jump right in," I said. I sat down and waited as Janet began to read through her notes.

"Janet?" I said, after a couple of minutes of her not saying anything.

"Yes, I just wanted to..." She extracted a photograph, jumped to her feet, and slapped it up on the board over the blank square that I'd just drawn on the board.

"This is Samuel Tiegh Wheaton." She stood with her back to the board, iPad in hand, and began.

"Josh took his lunch break and..." She caught the look I was giving her and quickly got back on track. "Wheaton is the founder of a business consulting firm that works primarily for smaller companies, usually start-ups, and he's very good at what he does. However, his main bread-and-butter comes from CDE International Finance Company, the flagship of the Chesterton group of companies where he's affectionately known by the staff as Uncle Sam."

She paused and flipped through a couple of screens on her iPad.

"I came into the office yesterday morning, after I'd talked to Lenny, and did a search of criminal records. Sam Wheaton does not have a record per se, but Josh found that back in 2008 he'd settled a couple of sexual harassment claims by members of his own staff. He was never married, but he did father two children, a girl aged twelve and a boy aged thirteen, by different mothers. Both were adopted at birth," Janet said.

"So, he likes the ladies," I said smirking.

"Younger ladies," Janet said.

"How young?"

"Legal age, barely. But as far as I could tell, he's never crossed the line. We should probably do a thorough background check on him," she said, looking at Lenny.

"So what's his connection to Regina Mae?" I asked.

"Samuel Wheaten is a close friend of old man Chesterton; a very close friend. It was him that bailed him out of his sexual harassment problems. In fact, Edward Chesterton the Second is quoted as saying that 'Uncle Sam is a good man and a trusted confidant.' Apparently, he's run every major financial decision past Uncle Sam for the past two decades and has yet to regret a single one." Janet pinched her lips together like a fish as she continued to look over her notes.

"Oh," she said, almost as an afterthought, "and Genevieve worked for CDE prior to her marriage to Eddie, so Uncle Sam must have known her even back then."

"So," I mused aloud. "Here we have a guy, not related to the Chesterton's, but who has intimate knowledge of all their financial dealings and probably most of the family secrets as well. He's a man with a penchant for young women. He's introduced to Eddie's lovely new bride and likes what he sees. He makes a pass at her, and she rejects him. Or maybe she didn't. Maybe she had an affair with him and then broke it off—for somebody else maybe—or maybe she was about to expose him... Who knows? He's been on his best behavior for a decade. Hmmm." I was liking the sound of this.

"Hmmm indeed," Janet replied. "Here is his contact info." She placed a sheet of paper on the desk in front of me. "He rarely goes into the office," she continued. "Spends most of his time at the golf course or at the gym."

"Well," I said, brightly. "What do you say, Janet? You want to question Uncle Sam?"

Although I wasn't at all disappointed in my own looks, if I wanted to extract information from a pervy guy who was into young girls, I knew younger was better.

"Absolutely," she bubbled.

I thought she was going to start clapping she was so excited.

I checked my watch. It was almost nine.

"Hawk," I said, "I want you and Anne to go check out the crime scene. See if you can figure out what she was doing down there by herself at that ungodly hour of the morning. I figure she must have been coming from a club or bar or... party, whatever. Ask around, see what you can find out; who she was with... you know the drill. Go talk to people."

I turned to Lenny and said, "I want to know everything about everybody, but start with Genevieve Chesterton, then the close members of the family and... okay, I don't have to tell you."

He nodded. "I'm on it, boss. I'll have something for you when you get back."

I stood, grabbed my iPad, my purse, phone and weapon, and walked to the door.

"We'll meet back here this afternoon at two-thirty and compare notes. Maybe between us... well, we'll see."

10

SAMUEL TIEGH WHEATON'S HOME WAS ALL YOU'D EXPECT IT TO be for a man of his status: a beautiful, three-story house in an exclusive, high-status subdivision with what the realtors sell as "curb appeal." To me? It looked like one hell of a lot of expensive landscaping.

I parked my unmarked cruiser in the driveway and together, Janet and I walked to the front porch and up the steps to the front door.

"I shouldn't ask you to do this, Janet," I said as I rang the doorbell, "but you said that this guy has a penchant for young girls, so I need you to..." I took a deep breath and continued, "I need you to do me a favor. I need you to act like you're impressed by him, that you're attracted to him. Yes, I know. It's not professional and—"

"I can do that," she said, interrupting me. "Don't worry, I love it; it'll be fun. You'll see." I could almost hear the wheels turning in her head. "I know just how to handle a guy like him."

I was about to ring again when I heard hard-soled shoes on hardwood floor within. The door finally opened.

"Can I help you?"

"Mr. Wheaton?" I asked.

"Yes, can I help you?"

"I'm Captain Gazzara, Chattanooga Police," I said, showing him my badge and ID. "This is Sergeant Toliver." Janet did the same, smiling sweetly. "We need to talk to you for a minute. May we come in?"

"Yes, of course."

I let Janet enter first. He shook her hand, holding it tightly, quickly scanning her face. He did the same to me, holding my hand firmly as he gently tugged me through the opening into the house.

When he let go of my hand, shut the door, and squeezed past me, his smiling face was a little too close for comfort.

I had to admit it, he was a handsome man. In his late fifties or early sixties, he was tall with broad shoulders, a full head of salt-and-pepper hair, a slim waist. I don't think there was an ounce of extra fat on his body. He was wearing a white button-down shirt with cuff links and a pale blue tie. We'd obviously caught him as he was about to leave.

"Please, won't you come on through and sit down. What's this all about?" he asked, leading the way down a long narrow hallway to what was obviously a sitting room where he stopped, turned and waved us on through into the room, leaning a little closer to Janet as she passed. It was as if he was trying to sniff her hair.

The room was quite small compared to those in the grand penthouses belonging to the Chestertons. It was also more homey, more comfortable. The dark leather furniture was soft and complemented the antique feel of the home. To the left, a window overlooked the street; to the right a wall covered with framed photographs of Sam with various politicians, sports stars, the Dallas Cowboy cheerleaders, and even one with a Miss America contestant. It was, in fact, a bachelor pad.

"I'm afraid I have bad news," I said, taking a seat opposite Wheaton as he sat down on the large leather couch —Janet remained standing. "I'm afraid your employer's grand-daughter-in-law is... I'm afraid she's dead."

The news didn't seem to shake him very much.

He frowned. "You mean Genevieve?"

"Yes," Janet replied. "Genevieve. She was found on the River-walk early on Saturday morning. She was strangled to death."

I watched my sergeant look at Uncle Sam a little longer than necessary when she replied and then walk over to admire the wall of photos.

"I see," he replied, quietly, his face now a mask. "How can I help?"

I nodded, turned on the recording app on my iPad and said, "Mr. Wheaton, if you don't mind, I'd like to record our conversation. It's so much easier than taking notes."

"Yes, whatever you like. Go ahead."

"How well do you know the Chestertons?" I asked.

Wheaton was silent for a moment, staring down at his hands, then he looked up and described his lifelong friendship with the senior Chesterton. He described the family as tight-knit. He talked about what a great man Chesterton was, how he'd provided for his family, all of them, and how he expected them all to wear the Chesterton name with pride. If they didn't, they could kiss their inheritance goodbye and go off on their own; no one ever did.

"But you're not a Chesterton, are you, sir?" I asked. "How does he treat you?"

He smiled, somewhat modestly, I thought, then said, "Well, I must admit that I'm more than a little blessed. He treats me like family; they all do. They call me Uncle Sam. Kind of corny, I know, but it stuck. I attend all the family functions, the get-togethers and all of the company board meetings. I handle most of Edward's financial affairs."

"When you say Edward, you mean the senior Mr. Chesterton, correct?"

"Yes, that's right. Why don't we call him Grandfather? It's much easier."

I nodded, then said, "How well did you know Genevieve?"

"Everyone in the family knows Genevieve," he said. "By the way, can I get you anything, some coffee, perhaps?"

I declined for both of us.

He tilted his head to one side, closed his eyes, smiled, opened them again and said, "The girl was a breath of fresh air. I wouldn't say this to anyone else, but I thought she was the best thing to ever happen to Eddie."

"How so?" Janet asked, still staring at the photographs on the wall. She was standing with her back to him, arms folded, legs slightly apart.

He glanced round at her, his eyes lingering on her backside a little longer than perhaps they should have.

Is she doing that on purpose? I wondered.

"He was a playboy," Wheaton replied. "But I guess it would be hard not to be when you're getting an allowance of almost twenty-five thousand dollars a month... He's no great catch, you know, besides the money, that is. He's not a handsome man, not like his father, or grandfather; he's something of a throwback, I think. I don't think, even in his wildest dreams, would he have seen himself marrying a beauty like her. Hell," he said and looked sideways at Janet, who was now facing him, "I'd have sacrificed my inheritance for that, too."

"You don't really mean that, Mr. Wheaton... do you?" Janet asked, looking back over her shoulder at him.

Oh, that's a little over the top, Janet, I thought, but he didn't seem to notice, though I did see the look of interest he gave her.

"For that?" I asked. "What do you mean, *that*?" Of course, I knew exactly what he meant, but I wanted to hear him explain it. Could there have been anything between them? Had he given it the good old college try... had she? His answers, so I hoped, might give him away.

"Look," he said, leaning forward, his elbows on his knees, hands clasped together in front of him, "Genevieve was all woman, a real woman in every sense of the word, and that didn't go down well with the belles in the Chesterton family, or the rest of their upper-class, snobby friends. She was unconventional. Traditions and routines weren't her style, meant nothing to her. She was a free spirit. I liked her."

A free spirit? How many times have I heard that today?

"Did you have any dealings with her that were... let's say, more than just familial?" I asked.

He turned and looked at Janet then back at me and chuckled.

"No. I didn't, but if the opportunity had arisen, I wouldn't have said no."

He chuckled again, glanced again at Janet; she smiled sheepishly at him.

"Look, Genevieve was a player, a manipulator. She knew exactly what she was doing. Every time she walked into a room, she was the center of attention, and she loved it. It didn't matter if they hated her or loved her, she played it like a pro."

He paused, looked hard at me, then said, "Genevieve was no angel, Detective. Let's face it. Most women who come from her side of the tracks aren't. She could smell money a mile away and everyone knew it. I'm not saying she deserved to die; she didn't, but you can only tease a dog for so long before it bites."

"What on earth is that supposed to mean?" I asked. "Are you saying you believe she was murdered by a member of the family?"

He shrugged, smiled enigmatically, and said, "I'm afraid that's your job, Captain.

"Did you know she was black?" I asked quietly.

The man looked at me like I'd just slapped him.

"What? Are you kidding me?"

"Absolutely not. The medical examiner has confirmed her ethnicity."

"Lordy, Lordy, I had no idea." He chuckled. "I bet Regina Mae loved to hear that."

"Why do you say that?" I asked.

"Uhm, you *are* familiar with our Southern heritage, are you not? Very little has changed among the great Southern families. The old traditions, the old antebellum ways are as deeply rooted in this part of the country and, of course, the Chestertons. I never heard any mention of her being of African American ancestry, and if anyone would have known, it would have been me."

"So," I said, "being all-knowing, as you seem to imply, do you know of anyone in the family that might have wanted to do her harm... or made unwanted advances?"

"Since no one knew she was black, I'd say you can take your pick from anyone that had a penis." He chortled. "I'd even say there might be a few ladies in the mix who had unrequited feelings for her. The Chesterton family is big and not nearly as prim and proper as they'd have you believe."

"You saw her flirting with other men besides her husband?" I asked.

"Let's just say I saw her using the gifts God gave her to get what she wanted. Whether it was the last slice of peach pie or the keys to a new sports car, she never had to ask twice," Wheaton replied.

"Where were you the night before last, Mr. Wheaton, between two and three a.m.?" I asked.

Janet, continuing to wander around the room, her hands clasped behind her back, lingering at each picture, seemingly studying everything, didn't see the change in Wheaton's expression.

"That's an easy one," he said. "I was... shall we say... visiting with a lady friend. I stayed the night at her place."

He smiled, tilted his head slightly to one side, and his eyes twinkled devilishly as he turned and looked at Janet. There was no mistaking it: he was interested in her.

"I'll need to talk to her, your friend," I said. "Would you mind giving me her name and phone number?"

"Of course not. No problem. I'm sure she'll be happy to tell you all about our evening together, but I must ask you to be discreet. She has her reputation to uphold."

"I'm sure she does," I said, dryly. "Does she know the Chestertons?"

"Who in Tennessee doesn't?" Wheaton replied, looking again at Janet.

"That's not what I meant, Mr. Wheaton. I meant does she *know* them, on a personal level."

"Yes, she knows Regina Mae quite well, and her husband, which is one of the reasons I asked you to be discreet."

"Right," I said. "So, the name and phone number, please?"

He gave them to me, somewhat reluctantly, I thought. I made a note of them and continued.

"You have something of a reputation yourself," I said. "Is that not so, Mr. Wheaton?"

"I'm... not sure what you mean, Detective."

"Oh, I think you do. Let me ask you this: why did Mr. Chesterton cover up the sexual harassment complaints against you? They were, I believe, settled without publicity. How, exactly did you pull that off?" I watched the smile drop from his face. Behind me, I heard Janet's sharp intake of breath.

I didn't really want to know, but I was getting tired of his holier-than-thou attitude, so I figured I'd drop the bomb and watch his reaction.

He looked at me without speaking for what seemed a long moment, obviously taken aback, and then scoffed, "That was a long time ago, Detective. I was young and stupid, stepped over the line. I was already working for Edward and I... He... Well, it's all ancient history now and has nothing to do with Genevieve, so please, let's move on." He licked his lips.

"You stepped over the line?" I asked, skeptically. "That, I think, is sugarcoating it a little. Isn't it also true that the old man settled several paternity suits for you?'

"Two, there were two. Both children were adopted, went to very good families... Where the hell are you going with this, Detective? So I screwed up a couple of times when I was a kid. Who the hell doesn't? It was not a big deal."

"For you," I said with an attitude. "I'm sure it wasn't. For the women... well."

I looked him in the eye and continued, "Where am I going with it? Old habits die hard, Mr. Wheaton, so they say and..." I paused, then dropped another one on him. "Did you know that Genevieve was pregnant?"

He looked like I'd punched him in the gut.

He swallowed hard, then barely whispered, "No. No, I didn't."

Don't let up, Kate. Hit him again.

"Were you having an affair with Genevieve, Mr. Wheaton? Did you get her pregnant and then turn again to your best friend and confidant Edward Chesterton to help you one more time? It would, after all, be"—I made air quotes—"'no big deal,' would it, especially if everyone in the family, including the old man, thought Genevieve was a slut? Did... he... have her killed, Mr. Wheaton?"

It was at that point that Janet jumped in.

"I think that's a little out of line, Captain—"

I smiled inwardly as I interrupted her. "Excuse me, Sergeant? What did you say?"

She shrugged, then said, "I'm sorry, it's just that... well, I'm sorry."

Wheaton looked at her like she was dipped in chocolate. When he looked back at me his expression had hardened, his eyes narrowed, lips drawn tight. Yep, he was pissed. I decided to give him a pass.

I nodded and said, "Mr. Wheaton, I think she was killed by someone she knew, so I'll ask you again, can you think of anyone in the Chesterton family who might want to hurt Genevieve?"

I changed my tone, softened it to one bordering on sympathy. "Look, that baby is, I think, pivotal to my investigation. Edward Chesterton, either one of them, second, or third, would not have been happy about the possibility of her giving birth to a black grandchild, now would they?"

"Are you out of your mind, Captain?" he snapped. "Edward Chesterton is a saint, a great man. I wouldn't be where I am today if it wasn't for him."

"No, you'd probably be in jail or broke and up to your ears in child support. He saved you from yourself more than once. Why wouldn't he do it again?"

This time, I'd gotten to him. He was barely keeping his rage under control.

"Captain," Janet said, very quietly. "I think we've bothered Mr. Wheaton enough. It's time we left, I think."

She was standing with her back to the mantelpiece. I looked up at her. So did Wheaton. She looked back at me, defiantly, and again I had to smile to myself.

"Maybe you're right," I said, and nodded as if I was tired, trying to look defeated.

"Mr. Wheaton," I said, standing up. "Thank you for your time. We'll be in touch." And, without another word I walked out of the room, leaving Janet there to make apologies and excuses for me.

Just as I got to the front door and was about to open it, I heard her let out a quick laugh and then silence. I let myself out and waited for her on the front porch; she appeared a few minutes later.

"Okay," I muttered as we walked back to the car, our heads down. We had to keep the act going in case he was watching us from the window. "Spill it, Janet. I am dying to know what he said to you."

"Oh, that guy is a pussy cat," she said. "When you left the room, I handed him one of my business cards and told him that if he thought of anything else, he could give me a call. Then I told him that if he ever felt he needed someone to talk to, I'd be happy to listen."

"That's all it took?" I said, smiling.

"Yup! 'Oh, I'd like that,' he said. 'I'd like to talk. And then maybe we could have dinner or something.' I had to laugh. You heard me, right?"

"Yes, I heard you. Wow. He doesn't waste any time, does he?"

I put the car in drive and headed back toward Amnicola

Highway and the PD. The sky was an ominous dull gray blanket so low it shrouded the peak of Lookout Mountain and offered a promise of imminent rain.

"I bet I hear from him before the end of the day," Janet said.

"Okay, but just be careful if you decide to meet with him. Make sure it's in a public place and don't let your guard down. We'll check his alibi, but I don't get the feeling he's a murderer," I said.

"You don't?" Janet said, her eyes wide.

"No... No, I don't. Do you?"

"I don't know... maybe. He reminds me of a guy I busted back when I was in uniform. He was a real smooth talker, dressed nice, smelled good. At first glance he could be a suit right out of the nearest bank, harmless, right?" She shook her head slowly. "Turned out the guy was a serial date rapist. I believe that he actually thought, even as I was putting the cuffs on him, that he could sweet-talk his way out of it. I get the same kind of vibe from Samuel Wheaton. I believe he could be... I dunno, overpowering? Yes, that's it, overpowering, literally."

"Before you go to meet him anywhere," I said, "you let me know where you are going and when. I'll have an off-duty officer keep an eye on you."

"You don't think I can take care of myself?" Janet looked hurt.

I grinned at her as I pulled the car into my designated space at the rear of the PD.

"What do you think?" I asked.

Janet simply smiled, took her right foot off the dashboard, unfolded her arms, and opened the car door.

"Never mind what I think, Cap. It's what you think that matters, right?"

"Damn right!" I said as we walked together into the PD.

11

WE WALKED INTO THE PD AND JANET PROMPTLY DISAPPEARED, said she had to follow-up on her leads and would get back with me as soon as she had something to report. That was fine with me. There was a lot of chatter and a lot of information to digest, and it was barely eleven o'clock in the morning. We weren't scheduled to meet again until two-thirty that afternoon, so I figured I had at least a couple of hours to myself to think things through. That being so, I headed across the road to get a decent cup of coffee, and fifteen minutes later, I was back in my office ready to begin, but it was not to be.

No sooner had I sat down at my desk when Janet burst into my office, followed by Lenny Miller. She was wild-eyed, flustered, excited, all at the same time, waving her yellow notebook like she'd just discovered a cure for cancer.

I leaned back in my chair and stared up at her. "Okay, tell me. What did you find?" I asked, waving for her to shut the door.

"You aren't going to believe this, Kate," she said excitedly.

Only rarely did she ever call me that, so I knew immediately that she'd discovered something significant.

"I'm going to let Lenny tell you. He found it. It was shock enough that Genevieve was black, but... Go on, Lenny, tell her."

"Sit down, both of you," I said, and they did.

"Now," I said, "Lenny?"

"Well, I did as you asked. I did a little digging into Genevieve's past. It turns out that not only was she black, but she also has a family."

He flipped through several screens on his iPad and then began to read from his notes.

"Her real name is Naomi Washington, not Genevieve, nor Bluford. And her parents, Benjamin and Alisha Washington are alive and well in Baton Rouge, Louisiana. She also has a brother, Nathan Watkins."

Janet smiled at me and said, "You see what I mean? I've read several news and magazine articles that quoted Genevieve directly, saying that she had no family and was a 'pull-yourself-up-by-your-bootstraps' story of survival. She fell in love with a literal heir to the throne and they were supposed to live happily ever after. And then she was murdered. I'm sorry, Cap, but the suspect pool just got a little deeper."

Did it ever. I looked at the two of them, then shook my head. Now, not only was this case not going to be closed quickly, but I was going to have to ask for permission to go down to Baton Rouge to question the family. Chief Johnston was not going to be happy. He didn't part with department funds easily.

The case was beginning to frustrate me. I'd already interviewed three people, all of whom, to put it mildly, had an issue with Genevieve for one reason or another, but in common all three couldn't forgive that she was from "the wrong side of the tracks." I had a prime suspect, maybe two—Eddie and Wheaton—but without any direct evidence they were, both of them, tenuous at best.

Lenny continued to fill me in on the life and times of Naomi Washington AKA Genevieve Bluford-Chesterton, and it turned out she really did come from the wrong side of the tracks, street actually.

She'd attended predominantly black schools from kindergarten through high school graduation. She'd briefly attended BRCC—Baton Rouge Community College—on a Pell grant and a small student loan but had dropped out after only fifteen months.

She'd worked as a waitress during her time in college, and then as a salesclerk at one of the mall department stores. Her financial credit-worthiness, though, was never in doubt. From the day she began work, while she was still in college, she'd saved her money. Other than the student loan, which she paid off in six months, she'd never been in debt. At the time of her move from Louisiana, she was not quite twenty-four years old and had a little over twenty thousand dollars in savings and twenty-four hundred in checking.

She and Eddie were married a year later. She was two months past her twenty-sixth birthday when Cole Meredith found her body on the Riverwalk.

It was a sad, sad story of a promising young life snuffed out on a whim. Some evil son of a bitch had decided —and I had no doubt about it—that because of her color and her infiltration into one of the most influential families in Tennessee, she no longer deserved to live. And, when I thought about it like that, I became angry, very angry. So angry I could see nothing but that poor girl fighting for her life on the dark walkway, knowing all the time that it was futile.

Lenny stopped talking. Janet said nothing. I was temporarily out of it. I was leaned back in my chair, my eyes closed, a silent observer of the events that night on the banks of the Tennessee. All I could see was Genevieve, bent half over backward, clawing at the garrote as the indistinguishable shadow twisted his fists against her neck, pulling it tighter, tighter, tighter...

"Cap?" Janet's voice jerked me violently back into the present.

"Yeah... yeah, what?"

"What now?" she asked.

"What now, indeed?" I said, trying to pull myself together. What had just happened to me was a first. Never had I been transported into... Even now, I don't even know what to call it. A window to the past? A stupid vision? I don't know.

"I'm going to Baton Rouge," I said. "I need to interview the family. I'll need to talk to the chief first. I know he's not going to like it. Still, I don't see how he has a choice, not considering who the victim is."

I stood up and walked around my desk. "Lenny, thank you. Great job. Now go see what else you can dig up." And he left the room.

"Janet," I said. "Bring your notes and come on."

Chief Johnston was in an unusually good mood that morning. Cathy, his secretary, ushered us straight into his inner sanctum. He rose from behind his desk to greet us with a thin, though somewhat intimidating smile on his lips.

He came around his desk and extended a hand to Janet. "How is Captain Gazzara treating you, Detective?" he asked.

"Oh, terrific, sir. We're working on a humdinger right now," Janet said enthusiastically.

"So I understand," he said, turning to me, his hand extended.

I shook it.

"Please, sit, both of you," he said. "You have an update for me, Catherine?" he asked, returning to his chair.

I brought him up to date with the investigation, told him about the victim, my interviews with the Chesterton family, and the revelations concerning Genevieve's hitherto unknown family.

"So," I said finally, "I need to go to Baton Rouge and interview her family."

Wait for it, Kate, I thought, expecting him to argue about budgetary nonsense, but he didn't.

"Well, you'd better get going then," he said. "It goes without saying that this is a high-profile case, and we need to wrap it up quickly and discreetly. This is no time to argue over a couple of dollars the budget isn't going to miss." He looked hard at me. "You'll go on your own, though, and I don't have to tell you: no expensive dinners or visits to the spa."

"I'll be sure to cross those off my to-do list, Chief." I smiled at him, nodded and continued, "I'll leave this afternoon and be back as soon as possible, a couple of days at most."

"You'll keep in touch; daily updates," Johnston said. "You have my cell phone number. If there's anything you need, don't hesitate to call."

"Of course, sir," I replied.

"That will be all, Captain, and good luck."

"Thank you, sir," I said.

I stood quickly and left his office. Janet followed behind me excitedly.

"Anything special you want me to do while you're gone, Cap?" she asked.

"Just keep your phone on. Take your lead from Hawk; he has a world of experience and you can learn from him. And don't forget what I said about Sam Wheaton. If he calls and wants to meet... Never mind, I'll talk to Hawk myself. If he does call, you bring Hawk in, understood?"

She didn't look at all happy about what I'd said.

"I don't think that's necess—"

"It's not up for discussion, Janet," I snapped, interrupting her. "The man is a prime suspect in a murder investigation, and he has a history of sexual abuse; he's a predator. You will *not* disobey my order. Understood?"

She heaved a huge sigh, looked up at me, her eyes wide, and said, quietly, "Understood, Captain."

I could tell she was disappointed, but it was for her own good. She had just enough experience, and more than enough self-confidence to get herself into a world of trouble.

I booked a seat on the afternoon flight out of Lovell Field to Nashville, spent an hour debriefing Hawk, Anne, and Lenny, then I took Hawk aside and briefed him about my upcoming trip and the admittedly half-assed plan for Janet to get inside Sam Wheaton's head. He didn't like the idea at all. In fact, he argued strenuously against it. In the end, however, he reluctantly agreed to keep an eye on my enthusiastic but potentially wayward sergeant.

Finally, not feeling at all confident that Janet would play by the rules, I left Hawk in charge, headed home, packed an overnight bag, and drove to the airport. Two hours later, I was on a Southwest Airlines plane out of Nashville heading to Baton Rouge, Louisiana.

12

THE PLANE LANDED IN BATON ROUGE RIGHT ON TIME, AND I was able to get to my rental car without a hitch. The sun was already setting by the time I got to my hotel, a bare-bones place, but it had room service and a minibar.

I showered, dressed in my PJ's, ordered a burger with fries, cracked open an overpriced bottle of red wine, spread my files out on the bed, pulled up a chair and began to read.

Naomi Washington AKA Genevieve Bluford Chesterton came from a lower-class neighborhood of Baton Rouge, not a ghetto, but not Nob Hill either.

According to the information Lenny had provided, Genevieve had barely squeaked by in high school and not at all in college. She didn't have a criminal record, but she was known to associate with some individuals who did.

"Same old story," I said to myself as I continued to read through the profile. *How many of these kids go astray simply because of where they live, or the school they attend?* I wondered.

Actually, living as I did in Chattanooga, I had a pretty good idea: you only have to drive around the projects, any time of day or night, to find out. They're out there for all to see: pushers, addicts, pimps, prostitutes, gangbangers, most of them barely old enough to drive, much less drink a beer.

It seemed, though, that our girl had managed to rise above the temptations of the simple life. She'd worked hard, saved her money, and gotten out of town.

According to Lenny's research, the last time Genevieve had lived at her parent's address was in January 2017. Her mother and father seemed to be good folks. Both were gainfully employed and, apart from a mortgage and a small car payment, were debt free. There was nothing in the file about the son, Genevieve's brother, Nathan, and I wondered why.

Damn it. Tim wouldn't have left a gap like that.

It was then that another horrible thought struck me. *Holy crap! I bet they don't even know what's happened to their daughter.*

"Why would they?" I said to my empty room.

No one in Chattanooga knew who the hell Genevieve really was, so the family wouldn't have—couldn't have—been notified. And I guarantee no one in Baton Rouge has any knowledge of her other life.

I suddenly felt weary beyond words. If there's one job a cop, any cop, hates, it's having to give the parents the news their child is dead, and now I was going to have to do it for the... oh hell, I lost count so long ago I've no idea how many times. Why didn't I think of it before?

Well okay then, I thought, sadly. *That's just how it has to be.*

I closed the file. It was slim, and I'd read it through from cover to cover. There was nothing in it that would make my job any easier, or less painful for them or for me... and I wished I'd handed Naomi Washington's family over to Janet to interview... Nah, not really.

I lay the folder on the nightstand next to the bed just as my food arrived, but somehow, I just wasn't that hungry anymore.

I set my iPhone alarm for five-thirty, crawled into bed, turned off the light, and closed my eyes, the burger and fries uneaten.

13

I WOKE UP WITH A HEADACHE AT THREE-THIRTY THAT MORNING not knowing where the hell I was, and no, it wasn't because of the wine. That twelve-dollar bottle held only a single glass. So I tossed and turned the rest of the night, lost in a half-world between dreams and reality populated with visions of me telling the Washingtons their daughter was dead.

I lay there sweating. The air conditioner wasn't working worth a damn, so it must have been eighty degrees or more in that hotel room.

Why I was having so much trouble with the idea of telling them was a mystery to me. I'd done it before, hundreds of times and it never got any easier, but this time it was different... And then it dawned on me.

Oh geez! It's the baby.

You see, I just couldn't imagine receiving another response like the one I'd gotten from Regina Mae when I gave her the news. If it happened again, I'd probably slap one or both of them. With that thought and a smile on my lips, I closed my eyes again and fell into a deep sleep only to be awakened some thirty minutes later by the strident voice of Bobby McFerrin urging me, "Don't Worry, Be Happy." It was five-thirty and I felt like sh—

Fortunately, I didn't feel like that for long. I took a long hot shower, washed my hair, and dried it with a piece of blue and white electric junk I found in one of the bathroom cupboards. Then I dressed in my second-best pair of jeans and a clean white blouse, hitched my Glock and badge to my belt, slipped into my signature tan leather jacket, and headed out across the road to the Waffle House. There I blew a week's calories on a heart-attack breakfast, but oh how good it was; and oh how guilty I felt.

Then, feeling ready to face the day, I entered the Washington's address into the GPS app on my iPhone and drove my rental car to the address in the Garden District.

The neighborhood was much as I expected it to be, quiet, older homes but, for the most part, the streets were clean and tidy as were the white frame houses. The lawns were neatly trimmed and the paint on the homes fresh and bright. The only indication that all was not quite as safe in the neighborhood as it might be were the black bars on the front doors and basement windows of many of the homes.

I found the house I was looking for, just one small, single-story home on a long street of 1930-something look-alikes. I pulled into the driveway and noticed the curtains of the next-door neighbor's house twitch and then part just enough to reveal a pair of dark, curious eyes. The curtains closed as soon as the owner of the eyes realized he or she had been spotted, and I smiled to myself as I turned off the engine and put the car in park.

"Here we go," I muttered, as I slammed the car door and walked to the steps and up to the front porch.

While the little home was nice enough, it was a far cry from what Genevieve must have gotten used to, a world of difference from Eddie's and Regina Mae's homes.

The windows were tightly closed, the drapes too, and I could hear the air-conditioning unit at the left side of the house running. I took my creds from my jacket pocket and knocked on the front door.

"Who's that outside this early in the morning?" a male voice said.

I looked at my watch. It wasn't quite eight-thirty.

"How should I know? Go see," a female voice said.

"Not me. I gotta finish gettin' ready to go to work. You go."

I heaved a sigh and knocked again. I already had a headache coming on behind my right eyeball.

The door opened a crack.

"Can I help you?"

I flashed my credentials and introduced myself.

"Are you Alisha Washington?" I asked.

The door opened wide enough to reveal a once-lovely white woman, an older version of Genevieve except she had a front tooth missing.

She must have been something back in the day.

"Yes." She had an attitude and didn't look happy that the police, any police, let alone police from Chattanooga were knocking on her door. "Chattanooga? You far from home, lady. What you want?"

"Mrs. Washington, I have some news about your daughter. May I come in?"

Alisha Washington looked at me suspiciously. Then she looked up and down the street, nodded, snapped open two deadbolts on the barred screen door, pushed it open, leaned out and looked up and down the street again before stepping back into the house and holding the door open for me.

"Listen to me, woman," she said as she led the way into the darkened living room. "I don't care what that girl has done. She's over eighteen, and she ain't my responsibility no more."

There was a faint smell of marijuana in the living room, but it wasn't that strong. The place was tidy with mismatched furniture and a huge flat-screen television in the center of the wall facing the heavily draped window.

It was at that moment that a huge man in a suit and tie with coffee-colored skin appeared from the hallway. He stood stock-still, staring at me intensely.

"You must be Mr. Washington," I said. "If you have a minute, what I have to tell you concerns you both."

He just nodded, said nothing.

"Yes. What is it, then?" Alisha said.

I took a deep breath and said, "I think you'd both better sit down."

She looked at me curiously; he continued to stare at me. They sat down together on an obviously quite new sofa opposite the TV and stared up at me.

"May I sit down too?" I asked.

They both nodded as one.

"Mr. and Mrs. Washington, I'm afraid I have bad news: your daughter, Naomi, is dead. She was murdered four nights ago."

For a moment, the news seemed to just hang in the air as they both stared at me. I had the strangest feeling Alisha was waiting for me to continue.

"Mrs. Washington, are you all right?" I asked.

Very slowly, she began to shake her head.

"No... How, where?" she whispered, now holding her husband's hand in both of hers.

"In Chattanooga," I said, quietly. "She was... We think she must have been to a party. She"—I didn't want to say *her body* or the word *strangled*—"was discovered beside the river by a dog-walker." I waited. "I'm sorry to have to tell you that she was seven weeks pregnant."

Mrs. Washington nodded as tears filled her eyes. But they didn't spill over. She sniffled a little, jerked her head back, turned her head to look at the man sitting beside her, let out a deep breath, and licked her lips. The man still hadn't said a word, but I could tell that the news had hit him hard, harder than his wife, perhaps. His eyes were glistening, and his lips were trembling.

She laid her head on his massive shoulder, still holding his hand in both of hers, only now his other hand was on top of hers.

"Have you caught him, the man who killed her?" His deep voice reminded me of James Earl Jones.

"No, not yet, but we will."

He nodded, looked up at the ceiling, and whispered, "Yes, I bet you will."

I didn't know if he meant it or if he was being sarcastic. My bet was on the latter.

Sheesh, I need to move this along.

"I know this is a really bad time but, if you could... I have some questions that only you can answer."

He sighed, nodded and said, "I'm Benjamin Washington." The attitude seeped out of him like air from a punctured tire.

"I'm supposed to be at work," he said. "I'll call and tell them I won't be in today. They'll understand. I'll do it in a minute."

He squeezed his wife's hands, then let her go and put both arms around her and pulled her to him; she sobbed silently into his shoulder.

"Please," he said. "Ask your questions."

I nodded, opened my iPad, and asked their permission to record the interview. They gave it readily.

"How long have you been married?" I asked, looking at the man—her face was still buried in his shoulder; her shoulders shaking. She was obviously crying.

"We're not actually married," he said softly. "Didn't see no need to."

I nodded.

"We've been together for almost thirty years." He stroked the back of Alisha's head, gently smoothing her graying hair.

"How old was Naomi when she left home?" I asked.

"She left in 2017. She was twenty-four."

"Did she visit often?" I asked.

"No," he said. "Just at Christmas, usually to flaunt her new things. She'd drop off her bags, then run off to visit her friends... Some friends... She didn't even spend the night with us. Then, when she'd had enough, she'd kiss us goodbye and head off back to Chattanooga."

"We saw her one Easter," Alisha said. "Ain't that right, Ben?"

She looked up at him; he slowly nodded his head.

"Did you know she'd changed her name, and that she was married?" I asked.

"No," Alisha said, sitting up and wiping her eyes. She pressed her lips together, then shook her head. "But that don't surprise me. That girl!"

"We ain't rich, Detective, but we're honest," Benjamin Washington said, "and I'll tell you, I had some wild days in my youth, but I show up at work every day. And Alisha, she works at the church, has for almost ten years. But that girl, she something else."

I looked at Alisha, but she didn't offer any further information.

"What was she like?" I asked.

"Like? She was like..." Mrs. Washington shook her head. "Detective, Naomi... she beautiful outside, ugly inside; broke my heart, but I loved her. My daughter... she hated it here, was ashamed of where she come from. I don't know why, considering she ran with every local punk in town. I took her to church with me. I tried to get her to have a little God in her life. It wasn't no use. A mother should never say this, but I was ashamed of how she turned out. I didn't raise her to be like that."

"What do you mean?" I asked.

"What do you think I mean? She was a hood rat if ever there was one. She liked them bad boys who wear their colors and flash their hand signals, making themselves look like they having some kind of palsy fit."

Alisha had obviously spent a lot of time in the hood herself. Her accent was thick and seemed to me to clash with her lily-white skin.

"When was the last time she visited?" I asked.

"Last time she was here?" Alisha said. "Christmas, five months ago."

"And she didn't tell you she was married?"

"Lord, no she didn't tell me she was married," Alisha said. She said it like it was the last thing on earth her daughter would tell her. "I can only imagine the kind of man she told 'I do' to. Was it him what killed her? Who she marry anyway?"

"His name is Edward Chesterton. She married him under the name of Genevieve Bluford, which is why we had such a hard time finding you folks. I don't know if he killed her. The investigation is ongoing, so I can't tell you very much. What I can tell you is that he's very well-off, and he comes from a long line of old money. I'm not sure how much he knew about Naomi; probably not much, since she'd changed her identity. None of his family knew she was black. Did you know she was passing herself off as white?"

"No, but it don't surprise me none," she said, shaking her head. "We had some terrible fights about her color. She hated her father because he was black." She turned her head to look up at him fondly. "He isn't perfect, not by a long way, but he was a good daddy to her and Nathan. When she told us she was leaving, he gave her two hundred dollars so she could buy some clothes as soon as she got to Chattanooga." She chuckled bitterly.

Me? I didn't have the heart to tell her about Genevieve's bank account.

"He was good enough for her to take his money, but he wasn't good enough to keep her daddy's name, take pride in her family. Wasn't good enough to accept that she was black."

I nodded, thinking how Genevieve and Eddie were slowly being revealed as a match made in hell. He knew what to do and how to do it, to upset his family and, in her own way, she was no different.

I scribbled my thoughts in my pocket notebook then looked up. Alisha had taken Benjamin's hand in hers. It was also an unusual fact that Benjamin and Alisha Washington had been together for both of their children—a rarity in the black community. Studies have proven that children who grow up with both parents tend to succeed in life. Naomi certainly did; she married a millionaire. But someone—*hell, everyone*—wasn't happy about it.

Hmm, I wonder if Nathan did as well as she did. I doubt it.

"Can I offer you something to drink, Detective, tea or water?" Benjamin asked.

I shook my head and said, "No, but thank you."

"We haven't heard from Nathan either," Alisha said.

She must have been reading my thoughts.

"He ain't nothing like Naomi. He's a good boy. We thought that if he went to Chattanooga with Naomi, he might be able to keep an eye on her," Alisha said.

She let go of her husband's hands, looked down at her own hands, and worried a hangnail as she spoke.

"Nathan is your son?" I asked.

"He's Naomi's half-brother. I had him just a year before I met Benjamin. That boy was a joy from the minute he come into the world."

She chewed her lip thoughtfully. The thin lines that were her eyebrows pinched together in the middle as she continued.

"He and Naomi grew up best friends, but then she got a taste for hoodlums and her brother didn't like that. She tried to balance the two, but those thugs don't like family. They didn't like Nathan, who just wanted to go to work and come home and play his video games."

"He loved his video games." Benjamin chuckled.

"He sure did," Alisha said. "Nathan Watkins. That's his real daddy's last name. Although he grew up with Benjamin as his daddy. That's why he turned out so good." A tear rolled down her cheek.

"Do you have Nathan's address, Mrs. Washington? I'd like to talk to him. If he was keeping an eye on his sister, maybe he'll have some idea of what happened to her." This was a promising lead.

"Yes. Ben, get that card on the fridge with Nate's address on it."

He squeezed her shoulder, rose, and walked into the kitchen.

"Detective Gazzara, can I ask you a question?" Alisha continued to worry the hangnail on her finger.

"Of course."

"Did she suffer, my Naomi? Was she in a lot of pain when she died?" she asked, holding her breath as she waited for me to answer.

"No," I lied.

Naomi/Genevieve knew what was happening to her. I was sure of that. I was also sure that the pain must have been excruciating... I thought about those two thin ligature marks around her neck and the bruises where the killer's knuckles had dug into her flesh as he pulled and... I could only imagine the terror she must have experienced as she clawed at the ligature as the life was slowly squeezed from her body. Oh yes, I knew, but I couldn't tell her mother, not then.

"Thank God," she whispered, and I felt like shit for lying to her. "My poor baby... And I would have been a grandma." Her bottom lip quivered.

Benjamin reappeared with a small card. He must have heard because his eyes were filled with tears.

"Here you go," he said, handing it to me.

I took the card, made a note of the information in my pad, and handed it back to him.

"I have one more question to ask," I said. "Do you know of anyone in Naomi's past that might have wanted to hurt her? You said that she was involved with some bad people. Did she break up with one of those thugs... or maybe knew something that could have cost her her life?"

Alisha looked me in the eye and said, "Yes, ma'am. Could be all that, and then some. I don't know none of their names. They a raggedy-ass bunch, all dress alike with their bandanas and do-rags and pants hanging below the cracks of their asses. I don't know if she crossed one of them bangers. If she did, I don't know about it. Best it stay that way too. We still gotta live here."

I'd heard that before, so many times, and it made me furious. I knew theirs was a difficult situation, but not unusual.

"I understand," I said and took out a business card and handed it to Benjamin. "If you think of anything, even if you think it is unimportant, please, give me a call anytime day or night. And... if you need help, I'll do my best for you."

"Can we see her, Naomi? Can we come to her funeral?" Alisha asked.

"Yes, of course," I said, wondering how the Chesterton family would react when they met their in-laws.

Sheesh, I'd like to be there for that one.

"It may be a while before we can release the... release her to the family for a funeral, but you're welcome to come and see her whenever you like."

She looked at her husband. He said nothing, just nodded, as if to say, "whatever you think is best."

"Can I think about it for a few days and then call you?" she asked.

"Of course, anytime."

"And if you find our boy," she said, her eyes wide, pleading, "tell him to call home. I just want to make sure he's okay, too."

"I'll do that. I promise. By the way, do you have a recent photo of him I could borrow?"

"Not recent, no. Just an old school photo. He doesn't like having his photo taken." She went to the sideboard, opened one of the drawers, and then handed me a five-by-seven photo of a grinning kid. "He'd just turned sixteen when that was taken," she said.

I stood and extended my hand. Alisha took it in both of hers and squeezed it hard. Benjamin did the same, and I left them. I stepped out into the warm air, felt the small hairs on the back of my neck begin to rise. I stood on the porch, my back to the door and looked across the street, then to my left then my right. All was quiet... no, all seemed eerily still. Suddenly, I had the feeling I was being watched.

Faintly, even through the closed door, I could hear Alisha sobbing and Benjamin's deep voice.

"Let us pray for her, Alisha. Let us pray that she's in a better place."

"My baby. My poor baby," Alisha cried quietly.

There was a moment of silence, and then he began, "Dear Lord, we pray that you have taken our beloved daughter into your keeping and..."

That was a first for me, and I could listen no more.

I went quickly to my car and drove back to the hotel, stopping only to pick up a large coffee.

Once again I needed to think, to focus. One thing I knew for sure was that I needed to call Janet and have Lenny do a full background check on Nathan Watkins. And that was where I was stuck. It was not yet ten-thirty and I was exhausted, my stomach was growling. I was hungry and needing a break to eat, think, and regroup.

I'd just parked the car outside the hotel and was about to get out, when I changed my mind. Instead, I reversed back out and then swung out onto the highway, looking for a "nice" restaurant where I could eat a second breakfast. I felt... I dunno, washed up, drained... whatever. Anyway, I didn't call Janet until I left for the airport a couple of hours later.

I'd felt like that before. It was all to do with the duty I'd just performed. It always left me feeling a little less than human and, as I drove, I recalled the last time I'd done such duty. Less than a month ago, I'd had to inform a mother her son was dead. He died from an overdose of heroin. Oh yeah, he was just a junkie, and we cops all knew him well. "Just a junkie?" How's that for inhumane?

How many times had I or someone else told him, "that shit will kill you"? Too many to count, but it didn't stop him. Some other kid found him lying in a front yard, dead. The kid's mother called 911, and I caught the case. All suspicious deaths are treated as homicides until proven different, but I knew what it was. I didn't have to, but I took it upon myself to tell his folks... his single-parent mother. The kid had just had his nineteenth birthday.

I felt like shit then, too. Who wouldn't?

And now I had the same kind of feelings, the kind of hangover effect I was experiencing as I drove. It was as if... Well, it was like I'd stayed up all night staring at the television: my eyes hurt and I was all-over tired.

I pulled into what looked like a halfway decent diner, stepped up to the counter, and took a seat next to a kindly looking black guy wearing a red baseball cap.

"Morning," he said as I sat down.

"Good morning." I looked sideways at him and smiled.

I ordered a cup of coffee, two scrambled eggs, and a well-done T-bone steak. *So much for Chief Johnston's warning,* I thought. *Actually, if I remember correctly, he said steak dinners.* This was breakfast so, as far as I was concerned, I was still obeying orders, even though I knew it was all a matter of semantics.

By the time I finished my food it was almost time to leave for the airport. I rushed back to the hotel, grabbed my overnight bag, and checked out.

The drive to the airport was easy enough, but I don't remember it. I was awash in thought. Over and over, in my mind, I watched as the killer strangled Genevieve. Not once did I manage to get a glance at his shadowy face. I checked my rental in and took the shuttle to the terminal. By the time I was inside and at the gate, I was a dithering mess, my mind, churning. All I wanted was to get back home and to my apartment and go to sleep.

It was just after seven o'clock that evening when I walked through the door and, of course, my phone was ringing inside my purse. I didn't recognize the number, so I let it go to voicemail, went to the kitchen, poured myself a large glass of red, and headed for the shower.

The hot shower did me a world of good. The wine was cold and wet, my sofa was waiting for me like an abandoned lover and, as luck would have it, *Pretty Woman* was playing on television: exactly the kind of brain-numbing, no-thinking kind of movie I needed. I did make it to the end of my glass of wine, but not the movie.

When I awoke, still on the sofa, the sun was already high in the eastern sky and shining in through my open drapes, and I felt better, so much better I decided to forgo my morning run. Instead, I drank a cup of coffee as I listened to the news, then I slipped into a pair of jeans, a simple white shirt and my sneakers. I tied my hair back in a ponytail and, with the exception of a little lip gloss, I decided not to wear any makeup... let my skin breathe for a change. I checked myself in the mirror and was quite pleased with what I saw.

I'd driven all the way to the station on Amnicola before I remembered the phone call of the night before. I parked my car in my designated space and checked to see if the caller had left a message. He had. Edward Eaton Chesterton the Second had indeed left a message, a message that was to be the beginning of a very strange relationship.

14

"How did it go?" Janet asked.

She placed a large cup of coffee on my desk in front of me. I looked at it dubiously, then at her.

"Where'd this come from?"

"Starbucks. I got it on my way in this morning."

I looked at my watch. It was just after eight-thirty.

"And at what time was that?"

"Just after seven, but I warmed it in the microwave. It should be okay... shouldn't it?"

I picked it up, sniffed it, sipped, sipped some more, and some more, then put it down. "Yes, it's good, and thank you," I said. "Janet, you don't have to live here, you know. Your shift starts at eight, like mine." Yeah, that's right, though mine was more than a little flexible...

Hah, that's a freakin' joke if ever I heard one.

"My trip to Baton Rouge? I love how they say that name. It went well, considering I had to inform them of their daughter's death, and that she was pregnant. None of that went well; it never does... I think I'll let you do that duty from now on." I knew I wouldn't, but to see her expression when I said it was... enlightening: the color all but drained from her face.

"Sorry, Janet," I said, "but you're going to have to do it sometime... Oh, forget it. What about Genevieve's half-brother, Nathan?"

Janet grimaced. "I haven't seen Lenny yet. I'll go and see—"

"According to the mother they were close," I said, interrupting her, "and that he came to Chattanooga, ostensibly to keep an eye on her." I took a sip.

"He didn't do a very good job then, did he?" Janet replied.

"From what I heard from the parents, he didn't have a lot of choice. She was... independent," I said, "which didn't leave him with too many options."

I took out my notebook and wrote his address on the back of one of my business cards and handed it to her.

"Here's his info. That's his last known address. I don't think it's any good, so I need you to find him. He might know who Genevieve was hanging out with, other than her husband."

"Got it." Janet was up and almost out the door when I stopped her.

"Whoa, hold on there, young lady. What about Wheaton? Did he contact you? Did you meet? Did Hawk go with you?"

I could tell by the look on her face that she had indeed met with him. I pointed to the chair for her to sit back down. She pursed her lips like Daffy Duck and rolled her eyes.

"I did meet with Sam Wheaton, or Uncle Sam as he asked me to call him. And yes, Hawk went with me, but I made him sit outside in the car... Oh, don't look at me like that. I met him for lunch, at Chantelle's. Hawk watched through the window." At that, she giggled. "He wasn't too happy, but I needed to talk to Wheaton alone, loosen him up. It didn't work. I tried to finesse my way onto the topic of the Chestertons, but he was much more interested in partying." Janet clicked her tongue. "It was all rather embarrassing."

"He didn't give you any information?"

"About the Chestertons? No. He's too smart for that. I think he knew what I was after. All I could squeeze out of him was that he'd"—she did the air quote thing—"'never say a bad word about Edward Eaton Chesterton the Second.' Not because Granddad was a good guy but because he was the Golden Goose, the cash cow that just kept on giving." She paused, gave me a shifty look, then said, quietly, "He offered to take me to his summer home in Barbados."

"*Shut... Up!*" I said. "And you're telling me you're not interested? I'm shocked," I teased, then said, seriously, "Well, that's good to know. He's a predator and might just be the weak link. Have Lenny dig deeper, see if he can find any of Wheaton's victims. I want to know where he goes and who he goes with, if he has any regular girl-friends... or boyfriends. That, Janet, would be the *chef-d'oeuvre*."

"The chef dee what?" she asked, screwing up her face.

"Oh, dear," I said in mock frustration. "It's another way of saying 'the icing on the cake,' or 'the crowning glory.'"

"Oh, yeah." She half-closed her eyes, primped the back of her hair, then smiled sweetly at me and said, "He also said that I have the face of an angel and the body of a devil." She polished her nails, both hands, on the lapels of her jacket.

"No-he-didn't," I ran the words together, mocking her, grimacing.

"Oh-yes-he-did," she mimicked me, "and then he teared up. I thought he was going to cry. He told me he was lonely, and that he hadn't felt such a close connection with anyone like me... ever." She tilted her head to the side, lifted her chin, turned down the corners of her mouth, and then burst out laughing.

"You know what my father, God rest his soul, would say about that?" I chuckled. "When you got it... you got it."

"I don't got it." She laughed. "But Wheaton sure wanted to give it to me... Truthfully, though he was quite harmless. I never felt in any danger. I just felt embarrassed for the guy."

"Right?" I said. "He looked so... well put together, and he's not ugly," I added.

"He's ugly when he cries." Janet continued to chuckle as she wrinkled up her face like she was crying.

I laughed too, and I was still laughing when Chief Johnston appeared in the doorway. He was not laughing.

"I'm pleased to see you ladies are having a good time, Captain. Is there any chance you might tell me about your trip? I can only imagine what that last-minute flight to Baton Rouge must have cost."

Janet saw her cue to leave. "I'll get that information for you ASAP," she said, waving the piece of paper with Nathan Watkins's name and last known address on it.

"I haven't had a chance to type up my notes, but I did get a promising lead. The victim has a half-brother and, according to her parents, she liked to hang out with a rough crowd. It might just be gang-related; retaliation, perhaps. I just don't know yet. I'll have everything typed up for you as soon as possible, by this afternoon, sir?"

He nodded, then said, "We have to solve this one quickly, Kate. Number Two has called me twice already."

"Number Two... Oh, yes, you mean old man Chesterton," I said, smiling. "I wonder what kind of man Number One was?"

"From what I hear," he said, "this one is a chip off the old block... This afternoon then, I'll expect an update."

"Yes, sir. As soon as I can type it up."

"Don't bother with that. Takes too much time away from the job. A verbal report will do nicely." And he turned and left me sitting there, my mouth wide open.

Geez... Oh joy! I think I'm in love. What a freakin' difference to Finkle.

And then I remembered the phone call I'd ignored the night before. I flipped the screen on my phone and listened to the message.

"Detective Gazzara, this is Edward Chesterton. I've been informed that you're investigating the death of my grand-daughter-in-law. I'm ready to talk to you. Call me."

I had to chuckle at the man's self-importance.

How nice of him to clear a space on his calendar for me, I thought. *I bet he'd have a fit if I were to call and tell him I didn't need to speak to him at all.*

But I did need to speak to him, so I made the call.

"Yes?" It was the same grouchy voice that had left me a message.

"Mr. Chesterton?"

"It is. Detective Gazzara, I have time to talk to you now. I'll have my car pick you up. Where are you?"

"Excuse me, sir," I said, mildly. "That's not the way it works. I have several cases I'm working on that also need my attention. I can't just drop what I'm doing to come to you," I lied.

"Like hell you can't!" he snapped.

"Second," I said. "I don't get in cars with strangers, Mr. Chesterton. Mrs. Gazzara didn't raise no fool, so I will drive myself, thank you."

I waited for him to speak, but he didn't, so I continued, "Now that we've laid down some boundaries, I would like to talk to you, if you are available, this afternoon, say between three and four."

I smirked. The guy had probably never waited for anyone, ever, so maybe my tactic was a bit over-the-top, but I didn't care.

He'll send his car to pick me up? What an ass.

"I'm a busy man, Detective. I don't have time to wait around and—"

"Mr. Chesterton," I interrupted him—something else he wasn't used to, "you're welcome to come to the police department and speak with me here, at your convenience. I don't see any members of the press around here right now, but those guys do have a way of finding things out. There could be a mob of reporters here when you arrive. Reports of Genevieve's death are all over the media." I swear I could hear him gnashing his dentures.

"Fine, between three and four, then. My secretary will give you directions."

There was a click and a buzz, and then a pleasant-sounding woman picked up and politely gave me directions to the main

Chesterton Estate on Elder Mountain. It would take me about thirty minutes to get there, depending upon the traffic.

I hung up, put my hands behind my neck, closed my eyes, leaned back in my extra comfy leather chair, and was soon lost in thought. I could see my day was already shaping up to be an interesting one.

15

I PICKED UP MY DESK PHONE AND BUZZED JANET AND ASKED HER
to bring in the troops. I needed to find out what had been happening
while I was gone, and I needed to know about Nathan Watkins.

*I wonder if Tim would like to be a cop? I sure as hell could use
him... Nah, Harry would never let him go... besides, he has too much
freedom where he is. Oh well, it's a nice thought.* It wasn't the only
nice thought I had. *Thanks for the memories, Harry.*

They wandered in, coffee in hand, iPads under their arms, one
after the other, Janet first. I waited until they were seated and then I
began.

"Okay people, we're in trouble. We're now into the sixth day and
you know what that means: the first forty-eight hours and all that
good stuff have expired and, according to the theory, we're looking at
a potential unsolved case. That is unacceptable. So what do we have?
I'll tell you. As far as I know, we have *nothing*, nothing but a bunch of
half-assed theories and a couple of suspects but no evidence that ties
any of them to the crime scene."

I looked around the group. Janet shifted uncomfortably in her
seat. Anne was looking at her fingernails, turning her hand up, then

down, spreading her fingers. Lenny stared at his still closed laptop. Hawk stared stoically back at me.

Geez, I was better off when it was just Janet and me to worry about...

"This is a high-profile case," I said sternly. "We have to solve it, and quickly, no two ways about it. If we don't make progress, the chief will take it away from us. That's not going to happen. Understood?"

They nodded, all except Hawk, who continued to stare at me. *What's with that guy?*

"As you know," I said, "Genevieve Chesterton is... was... she was not who or what she claimed to be. And, as you also know, she had a family in Baton Rouge who I interviewed yesterday. The parents are good folk, working-class, black father, white mother. They knew nothing of their daughter's subterfuges. They did know that, at least until she left home in 2017, she was something of a wild thing, but even that could have been a subterfuge. When she arrived in Chattanooga, she had good credit and money in the bank, which means that even while she was Naomi Washington, she was cultivating her new identity, Genevieve Bluford, and must have been doing so, quietly, for at least a couple of years."

I paused, stood, stepped over to the big board, picked up my plastic ruler, and tapped Genevieve's photograph.

"Look up the word enigma in a dictionary and you'll see a photo of this young lady. Who the hell knows what she's been up to the past four years, or who with... She does have a brother, that's a half-brother, Nathan Watkins. Lenny, how about Watkins? If you have anything, I'd like to hear it."

He opened his laptop and began flipping through his files. I picked up my empty coffee cup, shook it, put it down and muttered, "Damn it!"

"There's some swill left in the break room," Janet said, sadly. "Would you like for me to go get you a cup? Bottom of the pot, I'm afraid."

"Maybe I should just start drinking tea," I muttered.

"There's plenty of that in the break room. No one drinks it. But I think it might have been here since the Reagan Era."

"Forget it. I'll go out and get myself a cup later. Come on, Lenny. Tell me what you've got." I leaned back in my chair to listen.

"Nathan Watkins travels below the radar," he began. "He's clean. No criminal record, not even a parking ticket, which is strange if what you told me is true... Oh, I'm not questioning you, Captain. Anyway, he's never had a job, that I can find, has no credit record whatsoever. Captain, the man has never owned a credit card or borrowed a dime. He does have a social security number, but he's never applied for a driver's license, never filed a tax return. It's almost as if he doesn't exist. That's it. That's all I have. Sorry."

I looked at him, my mind in a whirl. I didn't know what to say to him.

Finally, I said, "That can't be right, Lenny. He was born in Baton Rouge, went to school there. I have a photo of him."

I rummaged through my file, found the old five-by-seven Alisha had given me.

"See?" I said, "That's him, when he was sixteen." I stood and fixed the photo on the board below Genevieve's. "Janet, have copies made please." I turned again to Lenny.

"Right," Lenny said, "I hear you, but that's *all* there is. He graduated high school, but he was a mediocre student. That's it. After graduation, he dropped off the map; nothing."

"How about his address?" I asked.

He shrugged. "The one you gave me doesn't exist. No such street, no such number, and could not find him listed as owning or renting anywhere in the Tri-State area. The phone number doesn't work either: burner, purchased at Walmart in Baton Rouge two years ago."

"Well, damn!" I muttered. "Keep digging, Lenny. There must be something."

"Captain," Janet said. "I have something. While you were gone I went to Club Suave... No, wait, I think you'd better hear what Hawk and Anne have to say first."

I looked at her, she shrugged. I looked at Hawk, he shrugged. I looked at Anne, she did the same. I was rapidly becoming frustrated. Dealing with these people was like dealing with a bunch of closed-mouthed informants.

"Oh, for Pete's sake," I said finally. "Do I have to drag it out of you? Hawk, I asked you and Anne to check out the crime scene, and then do the rounds of the clubs... So? Did you figure out what she was doing down there on the Riverwalk by herself?" I asked.

"It's hard to tell. It was Friday night, and you know how that can be. There were several clubs close by, some of them open until one or two o'clock in the morning, four in fact. We visited them all, showed her photo to everyone who would look at it, but no one working at any of them remembered seeing her, except for just one guy at a place called Club Suave—it's on Delta—but even that one was iffy.

"One of the bartenders, a John Cooper, thought she might have been there, late, but he wasn't sure; the place was busy, noisy, full to capacity. I mentioned it to Janet, figured she might want to follow it up."

"So you don't know who she was with?" I asked.

"Nope," Hawk said. "Those people don't like cops, much less do they like to talk to them."

"Janet," I said, turning to look at her. "You mentioned Club Suave. You want to tell me about it?"

She perked up, sat up straight, opened her iPad, shuffled through several notebooks, and looked up at me.

I almost rolled my eyes but nodded instead.

"Club Suave," she began. "I went there last night, at about nine o'clock. There weren't many people there at that time of night, it being a Wednesday and all..." She caught the look on my face and changed tack.

"Club Suave is an exclusive dance club. It caters to the young and the beautiful. You know, the kind where the bouncers let you in based on your looks and the quality of your clothes... Anyway, I talked to John Cooper. He's a really nice guy and..." Again, she caught the look.

"It turns out," she continued, "that not only was Genevieve a regular there but so was her brother and his friends," Janet said.

"Wait a minute," I said. "Her brother?"

I looked at Lenny. He shrugged.

"Yes," Janet said. "He goes there often, but always with Genevieve. The bartender didn't know what Nathan's name was—not until I told him—just his street name... Boo, but he did know he was Genevieve's brother. Apparently, Nathan, or Boo, lives in a crib —his word, not mine—in an old house on Bailey Avenue. I drove by it this morning. It's not a very nice place."

Boo? I thought. *What the hell kind of name is that?*

"Club Suave!" I said it like I had eaten a raw onion. "I've never been there, but I've heard of it. It's over on the North Side, right? It's owned by a black guy, name of... Rolland something."

I looked at Lenny. He nodded and made note.

"That's it," Janet said.

"High-end, you say? Yeah, right," I said sarcastically, "and how many times have we been called out to that place?"

"Like every weekend," Janet said. "Well, in the summertime anyway."

"So," I said, thoughtfully, "Genevieve and her brother frequented the same club, moved in the same circles... I wonder if Eddie knew about that? I find it a little hard to believe that he didn't. One more thing he isn't telling us. More to the point, I wonder if he was there last Friday night?"

"It's not a great neighborhood, where he lives, her brother," Janet replied. "I've been in worse, but I'm just letting you know. With a street name like Boo, I have a feeling he's dealing to make a living, but street level, nickel and dime sales. Well, not exactly nickel and dime, but... oh, you know what I mean."

I smiled at her and said, "Enough to get him into the clubs," I replied.

Janet nodded and said, "I guess."

"You want to go pay him a visit?" I asked.

"Oh, yeah," she said, leaping to her feet and heading for the door.

"Be careful," I shouted after her.

"Bad idea, Captain," Hawk said as the door closed behind her.

"You think?" I said. "Why?"

"She's just a kid; more moxie than experience. I know that area, and so do you. It's not safe for her to go there alone. She'll talk herself into deep shit."

I let the words sink in, looked at Anne, then again at Hawk and nodded my agreement. I picked up my phone and called Janet's iPhone and told her I'd had second thoughts and that her project was on hold until tomorrow, that I wanted to be there to confront Nathan-slash-Boo, so we'd go together. I could tell she was pissed, and I didn't blame her. As a distraction, I told her to team up with Anne to check into Eddie's alibi.

"You heard that, Anne?"

"Uh... yeah, and thank you ma'am, but I'm not sure I can stand too much of that perky little shit. She'll drive me frickin' nuts. Can't you find her something else to do?"

I grinned at her and said, "Let her have her head, Anne. She's perky, yes, but she's also very bright. She's fun and has a nose for rooting things out."

"She's a pig, you mean?" Anne grinned at me as she said it, but I could tell she wasn't happy.

Well, she's part of the freakin' team now, so she needs to suck it up.

"Hawk," I said. "You're with me. Give me an hour and then we'll go visit Granddad. I'll buzz you when I'm ready to leave."

They left and I settled down to work on more mundane things, to clear away some of the crap that had accumulated over the past week. I answered a couple of emails and managed to plow through a half-dozen files that I could then close and, thankfully, send them to the place where closed cases go to die.

When I finally looked up from my work, it was almost three o'clock. I didn't want to get to Chesterton's place until just before four o'clock. I'd realized during that first phone conversation that if I wanted to make any headway with the old man, I first had to establish control. He'd be angry that I'd wasted most of his day, but that was the plan. He was used to having things done his way and that was what made him strong, intimidating. I had to show him from the outset that I was no pushover either. He needed to learn that I was not impressed by either his social or business status; that alone should have been enough to render him powerless.

So, at approximately three-fifteen I stepped out of my office and went to find Hawk.

"Grab your iPad and let's go," I said.

16

It was exactly three-fifty-five when we arrived at Chesterton's beautiful, multi-million-dollar home. I'd followed his secretary's instructions to Elder Mountain and found the great house hidden from view by a couple hundred acres of trees. We drove through the open wrought iron gates to a large, ornate fountain where the driveway divided and went off in two different directions. We took the right-hand fork and drove through beautifully manicured lawns until we eventually found ourselves in front of a magnificent, natural stone three-story antebellum palace complete with the obligatory columns each of which had to be at least six feet in diameter.

Seven steps of smooth gray slate led up to a front porch big enough, I was sure, for the whole family to get together. I tried not to gawk, but I couldn't help it. It reminded me so much of Robert E. Lee's great house at Arlington.

Geez, I thought, as I slammed the car door shut, *what can't you do when you have an unlimited supply of cash?*

I parked the car at the foot of the steps and stepped out into the late afternoon sunshine. I stared, for a moment, up at the great edifice in awe, and then mounted the steps with Hawk at my side. It wasn't until we were almost at the front door that I saw him.

"It's about time!" he said loudly.

The man was sitting in a rocking chair outside a massive pair of open French doors—they had to be at least twelve feet tall. A small white table was positioned between him and three more seats. A cup of coffee and a cigarette smoldering in an ashtray along with several butts completed the picture.

"Who's that with you, your father?"

"Mr. Chesterton?" I said, waving, smiling brightly. "This is Sergeant Hawkins—"

I was interrupted when an elderly bloodhound emerged from the house, his head down, front feet wide apart, growling menacingly at me.

"Jack! Heel!"

The dog instantly laid down at his feet but didn't take its eyes off me.

"I'm sorry, Mr. Chesterton, I'm going to have to ask you to put the dog away," I said with one hand in my purse, on my mace, and the other instinctively stopping Hawk short. "It's for your safety and mine."

So, I thought, *the old man wants to play games of his own. This is going to be an interesting afternoon.*

"Jack won't hurt you, ma'am." Chesterton smirked, leaning forward to pick up his cigarette. He was indeed a handsome man, and he looked just like he did in the newspaper clippings in the file. He had a full head of gray hair and a thick mustache, cowboy style.

Damned if he doesn't look just like Sam Elliott.

He wore boots, too, but I doubt they'd ever kicked a cow patty or had been adorned by spurs. His posture was relaxed, reclined in a white wicker rocking chair that looked as if it had been plucked from a Tennessee Williams novel. The wicker was intricately woven, the jade-colored cushions thick and comfortable. The man looked totally at ease.

"I'm afraid I must insist," I said, batting my eyelashes, smiling at him, tilting my head.

He glared at me for a moment, then raised his voice and without taking his eyes off me, said loudly, "Pauline, come and get the dog."

A small woman, about five feet tall, dressed in a gray maid's uniform appeared almost instantly in the doorway, snapped her fingers, and patted her thigh. Jack rose to his feet, presented his head to his master for a pat, then circled around the old man's chair and followed the maid into the house.

We approached the table, and he motioned for us to sit.

"Jack is a good-looking dog," Hawk said, pleasantly. "Is he a pure-bred bloodhound?"

"She," Chesterton replied. "Jack is a she. And yes, she's got purer blood than some of the folks in my family."

He took a final drag of the cigarette then stubbed it out.

"Ah... yes," I said. "You must be talking about Genevieve." He'd opened the door and I walked right on in.

"That's right. I am," he snapped.

Okay, he surprised me with his boldness. I should have seen it coming.

"Why don't you get down to it, Detective," he said, without rancor. "I know why you're here, and I ain't got all day. So either shit or get off the pot."

"My mother used to say that," I replied, and it was true. "Mr. Chesterton," I said, taking my iPad from my purse. "I'm informing you that I'll be recording this conversation. If you have any objection, please tell me now and we can do this another day at the police department."

He shrugged, leaned back in his chair, smiling, steepled his fingers in front of him and shook his head, and again I was taken by his good looks. Unlike so many other good-looking men, however, he had that steely glint in his gray eyes that told me he could be just as vicious as he could be charming. I wasn't sure what side of himself he was going to present, but I took him at his word and wasted no more of his time.

"Mr. Chesterton," I began, "your grandson has accused you of killing Genevieve. Do you know why he might have said that?"

He didn't flinch.

"That boy has always thought with his pecker," Chesterton said. "I'm not surprised. I told him that if he didn't get the marriage annulled within the year that I was going to cut him off, and I meant it. I had already begun proceedings to make good on my promise. He was... angry. Still is, I guess."

Damn, something else little Eddie neglected to tell me.

"Why did you want the marriage annulled?"

"Gazzara. What is that, Italian?"

He pronounced it I-talian. "Yes, sir. On my father's side."

"What's your mama?" He smirked.

"She was Danish," I replied.

"Well now, that ain't so bad. You see, Detective Gazzara, Sergeant Hawkins," he said and nodded at Hawk, "the Chesterton family traveled to this great country from England on the Mayflower, but our ancestry goes back much further than that, to the Dark Ages, in fact. We're Anglo Saxons; we invaded England in the fifth century. There are Chesterton's all the way from Maine to Florida. We built an empire here, and I'm not about to have generations of hard work watered down by the blood of inferiors."

He coughed, cleared his throat, then said, "I know what you're thinking. Why that racist SOB. Who the hell does he think he is? Ain't I right?"

"My opinion of you isn't the issue, Mr. Chesterton," I replied. "I'm trying to find out who killed Genevieve. I will say this, though, that kind of rhetoric doesn't do anything to eliminate you from the list of suspects."

I glanced sideways at Hawk. His expression was stoic as he stared unblinking at the patriarch.

Whew, he looks pissed, I thought. *I wonder what the hell he's thinking.*

"It ain't a crime to decide who gets my money and who doesn't," the old man growled. "If my grandson loved that... that piece of trash enough to marry her, then he doesn't need me to be financing him. It's my money. I can toss it in the fireplace to keep warm if I so choose."

He shook another cigarette from a pack on the table, tore a match from a book, lit it, then let it dangle for a few breaths from the corner of his mouth before coughing violently and setting it in the ashtray.

"It's quite obvious that you knew she was black," I said. "How did you know?"

There's no way he could have known about her blood type. It's impossible.

"Detective Gazzara, of all people, you should know that you can take the girl out of the ghetto, but you can't take the ghetto out of the girl." He smirked.

"You mean that somehow you just knew, that you have some kind of sixth sense that can identify racial traits that are invisible to the rest of us? Is that what you are saying? I don't believe you." I shook my head, frowning.

"Ha, that sure would save me a fortune in private investigators. You never heard the girl talk. She'd mastered the accent but, every once in a while, she made a slip, just a small one to be sure, but I knew... As soon as Eddie told me he was going to marry that slut, I had my people do a thorough background check on her. I know her daddy is black and her momma white, and that they live in a five-room shack in the worst part of town." He picked up his cigarette, took a drag, and began to cough as if he was about to lose his lungs.

"Most of what you say isn't true," I said. "It's a fairly nice home in an older neighborhood. I know, I was there only yesterday."

He ignored my comment and continued as if I hadn't spoken, "I knew where she went to eat, sleep, screw, who she ran with. I had her followed every minute she was awake."

"If that's true," Hawk said, "somebody really screwed up, didn't they? Or did they?"

"Screwed up?" The old man glared at him.

"They weren't watching her the night she died, or whoever you had following her, killed her."

"That's bullshit," he snapped. "You're fishing."

"So what the hell happened then?" Hawk persisted. "Your people just stood by and watched as some asshole strangled the life out of the poor kid? People like you, old man, sicken me. You represent the worst of your kind, a past you can't let go. You're a sad—"

"You... you... you arrogant son of a bitch," Chesterton snarled, interrupting him, sitting upright in his chair. "You watch your damn mouth or get the hell off my property."

"Screw you, you overprivileged, self-righteous—"

"That's enough, Sergeant," I snapped, more for effect than out of outrage at my partner's outburst. Truth be told, I wish I could have said those things myself, but with rank comes responsibility.

I turned back to Chesterton. He was once again reclining in his chair. He crossed his legs, took a huge drag on the cigarette, lifted his head and blew a perfect smoke ring, watched it rise, then lowered his eyes, looked at me and said quietly, "You should teach your half-wit sergeant some manners, Captain, before someone does it for you."

Hawk opened his mouth to speak, but before he could, I held up my hand, silencing him.

"I think you both need to calm down," I said. "How did your grandson and Genevieve meet?" I asked, changing the subject in the hope I might drag the interview back on track.

The old man stared at me for a moment, two thin tendrils of smoke drifting out of his nostrils. He looked like a sleeping dragon.

"I don't know," he said finally. "He never would tell me. All I know is, he met her... somewhere, then put her to work at my company," he said. "Three months later the idiot asked her to marry him. The rest, as they say, is history."

"So," I said, "you found out her real name and that her parents were still alive, but you never told him, and you allowed him to marry her anyway? I don't get that."

"Detective, I'm going to school you on people... and life. Listen to me. It might do you some good. It is better to know a little dirt about someone than to know all the good deeds they may have done because, in the end, no one cares about the good deeds." He stared at me, quietly for a short moment, then continued, "But they will burn you at the stake for even the smallest indiscretion. You see, I was able to keep Genevieve in line with that little bit of information."

He was obviously very pleased with himself.

"And don't kid yourself," he said. "Eddie might not have known who she was, but he sure as hell knew exactly what she was. Sure, when he was growing up he did his duty, dated the local bluebloods, but they weren't his flavor, not at all. I lost count of the number of times his daddy caught him sampling the local color, if you get my meaning."

Holy cow! Really?

"What did Genevieve do when you confronted her, told her that you'd found out about her?" I was intrigued. This whole scenario was better than *Gone With The Wind*. Hawk seemed to be as engrossed as I was.

"What do you think?" he snapped. "She lost it, became hysterical. She begged me not to tell anyone. She said that she was more ashamed of her heritage than I was. Can you believe that?" He chuckled.

"But she wouldn't leave?" I asked.

"No. She promised to treat Eddie well and said she'd be quiet and not cause any trouble with the rest of the family, especially Regina Mae. Not that I gave a shit if she made trouble with her, the loopy bitch. So I gave her a chance."

He frowned, shook his head, then said, more to himself than to us, "I should have known better. Those people can't keep their mouths shut. It's only a matter of time before they expose themselves, and she did, which is why I told Eddie to get rid of her, or else." He launched another smoke ring and watched it rise.

I waited, but he just continued to stare at the smoke, so I said, "So, what did she do... to expose herself?"

"She must have had... she liked goin' to the clubs where her kind... you know, those places. The clubs where her kind get together. Places where we can't go. Those people see my grandson there and the next thing I know he's the one who's dead..." He paused, then, almost as an afterthought, said, "He went with her, one time that I know of, and some big goon literally handed his ass to him."

He shook his head, obviously exasperated, or maybe it was disappointment he was feeling.

"My grandson isn't a fighter. He isn't good with numbers, either. Ha, and he sure as hell's not good with women. Damned if I didn't get stuck with the runt of the litter. I need some great-grandsons and quick."

I got the impression that he was thinking out loud.

"Did you know Genevieve was pregnant when she died?"

That was the only time I saw Granddad Chesterton pause.

He looked at me and squinted, took one last deep drag on his cigarette and stubbed it out. He blew two more tiny smoke rings into the air tilting his chin up but never taking his eyes from mine.

"No, Captain, I didn't." He shook his head, slowly, then looked me in the eye and said, "I *am* sorry that the child had to die, as I am that Genevieve did, but it's probably for the best. You see, dollars to donuts the child wasn't Eddie's anyway. And even if it was—oh yes, I'd have had a DNA test done—and even if it was, I wouldn't have accepted it. Call me what you want, but I'm telling you the truth."

I looked down at my iPad, then at Hawk—he was staring at the old man with something akin to hate in his eyes. And then Chesterton, the old bastard, was smiling at me.

"Don't you dare judge me, Captain. You think I just woke up one morning feeling the way I do about these people? Well, I didn't. I grew up here, worked hard to keep what my father handed to me, not like that idiot grandson of mine." He swallowed and the smugness left his face. "Let me tell you a story, a true story... my story."

He didn't wait for an answer.

"My best friend all through grade school was a boy by the name of Reginald Hobbs, Reggie. Black as the ace of spades, he was. A good kid who came from a good, hardworking family. But all that changed when we went to high school. I went to a private school, Reggie to a public school. It didn't bother me, not one bit, that he went to the black high school and I went to the white one. This was back when kids of color weren't supposed to mix with whites.

"Anyway... one Saturday afternoon, it was, I saw him walking with four other boys, all about the same age, all black like Reggie. I went running up to him to, I don't know, maybe to play some ball or go swimming; it was what we'd always done. Those boys, including Reggie, said yeah, sounds like fun, said we'd take a shortcut to the ball field down a dirt path. I didn't think anything of it. We were all laughing and talking and the next thing I know, when we were away from the road and no one could see or hear us, those five boys jumped me.

"Back then I could take a punch as well as any other kid, but you see, Detective Gazzara, what I couldn't take was that Reggie had turned on me: he was in it just as deep as those boys who didn't know me. He didn't even hesitate. It was like all those years of friendship between us were just pretend. And I'm supposed to forgive and forget? Hell no! I'm supposed to not judge a book by its cover? Hell no! Those five little bastards beat me up because I was white; no other reason. He's dead now, Reggie. Shot in the head by one of his own kind. Go figure."

He looked... sad, yes, that's it sad.

"So you had Genevieve killed as payback?" Hawk said, quietly.

"No! I didn't. I had them arrested, Reggie along with them, crying and bawling for his mama the entire time! That day I learned that the only thing people, any people, respect is someone bigger and more powerful than they are, and I made my mind up right there and then that I was going to make damn sure that anyone who had any thoughts of taking me down would think long and hard before they made a move. I made up my mind I would be twice as big, twice as powerful as anyone on the planet, and I am, Captain. You know it and so does everyone else. Why do you think you were able to roll right onto my property without having to pass through some sort of security?"

I took a deep breath but said nothing.

Chesterton leaned forward and looked me square in the eyes. "I'll tell you why. It's because everyone within five hundred miles of this place knows I'll shoot them dead if they try anything on my land, and that I've got the money to get away with it."

"Genevieve wasn't shot. She was strangled," I said.

"That's right. She was. But not by me. Like I told you, I was going to make good on my threat to take away Eddie's allowance, his inheritance, all of it. I didn't need to kill anyone. It was my money to take back. She wasn't standing in the way. She was the cause of it. Maybe you should take another look at my grandson. He's the one with reason to kill her." He pointed at me then leaned back in his chair.

"So you think your grandson killed Genevieve? Her husband?" I asked.

I have to admit I was more than a little flabbergasted, unsure of what to say next. I arrived at the party thinking I was so smart to make the man wait and throw him off his game and well, he'd aced me.

"Isn't that usually who the guilty party is, the husband?" Chesterton smirked, then called for Pauline.

She came bustling out to the porch. Without uttering a word, she picked up the ashtray, took it back inside, and returned a moment later with a clean one.

"It has been known to turn out that way," I replied. "Mr. Chesterton, where were you the night Genevieve was murdered?" I knew he'd have an alibi; of course he would and it would be airtight, but so what? He could have paid someone to do it for him.

However, as I sat there watching him, looking for tells, and as much as I hated to admit it, my gut was telling me he wasn't my man. It was telling me not only that he didn't kill Genevieve, but he also didn't pay anybody to do it for him. He just wanted her gone, and he was using his money to force his grandson to get rid of her.

"I was having dinner with one of the board members of my company at St. John's," he said lightly. "I know the owners so you can verify it with them. I also ran into one of our State Representatives and his lovely wife, who will also verify my whereabouts." He seemed to be enjoying himself.

"I do appreciate your time, Mr. Chesterton," I said as I stood up.

I turned off my iPad and took a business card from my pocket and handed it to him.

"If you think of anything that might shed some light on what happened to Genevieve, I really would appreciate a call."

"Will do, Detective. You and Sergeant Hawkins have a lovely evening, both of you, you hear?"

He remained seated, took another cigarette from the pack, lit it, and blew the smoke up in the air with all the satisfaction of a sailor on shore leave.

I turned as if to leave, then made as if I'd changed my mind, turned back to him and said, "By the way, Mr. Chesterton. Who's the Frenchman?"

He didn't even flinch. If there was a tell, I didn't catch it.

"Frenchman?" he said. "What Frenchman?"

"Your grandson suggested I ask you about the Frenchman," I said.

He shook his head and said, "The lad's mind must be wandering. Maybe he's talking about someone who works for me. There were more than six thousand, worldwide, at the last count. I can't keep track of them all."

I nodded, and we left him blowing smoke rings.

I let Hawk drive us back to the PD. I was exhausted, dumbfounded, my head whirling. I'd planned to take control of the interview, but it hadn't worked out that way. I felt like I'd just gone twelve rounds with a heavyweight... and, on thinking about it, that's exactly what I'd done. It dawned on me then, that Chesterton probably had more experience dealing with law enforcement than I'd given him credit for. Oh yeah, where there was money there was scandal, corruption and crime, and there I was treating him like he'd never dealt with the law before, and the guy probably reveled in my naiveté.

Oh well, there's no point beating myself up. The man played me, and I let him. But, as Scarlet said, tomorrow is another day, and he won't catch me lacking next time. I'll take his advice: bigger is better, and the police department is bigger than he is, and it's all mine.

"So? What are your thoughts?" I finally asked Hawk.

"Where the hell do I begin?"

"Well," I said, "he might be repugnant and crude, but a guy that honest about his feelings is a guy who knows who he is."

"He's a son of a bitch, is what he is," Hawk said.

"Yeah, that," I said. "That's what I was thinking too, but a forthright son of a bitch, and a racist, but I don't think he killed her, or had her killed, and he has an alibi that can easily be verified."

I looked at my watch. It was almost six. It had been a long afternoon.

"I don't know about you," I said, "but I'm beat, in more ways than one. He's a tough old bird, is Chesterton. I think we need to call it a day... Be sure to check his alibi. I'm sure it will be solid, but you never know and if we don't... well. Hey, you see how he looked like Sam Elliott?"

Hawk cut me a dirty look but said nothing.

17

THE FOLLOWING MORNING, FRIDAY, I MADE GOOD ON MY promise to go with Janet to interview Nathan Watkins—or Boo as he was known on the street. But first I needed to bring the rest of the team up to speed and see what they had found out the previous afternoon. Thus, we assembled in my office at eight o'clock that morning.

"So, what have we got?" I asked when everyone was settled. "Anne, what about Eddie's alibi? You checked it out, right?" I asked. Eddie, I already knew from my own interview, was a narcissistic kid with a drinking problem and a severe case of affluenza.

"We did, and he doesn't have one, not for the hours between twelve-thirty and two, but I doubt that it matters. His relationship with the truth is strained, to say the least... Okay, so we went to the Sorbonne and spoke with Laura. She said Eddie and two friends entered the bar at around ten-thirty and all three were already drunk out of their minds. She said it was just after twelve when they left, staggered out of the bar, all three of them. We talked to both of the friends, Alex Pruitt and George Martinez. They both said they left the Sorbonne around one-thirty, which was either a lie or they were too drunk to know. Either way, none of them have an alibi."

"Well," I said, "if anyone's to be believed, it's Laura. Did you ask him about Club Suave?"

"We did," Janet said. "Well, I did. He said they didn't go there. He said they ate barbeque at Rusty's—Rusty doesn't remember them, I checked—and then they went to the Mellow Mushroom—I couldn't find anyone there that remembered them either—and from there they went to the Sorbonne..." and then she ran out of steam, glanced at Anne and shrugged.

"So that means the suspect pool just grew by two," I said. "They could have gone from the Sorbonne to Club Suave, all three of them, and all three could have been involved in the murder. Hawk, you and Anne go talk to the people working in that arcade under Eddie's apartment. Maybe that coffee shop is an all-nighter and somebody saw them come home. Maybe you can provide them with an alibi."

I turned to Lenny. "What've you got for me, Lenny?"

"Well, I did some digging into Sam Wheaton's background, like you asked."

"Okay," I said. "Let's hear it."

"Well, yeah, okay," he said as he flipped through the screens on his iPad, and then put it down on his lap.

"I have it all written up for you," he said, handed me three pieces of paper clipped together, and like sets to each of the others in the room, then picked up his iPad and began.

"So Sam Wheaton got his start on Wall Street right after he graduated from NYU—New York University—with a degree in Risk Assessment, but in 1988 he was fired for an unspecified Regulation D infraction... My guess is that he was manipulating funds, but what do I know? He was unemployed for almost six months until he founded a business and financial consulting company, STW Risk Management Company.

"STW Risk is unique in that it was formed, according to Wheaton's blurb, to manage the assets of small loan companies—à la some of the more substantial payday loan vendors—and clients with assets of more than twenty-five million dollars. But there's one notable exception, CDE International Finance Corporation, Chesterton's company, whose assets are estimated, though I couldn't confirm it, to be in excess of three-billion dollars."

Holy Cow, I thought. *Three billion. That really is motive, and not just for Eddie.*

"Any word on how well Eddie and Wheaton get along?" I asked, interrupting Lenny's flow.

Lenny shook his head and said, "No, not really. I found nothing to suggest any differences between them. Eddie works for CDE so they must interact... when Eddie bothers to show up, I guess."

"How about Number Three, Eddie's father?" I said.

"Same. Wheaton, so it seems, is everybody's friend."

I looked at Janet. She smiled self-consciously. Fortunately, no one else caught it. I nodded for Lenny to continue.

"Okay, so Wheaton met Edward Chesterton the Second, the chairman and CEO of CDE international in 1986 through a mutual acquaintance, Robert Marks, an insurance executive, and his wife, in Naples, Florida, and the two of them hit it off. A year later, Wheaton became Chesterton's financial adviser and right-hand man. In less than a year, Wheaton had sorted out Chesterton's somewhat expansive enterprises and was given power of attorney that allowed him to hire people, sign checks, buy and sell properties, borrow money, and do pretty much anything else of a legally binding nature on Chesterton's behalf.

"If ever there was an arrangement that offered an opportunity for abuse, this one has to be it," he continued. "I was, however, unable to find anything that would indicate that Wheaton has ever abused the privilege. True, he lives extremely well, but his company is successful and Chesterton pays him an 'exorbitant amount,' said to be one percent of CDE's net profit."

He paused, flipped through several screens on his iPad, and then continued, "In 1996, Wheaton relocated STW Risk to the island of St. Thomas in the US Virgin Islands. By relocating to the US Virgin Islands, he was able to legally reduce his clients'—and his own—

federal income taxes by 90 percent. The US Virgin Islands are, in fact, a US Government, officially sanctioned offshore tax haven, which makes it one heck of a good deal considering that the USVI offers all of the advantages of being part of the United States banking system, but with a three-and-a-half percent income tax rate. I read somewhere, in Newsweek, I think it was, that the USVI is a slice of paradise that some experts consider the nation's one and only, officially sanctioned, full-blown offshore tax shelter."

"No dirt?" Anne asked skeptically.

"No. That's it. I have nothing else for you. As far as I can tell, except for the two sexual harassment suits and his paternity problems, he's clean."

"So what does all this mean, then?" Anne asked, flipping through her hard copy.

I was wondering the same thing myself.

"It means," Hawk said, "that this man Wheaton knows all of the family's dirty little secrets, which makes him a very powerful man; and a very dangerous man, a man to be wary of. Did he know the girl was black, I wonder, and that she was pregnant?"

"He says he didn't," I said, "and I understand what you're saying, Hawk, but does any of it give Wheaton a motive to kill the girl, other than a possible rejection of his sexual advances?"

"Sexual advances?" Anne asked. "That's a bit of a stretch, isn't it? How old is he?" She looked up at Wheaton's photograph and smiled. "Good looking dude, though."

I looked at her, then at Janet, who blushed and looked away, but not before Anne caught it.

"Ahhh," Anne said, "I see. Are you going to tell us about it?"

Janet opened her mouth to speak, but before she could, I interrupted her.

"There's nothing to tell yet," I said. "We offered the bait, and he's nibbling but we have yet to set the hook. You'll know, all of you, when we have something... or nothing."

I looked up at the board, shook my head, and wondered how the hell I was going to sort it all out. I stared at the blank square that represented the Frenchman for a couple of seconds, and at the big black question mark I'd drawn beside it and then, still looking up at it, I said, "Lenny, Hawk, see what you can find out about this Frenchman that Eddie dropped on us. There could be something to it, or it could simply be a red herring." I shook my head and sighed and checked my watch. It was already after ten.

I need a break, I thought. *I need to get out of here.*

"So we all know what to do right?" I asked, then looked at each of them in turn. "So let's go to it. Janet, grab your stuff. Let's go find Nathan Watkins, or Boo, or whatever the hell his name is."

18

It took us little time to find the address where Nathan Watkins was supposed to live. It was actually off Bailey on Caxton in the Highland Park area where the homes were not that much different from the Washington home in Baton Rouge: older homes, most of them, simple, ranch-style frame houses with security bars on the windows and doors.

When we found the address I wasn't too surprised by its appearance. A two-story, wood-sided house built around the turn of the century. It wasn't unique. I could think of dozens just like it, most of them turned either into apartments or offices. This one appeared to be unchanged, though it was obvious that more than one family was living there.

Nor did it appear to be the home—headquarters—of a drug lord. There were no members of a "crew" watching from the front and back porch, no suspicious looking expensive cars with custom rims or tinted windows parked either in front, at the rear, or even nearby. It was, to all intents and purposes, just another old house in a depressed section of the city. It was, I hoped, where the kid we needed to talk to lived. He wasn't going to like it; of that I was certain. Highland Park is where an unofficial neighborhood watch keeps a wary eye out for unwelcome visitors, and once word got out that we were here, Nathan would have some explaining to do.

We parked on the street one house down from Nathan's and walked the short distance to the front porch. The front door was closed, but as we mounted the steps we could hear raised voices coming from inside.

"I don't care!" a female voice shouted. "I want it out of this house! I live here, too and I don't want nothin' to do with you or your honky friends!"

"That's not happenin'," a male voice replied. "If you don't like it you can get the hell out!"

We stood for a moment on the porch, listening.

"You in too deep," the female voice pleaded. "You gonna take everyone else with you and that means me. I can't leave my baby just cause you done somethin' stupid. My brother in jail. My cousin in jail. Now my baby-daddy gonna be in jail. What am I supposed to... Who the hell is that?"

"That's our cue," I said to Janet. "You take the back. I'll go this way."

She nodded, drew her weapon, ran down the porch steps, and headed to the back of the house. I drew my Glock, held it down by my leg and knocked on the door. There was a sudden rush of feet on hardwood floors somewhere inside.

"Police!" I shouted. "Come on out with your hands up."

The occupants, already in an elevated state, would, I hoped, calm themselves down and comply. That was what usually happened when the police arrived. Domestic situations of any kind are extremely dangerous. You never quite know what to expect: an irate husband or boyfriend armed with an AR15, or worse.

And, of course, these two didn't open the door, but I knew they were in what I supposed was a living room off to the right.

"Miss, sir, please open the door," I said, my Glock still at my side.

"My name is Detective Gazzara. I just want to talk to Nathan Watkins. Is he here?"

Before either of them could answer I heard Janet shouting from the backyard. "Show me your hands! Get down on the ground and show me your hands!"

Oh crap, what the hell has she done?

I ran down the steps and around the back of the house to find my partner, all one-hundred-fifteen pounds of her, straddling a young man twice her size and face down on the floor as she yanked one arm behind him, slapped a cuff on his wrist, and then did the same to the other.

The back door flew open and a young woman stepped outside, her face streaked with tears.

"Get your hands up!" I shouted, pointing the Glock at her.

She did as she was told, slowly sat down on the concrete step, and said not a single word.

She looked to be about twenty years old and at least seven months pregnant if not more.

"Keep your hands up where I can see them," I said. "Is there anyone else inside the house?"

She shook her head.

"Stand up. Do you have any weapons on you? Any needles or anything that might stick me?" I asked as I patted her down.

"No, ma'am." The voice was subdued, shaky, nothing like the strident voice I'd heard from the front porch. She sounded scared, and that was good.

"Sit down," I said to her, "and keep your hands where I can see them."

"Nathan Watkins?" Janet leaned down and shouted in the man's ear. "Is that you?"

"I don't know no Nathan Watkins," he muttered defiantly.

"You don't know who you are?" Janet said, smiling widely at me. "Well, that's okay. I guess we'll all find out who you are together. Come on, get up and have a seat next to your sweetheart."

She helped him up by pulling on his handcuffed arms. He grimaced and grunted and let out a couple of gasps.

"I'm not hurting you, am I?" she said. "A big tough guy like you, diving through a window just to get away from little old me, and I'm hurting you? Boy, are you ever going to have a fine time in the tank with the other bangers. They'll eat your lunch."

"Keep an eye on them both while I clear the house," I said as I brushed past the woman and went inside.

The girl was right; there was no one else inside, though it was obvious that the place was occupied by at least a half dozen people besides our two. I also found a small amount of weed on the kitchen table. Not enough to charge them with possession for resale, but enough for an excuse to take them both in if they didn't play ball.

When I stepped outside again, Janet had them both seated together on the back stoop. The man looked at me defiantly, his eyebrows pinched together in the middle. Inwardly, I smiled. *And here we have yet another one,* I thought. How many just like him I'd run into over the past fifteen years or so, I'd lost count. They're all the same, so predictable. I was sure we weren't going to get very far with this one.

"Nathan Watkins?" I said as I stepped around him so that my back was toward the sun and he had to look up at me. "That is you, right?"

He didn't reply. He just continued staring up at me, his eyes narrowed to mere slits, his forehead one huge frown.

I glanced at the girl. The tears were gone. Her face had hardened. She said nothing.

I didn't care about the woman at all, but if the guy was indeed Nathan then I wanted to talk to him, and if he wasn't going to cooperate... well, I was just going to have to persuade him that it was in his best interest to do so. But first, I had to find out if he was... Nathan.

I stared down at the woman, thought for a moment, then said, "Well, it seems that you have a problem, ma'am. Stand up please." I helped her to her feet and then led her to the far end of the stoop, just out of earshot of the man I figured was Nathan Watkins.

I held the baggie up in front of her and said, "I found this on your kitchen table and we both know what it is, don't we? It's not a whole lot but, DCS takes a dim view of expectant mothers using illegal substances, but you knew that, right? This," I said, wagging the baggie in front of her nose, "is enough reason for them to take your child away from you. Is that what you want?"

Her eyes filled with tears again.

"Look, this ain't my house. I just live here with Nathan," she said quietly. "That his weed, not mine."

"So, he is Nathan Watkins?" I asked.

The girl nodded her head.

"And what's your name?"

"Sheila Teverson," she muttered.

I nodded, making a mental note of her name, then said, "Why did he take off running when we arrived?"

I watched her face. She shrugged and shook her head.

I continued, "You're sure? He didn't tell you he was in some kind of trouble?"

"No," she said. "Boo don't do nothin'. I mean, he ain't no thug."

Sheila Teverson's definition of a thug was probably a lot different from mine, and I wasn't about to take her word for it that Nathan wasn't one. He'd tried to run, so he was obviously up to something illegal, or he had something else to hide. I was sure that she knew what it was, but she was putting on the innocent act, hoping I'd fall for it. As if!

"You're sure?" I asked.

She nodded enthusiastically. I turned and looked at Janet. She was talking quietly to Nathan. He wasn't looking at her. His replies were mumbled and he barely moved his lips. And then I looked toward the sidewalk. Several neighbors were approaching.

Uh oh! I thought. *Time to get out of here.*

"Sergeant," I said, "please escort Mr. Watkins to the car."

"But I told you," Sheila pouted. "He ain't no thug. He didn't do nothin'."

"Just keep your mouth shut, Sheila!" Nathan yelled.

"This ain't right. He didn't do nothin'," Sheila continued to protest. She glared at me. "You said you'd let him go."

"I said no such thing! I told you what would happen to you if I decided to turn you both in. He was coming with me no matter what. Now you can go back inside and maybe you'll get to keep your baby."

Sheila was pissed, I could tell. She'd figured she had me when she confirmed his identity, and now she was taking it personally.

"You lied to me," she screamed. "You made me think you was trying to help. Better watch your back, bitch."

By then the small group of neighbors had gathered on the sidewalk. Several were mumbling angrily, and I had a feeling things were about to get nasty. If the group grew any bigger... I knew things could deteriorate fast. Sheila knew it too, and she kept shouting about how bad her man was being treated, how she'd been lied to.

It wasn't an unusual situation, and it's why we all hate having to deal with domestic calls. A woman calls 911 claiming she's being abused. We respond, arrest the boyfriend, and the abused female complainant pitches a fit and starts screaming at the officers. Inevitably, the cops are the bad guys. It never made any sense to me.

I left her to it, joined Janet at the car, and loaded Nathan into the back seat before the situation escalated further, and we headed back to the police department.

"You know, Nathan," I said, glancing at him in the rearview mirror, "if you'd just given us a minute of your time you wouldn't be in this mess. Tell me, why the hell did you run?"

He said nothing, just stared truculently up at the mirror.

"We just wanted to talk to you about your sister, Naomi, to tell you that... to tell you that she's dead."

I watched for his reaction in the rearview mirror. There wasn't one. Either he already knew, or he didn't care.

"I see," I said. "Think about it, Nathan."

19

Unlike his sister, Nathan looked black. His skin was the color of lightly creamed coffee, his hair straighter than you might expect, but also black. He was tall, well-built... ripped, some would say. He did have his sister's eyes though; the eyes that glared at me when I pulled him from the back seat of my car were the same as those I'd seen on Doc's examining table, staring up into nothingness.

"What the hell's the matter with you?" I asked him as I paraded him past the duty sergeant's desk to the nearest interrogation room. "You could still be home right now. But no, you had to do it the hard way. You happy now?"

I pulled out a seat for my guest at the plain steel table in the center of the room. He flopped down onto it, all attitude and screw you. And don't they all? From high school kids trying to act tough in the principal's office knowing that their parents weren't going to do anything about their shenanigans to the idiots like Nathan with street cred to protect and expand. Except this wasn't the principal's office. It was a murder investigation, his sister's murder, and the way he was acting was suspicious to say the least.

"You want anything to drink? Some water? A Coke?" Janet asked loudly making Nathan jump slightly.

He shook his head no.

I tapped Janet on the shoulder and beckoned for her to follow me out into the observation room. She did and shut the door behind her.

"Go see if any of the others are in the building," I said. "If they are, I want them to watch this interview, okay?"

She nodded. "I'll go check. Back in a few."

She returned a few minutes later followed by Hawk and Anne. I explained what I was about to do and then I reentered the interrogation room alone, leaving the three of them to observe. And so it began.

"Now, Nathan. This can be as easy as you want to make it," I started. "But let me warn you: I don't have all day, so don't waste my time. Let's get on with it, shall we?"

He didn't answer. He just stared harshly at me.

"Tell me about your sister, Nathan. You already knew she was dead, right?"

I thought for a minute he wasn't going to answer, then he looked up at me, his face had softened a little, and he looked down at his cuffed wrists.

"Yeah," he said. "I got the word, on the street. Look, I didn't have nothin' to do with Naomi. I ain't seen her in weeks, more'n that."

"But your parents sent you here with her to keep an eye on her. What did you tell them when you found out she was dead?" I asked.

He took a deep breath, shook his head and said, "I didn't tell them."

"Why not? Don't you think they have a right to know? They're her parents. She was their only daughter," I said, trying to get him to open up.

"They didn't need to know."

He leaned back in his chair. "She broke their hearts, forgot all about them when she married that white boy. She forgot where she came from and who her people was."

"How about you, Nathan? Did she forget about you too?"

He shrugged. "Yeah, mostly... but I was here; they wasn't. I tried to stay in touch, but... I saw her now an' then, when she was out partyin', sometimes. How'd she die anyway? Can I see her?"

"Do you want to see her?"

He nodded his head, slowly.

"I can arrange that, but first I need you to cooperate."

"I'm cooperatin', ain't I?" he said, his voice two octaves higher.

"Nathan," I said, "to all intents and purposes, you don't exist. You haven't filed a tax return in years; you haven't applied for a driver's license since you arrived here. Your girlfriend said you owned the house where we found you, but there's no record of you owning property anywhere. Can you explain that?"

"Yeah," he grinned at me, "I can. I like to stay under the... like the radar. That way I stay clean."

"Stay clean?"

"Yeah, do what I want, whenever, whatever, see?"

"So how do you earn money, make a living, provide for your family?"

"Odd jobs; this an' that, for cash, you know."

"No, I don't know. I do know you don't leech off the welfare system so I imagine you do a little dealing, right? Sell a little weed, some coke, a little meth? Is that why you like to stay 'under the radar'?"

"You the smart one, Detective. You figure it out."

I nodded, stared hard at him. He didn't flinch; he just grinned up at me, totally in control of himself.

"Nathan, did it bother you that your sister married into big money and then... how shall I put it... disowned you and the rest of her family, cut you all off?"

"Hell, yeah. I mean, I covered her ass, right? Kept her out of trouble, saved her ass more than once. If not for me, she be in serious trouble."

"It doesn't come any more serious than dead, Nathan. Where were you that night... when she needed you most?"

He looked sour, like he was about to sneeze, then looked up at me and said, "I told ya, I ain't seen her in weeks. I didn't know she was inta that kinda shit. Look," he said, seriously, "early on, when we was not long come to town, I saved her from getting into serious trouble with some bad dudes, a couple of times, before she hooked up with her sugar-daddy. She liked her dope, but she didn't like payin' for it, not even when she had money. She partied all the time an' she didn't care who with."

Nathan folded his arms across his chest. "She hooked up with her man, and then she didn't bother with her brother no more. So I don't bother with her; simple as that."

"Nathan, were you jealous of your sister?" I asked softly.

"Naw. It's just that I knew where she came from, what she was. I could have blown the whistle on her any time, but I didn't. You'd think that count for somethin' right? Well it didn't. She cut my ass off. Don't want to know me no more." He looked down at his cuffed hands, then looked up at me and continued. "Look, Naomi could pass. She used it. She wanted to be white, and this is what it got her. Serve her right," he mumbled.

I sensed a heavy dose of sibling rivalry in his tone whether he wanted to admit it or not.

"So where were you?"

"When? When she got killed? I don't know... When exactly was that?"

"Sometime between midnight and two in the morning, Saturday morning."

He shrugged. "Hangin' out, prob'ly, at Sheppy's, like most nights: play a little pool, smoke a little dope, just chill, you know?"

"Can anyone corroborate that for you?"

"Corrob'rate? You mean say I was with 'em. Sure, a half-dozen dudes, at least."

Oh yeah, and if you'll believe any one of them, I have a hundred acres of swampland in Florida I'll sell you.

"Names?" I asked.

He rattled off a half-dozen. I made note of them, and we'd check his alibi, but it would mean little to nothing. The street looks after its own.

I thought for a minute and then changed tack.

"Did you go to her wedding?" I asked.

"What? Me? Are you kiddin'?" He gave me a weird look then said, "Wasn't invited."

"So when you moved here from Baton Rouge, despite your promise to your parents, you went your separate ways?" I asked.

"No, not right away. She made 'friends' in the neighborhood; me too." He made air quotes with his fingers when he said the word friends.

"What do you mean?" I asked.

"She wanted to be high society, but she couldn't give up the hood." Nathan smirked. "She liked to get dirty. Be seen at the club. Get high. You know. You find any white friends she had? Nope. You didn't, did you? Just that honky she married."

It was true. We'd found no friends, white or black. She was almost as much of an enigma as was Nathan. The only one who really knew anything about her was Chesterton Two, a bigot who put a private investigator on her tail.

"I heard when she got married it was all white women in the bridal party. Like a regular Klan rally. That musta been some booty call." Nathan snickered.

"Spare me the Malcolm X speech, Nathan," I said. "So you're saying you didn't know any of her new friends?"

"No, I ain't sayin' 'at. I knew the black ones. The hoes didn't like her, but the bros... she fine with them. She had a couple of boys she'd hook up with regular at the clubs. She liked that black—"

"Did you see your sister with these men?" I said, interrupting him before he could finish the thought.

Nathan nodded. "Yeah, I did."

"Give me their names, please."

"Nope."

"What do you mean, no?" I snapped.

"Lady, you know better'n to ask me shit like 'at. I mean, you want me to end up dead, like Naomi?"

I should have seen that coming.

"I ain't saying another word, sister." He held up his cuffed wrists, and said, "An' if I ain't under arrest, then you need to take these cop locks off."

I sighed, shook my head and said, "Come on, Nathan, this is your sister we're talking about. We need to find her killer."

He shrugged, looked down at the table, then back up at me and said, "Look, I'm sorry what happened to Naomi, but there ain't nothin' I can do. Lady, she asked for it. She a bitch; she lie, an' manipulate anyone to get what she want. Hell, she manipulating you now, from the grave."

"Why do you say that?" I asked.

"She wanted to be something she's not. She played white and got inta y'all's world, but she wanted to play bad girl too. She wanted the best o' both worlds; she did that. Now she's dead and playing the victim. And I'll tell you right now she ain't no victim. She deserved whatever she got."

"That's cold, Nathan. You think the baby deserved what she got too?"

"Baby? What baby?"

"She was pregnant, Nathan."

His mouth dropped open, his eyes widened, and his head moved slowly from side to side.

"Aw, man. You shittin' me, right?"

I shook my head.

"Oh, man, that's so messed up." He looked up at me, his eyes glistening.

So he does care.

"Anything you want to say, Nathan?" I asked.

He looked at me, then slowly held his hands up again and said, "Come on, Lady. Lemme go, huh?"

I removed the cuffs and said, "I need those names, Nathan. How about it?"

He just looked at me and shook his head.

I handed him my business card with instructions to call me if he changed his mind. It was a forlorn hope, but you never know.

"Nathan, your mom asked me to pass on a message. She wants you to call home. She just wants to know you are all right," I said, fulfilling my promise to Alisha Washington.

His eyes watered and he nodded his head once. Whether he'd call or not I didn't know.

I stood behind him and pointed at the one-way glass and then beckoned. Janet entered the room almost immediately.

"Show him out, Sergeant," I said, and she did.

"I don't know what's with him," I said when we all reassembled in my office. "His sister's dead, and he doesn't seem to care, although the news about the baby seemed to upset him, some. It's not natural."

"Maybe they didn't like each other," Hawk said, his voice dripping with sarcasm.

"He knows a lot more than he's telling," Anne said. "Her sex life, drug use, he's playing us. He was tight with her, had to be. If they weren't on friendly terms, he wouldn't know those intimate details. He said he hadn't seen her in weeks; I don't believe it. He's the key, right?"

"Could be," I said. "Hawk, any comments?"

"Yeah, the guy's a rat. Why don't you let me talk to him, alone?"

I smiled and said, "How long until you retire? You do want to hang onto your pension, right?"

He shrugged, then said, "All we need is names. Shouldn't be too difficult to get them from him. Just give me the word."

I stared at him. *Geez, he's cold!*

"Did you and Anne check out Eddie's alibi?" I asked him. "Did anyone at the coffee shop see what time he and his friends arrived home?"

It was Anne that answered. "Unfortunately, the café closes at eleven, so no."

"Okay," I said. "So, Hawk, you take Anne with you and go check out Nathan's alibi. You made a note of the people he said he was with, right?"

"I did," Janet said, handing a piece of paper to Anne.

"He also said Genevieve liked to visit the clubs," I said. "I want to know which ones, who she went with, who she met, who she left with. I also want to know if Nathan went with her. I want to know who she was screwing. Go talk to people. Start with Club Suave. It's where she was the night she died so it's as good a place as any."

Hawk nodded and rose to his feet; so did Anne, and they left.

"Janet," I said, after the door closed behind them, "Anything you want to add?"

"I think he's hiding something. I just can't figure out how to find out what it is."

"Maybe he's clean... well, as far as his sister's death is concerned," I replied. "But you're right, and so's Anne. I think he's the key."

"It didn't bother you that he didn't seem upset that his sister was dead, murdered?" Janet asked. "I wanted to come in there and slap him silly."

I smiled at the thought of Janet slapping big bad Boo.

"No," I said, "because I think he actually was upset about it, very upset, and he was hiding it. I'm thinking we need to find out exactly what Nathan is into. You up for a late night?"

"Always." Janet rubbed her hands together.

"Great. Go home and get something to eat and put on some comfortable clothes. It might be a long night. We'll meet back here at eight." Little did I know how long a night it would be.

She left, and I set aside the Genevieve Chesterton file and set about catching up on some paperwork. It never seemed to end. By six o'clock that evening, I was done, and I headed home to shower, change clothes, and get ready for... a night I'll not easily forget.

20

"To say that the freaks come out at night would be an understatement in this part of town," Janet said as we sat in the car parked under a tree two blocks from Nathan's house.

"Yeah," I said, "and it's not even that late... His house is kind of quiet, though; the lights are on in the living room, but... Maybe he decided to stay home. If nothing happens by one o'clock, we'll get out of here."

I was watching Nathan's home through a powerful pair of binoculars, watching the windows for signs of life, moving shadows on the blinds. I'd been at it for almost two hours, seen nothing, and my arms were aching. Janet was right though: it was only fifteen minutes after ten o'clock, still a little early for a Friday night street party, but the neighborhood was already coming to life.

People were out on their stoops, doors wide open, music playing loudly. Any other night I would have been worried about sitting there in the dark; it was asking for trouble. Thankfully, though, there was a party going around the corner and cars were parked on both sides of the street for a half-block in each direction. Even so we still had to duck down out of sight when someone drove by. Let's face it, two white women in a parked, unmarked white Dodge Charger screamed cops. If we were exposed, well... these days, who knows what might happen.

So, we'd been sitting there for a while; the twenty-two-ounce coffee Janet had brought was just about done and what little was left was cold. I put the binoculars down and finished it off; cold coffee is good, especially when there's nothing else.

"How come you've never married, Cap?" Janet asked.

"What?"

"Well, I don't get it. You never date, not that I know of, and you're hot when you... well, I've seen you. You can't be short on offers... to go out, I mean."

"Getting a little personal, aren't we, Sergeant?" It wasn't the first time I'd been asked the question, so I supposed I shouldn't have been surprised.

"Well, yeah, but I'm your partner, right? It's kind of... Okay, I'm being nosey. Just askin'," she said, taking some kind of granola thing from her pocket and offering it to me.

I shook my head. If it had been a cheeseburger I'd have snatched her hand off, but I wasn't in the mood for healthy.

"Oh, I don't know," I said, a little reluctantly. I wasn't comfortable talking about my personal life. "It's a cop thing, I guess. None of the guys I know could make marriage work, so how the hell am I, a woman, to make a go of it? I've been a cop so long now I can't remember being anything else." I chuckled.

After pondering her question, I continued, "Yes, I get asked out, now and then, but I don't often go. Maybe I should? I dunno. It's a whole lot of hassle for... nothing?"

"But don't you, you know, miss it?"

"Miss what? And before you answer, if you're asking about what I think you are, that's way too personal. Change the subject, okay?"

"Oh come on, Kate. It's me, little old Janet. I know you must have needs. I sure as hell do."

"*Enough*," I snapped.

"You still haven't answered my first question," she persisted, undaunted.

I turned in my seat and stared at her. The little b... didn't flinch, stared right back at me, smiling sweetly.

"Look," I said, giving in a little. "I don't know why. Maybe I haven't met 'Mr. Right' yet," I said, sarcastically, making air quotes with my fingers.

And then she really stepped over the line.

"Tell me about Harry Starke," she said, no longer smiling. "How come you let him get away?"

Suddenly, I felt flushed, angry. "That's enough, Janet! How the hell did you know about him anyway?"

"I'm sorry," she said. "I didn't mean to upset you. I was just asking to help pass the time."

Upset me? Hell, I thought I was beyond that after all this time... guess not. Damn!

"I'm not upset. Just change the subject."

She sat quietly for a long moment, staring out through the windshield, then said, "You said you'd been a cop so long you can't remember anything else. So can I ask, why did you become a cop?"

I heaved a sigh, turned my head to look at her. She raised her eyebrows and shrugged.

"I don't really know. I got the idea in high school, I guess. Who knows? After I graduated high school I went on to UTK and got a BS in forensic psychology... and then I applied for a job at the PD. It seemed like the right thing to do. How about you?"

"Retaliation. This redhead didn't make any friends in school, just the opposite, in fact. I was bullied... by the girls and the boys. So I decided I wouldn't take any more crap... not from anyone. What was it Al Capone said? 'You only get so far with a kind word. But you get a lot further with a kind word and a gun.' Maybe I didn't get that quite right, but you get the idea."

"Yeah," I said, "I heard that one too, but I'm not sure old Al is the best role model to quote. But I do understand... and I hate that you were bullied."

She shook her head, stared out through the windshield and said, "Thank you. There wasn't a whole lot I could do about it... not then, anyway. I mean, I'm barely five foot five. Some people think it's fun to push people like me around. I think it's the red hair that makes them do it. Well, I decided to do something about it. I took karate and became a cop."

The way she said it was deadly serious, but it came across as kind of funny.

"Karate?" I smiled. "Are you serious?"

"Oh, I am. Really. I have a black belt, first level, shodan." She turned to look at me and said, "I'm going to tell you a secret. If you repeat it, I'll have to kill you."

"And I believe you," I joked.

"My first day as a rookie cop, when I put on my uniform to go to work that day, when I first put on my weapon and my badge, I stood in front of the mirror in my bedroom and just stared at myself. I don't know how long for. It could have been just a few minutes or twenty minutes before I left and went to work. Isn't that weird?"

"No, not really. And I get it," I said. "I do it myself, usually before I go out on a date which, as I said, isn't very often."

"And then, they paired me with Keith Manners," she said and shook her head, chuckling.

"Keith Manners? He's huge... like almost seven feet tall."

"I know, right?" she said. "We looked like a freaking circus sideshow, but he's such a treasure and I learned a lot from him. I'm not sure if they put me with him to make sure I didn't get hurt or if it was a joke, but he sure kicked this baby bird out of the nest. It was a case of fly or the cat will get you. The key to being a good cop, Keith always said, is doing the unexpected, and that's what I try to do. That's why I was able to take Nathan down. He wasn't expecting it."

Janet looked wistfully out of the side window, then said, "I miss

Keith. I was only with him for a few months before he retired what, three years ago? Then the chief kind of took me under his wing."

"Did you let him know you made detective?"

"Hell yeah. He was the third phone call I made after my mom and my boyfriend," she said, raising her own binoculars. "Uh-oh."

"What, what do you see?"

"Looks like our boy is on the move." Janet pointed.

I put my binoculars to my eyes and watched as Nathan descended the front steps and strutted along the sidewalk toward us, then made a right turn just before reaching the block where we were parked.

"I'll follow him," Janet said.

Before I could stop her, she'd hopped out of the car. She may as well have been holding up a neon sign that read "COPS." Her red hair and pale skin were a beacon in the darkness.

I scanned the street and saw that I wasn't the only one who thought she looked out of place. An old woman in a jogging suit sitting on a porch swing at a house across the street tapped her companion, a female in her early twenties, on the shoulder and pointed at Janet. The younger girl was wearing a tank top and short shorts, both of which left very little to the imagination. The younger woman stood, craned her neck to look, then took out her phone, punched in a number, and began talking.

Janet stood at the corner for a few seconds, looking this way and that, as if she was lost, then bent down, tied her shoe, looked around again and then checked her watch. She stood up, put her hands on her hips, shaking her head, then walked back to the car.

Not bad, Janet, I thought, *but beyond stupid.*

I'll admit she did look lost, like some dumb ass looking to score some weed, or maybe find her boyfriend who told her to meet him at some house party. It was plausible. But what she did wasn't how it should have been done. I had my own rules of surveillance—safety being the priority—and jumping out of the car in a dangerous neighborhood, at any hour, even to shadow a murder suspect, was not one of them.

When she got back in the car, I laid into her.

"That was damn stupid," I said angrily. "Do it again and you'll find yourself back in records as a filing clerk. That pair on the porch spotted you before you got across the road. We're blown now, damn it."

"I'm sorry."

She didn't sound at all sorry.

"I just didn't want to lose him. He went into a convenience store on the corner of the next block. That way," she said as she pointed.

"I mean it, Janet. I don't need for you to get yourself killed. Do it again, and you're gone."

I didn't look at her as I started the car, but I could feel her discomfort.

Too damn bad. Maybe it'll teach her a lesson.

Ever conscious of the pair of women on the porch, I turned on the lights, eased the car forward, made a left, and parked the car a half-block away from the convenience store.

I raised my glasses and took a peek. There were three guys out front, two seated on the floor with their backs against the front wall of the store, and one standing in front of them smoking a cigarette. And so we waited, watching.

We didn't have to wait long. Just a couple minutes later, Nathan appeared through the open door, tapping a pack of cigarettes against his palm, then shaking hands and doing that complicated high five thing with the smoker.

All four were dressed similarly: jeans at half-mast, baggy T-shirts and tennis shoes that probably cost more than a set of tires for the Charger.

A car turned the corner behind us. Bright lights lit up the interior of the Charger. I could actually feel the thud of the bass as the vehicle slowly approached. My heart started to race.

"Get down," I hissed to Janet. When she looked at me like I was crazy, I added, "Do it."

The huge, black SUV rolled slowly by and I suddenly had a horrible feeling that we were about to receive a hailstorm of bullets, but of course that didn't happen. Oh yeah, I reached for my weapon, just in case, but I didn't need it. The huge car cruised on by without incident. I peeked out through the side window, but their tinted windows blocked my view, but not theirs, I was sure.

It was a Cadillac Escalade, one of those huge luxury monstrosities, and it slowly made its way down the street, the rims on the wheels glittered in the light from the streetlamps. The behemoth came to a stop outside the convenience store, and Nathan hopped in through the rear door. The smoker dropped his cigarette, ground it out under his foot, then joined Nathan inside the Caddy. The car pulled away immediately, its tires squealing softly, and turned right onto McCallie Avenue.

"Wow," Janet said, "a Cadillac like that in this neighborhood? Some people pay less in rent than the car payment for that thing. What's it doing here?"

"Hell," I muttered, more to myself than to her, "I bet my rent is less than the car payment... I think it came by specifically to pick up Nathan and his buddy. What do you say we see where that party bus is going?"

"Yes, ma'am," she said, brightly, my earlier admonishments seemingly forgotten. "I know it makes me sound racist, but come on, you don't have to be a genius to figure it out that a hundred-thousand-dollar car in this neighborhood isn't being driven by Mother Teresa."

"Really?" I asked her, dryly.

"You know it."

I didn't turn the headlights on until I saw the Cadillac's taillights disappear around the corner, then I slowly pulled away and followed the Caddy heading north on McCallie toward the Missionary Ridge Tunnel. We exited the tunnel and the Caddy drove on for maybe a mile then made a right onto Germantown Road and headed for I-24.

"Ok, let's see who owns that puppy," Janet said as she radioed in the license plate number.

21

WE DIDN'T SPEAK AS I FOLLOWED THE CADILLAC ONTO THE interstate. I was focused on the cars around me, trying to keep a safe distance while making sure I didn't lose the Caddy. They were driving fast; speeds in excess of seventy-five. The speeds didn't bother me: the Charger Interceptor could handle speeds far in excess of a hundred. It was the speed limit—fifty-five—that did.

"Do you think they know they are being followed?" Janet asked, clicking off her mike.

"No. I think it's just the way they like to drive," I muttered.

The adventure on the expressway lasted only a few minutes until the Caddy swung right at Exit 178 onto Highway 27 toward downtown. We crossed the river heading north and then took the Manufacturer's Road exit at a sedate forty-miles-an-hour... And I knew right then where we were headed.

"Club Suave. I should have known," I muttered. "Hell, we could have saved ourselves the aggravation and just staked the place out. We certainly would have blended in a little better... and why didn't they just take McCallie to the Market Street Bridge? Would have saved them time and a ton of gas money."

Just as we pulled in behind the suspect, dispatch came back with the name of the owner of the car, one Reverend Talbot Montgomery.

Club Suave was located just off a busy street on the North Side. The parking lot was nearly packed so it was much easier for us to blend in.

"Whoa. Did dispatch say the Caddy is registered to a Reverend?" Janet asked, as we watched the car doors open and a half dozen boys from the hood pile out.

"Confirm that," I ordered.

She radioed in and received an immediate confirmative from dispatch.

"I don't care who owns it," she said, setting the mike back in its holder. "I don't believe any of those boys are reverends. You think it's stolen?"

"Stolen?" I said. "Maybe, check with dispatch and see if it's been reported." She did, and it hadn't.

From a row farther back we watched as the driver, a tall skinny kid, Nathan, and the smoker hopped out of the car followed by three other similarly dressed dudes. They looked like a bunch of guys who were out to meet girls, drink some booze and party.

A group of five young women were also heading toward the club entrance. Our six heroes stepped up behind them and the catcalling started.

"Nathan's not acting like a guy who just found out his sister's been murdered," I said. "We've got nothing we can bust them on, other than speeding, and I don't think it would be wise for us to follow them into that club. As I recall, the owners are not big fans of the badge. No matter, let's just sit and watch for a minute." And we did.

I watched as our group approached the entrance. The bouncer looked happy to see them and quickly unhooked the rope allowing them to enter without having to stand in line.

"Looks like they're well known," I said, as handshakes were exchanged. I'd learned early on in my career that it's not what you know that opens doors in this town, it's who you know. And whoever that driver was, the bouncer knew him and the rest of the group well.

Like the Cadillac, Club Suave pulsed with the sound of thudding bass oozing out through the walls. A line of maybe thirty people waited in front of the crimson rope, hoping to be allowed to enter. Young women, most of them black, fidgeted, shifted from one high heel to another, tugging at their short skirts, adjusting and readjusting ample bosoms that were, in most cases, barely confined to the outfits they were wearing.

There were men too, though not so many as the women. Those that weren't with a woman smoked nonchalantly, arrogantly, constantly hitching up their jeans and rubbernecking along the line.

The bouncer, a mountain of a man, was the sole judge, jury, and executioner at the head of the line making sure that no one crossed the velvet rope without his permission.

I checked my watch. It was almost ten-thirty. I shook my head. I'd had enough. I decided Nathan either just didn't give a damn about his dead sister, or he was somehow involved in her death, and so would join my growing list of suspects.

"So what do we do now?" Janet asked as I started the engine.

"We sleep on it," I said. "I'm beat. All tonight has done for us is to confirm Nathan as a suspect and provide us with yet another group of possible suspects: that group that just went into the club with him. We need to find out who was driving the Cadillac. Nathan wouldn't say who his sister's friends from the hood were; maybe we just caught ourselves a break and that's them, though they probably won't be as polite as her new family."

"Some of her new family weren't all that polite either," Janet said, dourly, making me chuckle as we pulled out of the parking lot.

"Ain't that the truth?" I said. "Maybe in the morning we might have a better grasp on things. Right now, I'm bushed."

Janet yawned, nodding, and said, "Yes, ma'am."

And I drove back to the PD to get her car.

"I thought you were tired," she said as I parked and climbed out of the car.

"I am, but after all that coffee..." I shrugged. "A quick bathroom break and then I'm heading home."

"Are you sure you don't need me for anything?"

"No, Janet. Go on home. I'll see you bright and early Monday morning."

She nodded, walked to her car, started the motor, revved it, honked the horn at me, waved and peeled out of the parking lot. I shook my head as I watched her go.

Good thing the chief didn't see that, I thought, smiling to myself as I walked to the rear entrance of the building.

I did need to use the bathroom, but I also wanted to be alone for a while, to mull over what we'd seen that night. I was having a tough time relating Nathan to the owner of that Cadillac Escalade. He didn't belong in it any more than Genevieve belonged in the Chesterton family.

The idea that the Caddy was registered to a Reverend Montgomery was stuck in my head. There was something about that name that was familiar. I'd never been to one of his services, but I knew I'd never get to sleep if I didn't do a little digging. I looked at my watch. It was ten-forty-five.

I need to get on with it or I won't get any sleep anyway. Not that it would matter. I had almost a whole weekend to chill out and rest... and I was ready for it.

You may not believe this, but when I walked into the PD that night, the place was jumping. Janet's words were never truer: the freaks do indeed come out at night, especially on a Friday night. From what I could tell every last one of them was in the police station.

I elbowed my way past the front desk and through a sea of blue uniforms to my office. It was noisy but invigorating. Yeah, that's right. There's something about a police station full of cops and their suspects: drunks, hookers, youngsters with attitudes—male and female, rednecks and the homeless. The noise was louder than it usually was during the daytime. The smell of bad cologne, body odor, and cigarette smoke on the perps mingled with the scent of burnt coffee. The conversation, if you can call it that, was loud and often profane. Shakespeare, I'm sure, would have learned a thing or two had he been present that night.

I grabbed a mug of the crappy coffee, did my thing in the restroom, then went to my office and slammed the door shut, leaned my back against it, laid the back of my head against the wood, closed my eyes, and breathed deeply, the cup of coffee still clenched tightly in my fingers. The quiet inside the room was deafening; my head was throbbing, but only for a minute. I opened my eyes and stared across the room at the storyboard, my back still against the door, and I sipped the scalding hot liquid in the cup... Nope, can't call it coffee; it had to have been made at least a couple of hours ago.

Where the hell do they buy these crappy grounds? I wondered.

Slowly, I began to feel my second wind kick in and I went to work.

I dove into Reverend Talbot Montgomery's background, and it didn't take but a couple of minutes for me to find a very interesting, and perhaps coincidental, link to the Chesterton family. I typed his name into People Search and found that the Reverend "Monty" Montgomery lived... Come on, guess. Where do you think? Yeah... He lived in the same exclusive building as Regina Mae Cottonwell-Chesterton.

Now, maybe I was being a bit ageist, if there is such a thing, and maybe my thinking was getting a little jaded, but I didn't think any of the men that piled out of that Cadillac at Club Suave looked like they were men of the cloth.

Hmm, I thought skeptically as I checked my watch. *It's not quite eleven... I'm thinking it might be worth me paying the Reverend a late-night visit. I wonder if he knows where his Cadillac is? I think he should know, and I think I should be the one to tell him; it's the right thing to do.* I smiled to myself at the thought.

22

"How can I help you, Detective?"

The night doorman at Regina Mae Cottonwell-Chesterton's apartment building looked like he'd stepped out of a beautiful dream. He was tall, with a broad chest, blue eyes and a five o'clock shadow the likes of which you see only in the movies. The sleeves of his jacket stretched tightly as his muscles moved beneath them. His hair, a gorgeous golden color, but close-cropped, suggested he might have done some time in the military.

A marine, maybe? I wondered. *Whatever, he's a fine-looking...*

"I need to talk to one of the tenants... Daniel," I said as I glanced at his shiny brass name tag. "The Reverend Talbot Montgomery."

As much as I wanted to stay and chit-chat with this amazing specimen of the male species I didn't, nor did I ask him for his phone number; nor, unfortunately, did he ask for mine, not that I'd have given it to him... I think. Mixing business and pleasure was never a good idea.

He reached for the phone, but I stopped him.

"I'd prefer that you not notify him. If it won't get you in trouble."

"Would I be placed under arrest for obstructing a police officer?" His blue eyes twinkled.

"You might be," I replied, unable to stop myself from smiling at him.

"Well, that might not be so bad, right?"

His eyes never left mine, but I suddenly had a horrible feeling he knew exactly what I looked like naked.

He swept his hand in the direction of the elevators, indicating I was being allowed to pass, and said, "Second floor, number one."

I thanked him and walked across the hall knowing damn well he was checking me out. It was all I could do to stop myself from doing a runway walk. I pushed the elevator button—it opened immediately—stepped inside and turned around. He smiled and waved playfully. I did the same, and then I felt like an idiot.

"Focus, Kate. This isn't the Dating Game," I scolded myself.

The elevator door opened and I stepped out into a lobby, similar to Regina Mae's, but smaller. The reverend's door was to the left. A small, gold cross hung next to a small brass plate upon which the legend, Rev. Talbot (Monty) Montgomery and Family, was engraved.

And Family? Hmm.

I stepped up to the door and pushed the button. It was one of those video doorbell things. I put my hand over the lens, wondering if the man was already sound asleep.

"Who is it?" a deep voice echoed tinnily through my fingers.

I removed my hand, held up my badge, and identified myself.

The sound of locks opening echoed across the hallway. The door opened to reveal a... let's say, a robust man whose stomach made its appearance before his face.

"Reverend Montgomery?' I asked, holding up my badge.

He nodded. "Yes," he said, frowning. "It's very late, Captain. What can I do for you?"

"It is," I said, "and I'm sorry..."

"It's my son, isn't it? Is he all right? Please tell me he's all right." The man's eyes bugged with worry.

"Is your son driving your Cadillac tonight?" I asked.

"Oh, dear God, don't tell me. Was he in an accident?"

"No, sir," I said firmly. "Your son is fine. May I come in?"

The reverend took a step back, wrapping his maroon silk robe tightly across his flannel pajamas, then stepped aside for me to enter.

Oh... m'God. Are you serious? I thought as I looked around the apartment.

It was all glass, brass—gold paint and plate, I was sure—and mirrors. I felt like I was walking into the Presidential Suite at the Flamingo Hotel in Las Vegas. There was no southern charm about the reverend's residence... more a rather tacky display of the wealth he'd siphoned from the pockets of "the faithful," his congregation.

"What's this all about, Detective? Has my son been arrested?" he said as he led me to a gray leather sofa in the living room. "Please, sit down."

"Arrested?" I asked as I sat down. "That's a strange question. Why would you ask that?"

"Well, you... you're here; it's late and—"

"No, he's not been arrested," I said, interrupting him, "not yet anyway, but I do have a couple questions for you, Reverend. Do you mind if I record our conversation?" I asked as I took my iPad from my bag.

He nodded and sat down opposite me, his back to the wall of windows that overlooked the city.

"Please call me Monty."

"Thank you," I said, uncomfortable with the idea. "I'm investigating the murder of Mrs. Genevieve Chesterton. Her body was found last Saturday morning on the Riverwalk, and I'd also like to talk to your son. Is he here, or is he out driving your Cadillac?"

I watched the color drain from his face.

"Oh, dear Lord. That poor, poor woman," he muttered. "No, Treyshawn, my son, isn't here, and yes, he has my car, with my permission, of course. He went out with some of his friends. He's a popular boy. It comes with the territory when you have a rather well-known family name. I'm sure you understand."

"Yes, sir, I do understand. Who is he with, do you know?"

"No, ma'am. He's basically a good boy, and I trust him. Well, you have to, don't you?" He shrugged, and his belly shook. "I know that it may not be the right thing to do, but his mama, God rest her soul, kept a tight rein on the boy... too tight, I think. Now that she's gone... he's making up for lost time, enjoying life, with his friends, on the streets, unfortunately. I don't like it, but he's an adult and can do pretty much as he wishes, and he has to learn."

He paused, thought for a minute, then continued, "And I feel that if he's to enjoy the Lord's salvation, he must be allowed the freedom... the opportunity to expel the gangster within. To do that he must learn that material things and a life of crime have nothing to offer but pain and damnation. And he *will* learn. I have faith in him."

As I sat there listening to his diatribe, I looked around the room, and it was all I could do not to roll my eyes. I had to bite my tongue. Seated in his luxurious apartment, surrounded by expensive baubles and "material things," the man was the very definition of the word hypocrite, and I dearly wanted to call him out, but I didn't. I wanted him to talk to me, and I already knew that was something he loved to do, so I figured I'd give him plenty of rope, as they say.

"You mentioned his friends," I said. "Would you mind giving me their names?"

"Umm," he wriggled uncomfortably in his seat, as if he was sitting on something sharp. "Well, I don't really know who they are. I know there's Dewayne... and Jamar... but I don't know their last names."

Of course you don't, I thought. *You're full of it. You don't know crap about your son, nor do you want to: out of sight, out of mind.*

"How about Nathan Watkins?" I asked. "Is he one of Treyshawn's friends?"

Monty nodded. His eyebrows lifted. He looked pleased, like a kid about to give a tough schoolteacher the right answer.

This should be interesting.

"Yes, I think so. I met Nathan once. It was maybe three months ago. He came to one of my fundraisers as Treyshawn's guest. They didn't stay long. My son is not interested in my political affiliations. He doesn't understand how the squeaky wheel gets the grease."

I nodded. *So Monty thinks of himself as a politician, does he? Why am I not surprised? Okay, so let's try this…*

"Did your son know Genevieve Chesterton? Did he ever mention the name?" I asked, watching his face, looking for a tell. I was disappointed. He didn't even blink.

"No," he said. "Not that I recall. But then, he doesn't talk much about his lady friends." Monty replied, smiling bashfully. "Boys always think they know more than their fathers when it comes to women. Don't you agree?"

"I wouldn't know, Reverend," I replied, dryly. "I am a woman."

"But you're also a police officer, and I would have thought you'd have known about such things."

He was right. I have a degree in forensic psychology, so I did know, and I believed him when he said his son didn't talk about his girlfriends, but there was something about Monty that was rubbing me the wrong way. I pressed on.

"What does your son do for a living, Reverend?"

He hesitated, then said, "He's unemployed at the moment, but helps me out whenever I have a need; I give him a small allowance."

"Indeed, and how small is small?"

Again, he hesitated, then seemed to give in to the inevitable and said softly, "One thousand dollars a week."

Holy cow. Are you serious? That's almost what I make.

I stared at him, disbelieving, then finally, I asked, "How about Genevieve's mother-in-law, Mrs. Regina Mae Cottonwell-Chesterton? You must know her; she lives in this building. Have you ever spoken to her?" I watched his reaction.

"I've only seen her. I have never spoken to her other than to say good morning or good evening. She's usually escorted by her son. A tall fellow, rather skinny, and like Treyshawn, a bit of a mama's boy, from his appearance. But, there are worse things to be, I suppose." He chuckled.

"Does Treyshawn know Mrs. Cottonwell-Chesterton's son? His name's Eddie, by the way."

"I mean no offense, Detective, but my boy doesn't associate much with his white brothers. I like to think it's because it reminds him too much of his mama."

"His mother was white?" I asked.

He ran his hand over his short salt-and-peppered hair, smiled sadly, then nodded and said, "We met at church, oh, it would have been almost thirty years ago now. I knew she was to be my wife the second I laid eyes on her..." he paused, looked to be deep in thought, then continued, "She was a very Godly woman, my rock, you might say. And she had a way with people; she was not afraid to ask the local politicians to dig deep in return for our support... I do miss her so."

"What happened to her?" *Not that I care, but keep on talking, my friend.*

"Cancer. It runs in her family," he replied sadly.

"That's too bad," I said. "I'm truly sorry... Monty."

I looked at my watch. It was a quarter to midnight.

"Please don't be offended," I said, "but I need to ask you: does your son date white women?"

"I... er... I don't know. I don't think so. If he does, he hasn't met any worth bringing home."

"Has your son ever been arrested?"

"No, ma'am. Not that boy." He sighed and shook his head. "He's a good boy. He *is* a good boy. Not the brightest, I'll admit, but he stays out of trouble." He looked at me, must have seen something in my expression, because he said, softly, "I can assure you he had nothing to do with this girl's death."

"Your son was seen, earlier this evening, with Nathan Watkins. Did you know he was Genevieve Chesterton's brother?"

"I did not... no!"

"They were seen entering Club Suave, together. That's not the kind of place 'good boys' frequent. Genevieve also used to frequent Club Suave. Treyshawn, being Nathan's friend, must have known her. Therefore, you can understand why I am asking these questions." I watched his eyes, his face: nothing. He didn't seem to be too bothered that his son was patronizing a place like Club Suave.

"Yes, Detective. I totally understand," he said, looking down at his hands. "But Treyshawn is young, younger than his years. He's twenty-six years old and still thinks like a teenager, and not necessarily with his brain."

That's something to consider, I thought, as I watched his face. *I need to talk to this man-boy.*

"I'm sorry for Mrs. Cottonwell-Chesterton's loss, and her son's. I'll be sure to offer my condolences the next time I see her. And I'll say prayers for them and Genevieve. She attends a different church, but I believe God listens to all our prayers." He took another deep breath and stared at me.

"Do you know where Treyshawn was last Friday night?" I asked softly.

The Reverend Monty might have been a snake-oil salesman in the world of religion, but I didn't get the feeling he was trying to hide anything about his son. But I did get the impression they weren't close.

He thought about it before he answered, and then said, "He was out, with his friends, I suppose. I know, because I was up late myself, watching Mel Gibson's movie, *The Passion of the Christ.* I've watched it many times... Many, many times."

"What time did he come home?"

He shrugged, thought for a minute, then said, "I'm not sure. I do know it must have been very late because I was very late going to bed, and he wasn't home..." He didn't finish what he was saying.

"And what time did you go to bed?" I asked, keeping up the pressure.

He shook his head, then said, "A little after midnight, I think."

"Do you know where he was, where he went?"

He shook his head, then clasped his hands together in his lap and hung his head but said nothing more. He was thinking deeply about something. What, I didn't know. Maybe it was the movie. Maybe it was something else, something he didn't want me to know.

There was no point in trying to grill him further. The Reverend Talbot "Monty" Montgomery was, I think, being as honest as he could be, but I was pretty sure he knew he wasn't in possession of all the facts, and it was bothering him.

It was time for me to go. I tapped the button on my iPad to stop the recording, rose to my feet, and slipped the tablet into my bag.

"Thank you for your time and patience, Reverend," I said. "I really do appreciate it, and your cooperation. If you can think of anything that might help me with my investigation, please give me a call."

I handed him a business card.

"I will have to talk to your son. He isn't planning any long trips, I hope?"

"No, ma'am," he replied. "Treyshawn will be available to speak to you whenever you call. I'll make sure of it. And if you need me for anything further, please don't hesitate to ask."

I offered him my hand and thanked him, and I left him standing at the open door.

The elevator descended, the door opened, and I stepped out and looked around for the gorgeous doorman, but the lobby was empty.

Feeling a little let down, I made my way to the revolving exit door and was just about to step inside when I heard a noise behind me. Automatically, I turned and looked to see what it was, and got the shock of my life.

A door behind the front desk, just a few yards to the right, had opened and two people had stepped out of what appeared to be a maintenance room and suddenly I was staring, eye-to-eye, at Regina

Mae Cottonwell-Chesterton dressed in her robe. Behind her was a somewhat disheveled doorman.

23

OH YEAH, I THOUGHT, AS I STEPPED BACK OUT OF THE REVOLVING door. *Now that I need to investigate.*

Regina Mae Cottonwell-Chesterton said something I couldn't hear to the dreamboat who was now back behind the front desk, and then she sprinted to her private elevator.

"Mrs. Chesterton!" I shouted.

But Regina Mae took no notice. She tugged at her silk robe, strutted into the elevator, turned around, pressed the button, and then her eyes locked on mine and held them for a split second before the doors slid shut.

I saw panic in those eyes, or was it defiance? I whirled around and stepped over to the front desk where Mr. Muscles was fumbling with his shirt buttons and trying to tuck in his shirttails at the same time.

"Well," I said. "Just look at you. You should zip up while you're at it. So, Regina Mae? One of the perks of working the night shift?"

"It's not what you think," he said, jerking up on the zipper.

"You should be careful doing it like that," I said. "You could lose your... Well, you could hurt yourself. So, what is it you think I think?"

"Regina and I have known each other a long time. I've been a doorman here for almost six years and—"

"And you know when her husband's out of town," I said, cutting him off. "Just as you know the nightly routines of most if not all of the tenants. Tell me what else do you know and who else are you servicing, Mister..."

"Racine. Daniel Racine." His cheeks were flushed, and he was sweating profusely.

The result of getting caught or his wild interlude with Regina Mae? I wondered.

"Look," he said, smiling at me, "you've got it all wrong. I—"

"Of course I have," I said sarcastically, interrupting him. "So tell me, how often does Regina Mae visit you?" I asked as I took a small notepad from my bag.

"Am I going to lose my job?"

"That depends on how honest you are with me, Mr. Racine. Now tell me, how often does she come down here and what exactly is going on?"

Daniel Racine was as dumb as he was beautiful. He spilled the beans on poor Regina Mae as if he was trying to save himself from the electric chair. They'd been carrying on for almost eighteen months. It had started out as harmless flirting but quickly intensified when Regina Mae turned up at the front desk one night wearing nothing but a silk robe.

"It wasn't my fault," he said, self-consciously trying to tidy his hair with his fingers. "She, she initiated it," he stammered.

"Oh really?" I asked, with real interest. "And how, exactly, did that work?"

"I'm not lying. Look, women... they like me," he said, without a hint of modesty. "They do. I saw the way you looked at me when you came in, so I flirted with you. You didn't seem to mind. After all, you flirted back. It's in my nature to—"

"To sleep with the lonely females in the building?" I interrupted him.

"*No.* Not at all."

"Tell me something," I said. "How many women in this building are you sleeping with, Mr. Racine?"

He took a deep breath and ran his fingers through his hair. "Three, including Regina Mae... Are you going to have me fired?"

"On the contrary. I'm going to use you, Daniel. Not unlike the horny housewives in this, this Peyton Place are using you... Oh, now don't get the wrong idea," I said when I saw him begin to grin. "You'll be keeping your pants on. Understand?" I smirked.

"Yes, ma'am."

"Good, now listen up. When Regina Mae asks what we talked about, and she will, you're going to tell her that you didn't say anything to me about your affair with her. Understand?"

"Yes, ma'am." Daniel nodded, his eyes bulging like he suddenly understood a difficult math problem.

"I want you to convince her she has nothing to worry about," I said. "And I want you to call me when Treyshawn Montgomery comes home."

"Yes... *What?*" he asked, frowning. "Why?"

"Just be a good boy, Daniel, and do as you're told, and don't ask questions. You're in enough trouble with Regina Mae. You wouldn't want to add me to the mix as well, now would you?"

He shook his head, somewhat enthusiastically, so I thought, and I had to smile at him as I slid my business card across the top of the desk toward him.

He let out a deep breath, looked at the card, picked it up, then locked eyes with me and said, "So you're not going to rat me out?"

"Not tonight," I replied and turned and walked toward the front door.

"Wait," he called after me.

I stopped, turned around, and stared at him. "Yes?"

"I don't suppose you'd let me take you to dinner... No, of course you wouldn't."

I shook my head, smiling at his audacity, and then I left him. He truly was a lovely man.

What a shame, I thought as I walked to my car.

It didn't matter to me that he wasn't too bright. I could have easily overlooked that character flaw for two, maybe even three months. But I can't tolerate a cheater. The sad thing about it was, though, that I knew he didn't think he was cheating. No, he would argue that it was Regina Mae who was the cheater. He was just enjoying the ride... Sorry, no pun intended. He wasn't married, so he wasn't doing anything wrong. Yeah, I'd heard it before from a man even better looking and certainly smarter than Daniel Racine.

"But still not smart enough," I muttered to the night as I pushed the memory of my lost love out of my mind.

I got in my car and drove toward home. The streets were pleasantly quiet, just a few cars traveling along with me. I wondered how many of them were heading home after an illicit encounter. *Bastards!*

"That's a very negative way of looking at things, Kate," I said to myself as I spotted a twenty-four-hour liquor store. I pulled in and a few minutes later pulled out again with a couple of bottles of what I thought would be a nice red wine—it was on sale for six dollars, regular price fifteen—and two bags of pork rinds. Had they sold ice cream I would have snagged a pint of chocolate-chip—it would complement the red wine admirably. But they didn't so I figured I'd make do with what I had, and then go to bed.

Oh, dear Lord. What a way to live. I really do need to get out more.

Once inside the privacy of my own apartment, I decided to forgo the shower, pour myself a glass of wine and just flop. So I did. I unscrewed the cap on the bottle—now if that doesn't tell you something, I don't know what will—filled the glass, took a long slow sip, my eyes closed, and savored the taste of decadence... It crossed my mind to really pamper myself and drink and eat in a tub full of hot, scented bubbles, but I was too exhausted to make the effort. Instead, I sat down at my coffee table, my legs stretched out in front of me and, with an old episode of Star Trek playing on the television in the background, I wrote down my thoughts about what had transpired that evening.

It had indeed been quite an evening, what with our stakeout, the wild ride on Interstate 24, my interview with the Reverend Monty and finally my run-in with Gorgeous George... Daniel.

As I perused what I'd written, I realized my list of suspects was growing, almost exponentially, but I was still no closer to finding Genevieve's killer. And I didn't see that changing anytime soon.

I picked up the now empty bottle of red, looked at it, shook my head, felt my eyes click first to one side then the other, trying to catch up with my face. *Wow, that's some powerful stuff,* I thought as I walked a little unsteadily to the kitchen and dropped the bottle into the garbage can.

"So what if I'm buzzed?" I argued with the image of Captain Kirk. "I think I'm more honest, more forthright when I'm buzzed. Let's face it, the only people who are ever truly honest are drunks and children. Right? Hmm, maybe I should try plying my suspects with booze before I question them." *That's a great idea,* I thought, blearily. "I'll run it by the chief. Maybe he'll increase my budget to cover the cost," I giggled.

Oh, yeah? I thought. *And maybe he'll just kick your silly ass out.*

The sheer stupidity of the idea made me laugh out loud and say to Kirk, "I'd love to talk to Edward Eaton Chesterton the Second while he's under the 'fluence of a little extra sauce."

That was the last thing I remembered until I woke up in bed the next morning with a blinding headache.

24

THE WEEKEND PASSED UNEVENTFULLY FOR A CHANGE: NO CALL-outs, no late-night phone calls, not even one from Janet. I ran six miles early on Saturday morning, and again on Sunday. The rest of the time I spent relaxing, but always on the alert for the dreaded phone call; it never came, and I couldn't remember the last time that had happened. So, I should have been bright and perky when I arrived at my office early that Monday in May, but I wasn't.

Yes, I'd been able to relax. I ate sensibly, didn't drink a single drop of wine, or any other alcoholic beverage, and I slept well, but when I got out of bed that Monday morning, I was blessed with a headache that bordered on a migraine, so what was wrong? I couldn't figure it out. I took three aspirin, washed them down with black coffee, hit the shower, and then dressed for work: blue jeans, light blue blouse, light-weight tan blazer.

I stopped on the way to the office to grab a large coffee to go, then parked the car in my spot, and pushed my way through the rear door into the building.

"Hey, Captain," Randy Lewis called as I walked out of the elevator. "What's with the sunglasses? Paparazzi following you?" Randy was one of my favorite uniformed cops.

"Very funny," I snapped as I slowly made my way through the crowded room toward my office, trying to hang onto my bag and iPhone and to not slop the overfull, extra-large cup of steaming hot coffee. It had a lid on it, but you know how reliable those are, right? And it was so hot I didn't dare sip it for fear of losing all sensation in my taste buds.

"Rough night, Captain?" some wag at the far side of the room shouted.

"Who's the lucky guy?" another yelled. "I'd hate to see what he looks like this morning."

"No guy, asshole. I have a headache, so shut the hell up and find something useful to do." I rolled my eyes behind my sunglasses, then realized they couldn't see the move.

"Geez, you guys are hilarious," I muttered to the group of grinning uniforms hanging around the water cooler, waiting for their shift to start.

Finally, I made it into my office, my refuge, but wouldn't you know it, little miss perky was already there waiting for me.

"Don't start," I said, testily, before Janet could speak. "I have a headache, so sit quietly for a minute or go someplace else."

"Yes, ma'am," she whispered.

I immediately felt sorry for being so snarky.

"Sorry, Janet. Just give me a few minutes to drink a little coffee, okay?"

And so we sat there; me with my eyes closed sipping on the still scalding coffee, and Janet thumbing through Pinterest on her iPhone.

Finally, I opened my eyes, set the coffee on my desk, and looked at her. I closed my eyes again, rolled them under the lids so she couldn't see it, sighed inwardly and said, "Okay, Janet. I can see you're dying to tell me something. What is it?"

"So, I did some digging on Reverend Talbot 'Monty' Montgomery. He has a son named—"

"Treyshawn. I know."

I told her about my late night on Friday. I did, of course, leave out the part where I flirted with the doorman. I did tell her how I caught Regina Mae making a late-night booty call to avail herself of the amenities, the hunky doorman.

"*NO WAY!*" she shrieked, and pain speared through my brain. "You're lying," she gasped.

"What?" I asked, my eyes barely open. "I don't lie... well, only when I need to, but why in the world would I lie about something like that?"

"That kind of stuff only happens in movies," Janet squeaked. "So, are you going to use it to squeeze her for more information? No wait! I can do it... Can I do it, Kate, please, please? I could wear a wire or something?"

"Janet, I love your enthusiasm, but you need to calm down, take it easy. I need to—"

"I'll try," she said, interrupting me. I know she heard me, but she didn't hear me, if you understand what I mean. "This isn't nearly as juicy," she said, "but I ran the Montgomerys through the databa—"

"Please, Janet, stop," I said, putting my hands over my ears. "You're killing me. Go get the others. There's no point in going over everything twice."

She jumped to her feet and left and then returned ten minutes later, followed by the rest of the team: Hawk, Anne, and Lenny. I waited until they were seated and looking at me expectantly, and I told them to take notes. Then I related the events of the previous Friday: our stakeout at Nathan Watkins' home, the Cadillac, Treyshawn and my interview with Monty Montgomery... and I glossed over my encounter with Dirty Dan and Regina Mae.

While I talked, I stood and brought the storyboard up to date. I added the names of Nathan Watkins, the Reverend Monty, and Treyshawn.

"So," I said, stepping away from the board and staring at it, "this is what we have: six people of interest including our prime suspect,

Eddie Chesterton and the mysterious Frenchman he so obligingly dropped on us, but let's not forget that the murder could just have been a random act of violence... although the method would tend to negate that. And I think there's still something we're missing. The questions we have to answer are twofold. First one: who benefits from Genevieve's death?"

I looked around the room. Janet was nibbling on the eraser at the end of her pencil; Lenny stared at me over the screen of his laptop; Anne had her legs crossed and her arms folded; Hawk was leaning back in his chair, his eyes half-closed and I wondered for a minute if he was asleep. He wasn't.

"Well?" I prodded.

"I... don't think anyone does," Janet said hesitantly. "She had no money or property of her own. There was a small life insurance policy... well, small for that family, two-hundred-and-fifty thousand. That's a drop in the ocean for them, even for Eddie. Not a motive, I shouldn't think. It's less than his annual allowance. No one gains, in my opinion."

"That's true," I said, "so then the question becomes: Why did she have to die, and why did she have to die in such a gruesome way? Was the act premeditated, an act of opportunity, or a random act by a mugger? It wouldn't be the first time, would it? So, what could be the motive? Not money. Revenge, maybe? Hate? Love? Or just plain old rejection?"

I paused, waited to see if anyone would jump in. One did.

"You left one out," Hawk said.

Everyone turned to look at him.

"Oh?" I said. "Do tell."

"I think it was a professional hit."

"And why's that?" I asked.

"Look at the marks on her neck," he said, pointing at one of the autopsy photos.

"Okay, I'm looking, so?"

"Looks like it was done with a garrote to me, a short loop of thin twine, like this." He took a piece of black twine from his pocket and tied the ends together to make it a loop, then he threaded it around the fingers of both hands, and continued, "Also, see how the ligature marks are slightly angled upward from front to back, and notice the position of the bruises where his knuckles bit into her neck. He was tall, taller than her, and she was... how tall was she?"

I looked at the autopsy report and said, "five-ten."

Hawk nodded and said, "And she was wearing four-inch heels, as I recall. That puts her at six-two... Stand up a minute, Anne."

She gave him a funny look, but she did as she was asked. Hawk stood, left his seat and went to stand behind her.

"How tall are you, Anne?" he asked.

"Five-nine, why?"

"Five-nine," he said, nodding, and you're wearing..." he looked down at her feet, "flats. I'm five-eleven, so we're of comparable heights to the vic and her killer. Now look..."

He stood behind her, clenched his fists, the loop of twine still wrapped around his fingers, slipped the garrote over her head and pulled it tight, placing his fists on either side of her neck, his elbows down, his forearms against her back.

"See what I mean?" he said. "He would have used his forearms against her back and his fists against her neck for leverage. We're looking for a guy at least six-two, maybe even a little taller."

He removed the loop from around Anne's neck, and they both sat down again.

"That could be both Eddie and Nathan," I said.

"And Treyshawn," Janet piped up.

"Or the Frenchman," Hawk said, returning to his seat. "He could have been hired by either Wheaton or the old man. If Eddie knew about him, Wheaton would certainly have known too."

"We don't know how tall he is," I said, "or if he even exists. Janet's right, Treyshawn is tall enough, so are Nathan and Eddie."

"But you've just said, they don't have motive," Anne said. "Why would her brother want to kill her? Why would her husband, or some friend of her brother's? It makes no sense. A professional hit, though..."

"I told you," I said. "Love, hate, lust, revenge. We still don't know what's in any of their heads. We already know Wheaton's a predator, so he could have lusted after her, been rejected, and wanted revenge. So could Treyshawn, for that matter, or his two friends."

You'll be believing your own BS next, Kate, I thought, grimly.

I stared at Hawk, mulling it over. He was right, why would they want to kill her, and so horribly? But I still wasn't buying it.

"Okay," I said. "Let's suppose you're right. Who would want to hire a professional killer?" I already knew the answer, but I wanted to see what Hawk would say.

"Old man Chesterton, of course," Hawk said.

Oh yeah, I was right. I shook my head.

"I don't see it, Hawk. Why, what would be his motive?"

"You interviewed the bigoted, racist old bastard, so you tell me. You think he wanted a black grandson or granddaughter inheriting his stash? Hell no. My money's on him and his Frenchman."

I stared at him, as did the others. I hesitated, then said, "Okay, Hawk. I'll buy in. You and Anne find the Frenchman, and quickly."

He nodded but said nothing.

"How about Wheaton's alibi?" I asked him.

It was Anne that answered. She flipped through the screens on her iPad and then said, "He was with a Lucy Weston. She lives in a gated community off Highway 8. According to her, the subject arrived at her home around eight-thirty on Friday evening May third and didn't leave until after nine the following morning, Saturday. So, he's in the clear."

"Is she credible?" I asked, looking at one and then the other.

Neither of them answered, though Hawk shrugged.

"Oh come on, people. Either she is or she isn't. If she isn't, then—"

"I wouldn't trust her with my dirty laundry," Hawk said. "She's twenty years younger than he is and in it for his money. Sure, she's going to protect him; as in protecting her investment, if you can call selling your body an investment."

"Sheesh," Janet said. "Why don't you tell us what you really think."

"So," I said to Hawk, "was she lying or not?"

He lowered his head, closed his eyes and slowly shook his head, then he looked up at me and said, helplessly, "I don't know, Kate. Unless we can prove she's lying, we have to take her word for it and rule him out as the actual killer. But let's not forget, he could have hired it done."

I nodded. "I'm not ruling him out, not yet anyway. Lenny." I turned to look at him. "Any luck finding those two girls Wheaton supposedly assaulted?"

"Working on it," he said.

I stared at him, "Any idea when you might know something?"

"As soon as I can, Captain."

"I want you to dig into old man Chesterton's company. I want backgrounds on all his senior staff, especially any with French-sounding names."

"You got it."

Geez, I thought inwardly. I heaved a huge sigh. *This guy is tough to deal with... I wonder if it's me? Maybe he doesn't like me. Okay, tough; he's going to have to suck it up and deal with it.*

I sat down, swiveled my chair so I could see the storyboard, stared at it making mental notes, then I turned again to face my team.

"Okay," I said, making notes on a yellow pad. "Hawk, Anne, finding the Frenchman is your number one priority, but I also want you to check Nathan Watkins' alibi. He claims he was with friends at a place called Sheppy's. Do you know it?"

"Yup!" Hawk said, nodding.

"Good, and while you're at it, see if you can find Treyshawn's two friends..." I checked my notes, "Dewayne and Jamar and interview them both, separately. Find out what they were doing that night, who they were with. I want to know specifically what Treyshawn was doing that night. Janet and I will deal with Treyshawn himself. That doorman should have called me by now. If he... well, never mind." I didn't want to get into all the details right then.

"Janet," I continued and she looked up at me, expectantly. "What did you find out about the Montgomerys?"

"Well," Janet said, "as I started to say earlier, I ran the Montgomerys through the database. Neither one has priors. There are a lot of political affiliations, but—"

She was interrupted by my phone ringing.

"Maybe this is my doorman," I said, looking at the 'unknown number' flag on the iPhone screen. "I told Daniel to call the minute Treyshawn got home, but I have a feeling he's one slippery—"

I answered the call, "Captain Gazzara."

"*Captain Gazzara*, what in the hell do you think you are doing?"

Well, it certainly wasn't the doorman.

"Excuse me?" I snapped, sending spears of pain around the back of my eyes.

"I received a phone call from my daughter-in-law. She said that you were skulking around her apartment at all hours of the night spying on her. We're not talking surveillance here, Captain. We're talking downright harassment."

Geez, it's the old man!

"Mr. Chesterton?" I asked.

"Of course it's Mr. Chesterton! Who the hell else would it be? Now unless you have cause to be slinking around her apartment building, and I'm confident that you don't, you will leave me with no choice but to report you to your superiors."

"Mr. Chesterton, I go wherever the trail leads me. It just so happens that—"

"It just so happens, Miss Gazzara, that your trail crossed the path of the biggest man-whore in all of Tennessee, Daniel Racine. That doorman has been through more women than the revolving door in the lobby." Chesterton stopped talking, took a deep breath, cleared his throat, and then continued, "If you think you can pump that shit-for-brains for information by sleeping with him, I'll have both your jobs."

"What?"

"My daughter-in-law may not be running on all cylinders, but I won't tolerate my kin being harassed. Now, I know you've become quite comfortable working with the neighborhood darkies and that you're reluctant to arrest any of them. You're one of those "woke" cops I'm always hearing about, I'm sure, but I'm telling you now that I show no preference for men or women when it comes to throwing the hammer down."

"Are you threatening me, Mr. Chesterton?" I asked.

"It ain't a threat to tell an incompetent to do their damn job," he snarled. "If I find out you've been skulking around my daughter-in-law's apartment without probable cause, I'll have that shiny badge of yours and you'll be lucky to get a job as a security guard at Roscoe's Coat Factory." Then the line went dead.

I looked around the room. As far as I could tell, only Janet had heard the diatribe.

"Okay, people," I said, "go get 'em. I'll check in with you later."

I waited until the door closed and then looked at Janet and laughed out loud, suffering yet another stab of pain as a result.

"Oh... My... God," Janet said, her eyes wide. "What was that all about? He threatened you. We can arrest him for that. I'll go get him, right now. Just gimme the word, Kate."

I shook my head, then said, "Nope, that was just too funny. I needed a good laugh, and anyway I have a better idea."

"We're going to visit Regina Mae, right?" Janet asked. I swear she was almost salivating at the idea.

"No. Granddad Chesterton said to leave the poor delicate peach alone. We're going to go and talk to his grandson."

I stood, grabbed my iPad, adjusted my badge on my belt, and took a deep breath. Oh yes, I was pissed off that Chesterton had the temerity to make such a call, but I wasn't the least bit threatened by the old man. He didn't know why I was at the apartment building that night, and that was good. I intended to let it stay that way, at least for now.

Every once in a while, when I became angry, I'd channel my inner Dirty Harry. This was one of those times. Maybe it was my elevated state of emotion that finally rid me of the headache, but suddenly it was gone, and I was ready to take on the world.

But, like all good plans, this one went awry when the chief showed up in my office.

"Detective Toliver, I need to talk to Captain Gazzara in private, if you'd give us a moment, please."

My first thought was that Granddad Chesterton had indeed put in a call to the chief and threatened to file charges against me and the entire department if the chief didn't put a muzzle on me.

"I received a call from Mrs. Evelyn Karl yesterday. You remember her, of course. It seems she's nominated you for the Chattanooga Police Officer of the Year award."

"Evelyn Karl?" I said, just a little stunned at the news. "Yes, I remember her... What on earth?" *Officer of the year? Yay,* I thought sarcastically, *that's a first and one I can do without.*

"Oh, good lord, Chief. Do I have to?"

He smiled. "Of course you do. Why wouldn't you?"

I simply shrugged and basically accepted my fate.

Evelyn Karl's granddaughter, Molly, was a runaway. We, that is I, found her in a crack house and returned her to her grandmother. She went to rehab, I think. Quite frankly I was sure I'd be hearing from Evelyn Karl again, but only to tell me the girl ran away again. Molly was your typical problem child.

It was a sad story. The girl was a product of a broken family, a black family. The father had left them just after Molly was born. The mother had questionable and an insatiable taste in men so grandma stepped in and tried to raise the child.

It was a story we cops hear many times during our careers. Evelyn reported her missing and I caught the case, one of Henry Finkle's last favors, and I say that with tongue in cheek. Anyway, I didn't have much hope of finding her. I figured she was a runaway and if she was, I was pretty well certain she was in the hands of a pimp sex trafficker who had her drugged and for sale on the streets.

I can't say I did anything differently than I have for other parents who tell me their child hasn't come home. All I can remember is that I called Evelyn Karl every other day to tell her where I was going and what I was doing. It was only blind luck that I even stumbled across Molly. I was called out to an armed robbery, and wouldn't you know it; one of the witnesses was a scrawny girl that vaguely resembled Molly's photograph.

One of the uniforms took her statement, but she was gone before I could talk to her. It wasn't hard to find her though. When I walked into that crack house that afternoon they scattered like roaches, all but the scrawny kid. She wasn't high, but she would have been if I hadn't intervened.

"Molly?" I asked, crouching down beside her.

"Yeah?"

"You ready to go home?"

She looked up at me with tears in her eyes and nodded.

"Would you like me to take you to your grandmother? She's been looking for you."

"Yeah." That was all she said.

She didn't talk in the car on the way to the station. When we arrived I asked her if she'd like some water or a Coke, but she shook her head. When her grandmother walked in, however, it was like a gate opened. Molly ran to her, crying and babbling and apologizing... and so did Evelyn. It was very touching.

So I had Evelyn sign the papers, gave her the address of a rehab facility where she could get Molly some help, and suggested she take her to the hospital for a checkup. She said she would do just that, and I let it go. I didn't really think she would, but once I handed the kid over it was out of my hands, so I went back to working on the real cases, the murders, rapes, you know, the stuff that makes the news, good for the TV stations and ratings.

I never gave Evelyn or her granddaughter a second thought. Not until now

"Well, I can't tell Mrs. Karl what to do, but I don't need this, not now, Chief."

"Of course you do. You want my job someday, don't you? You need to sign a couple of forms and confirm her statement."

"Well, okay, I guess." Was all I could think of to say. *Me Chief of Police? That's a hoot.*

"They'll be in my office tomorrow morning. I've got to sign off on them, too. Any time you have a few minutes."

He put his hand on the doorknob and I had hoped that was the end of it. But, of course, it wasn't.

"Tell me, Kate: how's the Chesterton case going? Good news, I hope?"

"If no news is good news, then yes, Chief. Good news."

"Smartass," he said, smiling. "Keep me informed. No nasty surprises, okay?"

"Yes, sir... and no, sir."

He smiled again, nodded, opened the door and stepped out into the corridor.

"Everything okay, Cap?" Janet asked, opening the door and poking her nose inside.

"Grab your badge and let's go."

A few minutes later we were in the car and headed west in the direction of Eddie Chesterton's apartment.

25

"I don't think I'd like to live in an apartment building with an arcade in the lobby," Janet said as we walked inside.

"Oh, yes? Why is that?"

"Well, think about it. You can get your dry cleaning here. Your groceries here... well some, at that convenience store. You can get a coffee here, have a drink here. Drinks lead to talking to strangers. That can lead to hookups. If everyone in your building is staying close to home, it could become one big, nasty, incestuous group," she said with her lips pulled down at the corners as she studied everyone walking around. "Gross. I'll bet fifty percent of these people have slept together. If not literally then by two degrees of separation."

Oh yeah, I had to laugh at that, especially when I thought about Regina Mae and Dirty Dan.

"You don't need an arcade for that... Wow, Janet, you have a weird way of thinking. You came up with all that just by observing the convenience store and the dry cleaner?" I asked.

"I did." She lifted her chin proudly.

I grinned and said, "You amaze me, Toliver."

"I amaze myself," she said as she stepped aside for me to enter the elevator.

I stood outside Eddie's door, put my finger to my lips and looked at Janet, then put my ear to the door and listened. I could hear the soft sounds of cool jazz, and possibly the clinking of glasses, but no voices. Well, it was a little too early for drinks, although Eddie did offer me one the first visit.

I knocked on the door and covered the peephole with my hand.

"Who is it?" Eddie Chesterton barked; he sounded frustrated.

"Eddie? It's Captain Gazzara. We need to talk."

The door opened a crack, but the chain was still on.

"Come on, Eddie. Open the door. Let us in."

The door closed and I heard the sound of the chain being removed, then it opened again, and there he was in all his glory.

"My Lord, Eddie. Don't you ever get dressed?"

He tugged at the sleeves and the belt of the same robe he'd been wearing the first time I talked to him. His hair was disheveled, his eyes bloodshot, and he needed a shave.

"What do you want this time?" he said as he turned his back on us and walked unsteadily to the kitchen.

"I need answers to some questions," I said as I tapped my iPad.

"I'm going to record the interview. You okay with that, Eddie?"

He shrugged, and told me, "yeah, whatever," then he took a coffee cup from a small cabinet. His hand shook as he poured his coffee; the man was nervous. He kept glancing toward what I assumed must be his bedroom.

I read the date, time, and those present, into the recording app, and then introduced Janet. "This is Sergeant Toliver." I jerked my thumb toward Janet. "Sergeant, this is Mr. Chesterton, Eddie, as he likes to be called."

She nodded at him and said, "I'll start the Q and A with who's in the bedroom?" Janet asked.

"No one," Eddie snapped.

Janet wasn't about to play games.

"Well let's see, shall we?"

With her hand on her weapon, she stepped over to the bedroom door and knocked loudly on it.

"Chattanooga Police!" she shouted. "Come out with your hands up... Now!"

Seconds later the door opened and a young woman emerged wearing nothing but skimpy lace underwear. Her skin was flawless, the color of creamy coffee, and her hair was weaved into a fantastic French braid that reached almost to her waist.

"So soon, Eddie?" I asked. "What's your name, honey?"

"Camille Bolton." She kept her hands up. Her nails were long, bright green daggers.

"Camille," Janet said, "put your hands down and take a seat on the couch."

"She's just a friend," Eddie shouted. "She doesn't have anything to do with anything!"

"Hush," I said. "The neighbors will hear you."

I sat down opposite the girl. She was gorgeous. I couldn't take my eyes off her. *No... nothing like that, for Pete's sake. She was lovely, and I was wondering what the hell she was doing with a jerk like Eddie.*

"Camille, how do you know Eddie?"

"We just met last night," she said. "I mean, we knew each other from the club, but we just hooked up last night. He said he'd just broke up with his girlfriend."

Her eyes bounced back and forth from me to Janet and back again, then she seemed to gain confidence and said, "Look, I don't know what he's into, but I ain't got nothing to do with it. Can I get my clothes on?"

I nodded and said, "Go ahead. Janet, go with her. Keep an eye on her."

She looked harmless enough but looks can be deceiving, and I wasn't about to take any chances. Anyway, she didn't seem to mind the company, but she scowled at Eddie like an angry cat; he visibly withered under her glare.

"What are you doing here, Detective?" he said angrily. "I told you it was my grandfather who had my wife killed. Why haven't you arrested him yet?"

"Eddie, your wife has been dead little more than a week and you've already got some poor girl in your bed? And you lied to her. You told her you'd broken up with your girlfriend. That wasn't nice of you, Eddie, now was it?" I asked like I was a disappointed mother. "You can see how I might find that suspicious, can't you?"

And then I heard laughter coming from the bedroom. It sounded like Camille. It seemed that she and Janet were getting along quite well.

"I'm lonely," he whined. "You don't know what it's like, coming home to an empty apartment, waking up in the morning and Genevieve's not here. I miss her. I needed some company that's all. No big deal. I just didn't know what else to do."

"Some people go to church, Eddie. Some people join a therapy group. Some even take a few days, weeks, months just to mourn and grieve and get their mind around the fact that their loved one is gone. I'm just spit-balling here." I smirked. "In all the times I've had to break the bad news to a loved one, never once did anyone go right out and pick up a newer model. That's pretty damn cold, Eddie."

"I know how it looks," he stammered.

"Oh yeah? How does it look, Eddie? Tell me."

"Bad?" He put his hands on the counter of his kitchen island. "It looks bad. I know. But I'm just so upset. I loved Jennifer."

"Genevieve?"

"Genevieve!" he corrected himself, then screwed up his eyes and tried to cry.

It was an embarrassing display. He couldn't; he just looked constipated. I wanted to slap the cuffs on him and take him in just for bad acting, but I let him continue.

"You see? I don't even know what I'm saying. My heart is broken and I... wanted some relief. I just wanted to forget what my grandfather did for a little while."

Just then Camille came out of the bedroom. She was wearing a hot pink, spandex top and a tight black skirt that barely covered her butt; between them they highlighted every curve, and there were plenty of them. Without paying any attention to Janet or me, she stared at Eddie. He smiled up at her, sheepishly.

"Dead wife?" she snapped. "Are you serious? What kind of creep are you? I need cab fare." Camille put her hands on her hips.

Eddie sighed. "Uhm, can't we settle this later?"

"You think I'm going to take the bus dressed like this? Boy, you crazy."

"I don't know if I have any cash on me right now and—"

"I know you didn't just say that." Camille flipped her hair. "You got cash somewhere. Find it!"

I had to smile at Eddie's distress. Camille had moxie, that was for sure.

Eddie looked first at Janet and then at me.

"Don't look at me," I said. "I'm just a cop, remember?"

He rose unsteadily to his feet, hustled around the kitchen, opened a couple of drawers, looked bewildered, then went into his office. I, of course, followed him and watched as he knelt down in front of a small safe. After a couple of clicks and snaps he opened the safe door and took out several bills.

I followed him back into the kitchen and watched as he handed them to Camille. Judging by the flash of her eyes, they were big enough to get her home and then some, maybe even big enough for her to forget about what had just happened to her. She snatched them out of his hand, spun on her four-inch heels and, without so much as a word, flounced out of the apartment slamming the door behind her so loudly it made Eddie jump.

"That was nice of you," I said. "Now, can we get back to business?"

"I'm not feeling well," Eddie said, licking his lips, trying to look sick. "I think I need to lie down."

"You can do that later. I wonder what your grandfather would do if he knew you had a woman like Camille in your apartment?"

At first he just looked at me, then sighed, lowered his head, and said, "He doesn't care what I do."

He walked over to the sofa and flopped down on it.

"Oh, I think you are wrong there," I said. "He made it very clear to me that he doesn't like people of color."

"Yeah, well, screw him," Eddie snapped back, suddenly not so woozy. "What he doesn't know won't hurt him."

"Do you think he knew that Genevieve was black?" I asked.

Eddie froze, and I mean he *froze!*

"What? What are you talking about?" He practically choked on the words. "Genevieve wasn't black." Bless him, he tried, but I could tell by the look on his face that he knew that she was.

"Yes, she was." I explained Doc's findings and told him about my visit to her biological parents. "But you did know, didn't you, Eddie?"

"Her parents?" he asked, seemingly dumbfounded. "She told me she didn't have any family."

He stood, paced, then finally sat down on one of the bar stools at his kitchen island.

"Okay," he said resignedly. "Yes, I did know. I knew she was black, but I didn't know she had a family... She was the right kind of black, didn't look it, not at all, but behind closed doors she sure as hell acted like it, in all the right ways."

"Wow," Janet muttered. "Nice way to talk about your wife. You really are a piece of work."

"I meant it as a compliment," he said. "I loved her. What did my grandfather say? Did he say anything about my money?"

"He might have mentioned your *allowance*," I said. It was a cheap dig, but I couldn't help myself. What kind of grown man gets an allowance?

"Screw my allowance. Did he say anything about my inheritance?"

"Not a word... Eddie, you mean to tell me that your wife didn't tell you that she had a family in Baton Rouge? You want to tell me how your grandfather knew and you didn't? And you are aware he also knew Genevieve was black?"

"No. How could he know that? Genevieve looked like she'd just stepped out of an Irish Spring commercial for God's sake. When I met her in Baton Rouge, she was a nobody. No, the old man didn't know." Eddie swallowed hard. "You're lying. He would have no way of knowing unless you told him. I didn't, and I know Genevieve didn't. I even arranged for her to get that job at CDE." He started to pace again.

"You met her in Baton Rouge?" I asked.

"Yeah. I was with my mother on one of her fundraisers. My father was out of town, as usual. It isn't proper for a Southern lady to travel unescorted, at least, my mother doesn't think so." Eddie winced at the thought.

"That was when I met Genevieve. She was like an angel. We talked for hours on the phone... She was perfect. Sure, she was a little rough around the edges but nothing that couldn't be fixed. No one knew she was black."

"You obviously don't know your grandfather very well, Eddie," Janet said. "He had a thorough background check done on your wife."

"He would have said something to me. He would have told me. He would have gone ballistic." Eddie sounded terrified. "Oh, my God. I made sure everything looked right. What have I—"

"Had Genevieve told you she was pregnant?" I asked, interrupting him before he freaked out.

He shook his head but wouldn't look at me. Whatever came out of his mouth next was going to be a lie.

"No. No, I didn't know until Mother shared the news with me after you told her." He put his head in his hands. "I knew she'd be good at making babies. We spent so much time—"

"Eddie," I said, interrupting him, not wanting to hear what he was going to say next, "I need you to think for me. Do you know Treyshawn Montgomery?"

He looked at me as if I just dropped something nasty into his hand. His shoulders slumped. He took a deep breath and then released it in a long, defeated sigh and rolled his eyes.

"Yes, I know him. Everyone knows Treyshawn. He's a dealer. But he only deals to those of us who know how to keep a secret. He doesn't sell to Bubba down the street. You understand?"

"So you're telling us that you've bought illegal drugs from Treyshawn Montgomery?" Janet asked.

"Of course. Everyone I know has," Eddie said, wiping the sweat from his top lip.

"How about Genevieve?" I asked. "Did she buy from him?"

"Sometimes. I think so. I don't know what she did when I wasn't with her, but everyone who's anyone likes to do a little something special... and they get it from Treyshawn. I'm just saying."

"Well here's the thing, Eddie," I said. "Treyshawn and Genevieve's brother Nathan Watkins are known to be friends, good friends... Did you know about Genevieve's brother; did she ever mention him to you?"

"Nathan? I know him too. He's her *brother?*" Eddie asked, aghast.

"You didn't know?" Janet asked without looking up from scribbling her notes.

"No, she never told me about him, or that she even had a brother. I thought she just liked slumming it a little with them, that she was playing some kind of game."

"Did you ever suspect Genevieve of having an affair?" I said, interrupting his train of thought.

He looked at me, astounded, then said, hotly, "*No.* She'd never have cheated on me. Not because she loved me, which she did, but because I had money and will someday be a billionaire. She even had my initials tattooed on her back; you know that. But see, I held the purse strings. No, she'd never have cheated on me."

"Eddie, I think we should—"

"Nathan was her brother? You've got to be shitting me. I can't believe it. Do you know how much money I paid that piece of shit for pot and... he knew I was family..." his voice trailed off as he suddenly looked at Janet and me like he was hoping we hadn't heard what he'd just said. Before I could ask any more questions, however, he slammed his hand down on the kitchen counter.

"If those people think they have a claim on my money just because I was married to Genevieve, they can think again!"

"What?" I said and looked at Janet who was staring wide-eyed at him.

"Oh, I get it. I really do get it," he snarled, alert now and angry. "Those people think they've found them a gravy train, don't they? Well, Genevieve married me under false pretenses! She lied to me. She told me she had no family, no brothers or sisters. They won't get one red cent! I'll hire the best lawyers in the state and bleed them dry before I let a bunch of cotton-pickers get their hands on the money my family earned!"

"I guess the apple doesn't fall too far from the tree," Janet muttered.

"I guess not," I said, so taken aback I was wondering what the hell to say next.

"I know what you're thinking," he snapped, "and I don't frickin' care." Eddie's eyes began to water. "Genevieve," he whispered. "My Genevieve..." He looked up at me and continued, "We had a few problems, and she obviously had some secrets, but I loved her."

"Oh yeah, sure you did. We can see that," Janet said nodding, frowning. "I'm sure Camille could, too," she finished sarcastically.

"Go ahead. Make fun. I did love her. I could have married anyone I wanted. *Anyone!* But I chose her. And I'm not ashamed to tell you the sex was amazing!" He folded his arms and smirked.

"That's enough, Eddie, way more information than we needed," I said. "Will you be seeing Treyshawn any time soon?"

Once again, the man froze, and from the look on his face, I doubted we'd get anything further from him. I was only half right.

He shrugged, wiped his eyes with a paper towel, then said thoughtfully, "I don't know. Maybe... I mean no. Are you kidding me? No, I won't be seeing Treyshawn again. Not today. Not ever. Not that stinking brother either."

His Adam's apple bobbed up and down as he swallowed hard. "I think you need to leave now."

"Eddie," Janet said brightly, as she rose to her feet and snapped her notebook closed, "this conversation was really enlightening. I think it's safe to say we all learned a little something, right?" she said with a sweet smile. "My mom always said if you can learn from your mistakes it's all worth it... and boy, have you ever made some doozies."

"Words to live by, Eddie," I added as I stood up.

"I'm asking you both to leave, now," Eddie said, and then pinched his lips together so tightly they all but disappeared. "Don't make me call security."

"All right, Eddie," I said. "We've taken up enough of your time, and I thank you for it, but I'm afraid this isn't over. Genevieve's killer is still out there, and I'm going to find him."

He snorted, then said, "That's because you people are too timid to arrest my grandfather. I have to admit, though; he is one scary son of a bitch." And with that said, he stomped to the door, yanked it open and stood there with one hand on the knob, the other hanging limply at his side. He looked like a pitiful scarecrow wearing an expensive robe and pajama bottoms. I half expected to see a huge, black crow land on his bony shoulder. We hadn't made it two steps into the hallway when the door slammed shut behind us.

26

"I GET THE FEELING HE WAS HAPPY TO SEE US GO," JANET SAID AS she started toward the elevator.

I shook my head, put my index finger to my lips, took a tiny microphone with an earbud from my bag, put the bud in my ear and placed the tiny mike against the door and whispered, "This was not an interrogation, Janet. This was baiting the hook."

I listened for a few seconds and then heard a panicked Eddie, loud and clear, talking to his mother on the phone. Just as I'd hoped, our visit had scared the pants off him.

"The police were here," he shouted. "They were asking me all kinds of questions about... no... no, they didn't say anything about you! Why aren't they questioning Granddaddy?"

I grabbed Janet's pocket notepad from her hand, gave her the mike, signaled for her to hold it against the door, and I began taking notes. Well, I tried to, but it wasn't easy.

"Mama, I feel sick... Yes. Yes, I want you to come over. But when? When is this all going to be over with?" He sounded like a spoiled child, and I guess that's exactly what he was.

"Can we go to Miami? Yes, yes, I'd like to go again. No. No,

Mama, I promise I won't go clubbing without you. We can go together, just like we did when I was on spring break."

Janet had her ear to the door, and she looked sideways at me with her jaw hanging open.

"As soon as this problem with Genevieve is resolved we can go? You promise? Yes, I feel better. Do you really mean it, Mama? Yes... Yes, I know. Yes, I'll calm down. Do you think the police will arrest Granddaddy soon?"

I wasn't sure what I was listening to, but whatever this exchange between mother and son was it was creeping me out.

"And it won't affect me, right? I mean, I won't have my inheritance cut back or anything, will I?"

And then something broke.

"You promised he wouldn't take away my money," he yelled. "How do you expect me to live? I can't believe this! No! No... No, you don't! You don't love me!"

Now it was my turn to look at Janet with a slackened jaw.

The shouting subsided and I could hear Eddie muttering, but I couldn't make out the words until...

"Just make sure it's a Ferrari—a black one! And when we go to Miami, I want the Penthouse Suite at the Setai. You had it last time and I had to take one on the floor below. No! It was horrible. No, you can't use the Jacuzzi unless I say so."

Janet mouthed the word "Wow."

I nodded my head, jerked my thumb toward the elevator, and we quickly made our way back down to the lobby.

"What's with those two?" Janet asked, shimmying her shoulders as a shiver ran over her. "I feel like I need a shower after listening to that exchange. Do you think they are... you know?"

"Well, I have to admit the conversation sounded a little incestuous. It also sounded like Granddad has cut his allowance. Can you believe she's buying him a Ferrari? I think that Eddie is a little too confident that Granddad is the one who did Genevieve in."

"Do you think he did it, killed his wife?" Janet asked.

"Me thinks little Eddie doth protest too much," I said. "When we get back to the station, I want you to have Lenny dig deep into Regina Mae... and Mr. Daniel Racine. See if there's anything there. It might be a good idea to apply a little pressure to both of them."

"Got it," Janet said. "What are you going to do?"

"I'm going to try and get a handle on some of my overdue paperwork, but while I'm doing that, I'm thinking that maybe Granddad will call me again, or worse, call the chief." I smirked. "I did, after all, ignore the old goat's specific instructions so I have a feeling I might be in for some serious scolding."

Back at the PD, Janet went her way and I went mine. I closed my office door and sat down behind my desk and looked at the clock on the wall; it was just eleven-thirty with the sun peeking through the slats of my blinds.

I wished it were a little more overcast. Gray days somehow made the work easier. Well, maybe that was just me. But, regardless of it shaping up to be a bright afternoon, I did manage to wrap up several open files and answer a half-dozen emails. *Good job, Kate!*

By three-thirty I was done with office work—not finished with it, just done for the day—and was kind of surprised that Janet hadn't returned with a status report on her findings. And I hadn't heard from any of the others either. So I went looking.

Janet was not in her cubicle. Hawk and Anne were missing too. *Strange,* I thought. *I wonder where everyone is? I could call them, I suppose... Nope, I have to give them the freedom to do their jobs, not keep looking over their shoulders, trying to micro-manage them. Okay, so it's getting close to four. I need some fresh air. A jog around the park would work wonders.*

I made up my mind to cut class and was just about to leave and go home, change, and then go to the park when my phone rang; it was Janet.

"Sorry I bailed on you, Cap," she said, "but I've dug up some great information about Regina Mae." She sounded excited.

"Well, okay, but we've had a couple of late nights and I was just about to go home. How about you give me the Cliff Notes version now, and we can discuss the details tomorrow morning when the others are present?"

"Okay, I'll start with Regina Mae's boy-toy, Daniel Racine. Oh Lordy, is he ever a ripe one. He went to UTC and majored in business administration but dropped out in the middle of his junior year to work at a gay bar, Randolph's."

"Randolph's? Okay, that doesn't surprise me as much as it should," I said, more than a little disappointed. Not that I was remotely interested in him, but boy was he ever good-looking.

"Any priors?" I asked.

"Nope. He has a clean record," she said.

"You sound sad about that," I joked.

"Not really, but you know how much easier it is to question someone if you have a little dirt on them. Well I think it is, don't you? I also saw his pictures online. Whew, I wouldn't mind fifteen minutes alone with him in an interrogation room. Meow."

"Why Janet." I smiled at the thought. "What would your boyfriend think?"

"Hey, I'm not exactly dead," Janet said, "and don't tell me you'd turn him down either. And he's not gay, now is he? Not based on the info you gave me about his late-night antics with the divine Mrs. Chesterton. From what I was able to gather from his profile, and online, he's one giant puff piece, as BI as they come; goes both ways and doesn't seem to care whether he's coming or going."

I opened my mouth to speak, but Janet being Janet, continued on at her usual rapid-fire rate.

"Crazy as it may seem, Kate, I like a guy who can think on his feet, not his back, and that's not Daniel Racine. Besides, a doorman who's also a bartender doesn't sound like a winning combination, even if I didn't know he was banging some, if not all, of the residents. I wonder how much he makes... from the residents? I wonder if he services the male residents too?" And then she finally ran out of steam and took a breath.

"Ouch. Poor Daniel." I chuckled. "So, is he still bartending?"

"According to his credit report he is. He quit Randolph's about a year ago and is now working at a place called Angelo's. It's inside the Monaco Hotel, just a hop-skip-and-jump from Regina Mae's residence. How convenient. I guess he walks to work, if you can call it that, from there."

"Okay, that's enough about Dan. Now tell me about Regina Mae."

"She's got a clean record too, and good credit. Well, she would, wouldn't she? But here's the thing: she's involved with several charitable organizations that... well, you wouldn't really expect her to be helping them. Some are out of town in Baton Rouge, Louisiana."

"Oh really?" I said. "Now that is a surprise, and a coincidence, and I don't like coincidences, and especially this one."

"Right. I hear you," Janet said. "And here's another one for you. It turns out she has family there, in Baton Rouge, a cousin. What was it I heard? Once is chance, twice is a coincidence, three times and you have a pattern." She took a breath and before I could speak, continued.

"The cousin is a Mrs. Sally Booker. She's clean too. She's on the board of directors for an organization called the Louisiana Partnership of Women in Nursing. I haven't looked into them yet... Maybe I'll get Lenny to do it in the morning. Anyway, they have quite a few fundraisers and charity events every year, and last year they donated fifty grand to a women's clinic... reproductive rights, if you know what I mean. Well, it turns out that Regina Mae gives a substantial amount of money to her cousin's charity and participates in some of their fundraisers. You know?"

"Yes," I said. "I'm following you so far."

"Okay, well, you're gonna love this. You sure you don't want to wait till morning so I can tell the others at the same time?" she teased.

"Tell me now, dammit."

"Yes, ma'am. So, Talbot Montgomery's church has a sister church and it's also located in Baton Rouge and, get this, it's the same church that Sally Booker belongs to, and where, according to her income tax returns, she donates almost a fourth of her annual income. Ain't that cozy? Coincidence number four? I can't understand why she hasn't been audited."

"Oh, yes. Now that really is something," I muttered. "How long has she been a member of that church and where, exactly, is it located?" *As if I don't already know!*

"Hold on to your panties, Cap. It's about seven blocks from where the Washingtons live. Don't you think it's kind of strange that money is going to a church from one entity that is also affiliated with encouraging women to, well, you know?" Janet asked.

"I do. But politics make strange bedfellows."

I thought for a moment. This was starting to get a little too radical for my taste. "What's the name of the church?"

"The New Light Missionary Church," Janet replied.

I felt my heart jump in my chest.

27

_____

WITH JANET'S VIRTUAL TSUNAMI OF NEW INFORMATION ALMOST drowning me, I told her to go home and get some rest—fat chance of her doing that. I was going to spend some time processing what she'd told me, and we'd discuss our next step the following day.

It was going to require some sorting out, so now the idea of going home was out of the question. I did, however, need a change of scenery, which I figured would be as good as a rest. A glass of red would go down quite nicely too; I could kill three birds with one stone. *Cool!*

So I grabbed my bag, my iPad, and my phone, slipped my jacket on to cover my gun and badge, and I headed downtown to Angelo's in the Monaco Hotel.

"What are you doing here?" Daniel said in a loud whisper when I stepped up to the bar. "Are you trying to get me fired from this job, too?"

"They fired you from your doorman job?" I froze for a second.

"Yeah. Someone told the administrator that I wasn't at the front desk during my shift, and that I left it unattended for half the night. Did you do that?"

"I don't live there, Daniel. I don't care what you do. Did it ever cross your mind that it might have been Regina Mae that threw you under the bus?" I folded my hands and leaned against the bar. "I'd like a glass of pinot noir, please."

Angelo's was a nice little place with red and white checkered tablecloths, some obviously expensive prints of the great master Michelangelo's artwork framed on the walls along with colorful maps of Italy and some of its provinces.

There was a couple seated to the right of me at the far end of the bar—which wasn't really so far I couldn't hear them talking, and boy were they talking. They seemed to be oblivious to the idea that there was anyone else in the world but each other. She was lovely in a white dress and red shoes, sparkling bands of gold around her neck, her wrists, and her fingers. He was equally lovely, for a man, in a shirt so white it seemed to give off its own light. They spoke in whispers; bossa nova music played softly from hidden speakers.

Nice.

Daniel grabbed a bottle of pinot from behind the bar. Next he grabbed a glass from the rack, turned it right-side up with a deft flick of his fingers, held it up to the light and inspected it, a delicate piece with a needle-thin stem and a huge bowl.

He poured the wine, turning the bottle as if spilling a single drop would be a sacrilege. He pushed the glass toward me across the bar top. I picked it up, swished it a couple of times, gave it the obligatory sniff, and took a sip.

Not bad, I thought. *Almost as good as the two bottles of crap I bought at the liquor store the other night.*

"Regina would never do that," he whispered.

"Do what?" I asked, looking at the glass. "Oh, you're talking about your job. You don't think she'd turn on you? Really? She got caught, Daniel. She got caught with her hands in the cookie jar, or should I say with her panties around her ankles." I smiled. "She can't get rid of me—I'm a cop—but you?" I shrugged. "You're just another toy; plenty more where you came from."

"Do you think it really was her?"

"Daniel, she lives in the penthouse. Their names are in the papers at least once a week. You were banging the wife of Edward Chesterton the Third, and you got caught... by me. Just think about that for a minute."

I watched his face, and even though he was so very, very pretty to look at, I could tell he was having trouble putting the pieces of the puzzle together. Deep, or even light, thinking was not his strong suit.

"Okay," he said. "So maybe she did drop me in it. Now that I'm no longer the doorman, you have no reason to keep harassing me for information," he said as he wiped down the bar.

"Oh, but I do, Danny, I do... and by the way, why didn't you call me when Treyshawn Montgomery arrived home?"

"Because I wasn't there, of course."

Okay, can't argue with that, I suppose.

"Good enough," I said, "but you're not off the hook. Tell me, did Regina Mae ever mention Baton Rouge during your.... conversations together?" I clicked my tongue. "Did she ever tell you she was going away and wouldn't be able to see you for a while?"

"Oh, come on Detective, I wasn't banging her all the time. Yeah, Regina goes to Baton Rouge, quite often, in fact. Maybe once a month, and usually with her son Edward, until he got married. After that she stopped taking him."

"Did she say why?"

He actually chuckled, then said, "She said he'd caught something nasty down there. I assumed he'd gotten himself a dose of the clap."

Now that's funny, I thought, smiling to myself. *Genevieve an STD!*

"Did she talk much about Eddie and his new wife?"

"She talked about him all the time. How he'd never grown up. How he needed someone to take care of him, but no one could do it like she could. She was constantly bragging about the trips they went on together, how close they were, like she was trying to make me jealous or something. Kinda creepy, I thought."

"Eww," I said, playing along, frowning. "You think she... they might be..."

"Hah, I don't know what they were up to. I never asked. I'm not the jealous type." He winked at me.

"Did she ever talk about her daughter-in-law, Genevieve?"

"Not that I can remember. I know the wedding was a big deal. She talked a lot about the wedding, but... hmm, how shall I put it? Okay, it was like, other than a huge social event that her son was starring in, it didn't mean a whole lot. Like nothing had changed. Not like he was sharing a new life with someone else."

"Did that seem weird to you?" I asked.

"I thought she was talking about it because we were close. We were, like, having an affair, but on thinking about it, she was pretty closemouthed where the family was concerned... or their affairs. It was, like, the less I knew about her family, the better." He shrugged then continued. "I guess maybe she thought I'd ask for more money if I knew any real family secrets."

He leaned closer to me. He smelled really good of orange and spice.

"She was paying you?" I leaned back, away from him.

"Well, it wasn't like there was a set fee. Sometimes she'd give me cash. Other times she'd give me tickets to a ball game. It just depended on her mood."

He stood back a little, folded his arms, and said, "Hey, I know what you're thinking. I'm not a prostitute. I was getting something out of it, sure, but she was getting a whole lot more."

"She sure was, a romantic rendezvous in the broom closet with Chattanooga's version of Bradley Cooper," I jabbed.

He leaned back on his heels, his arms still folded, and gave me a dirty look.

"Did she ever invite you to go to Baton Rouge with her?" I asked.

"No. She always took her son," he said. "Look, I don't know what you think Regina did or didn't do. But I know her really well, and I can tell you she's a good person. She's smart, attractive, intelligent, and she has an amazing body for a woman her age and—"

"And she's cheating on her husband which means she's not afraid to lie, right?"

I watched Daniel's lip twitch nervously in the corner.

He shrugged. "That's different."

"You think? Maybe. Maybe it is, Daniel, but let me tell you something: during my long experience as a cop, I found that people who lie about one thing, no matter how small, will lie about everything. Regina Mae is no different. What do you think she'd tell her husband if he finds out you've been screwing her? Rape? Blackmail?"

"She wouldn't... He's not going to find out, not unless you tell him." He glared at me then said, "I can't wait for her to prove you wrong, and I know she will. She'd never rat me out, especially when we were having such a good time. You think she can do without this?" He grabbed his crotch and moved it slowly up and down. "Not hardly. She'll call me. You'll see. She always does," he bragged.

I took another sip of my wine and slid off the barstool.

"What do I owe you?"

"Oh, it's on the house."

"Sure it is," I said, throwing a twenty onto the counter. "Now ring it up and give me a receipt."

He did as I asked. I grabbed the receipt and smiled sadly at him, tilting my head a little, and said, "Thanks for the chat, and good luck hunting for a new gig. I'm sure a resourceful fellow like you will find something soon."

"Maybe I should consider being a cop?" He smirked.

"Maybe," I replied. "Goodbye, Daniel... Oh, and don't think you're off the hook. I *will* see you again soon."

I left him standing there, frowning, watching me leave. I could almost feel the power of his stare.

When I reached the door, I paused, then turned and looked at him. He was smiling. He inclined his head slightly, nodded, then raised his forefinger to the side of his nose and tapped it. I raised my right hand, made a gun of my forefinger and thumb, pointed it at him, and dropped the hammer. Then, without waiting for a reaction, I turned away and walked to the restaurant door.

The aroma of garlic, peppers, and Italian sausage cooking was tempting, but the menu on the stand next to the door had no prices, and we all know what that means. It was out of my league. So, it was going to be a greasy burger with cheddar fries from a joint on East Brainerd, which was on my way home.

When I arrived home, I poured myself a glass of sweet tea—no more wine for me—and drank deeply; I was parched. Next, I inhaled the most delicious charbroiled burger I'd eaten in a long time and washed it down with more tea. Then I stripped and headed straight for the shower. I spent maybe ten minutes under the hot water, washing away the cares of the day, then I dressed in sweats and settled down to work. I intended to do what I said I was going to do, and I did. I sorted out all the new information, assimilated it and, by the time I'd finished, I had a rough idea of what I needed to do next.

28

I AWOKE THE NEXT DAY TO THE EARLY MORNING SUNSHINE streaming into my bedroom and a heavy feeling in my gut.

I knew that greasy burger was a mistake, I thought. *I need to go for a run. What the hell were you thinking, Kate? Eating that crap food like you had a twenty-one-year-old's metabolism.*

I slipped back into the sweats I'd abandoned the night before, stepped out of the apartment into the fresh air, did some stretches, and then set off at a brisk jog out of the complex onto East Brainerd Road. It was still early; the morning rush had barely begun, and the air still had a chill to it. I had gone only a couple of blocks before I began to feel better.

I ran my usual route: west toward Banks Road and, by the time I'd made it to Morris Lane and made the turn, my brain was firing on all eight cylinders, but I could think about nothing but the Genevieve Chesterton case. Yes, I had other cases to worry about, including the murder of a twelve-year-old girl, but my priority, because of its high profile and the people involved, had to be Genevieve.

Things had been moving fast the past couple of days, and I had a feeling they were about to go even faster. My mind was in a whirl.

Hawk and Anne, I thought. *I wonder if they found the French-man. Who is he? Need them to go interview him. Alibi?* I upped the pace. I was feeling the burn, breathing hard.

And what about Wheaton? Is his alibi legit? Could his "date" have made a mistake? Is she lying to cover for him? I'll have 'em go door to door, talk to the neighbors.

Is Regina banging Treyshawn? Surely not. Although... Nah. She's got her hands full with Dirty Dan... literally, ha ha ha. It's worth digging into, though.

My thighs were beginning to ache as I pushed myself to keep up the pace. My lungs were burning as I panted in rhythm with each footfall.

What about Regina Mae's trips to Baton Rouge? I wondered.

It all kept coming back to Regina Mae's visits to, and contacts in, Baton Rouge. Something was bugging me, though, and I couldn't get a handle on it. And I couldn't get my head around her relationship with her son. Was she doing the nasty with him too? Ugh! The idea was unthinkable, but it wouldn't be the first time a mother had an unhealthy relationship with her son.

What was it really about—Baton Rouge and Regina Mae's work down there? Why did Eddie go with her, on every visit, and then suddenly stop? Was it out of respect for his marriage, or was she ashamed that her son had married a gal from the "ghetto" instead of a local debutante? *And an African American, too!*

I turned left into my apartment complex, my legs rubbery, but I felt alert and sharp and like I'd burned enough calories to rid my system of the fat and grease from last night's food fest. Now I was really able to concentrate.

"Kate, what are the chances that Alisha Washington knows about that church?" I muttered while wiping sweat from my forehead.

I slowed to a brisk walk the last hundred yards, thinking hard, and by the time I reached my front door I'd come to a decision: today I would make a bold move. It would be little more than a shot in the dark, but what did I have to lose?

I poured myself a cup of strong black coffee, took a couple of sips, then showered and dressed for action: white blouse, tailored business suit with a knee-length skirt, and black pumps with two-inch heels. I put my hair up in a high-top ponytail, and then I called Janet.

She answered immediately.

"Janet, are you on your way in yet?" I asked.

"Yes, I'll be there in five minutes."

I looked at my watch and shook my head; it was twenty-five after seven.

"Good, as soon as you get there, get hold of the others and have them in my office ASAP. I'll be there by eight."

I stopped at the bagel shop just across the road from my apartment complex, picked up a large coffee for me and a to-go travel container of dark roast coffee for the team, then slid into the heavy traffic on I-75, took Highway 153 to Amnicola and was in my office twenty minutes later.

"Wow, look at you," Janet said as I walked in.

I smiled and set the coffee container on my desk. Even Hawk looked surprised. Lenny too. Janet started filling coffee mugs.

"What's going on?" Anne asked.

"Nothing, not right now anyway," I said, taking my seat behind my desk.

It was at that moment Chief Johnston walked into the room and took a seat at the back and folded his arms.

"Carry on," he said. "Don't mind me."

I looked nervously at him but relaxed when he honored me with the beginnings of a smile. Janet hustled a coffee over to him, but he declined the offer with a shake of his head.

I nodded at the chief and said to the group, "Well, first I need you to bring me up-to-date on what you've been doing. Lenny, were you able to find the two girls that obtained judgments against Sam Wheaton?"

"I did: Lesley Cooper and Leigh Mason. I gave the names to Anne." He looked at Anne, as did I.

"Anne?" I asked.

She nodded, leaned back in her chair, folded her arms and said, "I talked to both of them. No help there. They are both bound by confidentiality agreements that were part of their settlements so they couldn't talk. Sorry." She shrugged.

"I also found the Frenchman, I think," Lenny said.

Now *that* I was interested in hearing about. "Okay," I said. "Let's hear it."

"His name, if it is him, is Gaspard Boucher, which is kind of ironic since the word boucher is French for butcher. Anyway, he's a naturalized American citizen and works out of CDE's New York office. From what little I was able to learn, he's some kind of fixer. His official title is Senior VP of Special Operations. He doesn't have a record, per se, but before immigrating to the United States he was a French police officer, an Inspector with Interpol. I was unable to access those records, but I think it's him. I turned what I had over to Hawk yesterday."

I looked at Hawk.

"I made a call to a guy I know," Hawk said. "A lieutenant in the NYPD. I met him while we were both attending a three-week course at the FBI Academy... Anyway, he said he'd check out Boucher's movements from May three through five and get back to me. He hasn't, not yet anyway, but he will."

I wasn't that excited at the news, mainly because I figured it was a red herring thrown at me by Eddie to get me off his tail and implicate his grandfather, but who knows. In our game, anything can happen—ordinary or extraordinary.

"Good," I said, nodding and flipping through the screens on my iPad. "Let me know as soon as you hear anything. If we can eliminate him, fine. If not..." I glanced at the chief, "Someone's going to have to go to New York and interview him. That would be you, Hawk." Again, I glanced at the chief. He was sitting there like a stone statue.

"In the meantime," I continued, "we also need to follow up on

Wheaton's alibi. I'm thinking it's probably good, but you never know. Did it check out?"

"Hawk and I went door-to-door, yesterday afternoon," Anne said. "We talked to several of the neighbors. One old biddy I talked to put his car outside Lucy Weston's garage at around ten-thirty on the Friday, and it was still there the following morning. So he was there. Whether or not he was there all night we can't be certain. We still have only Lucy's word for that."

"So, Wheaton has an alibi," I said, "but it's questionable. Okay, keep digging. Maybe you'll find something. Hawk, maybe you should give your buddy another call... No, give him a little time. We don't want to pi— upset him."

I thought for a minute, looked at the chief, and then said, "I have a couple of ideas, but I'm not ready to share them, not yet. I have a couple of things I need to follow up on and, by the looks of it, several messages.

"Janet, I need a photo of Regina Mae Chesterton. Can you find a good one for me?"

"Of course. She's all over the Chattanooga magazine for her philanthropic work and attending all the posh parties. What are you going to do with it?"

"You'll see," I said.

"Okay, people," I said. "Go to it. We have a busy day. Stay in touch."

And they left me alone there with the chief still sitting with his arms folded staring at me enigmatically.

The door closed and he rose to his feet, approached my desk, and sat down in the seat Janet had just left.

"I want you to know, Catherine," he said, "that I have every confidence in you, but I need a result, and quickly. Old man Chesterton is all over me. He wants to file a harassment charge against you. I'm holding him off, but for how long... well, I'll do my best. Are you any closer to a solution?"

"Yes, sir, I think I am. I may even have it done by the end of the day."

At that, he brightened, not just a little but a lot.

"You want to tell me about it?" he asked.

I hesitated, then said, "If you don't mind Chief, I'd rather not. If I'm wrong... I don't think I am, but..."

He nodded, stood, walked to the door, opened it, then turned to look at me and said, "Good job, Kate. Let me know as soon as you have something. I want to be there when charges are made." And then he left, closing the door gently behind him.

29

THERE WERE A HALF A DOZEN MESSAGES FOR ME IN THE SYSTEM, several of them from Edward Eaton Chesterton II. I tapped the button and listened to the crusty voice.

"My tax dollars at work," the old man snapped. "Of course, when I call you don't answer the phone. Detective Gazzara, I thought I made myself clear that I wanted you out doing your job and not harassing my family."

He left a total of three messages, all stating the same thing in three different ways. If I didn't stop harassing his daughter-in-law and his good-for-nothing grandson, I was going to hear from his lawyer.

"If you feel you have to solve the murder of a good-for-nothing, lying piece of trailer trash then, by all means, have at it. But harassing members of my family because we happen to have money is unacceptable," he growled. To me it sounded like he'd said this kind of thing before. "I will have charges brought against you if you do not conclude this persecution of the Chesterton family."

The message ended and the next one began.

"Captain Gazzara, this is Sam Wheaton."

You can imagine my surprise when I heard that voice.

"I must tell you that your investigation has gone on long enough. It seems to me that you have resorted to intimidating members of the Chesterton family. I'm warning you, Captain, complaints will be filed against you stating that you have overstepped your legal boundaries," Uncle Sam continued.

I sat there, stunned at what I was hearing. The worst part of it was that these same people who claimed they wanted the case solved were stonewalling me. And now I had no choice but to inform the chief that complaints from the Chestertons might be pending. He wasn't going to like that, not one bit.

But I didn't have time for that, not then. If I was going to do what I'd planned, I was going to have to work fast.

I picked up the desk phone and buzzed Janet.

"Janet, where the hell are you?"

"Almost done, Cap."

"Well, step on it. I need to get out of here."

Two minutes later she came hurrying into my office. I stood and held out my hand.

"Do you have the picture?" I asked.

"Oh, yeah. I have a really nice one. I downloaded it onto my phone. See?"

She showed me what was indeed a lovely photograph of Regina Mae. She was at the center of a group of three women at some charity event. She looked very much at home in a designer dress and wearing a collection of jewelry that would have rivaled the Queen of England's: her wedding ring rivaled the North Star.

"Send it to my phone," I said, "and then go back to your desk and wait for my call. There's something I need to do, then we can get out of here."

"You got it," and she was gone. It was as if illusionist David Blaine had snapped his fingers and then... poof!

The door closed and I picked up my iPhone and dialed Alisha Washington's number.

"Hello? Who is this?"

"Alisha, this is Captain Gazzara."

"Oh... Hello. Have you got news?"

I took a deep breath. I knew I didn't have the news she was hoping for, but I had a feeling I was getting closer.

"Alisha, I will have, very shortly, but right now I need your help with something. I'm going to send you a photograph, and I want you to tell me if you recognize anyone. Hold on... I'm sending it now. There. Did you get it?"

She didn't answer.

"Alisha? Mrs. Washington?" I looked at my phone expecting to see the call had disconnected, but it hadn't.

"I don't believe it," she said finally, quietly.

"Alisha, do you know any of these women?"

"Yes, the one in the middle. I only met her once, but I'll never forget it." She paused, for a long minute.

"Detective," she continued, "I don't know what your opinions are on a woman's reproductive rights—hah, they call them rights—but I have a problem with people and organizations that focus on the black community and try to force their own opinions and beliefs on us. Yes, I'm white, but I *am* part of this community, and I support my church and its teachings." She cleared her throat again. "So, it was when I joined the ladies of my church and we went to say prayers... to protest outside a clinic in Baton Rouge. Well, that was where I ran into that woman."

Oh, yeah, I thought, *now we're talking!*

"You're sure it was her?"

"I'll never forget her. Never, not as long as I live. Our church holds regular vigils there. We pray for the unborn souls and I'll admit, we try to persuade women to change their minds. Well, that particular day that woman came stomping up to me—I do believe she singled me out—and began cussing and screaming at me."

"What was she saying?" I asked quietly as I made notes.

There was a pause, then she said, "She was ranting that I was breaking up families, that I had no idea what damage I was causing.

'What the hell are you talking about?' I shouted back at her. Yes, those are the words I used. I cussed. I admit it. I've dealt with angry people before, but this woman was... Well, she was like... crazy, or something."

"Did she attack you physically?" I asked.

"No. I thought at first that she was going to, but she didn't. She was just a shrill voice shouting obscenities. I don't think she dared to hit me. She got close to me, but never too close. I may be a believer, Detective, but that don't make me a doormat. I think that woman got the message."

"Yes, ma'am." I smiled. "Go on."

"Well, she continued to scream at me, us, on the sidewalk. She told us we were all no good. Then she said something truly evil..."

I heard her take a deep breath, then say, "She said... 'I hope your children die before they can have babies.'"

"You're not serious?" I said, not sure about my own feelings. *That's a direct threat, and if Regina Mae was involved it would make Genevieve's murder premeditated.*

"Oh, I'm serious, Detective. That bitch is crazy, pardon my language," Alisha said, with a hint of amusement.

"Was she alone or was she part of a group?" I asked.

"She was with some people from the clinic, but there was a car waiting for her, and there was a man in it. He didn't get out, though, and I don't blame him."

"Do you remember what he looked like? Could you describe him?"

"Not really. But he had reddish hair... Slim, for sure."

Could it be that Eddie drove his mother to this clinic so she could verbally abuse his mother-in-law? My head was spinning.

"When did this take place, Alisha?"

"If I had to guess, I'd say maybe three months ago." Now it was my turn to just sit there for a moment and let it all sink in.

"Alisha," I said, "I'm going to ask you one more question, and I want you to think very carefully before you answer it."

"Okay," she said.

"Do you think that the woman knew who you were?"

"Oh!" She sounded surprised. "I don't know. I never thought about it before, but she did make a beeline for me, and it was me she was screaming about. That part about breaking up families... What did that mean? I don't know, Detective. I really don't."

"It's fine, Alisha. You've been more help than you know. Thank you for your time. I'll be in touch real soon."

"It's all right detective. Who... who is she? Did she kill my baby?" Alisha's voice wavered. I could imagine her sitting on the edge of her couch, her eyes filled with tears.

"I'm sorry, I can't talk about an ongoing investigation, but as soon as I have something, I'll call you."

"You know," she said, "when you first came to our house, I thought it would be the last time I'd hear from anyone about Naomi's murder. We're not rich folk and, well, it's not like we don't know what some people think of us, of me being white and married to a black man. So I just want to say thank you." Her voice caught in her throat, and I heard her sniffle.

"I'm just doing my job, Alisha," I said. "I'll be in touch. I promise."

Regina Mae freakin' knew who she was. She verbally attacked the woman she knew to be Genevieve's mother. Damn! That's a whole lot more than I hoped for.

I suddenly realized how tensed up I was. My body felt more exhausted than it did after my morning run. But hell, I'd just gotten a major break in the case.

I had to relax for a minute, loosen up and think, try to figure out how everything fit together. One thing I was sure of: it was more than just a coincidence that Regina Mae had showed up at the same little clinic in Baton Rouge where her son's mother-in-law jus* ᴸ to be protesting, and on the same day.

But how did she know, I wondered. *Did Grand, when he said he'd kept his knowledge to himself? L*

Mae about Genevieve's racial background and her family? Maybe he accidentally let it slip... Nah, it's more likely that as soon as she found out that little Eddie was bent on marrying Genevieve she, like old man Chesterton, did her own background checks which is how she found the Washingtons and, voila, that's how she found out that the girl was black.

I shook my head. There was a piece missing. Somewhere in this incestuous little cell there was someone, an outsider maybe, who held the key. And then something—a dose of Harry's sixth sense, maybe? —made me circle back to the two real anomalies in the story: Nathan Watkins and Treyshawn Montgomery. One a disenfranchised brother of the victim; the other a preacher's son who was also a drug dealer to Chattanooga's elite. And Regina Mae's cousin, Sally, belonged to Reverend Monty's sister church in Baton Rouge; that was another fact that picked at me.

Okay, Kate, it's time to kick it up a notch, hit the bricks and move on.

I buzzed Janet and told her to meet me at her car, a blue-and-white police cruiser. Wouldn't you just know it, she was already there when I arrived, leaning on the hood of her car looking at her phone.

"Let's go," I said, as I got into her car on the passenger side. "Hit the gas, to Reverend Montgomery's apartment to talk with Treyshawn. I think things are about to break wide open."

30

"CAN I ASK WHAT THIS IS ALL ABOUT?" THE REVEREND Montgomery looked genuinely bewildered when he opened the door. He was dressed in a designer sweat suit and a pair of Air Jordan's that must have cost more than my monthly rent.

"We'd like to talk to your son," I said lightly. "Is he home?"

"Yes, he's home, Detective. Again, I must ask you, what is this all about?"

"We just need to ask him a couple questions," Janet said.

"Is he in trouble?"

"Not at the moment," Janet replied with a sweet smile. The briefing I gave her on the way to the apartment had her chomping at the bit to get started. I'd already decided to let her take the lead; the thought being that her youthful appearance might put Treyshawn at ease, and maybe he would open up a little more to her than he would to me.

"Just one moment. I'll go and fetch him. He's still in bed."

Involuntarily, we both looked at our watches.

"It's after eleven," Janet mouthed at me, as Reverend Monty

walked along the hallway and gently knocked on a closed bedroom door.

I nodded but didn't answer. *What is it with these people?* I thought. *If the police had shown up at my house, wanting to ask me questions, my mother would have been shouting, demanding to know what the hell I'd done to bring the cops to her door. I'd have been more afraid of her than the police, that's for sure.*

The Treyshawn that finally appeared looked a lot different from the gangster who climbed jauntily out of the Cadillac in front of Club Suave. It was the same kid, I had no doubt. He was tall, muscular, abs like the proverbial washboard—that was easy to see because he was bare-chested wearing only pajama bottoms—and he had one of those haircuts where the sides and back are shaved leaving a tuft on top of his head. His eyes were half-closed, his mouth hanging open slightly. He couldn't have been a day over twenty-two, maybe twenty-four at the most. He didn't come across as the hardened thug we knew him to be.

"Please sit down, Detectives," Pastor Montgomery said, then turned to his son and continued, "Now, Trey, you tell the detectives what they want to know." Then he looked at me and said, "I'll be in my study if you need me."

We sat together on the sofa; Treyshawn sat opposite us.

Janet introduced herself, then me, then informed him I would be recording the interview, and then asked him if he had any objections.

He shook his head, said no, and waited until I had the recording app running and the details read in for the record.

Before Janet could ask the first question, he asked, "Am I going to be arrested? Do I need a lawyer?"

"We just need to ask you about your relationship with Regina Mae Chesterton and her son, Eddie," Janet said.

"Oh. Well..." He shrugged. "Okay, I guess."

"Treyshawn, does the name Genevieve Chesterton ring any bells?" Janet asked, keeping her voice soft and gentle.

"No?" he replied immediately.

"How about Nathan Watkins? Do you know him?"

"No?" He shook his head, his bottom lip still hanging loose flopped sideways, back and forth.

Janet looked at me. I said nothing.

"That's funny, Treyshawn," she said, "because..." She flipped through her notebook, more for effect than her need for information, and said, "on the night of May 10 at ten-forty-three, Captain Gazzara and I saw you pick him up in a Cadillac registered to your father in front of a convenience store. Or was someone else driving your father's car that night?"

Treyshawn shook his head.

"So you do know Nathan Watkins. Why did you lie?" she asked.

He shrugged. "Yeah, I know him. We went to the club that other night. So what?"

He looked down, focused on the cover of a BET magazine on the coffee table.

"Fine," Janet said. "No more lies, okay?"

He nodded but didn't look up.

"What about Eddie Chesterton? How well do you know him?"

"He was at the club sometimes," he said, truculently.

"Good. That's better, Trey. Now, how about his wife, a pretty white girl, did you ever see her? You would have noticed her. I don't think too many white women go to Club Suave."

"Yeah. Sure, I seen her."

"So you did know Genevieve Chesterton. Another lie?"

"Nah, I mean... I didn't know that was her name," he said, licking his lips. A thin layer of sweat had begun to form on the young man's forehead. He was also bouncing his right knee as he looked up at Janet.

"Did you ever see her anywhere else, like at other clubs?" Janet asked.

"Sometimes she was here," he said.

"Here? In this apartment?" I asked, surprised.

"No. Here in the building. She said she knew people here, but I think she was coming around just to see me." He leaned back in his chair, folded his arms and smirked.

"Why would you think that?" I asked.

"She told me she was having problems with her husband. That he wasn't paying no attention to her no more; know what I mean?"

"You mean sexually?" Janet asked, wincing as if she was embarrassed.

"Yeah, that... sexually." He smirked.

"Did you sleep with her?" I asked.

"Nah. I just sort of played the game, you know. I talked to her and stuff."

"Eddie Chesterton," Janet said, very quietly, "told my partner that you, Trey, are the connection for party favors for the rich and famous of Chattanooga. What do you have to say about that?" She asked the question as if she didn't believe it herself.

"Naw, man. I don't do dat." Treyshawn smirked, shook his head, but didn't look at either one of us. He was obviously lying.

"Why do you think Eddie Chesterton would say something like that if it wasn't true?" Janet pressed him.

The only answer she got was a shrug of the shoulders.

"Did you ever see Genevieve take drugs when she was at the club or here in the building?"

"Naw. She was just a freak," he said. It was obvious he was making it up as he went. It was the go-to response of any guy who wanted to make a woman look bad.

"She was a tease, man... She liked to tease, you know? When I seen her here in the lobby and she rode the elevator up with me, we talked about hooking up, but it never happened. She probably found some other dude." He blinked, looked to the left and licked his lips again.

"Okay, so we've established that you knew Genevieve and her brother Nathan, and that you knew Genevieve's husband, Eddie." Janet scooted to the edge of the couch. "How about Regina Mae Chesterton, Eddie's mother? Do you know her?"

"No," he snapped quickly; too quickly.

"Really?" Janet said, sounding surprised. "I don't see how that's possible. She lives in this building, in the penthouse. Are you sure you haven't seen her?"

"Oh yeah, I seen her, but I never spoke to her. We never talked." He rubbed his hands together and continued, "I've never been to the penthouse."

"I didn't ask any of that, Treyshawn." Janet chuckled. "I asked if you knew her. She said she knew you."

Oh dear, Janet. That was a lie. A big fat lie.

And so it was, but it worked. The look on Treyshawn Montgomery's face told us both that he did indeed know Regina Mae and not just in passing. Janet had pulled a rabbit out of the hat.

I could almost see the wheels in Treyshawn's mind, turning so fast they must have been making his head spin. How was he going to explain to us why Regina Mae was telling the police they knew one another when he'd been telling us they didn't? He'd backed himself into a corner and there was no way out. He'd already screwed up once when he lied about knowing Nathan, and again when he said he didn't know Genevieve.

"Treyshawn," I said, impatiently, "you seem to have a very loose relationship with the truth, either that or you're in the early stages of dementia and suffering from memory loss. Which is it?"

He looked at me, sullenly, but his face was expressionless.

"It's okay, Captain," Janet said soothingly. "Treyshawn. Let's try one more time, shall we? You do know Regina Mae Cottonwell-Chesterton, don't you? You might as well tell us because she's already told us everything. She made herself a deal." *Another fib.*

"Deal? What kind of deal?" Treyshawn clenched his fists.

"The kind of deal someone makes when they need to clear their conscience," Janet said, ambiguously.

"I didn't do nothing!" he shouted. "Whatever she's telling you is a lie!"

"Okay, Sergeant," I said. "I can see where this is headed.

Treyshawn, I think we'd better continue this conversation at the police department. In fact," I said and looked at Janet, "I think we need to bring Regina Mae in, too. We'll need to clear this mess up. Right, Trey?"

He didn't answer, the wheels in his head were slowly grinding away, trying to figure a way out for himself. They were losing the battle. He was about to lose it, I was sure.

"Go ahead and get dressed, Trey," Janet said. "We'll sort it out, I promise. It shouldn't take very long." More ambiguity. Sure, we'd sort it, but she didn't tell him how.

Treyshawn chewed his lower lip, made some sort of decision, pushed himself angrily up from the chair and stomped to his room.

Janet followed him and stood near the door, listening to make sure there wasn't going to be a problem. When Treyshawn yanked his bedroom door open just a couple of minutes later, he was wearing clean jeans and a T-shirt; the jeans, however, fit him perfectly, snug around his hips; the absence of his signature droopy, cargo shorts was notable.

31

I WAITED WITH REVEREND MONTY UNTIL JANET HAD ESCORTED Treyshawn to the elevator, then I took a few minutes to speak with him. I explained the situation and my suspicions that his son was somehow embroiled in a scheme perpetrated by Regina Mae.

"I don't believe it," he said angrily. "What has my son got to do with her?"

I thought hard before I answered that. I had to be careful because one, it was an ongoing investigation and two, I had a feeling that the reverend was about to show his true colors and start calling my superiors.

"I really can't talk about..." I began, and then I saw the pain in his eyes.

I sighed and shook my head. "He's a drug dealer, Reverend. Did you know that?"

He put a hand to his head and closed his eyes.

"I tried to keep him off the streets. I gave him every opportunity, and now look where we are." His eyes filled with tears. He put his hands together, looked up at the ceiling and said, "Dear Lord, please help me in this my hour of need."

Then he looked at me and said, "You know how it is, Captain. You can take the boy off the streets, but you can't take the streets out of the boy, or something like that."

I nodded sympathetically. How many times had I heard that, or a variation of it?

"Should I get him a lawyer?" he asked.

"I think that might not be a bad idea, Reverend."

I could have told him no, but that would have been unethical and denied the boy his constitutional right. The problem was, I needed to get Treyshawn to talk, and there was no way that would happen with a lawyer present. I needed to get a move on.

When we arrived at the PD, Janet settled Treyshawn in an interview room. As we watched him through the one-way glass, I could tell by his body language that he'd come to some sort of decision. It looked to me like he'd decided not to cooperate.

He'd folded his arms, stretched his legs out straight under the steel table, slouched down on the uncomfortable steel chair, and was sucking on his bottom lip.

"We don't have any reason to hold him," Janet said as we stood together watching him. "Not unless we can link him to Regina Mae... Are you sure about her, Kate? How did you connect the dots?"

"It's a convoluted series of events and coincidences, some of which you already know, some you don't." I paused, staring at Treyshawn, thought for a minute, then continued, "See, I think Regina Mae knew all along that Genevieve was black. I think it upset her so much that she tracked down Alisha Washington and confronted her, without letting on she knew who she was. And I think she probably met with Treyshawn, on several occasions, when he was coming home late at night, and when she'd just got done visiting Daniel... maybe even with Nathan tagging along.

"Her opinion of black people is pretty radical, we know that. So when she sees this wanna-be thug, she makes some inquiries—maybe she even questioned her son Eddie about him. So she finds out who and what he is. Then she pays him to do her dirty work: get rid of her pregnant, black daughter-in-law."

Well, it sounded good to me... And it was right at that moment when I began to wonder if maybe I was assuming too much, had it all wrong. No matter, the die was cast and I was committed to follow it through.

"But where's the smoking gun?" Janet said. She looked at me and her expression morphed from pensive to shocked.

"Wait. I'm so stupid. You're right, Kate. Treyshawn would *not* do her a solid out of the goodness of his heart, now would he?"

"What? No!"

"He's not the type to volunteer his services for free." She smiled. "In your scenario you said she probably paid him, right?"

"Yes, but I don't know that..."

"How much do you think she would have paid him to kill Genevieve?"

"I couldn't say, not without—"

"*The bank statements,*" Janet all but shouted. "That's right, and that's what I mean about me being stupid. I pulled everyone's bank statements except Regina's. I only pulled her credit report." She smacked herself in the forehead with the palm of her hand.

"I got bank statements for Eddie, Wheaton and old man Chesterton, but she slipped through the cracks. I didn't think she was seriously a suspect because she's so—"

"How long will it take you to run the report?" I asked.

"Give me fifteen minutes."

"You have ten."

She nodded, turned on her heel, and dashed out of the room. She must have pulled in some favors to get the bank statements as quick as she did. I clocked her in at just over eight minutes when she returned, smiling from ear to ear.

"I didn't think Treyshawn would have a bank account, but he does," she said excitedly. "I pulled that one too. I think you'd better send a car to pick up Regina Mae."

Janet showed me the paperwork, explained it to me quickly, and then asked the question, "Can I do it, Kate? Let me talk to him, please."

I smiled at her and said, "You got it, Janet. Go get him. Wait, hang on while I send a car to pick up Regina Mae."

She nodded excitedly, waited while I made the call, then took a deep breath and led the way into the interrogation room where Treyshawn had decided he'd had enough.

"Look," he said, sitting up straight and unfolding his arms, "if you ain't going to charge me I'm getting out of here. This is bull—" He started to his feet.

"Sit down, Treyshawn," Janet snapped at him.

He sat down again, not quite so sure of himself.

"What did you do with the ten thousand dollars that Regina Cottonwell-Chesterton transferred into your account?" Janet asked.

"I don't know what you're talking about," Treyshawn said and rolled his eyes.

"Oh, you don't?" Janet replied sweetly. "Let me show you." She sat down across from Treyshawn, placed the bank statement on the table in front of him, and pointed to the columns.

"These here are deposits into your account, see? There was a deposit of five thousand into your account on May 1, three days before Genevieve was murdered, and another five thousand on Monday, May 6, two days after. Now where could they have come from, I wonder... Oh, I know, let's look here." She swapped statements and continued.

"Now, this is Mrs. Chesterton's account, and these are her withdrawals: there's this one for cash, five thousand on May 1... and here's another one, also for cash on May 6. That's quite a coincidence, don't you think, Treyshawn?"

He didn't answer. He just stared sullenly at the sheets of paper in front of him.

"No comment, Trey? Can't say as I blame you. Now, if you look at those two withdrawals, you'll see the stupid woman made notes...

so..." She looked him in the eye and said, "I'm sure you'll correct me if I'm wrong but doesn't that say 'T. Montgomery'? Oh, but maybe I'm wrong. Could that be a reference to your father, Talbot? Hmm, maybe we should go pick him up. What do you think, Trey?"

We watched as his jaw fell open and his face turned gray.

"That money was supposed to go to my dad's church. That's all," he stuttered. "She told me she made a mistake and deposited it in the wrong account, that it was supposed to go to my dad, a donation to the church. That's what she said, honest."

"Oh, no," Janet said. "That's not what happened. People like Regina don't make that kind of mistake. I know, maybe she was going to launder the money through you, and you were supposed to give it to your dad? If so, that's too bad. I thought your dad was a stand-up guy. This isn't what we'd expect of a pastor. I think we'd better bring him in, Captain."

"No. Wait. My dad... he's not involved." Treyshawn's knee started to shake and his expression changed to one of fear.

"Do you want to talk about it, Treyshawn?" Janet asked quietly. "You can spare your father the humiliation of being dragged down here in handcuffs. She didn't make a mistake, did she, Trey? Maybe she did tell you to donate it to your father's church, but you were supposed to read between the lines, right? She was just covering her ass, but you and I, we both know what it was really for, don't we?"

He didn't answer, just stared at the tabletop.

"Your father," she said. "He's a man of God, and you know what he'd tell you."

"The truth will set me free?" he asked.

"Yeah. That's what he'd tell you," Janet said.

The boy nodded but hid his face from us.

Then, in a sweet voice that I believed was truly genuine, Janet asked him if he'd like a drink, Coke or water. He shook his head. She offered him a cigarette. Again, he shook his head. She asked if he needed to use the bathroom. This time he nodded. A uniformed officer accompanied him while she and I talked.

"Good job," I said. "Really. Well done, Janet."

"Yeah, well," she said wryly. "That was the easy part. Now we need to have Regina Mae brought in. We need to put her in the hot seat."

"Just a few minutes more," I said. "Patrol is already on the way to get her, and she's mine. I can't wait." And I couldn't.

Sometimes, when solving a case, there's a clear path to the solution: you simply follow the evidence from point A to point B, and everything falls into place. But this wasn't one of those cases. There was almost no evidence at all. Sure, we followed the leads, but then I'd made a really big leap of faith and still didn't have what I needed. All I had was a whole lot of supposition, coincidence, and intuition. You can't convict on any or all of those things. Sure, the bank statements helped, but they were circumstantial, and if they stuck to their story—that the money was supposed to go to the church—the only thing they proved was that Treyshawn had stolen it.

We, that is I, still had a hell of a lot of work to do before I could make an arrest.

32

"THIS IS PREPOSTEROUS!" REGINA MAE SHOUTED, CAUSING everyone within fifty feet to stop what they were doing and gawk at her. "I've never been treated so rudely in all my life!"

"Calm down, Mrs. Chesterton!" Randy, my favorite uniformed officer ordered. "Or I'll put you in the holding tank until you can regain your composure."

"Regina Mae," I called out and waved across the station. "Thank you for taking the time to come on in and talk to us. I can imagine what a bother it must be."

"You! I should have known," Regina Mae hissed.

"Should have known what?" I asked innocently. "Look, this is just routine, a few questions for the record. Please... come with me?"

"I want you to know that I've called Grandfather Chesterton, and he's not at all happy." She squinted as she approached me.

Oh, I bet he isn't, I thought.

"You can believe me when I tell you," she continued like some superior being, "he's already speaking to our family attorneys. You, Captain, are an unmitigated disaster."

"Can I get you some coffee or water, Mrs. Chesterton? I'm sorry I can't offer you sweet tea," I said as I led her to the interrogation room next to Treyshawn's.

As planned, Janet had left the door to his room open so Regina Mae could see him, and boy did she ever.

"What is he doing here?" she shouted.

"Who?" I asked.

"That boy," Regina Mae snarled.

"Treyshawn Montgomery?" I asked, acting surprised, closing the door behind me. "You know him? Oh, yes, of course you do. He lives in your building, with his father. Have you ever met Reverend Montgomery?" I asked, conversationally.

She hesitated, then snapped, "No! Well, just to say hello to."

"Hmm, please sit down, Mrs. Chesterton. I should tell you that our conversation is being recorded: sound and video. Have you ever attended his church?" I asked, without skipping a beat from one subject to the other.

"Absolutely not."

"Treyshawn mentioned that only last week you made a substantial donation to his father's church, ten thousand dollars, I believe. Why would he say such a thing?"

"I don't know. I'm sure the nasty creature would lie about anything. You know how those people are."

"Those people? You mean Christians?" I asked.

"You are in law enforcement, Detective. You know what kind of people I'm talking about."

She folded her hands together in her lap and sat there looking demurely at me. I had the feeling she expected me to agree with her. Her polished nails and expensive jewelry looked completely out of place in the plain, dreary room.

"How often do you go to Baton Rouge, Mrs. Chesterton?"

That took her aback.

"Quite... often," she said hesitantly. "I have kin there. I go at least once every couple of months. My cousin and her family do excellent work for the unfortunates of the inner city." She cocked her head to one side and squinted at me.

"And you attend fundraisers there?" I asked.

"Of course. They organize fundraisers for her charity, the Louisiana Partnership of Women in Nursing." Regina Mae raised her chin with pride. "I'm proud to be involved."

"Do you ever take anyone with you to Baton Rouge?"

"Yes, I do. My son, Edward, usually accompanies me. I don't like to travel alone. So many men get the wrong impression about a lady traveling on her own."

I wasn't sure if she'd forgotten I'd caught her with Daniel only a couple of nights ago, or if she was intentionally ignoring that fact. Either way, her babe-in-the-woods act was falling flat.

"That's where he first met Genevieve, isn't it?" I leaned back in my chair and crossed my arms and stared at her, watching her eyes for any sign of a tell. "He was with you at one of your charity events, wasn't he?"

Regina Mae pinched her lips together so hard they turned white.

"So," I said, lightly, "you could say it was you who brought them together. That must have made you very proud." I smiled, then hardened my voice and said, "Until it didn't."

"I am telling you, Captain, that I had nothing to do with that girl's death and—"

"You mean your daughter-in-law," I interrupted.

"I had nothing to do with my daughter-in-law's death, but I understand what you're trying to do. Well, you won't get away with it. You're a lowlife targeting the wealthy of this city, to show the world that Chattanooga isn't racist." She paused, smirking. "You hate people of privilege, like me. You're just as bad as the rest of them."

"Funny you should mention hate. When was the last time you were in Baton Rouge? I ask because I have a really funny story to tell you." I watched for a reaction. Other than a slight lowering of her head, there was none.

"As you know, Genevieve's mother and father are both alive and well and living in that city. You did know that, didn't you? That's why you went with your cousin... Sadie?"

"Sally," Regina Mae hissed.

"Sally." I snapped my fingers. "Right. You went with Sally to confront a group of peaceful protesters in front of a women's clinic. Do you remember that?"

She shrugged. "No. I've attended a lot of such events in Baton Rouge. One event is much like another."

"In fact," I said, "you verbally attacked a woman there, one of those protestors, Genevieve's mother. She positively identified you, so please don't deny it."

Regina Mae's face turned bright red, but she said nothing.

"You also threatened her children. You said, and I quote, 'I hope your children die before they can have babies.'"

I stood, walked to the wall opposite the one-way glass, leaned against it, folded my arms and stared at her. The bitch stared right back at me, unflinching.

"And then guess what?" I asked but didn't wait for an answer. "Her only daughter is horribly murdered and... she just happens to be pregnant. Wow. That's a horrible thing to say. I wouldn't want to have that on my conscience. How do you live with yourself, Mrs. Chesterton?"

She sat stone-still, glaring at me.

Before I could continue, there was a knock on the door and Janet stepped in.

"Sorry to interrupt, Captain. Oh, hello, Mrs. Chesterton," she said politely.

"What is it you want, Sergeant?" I asked.

"Well, let me tell you... and, Mrs. Chesterton, you might like to hear this too. I was just talking to Treyshawn Montgomery in the room next door and, well... what have you been saying to him, Mrs. Chesterton?"

"I haven't said anything to him. I don't speak to that kind of creature," she hissed, glaring first at Janet, then at me.

"Oh dear," Janet said. "I wish you hadn't said that. You see I believe him, so we've subpoenaed your phone records which means... well, we'll be able to confirm his statement easily enough."

"Wait, I'm lost," I said, playing the game along with Janet. "What did he tell you?"

"Treyshawn said that Regina Mae arranged for him to meet up with Genevieve," Janet said.

"Now that I find really hard to believe," I said sarcastically, "since Mrs. Chesterton is such an upstanding citizen, and Treyshawn is a known drug dealer. And she claimed that she doesn't talk to... What was it you called him? 'A creature like that,' wasn't it? You can't tell me that she would introduce her daughter-in-law to him. I don't believe it."

Now she was angry, close to exploding.

"Look, I'm not trying to embarrass you, Regina Mae," I said as if trying to placate her, but then I paused for a moment before I dropped the hammer on her.

"When I interviewed Daniel Racine... you know him, don't you?" I said, smiling at her.

She didn't answer.

"Well," I continued, "he said that you often waited for Treyshawn, in the lobby, at all hours of the night, and that you knew him quite well." It was a bit of a stretch, but what the hell?

"That was how you and Racine became so well acquainted, wasn't it?" Janet asked. "Your affair with him helped pass the time while you were waiting for Treyshawn. Good-looking guy, Racine; not bad if you can get it, I suppose, but that was a mistake, wasn't it? Racine will look good on the witness stand." She paused.

I watched Regina. Her face was expressionless, but I could see the hate in her eyes.

"Then," Janet continued, "you somehow managed to persuade Treyshawn to kill Genevieve. You offered him ten grand; hard for a creature like him to turn down. And no one, so you thought, would ever connect the two of you. It was perfect... but it wasn't, was it?"

"You're going to take the word of a drug dealer?" Regina Mae scoffed. "I don't think so. My daughter-in-law was a liar and a whore who latched onto my son in the hopes of getting her dirty black hands on our family's money. That's what you've got? That's what you've pieced together? Pathetic! I'll have both your jobs before this day is finished."

"Oh, I don't think so," I said.

Just then Randy knocked on the door. I stepped over and opened it, and he whispered to me.

"Oh, thanks. Regina Mae, there is someone here to see you. I'll go get him. Randy, please ask the chief to come to the observation room."

Janet stayed with Regina Mae. She told me later that the woman kept rolling her eyes and mumbled degrading comments about her, Janet's, financial status, cheap haircut, clothing, and so on. But that stopped when Edward Chesterton the Second stepped into view.

Janet and I left the two of them alone to talk, retreated to the observation room and joined the chief behind the one-way glass. I had no idea how their conversation was going to go. It was being recorded, but I didn't want to miss a second.

"Oh, Granddaddy, thank goodness you are here," Regina Mae twittered, rising to her feet and hugging his neck. "I tell you, you'll own half this city before this is all done."

"I already do," he said, pushing her away from him. "Shut your stupid mouth and sit down."

She sat down on the steel chair with a thump.

He scowled at her and said, "What in God's name have you done, Regina? It was bad enough that my son married you, but I always thought you had enough good sense to stay out of grown-up matters. I was wrong again."

"Granddaddy, this is all a huge misunderstanding," she said firmly.

"That boy in the next room said you paid him to kill Eddie's wife... And damned if you didn't do it with my money. He said you arranged it, transferred the money—from the bank I've used since I was thirteen—to your bank account, and then deposited it in *his* bank account, thinking that no one would figure out the connection."

"You said it yourself a hundred times, Granddaddy, that those people can't be trusted. No one will believe him. He's a drug dealer and comes from—"

"His father is a pastor, you silly bitch. More God-fearing than you," Chesterton whispered as he stared at his daughter-in-law.

"I did the world a favor," she said defiantly.

And there it is, the confession. I have her.

I looked at the chief. He nodded, but held up his hand, placed a finger to his lips and nodded at the scene still unfolding before us.

"Can you imagine," Regina Mae continued, "the shame that would have come with a half-breed baby? What if the child was darker than Genevieve? Suppose some retarded gene popped up. How would we explain it? How would you have looked to all the men who look up to you? They'd see you had poisoned blood in your family tree. I had to do what needed to be done, and I did."

He sat down opposite her, shaking his head, unbelieving of what he was hearing. "I've put a call in to Edward. He's on his way home. I've also called my attorney."

She still didn't get it.

"That sounds fine, Granddaddy. The sooner I can get out of here the better. We'll make this department crawl on its belly before this is over." She pushed herself up to stand, but the old man held up his hand.

"Not so fast. Sit down. The lawyer is for Edward, not you." He clenched his teeth. "No son of mine will remain married to a murderer. The divorce papers will be ready by tomorrow morning."

"Granddaddy, you can't be serious. This lying little piece of garbage has you hoodwinked." And then it hit her what was happening to her. "*You're turning on me?*" she said incredulously. "After everything I've done for this family. I gave you your only grandson and this is the thanks I get?"

"That you did, and maybe now the boy will learn how to be a

man," he growled. "You ruined him. You treated him as if he was your property. You babied him, ruled him, covered for him and, even when he did make a decision on his own, even if it was a bad decision, you went right ahead and made it worse. *You made it worse! You ruined the family name!*" He glared across the table at her.

"This all could have been dealt with," he said. "The girl's ethnicity, the child she was carrying, it all could have been handled and the Chesterton name would have remained unsullied, but not anymore. For all I care you can rot in here, or in hell where you belong."

Old man Chesterton stood, walked to the door and banged on it. Officer Randy opened it immediately and the old man, taller and meaner looking than he'd been when I first interviewed him, stormed out of the building without saying another word.

I looked at the chief. He had a grim smile on his face, made even more so by his huge mustache. He nodded to me, then turned and left the room.

I turned to Janet and told her to go and charge Treyshawn with capital murder, then I returned to the interrogation room and told Regina Mae to stand.

"Stand up, Mrs. Chesterton."

Slowly, she rose to her feet, both hands on the table.

"Regina Mae Cottonwell-Chesterton, I'm arresting you for conspiracy to murder in the death of Genevieve Chesterton and her fetus. You have the right to remain silent..." And so it went on.

When I guided her out of the small room and handed her over to Randy, Janet already had Treyshawn in handcuffs. He looked angry, probably blaming Regina Mae for the decisions he'd made. I'm sure his public defender would present him as an impressionable young man who just wanted to prove himself, and that Regina Mae was the real culprit, the real mastermind behind the plot to kill Genevieve Chesterton, as indeed she was.

I also had no doubt that Regina Mae's defense attorneys would try to cut her a deal; that wouldn't happen; not in today's racial climate. This trial was going to be as big a media circus as Genevieve's wedding was just a year ago.

"What's the matter, Cap?" Janet asked after the two suspects had been taken away to booking.

"I don't know. I'm afraid of how this is going to play out in the media. We're going to have a tough time if it turns into a big racial issue." I shook my head. "I gotta go call the Washingtons, tell them we've made an arrest."

EPILOGUE

Two weeks had gone by since I'd wrapped up the Genevieve Chesterton murder, and the case was in the hands of a passel of overpriced lawyers and sleazy reporters. I was pretty happy with the outcome: the perps were going to get what they deserved, but there were a couple of loose ends: Eddie Chesterton and Nathan Watkins. What part did they play in Genevieve's murder, if any? I'm pretty sure that Eddie knew that Regina and Treyshawn murdered Genevieve, and that would have made him an accessory, but I couldn't prove it. Eddie denied it, of course, and his mother was adamant that he didn't know. Nathan? I don't know. Maybe he knew what his friend did, maybe he didn't. He denied knowing anything, and Treyshawn wouldn't snitch. So, both Eddie and Nathan walked.

Me? As I said, two weeks had gone by and I was in my office sipping coffee when there was a gentle knock on the door.

"Yes!" I shouted.

The door opened and Randy said, "Someone to see you, Captain."

I nodded, and a nervous young woman entered.

"Can I help you?" I asked, puzzled.

"Detective Gazzara, you probably don't remember me. I looked a bit different the last time you saw me," she said. "My name is Molly. Evelyn Karl is my grandmother."

"Oh, yes," I said and smiled at her. "You're right. I wouldn't have recognized you. How are you doing, Molly? Come on in. Sit down."

I stared in disbelief at the girl sitting in front of me. Just a few months ago she was a scrawny, pale punk on her way to the junkyard, and when I say junk, I mean she was a junkie. Now, she was a healthy young lady with color in her cheeks and her hair in pretty pigtails.

"I don't want to take a lot of your time," she said, looking down at her shoes. "Grandma told me she nominated you for the policeman of the year award... but you didn't get it."

"Oh, that's okay. The cop who did get the award saved a baby from a hostage situation at a convenience store, and he got shot in the process. I was happy to see him get the honors." I smiled.

"Well, I think you should have gotten it and so does Grandma," Molly said, shaking her head. "She said that no one else worried about me running away except her and you. No one else gave a damn except you, were her exact words, and that it's cases like mine, cases that don't have any glory, that matter. That's what Grandma says."

"Well, you can tell your grandma I appreciate that. Where is she, by the way?"

"She's getting her hair done. She's at Adele's, downtown," Molly said. Then she sat there awkwardly twiddling her fingers, then said, "Why did you do it?"

"Do what?"

"Why did you go out of your way to find me?"

I didn't tell her that it was just a random stroke of luck that she just happened to be at the scene of another crime. I didn't know what to tell her, but then...

"I could tell you that I just happened to be at the right place at the right time. And so were you. But I believe there's no such thing as an accident. I believe we crossed paths at the exact moment that fate, or God, decided we should. I can't explain it, Molly. In my line of work, we take the miracles when and as they come, and we don't question them."

Molly smiled bashfully and nodded her head.

"Are you in rehab?" I asked.

"Yeah."

"And how is that going?"

"Pretty good. I'm feeling better and I've gained weight." She rolled her eyes.

"Don't worry about that. You are supposed to have some weight on you. Look at me. I'm no skinny mini. But I think I do okay." I patted my stomach. It looked a whole lot bigger than it was because of my pants, and my blouse tucked inside them. They made me look fat, but I didn't need to flaunt my runner's body, especially not to her.

"Detective, when did you decide you wanted to become a cop?"

It was the second time I'd been asked that question inside of a week.

"Tell you what," I said, "why don't you give your grandma a call and let her know where you are? I'll get us a couple of Cokes and tell you all about it." I smiled.

"Are you sure? You don't have bad guys to catch or something?" she said, her eyes bright and clear.

"I'm sure. Because that's the thing about police work. It's never done." I laughed. "There will always be bad guys."

"Okay then, that sounds great."

I got up from my desk and watched as Molly took out her phone and proceeded to text her grandmother.

"Anything I can help with, Cap?" Janet asked as I walked by her cubicle on my way to get the Cokes.

"No. Just hold my calls for half an hour or so."

Thank you for reading this 2nd collection of three Kate Gazzara

novels. I hope you enjoyed it. If you did, I'm sure you'll want to read the next three books in the series together as well,
The Lt. Kate Gazzara Series - Books 7 - 9
Available Direct from the author and at retailers.

First, I'd like to thank my editor, Diane. Her suggestions were always thoughtful, insightful and helpful, and I am truly grateful. Thank you, Diane.

When an author needs help with forensics, he or she usually turns to the Internet for that help, but there's really nothing that can compare with the real thing. So, I'd like to offer a special thank you to Detective/CSI Laura Lane of the Bradley County TN Sheriff's Department. Many thanks for your help, Laura.

The people of Chattanooga: I love you folks. Thank you.

To all of my fans, and I can't believe how many there are of you, thank you for your loyalty and support. Without you, I couldn't do this.

Ron, Gene, David – you know who you are – thank you for your firearms expertise, and your friendship. I love you guys.

Finally, I'd like to thank my wonderful wife, Jo, for putting up with me and my obsession for almost forty years. I love you. You're the best. And of course my constant companion, even if she does eat everything that's not tied down, Sally.

ABOUT THE AUTHOR

Blair Howard is a retired journalist turned novelist. He's the author of more than 40 novels including the international best-selling Harry Starke series of crime stories, the Lt. Kate Gazzara series, and the Harry Starke Genesis series. He's also the author of the Peacemaker series of international thrillers and five Civil War/Western novels.

If you enjoy reading Science Fiction thrillers, Mr. Howard has made his debut into the genre with, The Sovereign Stars Series under the name, Blair C. Howard.

Visit www.blairhowardbooks.com

You can also find Blair Howard on Social Media

From Blair Howard

The Harry Starke Genesis Series
The Harry Starke Series
The Lt. Kate Gazzara Murder Files
The Randall & Carver Mysteries
The Peacemaker Series
The Civil War Series

From Blair C. Howard

The Sovereign Star Series

Made in United States
Troutdale, OR
01/20/2025

28132882R00425